THE
GAME OF
STARS AND
COMETS

Baen Books
By Andre Norton

Time Traders
Time Traders II
Star Soldiers
Warlock
Janus
Darkness & Dawn
Gods & Androids
Dark Companion
Masks of the Outcasts
Moonsinger
Crosstime
From the Sea to the Stars
Star Flight
Search for the Star Stones
The Game of Stars and Comets

THE GAME OF STARS AND COMETS

BY

ANDRE NORTON

THE GAME OF STARS AND COMETS

This is a work of fiction. All the characters and events portrayed in this book are fictional, and any resemblance to real people or incidents is purely coincidental.

A Baen Books Original

Baen Publishing Enterprises
P.O. Box 1403
Riverdale, NY 10471
www.baen.com

ISBN 10: 1-4165-9155-9
ISBN 13: 978-1-4165-9155-9

Cover art by Bob Eggleton

First Baen paperback printing, April 2009

Distributed by Simon & Schuster
1230 Avenue of the Americas
New York, NY 10020

Library of Congress Cataloging-in-Publication Data

Norton, Andre.
  The game of stars and comets / by Andre Norton.
     p. cm.
  ISBN 1-4165-9155-9 (trade pbk.)
  1. Science fiction, American. I. Title.

PS3527.O632G27 2009
813'.54--dc22

2008051052

Printed in the United States of America

10 9 8 7 6 5 4 3 2 1

✦CONTENTS✦

THE SIOUX SPACEMAN

☆ CHAPTER 1 ☆

ON LODI, a crossroad station of the space lanes, the Outworld Traders Base had been set up to accommodate transient servicemen on their way to and from assignments. It had the calculated comfort of a leave post, combined with the impersonality of a space port caravansary, that very impersonality a goad to flight if one had an uneasy conscience.

In the reception lounge of the assignment officer, a young man was seated in an easy rest which embraced his lanky body with an invitation to relaxation he plainly did not accept. One brown hand moved across the breast of his garnet red dress tunic. A twinge of pain followed that faint pressure. He would carry more than one scar for the rest of his life reminding him of his failure at his first post.

Only a stubborn spark of rebellion far inside Kade Whitehawk still insisted that he had been right. He frowned at a wall he did not see and freed himself from the foam cushion with a twist of his shoulders, planted his boots squarely on the floor, again baffled by a contradiction he had been facing for days. Why *had* the Service tests assigned him to outpost duty when he manifestly could not emotionally adjust to meeting Styor arrogance with the necessary detachment and control?

Service tests were supposed to be above question, always fitting the right man to the right job. Then why hadn't it been clear that one Kade Whitehawk, Amerindian of the Northwest Terran Confederation, under the right provocation would revert with

3

whirlwind action to less diplomatic practices of savage ancestors and handle a Styor lordling just as that alien's decadent cruelty demanded?

What if the tests were not infallible? Blind faith in them was a part of the creed of the Service. And if the tests could so misfire, what about the sacrosanct Policy?

Kade's hand balled to a fist on his knee. That Policy of neutral coexistence with the Styor rasped, or should rasp, every Terran. Suppose one could challenge the Policy, upset the Styor rule somewhere along the Star lanes and make it stick! Given a chance at the right time—

"Whitehawk!" The metallic voice of the call-box hissed the whisper through the lounge. He stood up, jerked his tunic smooth, and tramped into the next room to face a man who displayed no signs of welcome.

"Whitehawk reporting, sir."

Ristoff regarded his subordinate with detachment, his broad face impassive. Just so did Kade's own tribal elders confront an offender.

"You realize, of course, that your recent actions have thrown grave doubt on your eligibility for reassignment?"

"Yes, sir."

But I wouldn't have been called here, Kade thought, if that first official verdict had not been set aside. I'd already have been shipped out on the transport which lifted for home yesterday. Which means something has changed!

"We can not prevent the rising of emergencies." Dislike, cold and deadly, underlay those formal words. "And sometimes our hand is forced. A mixed Team on Klor has just lost one of its members by an act of violence. As you are the only one of your race unattached on Lodi at the moment, we are obliged to send you. You understand that this is a concession almost without precedent, considering the charge against you, Whitehawk, and that any future mark on your record will mean immediate dismissal, perhaps further proceedings under our charter?"

"Yes, sir."

Mixed Team! That was a jolt. Mixed Teams were special. Why, with his record smeared apparently past redemption, had he been given a mixed Team status, even temporarily?

"You will ship out at fourteen hours on the *Marco Polo*, with a personal kit not to exceed one shoulder bag. The Team has been established dirt-side five months now and are fully supplied. And, Whitehawk, just one more mistake and it may mean the labor gangs for you."

"Yes, sir."

Of course, mixed Team work was dangerous. Kade wondered if they used such duty as a form of discipline now and then. Exile and possible execution in one? No, Team responsibilities were too important to suggest they were a disposal for the unwanted. Mixed Teams were sent to open up trade on those primitive planets ruled, but not colonized, by the Styor; undeveloped worlds with native races held in peonage by the alien lords.

Kade thought about the Styor as he sorted gear in his quarters, trying to be objective, not influenced by his personal dislike for the aliens. Physically they were humanoid enough to pass at least as cousins of the Terrans. Mentally and emotionally the two species were parsecs apart. The Styor had built their star empire long ago. Now it was beginning to crack a little at the seams. However, they still had galactic armadas able to reduce an enemy planet to a cinder, and they dominated two-thirds of the inhabited and inhabitable worlds.

So far their might could not be challenged by the League. Thus there was an uneasy truce, the Policy, and trade. Traders went where the Patrol of the League could not diplomatically venture. In the beginning of Terran galactic expansion some Styor lords had attempted to profit by that fact. Traders had died in slave pens, been killed in other various unpleasant ways. But the response of the Service had been swift and effective. Trade with the offending lord, planet or system had been cut off. And the Styor found themselves without luxuries and products which had become necessities. Exploiting the wealth of worlds, they needed trade to keep from stagnating, and to bolster up their economic structure—the Styor themselves now considering such an occupation below their own allowed employments of politics and war—and the Terrans were there to be used.

With an inborn belief in their godship, and weapons superior to any possessed by the Terran upstarts, the Styor continued their empire. Styor lords dealt with any rebellion by a subject race drastically. Believing themselves invincible, they tolerated the Terrans.

But fire smoldered, never quite dying into ashes. Let one subject world make a successful resistance—Kade detoured about a mound of crates on his way to the ship pickup platform. He caught the pungent reek of animal odor and glanced at the contents of the nearest, making out a furred ball three-quarters buried in soft-pack. The prisoner of the cage had already been needled into sleep for the take-off, but it was plainly live cargo, and Kade was surprised. Not many shippers could afford the high rates for animal cartage across the star lanes.

Aboard the *Marco Polo* he found his own cramped cabin, endured the discomfort of take-off impatiently. When free to shuck his acceleration straps, he reached eagerly for the portable tape reader which could supply him with all the Terran information on Klor.

The instructive sequence of pictures crossing the palm-sized screen absorbed him. This was an encyclopedia of knowledge stripped to the essentials. As he studied, Kade was teased by an odd sense that something in this combination of history, geography and trade lore was hauntingly familiar. But he could not single out any fact he was sure he had known before.

Along his spine crept that chill which warns the fighting man of an ambush ahead, one no other sense has disclosed. Yet there was nothing more dangerous on Klor, as far as these records went, than on half a dozen other frontier worlds he could name.

The man whose place he was filling—how had Rostoff put it?— "Lost by an act of violence." Kade considered those stilted words. Had the Styor played one of their old tricks? No, a Terran's death at the hands of the Styor could not have been kept a secret, in spite of all hush-hush precautions. Such a rumor would have spread with speed across the whole Lodi base. Act of violence did not mean accident either.

Klor: climate in the temperate zones similar to that of northern Terran continents; three land masses, two lying north and south of the equator in the western hemisphere, and one, long, narrow, shaped roughly like a hook, occupying both hemispheres in the east. The south-western continent was so twisted by volcanic action that the land mass was largely a waterless, uninhabited desert, having no assets to attract the Styor. A handful of squalid native fishing villages clung tenaciously to its northern tip.

The hook land of the east was the most important to the Traders. Though there was a spine of sharply set peaks running diagonally the length of the continent and those peaks conventionally equipped with a fringe of foothills, the major portion of the land consisted of grassed plains. In fact, that section bore a fleeting resemblance to the ancient maps of his own home before the atomic wars had ended one civilization and allowed the return of his own race from backwaters of desert and mountain land where they had been driven earlier by the encroachment of a mechanized culture which had at last blown itself out of existence. The plains of Klor stirred ancient racial memories in Kade.

About halfway down the spine of the main mountain range, but set in the level country, was the Terran Trade Post. Its site marked a mid-point between the two major Styor centers. One housed the giant smelter-producer of kamstine, the other, Cor, the administrative headquarters for the whole planet. The rest of the country was carved into strips and patches which were the individual holdings of the lords. But Klor, except for the mines which were counted as personal holdings of the Emperor, was not rich picking. With the possible exception of the High-Lord-Pac, the aliens in residence on this frontier planet would be men of new families, or failures sent into limbo by clan exile, men under a cloud at home.

Terra's import was not kamstine, they had no use for the stuff, but fur. Those jagged mountains, showing their dull gray rock bones through patches of ochre vegetation, were honeycombed with caves, and most of those caves harbored musti in seemingly inexhaustible flocks.

There were bats of Terra whose silver-silk fur, had it been in sizeable skins, would have excited the trades with their beauty. But a pelt only fingers wide had no value. Man prospected the stars before he discovered the musti. Like the bats of his home world, the leather-winged flyers of Klor were nocturnal, but their wings had a spread of ten feet and the furred bodies they supported were in proportion. The fur was silky, with a delicate ripple-wave, or, as with the musti of the upper heights, a short spring-curl, shaded in color from the silver-grey of Klorian rock to the dark blue of her night sky. And one season's catch could raise the leave-pension bonus of a Trader to an upper-bracket income.

Musti were hunted by the Ikkinni, the natives. Each Styor lord had as many Ikkinni slaves as he could capture in the mountains or buy from a professional slaver. Kade pressed the repeat button on the reader, studied the image which appeared on the screen.

Humanoid, yes—but certainly X-Tee—although more alien physically than the Styor who argued by that premise that the Ikkinni were mere animals. And certainly in contrast to their oppressors they were weirdly different.

The specimen on the viewer was perhaps Kade's height, but the length and slenderness of arms and legs gave an illusion of added inches. Body and limbs were covered with fine, long black hair through which white skin showed pallidly. The hair was heavier on shoulders and chest, rising on top of the head into a peak of coarser, stiffer growth. On the cheeks and chin the sprouting was a soft down from which a hard beak of nose protruded in a bold curve, overshadowing the rest of the features. A wide, seemingly lipless mouth was a little open, and teeth, certainly those of a carnivore, matched the skin of whiteness.

For clothing the native wore a sash-like length about the hips, the ends brought between the legs and drawn through the front band, to hang free to knee level, the material a tanned hide. But the collar about the native's neck proclaimed his slave status.

About three inches wide, that article fitted smoothly to the flesh, and Kade knew that its presence doomed the unfortunate Ikkinni to the lifelong servitude from the moment it was welded on. For that band was a guard, a taskmaster, a punishment in turn, by the whim of the Styor owner. Impulses broadcast miles away could transmit jolts of pain, or killing agony, to the slave. One could not escape by running.

Before the coming of the Styor, as far as the Terrans could learn, the Ikkinni had lived in loosely governed tribes, mostly in collections of two or more family clans. Intertribal war had existed, usually as a means of obtaining new wives or raising the prestige of the competing tribes. They had been wandering hunters, with the exception of some coastal fishermen and a handful of families who had settled in the highly fertile river bottoms to plant and harvest fruit and grain.

The farmers had been the first victims of the Styor aggression, the hunters retreating after a series of disastrous skirmishes into the mountains where freak air currents prevented the use of Styor air-craft. Slavers still led raids into those vast mountains and trapped Ikkinni with the same dispatch as the natives in turn netted the musti of the caves.

Kade noted the two spears and coiled net that the primitive in the tape scene carried. They were no defense against a blaster, a needler, or the supposedly innocuous stunner allowed Terran Traders on Styor-held worlds. And without any effective weapon, what chance had the poor devils ever had?

The Terran's hand had gone to the grip of the weapon riding on his own hip before he realized where that line of thought led. Tadder could happen all over again. He was thinking in the same pattern which had led to his disgrace there. Traders did not meddle. At the slightest hint of any involvement with local affairs outside the strict bounds of the service duties, their commanding officer shipped them back to base. He must remember. Remember and control his temper and instincts.

Kade adjusted the reader, called into being on its screen the list of Team personnel. Not that he could hope for any backing from those veterans if he blasted off orbit a second time.

"Shaka Abu, Commander." The click of words introduced his new superior officer. An Africo-Venusian, tough-looking, the slightest tinge of gray showing in his head lock. Perhaps not a particularly successful man or he wouldn't still be a Team leader in the field, but rather would occupy some position of greater authority at one of the sector bases.

"Che'in Lan." Younger, placid, something self-satisfied in his sleepy-eyed face.

"Jon Steel."

Kade curbed a start of surprise as he viewed the picture of not just a fellow Amerindian, but one, by the faint touch of paint between his brows, of the Lakota; a tribesman of the Sioux! This must be the man he replaced, the one who had died by violence. No team had more than one representative of any Terran race.

"Manuel Santoz." Kade hardly glanced at the last man on the list. He was too intent on Jon Steel, who had died on Klor. Again that sensation of a waiting trap. There were too many coincidences in all this.

Sure, many Armerindians were enlisted in the Service, the adventure of out-world duty was welcomed by the youth of the Federation of Tribes. But there were twenty or more of those tribes with numerous subdivisions. For a Lakota to replace a Lakota seemed hardly to come about by chance alone.

And Ristoff, because of his position, must have known that to send Kade to take the place of a dead tribal brother was to unleash an avenger. Or was this sequence of events a new and stiffer testing set up on purpose? If Kade followed the dictates of tribal custom and made trouble on Klor, then Ristoff would have him, space cold.

He slid his stunner from its holster, checked the charge now activating that side arm. The weapon could not kill, not with the diluted energy issued to Trade men, but it could knock an enemy insensible, to be dealt with in a more fatal fashion when and if opportunity offered.

However Kade had learned one lesson on Tadder: the need for caution. In the old, old days his kind had had a standard to measure skill and courage. One entered a hostile camp and exited again unharmed, undetected, bringing along an enemy's favorite war mount into the bargain. He'd play his own game. If Ristoff had set up a frame for some murky reason, he'd learn the why of that, too. Again there was that chill along his back, almost as if a coup stick had thudded home. And not a friendly one, no, not a friendly one at all!

When the *Marco Polo* broke out of hyper over Klor, Kade knew all the Terran records could tell him about that world. He could trace an accurate course from the most detailed maps available to the Traders, which included the musti hunting grounds in the mountains. For the Styor allowed hunting passes for periodic inspection of the trapped caves, to make certain that one section was not being denuded of breeding-stock. Such details were beneath the attention of the local lordling whose income might depend upon the result of a season's net work in the caverns.

In addition, the Terran had added to his storehouse of facts all points dealing with the Ikkinni, although limited, since the Styor did *not* encourage any anthropological research on the part of off-worlders. And he had tabulated his own findings concerning the methods and manners of the Styor, together with any modifications of those as listed by Terran observation on Klor. He had no idea of what lay ahead, save that the problem of Jon Steel's death was part of it. But in some way the doubts he had had in the waiting lounge on Lodi were backing his determination to do some investigating on his own.

He might have guessed that that was not going to be too easy, Kade thought a twenty-seven hour day later when he did at last have a measure of privacy. With a small staff, every member of the Team had been engaged in high-pressure work seeing to the disposition of the *Marco Polo*'s cargo and the mountain of paper work to be discharged before the transport lifted again. Kade, with only hasty introductions to his fellows, had been so buried in details that after a full day and night on Klor, he still had only a confused impression of post and personnel.

There were Ikkinni porters in service, hired out from their Styor masters. And one of them now stood just within the door panel of Kade's room, his eyes with their ruddy pupils gathering extra fire from the atom lamp, his long fingers hooked into the front of his sash kilt.

"It wants?" Kade asked in the tongue he had learned as well as he could from the Hypo-trainer on ship board.

"It has." The Ikkinni reached back a foot, hooked limber toes about a package and pushed it from corridor to room, showing the usual reluctance of his people to the carrying of burdens. A Styor would have instantly punished that act of rebellion. Kade made no show of knowing the subtle defiance for what it was.

Neither did he move to pick up the packet, knowing that to do so would be to admit inferiority.

"It has where?" He looked carefully beyond the packet lying on the floor. Then, turning his back to the native, he busied himself with placing a pile of record tapes in a holder.

"It has here."

Kade glanced around. The packet now rested on his bunk. Since no one had witnessed the action which had put it there, honor on both sides had been maintained.

"It has my thanks for its courtesy." Deliberately the Terran used the warrior intonation.

Those red eyes met his. There was no change of expression which Kade could read on that down-covered face. With a quick movement the native disappeared through the half-open panel of the door. He might never have been there, save that the packet was on the bunk. Kade picked it up, read the official markings of the Research and Archives Division. Below them was a name: STEEL.

For a long moment he weighed the package in his hand. But the communication was not personal. And officially the contents might well be his business. He smothered a small twinge of guilt and stripped away the wrapping, eager to discover what had been so important that Jon Steel had sent to Base for aid.

Ꮚ★ CHAPTER 2 ★Ꮚ

Sample submitted has the following properties, Kade read in the code-script of the Service. There was a listing of chemical symbols. *It will therefore ably nourish and support Terran herbivores without difficulty, being close in structure to the grama grass of our western continental plains.*

Grama grass, suitable nourishment for Terran herbivores—Kade read the symbols a second time and then studied in turn the two accompanying enclosures, each sheathed in a plasta-protector. Both were wisps, perhaps a finger long, of dried vegetation carrying a seed head. One was a palish gray-brown. It could represent a tuft of Terran hay. The other was much darker, a dull, rusty red, and Kade thought it might have been pulled from roots in the plain stretching away beyond the outer wall of the Klorian post.

So, Steel had sent a selection of native grass to be analyzed. And, judging by the wording of this report, analyzed with a purpose in mind, to see if it could nourish some form of Terran animal life. Why?

Kade pulled down one of the wall-slung seats and sat before the desk, laying the grass on its surface. He knew this must be important. Important enough to be paid for by a man's life? Or did the report have anything at all to do with Steel's death? And how *had* he died? So far, none of the men Kade had met here had mentioned his predecessor. He must get access to Steel's report tapes, discover why a finger-thick roll of Klorian wild grass had been sent to Prime Base for analytical processing.

13

The clear chime of the mess call sounded and Kade unsealed his tunic, tucking the contents of the packet into his inner valuables belt for the safest keeping he knew.

To join any established Team was never easy for the newcomer. In addition Kade knew that Abu had been duly warned concerning his glaring misdeed of the immediate past. He would need strong self-control and his wits to last out the probationary period the others would put him through. And, had he not had this private mystery to chew upon, he might have dreaded his first session with his new Teammates more.

But there was no outward strain in the mess hall where the odors of several exotic dishes mingled. Each man ate rather absently while he dealt with his own newly arrived pile of private message flimsies, catching up with the concerns off Klor which had meaning for him. And Kade was free to study the assortment of Terrans without having to be too subtle in appraisement.

Commander Abu ate stolidly, as an engine might refuel, his attention held by the reader through which a united strip of flimsies crawled at a pace which suggested that either the Team leader was not a swift-sighter, or else that there was enough solid meat in his messages to entail complete concentration.

On the other hand, Che'in's round face betrayed a variety of fleeting emotions with the mobility of a Tri-Vee actor as one flimsy after another flicked in and out of his reader. Now and then he clucked indignantly, made a sound approaching a glutton's lip-smacking, or chuckled, entering all the way into the spirit of his personal mail.

The third man, Santoz, had yet another method. Reading a flimsy selected from one pile before him, he would detach it from his machine, place it on a second heap, and stare at the wall while he chewed and swallowed several mouthfuls before beginning the process all over again. Kade was trying to deduce character traits from the actions of his three tablemates when one of the Ikkinni materialized by the door. Without turning his head Abu asked in the Trade speech:

"It comes. Why?"

"It has concern." But no inflection of that slurred speech suggested great emotion.

"It has concern. Why?"

"The furred thing from the stars cries aloud."

Abu looked at Kade. "This comes under your department, Whitehawk. I understand you have had vet training. That bear is important to our relations with the High-Lord-Pac. Better take a look right away."

Kade followed the native to the courtyard, close to the smaller warehouse where the more valuable trade articles were stored. Now he could hear the whining snuffle of his patient. The cage crate he had seen ready to be loaded at Lodi stood here under the protecting overhang of the warehouse roof, and its inhabitant was not only awake but distinctly unhappy.

The Terran squatted on his heels before the cage to see that the captive was indeed a Terran bear, about half grown, a white collar of fur across the chest showing in contrast to the rest of a dark pelt now linted with wisps of protective bedding.

Any bear shipped off-world would have come from one of the special breeding farms, the docile descendant of generations that had lived with mankind and been domesticated to such cohabitation. But no space trip, even taken in a drugged state, could have left the animal anything but nervous. And the captive in the cage was decidedly woebegone.

At Kade's soothing hiss the animal crowded closer to the restraining bars, peered at him, and uttered a whine, low pitched and coaxing.

The Trader read the label sealed to the top of the shipping cage. The bear was consigned to the High-Lord-Pac himself. No wonder it was necessary to see that such an astronomically expensive shipment arrived in the best condition. Kade fingered the lock, eased the front to the pavement of the courtyard. He heard a stir behind him, guessed the Ikkinni had lingered to watch.

Would the distinctive, strange body odor of the native have any effect on the bear? Kade motioned with one hand, hoping that the Ikkinni could properly interpret the order to withdraw.

Even though the cage was now open, the bear hesitated, pacing back and forth as if still facing a barrier, and whined.

"Come, boy. Soooo. There is nothing to be afraid of," Kade coaxed. He held out his hand, not to touch but to be touched, to have that black button of a nose sniff inquiringly along his fingers, across the back of his hand, up his arm, as the bear, as if pulled by a familiar scent, came out of the cage.

Then, with a sudden rush, the animal bumped against Kade, sending the man sprawling backward as the round head drove against his chest with force enough to bring a grunt of protest out of him. The Terran's hands went to the bear's ears as the moist nose, a rough tongue met his chin.

"Now, boy, take it easy! You're all right."

The man squirmed free of that half embrace, found himself sitting on the pavement with three-quarters of a heavy body resting on his thighs. Then he laughed and scratched behind the rounded ears. There was nothing wrong with this particular specimen of Terran wildlife except loneliness and fear. He fondled the bear and spoke to the hovering Ikkinni.

"Has the furred one from the stars eaten?"

"It gave the furred one food. But the furred one did not eat."

"Bring the food again."

Kade sat on the stone watching the round head bob, listening to the slurp of food disappearing as the bear now greedily dug into the contents of a bowl.

"The furred one wears no collar."

Kade glanced up. The Ikkinni's right fingers swept along his own haired shoulder inches away from the badge of his slave state.

"Only the one it was born with." Kade touched the white markings on the bear's dark coat.

"Yet the furred one obeys—"

The Terran understood the puzzlement behind the other's half-question. There were animals in plenty beside the musti known to the natives of Klor, but none were domesticated. To the Ikkinni a beast was either to be hunted for food, fought for protection, or without value at all, and so to be ignored. There were no dogs on Klor, no cats to guard a hearth, no horses—

No horses! Kade's mind caught at that, a faint glimmer, something—but he had no time to pursue it. Abu came across the courtyard.

"Everything all right?"

"Yes. Just a case of homesickness, I would say." The younger man got to his feet and the Ikkinni faded out of sight. Having finished licking his supper bowl the bear sat back on his haunches, rocking a little, round nose up to test new scents.

"What's a bear doing here anyway?" Kade asked.

"A new toy," the Commander snorted. "The High-Lord-Pac Scarkan is organizing a private zoo. It was Steel's project. He brought an assortment of animal tri-dee shots and showed them to Scarkan the last time he went to Cor for permit renewal. New things always enchant the Styor, but the enthusiasm probably won't last, it seldom does." Abu regarded his new Team recruit shrewdly, "Unless you can keep him stirred up to want some more. We won't transport elephants, remember. And no animal that cannot adapt to Klor."

The report on the grass made sense now. Steel had had another sale in mind when he had asked for that. Deer? Cattle? Some animal decorative enough to hold jaded Styor interest.

"If I could see his report tape," Kade ventured.

"There's one thing, Whitehawk. If you do deal directly with the Styor—" The Commander left that sentence hanging unfinished though Kade could provide the missing words. Dealing with the Styor, considering his past record, might be out of the question. He shrugged.

"You said it yourself, Commander, animals have been my special training. I can work up the sales pitch, let someone else deliver it."

Abu unfroze. "Fair enough. And, since animals are your business, you'd better take trap duty on the next expedition. Give you the lay of the land and break you in at that same time. Come along."

When Kade followed, the bear shuffled behind him. Abu glanced around once but did not suggest that the cage was a more fitting place than the corner of the room into which he led the younger man. Then both forgot the animal as they turned to the maps on the walls.

"We lease our hunting teams from three different lords. It makes for competition and prevents any monopoly of funds. And we rotate leases every other year, which spreads the credit around even farther. The locals may growl about the system, but the High-Lord-Pac agrees. He gets his cut as export duty regardless, and he doesn't want any other lord getting too prosperous."

"Some local trouble?"

"No more than usual. They're always trying to build up their own blast power at the expense of their neighbors. This is a scrap world where every district lord dreams of making a good run so he can emigrate into a bigger game elsewhere. It's the High-Lord-Pac's duty to keep the winnings fairly even—or that's the idea. Sometimes the scheme doesn't work. But so far on Klor there've been no favorites. Anyway, we take the hunting teams out in rotation, and Smohallo's is next. He's got a head tracker who's really expert, an Ikkinni of the Cliffs—"

"*A live one!*" Kade recalled his indoctrination on the *Marco Polo*. Of all the free natives on Klor the Cliff colonies of the highest and least accessible mountains were the hardest to enslave and had offered the Styor the most cunning and effective resistance.

"Yes, a live one. And Smohallo knows his value too. He's been offered what is equivalent to a small fortune for the fellow. Anyway, he put a double thick collar on the poor brute, and so is safe in working him even in the outback. He has a breed from Tadder for his Overman." Abu pulled at his long upper tip with thumb and forefinger. "Lik's a nasty blot on the landscape, but he's Smohallo's right hand and probably about two fingers on the left into the bargain. You'll remember that, Whitehawk."

The words were not a threat, just a stern reminder of fact, a fact which Kade must swallow. His outbreak on Tadder would undoubtedly continue to follow him for years to come.

"I'll remember," he replied shortly.

"So there'll be this tracker, Lik, and six net men, all from Smohallo's estate. You'll take one Ikkinni from here as carrier. Keep clear of Lik. He knows that the count sheet is your work, but because you're new, he may try to run in some half-growns."

Kade nodded. An old practice. To befool the Terrans was the hope of every Styor employee, openly expressed, of every Styor Lord, not so publicly admitted.

"You'll try new ground up north, into this district," Abu traced a map route with the nail of one dark finger. "Lik'll have a sonic which will ward off any attack by lurkers or animals. You may run into a slaver up there. If so, keep your eyes and ears shut and look the other way, understand me!"

"Yes." But he didn't have to pretend to like it, Kade added silently.

"They may be in tomorrow. In the meantime," the Commander went to a file, brought out a disc of tape. "Here's Steel's report. If you can get any ideas from it, they'll be welcome." It was plainly a dismissal but Kade did not leave. Tossing the disc from one hand to the other he looked straight into the harsh face of the other man.

"How did Steel die?"

"With a spear through his middle." The answer was curt.

"Wild Ikkinni?"

"It would seem so. He was out on a trapping trip. There is reason to believe that lurkers were in the neighborhood. So we reported officially."

But you don't believe it, Kade returned silently. And you're just as hot about it as any Lakota. He did not say that aloud for he guessed that the Team Commander was walking very quietly and cautiously along a path which might be mined. Every intonation in the other's voice suggested that. Yes, there was something wrong on Klor, and more than just the usual brutality and tyranny of the Styor.

As he tolled the bear back to its cage, a shadow moved. In the faint reflection of light from a window Kade saw an Ikkinni rise to his feet, wait for the Terran. Perhaps the courtyard watchman.

"It has waited."

"So? Why?" Kade led the bear into its quarters.

"To ask why does that animal which wears no collar answer to the words of the starwalker?"

"Because in the world of the Starwalker there is—" Kade sought for a word for friendship, could recall none in the limited trade language and substituted the nearest possible phrase. "There is a common night fire."

The bear whined, pawed at the barrier now between it and Kade. Kade made soothing noises and the animal curled up in the thick bedding.

"A common night fire for starwalker and furred one," the Ikkinni repeated. And then, with apparent irreverence, added, "It is Dokital."

Kade stood still. It took him a second to realize that the native had told him his name. His knowledge of the Ikkinni was limited to what he had learned from tapes. And he didn't know how to interpret this unusual confidence. Now he must feel his way.

"Swift is the spear arm of Dokital," he improvised. "It is Kade." He judged that his first name would mean more to the native.

"There is no spear in its hand," the words poured swiftly from the patch of darkness into which Dokital had stepped. "It wears a collar. It is no longer a man of spears." There was a note in that which brought an instant reaction from Kade.

"Swift is the spear arm of Dokital," he repeated without any emphasis, but firmly. Only that shadow in the shadows was gone. He stood alone by the bear cage.

A shadowy Ikkinni moved through the Terran's dreams that night and he awoke feeling stupid and thickheaded. But he applied himself doggedly to the study of previous trapping reports, striving to add all he could to his general knowledge before he went to the practical testing of the field.

He saw Dokital sweeping in the court, trailing in and out of warehouses pulling the supply carts. However, since the native ignored him, Kade made no move to speak to the other. There were quite a few leased slaves at the post. Kade counted more than a dozen throughout the day, and to them the Terrans paid no attention, except to give an order or two. He did not see any Overman and mentioned that fact to Che'in at lunch.

"Yes, we do not see Buk too often. He has a liking for cabal smoking and so keeps his quarters, except when he gets the signal for a Styor visit here. But that fact works to our advantage. Buk draws his pay and doesn't stir himself, we have no trouble with the Ikkinni, and the Styor get their lease credits on time. What they don't know doesn't hurt. Well—It looks as if I spoke a little too soon. There is the post Overman now."

He waved at the viewplate which afforded them a view of the courtyard. A corpulent humanoid, his yellowish skin stretched in a greasy band over a wobbling paunch, was standing beside the bear cage inspecting its occupant in bemused surprise. As all the Overmen, Buk was a half-breed, probably from Yogn, Kade decided. His hairless head had three horn-like bumps across the forehead, and his sharply pointed chin retreated as thick wattle of loose skin into his big neck. His scanty clothing—tight breeches, high boots, loose sleeveless vest—was a travesty of Styor hunting clothes, and he wore the long knife of an underofficer strapped tight to his left thigh. On the whole he was an ugly looking customer, until one saw the slight lurch with which he walked, noted the cloudiness of his pale eyes, and knew he was rotted by cabal addiction—but still to be counted dangerous if he had the advantage in an encounter.

The same gong which usually marked the passing hours at the post now rang a deep toned note and Che'in pushed back his stool.

"Visitors," he informed Kade. "Maybe Smohallo's come along with his gang to see what the *Marco* landed. They're always eager to get something new from off-world to show off first and there's a Dark Time Feast due in about a week where all the local brass will strut."

The Trade Team assembled in the courtyard, wearing red dress tunics, but also stunner clips in their weapons. Out-world Trade was not a collection of natives to be bent to Styor whims. And while the fact was never allowed to come to a test, both sides recognized it.

A second note from the gong was answered by a rasping squall which bit at Terran eardrums. Abu signalled and the force barrier guarding the post flashed off, to disclose an approaching party of some size. The Ikkinni with the nets were, of course, the hunters supplied to the post. Four more slaves pounded along at a trot, carrying on their bent shoulders poles supporting a small platform on which sat crosslegged an Overman who must be Lik. Yes, his big frame and handsome but cruel features were reminiscent of Tadder.

There came a line of Ikkinni bearing burdens, and behind them an elaborate half-curtained carry-chair in which a Styor lounged, his delicate, almost feminine features masked to lip level by a strip of gemmed lizard skin which matched the crested headdress he wore. He played with a needler, the most deadly side arm among the stars. His dress was the semi-military one of a reserve soldier though nothing about him suggested that he had ever seen service with the Fleet.

The Ikkinni hunters entered the courtyard, backed against the wall, their chests heaving with the exertion of their pace. Lik arose from the seat and stood watching the Terrans insolently, his thumbs hooked in his belt, his fingers playing about the edge of that control box which could lash out swift pain to any of the collared natives about him.

Abu stepped forward no more than two paces. That, too, was

correct. The post was Terra, here Smohallo was a guest and, in a measure, an equal, which fact most of the Styor tried more or less successfully to ignore. Kade, who had been watching the entrance of the local lordling, suddenly noticed a slight movement on Lik's part. He did not quite touch the hilt of his thigh knife, but there was the murderous wish to do so mirrored for a hot instant in his eyes.

And the Tadderan breed had been looking at Kade in that moment. The Terran's own hand dipped so that the grip of his stunner fitted neatly and comfortably into his palm. But that half-challenge occupied less than a second of time. Lik's eyes slid past Kade, were now fixed with wonder on the bear cage.

❂★ CHAPTER 3 ★❂

KADE TOPPED THE SMALL RISE, stood for a moment in the pull of a wind which held some of the damp breath of peak snow. Ahead the line of Ikkinni hunters trotted, heads down, shoulders hunched, followed by Lik, this time on his own two feet. They were striking up a valley which narrowed into a gorge, a tongue of plains land licking into mountain territory. Another few Terran miles, perhaps by midday, and they would reach the end of the known country, heading into wild lands which had not been before prospected by the musti trappers.

Even in this place the grass growth was calf high. By midseason it should reach well up a man's thigh. The grass equaled the grama covering of the Terran plains. Why had that been so important to Steel? Kade had had no chance to check the other's report tape before leaving the post. But there was one fact he did know, that Steel had been on just such an expedition as this when he had been found with an unidentified Ikkinni spear through him. Only last night Lik had made reference to that happening, had suggested the folly of any Terran leaving the hunting camp or wandering from the party on the march.

"These animals," the Overman had indicated his charges with a hooked thumb. "We can make them squeak to our piping." He patted his belt control. "But the lurkers in the mountains. Unless a man has a sonic, he is easy meat for them, never seeing his death until he has swallowed it."

23

"I thought all hunting parties were equipped with sonics," Kade observed.

"That is so. But such is the property of the Overman. Should one wander away too far—" Lik made a gesture like a Terran shrugging off the responsibility for such folly.

"I am warned." Kade had kicked his bedroll to the left, well away from Lik's vicinity. As he unsealed his sleeping bag he heard a faint rustle in the grass, guessed rather than saw Dokital had bedded down with the same avoidance of the Overman. Luckily since the Ikkinni was of the post crew Kade was reasonably sure Lik could not cause the young native trouble without his own knowledge and chance to interfere. Dokital's collar had been triggered by Buk against any run for freedom, but he could not be controlled by Lik's box.

Now, the morning after, the native drew even with Kade. Unlike his fellow slaves he held his head up, his eyes were fixed on the mountain peaks glistening white against the clear sky. Kade considered those peaks. There were three, set almost in a straight line, or so it appeared from the point where they now stood. And the Terran noted that their outlines suggested figures: Men, muffled in cloaks, folded in wings? He almost could believe that their party was under observation from that quarter, and for no friendly purpose.

"There is a name?" He nodded to the three sky-crowned giants.

"There are names," Dokital agreed. "Yuma, the Planner, Simc, the Netter, Homc, who strikes with a spear." He shifted the band which held Kade's field kit to his shoulders. "They wait."

"For us?" Kade asked on impulse.

"For that which will be." The Ikkinni's head came down, now aping the dull endurance of his fellows. But Kade had caught that half promise. Or was it a threat?

They camped at noon beside a stream which widened to pond proportions. A wiry Ikkinni, who had kept well to the fore all morning and who must be Iskug, the cliff man Abu had mentioned, hooked a fish out of the water. The creature was not scaled. Its rough, warty skin resembled that of a Terran toad, but bright red in color, and it had a spiky growth of hard blue mandibles about a narrow snout. Broiled over a fire it smelled far better than it looked and, feeling confidence in his immunity shots, Kade accepted a portion, discovering that the pinkish meat tasted better yet.

The Terran was alert to every sign of animal or bird life about them, making notes on his wrist recorder of two species of grazers they had sighted that morning, one equipped with a nose horn, the other apparently without any form of defense except fleetness. There were rodent things in the grass, and a flightless, feathered bird as fleet as the grazer but twice its size, which Kade was glad had not tried to dispute their passage. The spurs on its huge feet had been warning of a belligerent nature and, when it had opened its bill to squawk at them, he was certain he had sighted serrations like teeth set along the edges there.

But the impression remained that this was a rich game land not overcrowded with inhabitants. The Styor hunted some for sport, the lurkers for food, neither of them making big inroads on the native game. How true that was Kade learned a couple of hours later when they had made their way into the heights.

They had lingered for a breather on the top of a ridge, and ahead was a drift of mist—no, dust rising. Lik turned and two of the Ikkinni hastily moved to give him free passage.

"We stay."

"What is it?'

"One of the big herds of kwitu making the spring passage."

Kwitu, the horn-nosed creatures. But hundreds, thousands of them would have to be on the move to raise such a cloud as that. Lik sat down on a convenient ledge.

"They pass from south to north with the seasons. Sometimes it takes two days for a big herd to get through a gap." He watched the cloud of dust through narrowed eyes. "They head now for the Slit." His fingers went to his control box. Iskug, at the other end of the line of natives gave a convulsive jerk, his hands rising toward his collared throat, but he made no outcry in answer to that unnecessarily brutal summons.

Kade's hand balled into a fist, until he saw Lik's sly amusement spark in his yellow, reptilian eyes. Watch out! Lik might just double his collar pull for the pleasure of making the Terran show useless resentment. Kade's fingers relaxed, he brushed his hand across his hide field breeches, removing a smear of rock dust.

"There is a way into the mountains." Lik was not asking a question of the chief hunter, he was stating a fact. Iskug had better answer in the affirmative or suffer consequences.

"Such a one climbs high," the native's voice was husky.

"Then we climb high." Lik mimicked the Ikkinni. "And at once." He added an unprintable emphasis, but he did not give his guide a second collar jolt.

They did climb, from the back of the ridge, up a higher crown, and then by a series of ledges and rough breaks to the first slope of a mountain. The cloud of dust still hung heavy to the east and Kade thought that now and again the wind brought them a low mutter of sound, the bawling of the kwitu, the clamor of countless numbers of three split hooves pounding along the same ribbon of ground.

Close to sundown the hunting party reached a plateau where a stunted vegetation held tenaciously against the pull of the mountain winds to afford a pocket of shelter as a spring. Kade, kneeling beside the small pool that spring fed, was startled when he raised his eyes to the rock surface facing him. Carved there in deeply incised strokes into which paint had been long ago splashed, was the life-size representation of a kwitu, its broad nose-horned head bent until the pits which marked the nostrils were just above the surface of the lapping water. The unknown artist, and he had been truly an artist of great ability, had so poised his subject that the kwitu was visibly drinking from the lost mountain pool.

Kade sat back on his heels, held up his wrist so that he could catch the image, as it was now suitably lighted by the setting sun, on the lens of his picture recorder. Surely this was not Styor work; the aging and erosion of the stone on which it had been carved argued a long period of time, maybe centuries, since the figure had been completed. Yet who climbed to this inaccessible place to spend hours, days, perhaps months scraping into a natural wall of stone an entirely naturalistic representation of a plains animal drinking?

"Who made that?" His usual dislike for Lik's company did not hold now. The Terran asked his question eagerly as the Overman came down to pour water over his head and shoulders.

The other regarded the drinking kwitu indifferently. "Who knows? Old, of no value."

"But the Ikkinni—"

Lik scowled. "Maybe the animals make hunt magic. This is of no value. Phaw." He pursed his lips, spat. The drop of moisture carried across, to spatter on the rump of the kwitu. Then he grinned at Kade. "No value," he repeated mockingly.

Kade shrugged. No use trying to make the Overman understand. Filling his canteen the Terran tramped back to their camp. He watched the natives, apparently not one of them noted the carving. In fact that blindness was a little too marked. Once again his fighter's sixth sense of warning stirred. Suppose that drinking beast had some symbolic religious meaning? Kade's memory provided bits of lore, that of his own race and others, Terra born and bred. Far back in the mists of forgotten time were the men of his world who had wandered as free hunters, tribesmen who had drawn on the walls of caves, painted on hides, modeled in elastic clay, the shapes of the four-footed meat they wished to slay. And then they had made powerful magic, sending the spears, the arrows, the clubs later to be used in the actual hunting, crashing against the pictures they had fashioned, believing their gods would give them in truth what they so hunted in ritual.

He would not have credited the Ikkinni with the artistic ability to produce the carving he had just seen. But what did the off-worlders know of the free Ikkinni anyway? Their observations were based on the actions of cowered and spirit-broken slaves; on the highly preju-diced comments of masters who deemed those slaves no better than animals. Suppose that practices of that ancient hunting magic would linger on in a remote spot such as this, where perhaps no alien had ever walked? Lik had mocked such a belief in as filthy a fashion as he knew. But sometimes it was not a good thing to challenge the power inherent in things once venerated by another people. Kade had heard tales—

The Terran smiled quietly. An idea, an amusing idea was born from that point of imagination. He would have to know more of those Overman personally. Lik had mocked an old god thing. Kade began to fit one idea to another.

It was Lik himself who gave the Terran the first opening. They had eaten and were sitting by the fire, the Ikkinni banished to a suit-able distance. The Overman belched, dug a finger into his mouth to rout out a shred of food eluding his tongue. Having so asserted himself, he stared at Kade.

"What matter old things to you, off-world man?" he demanded arrogantly.

"I am a trader, to a trader all things which are made with hands are of interest. There are those on other worlds who pay for such knowledge. Also . . ." he broke his answer with a calculated space of hesitation. "Such things are worth knowing for themselves."

"How so?"

"Because of the Power," Kade spoke with a seriousness gauged to impress the other.

"The Power?"

"When a man makes a thing with his hands," Kade held his own into the light of the fire, flexing his fingers slightly so that the flames were reflected from the rings which encircled the fore digit of either hand, "then something of himself enters into it. But he must shape it with his own flesh and not by the aid of a machine." A flicker of glance told him that he had Lik's full attention. The Overman was of Tadder and Tadder was one of the completely colonized worlds long held by the Styor. However, a remnant of native beliefs could still linger in a half-breed and Kade knew Tadder only too well.

"And because this thing has been made with his hands, and the idea of it first shaped in his mind, it is a part of him. If the fashioner is a man of Power and has made this work for a reason of Power, then it must follow that a portion of the Power he has tried to put into his work exists, at least for his purpose."

"This you say of those scratches on a rock?" demanded Lik incredulously, aiming a thumb at the shadows which now enveloped the spring and the carved wall behind it.

"So it might be said, if the fashioner of that carving intended it to be used as I believe he might have done." Because there was a measure of belief in Kade's own mind, his sincerity impressed the alien and the other's scoffing grin faded. "A man is a hunter and he wishes meat to fall before his spear. Therefore he makes an image of that meat, as well as he can envisage it, setting his choice of prey beside a pool where there is good water. And into this picture he puts all the Power of his mind, his heart, and his hands, centering upon his work his will that that prey come to where he had made such a carving, to fall beneath his weapon. So perhaps that happens. Wiser men than we have seen it chance so."

Lik played with his belt. His grin was quite gone. Perhaps he had a thinking mind as well as a driver's callous heartlessness. A bully was not necessarily all fool. But inducing uneasiness was a delicate and precise bit of action. Kade had no intention of spoiling this play by too much force at the start.

"It remains," he yawned, rubbed two fingers across his chin, "that there are those who have a liking for the records of such finds. And I am a trader." He returned the matter to the firm base of a commercial transaction, sure Lik would continue to think of the carving, consider its possibilities, in more than one field.

Kade succeeded so well that the next morning when he went to the pool to rinse and fill his canteen he discovered Lik standing there, studying the carving. In the brighter light of day the kwitu was less impressive, more weatherworn, but the artistry of the conception was still boldly plain.

That unknown artist had left no other trace of his passing or his living on the plateau which had survived the years. Although Kade examined every promising rock outcrop, there was not the slightest hint that anyone had crossed that expanse before their own party, though Iskug took a guide's lead with the assurance of one who knew his path.

On the far side of the plateau they descended an easy zigzag stairway of ledges to the bottom of a canyon where the sky was a ribbon of pale silver-green far above, and their boots gritted in a coarse amber sand which identified a long-dried river bed. Their journey in the half-gloom of the depths took on an endless quality, but when they halted for cold rations at mid-day Iskug indicated a new trail, another climb toward the heights. This was the hardest pull they had so far had and the ascent brought them to another ridge.

A murmur of sound filtered up, and with the noise a haze of dust thick as fog, not yet close enough to torment throats and eyes, hanging in a murky wave about a hundred feet below. Now and then the curtain wavered and Kade could see the bobbing, dust-grayed backs of the kwitu still headed north, filling the slit below from wall to wall, the constant complaint of their bellows echoed and reechoed into a sullen roaring.

From here on their path followed ridge and ledge, gradually descending until the dust hid the road ahead. But Lik did not question Iskug, probably believing that with Lik's control of the collar, the native would not dare to lead them into danger.

They found it easy enough to thread along until they hit the level of the dust. There Lik called a halt, stationing himself behind Iskug, his fingers on the control buttons in warning. Linked hand to hand in a line, water soaked strips of cloth tied over nose and mouth, they shuffled on, the sound of the kwitu loud enough to drown out all other noises. Now and then Kade caught a glimpse of a bull's head tossed high, heard the squall of an out of season calf, louder and more shrill than the plaint of its elders. But for the most part there was no individuality in that live ribbon.

Escape into a side pocket came before sundown. But the dull murmur of the herd continued to be heard as the hunting party made their way back into the mountains. Kade knew that the thousands of migrating kwitu would not halt because of the end of daylight. The animal trek took on awesome proportions and the Terran was duly impressed.

Iskug led them into a basin where there were trees of respectable size and the grass was as lush as on the outer plains. Before the light had quite faded, Kade noted movement to the far end of the valley and turned to Dokital, patiently waiting behind him, for an explanation.

"That is?"

"The kwitu bulls. Old. Bad. Bad here," the Ikkinni tapped his hairy forehead. "No more want female, no want clan brothers. Only want to fight. Bad."

Bulls outcast from the herd, dangerous, right enough. But Lik must have noted them too for the Overman placed the cube of a sonic in the middle of their improvised camp, setting its dial. That guardian devised by the Styor had been adjusted to those it would protect, but any newcomer would be met by sonic blast which would be wall-like in its defense of their party.

Kade awoke in the first pale suggestion of dawn, awoke to instant consciousness. And that act in itself was a warning. Under the flap of his bedroll, he drew his stunner. Then, turning his head slowly, he tried to evaluate the sound which must have alerted him.

There was a crash in the brush, followed by the enraged bellow of a kwitu bull that must have tangled with the sonic shield. Yet Kade could not accept that as what had awakened him. Something more stealthy and from a closer point—He rolled on his side as might a disturbed sleeper. Then his knees were under him and he made his feet, stunner ready.

A flick from the brush cover, and the curl of a lash caught his wrist with force enough to jerk the weapon half out of his grasp. Had Kade not been alert he might easily have been disarmed. Jerking away from that clutch, he caught his heel in the tangle of his recently quitted bag and staggered back, out of the path of sudden and certain death.

For the bellow which he had thought marked the meeting of the kwitu with the sonic protector was not that at all. A horned head thrust through a bush, small eyes red with rage and pain centered on the campsite. A horn dug turf, threw clods over humped shoulders, and a ton of mad anger on four feet plowed directly across the ashes of last night's fire toward the Terran.

Kade threw himself to the left to avoid that rush. He was enmeshed in a tangle of grass and vines and held long enough to see the kwitu stop again to paw and horn the ground. There was not an Ikkinni in sight. And Lik—where was Lik?

The chill of premonition fathered a guess. Steel had died in this wilderness. Now his successor in turn threatened. By chance, or by careful arrangement?

Kade tore his arm free of a vine, snapped a beam-shot at the kwitu. The bull had wheeled for a second charge, moving with an agility which belied its bulk. The invisible ray of force caught it across the top of the domed skull. The result was not unconsciousness for the animal, but a complete break with sanity. At a dead run the kwitu tore straight ahead.

A small tree gave under that blind attack and Kade looked as through a window at the next act of the drama.

Lik stood in the open, a queer expression of surprise and horror distorting his handsome face. He could see the bull coming, but he made no move to avoid the headlong charge of the insane beast.

✦ CHAPTER 4 ✦

KADE SHOUTED, swung the stunner up for a second shot at the bull. But an amazing burst of speed by the heavy animal defeated his hasty aim. The head scooped, tossed. And Lik, big as he was, arose in the air, his agonized cry shrilling above the bellow of the kwitu.

The bull whirled as the Overman hit the ground and lunged again at the feebly struggling man, its hooves tearing through the plains grass. Kade steadied on one knee, the barrel of his stunner resting on his forearm, the strength of the beam pushed to "full" as he fired.

That blast of energy must have caught the kwitu between the small eyes, and the result was the same as if an axe had cracked open its thick skull. It went to its knees, round head plowing forward so that the under jaw scraped along the earth. Then the body struck Lik, bore him along with the impetus of that now undirected charge.

The Overman screamed once again. And his thin cry was echoed from the bushes. Out of one rusty clump an Ikkinni burst free, staggering, his hands tearing at the slave band about his throat, while the violent shaking of other bits of brush told of the agony of his fellows still governed by the control box on their injured driver.

With a groan the Ikkinni fell to his hands and knees, began to crawl painfully toward the tangle of kwitu and Overman. Kade tore at the twisted branches and vines which held him. Before he had kicked loose from that mesh the crawling native had reached the bodies, was pulling feebly at Lik.

32

Kade ran across the trampled ground and the Ikkinni looked up. It was Iskug, his lips drawn tight against his teeth, his eyes holding something of madness in their depths as he fought the pressure about his throat. Kade shifted the limp body of the Overman, was answered by a moan, a faint stir. The broad head of the kwitu rested on the man's middle, the weight of the heavy skull must be pressing directly on the control box.

The Terran wrestled with the bull's head, using the nose horn for a grip. At last he was able to lift it away from Lik. Blood welled from a ragged tear in the alien's thigh. Kade made an examination, using the materials from his aid pack to tend the gore. Lik might also have suffered broken bones or internal injuries, but this was his only visible wound.

Kade heard a whistling gasp of breath. Less than a foot away Iskug lay spent, a drabble of pale, pinkish blood flowing from nostrils and the corners of his now slack mouth. Beneath the down on his cheeks his naturally white skin was flushed to a purple dusk.

The Terran tightened the temporary packing on Lik's wound. The Overman was still unconscious but his breathing seemed better than Iskug's and the off-worlder sat back on his heels, making no move to touch the control box. With a laborious effort the native levered himself up. His ribs heaving as he sucked in great gasps of air. He crawled to the Overman, watching the Terran warily.

Obviously he expected opposition from Kade, but still he was going to make an effort to secure the box. What the off-worlder did then must have surprised the Ikkinni. For he moved, not to defend Lik, but to slide his arm about the hunter's shoulders, putting one hand over Iskug's to guide those hairy fingers to the belt about Lik's middle.

"Take!" he urged.

Iskug's fingers moved, fastened on that belt in a convulsive grip as a shadow struck them both. Dokital knelt on the other side of the prone Overman, went to work on the belt buckle. As he did so Kade saw a loop of rope hanging from the native's wrist, saw, also, the patch of raw skin where too tight bonds had chafed.

"What chanced?"

Dokital pulled the loop off, flung it into the grass.

"It was tied."

"Why?"

"There was a plan. It would not aid that plan."

"A plan for a killing?"

"For a killing," Dokital agreed. "There were two plans. One different from the other."

"And one was made by this one," Kade pointed to Lik. "The other by these." The Terran nodded at the natives.

"That is so. This collar master had the saying of one plan. To kill the starwalker with a bull."

"And the other plan?"

"To let the Planner—" Dokital nodded toward the distant triple peak still visible, "decide who died."

"True spoken." Iskug's voice was a croaking whisper. He sat with the control box tight within the circle of his arm. From the bushes the rest of the hunters crawled or staggered.

Kade watched them warily. He had the stunner, a cross blast of that weapon could bring them all down before they reached him, weak as they now were.

"The Planner decided, the Spearman thrust," Dokital said. He went down on one knee again, slid Lik's knife from its sheath, his purpose very evident.

Kade deflected that blow, sending the blade home in the trampled earth a good six inches from the chest which had been the target. Red eyes smoldered as they met his.

"Will the starwalker take on a blood feud for this one?"

"It does not. But also it would know why a killing was planned."

Dokital pulled the knife from the ground, ran his finger along the clean sweep of the blade. Then from that length of perma-steel he looked to Iskug.

"It has said that these two are not as one," the native from the post remarked.

Iskug fondled the control box. "Let the starwalker break this thing so it and it and it," he pointed to his men, "no longer must crawl at a lifted finger, but may once again walk straight in the sun as warriors."

Regretfully Kade shook his head. To meddle with the intricate control box might mean death for all those so tragically linked with that diabolical thing. He said as much, trying to make it clear.

"This still lives." He stooped to adjust the bandage about Lik's thigh. "It may have an answer to the box."

"Not to go back!" Iskug cried, was echoed by an affirmative chorus from the hunters.

Dokital fingered his own collar. The capture of this control meant no freedom for him. But he did not question Iskug's decision.

Kade asked another question as the Overman moaned.

"And for these?" He pointed to Lik, himself, Dokital.

Iskug hesitated. It was plain that at least two of the three offered a problem for which he had no quick solution. Yet it was also apparent he had no ill will for either Kade or the post native.

"For this," he turned almost with relief to Lik and drew his finger down his chest in a motion which needed no clearer translation.

"Not so. Perhaps it can break the magic of the collar," Kade countered. "The kill was mine," he slapped one hand on the dusty head of the kwitu. "It is mine," he nodded at the Overman whose life he had saved, at least for a space, by that same lucky shot. Whether such reasoning would hold with the Ikkinni he had yet to learn.

Dokital struck in. "It is now slave to the starwalker, taken as in a net."

The justice of that appeared to appeal to Iskug.

"It is broken," he observed without any concern. "So it can not serve."

"But it can talk, as the starwalker has said. Now come wet winds." Dokital gestured at the mountains about them. "We must have fire, cover."

There were clouds massing about the peaks, a fog creeping down to blot out the heights. Even Kade, knowing little of Klorian weather, saw there was a change for the worse in the making. Iskug studied Lik. With very obvious reluctance he gave orders for a litter to be fashioned out of the alien's sleeping bag and saplings from the grove. Hoping that the Overman could survive the handling, Kade got the inert body on the litter with Dokital's aid, and together they were left to carry on at the end of the procession heading for the nearest mountain wall.

By the time the rock escarpment was just before them the hesitant sunshine of the morning had gone and a murk close to twilight settled in. Iskug appeared to have some goal in view. He turned northwest at the edge of the slope and his pace became a trot Kade and Dokital, the litter between them, could not equal. As they lagged behind the Ikkinni dropped back, his impatience plain, to order the hunters to help at the litter poles.

Kade trotted beside Lik. He was sure that he had seen the Overman's eyes open and close again quickly, and he had not missed the movement of the hand groping for the control no longer there. Lik was not only conscious again, but enough in command of his faculties to want to assume leadership of his slaves once more. Yet now he lay once more with closed eyes, the more dangerous for that ability in his present condition to act a role.

The litter bearers passed between two pillars of rock and Kade dropped back. Then the storm broke in great pelting drops of rain, stinging as might pellets of ice against their skins. With a burst of speed they came into the shelter Iskug had sought where an overhang of rock shielded a hollow in the mountain side. The place was not a cave but the roof arched well over their heads and kept out a good measure of the rain.

Kade watched Iskug dig into the gravel at the rear of the hollow, bringing out of hiding an armload of the greasy, long-burning river reed stalks which were the best fire material on Klor. Since there was no reed-bearing river within miles as far as the Terran knew, such a cache meant that there must often be occupation of this shelter.

His own problem was Lik. The Ikkinni had set the litter well to the back of the half cave and left its occupant strictly alone. Iskug still hugged the control box to himself, having rigged it in an improvised belt of trap net against his middle. As far as Kade could see there was no chance of the injured Overman regaining his power. But he was also certain that Lik would try just that. Now the Terran squatted down beside the litter, ostensibly to inspect the other's bandages.

There came a crack of light and sound mingled, slashing down just outside the overhang. Kade started. Then his hand swept around to strike at the wrist above those fingers closing on his stunner. His gaze met that of the alien on the litter with a grim warning.

"Do not try that now."

Knowing that Lik would never accept him as an ally after this small defeat, Kade counterattacked swiftly, hoping to surprise some morsel of information out of the other.

"I am not meat for your killing, Overman!"

Lik's hatred was plain, and now nakedly open in the glare of his yellow eyes. The lips, feline flat against his teeth, were in a snarl of rage. Kade pushed his point.

"Why? Because I am Terran, or because I am I?" He could conceive of no reason for a personal feud between them, though he had disliked the other from their first meeting. Perhaps that instinctive revulsion had been mutual, and carried to an extreme by the alien's temperament.

Lik did not answer. His hands now lay clenched upon his middle where once they had played over the keys of the control and he closed his eyes, his whole body expressing his stubborn refusal to reply.

Iskug's fire blazed, driving out a portion of the damp storm chill with welcome heat. As the hunters gathered about it, their leader placed the control box between his knees, turning it this way and that in the light of the flames. Once he raised it in his two hands as if to cast it into the heart of the fire and from behind Kade heard Lik's small, evil chuckle.

Spurred by that sound the Terran shouted, "No!" Ikkinni heads turned. He added swiftly, "The Overman wishes that!"

Iskug stood up, tucked the control box back in his net sling, came to stand over Lik. Kade saw the alien did not flinch even when a spear pricked his flesh at heart level.

"Strike, dirt eater," Lik's lips shaped a grimace which might have been meant for a smile. "Strike and then guard that box, for it will bind every one of you!"

One of the other hunters came hurrying across, loomed over the wounded alien.

"Make that not so!" He ordered.

Again Lik laughed. "It could not if it would," he retorted, spirit undiminished. "The secret is not its—"

"It may be right," Kade pointed out. "This is a Styor thing. And Lik is not Styor."

The Overman's reaction to that was unexpected. Kade might have struck purposefully at a half-healed wound, bringing again agonizing pain. Lik jerked up on the litter, his fist striking the Terran on the shoulder, knocking Kade off balance so that he sprawled back.

Again those fingers snatched at his holstered weapon, and this time the off-worlder was too late to prevent loss. But he was leaping again for Lik as the alien snapped the beam button. There was no visible answer to that half aimed shot. And a moment later Kade's hold was on the other's wrist, twisting.

As suddenly as he had attacked the other, Lik surrendered, panting under the Terran's weight. And Kade had freedom to see what the stunner had done.

Iskug rolled on the gravel, his face again dusky, his hands tearing at the collar. Beyond him the rest of his fellows were down in the same torture. Then the head tracker gasped, half leaped, to fall back, but he was still breathing. The hands at his throat tugged again at the collar. And under that grip, feeble as it must have been, the band of silvery stuff broke.

He dropped the broken circlet, rubbed his throat with his fingers. Two of the other hunters lay still, one with his knees drawn up to his chest in a silent expression of his death pain. But the others moved sluggishly, almost as if they could not believe they were still living. Each, witnessing Iskug's luck, put hands to their own collars, snapped the bands easily.

Iskug cradled the control box between his hands once again. Cautiously he raised the cube to the level of his ear, shook it with increasing vigor. Then, in his fingers, the thing came apart, showered a rain of crumbled container and small, unidentifiable interior parts. Kade began to deduct what had happened.

Lik had struck that control with the beam from the Terran stunner. And that force thrust had reacted violently upon the Styor mechanism, not only deadening the collars—after one intense, final attack on their wearers—but ending by burning out completely the whole installation. In that same instant that the off-worlder realized the possibilities of the weapon now in his hand, Lik must have followed the same line of reasoning. For the alien lost his head.

He heaved under Kade's hold, fingers gouging and tearing at the Terran's eyes, his teeth snapping as might an animal's on the flesh of the other's forearm. And such was the wild passion of that attack that, for a second, Kade was forced on the defensive. Lik was pounds heavier than his opponent, and much of that poundage was well-developed muscle. Unlike Buk at the post, this Overman had not followed the slothful existence of the usual slave driver. Rather, his hunting expeditions had kept him in good physical condition.

Now, because he had lost all desire for self-preservation, he was intent only on destroying Kade, Kade's knowledge, Kade's suddenly vital weapon. Lik was as dangerous as the kwitu bull. And the Terran sensed that he was now fighting for his life.

He broke Lik's hold on his throat when by lucky chance he drove his knee down upon the other's wound. With a yelp, the Overman twisted, relaxing steel-tight fingers for a moment. Kade brought into play the scientifically taught infighting, part of the Service's training. He made connections with the other's square jaw at just the right angle, rolling away as a spear flashed over his hunched shoulder bit deep enough to send the answering spout of blood up on the breast of his own tunic.

"Why?"

But there was no reason really to ask why Iskug had killed. The Ikkinni was exacting payment for all the months, perhaps years, that he had lived under Lik's control. Now that the box was dead and he no longer needed Lik's knowledge of it, the Overman ceased to exist. But he took with him into the dark the answer to Kade's own questions. Why had the Terran been set up for the kill, and by whose orders?

In return they had the reply to the Styor's dominance on Klor. A drastic remedy though. Two out of seven died to achieve freedom— too high a price. Or did the Ikkinni think that way? Kade found an extra undershirt in his bedroll, collected every bit of the disintegrated control box from the gravel, adding to that the remains of one of the collars, which also crumbled at his touch. The Ikkinni watched him, still massaging their throats. Dokital, his collar conspicuous in that company now, joined the Terran in his task, his long fingers shifting out bits of wire, small wheels, a fragment of what might have been a charge disc.

"This is broken," he commented.

"There are those who perhaps can understand even a broken thing."

"Those in the stars?"

Kade nodded, knotted his improvised bag carefully. "If such is understood, next time there may be no more who die."

"A next time there?" Dokital's eyes were alive, brilliant flames of awakened fire.

"A next time, when we know more, yes." Kade promised.

"The starwalker returns to its kind?" Iskug broke in.

"It returns to the fire of its kind," Kade spoke firmly. He hoped the newly liberated men would not try to hold him prisoner.

"It returns, then hunters come—they who hunt men." Iskug looked stubborn.

"Not so," Kade objected. "It will have a story."

"What story?"

"That there was trouble with the kwitu and much killing by horn and hoof. This is the time of the great trek to the north and there is the storm. The kwitu were maddened by the storm, they came upon the camp where the sonic did not work. All died save it, and it." He pointed to Dokital and himself. "It and it were sleeping apart. And those who have planned for some deaths will be told of others come by ill chance. Who shall say this is not true?"

Iskug considered that. For the first time he smiled, thinly.

"The tale is good for it is mixed truth and careful thought. Who not in the mountains can prove the forked words are not straight? The collar master meant death for the starwalker, so arranged that we leave camp, that the sonic was silent. Then came the death, but not as it was planned. Yes, those," he spat, made a sign of vileness with two fingers, "could believe. And who seeks the dead to wear slave rings? The trail is open." He reversed his spear, driving it head down in the gravel.

"It says this also," he continued. "Discover what that weapon from the stars can do, and then give life to more slave ones. It lays this on you as a fire oath."

"So shall it be, as Iskug says," Kade agreed. He had gained his point, now he was eager to return to the post where he could start to work the affair of stunner against so much from him?

✦ CHAPTER 5 ✦

"BUT WHY WAS THE SONIC OFF?" Santoz leaned across the mess table to ask almost querulously. "Those Overmen know their drill out in the backs. Why, the camp could have been overrun by lurkers."

"Yes, why did the sonic fail?" But when Abu echoed that he was not asking a question of the defensive Kade, rather of the whole Terran Team. "Did you examine it afterwards, ascertain whether it failed through any mechanical defect?"

"You can't tell anything about a machine crushed by an angry kwitu bull," Kade pointed out, treading this conversational trail as warily as he might have lurked on the fringe of a hostile camp. He had had three days during his march back to the post with Dokital to prune and polish his story, working up bits of collaborative detail with the Ikkinni. And he hoped they both had the proper answers for any question which would come from either Styor or Terran.

"Very true," Abu agreed. "And you were asleep when the invasion of the camp occurred."

"Yes." So far he had woven truth into later fiction.

Che'in voiced a faint giggle. "Almost one could imagine," he drawled, "that your young Teammate here was in the greatest danger of all at that moment. How fortuitous, Whitehawk, that you should have awakened in good time. The Spirits of Outer Space would seem to favor you. Also, of course, Whitehawk could not determine, even if he had had it for inspection, whether the sonic was functioning

41

properly. Those are a product of the Styor and so another of the
small mysteries which so tantalizingly spice a Trader's life." He
lapsed into silence, still smiling, a smile which urged them all to
enjoy a subtle joke unnecessary to put into crass speech.

"The sonic's failure had been reported to Cor," Abu remarked in
the tone of one making an official statement.

"Yes, it might almost seem that someone paid a high price for a
bad bargain." Kade tried to needle some response from these three
who certainly possessed more knowledge of Klorian affairs.

Santoz looked baffled, Che'in amused. The reply was left to their
commanding officer.

"We will not go into that." The Commander's retort had the snap
of an order. "The High-Lord-Pac will conduct the investigation. It is
out of our hands, since the dead and missing are not post personnel."

Proper investigation for which side, Kade wanted to ask and
knew that would be fruitless. He got up.

"That is exactly what happened." He caught a measuring glance
from Abu, and was no longer so sure of himself.

"The report has gone to Cor. Undoubtedly we shall hear more."

Again Che'in giggled. "When one digs too deeply into the bottom
of a still pond, one stirs up a quantity of mud," he observed. "And the
High-Lord-Pac is not one to dirty his gloves of justice. Stalemate,
commander?"

"We may be glad for that. You," Abu regarded Kade straightly,
this time with a critical and unsympathetic eye. "Walk softly, my
friend. You will take over the com transmitter. I have a wish for you
to be at hand if your testimony should suddenly be needed."

To tend the transmitter, in a station where off-world messages
were few, might have meant a period of unrelieved boredom. But
Kade brought with him the tape which had been Steel's record, and
sitting where he could see the alarm light above the relay board,
plugged in an ear-reader to hear the words of a man who had been
killed somewhere on Klor—just as he might have been killed four
days ago.

The expressionless words which spun long sentences of trade
detail, descriptions of the country and the natives into his ears were
monotonous, and he had to guess what should have been in the
gaps. This tape had not been edited for a stranger's use, a man's

record was for his own advantage, a reminder of details pertinent to his particular post job. Kade had not expected a concise listing, just a leading hint or two.

He judged by the abundance of notes on flora and fauna that Steel had had a keen interest in the biology of the planet, narrowing eventually to observations concerning the plains vegetation, the kwitu herds, and the mountain valleys.

When those two unusual words were mentioned, Kade did not at first realize their significance. Then he straightened, his swift movement jerking loose the reader cord. Had he really heard that? The Terran thumped the small plug back into his ear, waited tensely for a repeat of that unbelievable phrase. Unbelievable because it had been uttered in another tongue, one perhaps twenty men in the Service, and those men scattered on like number of planets, could have translated.

"Peji equals sunkakan!"

So he had been right! Those two words in Lakota Sioux had cropped up in the middle of a description of a mountain valley Steel had surveyed, planted there perhaps to conceal their importance from any future user of the tape, save one of his own tribe. But had Steel then been expecting trouble, or personal danger? And how could the other have foreseen he would be replaced on Klor by a fellow tribesman. No, Steel must have used that phrase because the words themselves had a strong meaning for him, a meaning connected with his own racial past.

Peji: grass, the grass of the North American plains where Sioux warriors had ruled. *Sunkakan:* horses, the horses which the white man had brought, but which turned drifting primitive hunters into the finest irregular cavalry his home world had ever seen, aided them to hold back an encroaching mechanical civilization for a surprising number of years. Hold back conquerors! Kade pulled the plug from his ear, stared at the com board without seeing one of its buttons or levers.

That was history, and history was repetitious. The Amerindian, mounted, had held back the American Frontiersman, for a time. But earlier he had done something else. He had driven back, almost annihilated an older culture, based on domination and slavery. The Comanche, the Apache, the Navajo, mounted, had pushed their would-be Spanish rulers out of the Southwest, spoiled, removed from the earth the haciendas spreading northward, the mission-held lands, liberating the slave-peons either by death or by adoption into their own savage ranks. The Spanish, secure with their superior weapons, their horses, had crept up into the deserts and plains. The Indians had seen, had taken mounts from the Spanish corrals, had come raiding so that in less than a century, perhaps a half-century, the Spanish wave northward had broken, washed back, been put on the defensive even in the strongholds of Mexico.

The horse put by chance and blindness into the hands of born horsemen!

Had that been Steel's dream too? Feverishly Kade went back to his listening, ran through the whole tape. He was sure now he could pick out hints, that something of that idea had been in the dead man's mind. But only that one phrase was clear. Introduce horses into a horseless world, a world of plains where the grass would sustain the breed. Put the horse into the hands of natives now immured in the mountains. Make of them lightning raiders who could hit and run, darting back into mountain hideouts where the airborne reprisals of the Styor could not follow. A band of attackers who could split into individual riders only to regroup when the danger of pursuit was past, and how could an air patrol cover the scattering of half a troop of men all riding in different directions? Just as the outlying haciendas of the Spanish had fallen one after another to whittling raids, enemies striking without warning out of the plains, so could the lords of Klor, in their widely separated holdings, be victimized by raiders who had at their command a method of swift transportation which was not a machine to be serviced or to lack fuel, which would reproduce itself without any need for technologists or factories.

Kade's enthusiasm grew as his imagination painted a host of details. He believed he saw a way in which the High-Lord-Pac could be used to initiate the Styor downfall. A selection of tri-dees of horses, shown to an alien already enough interested in off-world animals to pay the fantastic fee for the importation of a bear, ought to do the trick.

Kade's enthusiasm grew as his imagination painted a might-be-easy. But horses for the Ikkinni—What proof had he that the native hunters of Klor would take as readily to the use of alien animals as his ancestors had done? Suppose the Ikkinni were neither natural born riders, nor could be made into passable horsemen? And they had no history of domesticated animals, even the dogs and cats which had accompanied his own Terran kind for so long were not to be found on Klor.

Yet Dokital had been fascinated by the bear, had asked about the relationship between it and the Terran. He could try some propaganda on the one Ikkinni with whom he had a tenuous bond approaching friendship.

Since their return from the hunt Kade had avoided the native mainly for Dokital's protection, since Buk, aroused by the death of his co-worker, had thrown off his lethargy and was now playing the slave driver with a harshness Abu did not challenge. Kade sensed that any special notice of the young Ikkinni now would bring him to the unfavorable attention of the Overman.

When at last Santoz came to spell him at the coms, he answered the other's small talk absently, eager to get to his room. But as he crossed the courtyard he caught a glimpse of faint light in a window slit which should be totally dark. And he threw back the door panel, to confront an Ikkinni, hairy back toward him, on his hands and knees beside the wall bunk, striving to open the storage place in its base.

Kade stood still, his fingers flexed not too far from the butt of his stunner. Then, without turning his head, the other spoke.

"It has been waiting."

"And searching. For what?"

"For that which was brought from the mountains." Dokital arose. As all the post slaves he was unarmed, spears issued only for hunting trips. Kade did not believe the other would attack against a stunner or attract a swift vengeance from Buk, but his attitude was far from friendly.

"And what does it want with the remains of the slave box?" Kade came into the room, shut the door panel.

"Buk wears a box also." Now Dokital turned, faced Kade, his shoulders slightly hunched, the look of an untamed thing about him, ready to offer battle if he could get what he wanted. "The starwalker can break the box of Buk, he has not done so. Nor has he given the box which was broken to others." The hostility was now in the open.

"Does it forget what happened when the box of Lik was broken," Kade kept his voice low, fearing that even a murmur might carry beyond the walls. Let a hint of what he had hidden reach Abu and he would be bundled off planet, his career ruined, perhaps a labor gang sentence waiting. And let that same rumor, even distorted, carry to the Styor and it could mean the death of every Trader on Klor, the banishment certainly of the only weapon the rulers allowed the Terrans to handle. "Some died because the box was broken," he tried to impress the native. "Let Buk's box feel this," he tapped the holstered stunner, "and maybe Dokital will be it who this time loses breath."

But the Ikkinni appeared unmoved by that argument. "Better it dies and some live." He held up his fingers and then deliberately folded those of one hand under. "Let this be so, starwalker. Yet still are these free." He wriggled the raised ones vigorously. "To lose breath is better than to run back and forth while Buks says 'do this, do that.'"

"Dokital says so, but will the others here agree?" Kade pointed to the fist of closed fingers. "Has it spoken to them concerning the broken box?"

"Had it spoken," Dokital answered with a deliberate spacing of words which gave a weight beyond their simplicity, "the starwalker might have lost breath—all the starwalkers—so that what they carry could lie here," he slapped the fingers of one hand across the palm of the other. "It waited but the starwalker had not broken Buk's box. Now it will talk, and things shall be done."

Kade slammed the full weight of his body against the Ikkinni, bore the native back to the bunk and held him there in spite of his struggles.

"Listen!" He almost spat into the rage-darkened face inches away from his own. "Buk will be taken at the right time. Move now and the Styor will blast us all into nothingness. Let me find out how the box is broken and perhaps we can move without men dying."

"Time! There is no time left, starwalker. A message comes from Cor. The starwalker is to go to the collar masters. When they discover what has happened it will lose breath and no starwalker can save—"

A message from the Styor city. But he had heard nothing of that.

The Ikkinni might have read the Terran's puzzlement in the slight slacking of his hold.

"It speaks the truth!" Dokital's body arched under his in a last frantic attempt to gain freedom. Then they both froze at a sound from without, a rap on the door panel.

Kade loosed his hold on the native, pulled away from the bunk, edged to the door, his stunner out and centered at a point between Dokital's red eyes.

"Who is there?" he called over his shoulder.

"Buk."

Dokital, still sprawled on the bunk, tensed, his head turning from right to left as if he searched for sight of a weapon he had no hope in finding. Kade gestured imperatively. The Ikkinni slipped to the floor, opened the base storage space and pulled himself into hiding.

The Terran took his time about freeing the thumb lock on the corridor door, waiting to see that space closed. Dokital would have to double up painfully in such a small cranny, but discomfort was better than having Buk discover him here.

To Kade's surprise, the Overman, hesitating on the threshold, made no attempt to look about the room. If he had come hunting a missing slave he did not disclose that fact. Instead his attitude was uneasy and Kade's confidence grew.

"The Overman wishes?" the Terran demanded with chill crispness.

"Information, starwalker," Buk blurted out with little of his usual assumption of equality with the Traders. He slid one booted foot into the room and Kade guessed that he did not want to state his business in the open. The Terran stood aside and Buk oozed in, shut the door panel and set his plump shoulders against it as if to stave off some threatened invasion.

"There is a story," he began, looking none too happy. "Now there are those who say that Lik saw a certain thing by the water and mocked that thing openly, then he was slain by that which he mocked."

Kade leaned back against the end of the bunk. "There was an old, old carving on a rock by the pool," he spoke gravely, "which Lik spat upon and mocked, yes. Then with the next dawn the kwitu which was like unto that pictured by the pool, came and rent him. This is no story, for with my two eyes I saw it."

"And the thing by the pool. Who made it so?" Buk persisted.

"Who live in the mountains, Overman?"

Buk's tongue, thick and a brownish red, moistened his blubbery lips. His fat rolls of fingers played a tattoo on either side of the control box at the fore of his ornate belt. His uneasiness was so poorly concealed that Kade's half plan, shelved at Lik's death, came to life again. Now he decided upon a few embellishments. If Buk was superstitious the Terran could well add to his growing fears.

"I have been asking myself," Kade said, as if he were musing aloud and not addressing Buk, "why it was that the kwitu did not turn horn and hoof on me, for I was easy meat when the sonic failed us. However the hunt was not for me, but for Lik, and he was not the nearest nor the first that the bull sighted. It is true I had not mocked that which was carved beside the pool, rather did I speak well of it, since such old things are revered among *my* people."

"But to believe so is the foolishness of lesser creatures," Buk's tongue made its nervous lip journey a second time. "Such thinking is not for masters."

"Perhaps so," Kade made polite but plainly false agreement to that sentiment. "Yet among the stars many things come to pass which no man can explain, or has not found a proper explanation to fit the circumstances. All I know is that I breathe and walk, and Lik does not, where Lik mocked and I did not. Perhaps this adds to something of meaning, perhaps not. But while I am on Klor I shall be careful not to mock what I do not understand."

"Foolishness!" Buk grinned sickly. "The collared ones can not slay with a picture!"

"Not they, perhaps. But I have heard also of a Planner, a Netter, and a Spearman."

Buk laughed again, but this time there was no mirth in that sound, it was close to the snarl of a rat cornered and knowing fear.

"Rocks! Mountains!" he jeered.

Kade shrugged. "I have told you what I know, Overman. Is this what you would have of me?"

Buk fumbled with the door panel, stepped back into the courtyard corridor, still facing the Terran almost as if he feared turning his back upon the off-worlder. He muttered something and was gone, slouching, his bristly head sunk a little between his shoulders.

Kade slammed shut the panel as Dokital crawled out of his hiding place. For a long moment they eyed each other, but the will to struggle was gone. The Ikkinni whipped out of Kade's room, heading in the opposite direction to the one Buk had taken.

The Terran turned back to his tapes. Since the High-Lord-Pac had purchased the bear for collection there must exist some tri-dee from which the Styor had made his selection. And among them might just be one of a horse. Equines had been exported to a score of Terran colonized planets and should be listed on the Trade tapes.

Only a small portion of his mind was occupied by that search. Dokital's demand for action, Buk's display of superstitious fear, the attempt to murder him by the sonic failure; a hint there, a half-disclosed fact elsewhere—Kade had the breathless sensation of one confronted by a complicated tangle and ordered to have it unraveled within an impossibly short time.

How limited that time might be he learned only a few moments later. Commander Abu came across the courtyard with the news.

"They are sending a hop-ship from Cor to pick up the bear," he announced. "And since the High-Lord-Pac has asked for a report on the hunt trouble, you might as well go along with the transport. Here," he held a box of tri-dees. "We'll suggest to his lordship that, because of the trouble, the Service will be glad to offer him his choice of any of these items. But don't be too blatant. The Styor want their bribes shoved in their pockets around some corner when no one is looking, rather than slapped into an outheld hand."

"You are going, too?"

The other nodded. "Pomp and ceremony," he said wearily. "Commander speaks to planet governor. Oh, check your stunner in before you leave. No one wears an off-world weapon in Cor."

As Kade hurriedly packed his jump bag he had no time to check the box of tri-dees. Nor did he see Dokital when he went to leave his stunner.

When the Terrans reached the landing apron Kade stood aside to allow Abu to proceed him up the ship's ramp. And, as the younger man set foot on that slender link between ship and ground he experienced a sudden sharp pull at his scalp lock. Kade's trained body went into action, falling back at the pull, but not quickly enough to carry his attacker with him. The grip was released and he sprawled clumsily on his back. As he scrambled up he looked around.

There was nothing to be seen, his assailant had vanished. He examined his small twist of hair with his fingers. The tight braid worn by his people was intact, and he could guess no reason for that odd assault at the foot of the Styor ship.

☽.★CHAPTER 6.★☾

COR AROSE ABRUPTLY from the rolling Klorian plain with insolent refusal to accommodate alien architecture to a frontier world. The city might have been lifted entirely from some other Styor-controlled planet and set down here bodily with all its conical towers, their glitter-tipped spearlike crests pointed into the jade sky. Arrogantly, they were not a part of the ochre landscape on which their foundations rested.

Since Styor ships were not adapted to Terran physique Kade had spent most of the trip trying to control a rebellious stomach and screaming nerves. Now he cultivated as impassive a set of features as he could while waiting on the landing strip for the arrival of the bear cage.

Gangs of Ikkinni slaves were at labor, with Overman halfbreeds from half a dozen different Styor-controlled worlds in command. But the lords themselves were not to be seen. The pilot of the ship which had brought the Traders must be of the pure blood, none other ever being given a post of authority. And the Portmaster, invisible in his vantage chamber somewhere in the heights above them, would be Styor.

Kade, seeing no official greeters, knew again the prick of anger at this deliberate down grading of the Traders. The omission of such civilities was more pointed when a slender private-flyer set down half the field away from the freighter and an almost instantaneous swirl of activity there marked deference paid to some outplains lordling.

51

The Terran took tight grip on his temper, promising himself that this time nothing he saw in the Styor stronghold, no insult covert and subtle, or open and complete, would provoke him into answer. The only trouble was, as he knew very well, Kade Whitehawk was not and never would be a proper exponent of the Policy.

Styor traveled in carrying-chairs. Overmen were on platforms, borne by slaves. Terran Traders walked along the canyon-deep avenues of Cor. The polished surface of tower walls flashed, dazzling to off-world eyes. There were no windows to break their lower stories, simply an oval door recessed slightly, always firmly closed, to be sighted here and there. Not a scrap of vegetation grew anywhere about the bases of those towers. But when Kade tilted his head to look up, he could sight indentations masked in green-blue, in green-green, in yellow-green, marking sky-rooted gardens of exotics from the stars.

A protesting whimper from the cage slung between transport poles made known that the bear had again recovered from the journey drug. The Terran jogged forward to speak soothingly. He must not allow the animal to become so thoroughly frightened as to make a bad impression when it met its new owner for the first time, especially not when Kade's purpose was to urge that owner to consider more such imports.

In spite of his discomfort on board the transport, he had examined the contents of the sample box and was happily aware of the presence therein of a certain tri-dee print. He hooked that box to his belt, carrying nothing in his hands. At least in that he preserved a small measure of difference between Terran and burdened slave. The heart of Cor was the Pac Tower. More than one garden feathered its length and the Terrans, together with the bear, found themselves in the highest of those where the foliage was almost that of their earth. The strips of sod which formed its paths could hardly be distinguished from the green grass of their mother world.

Released by Kade, the bear stood in the middle of a small clearing, head up, sniffing. Then, its attention caught by the laden branches of a berry bush, it shuffled purposefully for that lure.

"This is the new one?"

There was no mistaking the slurred voice of a Styor. Into the simplest sentence, Kade thought, the older masters of the star lanes could pack an overabundant measure of arrogance, as well as the ever present underwash of ennui. The Terran turned to face one of the floating chairs, hovering a foot or two above the shaved turf, bearing on its cushioned seat a Styor of unmistakably high rank.

The jeweled, scaled mask of an adult male hid half of the face, and the headdress above that, as well as the noble's robe, was ostentatiously plain. Only the great gemmed thumb ring, covering that digit from base to nail, signified the exalted status of its wearer.

"As was promised, lord," Abu replied.

The chair floated on and the bear, hunched down to comb berries into a gaping mouth, looked up. For a long moment the animal from Terra regarded the chair, and perhaps the man in it, appraisingly. Kade was ready for trouble. He knew that the bear must have been conditioned at the breeding farm for all eventualities which its first owners could foresee in an alien home. But reactions to the unusual could not always be completely prepared for, or against.

Apparently floating chairs, and Styor lords in them, had been a part of the bear's training. It grunted, unimpressed, and then turned back to the more important occupation of testing these new and interesting fruits.

"This is acceptable," the Styor lord conceded. "Let those who have such duties be informed as to the care." The chair made a turn and then stopped dead. The occupant might have been suddenly reminded of another matter.

"There was a report brought to Pac attention."

Kade discovered that an utterly emotionless tone could rasp like a threat.

"A report was made," Abu agreed.

"Follow. Pac will hear."

The chair swept on at a speed which brought the Terrans to a trot. They passed under the arch of an open door, crossed the anteroom of the garden, and came into a bare chamber with a dais at one end, to which the Styor's chair sped, setting down with precision in the exact middle of that platform. And that landing was a signal which brought from two doors flanking the dais, Styor guards, to draw up in a brilliant peacocking of jewels, inlaid ceremonial armor and off-world weapons, between the Terrans and the High-Lord-Pac.

"There was a slaying in the mountains," the ruler of Klor observed, seemingly having no attention for either of the off-worlders before him, his stare fixed upon empty space a good yard or so above their heads.

"That is so, lord," Abu agreed with equal detachment.

"The saying is that a sonic failed."

"That is so, lord," echoed the Terran Commander, adding nothing to the formal words.

Kade, studying the half-masked faces of the Styors before him, especially that of the High-Lord-Pac, experienced anew the distaste which had always been a part of the old, old Terran distrust for the reptilian. Those visors, sharply pointed in a snout-like excrescence above the nose, imparted a lizard look to all Styor. And in the person of the High-Lord-Pac that quality was oddly intensified until one could almost believe that there *was* no humanoid countenance behind the scaled material.

"When the sonic failed, an Overman and some of his hunters were killed by kwitu," the High-Lord-Pac continued in flat exposition. "And after his death several of the collared ones fled to the mountains, his control over them being destroyed."

"The truth is as the great one says."

"The starwalker who was with these hunters, he swears to this?"

"He stands before the great one now. Let the asking be made so that he may reply with his own mouth."

That lizard's snout descended a fraction of an inch. Kade could not be certain whether the eyes behind those gem-bordered slits saw him even now.

"Let him speak concerning this happening."

Kade, striving to keep his voice as precise and cold as the Commander's, retold his story—his edited story. Faced only by the array of masks he had no hint as to whether or not they believed him. And when he had done, the comment upon his version of the disaster came obliquely.

"Let this be done," intoned the noble on the dais, "that all sonics be checked before they are issued for use. Also let the master-tech answer to Pac concerning this matter. The audience is finished."

The chair arose, moved straight ahead as the honor guard hurriedly snapped to right and left offering free passage. Kade had barely time to dodge aside as the Styor ruler passed. Was this all? Would they have no further meeting and a chance to offer the High-Lord-Pac more off-world curiosities?

An Overman guided the Terrans to a room not far above street level, close to the slave quarters. Kade waited for enlightenment as his superior officer crossed the chamber, dropped his jumpbag on a seat which was no more than a hard bench jutting out of the wall. A roll of woven mats piled at one end suggested that this also must serve as a bed when the need arose.

"What now?" Kade finally asked.

"We wait. Sometime the High-Lord-Pac will be in the mood for amusement or enlightenment. Then we shall be summoned. Since we do not exist except to supply his whims, such a time may come within the hour, tomorrow or next week."

Certainly not a very promising forecast, Kade decided. He opened the tri-dee holder and, kneeling on the floor, he set its contents out upon the bench, sorting the beautifully colored small slides. They were so lifelike that one longed to reach into the microscosm and touch the frozen figures into life and movement.

Here were the smaller, long domesticated animals, cats, dogs, exotic fowl, a curved-horned goat, a bovine family of bull, cow and calf. Then came the wild ones—or the species which had once been wild—felines, represented by lion, tiger, black leopard; a white wolf, deer. Kade discarded a bear slide, and eliminated the elephants and the rest of the larger wild kind which could not be shipped this far out into space. Then he took out the last slide of all, balanced it on his palm, examining it avidly. To his eyes it was irresistible. But how would the High-Lord-Pac see it.

Abu had no present interest in the display of trade goods and his continued silence finally drew his companion's attention. The Terran Team Commander got up from the bench, stood now by the door through which they had entered. There were no windows here. A subdued light, dim to their off-world senses, came from a thin rod running completely around the room where ceiling joined wall. But that light was not so dim as to disguise Abu's attitude. He was waiting, or listening, or expecting—

Kade arose, still holding his choice of tri-dees. They were without weapons in the heart of the undeclared enemy's territory. And

Abu's stance brought that fact home to the younger man. When the Commander spoke he hardly more than shaped the words with his lips, using the tongue of their own world rather than Trade talk.

"Someone is coming. Walking."

Not a Styor visitor then, unless a guard on duty. A second later the eyepatch in the door panel glowed. Abu waited for a moment, and then acknowledged with a slap from his open palm directly below the small screen. The light flashed off, they viewed a foreshortened snap of an Overman. Abu slapped a second time, granting admittance.

"Hakam Toph," the stranger announced himself. "First Keeper of off-world animals."

Abu made the same formal introduction in return, naming himself and then Kade.

Toph showed more interest in Kade.

"It is the one who cares for beasts?"

Abu sat down on the bench, leaving the answering to Kade.

"It is," he replied shortly. The Overman was using the speech of an Ikkinni driver, and that in itself was an insult to the Traders.

"This one would know the habits of the new beast."

"A record tape was sent," Kade pointed out. He held up his hand at eye level, apparently more absorbed in the tri-dee he had selected from his samples, than in a sale already made.

And the Overman, catching sight of the array of plates on the shelf, came on into the room eagerly, drawn to the strange exhibits to be seen. Kade, nursing that last tri-dee stepped aside, allowing Toph to finger the small vivid scenes of beasts in their natural setting. The Overman was plainly excited at such a wealth. But at last he began to glance at the plate Kade still held, while firing a series of questions concerning the rest. When the Terran did not put his plate down or mention it, Toph came directly to the point.

"That is also an off-world beast?"

"That is so." But still Kade did not offer him the plate.

"That is one which is rare?"

"One," replied Kade deliberately, "which on our world is and has long been prized highly. It belongs to warriors who ride, by our customs, not borne on the shoulders of men or in chairs of state but on the backs of these beasts. Even into battle do they so ride. And among us the warriors who so ride are held in honor."

"Ride on the back of a beast!" Toph looked prepared to challenge such an outrageous statement. "It would see!" He held out his hand in demand and Kade allowed him to take his plate.

"So." Toph expelled breath in a hiss which might have signified either admiration or contempt. "And warriors ride upon this beast for honor?"

"That is so."

"You have seen them?"

Kade plunged. "On my world I am of a warrior people. I have ridden so behind those who are my overlords."

Toph glanced from the Terran back to the tri-dee plate.

"These beasts could live on Klor?"

"On Klor, yes; in Cor, no." Kade proceeded with the caution of a scout on the war trail, fearing to push too much or too fast.

"Why so?"

"Because they graze the grasses of the plains just as the kwitu. They could not live confined in a wall garden of a city tower."

"But at the holdings they could? One could ride them where now only the sky ships pass overhead?"

Toph was certainly getting the point fast, perhaps almost too fast. But the off-worlder replied with the truth.

"That is so. A lord or the guardsman of a lord could ride across the country without slave bearers or a sky ship. My own world is plains and for hundreds of years have we so ridden—to war, to the hunt, to visit with kin, to see far places."

Toph looked down at the plate once again. "This is a new thing. The High One may be amused. I take." His thick fingers closed about the tri-dee with a grip of possession Kade did not try to dispute. The Terran had taken his first step in his plan, and by all signs Toph was snared. Surely the head animal keeper of the Pac would have some influence with the Lord of Cor, and the acquisitiveness of a zoo keeper faced with a new animal of promising prestige would be a lever in the Terran's favor.

When the Overman left without any further demands for information about the newly arrived bear, his hand still grasping the tri-dee, the Team Commander, who had taken no part in the exchange, smiled faintly.

"Why horses?" he asked.

"This is natural horse country. The plains will support them."

"You will have to have proof of that, an analytical report, before the Service will ship them."

Before he thought, Kade replied, "Steel had that made."

"Interesting," Abu commented. "You found that in his tape, of course. Horses—" he repeated thoughtfully. "They'd come high on import price."

"Too high?"

"For the High-Lord-Pac of a planet to indulge a whim? With all the resources of Klor to draw on? No, I think he can afford them if he wishes to. You might get a reprimand from the ecology boys however."

Kade had not foreseen that angle. To introduce to any alien world a plant, animal, or bird without natural enemies and with a welcoming terrain was a risky thing at best. To Kade the plains of Klor seemed a natural setting for horse herds. They would share those vast expanses with the kwitu, with the deer species, and with the large flightless birds. Natural enemies—well, beside mankind, or Styor and Ikkinni, who should consider horses prized possessions and not prey, there were several carnivores. But none in quantity. Yet that was what he had hoped to see; a horse population exploding as it had on the plains of his own home, unleashing wealth and war mobility for the natives. However, if he had to untangle red tape within his own Service—

Kade was startled by a sound from his superior which was suspiciously like a chuckle.

"A little too soon, Whitehawk. Don't ride your rockets up full blast until you are sure of your orbit! Horses for the Styor. I wonder how the Ikkinni will welcome them. The currents of air keep their lords' ships out of the mountains. On horseback their slavers could range more widely. And I wonder about that, young man. You did not join this Team recommended as a Styor lover. Horses—" He studied Kade as a man might inspect an intricate piece of machinery which he did not understand, but must be able to set working with smooth ease.

"You said to tempt the High-Lord-Pac with something new," Kade said, on the defensive. He had been so full of his idea that he had underrated the Commander, a mistake he could see might be a disastrous error.

"So I did, so I did. And Steel, asking for an analysis, put all this into your mind?"

That was partly true and Kade was glad he could admit it. But he knew that Abu was not wholly satisfied. For the moment he was saved by the return of Toph with an order for them both to attend the High-Lord-Pac.

When they entered the antechamber of the garden where they had earlier deposited the bear, they found the ruler of Klor, his carrying-chair grounded, viewing the tri-dee which a guard held at eye level for his master's convenience.

"Tell of these." The order was passed to Kade.

Using the Trade tongue, the Terran enlarged upon equine virtues, giving what he hoped were vivid and entrancing descriptions of appearance, action, the advantages of horses to be bred and raised on Klor. There was no answering enthusiasm visible in the Styor, though it was plain the waiting Toph was already a convert.

"But in Cor they could not be?" The Styor interrupted.

"That is so. They must have open land."

"And the great ones of your world ride upon their backs with ease?"

"That is the truth." He launched into a description of saddles and riding gear, of the development of cavalry, both as fighting units and as striking and colorful guards for ceremonial occasions.

"These shall be bought," the Styor made his decision in his usual expressionless way. "Also there shall be sent to Cor reports concerning these creatures, other representations of them such as this, or larger." He gave the faintest inclination of head to the plate before him. "All this shall be done as speedily as possible."

Abu bowed. "The will of Pac is the law of the land and sky," he replied with the formal speech. "As the wish, so is the action. Have we now leave to depart from Cor, since we must carry out the will of Pac?"

"Depart and serve."

It was so quickly decided that Kade almost distrusted his success. On the way back to the Styor ship Abu asked some questions of his own.

"Where are you going to get horses in a hurry? When Pac says he wants a thing speedily, he means just that. Horses brought from

Terra will be months on the way, and in quarantine and tranship-
ment as well."

"There are horses, for generations toughened by space hopping,
to be had on Qwang-Khan." Not his horses, the blooded breed of the
Terran plains, but another stock, tough, wiry, inured to new worlds,
developed from ponies which had once carried Tartar horseman not
only into battle, but on treks to challenge the rule of a quarter of the
world.

"You've already done your research on the subject, I see." Abu
again came uncomfortably close to the truth. But to Kade's relief, he
pried no deeper.

۞⋆ CHAPTER 7 ⋆۞

KADE AWOKE with that same feeling of present danger which had instantly aroused him into full awareness in the mountains. Yet behind him was the wall of his room at the post, beneath him the easi-foam of his bunk. He lay, schooling his breath to the even lightness of sleep trying to catch sound or movement.

The window slit giving on the corridor was a lighter oblong against the dark wall. He heard the feather-light scuttle of a hunting "eight-legs" crossing the surface. Then he caught a small sigh of breath released.

Another scurry from the "eight-legs," followed by the faintest of tiny squeaks as the Klorian creature captured one of the furry night moth-things. Then, from the courtyard, the sound of boots; sharp taps, rapping on the door of his senses.

A figure slid along the wall and the brush of passing was clearly audible. Whoever shared his room was almost within reach. He caught a trace of odor and knew that an Ikkinni crouched there, perhaps torn between the peril of the supposedly sleeping Terran by his side and the patroller in the courtyard.

Kade sighed as might a disturbed sleeper, rolled over so as to bring his forearms under him, ready to impel him off the bunk. Again he heard that catch of breath, felt rather than saw ruddy eyes fast on him. He had no idea of how keen Ikkinni night sight was, and he could take no chances. Though the post natives were supposedly unarmed, there were objects within this very room which could be improvised into deadly weapons.

With one hand the Terran drew his stunner from the night pocket of the bunk and threw himself floorward, rolling over, to come up with his back against the opposite wall, the weapon ready. And he heard a flurry of movement from his invisible visitor, movement checked as the other laid hand on the door panel. For outside those parading boots still tapped a message of danger.

Then Kade had his answer to the amount of night sight possessed by an Ikkinni. Before he could move another body crashed against his and a hairy shoulder dug into his middle, driving the air from the Terran's lungs, smashing him back against the wall with a force which half dazed him so that he was helpless against a second attack. A blow on the side of the head crumpled him to the floor, barely conscious, and a second brought with it complete darkness.

"Whitehawk!"

Pain was a red band behind his blinking eyes, a light adding to it. His head rolled loosely as someone tried to pull him up, and he tasted the flat sweetness of blood. Then, somehow, fighting the swift stab of hurt in his head, he focused his sight on Che'in. For once the other Trader was not smiling; in fact a very unusual grimness tightened the corners of his lips, brought into line the jaw structure which lay beneath the soft flesh of his round chin.

Kade's hand went uncertainly to his head and he winced when his fingers touched raw, scraped skin above a welt. They came away sticky red.

"What happened?" he asked huskily.

Che'in's arm slipped behind his shoulder, supported him so that he looked about a room which had been ripped apart. Every cupboard panel was open, forced where they had been thumb sealed. The foam of the bedding frothed through numerous rents in its outer skin, and a trail of record tapes crossed the top of the desk, ending in a confused pile on the floor. The evidence was that of a mad search, a search where the fury of the searcher had mounted with his inability to locate what he sought.

That could mean only one thing—or perhaps two!

Kade fought waves of dizziness as he tried to raise his head higher to survey more closely the debris on the floor about him. His boots were still standing at attention at the foot of the bunk.

And noting they were undisturbed he knew that one secret had been safely kept.

"Stunner!" He cried. "Where is my stunner?"

If his assailant was Dokital and the native had his weapon—Why, an attack on Buk using the stunner might well mean death for half the Ikkinni slaves at the post. And whether that sacrifice was willing or not, Kade must prevent it by telling someone the full story.

Che'in pulled a familiar object from under Kade's leg. And the younger man snatched at it with a second wave of pure relief blanketing out the pounding in his skull for a welcome instant or two.

"I don't think your untidy friend will be back," Che'in remarked. "Have you any idea of what he was hunting for?"

To answer that meant danger of another kind. Again Kade stared at his boots. No one could possibly guess what had been cached in their concealed top pockets. And his head hurt so that his thinking was fuzzy.

"Wait!" Che'in edged Kade's head forward delicately, gently, making an examination, not of the welt left by the blow, but of the other's scalp lock. "So. When your visitor did not find what he wanted—" the Trader's breath came out as a hiss and again all lazy good humor was wiped from his features.

"What's the matter?" Kade put up his own hand, felt for the customary short braid. But his fingers discovered only a ragged tuft left. He had been hastily shorn by the thief.

"Why?" Groggily he looked to Che'in for an answer.

Kade could understand the search for the remnants of the control which was still crumbling to smaller pieces in spite of his careful wrapping of the bits. And he could have understood the disappearance of the stunner. But why had the thief overlooked the weapon to take a few inches of human hair? The motive for that baffled him completely though he guessed it was clear to Che'in.

"The ordeal of the knots," the other spoke as if thinking aloud. "He did not find what he sought, so he would practice the ordeal of knots. But why? What did he seek here? This is important, Whitehawk. It may be deadly. Something Steel or you had?"

Kade took refuge in a collapse which was not more than a quarter acted, heard Che'in call out, and lying limp with closed eyes, heard the answering pound of feet. From his feigned faint he must have slipped into real sleep, for when he awoke again he was in the small post infirmary with the bright sheen of sunlight across the foot of his cot. They had probably drugged him for he discovered that thinking was a foggy process when he tried to put together into some sensible pattern the events he could remember.

What connection did those events have? He was almost certain Dokital had been his attacker. Since Kade's return from Cor he had seen almost nothing of the young Ikkinni, and a few offhand questions had told him that the native had been on a second hunting trip as Santoz's attendant. Kade's conscience had been none too easy. Out in the hills Dokital could put his dangerous knowledge to the rescue of another party of slaves. So the Terran had been relieved when the party had returned the day before, intact, and with an unusually good catch of musti in the bargain. If the Ikkinni had passed on his information, the natives had had no chance to steal a stunner and act upon it.

Unfortunately Kade was no nearer his own solution of how to have the broken control box investigated. The technical knowledge such an examination would require was completely out of his field and he had no contact at the nearest Trade Base who could make such a study and subsequently keep his mouth shut. To approach the Commander here was simply asking for his own dismissal. And with his plan beginning to work Kade could and would not jeopardize his service on Klor. The order for horses had gone through to Qwang-Khan and been approved. Horses were on their way to Klor. And he had already made a start with his project of introducing the Ikkinni to what might be their future secret weapon of liberation.

On the very plausible argument that horses could not be transported to their final destination by Styor planetary freighters, but would have to be driven or ridden overland, Kade was conducting a lecture course for the post Ikkinni in the care, feeding and nature of the new arrivals-to-be. Tri-dees blown up to almost life size served to make familiar the general appearance of the off-world beasts. And, with the aid of an improvised structure of wood and tubing, Kade had demonstrated some of the points of riding, the nature of a saddle pad, and the use of reins in governing the mount. The imported mounts would naturally be already well trained and docile, at least considered so by their Terran breeders. But Kade still had no way of telling whether horse and Ikkinni could and would learn to live together.

To his disappointment so far he had awakened no visible reaction in the natives. Herded to the place of instruction by Buk, who watched and listened himself with close attention, none of the slave laborers appeared to consider lesson time more than an interlude of rest, enduring the Terran's efforts at teaching as the price which must be paid for such a breathing spell. With Buk there Kade had to keep closely to the text concerning the welfare of the off-world animals, imported directly for the pleasure and benefit of the Styor which the Ikkinni so hopelessly hated.

He had been pleased to see Dokital in his audience at the last class meeting. Somehow Kade had expected a more alert response from the native who had been attracted by the bear. But the young Ikkinni had proved as stolidly unresponsive as his fellows.

And now, with a faint ache still behind his eyeballs when he tried to focus upon the band of sunlight, Kade was discouraged enough to admit that Dokital wanted just one thing, release from bondage. Undoubtedly he believed the Terran had that in his power to grant but would not.

He had not found and plundered the hidden pockets in Kade's boots, nor taken the stunner. Why had he taken most of the off-worlders short braid? As far as Kade knew there was no Ikkinni custom demanding that to disgrace an enemy. And what possible use could Dokital find for about three inches of alien hair?

What had Che'in said? "Ordeal of the knots." Kade repeated that aloud now, but the words meant nothing.

"Yes."

Kade turned his head on the foam support. Che'in was well within the door, walking with a cat's silence in spite of his boots. There had been a subtle alteration in this Teammate, no direct change of feature, or real disappearance of the basic placidity Kade had always seen the other display. Only now the Terran knew that serene expanse as a mask, under which a new pattern was coming to life.

The other stood looking down at Kade thoughtfully.

"Why do they hate you, Whitehawk?" He might have been inquiring about the other's health, only he was not.

"Who?"

"The Ikkinni," Che'in paused, and then there was a slight difference in his tone. "So you *don't* really understand after all! But then what a disappointment, what a grievous disappointment." He shook his head slowly.

"For whom?" Kade bottled his irritation. Trying to get any concrete information out of Che'in would seem to be a project in itself.

"The Ikkinni. And, of course, the Three Times Netter they employed to work on you. Or perhaps they have even hired a four knot man. From the disaster area they—or he—made of your quarters, I am inclined to believe your visitor was angry enough to go to a Four Netter—"

"Make sense," Kade's headache was returning. He was not amused by Che'in's riddle within riddle conversation.

"Magic," Che'in leaned back against the wall as if his usual indolence had caught up with him. "Take a tuft of an enemy's hair, knot it—with all the proper incantations and sacrifices—then each day draw those knots a little tighter—to be followed by subsequent bodily discomfort on the part of him whose personality is safely netted in your string of knots. If he agrees to your proposition, or you change your mind, certain of those knots can be untied again and his 'other self' released. If you get really thirsty for his blood, you tie your last knot firmly in a tangle and throw your net into a fire, or bury it in the earth, or dispose of it in some other final fashion which would provide a suitably unhappy end for your victim. Knotting is a local science of sorts I have been told."

Kade summoned up a grin. "And they expect this local magic to work on an off-worlder?"

Everyone knew that no one could be trapped by hallucination magic in which he was not conditioned from his birth. Yet the thought that somewhere a section of hairs, clipped in anger from his skull, was being skillfully and prayerfully knotted for the purpose of pain and revenge was not a pleasant one. Nor did it grow any less ominous the longer Kade considered it. Also there was always the chance that the hidden enemy, impatient at the ill success of his chosen scheme, might attack in a more forthright manner.

"If they discover their mistake," Che'in echoed Kade's last thought, "they may take more drastic, and quicker, steps. Why *do* they hate you, Whitehawk? What really happened during that mountain trip of yours?"

Kade was being forced into the position where he had to take someone into his confidence. If he went to Abu he believed he would be summarily shipped off planet. The Team Commander could not possibly overlook his subordinate's flagrant violation of Service orders. But Che'in—could Kade trust him? They had nothing in common, save their employment at the same post, and the younger man knew very little of the other. In the end it was Che'in who made his decision for him.

"Lik was not killed by a kwitu."

Kade stubbornly held silent, setting his will against the silent and invisible pressure the other was somehow exerting.

"Lik came to a doubtlessly well-deserved end by violence, maybe a spear."

Kade was quiet as Che'in in his careless voice picked for the truth.

"Somehow, somebody discovered that a belt control is not entirely infallible."

Kade had schooled himself to meet such a guess. He was sure he made no move, not so much as a flicker of the eyelid, to reveal how close that hit. Yet Che'in was on it instantly. The difference which the younger Trader had noted in the other at his entrance was nakedly eager, breaking through the mask. Che'in looked alive as Kade had never seen him. The face was not that of a Trader, a man who lived by the Policy, but that of a warrior being offered a weapon which would make all the difference in some decisive meeting with an old enemy.

"That is the truth! Say it, Whitehawk! That is the truth!"

And Kade's will broke down under that flash of real emotion.

"Yes."

"No wonder they're after you!" Che'in's head was up, that avid eagerness still in his features. "If there is an answer to the collar control every Ikkinni on this planet will want it." He took a step forward, his hands closed firmly on the foot of the infirmary cot. "What sort of a game have you been playing, Whitehawk?"

"None." Kade hastened to deny what might be termed trickiness. "Everything was an accident. Lik was trampled, gored by that bull just as I said. What happened afterwards was pure accident." He retold the scene with the terseness of an official report.

"A stunner?" Che'in repeated wonderingly, drawing his own weapon from its holster. Then he added a sharp-toned demand. "What was your beam quota at the time?"

Kade searched memory. "Must have been on full. I hadn't thumbed down since I shot the kwitu."

"Full! And it blasted the control and scrapped the collars!"

"And killed two Ikkinni," Kade reminded him.

"Suppose the quota had been on lower voltage?"

"Well," Kade began and then stared warily at Che'in, suspicious of being led into some statement which would damn him irrevocably. "There is no way of experimenting on that score. The Styor certainly are not going to let off-worlders play about with a slave control box for the purpose of discovering how such can be made harmless."

"Correct." Che'in was masked again. He stood weighing his stunner in his hand as if he would like to try such an experiment. "However, there is this also, Whitehawk. That sonic was tampered with and you were meant to be the victim, just as Steel was written off the rolls earlier. It is good for us here at the post to know a few things, to prevent other bright ideas from overwhelming the ones who dreamed that one out of hyperspace—"

"Why do they—whoever they may be—want me—us—dead?"

Che'in smiled. "An excellent question and one to which there could be several answers. First, a great many of these petty lordlings dislike Terrans merely for being Terrans. We are the first threat to their status which has risen in the long, comfortable centuries during which they have had the large part of the habitable galaxy in their own tight pocket. Just to eliminate some Terrans under a safe and innocent cover would be sport enough to appeal to certain of our unfriendly acquaintances. Then there is the rivalry between the lords here on Klor. A few judicious 'accidents,' the cause of which might be attributable to the negligence of the slaves of one Styor by his jealous neighbor, would make a difference when the next season's hunting rights were allotted. A dangerous game, to be sure, but greed often spurs one into taking bigger risks than the prize warrants."

"But," Kade said slowly, "there could be a third possibility?"

"Politics," Che'in reholstered his stunner, leaned once more against the wall. "The game of Styor against Styor on Klor is also carried on at higher levels. It could be planet Viceroy against planet Viceroy, jockeying for power within their empire. This is an outpost and the officials here are in two categories, the exiles with a black mark against them on the roles back home, and those who are ambitious but without power or backers. The first group want a coup to redeem their careers, the latter a chance to push their names. And use of carefully manufactured 'incidents' can help either."

"But too many Terran deaths—"

"Yes, if anyone is setting up that particular orbit he is locking his jets on danger, two strikes against his three-fin landing again. But some men are desperate enough for a tricky gamble. Someone, say, trying to unset the High-Lord-Pac."

"What are you going to do?" Kade came bluntly to the point.

"About this stunner business? Nothing just now. We need the raw material for an experiment. You still have the remains of the blasted control box?"

Kade nodded.

"That goes off the planet today, the supply ship is due in. That fact, by the way, is what brought me here, Whitehawk. Someone has really humped himself passing papers hither and thither. Your precious oat-burners are on board."

Kade had swung his feet off the cot and was looking about for his clothing, the pain in his head forgotten. Che'in laughed and handed him his uniform tunic.

"They're not sitting on the landing apron yet. You have about four hours grace, since they are still in orbit. You needn't run *all* the way to the field—and don't forget that control box, friend."

Kade bent down, unseamed those lining pockets in his boot tops and brought out the four small packets into which he had divided the remains of both collar and control box, some of it now only metallic dust. If the experts could make anything out of these bits and pieces he would be not only gratified but amazed. And giving the responsibility of that task to Che'in left him freer in mind as he went to the field where he found most of the post personnel waiting. Some of his enthusiasm must have spread outwards to the others after all.

There were five mares and a stallion. Although not the proud, sleek creatures of Kade's dreams—for the imports from Qwang-Khan were smaller, shaggier in coat—all were dun with black manes and tails, their legs faintly marked with dark stripes, reverting to their far off Terran ancestors. But when the young Terran personally freed them from their shipping boxes, led them, still dazed from trip shots, out into the corral he had had built, Kade was pleased to find fortune with him. Against the general ocher-brown of the landscape they would be hardly visible from a distance. And these ponies used to the hardy life of one frontier planet would make an easier adjustment to another.

The Terran's only worry was the attitude of the Ikkinni. Since he had chosen to handle the animals himself upon their landing, Kade had not at first been aware of the fact that the natives did not approach the corral at all. Only later, when he wanted help in feeding and watering the new arrivals, he met Buk, and the latter had a sly half-grin.

"Does the starwalker want a labor gang?"

"The animals need water, food—" Kade stopped speaking as he saw Buk's fingers seek the control box, touch buttons which meant punishment for the slaves.

"Why?" Kade demanded, knowing that the Overman was enjoying this.

"These earth worms say those are devils starwalker brought to devour them. Unless they are driven they will not tend the horses."

"No!" If Buk drove the Ikkinnis to handle horses under the lash of collar pain, Kade's plan would be defeated.

"I will lead the horses to the wide field," he said swiftly. "Let the Ikkinni then put the water and feed into the corral while it is empty."

Buk's grin faded. Kade allowed him no time for protest as he hurried to the corral gate. So far he had merely postponed trouble, but for how long? And was Buk telling the truth, or using his own power to make the natives hate and fear the horses?

◦★ CHAPTER 8 ★◦

"**THAT'S IT**, not one of them will willingly go near the horses," Santoz sounded as if he were relishing Kade's discomfiture. "This situation could blow up into real trouble."

"If," Abu answered from the head of the council table, "we don't fulfill our contract with the Pac we'll also be in trouble."

"What I am asking," Che'in struck in mildly, "is how this 'devouring demon' rumor ever got started in the first place. We've imported other, and much more potentially dangerous beasts in the past and never aroused more than some curiosity. Why this sudden antipathy for horses?"

Kade wanted an answer to that himself. It was almost as if someone—or something—had picked the plan out of his brain and set about an effective counterattack even before he had a chance to get started.

"Those other animals were smaller," Santoz pointed out with irritating reasonableness. "The only large animals native to Klor— the kwitu and the susti—are dangerous."

"So is the farg and that is just about the size of a half-grown bear. These Ikkinni were hunters before they were captured, we don't have any of the slaves from the breeding pens here. No, I would say that the rumor of demons did not spring full born from one of their crested skulls. I'd say it was planted."

"But why?" demanded Santoz.

Che'in smiled gently. "Oh, for any number of reasons, Manual.

71

Say that such a story could be used to inflame the post laborers into a revolt—"

Santoz sneered. "Revolt! With Buk having their lives under his finger tips every second of the day and night? They're not fools!"

But, Kade's own thoughts raced, *a revolt with a method of handling Buk and his box, however risky, was possible. Was this the time to make a general confession?* His lips parted but Che'in was already speaking.

"I don't believe that any of us are experts in Ikkinni psychology. The Styor have not encouraged such research. Perhaps our best move—"

Abu cut in. "Our best move, since we can not lift a contracted order off-world again, is to get these animals into Styor hands as quickly as possible."

Che'in grinned. "Give the 'demons' into the keeping of those already granted such propensities by the Ikkinni. But, of course!"

That makes good sense according to trade reasoning, yes. But Kade did not want a fast move in that direction.

"We'll have to take them overland," he pointed out. "And if the Ikkinni have to be forced to act as drivers—"

Abu frowned. "Yes, they might turn against the animals. Well, have you anything helpful to contribute?" His glance to Kade was direct, cold and demanding.

"Let me have one native to begin with, and no Buk. Two days of work about the corral may bring us a convert."

"I don't see how!" Santoz objected. "Any native would have to be collar-shocked to get him there and, without Buk, he could turn on *you.*"

"You have someone in mind?" Abu asked.

"Well, there is Dokital. He asked questions about the bear. He might just be interested enough in horses to stay around until he saw that they weren't dangerous."

"Buk is interested in them," Santoz suggested.

Kade's hands tensed under the edge of the table. Santoz was right, the Overman had hung about the corral, asked a multitude of questions. But he was not going to take any cross-country ride with Buk as a partner.

"Not practical," Abu's retort had the snap of an order. "Unless we also choose to send along the labor force in its entirety. We can not use the Ikkinni here without Buk. The Lord Sabatha would withdraw all of them immediately. They're his possessions, ours only on lease. I don't know, Whitehawk, why you think you might have any luck with Dokital, but you can try for another day or so."

Only they were not to have another day. They were to have less than five hours.

Kade was in the field beyond the corral. He had a light riding pad on the stallion, another on the back of the lead mare. Equine nature had not changed across the star lanes, nor through the centuries. The herd was as it had always been; a wise mare to lead the bands into new pastures, the stallion ready to fight for his mares, bringing up the rear while in flight, nipping at those who fell behind.

By the gate of the corral stood a black figure, every line of his thin body suggesting, even from this distance, defiance he dared not translate into explosive action. Kade swung up easily on the stallion, booted the horse into a trot back towards the pole wall. And he did not miss Dokital's answering crabwise movement which was halted only by the half-open gate. Now the Ikkinni stood penned as the horse and rider approached him, his hands opening and shutting as if searching the empty air before him for a weapon which did not materialize. The stallion stretched out his head, sniffed at the native, and blew gustily.

"The beast carries no spear against it," Kade said. "Across the star paths this beast serves warriors, wearing no collar but this," he lifted his hand, displaying the reins. "As the Kwitu, grass is for its eating, not the flesh of men."

The hostility he was certain he read in the native's eyes did not diminish. Kade knew that with time pressing he must force matters. He whistled, the stallion nickered, and across the field the lead mare answered inquiringly. He had taken the precaution of looping her reins to the empty saddle pad, and now she came at a canter to join them, her sisters drifting after.

Buk was nowhere in sight, but Kade could not be sure that the Overman was not watching. Should the alien use the collar controls now—At least after his first attempt at escape Dokital had not moved, although Kade left a way open for him.

"Warriors ride," the Terran remarked. He put out his left hand and drew his fingers down the mare's soft nose.

"There is no warrior." For the first time the Ikkinni spoke. "It wears the collar." The heat of anger was searing, though the native did not even glance toward the stunner at Kade's belt.

"That is perhaps so," Kade agreed. "A warrior fights with a spear, a slave with magic knotted by night."

Dokital gave no answer to that charge. He stepped out of his corner refuge as if he were being pushed toward the horses and the rider by his desperate need to learn some truth. "The net holds it not?"

"The net is of Klor, how could it hold it which is not of Klor?"

Dokital blinked as he digested that bit of simple logic. But he had intelligence enough to not only accept Kade's answer but come back with a counter-argument to cross as a fencer's blade crosses his opponent's.

"The beast is not of Klor, how then can such be slave to those on Klor?"

"There is magic, and magic. Some kinds sweep from star to star, others bind the men of one world only. There is nothing to be learned without trial. The knots were netted for it, and that was a trial. Now let another trial be made."

For a moment, a very long moment, there was silence. Kade heard the ripple of breeze through the grass, the distant call of a sky high bird. He loosed the mare's reins, gathered them into his own hand.

Dokital moved, raising his palm up and out, taking one step and then another toward the mare. She turned her head, regarded the Ikkinni placidly. Then her nose came down to lip the native's fingers and Dokital stood valiantly, a tremor visible up his arm, yet he stood.

"Up!" Kade ordered, with a rasp which might have come from Buk's lips.

If Dokital had not appeared to absorb the information of the impromptu class in horsemanship it was surface indifference only. He mounted the mare clumsily. But he was safely on the riding pad when Kade walked the stallion out into the open land, leading the mare, the other horses trailing.

The walk became a cautious trot and the mare pushed a little ahead, until Ikkinni and Terran were riding almost thigh to thigh. Kade could read no expression on the native's face, but he was certain a measure of the other's rigid tenseness had vanished. And now Kade dared to increase the pace to a canter. They circled, were heading back toward the clustered buildings of the post, and Kade cut the speed back to a walk.

"A warrior rides," he said.

Dokital's hand went up to the collar he wore. "There is no warrior wearing this, starwalker," his head came around, his eyes were again red flames of eagerness. "Break these from us and you shall see warriors! But this must be soon."

A note in that alerted Kade. "Why?"

"The word has been passed. These are evil." Dokital combed his fingers in the mare's cropped mane. "There is said kill, kill!"

"Who kills? Those of the collars?"

"Those of the collars. With more from beyond." Dokital pointed with his chin toward the land which cupped the Terran post. There was the scarred landing apron, the winding river, the drifts of fast-growing grass broken by groves of trees, but it was a land at peace as far as Kade could see.

"From beyond?" he echoed.

Again, not lifting his hands from the mare's neck, Dokital gestured with his head toward the river.

"There are hunters out there. The Overmen bring them to a killing."

Kade reined in the stallion, leaned over as if to examine the rein lying along the horse's neck. But instead his eyes went on to the river bank. Not too close to the post one of the small bat-winged flying lizards zoomed to what must be the extent of its limited flight range. And it headed, not along the course of the waterway, but into the prairie. For the first time the Terran heard a sound near to a chuckle from the Ikkinni at his side.

"They walk there like the kwitu."

"Hunters?"

"That?" Dokital spat accurately over the mares head, his opinion of such clumsiness in the stalk so made graphic. "No. One who drives."

"How many?"

"One who drives—six—eight—ten." The native recited the listing of belt controls indifferently. "Another who drives more, more."

His crested head turned on his neck as he conveyed the idea that the post was now ringed by unseen enemy.

"But why?"

"Over many say starwalkers bring demons. It fears. Also Overmen drive."

And the Overmen could only be taking orders from the Styor! The stallion obeyed Kade's reining, the pressure of his knees. Out of the grass, between them and the walls of the post courtyard, arose a line of men. And from the post Kade heard a shout—perhaps of warning, perhaps of outrage and surprise. Small figures boiled out of hiding, ripped loose from the grove, erupted from the face of the prairie. There was no time to reach the control of the post's force field. Kade could hear a distant clamor which argued that a fight had already broken out inside.

He booted the stallion into a dead run, flattened himself as small as he could on the animal's back.

The war cries came from all directions and a spear, too hastily thrown, arched over the Terran's back.

"Slay. Slay the demons!"

This time the spear scored Kade's shoulder, ripping the stuff of his tunic, its passage marked by a smarting red line. But he had broken through the line of natives which came apart, curling away from his mounted charge. He was by the corral, almost into the courtyard.

A red Terran coat made a splotch of color by the drab wall of the com room. But the man who wore it was propped on his arms, coughing out his life, as a spear shaft danced between his shoulder blades. Kade drew his stunner, sent one Ikkinni crashing into the dying Terran.

Then, out of nowhere, a mesh wrapped about his head and shoulders, and he fought wildly against a net, trying to keep his seat on the saddle pad. The throttling cords gave a little as Kade jerked at them. Against him the mare crowded and a knee ground into his thigh as fingers caught at his wrist, forced the stunner out of his hold.

"Kill! Kill!"

Buk shouted the order from behind a barricade of bales. The Overman was sweating and there was an avid eagerness in his face. His fingers were on his control box, he must be driving his gang frenzied by those jolts of force. And a handful of the Ikkinni were battering at the door of the com room, using spear butts fruitlessly against a substance only a flamer could pierce.

The haired hand which had pried the stunner out of Kade's grip steadied, as the thumb clicked a new charge into place. Somewhere, somehow, the young Ikkinni had picked up the oldest rule of hand gun shooting; to aim it as one points a finger. And the finger now pointed to Buk's control.

Nothing outwardly marked the impact of that arrow of energy until Buk tottered against the bales, his mouth drawn into a square of pain, his hands pawing at the air, while the control box shattered in a bright burst of unleashed power.

But Buk was not finished. Perhaps mere blind fear and pain sent the Overman at Kade, the largest target in his vicinity. He threw his knife and the Terran, still half-pinioned by the net, had no defense. One of those same net ropes saved the off-worlder's life, deflecting that wicked point to score flesh but not wound deeply.

For the Terran the rest of the fight possessed a dreamlike haze. Buk came on, wobbling uncertainly, his hands clutching air as if to tear at Kade. The stallion backed, snorted, and ran. While Kade, one hand over the bleeding cut in his side, clung to the saddle pad with all his remaining strength. Nor was he aware that another rider followed, while the loose mares, scattered and running wild, eventually gathered to their leader to head for the hills where evening shadows were already standing long and dark.

Kade remembered only one other thing clearly. The scene came to him for the rest of his life as a small vivid picture.

The horses and their riders were already screened by rising river banks, but they followed the curve of the stream, so that Kade, as their gallop fell again to a trot, was able to witness the act of a Styor ship coming from the north. The flyer was not a freighter, but a needle-slim fighting ship, undoubtedly one of the Cor garrison.

It circled over the Terran post where the rising smoke told of continued destruction. Then, with an ominous deliberation the flyer mounted skyward vertically. The pilot's return to earth was slow, deadly, for he rode down his tail flames which crisped everything. Had any Terran survived the initial attack by the controlled natives, there was little or no hope for him now. Attackers and attacked alike had been burnt from the face of Klor. To Kade the callous efficiency of that counterblast sealed the Styor guilt.

The Terran cried out, tried to turn the stallion back. But the reins were torn from his hold and, as a mist of pain and weakness closed in on him, Kade was dimly aware that they were headed on up the river into the mountains.

Arching sky over him was black, with the stars making frost sparkles across it, for the night was cold with the chill of early spring. Yet warmth and light were at his left, a warmth which was a cloak pulled over his half bared body. Kade dragged one hand across his left side, winced as its weight pressed a mass of pulpy stuff plastered on his wound.

He heard a low nicker, saw a horse's head, half visible in the limited light of the fire, toss with a flicker of forelock. And a figure came from the dark to loom over him. Dokital. Kade blinked, trying to see what was strange about the Ikkinni. A long moment later his dulled wits knew. The native's throat was bare, his slave collar was gone. As the other folded up his long legs to hunker down beside the Terran, Kade raised his hand.

"It is free."

White teeth flashed between dark lips. "It is free."

Those long-fingered hands went to work on Kade so he speedily forgot everything but the painful reaction of his body. The crushed mess was scraped from tender skin and a second poultice applied, patted into place with what seemed to Kade to be unnatural firmness. Unclenching his teeth he asked a question.

"We are in the hills?"

"The higher places," Dokital assented. "The collar masters can not come here. The Spearman brings down their fly-boats."

"And the post?" But Kade's memory already supplied the answer to that.

"There is no place. Those have left it only stinking earth."

Kade digested that. There was a chance, a very slim one, that perhaps Abu or Che'in, or both, had survived. He was sure that Santoz was the man he had seen die on the spear. Every Trade post was equipped with an underground emergency com. If the other two had managed to reach that in safety before the burn-off, there was a good chance they could hold out there until the help summoned by their SOS came. But the chance of such survival was indeed thin. Had they been above ground, still exchanging fire with the attackers when the Styor ship struck, then he was the last Terran left on Klor.

Meanwhile, for him, the mountains where the Styor ships could not patrol were the safest hideout.

"The horses?"

"One died from a spear," Dokital reported. "But the rest ran— faster than the kwitu, than the slog, faster than any Ikkinni, or any spear from an Ikkinni hand. Truly they are windswift ones!"

"Where do we go?"

Dokital fed a piece of rust-colored wood to the fire. "It is free. In the upper places there are many free warriors. It will be found."

"Iskug?"

"Iskug or others." He added a second piece of wood and the flames shot higher. Kade pulled himself up on one elbow, saw the horses stand, their heads pointing to the light, as if they, too, sought the promise of security, if not the warmth, of the fire.

But if Dokital meant that splotch of yellow-red in the night as a signal, there came no immediate answer. And at last the flames died, unfed, while Kade slept uneasily, but unstirring.

He awoke again cold, cramped, a chill slick of dew beading his good shoulder where he had pushed aside a light covering of twigs and lengths of dried grass. The throbbing in his side was only a faint memory, to be recalled when he moved stiffly to sit up. Last night's fire was burnt away to a handful of charred wood ends and a smear of ash. Seeing that, he looked around quickly, plagued with the thought he had been left in a deserted camp.

A sharp jerk jarred his wound into painful life again as he discovered that his feet were anchored, lashed together at his ankles, the ends of those bonds fastened out of sight and reach. The slab of vegetable plaster on his side flaked away as he leaned forward to pull at the cords. Certainly Dokital the night before had shown no signs of hostility. Why had he bound the Terran while he slept?

With a catch of breath at the hurt it cost him, Kade managed to finger the cords about his ankles. They were twisted lines such as were used to weave hunters' nets and he could feel no knots. The ends of the lines vanished between large boulders on either side, holding him firmly trapped. He remembered Che'in's talk of four fold knots to hold an enemy. But that had been a part of native magic. What he felt and saw here had very concrete reality.

☽★ CHAPTER 9 ★☾

ABOUT HIS BOOTS the loops were tight and smooth almost as if they had been welded on. And their substance was not that of ordinary rope, for his fingers slid greasily around without contacting any roughness of braided surface. Kade raised his head, tried to gauge by the amount of light now gilding the peaks how far the morning had advanced. The hour was well past dawn, for sun touched the upper reaches.

Standing strongly against the sky were those three impressive peaks, the Planner, the Netter, the Spearman, which told him that their flight the day before had brought them in the same general direction as the hunt had taken weeks earlier.

Last night's camp had been made against the flank of a rise where the debris of an old landslip had set up a backwall of boulders. Kade caught the faint gurgle of water flowing swiftly, so a mountain stream could not be too far away. And that sound triggered his thirst. Suddenly he wanted nothing so much as to bury his face in that liquid, drink his fill without stint.

Kade could see the space where the horses had stood in the dark, watching the fire. But there was no sign of those animals now, just as Dokital had vanished. Had the Ikkinni taken them and gone for good?

The Terran writhed, and in spite of the pain which clawed at his side, drew his feet as far toward his middle as he could before kicking vigorously. The bonds gave a matter of inches and that was all. With

81

his hands he dug in the loose soil and gravel beside and under him, discarding a length of charred branch, hunting a stone with which he could saw at those stubborn loops. If necessary he would try abrading them with handfuls of the gravel.

A first pebble was too smooth. Then he chanced on a more promising piece of rock, having a blunted point at one end. Pulling forward, his left arm protectingly across his wound, Kade worried at the cords. And rubberwise, those bonds resisted his determined assault.

Dripping with sweat, weak with effort and pain, Kade sat, shoulders hunched, the stone clasped in his hand. He was sure that an hour or more had passed since he had awakened, the sun was farther down the sundial of the mountain. And he was equally sure with the passing of time that he had been abandoned by Dokital, though why the native had taken the trouble of tending the Terran's wound before deserting him Kade could not understand. Unless the Ikkinni had left him staked either as an offering to the three stark mountain gods, or to be found by the pursuing Styor.

And the latter supposition sent Kade to a second attack on the ankle ropes.

The odor of the dried poultice, of his own sweat, was strong in his nostrils, but not strong enough to cover another scent. He became aware of that slowly, so intent was he on his own fight. The new stench was rank, so rank that he could no longer ignore nor mistake it. Kade stiffened, head up, nostrils wide.

Once that noisome odor had been sniffed, a man never forgot it. And the whiff he had had to plant its identity in his memory had come from a cured, or partially cured, hide back at the post. This was so ripely offensive it could only emanate from a living animal. Animal? Better living devil!

The musti of the caves were dangerous enough, they had claws to rend, fangs to threaten. But they had a cousin which was far more of a living peril, a thing which hunted by solitary tracking, which could spread wing or creep on all fours at will, with a man-sized body, a voracious hunger, an always unsatisfied belly. And because it feasted on carrion as well as live prey it aroused revulsion instantly. Kade cringed as he began to guess why he had been tethered here, though the reason behind that action still eluded him. It would have been far safer for Dokital to have used a spear and finished him off neatly and quickly.

That stench was now almost a visible cloud of corruption. But, though the Terran strained his ears for the faintest sound which might hint at the direction from which sudden death would come, he heard nothing save the sigh of wind through branches, the continuing murmur of that tantalizing stream. Only his nose told him that the susti must be very close to hand.

He squirmed around, jerking desperately at his bonds, managing to fight enough play into those ties so that he could pull himself up, put his back to a boulder. Half naked, with nothing but the stone in his hand, Kade looked around for another possible weapon. To his mind the outcome of the fight before him was already settled, and not in his favor.

His stunner was long gone, but he still wore the belt with its empty holster. Now Kade tore feverishly at the buckle, pulled the strap from around him. He held a belt of supple yoris hide, a buckle and the holster weighing down one end. And he twitched it in test, seeing that he could make it a clumsy lash of sorts. With that in his right hand and his stone in the left, the Terran pushed tight against the rock to wait for the lunge he was sure would be launched at him from one of three directions.

Straight across the ashes of the fire was an open space, the last path the susti would choose. The creature was reputed to be a wily hunter, and its species had been ruthlessly hunted by Ikkinni and Styor alike for generations. Stealth must have been bred into its kind by now.

To Kade's left the trail of debris made by an old slide made a gradually diminishing wall, a dike of large and small boulders, rough, climbable, but not a territory to welcome a rushing charge. And anything crossing it would be plainly in view for several helpful moments before reaching him. The Terran hoped that would be the path. He held his head high, trying to test the odor for a possible direction of source.

His right offered the greatest danger. There was a curtain of brush some five feet away. He could see broken branches where Dokital must have raided for wood and for the covering he had heaped over Kade before leaving. But the vegetation was still thick enough to conceal a full squad of Ikkinni had the natives chosen to maneuver within its cover. Was it too thick to allow the winged susti passage?

Kade swung the belt back and forth, trying to get the feel of that unlikely weapon. He could use the strap as a flail, with the faint hope that the holster might thud home in some sensitive spot, say an eye. But that hope was so faint as to be almost nonexistent. And his head turned slowly from boulder wall to brush, striving to catch some betraying movement from the thing which must be waiting not too far away.

Such waiting gnawed at the nerves. The belt ends slapped against the Terran's breeches. Kade braced himself against the stone, struggled again to loosen the cording at his ankles. Free he might have a chance, a minute one, but still a chance. Then his heart thumped as one of the two anchoring lines gave so suddenly he was almost thrown. The cord rippled toward him from between two rocks. That side was free!

But he was to be given no more time. The susti had assured itself that this was not a baited trap. With a blast of roar, partly issuing from a crocodile's snout—if the crocodile had worn fur and possessed tall standing ears—and partly from the ear-storming claps of leather wings, the nightmare which haunted Klorian wilds burst through the brush and came towards Kade in a scuttling rush.

The Terran hurled his stone as a futile first line of defense, before swinging with the belt, cracking against the snout in a vicious clip. The talons, set on the upper points of the wing shrouded forelimbs, cut down. Somehow Kade ducked that first blow, heard the claws tear across the rock against which he had taken his stand. There was only the chance for one more blow with the belt. Again he felt and saw the improvised lash crack against the creature's snout. Then one of those wings beat out and Kade was pinned helplessly to the stone, his face buried in the noisome, vermin-ridden fur. One of the powerful back legs would rise, a single rake would disembowel him.

There was a squeal which was not part of the susti vocal range. Kade, his head still crushed by the wing, felt the creature's body pressed tighter against his as if impelled by some blow from behind. Then he was gasping fresh air, his hands rubbing his eyes, the susti's weight no longer crushing him.

With a speed he would not have believed possible to a creature so awkward on the ground, the Klorian terror had moved to face a new antagonist. Kade saw hooves flash skyward, come down in the cutting blows of axe-fatality. One such landed full on a wing, flattening the susti from a crouch to the sand. Before the creature could struggle up, the Terran stallion, squealing with red rage, brought punishing teeth to snap trap-tight on the nape of the susti's neck, tearing free only with a mouthful of flesh.

Kade had heard of the desperate ferocity of stallion fighting stallion for the kingship of a herd. Once he had seen such a duel to the death. And here was the same incarnate rage, the same deadly determination to win, turned not against a fellow horse, but against the alien creature.

The susti had been unprepared for that meeting, and it never recovered the advantage lost at the first blow. Since the stallion was able to rear above his enemy, using sharply shod front hooves as a boxer uses his hands, he repeatedly flattened the bat-thing, each fall of those weapons breaking bones, each rake of teeth ripping strips of flesh. Kade had never witnessed such raw and bloody work and he could hardly believe that the animal that had moved quietly under his orders could have changed in a matter of seconds into this wild fury. Long after the susti must have been dead the horse continued to trample the body. Then all four feet were on the ground, the dun neck stretched so that distended nostrils could sniff at the welter of splintered bone, blood-matted fur. There was a snort of disgust from the stallion. He threw up his head, his black forelock tossing high, to scream the challenge of his kind triumphantly.

Kade tore at the last of the cords which held him, putting all his strength into that pull. The bonds yielded reluctantly but he was able to twist and turn the loops until he kicked free. The stallion was trotting away between brush wall and boulder and the man ran after him.

He found the horse, coat splotched with foam, a line of sticky red down one shoulder proving that the stallion had not come altogether unmarked out of that battle, with front feet hock-deep in the stream, drinking from the top curls of topaz water. There was a spread of meadowland, pocket-sized but rich in grass, on the other side of the water. But, contrary to Kade's expectations, it did not hold the mares.

The Terran moved up beside the horse. Again that head tossed, flicking droplets of water on Kade's arm and reaching hand, evading the man's touch. The horse still wore riding pad and the reins trailed loosely from the hackamore.

Kade hissed soothingly but the horse snorted, jerked away from the man's hand. It was then Kade realized he must still reek of the susti. Kneeling beside the stream-side, well away from the horse, he poured cold water over head, shoulders, chest where that rank fur had smeared against his flesh. He felt the sting in his wound. Gritting sand rubbed away the last foul reminder of that contact. And now the horse allowed him close, to dab at that shoulder scratch with a soaked wad of grass. The furrow was not deep, Kade noted with relief. But the arrival of the stallion without the mares, with no sign of Dokital, continued to puzzle the man. And what had so aroused the horse to that attack against a beast which had not threatened him?

Kade had heard tales of horses and mules on his planet battling mountain lions, thereafter developing such an animosity against the big cats that they deliberately sought the felines out with a singleness of purpose and desire for vengeance against that archenemy of their kind. That was close to the reaction of a human under similar circumstances. Yet the stallion could not have met a susti before and Kade had not attempted to condition the animals since their arrival on Klor. Either unusually thorough precautions and preparations had been made off-world to acclimate the newcomers to all possible Klorian dangers, or the susti by its vile stench and very appearance had aroused hatred in the new immigrant. At any rate, Kade's life had been bought in that encounter and he was duly grateful.

The problem of what to do now remained. Where would they go? Leading the stallion, the man splashed across the stream and found what he had hoped to see; hoof prints cut in the soft clay of a sloping bank. If the traces continued as clear as this he would have no difficulty in back-trailing the horse and perhaps so discovering where Dokital and the mares had vanished.

Mounting, Kade headed the horse across the valley, pausing to study the trail now and then, each time seeing traces. Either the horses had left those while running free, or the Ikkinni had not taken the trouble to conceal the evidence of their passing.

The strip of meadowland narrowed, overshadowed by rising mountain walls, and the ground began to slope upward, gradually at first and then at a more acute angle. Kade revised his guess that the animals had taken that path of their own choosing. With water and good grazing in the valley, they would not voluntarily have picked such a way into the heights. Yet here and there a deep hoofprint marked either the exit of the small herd, or the return of the stallion.

Kade halted at the top of the rise to rest his mount and, with the age-old training of his kind, slipped from the pad, loosening the cinch to allow air to circulate under the simple saddle, before he crept to the edge of the downslope ahead, taking advantage of all offered cover.

The downslope was wooded, masked with a bristly cover of the twisted dwarflike trees found in the heights. Wind stirred through them, roughed Kade's flesh with its bitter bite. But more than wind moved on that curve of hillside. There was no mistaking the nature of those moving dots coming up with the dogged persistence of animals driven by a homing instinct. The mares! And none bore a rider.

Daringly Kade whistled and some trick of air current carried that summons to the sensitive ears below. The lead mare nickered and quickened pace, her sisters falling in behind her. Rocks rolled and behind Kade the stallion sounded his own call.

When the mares reached the ridge they were sweating, their eyes strained, showing white rims, their coats rough with dried foam and sweat, bits of twig and bark caught in the rippling length of their tails. By all the signs they had traveled far and fast.

The lead mare still wore the riding pad and her rein was caught to it on one side, dangling loose on the other. Also the pad was twisted and across its edge—

Kade put out a finger. That smear of blood, differing in shade from his own, was already partly congealed. The drop must have been exposed to the air for some time. But its presence there argued that there was a more sinister reason for Dokital's absence. Had the native been killed? But where? And why had he ridden the mare, driven the horses away, leaving Kade helpless in the deserted camp? Every time the Terran tried to make a pattern out of the bits and pieces he knew or suspected, they did not fit.

In the end he led the horses back to the valley of the camp, sure

that they would be content there. The stream supplied him with
the first food he had had that day; a fish, flat, elongated, almost
unpleasantly snakelike, but one he knew was edible even raw, and he
finished it off with the dogged determination to consume food as fuel
for his demanding body.

The fish also supplied him with what he wanted almost as much
as food; a weapon, or at least the beginnings of a weapon which, with
some careful labor, would serve. The tough spinal bone, shorn of its
fringe of small projections and sharpened, made a poniard, needle-
slim and nearly as deadly as dura-steel.

How much that would serve him against a Styor blaster, or an
Ikkinni spear, he questioned. But with it in his hand Kade felt less
naked. And he worked at its perfection all that long afternoon as he
made some plans of the future.

The Styor, after their ruthless attack on the Trade post, would hunt
down any remaining off-world witness with speed and dispatch. Let his
survival be suspected and they would have hunting teams into these
breaks to comb him out, station squads all along the trails leading
back to the post to pick him up. The logical move would be for him
to contact the free Ikkinni, Iskug's band of escapees. That would have
been his first endeavor yesterday, before he awoke bound and easy
meat for a susti. Now he might have to fear the natives as much as he
did their oppressors.

Yet a third possibility was so dangerous, that to try such action
meant very careful planning, a period of scouting and lurking, of
learning the countryside. To reach the destroyed post Kade would
have to evade Styor patrols and natives alike. And even when he
reached that site he might not be able to find the concealed com, or
to summon the Service ship in time to save himself. But he could get
out a warning of what had happened on Klor.

Kade ground with small, delicate touches at the point of his bone
dagger. To scout the territory would commit him to no move and he
should so be able to gauge the Styor positions. That much he would
try tomorrow. He was fairly certain at the way west from here and he
should be able to reach some upper vantage point in the hills from
which to view the post by midday.

The Terran followed Dokital's example of the night before, heaping
a loose pile of grass into which he crawled, listening to the move-

ments of the horses until he fell asleep, knowing that they would give the alarm against alien intruders.

Kade awoke soon after dawn to hear the low whinny of the lead mare as she went down to the stream. He pulled free of his nest, went to the water also. Following the immemorial custom of hunt and war trail Kade drank only a small amount of water, pulling tighter the belt about his middle. As he swung past the boulder wall of Dokital's camp a gorged winged thing shuffled along the cleaned skeleton of the susti, and two smaller shapes turned angry red eyes on him before they scuttled away into hiding.

Taking his bearings from the three peaks, the Terran headed westward. He had to make detours around two unclimbable cliffs and paused now and again to erase the marks of his own passing. Slightly before midday he did reach his goal. As he crept along a ledge the sun was pleasingly warm on his shoulders and he did not regret the loss of his tunic. For against the hue of sand and earth here his own bronze skin and the drab shade of his breeches should be indistinguishable.

Although miles separated him from the post, there was no mistaking the scar which the Styor burn-off had left to mark the site. Not one of the walls still stood, only a round splotch of blackened earth gleamed under the sun, the terrible heat of the ship's flaming tail had cooked earth and sand into slag.

He could have hoped for nothing else. Had there been survivors, they must be sealed underground, their only hope of rescue to come from off-planet. Kade looked from that scar to more immediate landscapes. He had one small point in his favor: the Styor would expect a Terran to be completely bewildered if thrown on his own in the Klorian wilderness, and the Overmen of teams sent out to track any possible survivor would be overconfident.

That estimation of the enemy was borne out when Kade surveyed the foothills below his present perch. There were trackers out, right enough. He could sight two separate teams heading eastward, and they moved openly, strung out as might beaters sent to scare up game. There was no doubt that sooner or later someone down there would stumble on the trail left by the horses day before yesterday and follow it to the valley of the susti. Which meant he must move and find a better hideout.

But even as Kade started to crawl from his ledge, he stiffened, hearing that familiar clap of sound, the roar of a spaceship homing on a post land area. And, in the sunlight, the silver body of a descending Trade scout was a streak as vivid and elemental as an avenging bolt of lightning.

✧⋆ CHAPTER 10 ⋆✧

IF KADE HAD BEEN startled by the sudden arrival of the Terran ship in Klorian skies, the search parties below betrayed their agitation by the speed with which they took to cover. Although he could no longer sight them, the off-worlder knew they still existed, a barrier between him and that ship now making a perfect three-fin landing on the apron of the vanished post. He had not the slightest chance of reaching the rescue party.

But he continued to watch their activities with strained eagerness. Would the Styor attempt to attack the party from the ship? Or would the aliens bring up one of their fast inter-atmosphere cruisers from Cor and begin a running fight when the Terran scout took off again? Kade did not see how they would dare to let the ruined post tell its story to Trade. Had the Styor not blasted, but allowed the evidences of a native attack to stand, they might have successfully blamed it on rebellious Ikkinni, indirectly on the Terrans themselves because of the importation of horses. As he lay there on the ledge, his head supported on his forearm, Kade thought that made good logic.

But why had they spoiled such a plan with the burn-off? What had gone wrong? Unless—unless they had learned of the blasting of Buk's control! Had the Styor lords, safely in the background of that assault, been able to monitor events from a distance and observed that the Ikkinni had a weapon of deliverance at last? Had they ordered the burn-off to catch their own dupes as well as the Terrans for no other reason than to make sure that no more stunners would fall into Ikkinni hands, than if they moved fast and were lucky, no rumor of the weapon's use could reach the rest of their slave gangs? It could be an answer, if a drastic one—risking a blockade from Trade in order to keep their slaves. But how could he judge the thinking patterns of a Styor by his own processes? The risk to them might have appeared heavier on the other side of the scales.

At any rate someone had been frightened enough, or angry enough to order that burn-off. Would the next attack come against the newly landed ship?

Minutes passed and no Styor flyer arose above the horizon. There was no sign of life from the breaks below where those hunting parties had gone to earth. Kade could make out, despite the distance, figures emerging on the ship's ramp, descending to the congealed scar of the post. And he speculated again as to whether Abu or Che'in was sealed, still alive, below the glassy surface of that burn.

Renewed activity below his perch drew Kade's attention away from the splotch on the prairie. There was a new advance, not back toward the plains, but up slope, heading towards him. And for a moment or two he wondered if he had been sighted and Ikkinni slaves dispatched to pick him up.

If the newcomers knew the terrain well they could take a path around the spur on which he crouched, cutting him off. And Kade dared not chance that they were ignorant of that, too many labor gangs had been hired out for hunting in these hills. He had to leave at once.

The Terran gave a last long look at the scene about the ship. Those small stick things which represented his own kind had gathered in one spot on the scar. His guess that at least one of the Team was in a hidden underground com chamber must be right and they were preparing to break the prisoner out. Kade eyed the section of broken, wooded land below him, the long curve of open prairie. To try to cross those miles was simply asking to be speared—or blasted if the Styor had issued more potent arms to their Overmen. He had not the slightest chance of reaching the safety of the ship and that was a bitter truth to digest.

But suppose the scout took off successfully with the man or men who had been rescued? There would remain that now open com chamber and the possibility he could try for it later, send in his own call. That was the hope he must hold to as he retreated now.

Kade crept from his ledge, started downward with the ridge rising as a wall between him and the only aid he could count on, using every tactic known to a hunter—and the hunted—to cover his trail.

Once he wriggled under a fallen tree, lay still, fighting the rapid pump of his own heart, the rasp of his breathing, while an Ikkinni paused within arm's-length, head up, nostrils distended, as if he could pick out of the light breeze which was ruffling his cockscomb of hair the scent of the off-worlder.

Kade blinked when he saw that that particular tracker wore no collar. If the slave Ikkinni had been loosed in the hills, their free brethren were also on the move with a purpose which drove them into dangerous proximity to the Overmen and their governed squads.

The Terran watched the native fade into the brush, and lay long moments in hiding, until he was sure of a detour which would not bring him treading on the other's heels. So tangled a path did Kade follow that he was honestly surprised when he came again into the meadow where the horses grazed. And the hour was close to sunset as he stayed under cover watching the animals.

But the peace of the scene was reassuring, especially when the stallion betrayed quick vigilance with his own examination and then welcome for Kade. Had the Terran been Ikkinni or Styor he was certain the herd would have been in flight before the invaders could get within blaster range of the animals.

However, with hunters boring into the mountain valleys, man and mounts dared not remain there in spite of the coming night. Kade mounted the lead mare, headed her back along the trail he had explored the day before, and was glad that the others came behind willingly, the stallion playing rear guard.

The Terran pressed the pace, wanting to be over the rougher stretches of trail while the daylight lasted. But he paused every time they were forced out of cover to look behind. And he regretted he had no chance to erase their tracks.

They came back, in the gray of the twilight, to the wooded slope where earlier he had met the mares. And now the leader he rode whinnied nervously, had to be urged on. Yet Kade could see nothing but empty country below, and he was sure they had outdistanced the

hunting parties. There remained the free Ikkinni, nor did he forget
that blood which made an ugly blotch on the saddle pad not far from
his knee.

He let the mare pick her own choice of ways as long as she
obeyed his selection of direction. And she went cautiously, pausing
to sniff the air, survey the unending ocher vegetation ahead. Once or
twice the stallion snorted, as if growing impatient at that slow
advance, but he did not press ahead.

Kade was hungry, as he could never remember having been since
the ceremonial fasting of his adolescence, and here in the shadow of
the trees he was cold as well. Sooner or later he would have to choose
a camp site.

The mare stopped short, her ears pointed forward, and now the
stallion joined her, his whole stance expressing interest in something
hidden from Kade's less acute sense. There was nothing to be seen
save the trees, the sparsely growing underbrush, and countryside
being blotted out by dusk.

Then the breeze, which awakened a murmur of sound, failed and
Kade caught a quiver in the air—it was hardly more than that. Only
the rhythm of that faint beat was manmade, he became convinced of
that the longer he listened. And surely the Styor hunting parties
would not advertise their presence by such means.

A village or gathering of cliff Ikkinni? Some ceremonial in
progress? Or—His imagination supplied other explanations. He
pressed his heel against the mare's round side, urging her on. And, as
she obeyed, that faint pulsation grew louder. Then some trick of
shifting wind brought it to him as a regular up-down ladder of
sound. And his blood answered that alien cadence with a faster
coursing, his heart accelerated to keep time to that drumming.

Horses and man came out of the trees into a glade, and here the
drum was a hollow core of vibration which pulled, not only at the
eardrums, but at the nerves of the listener. The horses were uneasy,
nickering. Finally the stallion reared, gave his ringing challenge as his
front hooves beat into the sky. Kade caught for dangling reins too
late, aware that that fighter's scream of defiance could carry, echoed
as it was by the rises about them.

Yet there was no pause in the boom of drum or drums, no
answering move in the shadows to indicate that the drummer was

aware of strangers. And Kade knew that he must investigate the source from which that beat came.

He dismounted from the mare, tethered her by her reins, sure her sisters would not drift too far away. Then, trusting in the fighting powers of the stallion, Kade chose to ride the stud on, drawn by that rolling sound.

Luckily a measure of light still held. The horse struck into an easy canter which took them out over a stretch of bare earth pocked with scrubby plants, an abrupt contrast to the more luxuriant foliage of the upper slope. They came into a draw gouged out by some seasonal water gush but now dry, firm and smooth enough to ape a leveled road. The stallion's canter lengthened into a gallop. The horse shied as one of the long-legged wingless birds erupted from the right. But when the Klorian creature ran on straight ahead, Kade's mount appeared to accept that burst of speed from its strange racing companion as a goad and the stride of those powerful legs lengthened once again.

The drums were loud now, a continuous, thunderous roll. And perhaps they acted upon the horse with some of the same impact of which Kade was himself aware. But the man kept his head and tried to control his mount as a glow ahead told him he must be approaching the site of activity.

Running yards ahead of the stallion the bird uttered a mewling cry, gave a contorted sidewise leap which warned Kade. He loosened rein again, kicked the stallion into a bound, flattened himself as close as he could to the horse's back. There had been a shadow crouched in the dry water course, a figure which arose in a spring. The horse leaped and that shadow fell away with a cry of terror.

Now when Kade pulled at the reins he found that the horse was past obedience. Given time he might bring the stallion back under control, but for a time the Terran could only keep his seat and wait for this fury to run itself out.

Kade thrust his knees under the loose foreband of the pad, riding as had his ancestors during the excitement of a buffalo hunt on a world half the galaxy away, reasonably sure he would not lose his seat. As horse and rider rounded a curve in the stream bed, the glow brightened, shooting heavenward in two pillars of light.

Without his rider's urging, the stallion began now to curb his headlong rush as he drew closer to the fires, coming at last to an abrupt halt. As the horse reared, voicing a tearing scream, Kade knew his precautions against being thrown had been well taken.

And he guessed in part what might lie ahead for he would never forget that stench, a whiff of which came nauseous and pungent through the softer odor of smoke and burning wood. Somewhere behind the hazy gleam of those twin fires was a susti, either alive, or very recently dead.

At first those fires dazzled his eyes. Then, as the stallion advanced in an odd, sidling way, with suspicion and wariness in every move, the Terran caught the weird scene in its entirety.

Here some freak of nature had hollowed an almost perfect horseshoe-shaped amphitheater, three slopes rising from a bare floor of sand, the fourth open to the gorge down which Kade had come.

An audience filled those slopes, movement pulsated around the bend of the horseshoe with here and there a down-covered Ikkinni face brought into momentary sharpness as the flame pillars wavered. Yes, there was an audience; more natives than Kade had ever seen gathered in one place before. He pulled at the reins, to discover that the stallion would still not obey. Unless he dismounted he was going to be carried on into the channel of light between the fires.

Kade drew the bone knife, knowing the uselessness of that weapon against the spears which would meet him now.

With rein and voice he appealed to the stallion, hopelessly. For the horse was still sidling ahead, hooves moving in a dance of small advances, smaller retreats. Then the arched neck went down and a front hoof tore up a fountain of gravelly sand.

A figure moved at a point midway between the fires but still yards away from the two in the gorge. And Kade saw the focus of this entire assemblage.

An Ikkinni stood there, equipped with net and spear, though he held the net in his hands and the spear lay on the earth with one of his feet set upon its shaft. Kade's attention, caught by the wink of fire on that weapon's point, located a round ring of cord about the ankle of the waiting native; something he remembered well. This was a prisoner, his feet bound even as Kade's had been in the deserted camp. A captive and yet armed with the weapons of his people, tethered by his feet—

And the smell of susti!

The stallion advanced, his head still held at an awkwardly low angle, as if he were nosing out a trail which existed a foot or so above ground level. The steps the horse took were small, mincing, and Kade felt the roll of muscle between his own knees, sensed the power for attack building up there.

It was then that horse and rider must have been sighted for the first time. A cry, eerie, piercing, sounded from some point high up on the slope to Kade's left. He heard a chorus of answering hoots from the other half-seen sections of the amphitheater. The Ikkinni prisoner turned, crouching, and Kade saw him full face. Nor was he in the least surprised to see that the captive was Dokital.

How the former post slave had come here Kade did not know, but that he had been set in his present position for the amusement or edification of enemies of his own species was apparent. And the nature of the peril to be faced was more evident with every breath of tainted air which Kade drew.

Nor did the Terran doubt that the animal he bestrode had indeed been conditioned, either by nature or by off-world techniques, to seek out and attack the source of such a stench, a living susti.

The stallion continued his seemingly awkward advance toward Dokital. And the cries which had heralded the appearance of horse and rider abruptly died away. Nor did any spectator move to interfere with either Kade or his mount. Perhaps, thought the Terran savagely, taking fresh grip on his wholly inadequate bone knife with fingers which were sweat-sticky, they had settled to watch their entertainment increased threefold.

Dokital, after his first startled glance at the newcomers, half-turned from them again, his whole stance betraying preparation for action as he stared beyond the fires to the rounded curve of the horseshoe, plainly expecting danger from that direction.

The stallion was well into the firelight and Kade debated as to the wisdom of dismounting. He had seen the animal in successful action against one of the weird bat-things, and the weight of a rider might handicap the four-legged fighter. Loosening his knees from the pad, he leaned forward and stripped hackamore and reins from the horse's head. The head was up now, nostrils distended, small flecks of foam showing in frothy patches about the angle of the half open jaw.

Kade leaped down, landing a stride's distance from Dokital. The Ikkinni's right hand, fingers grasping the net ready for a cast, made a small gesture which the Terran could interpret neither as a welcome nor a refusal of aid, merely recognition.

Why he chose to stand with the native who by all evidence had left him helpless to face the same danger they were about to meet here, Kade could not have explained. Maybe it was that having been brought here by the stallion, manifestly eager for the coming fight, his warrior ancestors would not allow him any retreat.

The stallion halted, turned as the two men, to face the same curve of earth and stone. Now Kade could make out a barricade, a crosshatch of timber stakes. As that moved, the horse screamed such a vocal defiance as was echoed in ear-shattering sound from the walls of the bowl. Dokital crouched, the net coiled at his hampered feet. Kade, breathing faster, held his knife in readiness. With the three of them to face at once, one susti should be partly at a disadvantage.

The crude door was jerking upward, to display a dark hole, ragged enough about the edges to suggest a natural mountain cave. And the stench was now a choking wave of corruption, setting Kade to gagging.

How long would they have to wait? He remembered those dragging minutes back at the camp before the attack when he had been able to see his foe. Here at least, they knew the direction from which attack would come. Yet nothing save that overpowering odor had issued from the cave hole.

The drums, which had died to nothing since Kade's entrance, broke out in a wild beat. They must be stationed, the Terran thought, near the top of the amphitheater. The heavier roll on his left was balanced by a quick staccato tapping from the right. And that din would now drown out even the stallion's cries.

But the horse did not neigh, no longer tossed his head. He was as intent upon that hole as a feline might be at the hiding place of legitimate prey.

Maybe the beat of drum was acting as either an irritant or a summons. For the susti flashed out of hiding, not in the clumsy, wing-furled crawl with which its fellow had approached Kade, but in a leap which bore it into the air, wings beating.

For a startled second Kade believed the creature was more intent upon gaining the freedom of the night skies, than upon attacking its intended victim or victims. But if the susti was a captive, it was also trained in its role. For though that first flight carried it past the three in the arena, on to the throat of the gorge, it banked widely, its wings momentarily blotting out the streaming columns of firelight, to fly back.

The three were saved only by the peculiarity of the enemy's hunting habits. Had it roved falconlike, pouncing on its prey from aloft, horse and men might have had little chance. But the susti had to kill such large opponents on the ground. So the glide of its return brought it down in a swoop as it headed for the horse. Perhaps it had fought with tethered Ikkinni sacrifices before and had the rudimentary intelligence to choose from the three the prey which appeared the easiest to subdue.

Only the stallion whirled with the agility of a veteran warrior and the susti missed its strike, while the hooves swung until one thudded against a leather wing, knocking the flyer off course. Those wings tried to beat, to raise the heavy body. Kade had to leap to avoid the sweep of one threshing surface.

Then the susti came to earth behind them, and horse and men turned to face the thoroughly enraged creature.

✵✫ CHAPTER 11 ✫✵

DOKITAL'S NET LASHED OUT not in a cast to entangle the susti—he could not have managed such a feat alone—but to cut whip fashion across that pointed snout, flick punishment at the bulbous eyes. The thing squealed—the thin shriek partially drowned by the thunder of the drums and yet piercing enough to reach their ears through the din—gave way a step or two, an advantage the bound Ikkinni could not follow up.

But the stallion was not tied, nor was Kade. And now the Terran stooped, twisted the spear from Dokital's foothold before the native could stop him. With that in one hand and his knife in the other he circled to the right, trying to flank the creature.

And the horse, as if the animal caught a thought from the man, trotted back, came around to get behind the susti. One man against that horror would have had little chance, but the three who faced it now reduced the odds drastically.

Dokital lashed again, coming to the end of his ankle straps, striving to keep the susti occupied, occupied and grounded where they had the better of the battlefield. The beat of the drums reached a wild crescendo, deafening the men in the arena. Kade saw the stallion's open mouth, knew the horse was screaming, yet he could hear nothing of that equine rage. And the pounding beat was making him dizzy, attacking him with snaps of vertigo.

As yet the Terran saw no chance for a telling thrust against the susti. The creature used its wings as shields, holding him at a distance.

And a spear's throw under one of those flapping barriers was beyond his skill. Kade watched for the opportunity to stab into some part of that obscene body, but the stallion went into action.

Using the same tactics followed before with such excellent results, the horse came up behind the susti and struck out, aiming for the hunched back of the creature. But, as if it had sensed that onslaught, the bat-thing clapped wings and those sharp-shoed weapons struck fruitlessly against leather edges, sliding off without harm. As the stallion went to his knees, Kade rushed in, the haft of the spear braced between arm and ribs—thrusting with all the strength of his body to ram the point home.

He felt the queer sensation of the head tearing into flesh and then a blow struck him, flattening him to the ground. Dazed, gasping for breath, he watched one of those hooked-wing claws curl over him, and brought up his knife hand in feeble defense.

There was no cutting edge on that improvised dagger, it had been made to stab. And somehow he held it point up against that wing paw as it beat down. The needle tip he had ground into being skewed between fine bones, the force of that blow drove his own hand back against his chest with crushing brutality. But the wing snapped up and Kade rolled free.

Dokital had enmeshed one wing and the darting head of the susti in the widest folds of his net, and was bent almost bow-shaped as he fought to hold fast. Kade got to the other side, caught the straining cords. In the firelight they could see the dance of the spear haft in the side of the threshing creature. But the wing which was free beat wildly, its wounded claw-paw grabbing for the two men.

The horse charged, head down, mouth wide open, using teeth against the hide of the thing's back, tearing loose both pelt and flesh. And in a second rush he used hooves once again, this time landing squarely on the chosen goal between the hunched shoulders.

So driven to the ground the susti pulled Kade with it, tore the net from Dokital's hold. However, for the men, the fight was over. Brought shoulder to shoulder by the susti's struggles they half supported each other as the stallion, with the lightning swift action of his kind, smashed the thing as he had smashed its fellow, days earlier. And handicapped by its wounds the Klorian terror was now an easy kill.

Kade became aware that the clamor of the drums was dying, as if those drummers masked in the high shadows on the arena slopes were so bemused by the action below that they were dropping out of the infernal chorus which had summoned the susti. Now the Terran could detect individual beats in the once solid wave of noise, the rhythm was irregular as well as dying.

Yet no one had come from those serried ranks of watchers to interfere in the fight. Would a successful kill of the captive devil allow the three their freedom, or merely delay the vengeance of the watching natives? Judging by their treatment of Dokital they were hostile—

The susti was finished, a pulp beneath the dancing hooves of the horse. Kade pushed away from Dokital, circled about the mass on the ground to near the snorting, still wild-eyed four-footed fighter. He called softly, held out his hands.

For a second or two he was afraid that the animal was too excited to hear him. Then the head turned, the eyes regarded the Terran. Placing one foot carefully before the other as if he walked on some treacherous surface, the stallion came to Kade. That proud head was lowered until the forelock brushed against the man's bare chest, and the Terran's hands smoothed up the arch of the sweating neck, fondled the ears. Without hackamore he had no rider's control, yet this was a time to impress the native watchers and Kade must take it. Still caressing the horse, he mounted.

The stallion neighed, to be heard above the almost dead rattle of the few remaining drums. Kade, one hand on the stiff mane where the neck arch arose from the body, his other up, palm out and before him, dared to call out in the speech of the Trade post:

"Ho! Here are warriors!"

The last drum was dead. He could believe that he heard a sigh of concentrated breathing along those rows of spectators who were only a blur beyond the reaches of the firelight.

"Here are warriors!" He kneed the stallion, kept his seat as the horse obeyed with a high stepping prance of forefeet. And from the right he heard Dokital echo the boast.

"Here are the warriors!"

By all that he knew of Ikkinni custom, those in the darkness must acknowledge that cry and admit equality with the victors or send forth a champion to dispute a claim which was a dare to every fighting man in that half-seen assemblage. And what he would do if such a champion appeared, Kade had no idea. But among his own kind bravery and skill in battle were recognized passports to diplomatic relations, even between old enemies. And so it might prove in this other culture solar systems away.

"It is Dokital of the line of Dok the long-armed, of Amsog of the quick wit, of Gid of the red spear. It is Kade of the starwalkers from the far skies. It is Swiftfeet of the horse kind."

Dokital threw the words at the still silent throng.

"Here are warriors who have fought the devil kind, the devil kind of the collars, the devil kind who obey those of the collars, the devil kind of the stony places." Dokital jerked the end of net. The crushed head of the susti rolled in gruesome answer, and the stallion pawed the earth, danced a step closer to his trampled foe.

"Here are warriors!" For the third time the Ikkinni flung that into the faces of the massed tribesmen.

The crackle of the flames cut the night and below that small sound Kade thought he could detect another murmur, as the whisper of a breeze running along the slopes of the arena. They waited.

Then, from directly above the cave door of the susti, there was a stir in the shadows, a ripple of figures rising, giving place to a small group of natives who stepped out in the full light of the fires. They halted there, five of them, well built men with the glint of jewelry on their upper arms, their belts, but no telltale rings about their throats. And, as the three from the plains faced them, each raised his spear and drove it point deep in the sand, ceremoniously disarming themselves.

"Here are warriors—"

Kade relaxed. Dokital dropped his net. The stallion stood as a statue.

"It is Kakgil of the line of Akil of the stone arm."

"It is Dartig of the line of Tigri the wind-swift."

"It is Farqui of the Inner Cliffs."

"It is Losigil of the Bitter Water Place."

"It is Vuqic of the line of Stigi the strong heart."

Each announced himself in turn. Their names, their identifications meant nothing to Kade, but he memorized them, sure that none of these men were petty chieftains with only a handful of followers.

Their pride of bearing rather argued that he was fronting what might be the tribal leaders of the free interior, men on whom the Styor might have set fabulous prices. And if that were so, and he could make peaceful contact—Kade fought down his own soaring excitement, this was no time to hope for too much, to grow careless.

He who had named himself Kakgil made a quick downwards sweep with one hand. The cords holding Dokital twitched, loosened. With a kick the Ikkinni drew one foot out of an imprisoning circle, and then the other. The ex-slave stepped forward, leaving his bonds on the sand behind him.

"It greets Kakgil, as one who runs the high places to one who holds the spear over them."

"It greets the runner," Kakgil responded gravely. He plucked his spear out of the sand, reversed it with a graceful toss, and held out the butt to Dokital. The other took the weapon, spun it in a like fashion and drove the point into the ground again before his own feet. Kade guessed at the symbolism behind that action. If these two had been enemies, that enmity was now at an end.

"It has spoken true words," Dokital continued, and now there was again a hint of challenge in his tone. He put up one hand, drew his fingers lightly along the curve of the stallion's neck. The horse turned his head, regarded the Ikkinni, but accepted the attention with the same docility with which he had allowed Kade to mount.

"This is Swiftfeet, and the kind of Swiftfeet are for warriors, even as it said."

Kakgil looked at the Ikkinni, the horse and the Terran.

"It has spoken true words," he acknowledged. "The evil tale came to us out of the night, now we know that is evil. Swiftfeet is the friend of those in the heights. This is so!" His voice arose, carrying authority, the determination of his will, and again the murmur whispered about the arena. One by one the other chieftains echoed him. And so Kade found they had not only won the fight, but also acceptance among the free peoples of the hidden mountain valleys.

Before the dawn Kade, the horses, and Dokital were taken to one of those well concealed villages and the Terran witnessed for the first time the life of the Ikkinni who were not linked to the Styor will by the collars.

The architects of that village had taken advantage of a natural feature of the mountain side in their planning of what was in effect one great house set cunningly into a vast half-cavern where the over-hang of rock not only provided the erection of stone and fire-dried clay with added protection, but effectively concealed it from any but ground level detection.

"Once warriors lived in skin tents," Kakgil noted the Terran's interest. "For then hunters followed the kwitu. Afterwards there were hunters for hunters, and those who wandered away from the high places could be easily netted and taken. Thus we make these hidden places."

Kade studied the rough walls, the small, easily defended entrances, and smaller, high window holes. The structure was undeniably crude, put together by those who had worked only with a general idea of what they must accomplish and primitive, untaught skills. Compared to Cor, Kakgil's village was a child's sand castle set against a finely finished plasta playhouse. Yet it represented a vast, awesome step forward into another kind of civilization, made in only a generation or two by men who had been roving hunters. And the potential it suggested was startling.

"This is a fine place!" The Terran gave hearty tribute not only to the city-house but to the labor and the dream which had brought it into being. And his sincerity was plain to the chieftain, for Kakgil gave a small sound, close to a human chuckle.

"To us a fine place," he agreed. "There are others," he waved a hand to the spreading peaks of the mountains. "Many others."

Kade discovered that there had been no great consolidation among the free Ikkinni. They still lived in bands of a few family clans, and such a village as he was shown harbored no more than a hundred natives at the most. But several such were linked by loose alliance, and the gathering in the arena had been comprised of the adults of five such communities.

The Terran established a camp with the horses outside the cave of the village and he was not surprised when Dokital chose to remain with him. They were eating cakes of ground grass seeds supplied them by their hosts when Kade asked his first question,

"It was left tied . . . for the susti—"

Dokital swallowed, perhaps to gain time. But he did not evade a reply.

"Tied, yes; for susti, no."

"Why?"

"It was not friend. The starwalker knew secret to free Ikkinni but would not help. It was made safe."

Kade could follow that line of reasoning.

"So it was left while Dokital went for the free warriors?"

"That is so. It has said those are for warriors." He pointed to the horses.

"So Dokital took the horses to impress the free men, but they would not believe, holding the stranger prisoner?"

"That is so. It was struck from the back of the runner by a net. It was out of its body for a time. When it returned there were bonds, and it was judged a thing of the collar masters sent to bring monsters into the hills where the masters can not come on their flying things."

"But how did this tale of monsters spread so far from the flat lands?" Kade asked.

Dokital's lips shaped a half-smile. "Ask of the mountains where blows the force of the wind-breath. Drums talk among the hills, men tell false tales to those who have not seen with their two eyes, heard with their own ears, touched with the fingers of their hands. The collar masters spoke and the ripple of their speaking reached far."

Kade began to understand the pattern. The Styor had tried to make sure not only of the Traders at the post, but of any who might possibly escape into the mountains. The aliens had planted this story of monsters, seen that the rumor trickled back by "bush telegraph" into the holds of the outlaws, thereby making sure of a hostile reception for any refugees.

"Now warriors believe differently?"

Dokital selected another cake. "The warriors of five tribes have seen with their own eyes, heard with their lips. Soon they will come to this fire, ask for more talk concerning Swiftfeet and his wife ones."

But it was not about horses that the two Ikkinni who stepped quietly into the camp came to talk. Kakgil and the taller, thinner native who had introduced himself in the arena as Vuqic, stood waiting until Kade arose. And then, using the same ceremony as they had before, they pushed spear points into the earth.

"There is fire, and food," the Terran recited the formula he had learned at the post. "It is welcome," he inclined his head toward Kakgil and Vuqic, remaining on his feet until both were seated.

Kakgil came to the point brusquely. "There is a story that the one from beyond the stars has a new weapon to make collars into nothingness."

"Part of such a story is the truth," Kade admitted. "But there is this also; that when the weapon makes nothingness of the collars, some of those wearing them die."

"That is the truth," Dokital added. "Yet it is free." His hand went to his throat, rubbing the calloused skin where a collar had once chaffed.

"These weapons which make a collar nothing. Let us see one."

Kade held up empty hands. "One each of those did the starwalkers carry. It is gone blasted away, and so are the rest. For the masters of the collars brought the fire death to all my clan."

"So has that story been told also," Kakgil assented. "But if these weapons exist beyond the stars, then those who fly into the far sky can bring us more. Do they not give the masters many things in exchange for the skins of susti? And we know caves in which musti have never been troubled. We can build a mountain of skins in return for such weapons."

"There is this," Kade brought his own problem to the fore. "A ship of the starwalkers came two suns ago to the burnt place where its clan lived. When those in that ship find no life, they will depart again. Maybe to come no more. And already that ship may have returned to the stars."

"In the high places there are drums to send thoughts and calls from one clan holding to the next." Vuqic spoke for the first time. "Have the starwalkers no drums to sound among the star?"

"There is a chance that there is one. But between this place and that lies much ground, also many hunting parties of collared ones. Out in the open country the flying ships of the collar masters can capture or kill those who try to reach the burned place. And it can not be sure that the drum is still there."

Kakgil laid a stick upon the small fire. "This matter shall be thought upon," he declared. "Now what of this Swiftfeet who serves warriors without a collar? Why was it brought?"

Kade noted that the Ikkinni gave the horse the "it" designation of a man, rather than the "that" of an animal.

"There is a saying," Vuqic cut in once more, "that it was to be taken to a master of collars—the high master—for a new toy thing."

"So was the thought," Kade said cautiously.

"But not all the thought," Dokital corrected. "It," he indicated Kade, "said that the runners are for warriors. And what master of collars is a true warrior? Kill is the order, but there is no spear in the hand of such a one. A warrior kills for himself, not afar and by word only."

Kade relied on what he knew of Ikkinni customs. "There is a story—in truth a story," he used their own idiomatic approach of one of the honored elders of their kind, a born story teller whose phenomenal memory and powers of invention could recall one of their age-old sagas, or add a new tale fashioned out of the events of the latest clan hunt. And to the Terran's gratification he saw that they were giving him close attention.

"Where it dwells among the stars there were once those who were also in their way masters of collars. And these same animals were ridden into battle by their warriors, so that the other peoples who had no such helpers could be easily hunted for killing or caught to be made into collared ones. But the animals were new to the land which they found a good one, and they broke free from their masters, running into hidden places. And the Ikkinni of that land found the beasts were also friends to them, so they stole more from the city places of the masters." He simplified, made into a story they could understand the explosion of history which had marked the coming of the horse to his own plains-roaming race, and what had occurred thereafter. And seeing their gleaming eyes, Kade knew that the parallel was plain to them.

Dokital spoke first. "These are a treasure to keep!"

"Ha, so!" agreed Kakgil. "But that is locked in time. Now is now and there is the weapon of the starwalkers. Give such into the hands of warriors and no hunters or collar masters shall enter these lands!"

"The weapons are beyond the stars!" Kade objected, afraid they would demand which he could not possibly give them.

"Other things have come from the stars. This is a thing to be thought on." Kakgil arose, reached for his spear. "This star drum for your signaling must be thought on, too."

☾⋆ **CHAPTER 12** ⋆☽

THIS TIME THE TERRAN headed toward the plains by night instead of day, and he did not go alone. A picked band of Ikkinni trackers, seasoned to the alarms and cautions of the hunted, went as guides, and, he suspected, guards. The natives were determined not to lose the off-worlder until they had made some sort of a bargain for stunners. Although Kade had continued to argue that the Trade Ship might have long since left Klor.

The very slim chance of using the hidden com was one he did not like to consider. He could not push out of mind the doubt that he might now be an exile on the alien planet, without hope of rescue. So he tried to concentrate on the business of getting safely back to the destroyed post.

They threaded a more complicated route than the one he had used days earlier, once skirting a camp of collared men, sleeping feet to the fire, their Overman sheltered in a lean-to of branches. Kade's Ikkinni neighbor toyed with his spear as he eyed them thoughtfully. But any miss from a death stroke meant torture for the slaves and the native did not use his weapon.

"Two watchers," he whispered to Kade, his motion only dimly to be seen in the light of the dying fire as he motioned right and left.

The Terran could detect no sound except the usual ones of the night. A sleeping slave stirred, and both watchers tensed. Kade had a knife, a spear under his hand. But he longed for a stunner. The slave

109

muttered and rolled over, but his restlessness did not arouse any of his fellows.

With finger pressure on the Terran's shoulder, the Ikkinni signaled Kade to the right. And the off-worlder applied all his knowledge of woodcraft to melt into the brush as noiselessly as possible. Together they flitted into a small gully where another joined them.

"It on watch now sleeps?"

The low voice of Kakgil answered. "It does."

Again their party drew together and pushed on. False dawn found them in file along the banks of a stream where rank, reedlike grass grew. The Ikkinni put the natural features of the spreading bog to their use. Mud, grey-green, was scraped from holes, plastered to the haired skins, to Kade's breeches, chest and shoulders. Handfuls of dried grass laid into that sticky coating so that every man could fade undetected into the landscape.

They continued to stick to the bog, following a trail, the markers of which Kade could not discover. Perhaps they existed only in the memory of the native who now led. As far as the Terran could determine they were now to the north of the former post, well out into the plains region.

Looming up now and again were islands of firmer land on which they paused to rest. And, as the first lines of the climbing sun split the sky, they ate grain cakes, drank sparingly from the leather bottle Kakgil carried. It contained a thin, acid liquid which burned the tongue, but satisfied the body's desire for water.

The village chieftain smoothed out a stretch of clay, marked on it with a stick. A finger's whirl was the swamp about them, a dot the site of the post. Kade began to realize that, far from being kept to the mountains as the Styor had contended and the Traders believed, these free natives must have made countless scouting trips into the plains in which their fathers had been hunted, each carrying in a trained memory vast knowledge of the lost lands. What raiders they would make, given adequate weapons and the means for swift movement!

But this was not a matter of future guerrilla attacks against Styor holdings. It was their own safe visit to a site which could easily be patrolled from both air and ground level. The Terran digested that crude map, tried to align it with his memories of the countryside.

If the scout ship had been sighted by the Styor—and unless the aliens were possessed by a suicidal folly they would have left a sentry near the post—there could be a Klorian force at hand already, or on their way to the burn-off. Kade warned of that and found that Kakgil had accepted such a possible peril. If the Styor were at the side, the mountaineers would leave a scout in hiding and withdraw, to try again. And the Terran understood the monumental patience of these people who had fought for a century against drastic odds. The drive which had sent his own species into the star lanes met time as an enemy, these men used it as a tool.

The sun which had promised so brightly in the dawn hours, shone only for a space. Clouds gathered above the mountains. Dokital, pointing to the wall of mist hanging above their back trail, laughed.

"The Planner has planned, now the Spearman readies His weapon. This is a good day, a good thing, a good plan."

Wind rasped across the plains, struck chill, lifting the vapors of the bog, thrusting at the tangled covering of their island. The signs of the storm suggested one more severe than any Kade had witnessed on Klor.

With the push of the wind at their backs they obeyed Kakgil's order to move on. Half an hour later, cloaked in the deepening murk, they splashed from a shallow runnel of water onto a solid strip of earth marking the fringe of the plains.

A Styor flyer might just try to buck the wind, but Kade doubted it unless the pilot had definite orders to operate. This weather should ground all routine patrols. But the method of advance, in a zig-zag pattern with frequent halts to take cover, proved to the Terran that Kakgil did not intend to underestimate the enemy.

Lightning crisped in the sky, bringing the tingling smell of ozone. Another such flash halted them, half blinded, and Kade was sure that unleashed energy had struck not too far away. Could the burn-off scar, by some weird chemistry of the glassy slag, be drawing the electrical fury of the storm?

That whip of flashing death was merely the forerunner of rain. Rain and wind which beat, pummeled their bodies, washing away their mud disguises, leaving them gasping in a blanket of rushing water. They tied their weapons to their belts and linked hands, to stagger on, backs bent to the storm. The falling fury of the water, the dark of the clouds which held it, concealed from Kade whether the Trade ship still stood, fins planted on the landing apron.

The off-worlder stumbled and went to his knees, losing his hold on Dokital, his line partner. His palm came down on slick, wet surface, smooth yet rippling. What he had fallen over was the edge of the burn site. And there was no waiting ship.

They could not walk across that surface crust, running wet and too slippery for feet shod in either Terran boots or the hide coverings of the Ikkinni. On hands and knees the party crept over the glassy expanse, searching for the opening to the underground installation.

Kade found it difficult to connect this slick slab of crystallized earth and stone with the square of buildings, the inner courtyard, he had known. He could not even guess from what quarter of the compass he had approached the scar. Where their goal might now lie could be within inches, feet, yards, or the length of the scar.

It was not the Terran who located the break in the crust. Kade, alerted by the message running from man to man along the advancing Ikkinni, came to the pit he had to explore by touch rather than sight. One or two of the Team *had* refuged below, to be freed by the ship's crew. Whether the com was still there and undestroyed he must learn.

Water poured over his fingers, cascaded into the depths. That flood could ruin the com in a short time. Kade managed to make the Ikkinni understand what had to be done. One of the hunting nets was slung over the edge and Kade used it for a ladder. As he descended water rose about his feet, lapped at his calves, wet the breeches above the tops of his boots. Then his feet met solid surface, he could feel walls on either side but not ahead.

The passage, if passage it was, ran on. And the water, pouring from above, was rising. If that unknown path ahead took a downward way perhaps the flood had already sealed it.

Kade shivered. If the water reached the com he was exiled. Time was not on his side now. He released his hold on the net, waded forward, waves washing about him, splashing to mid-thigh.

The footing was good, although the flood hindered swift movement. He kept one hand on the wall as a guide. And when he had gone some twenty paces he knew that the water was not rising any more swiftly than it had in the entrance pit.

On his twenty-first step the black dark of the pocket was lost in a flick of light. Over his wet head shone the green glow of an atmo lamp. He must have crossed some automatic signal set in the wall. Ahead were two more such lights, their round balls reflected from the curling waves through which he labored. Three lights then a sealed door, a door with a locking hand hollow in its center panel.

Was that lock tuned to open to the flesh pattern of any Terran, or only to certain members of the Team? But who could select survivors in advance?

Kade wiped his right hand back and forth across his chest, tucked it into his armpit for a long moment, hoping to rid it of the chill moisture. Then he fitted fingers and palm into the mould and waited. The slow creep of water was now washing a fraction of an inch higher every time it slapped against his body.

There was no warning click. Kade snatched his hand away as the panel flipped back into the wall. Around him the water rushed on, lapping into the room, swirling around the few pieces of furniture. There were wall bunks, some open ration tins on a pull-down table, signs of hasty leaving.

But what Kade wanted was still there; the com. He splashed to that shelf. However as he reached for the starting button he saw another object, poised directly before the communicator. And he had been briefed in the proper use of that sectional rod mounted on a firm base.

Now he knew that the men who had waited in that room, or some member of the ship's crew, had suspected—or hoped—for his escape. There would be no answer to any message sent from the com. Perhaps the installation itself had been booby-trapped to prevent examination by native or Styor—but he did not need it.

Kade caught up that tube. Sealed into it were delicate works, the technology of which was beyond him. But it would work when and if he desired. Cradling it against him, the Terran made his way back along the waterlogged passage. He had only to locate a proper site, set up what he carried, and there would be a new landing field on Klor, one not supervised by the Styor.

"It has?" Kakgil pushed close as he climbed out of the pit.

"It has a Star drum!" Kade fended off the other's hand. "But only it can sound this drum."

"Sound then!" Dokital moved in from the other side.

Kade shook his head. "Not here. Not now. A safe place, in the mountains."

With what he carried he wanted to be as far from the post as he could get before the storm ceased to protect them from the threat of Styor sky sweeps. And he conveyed that urgency to the Ikkinni.

The rainfall lessened as they plodded on, their pace which had begun as a trot, dropping to a dogged walk. Towards sunset they gained refuge in a criss-cross maze of foothills and they camped wet and cold that night, not daring a fire.

Two days later they came again into the valley of Kakgil's village to find it deserted. Only the horses, still free, welcomed Kade. He mounted volunteers from his escort, Kakgil one of them, and they headed on, into the heart of the range where the most daring slave hunters had never ventured.

A full week of the longer Klorian days passed before their small party caught up with an Ikkinni war party. Kakgil called a conference of scouts who knew the land while Kade set up his signal tube in demonstration, explained the terrain needed and why. Hunters compared notes, grew heated in dispute, finally agreed and voiced their suggestions through Iskug, who had joined the band.

"Two suns, two sleeps away, there is a place where long ago the Spearman struck deep into the earth." He rounded his hands into a cup. "It has seen the ships from the stars. If it who drives such a ship is skillful, the ship could be set into this place as so." He inserted a finger tip into the curled fingers of his other hand.

"This is the only place?" Iskug's description was too graphic to be reassuring. The Ikkinni agreed that the described crater was the best and safest landing the range had to offer.

Later Kade, standing at the end of a grueling climb and looking down into that hole, was not sure. There was floor space enough, yes, to set a scout down. And the surface appeared as level as any ground. But the fitting of the ship into the hollow required skill such as only a veteran pilot would possess. However Trade pilots were top men.

They made their way to the floor of the crater. The eruption which had caused the blowout must have been a cataclysmic one. Kade held the signal at shoulder level, triggered a thumb button, and slowly turned, giving the hidden lens the complete picture of this rock-walled well for broadcasting. Then he walked to what he judged was the center of the open space and secured the tube on the ground with latching earth spikes. Last of all he brought his hand down sharply on the pointed tip of the cone. There was no way for him to know whether the broadcaster was really working; his answer could only come, in time, from off-world.

Kade sat outside the crude hut at the lip of the crater. His calendar was a series of scratches on the boulder which served as a section of wall. By that reckoning he had been doing sentry duty here more than a month.

His thoughts were series of *ifs* now. *If* the signal, lonely in the crater, had somehow been damaged during their journey here, then the broadcaster had never been beamed starward at all.

If the Ikkinni lost patience they might turn on him. Styor parties were raiding unceasingly into the lower valleys driving many clans. from their villages. The spring hunting was interrupted. Hunger stalked the refugees. Let some chieftain pin the blame on the presence of the off-world fugitive and Kade might be delivered to the aliens for a truce.

If the Styor continued to bore in they would force his own withdrawal from here.

If—if—if—

A whistle from below broke his moody thoughts. Dokital, his dark-haired body hardly distinguishable from the rocks until he moved, came up at a pace suggesting trouble.

"Slavers!" The Ikkinni reported curtly.

"Where?"

"The water valley. They make camp."

Never before had any Styor-controlled party come this close to the crater. And if the aliens were establishing a camp this early in the day, they meant a stay of more than one night's duration.

"Kakgil—the horses?"

"They move north taking the kwitu trail."

That was a slight lifting of the Terran's burden of responsibility.

Kakgil would move his people and the off-world animals they now cherished to safety, putting a stretch of rough and easily defended country between themselves and the invaders.

"It goes?" Dokital fidgeted by the hut. Having once worn a collar he was not minded to be trapped again.

"It must stay for a while." Within the hour, before sunset, at any moment, the Terran ship could land. He must remain here. "Let Dokital go."

"Not so." The Ikkinni sat down, laid his spear across his knee. "From this place the evil ones can be seen, they can not creep up as if they net the musti."

Maybe they could not bring a net, Kade thought grimly, but the aliens had other and more potent ways of bringing the hunted to terms. And he was sure that the Styor had provided these servants with them.

Once they sighted a group of collar slaves searching for fire wood. But there was no indication that their own perch was under suspicion. In the hut they had water, two day's rations of seed cakes. And they could stretch that supply if need be.

"One comes."

"Whereso?"

"By the rock of the kwitu horn."

Kade followed the line of Dokital's pointing spear tip. The new-comer was no Ikkinni, collared or free, nor the Overman of a squad. Away from a carrying-chair, the other marks of his Klorian godship, a Styor was climbing stiffly up the rugged slope. He held one arm bent at chest level and divided his attention between his footing and a band about his wrist. In his other hand he carried the ultimate in the aliens' armament—the needler!

Flight was cut off. The Terran judged that the wristband was some kind of tracking device, perhaps centered on his own thought waves. He could walk backward, step out into the space of the crater, and crash down to end near the signal. Only then the Styor might use that signal for bait.

On the other hand, suppose he was needled down. Would the alien pass the signal unnoticed? The Styor was astute enough to investigate why the off-worlder had camped here. Either way the bejeweled, slim humanoid had all the cards on his side. Kade had overestimated the sloth of the pampered lords, underestimated their desire to make sure of the last Terran.

About the Styor's middle was an anti-person belt. No overlord would risk his precious skin with the slightest chance of a counterattack. The spear in Kade's hold, any Ikkinni net, a rock thrown by a desperate man, would rebound from the aura now about the alien as from a dura-steel wall.

Unless—Kade searched the ground about him for some suggestion of offence or defense. The Styor could probably track them if they tried to run for it. He did not know the range of the instrument the alien wore. On the other hand he was not going to be needled down without some counterattack, no matter how feeble.

More to gain time than by any plan the Terran signalled Dokital away from the hut, along the edge of the crater. The rough terrain hid them from actual sighting by the Styor, though his locator would bring him on their track.

Single file the two walked a narrow line along the drop. An idea grew in Kade's mind. A chance he was now desperate enough to try.

The Styor reached the hut, did not even glance into its empty interior, but came on, treading the same way the fugitives had taken. Again Kade signed to Dokital, sending the Ikkinni away from him. Then the Terran halted, balancing his spear in his hand. A few feet beyond, the ancient bowl of the crater was split with a crack wide enough to offer protection to a slender Terran body. He marked that down.

He was waiting as the Styor's head arose, the alien's eyes raised from the device on his wrist to the man before him. Then Kade hurled his spear.

The aim was true, though the point struck that invisible guard a good six inches away from the Styor's chest. And the involuntary reaction of the other carried through even as Kade had hoped. A flinch backward set the alien's booted heel on a patch of smooth stone. There was a wide flail of arms as the Styor went backward into thin air.

His safety belt would save his life, but now he would have the inner wall of the crater to climb. The Terran's attack had bought them a measure of time. Kade sped to the crevice, Dokital joining him. The Styor was floating down, settling to the floor of the crater.

But they had only gained a few moments of time, no real escape. Only—

Kade's arm went about Dokital, he carried the native with him in a rush as from overhead came a clap of sound louder than any thunder. Stone scraped skin raw as they tumbled into the rock crack. Above there was a flare of blinding light, and Kade hid his eyes with one bruised arm. The roar of a ship's tail flames as it braked into the heart of the crater was deafening.

Perhaps the Styor had had one instant of horror, a second's realization of descending death—then nothing at all. The same end he or his fellows had visited on the Trade post had already been his.

As the Terran and the Ikkinni crawled from their refuge the fumes of molten sand arose from that cup. Set neatly in the center was the star-ship. Kade climbed to the rim of the rock wall, waved at that expanse of pitted metal although no hatch had yet opened. But the response came soon enough, a ramp swung out to ground against the mountain some feet below him. He slid down, hearing his boots clang against its surface, hardly yet able to believe in that opportune arrival.

Somehow he was not surprised to be met by Abu in the cabin adjoining the control section. Nor was he more than mildly interested in the fact that the Commander's companion there wore five ticks of gold on the collar of his tunic.

"That's about it, sir." He had cut his report to the pertinent facts as best he could. Reaction was beginning to undermine the exultant self-confidence which had accompanied him into that cabin. There was a black list of sins of omission and commission which could be charged against him. What had Ristoff said on Lodi? If he fouled this last chance—And now the Book-of-Rules boys could pick Kade Whitehawk into little bits.

"Most reprehensible!" The five tick VIP pressed the button to turn off his recorder. "Now," the officer pushed away the machine with a gesture of repudiation. "Let us consider our real business."

"Most satisfactory." Abu's tone mimicked that used only moments before, but the words were different.

Somehow the formality of their meeting was gone as if the VIP had skinned off a tight tunic. He grinned and punched refreshment keys in the tabletop.

"A nice piece of work, one to keep rolling, Whitehawk."

"Roll right along," Abu joined the approbation. "Harder to stop now than a meteor with a musti net."

Kade was almost brave enough to demand an explanation.

"The time has come, sir," Abu added, "to initiate another fledgling into the fold."

Kade accepted the drink bubble the VIP extended, sucked a full mouthful of *Stardew*, Mars-side proof, without knowing just what he swallowed.

"Yes, a tale to unfold." The VIP drank. He bore, Kade decided critically, a not too distant resemblance to Che'in at that Trader's blandest and most irritating.

"The answer to your leading question," the officer continued blandly, "is that you've passed a little test with all jets flaming. You were handpicked for a job, sent here to use your wits. And you did. You see, there is the Policy—and the Plan."

"Seldom do the twain meet," Abu intoned piously.

His superior chuckled. "Be glad, Commander, that the right hand and the left do not shake too often. This is the way of it, young man. We have our loyal servants of Trade, who live and breathe by the Book, never, never make a mistake, and are a shining glory to the Service. Then we have some black sheep who also serve in their rebellious fashion. We call them the warrior breed." He paused, sucked at his drink bubble. "Their first general testing is to be sent to a planet where the Styor are really unbearable. If they can scrape through an 'incident' without being too far damned by the resultant publicity, then they are promoted to a Team on such a world as Klor.

"As you know, each Team is selected from widely different basic Terran racial stocks with a few of the normal "Tradetype" for cover. It is always our hope that one of our undercover 'warriors' will find inspiration in his new environment and manage to pull off a *coup* which will give another nudge toward the upsetting of Styor power. A pinch here, a prod there, little irritations breaking out all over the galaxy, yet nothing they can actually connect with us or any plan. That is the Plan!"

Kade saw. It was looking at a familiar landscape from an angle so bizarre he might indeed be viewing a new world.

"But the Styor burnt the post. Why?"

"There is such a thing as coincidence. Here your bit of pushing worked into the High-Lord-Pac's own bid for fame and fortune. He is trying out a formula for getting rid of unwelcome Terrans and building up a reputation for law enforcement at one and the same time. We'll let him think he got away with it—for a while. Long enough for your experiment to get a good start. What have you in mind for these Ikkinni? Mounted raids and guerrilla warfare?"

Kade nodded. He had a feeling that the VIP was far ahead of him, that his one or two bright discoveries were a matter of kindergarten games in an obscure backyard playground.

"He might be persuaded to see it through," Abu remarked. "That's the third step in our real Service, Whitehawk."

"Five horses—and the mountains crawling with Styor. How many years do you think it would take to make Cor uneasy?" Kade roused himself to demand.

"Oh, you don't have to have it quite as rugged as all that." The VIP clicked open a wall storage compartment, brought forth a belt and holstered stunner. He drew the weapon, slid it across the table to Kade's hand.

"Now that is something you will find useful. We've pushed through a rush order at the base, and can let you have about fifty now, with a drop of more to arrange for later. Try that on a collar control and you'll see some pleasing results, without obnoxious side features. Horses—well, another drop of those will take some doing. But clear us a plains-side place and we'll oblige. That is, of course, if you stay on here."

Kade fingered the stunner. He did not in the least doubt that it would act just as promised. Fifty of those to hand—why, they could free the slave packs now hunting them here, use the knowledge of the freed men against their masters—Open a section of plain—Yes, it could be done. A raid in the outer fringe, a landing site far enough from Cor that they could keep it open for two Klorian days, maybe longer. He heard Abu laugh.

"The relay is clicking, sir. Already he marches to unmask the High-Lord-Pac."

Kade grinned. "Not quite as fast as all that, sir."

The VIP nodded. "Start small, and don't push too hard. This may be *your* big war, it's only a small skirmish in the Plan."

Kade buckled on the stunner belt. "Tell me, sir, how long has the Plan been in operation."

For the first time since he clicked off the recorder the officer lost his genial air of satisfaction. "For about two hundred years."

Kade stared. "And how long—"

"Until," Abu answered softly, "a push here, a push there topples a star empire. An event I am beginning to doubt any of us here will live to see. Not that that matters."

And, thought Kade, perhaps it did not. But one could get a lot of satisfaction out of a good stiff push—with the Styor on the receiving end.

EYE
OF THE
MONSTER

☽★ CHAPTER 1 ★☾

REES NAPER OPENED HIS EYES. He had come into almost instant consciousness from the night's sleep as he always did. But there was something about his awakening this time, and he lay without any other movement save the raising of eyelids, trying to hear, to sense, to think what was different this morning.

A faint breeze shifted through the sonic net across the window to stir the rustling inner drapery within touching distance. That was it! The sounds, or rather the lack of the right ones for this place and hour. Those he had awakened to hear about the mission for months were missing this morning.

Rees moved swiftly, his hand burrowing into the chink between the foam plasta mattress and the bunk frame, reaching for what he had put there last night after hearing the last urgent warning on the com. Leather, satin smooth and silk supple, curled about his fingers as he pulled out the blaster belt with its holstered weapon. He clasped it to his chest as he rolled off the bunk and went to look through the sonic designed to keep out jungle insect life.

The courtyard of the mission lay open in Ishkur's greenish sunlight. A hoobra hen pecked at a bug, then made a running leap to capture the escaping victim before it took wing. Otherwise that space between the buildings was empty, save for the small creatures that lived in the ornamental flower beds and circular pool.

Rees hurriedly pulled on shirt and the breeches with their attached jungle boots. He was chilled in spite of the day's warmth.

You could smell it, sniff it up as surely as if it were the perfume of the violet tipped toofaa reeds out there in the water garden. Trouble—bad! Uncle Milo was wrong, and they were going to have to face up to the result of that error in judgment, that ingrained stubbornness on the part of the head of the mission.

Now with the blaster riding on his hip, Rees glanced over his other emergency preparations; the trail bag he had packed last night. It was too late to hope to get away with more than a survival kit. Again, because of Uncle Milo and his refusal to face facts as they were and not as he decreed them to be.

Rees slapped his palm on the hand lock by the corridor door. In the hall he paused for a long moment, his back against the wall, to listen and smell. Six months as Duggan Vickery's hunting assistant had given him some training with which to face this crisis.

No sound of any the Ishkurians about nor any trace of the distinctive body odor of the natives, so easy to detect when their emotions were aroused. Instead the beckoning scent of Terran coffee. Rees followed that quickly. No Ishkurian would drink coffee. The off-world beverage was rank poison as far as they were concerned and even to smell it upset their insides. Which meant the natives must have cleared out of the mission completely or Dr. Naper would not be brewing a pot now.

Rees sped past three rooms to the door at the end of the hall. The man seated at the table in the room beyond glanced up from the recorder-reader, a faint trace of frown automatically lining the space between his deep-set eyes.

"Good morning, Rees." His tone was precise and, as always, disapproving. Milo Naper and the nephew who shared his quarters shared very little else, neither ideas, emotions nor interests.

"What's going on?" Rees halted by the table. The com unit stood in the corner but its message screen was dark. It was not even turned on. He hurried to flick the button, only to be greeted by a din of static. A mountain storm must be in progress, blanketing out any call from the port at Nagassara.

"We can certainly do without that," Dr. Naper snapped. "Turn it off at once. I do not care to hear any more of this foolish blithering about trouble with the tribes. The utter stupidity of those chair warmers at the port leads one to completely despair of the Forces. If those officers would leave their comfortable quarters once in a while to get out and really learn something about this planet and its people, we'd have no more of this howling about trouble to come when the Patrol pulls out. Trouble to come—faught! I've been on Ishkur for twenty years, and the tribes have always been peaceful and very grateful for what we have been able to do for them."

"What about what happened at Aklanba?" Rees curbed his impatience and exasperation. "And the Patrol's always been here to keep order."

"It has always been my experience that off-world traders cause disturbances. Their greedy grasping for profit can start any number of minor outbreaks, even on peaceful worlds. Aklanba should never have been established that close to the Places of the Old Forest. To permit that was just another typical ill-judged decision of the government, a perfect affront to the High Trees. And doubtless the garbled report we heard about the disturbance there was greatly exaggerated. This fear of an Ishkurian uprising when the Patrol leaves is an evil thing.

"I told Jawin yesterday when he chose to take himself and his family to Nagassara—the Fermals also—that neither of them need look for any further employment here after they discover how foolish their panic was. In fact, I have dictated to the recorder my condemnation of their desertion at the time. Fifteen years of labor and aid to these jungle tribes can not be cancelled out merely because a few troops are going off-world—as they should have done long since. The Council is only coming to their collective senses at last in breaking up such autocratic bounds of control. I have the highest confidence in the assurances of tranquility given by the High Trees. To send away the Patrol is the first step in righting the wrongs of colonialism."

"There was a burning a month ago, and Ishback, Ishgar and Ishwan, all High Trees, directed it." Rees held tightly to his self control. Uncle Milo accepted wholeheartedly the mission line when it came to administration polices.

Dr. Naper's thin cheeks showed a stain of red. "I will not have such falsehoods repeated in my house! That vicious propaganda of the military is enough to foul the mouth of any man who repeats it. I know Ishgar, he has been educated in our schools at Nagassara. To resort to those vile superstitious practices would be utterly foreign to both his training and his nature. If you cannot forget that asinine indoctrination you had at the academy then please do not attempt to spew out such stuff in public here!"

"Then you will continue to stay, in spite of the warning last night?"

"Stay? Of course I'm staying."

"Did the 'copter return yet?"

"I don't know, nor do I care."

Rees held to his temper with a maximum of control. "What about the Beltz family? And that Salarika trader, Sakfor?" he persisted.

"I am glad to say that Gideon Beltz has not been carried away by this irresponsible hysteria with which we have been deluged for the past few weeks. And what the Salariki do is no concern of the mission."

"None of the natives are here this morning."

"Certainly. And I do not expect to see any for at least three days. This is the First Fast of the Leaves. Which only underlines the crass moronity of those officers in Nagassara. The tribes will be fully occupied with planting rituals for the next ten days. And it would be impossible for Ishkurians to make any hostile moves now, which they surely don't wish to, as you will see. This, Rees, is all the result of that infernal meddling on the part of Survey and the other Services. All this clamor concerning trends and precognition reports—the fiasco will simply discredit such twaddle. You will thank me in years to come, boy, that I was able to make the necessary decision on your behalf before you became a real part of their justly disliked and mistrusted employment."

Rees' lips were a thin line, pressed hard against the teeth. He had learned to swallow a lot in the past three years, but this morning he knew he would have to get away from Uncle Milo in a hurry or he'd say the unforgivable and unforgettable. While he had nothing in common with Dr. Naper, and they did much better apart than together, still he had not been able to leave last night with the Jawins. That would have been standing by with a holstered blaster while his uncle, unarmed, faced the charge of a kaga bull.

He did not share Dr. Naper's belief in the good will of the tribes and their continuing friendship once the Patrol's pacifying strength was removed. And somehow he must get his uncle to see the truth and clear out in time. But he could not do it if they quarreled.

"Where are you going now?" Dr. Naper demanded. "You haven't eaten any breakfast."

"I still have a job, if Vickery didn't pull out," Rees said over his shoulder. "By the looks, I'm late at camp already."

The younger man hurried on into the courtyard. It was true that the First Fast could have drawn the mission people back to their villages. But the feeling of danger, which Rees had had weighing on him since his awakening, quieted his tread now, set his eyes to watching bushes, the shadows in doors and windows.

"Rees!"

He whirled in a half crouch, blaster out and ready. Then with the same speed he thumbled the weapon back in the holster.

"Hey, Rees, you're such a quick draw!" Gordy Beltz materialized from under the low hanging branches of a buppu bush, his face liberally smeared golden with the juice of buppu berries. "You going to the animal camp? Take me 'long, please, Rees! There's nobody to play with and I'm lonesome."

Rees hesitated. Gordy could be a pest at times. But at the moment his small form in the oval of the courtyard did have an oddly forlorn appearance. And it certainly wasn't wise for the small boy to be wandering about by himself today.

"Where's your mother, Gordy?"

"She's got lither fever. Dad gave her a shot and told her to stay in bed. And Ishbi and Ishky never came this morning. Dad gave me a pyriration out of the can for breakfast. Please, Rees, can't I go with you? I want to see all the animals again 'fore Captain Vickery ships them out."

Rees stood with his feet slightly apart, his hand on his hips. "And if I take you—what's the order?"

"Don't touch, don't touch anything. I promise, Rees." Gordy pulled a narrow leaf from the buppu bush, spit into its middle, twisted it into a knot which he threw into the pool. "By the Tree Blood I promise."

Kids picked up things and got them surprisingly right, Rees thought fleetingly. Gordy made that oath with the same gestures and intonation a Guardian would use. Sure, kids picked things up, they remembered well, too. Why, he himself could still do the fish dance of the Salariki and he was a year less than Gordy in age when they lifted off that world. But then he'd had special training from the time he was old enough to notice anything, intended to make him absorb points of alien culture. As the son of a Survey officer he was supposed to follow his father into that service.

If only Commander Naper had come back safely from the Volsper run. But he had not and Uncle Milo Naper had turned up relentlessly at the cadet school and jerked Rees out. Well, in spite of his efforts, Uncle Milo hadn't made a mission man out of his nephew, only left him dissatisfied and rootless, unhappy, a constant irritation, in a way, to the dedicated people of an antagonistic way of life.

"All right," he told Gordy now. "Come on." He knew what being lonesome meant, to a greater degree than he hoped Gordy would ever realize.

"You aren't going by the main path, Rees?"

"I want to look at the 'copter park."

"The 'copter isn't there. It didn't come back yet. Rees, what does a red alert mean? They were sending that on the com when Dad shut it off."

"Some trouble—maybe in Nagassara."

"'Cause the Patrol is leaving? Why'd the Patrol leave, Rees?"

One thing Rees had learned from his father's training; straight answers and truthful ones were due children. He tried to simplify this one.

"Ishkur has been a part of the South Sector Empire. That means a collection of different worlds under one government. Two years ago the Council decided that frontier planets, such as this one, should be allowed to set up their own ruling states. So they ordered the Patrol to withdraw by a certain date. And all off-worlders who thought they might need the protection of the Patrol were to go then also."

"But the Empire was bad, wasn't it, Rees? Dad says it was bad. The off-worlders shouldn't rule Ishkurians."

"Some things were bad. In every form of government we've used so far, Gordy, there are bad things. But on some worlds our ways were better than the rule the natives had for themselves before we came."

"Not here, though, Dad says that." Gordy grasped Rees' hand and varied the trot he maintained to match the young man's strides with a series of skipping hops.

"Perhaps—" Rees had reached the landing area. Gordy's report was correct, there was no sign of the 'copter. Yet neither Jawin nor Permal would have left the flyer on robo-control when they disembarked with their families at Nagassara. And so it should have ridden back the guide beam for a landing hours ago. Rees' fingers tightened on Gordy's hand until the boy gave a yelp and tried to pull free.

Vickery had a 'copter, one really larger than the mission's, since he had to transport the caged animals in it. They could pack in the Beltz three, and the two Napers easily in one trip. And perhaps the Captain could argue Uncle Milo into seeing some sense. To Dr. Naper, Rees was a boy, stubbornly wrong-headed, but Uncle Milo would be forced to admit Vickery knew the Ishkurians very well and his advice would mean something.

"What's the matter, Rees? How come we have to hurry so fast?" Rees had quickened pace until Gordy was running.

"I'm late, and if the guides and hunters have left, the Captain will need me to help feed the animals."

At first the clearing down by the river appeared normal. Except no Ishkurians squatted about checking on capture nets, or charring torkum leaves over the fire before they chewed them. The cages ready for transport were arranged around three sides of a hollow square, with the river to the west. But at second glance Rees saw that those cages' doors were now swinging wide open; their occupants had all been loosed.

He ran to the plasta bubble of Vickery's tent, pulled open the zip-close. The owner, his guns, his jump bag were all missing; Vickery had cleared out and in a hurry.

Rees fairly leaped past the line of cages to the clearing of the 'copter. Pulled to one side was the jungle roller car, but the flyer was gone.

"Rees," Gordy had followed him into the tent, now he came running with a folded paper in his hand. "This had your name on it. Where's Captain Vickery and all the animals?"

"Gone away." He grabbed the paper from Gordy.

"Notice from the port." The words were hurriedly scrawled. "No ship-off possible for the animals. Red alert, I have to answer militia call. Can't find Kassa, when she turns up, keep her for me, bring her in with you."

Rees swallowed. Kassa! Vickery had not delayed to hunt Kassa! He felt cold all through his middle, sick and cold. Kassa, the Spician hound, was Vickery's prized tracker. The hunter would not have left her except to obey the most urgent order. The off-world militia must have been called up to answer some trouble at the port.

"Gordy!" he called harshly to the boy who had wandered toward the river, "come here!"

"Rees—I can hear something! Please—come and listen!"

But Rees could hear it also, a low throb of whimper, a noise which added to the sick feeling inside him. Suppose—suppose Vickery had not lifted with the 'copter after all? Suppose what had happened at Aklanba had also chanced here? Rees swallowed down growing sick panic.

He caught Gordy's shoulder, propelled the boy to the jungle roller. Pushing him into the seat Rees climbed in also to make a check. Vickery had not even waited to dismantle the sonic screen or dismount the flamer.

"Sit still now!" Rees ordered, caught a glimpse of growing fright on the small face turned toward him. He set his boot heel down on the floor button and the machine came to life.

They smashed straight through a corner of the cage compound, moving to parallel the river. But they did not have far to go. At first Rees was so overjoyed to discover that he had not found Vickery, that he actually drew a deep breath of relief. Until Gordy's cry of horror aroused him to action and he used the blaster on the tortured creature still feebly struggling. That could not have been there long. If it had been in place before Vickery pulled out the Captain would have flamed the whole jungle apart to get even with Kassa's tormentors. Was it meant to be a warning or was it a signal of victory over one off-worlder, and that one a long-time friend?

Gordy was crying now, noisily as might an ordinary small Terran boy, but with dreadful sobs which shook his body. Both of his fists were locked on the fabric of Rees' shirt.

"It's all right!" Rees flung one arm about that shivering body, pulled the child closer. "It's all right now, Gordy." But it was not all right and nothing could make it so. Not now. He shouldn't have brought the child here, but neither could he have left him alone. Somewhere, out in the jungle, eyes watched, Rees was sure of that.

He kicked the roller into action again. Uncle Milo would have to listen to reason now. They could dismount the flamer from this machine, turn the main building of the mission into a fort, appeal by com for rescue. Rees' mind skipped feverishly from one part of a workable plan to the next.

Captain Vickery had stood very well, to all outward show, with the natives. He had drunk leaf beer with two local chiefs and witnessed the Felling Dances. You could not say that barbarity was visited on Kassa for any sin of his master. This was no matter of a trading station set up on the border of forbidden territory. This was here and now, an icy warning to every off-worlder in the immediate countryside.

What about the Salariki? Dr. Naper knew nothing about them. Had they been able to go last night? With the machine still turning around at his guidance, Rees hesitated. To cut down by their post would take more time. On the other hand, to leave the Salariki there unwarned was unthinkable.

Their felinoid ancestry did not make them any less "men" at a time such as this and he knew that Sakfor had women and children of his species with him. Rees made a full turn and jammed the speed of the roller up the scale. It took to the air in one of the ground covering bounds which exhausted far too much of its fuel charge but which cut minutes to seconds. The Salariki station and then the mission—and he could only pray that time would not run out for them all!

☽⋆ CHAPTER 2 ⋆☾

As were the buildings of the mission, the trading post was constructed of glegg stone blocks, cut, while the substance was still workable, in an excavation on the river bank, put then together to harden under wind and rain into metallic toughness. Short of a force flash such walls could not be razed. But that oily yellow smoke curling up into the sky, the throat catching scent of burning oganna, told Rees now that Sakfor's fort had not been a refuge. His season's gatherings were afire.

Rees slammed the lever on the controls. With a tooth-rocking force the roller halted behind a screen of bush through which the Terran could see the post set in a curve of river bank. There was activity there. Rees' hand flailed out, knocking Gordy off the seat of the machine, down where the boy could no longer view what was happening. For a moment the young man's fingers rested on the firing trigger of the flamer. But they were too far away to catch the looters in its beam. And to betray his own presence there would no longer help the Salariki.

The Terran kicked the reverse, glad that the purr of the sonic screen drowned out most the sounds. The reality of the massacre now ending there was worse than any description broadcast by com. Rees fought the revolt of his stomach as he edged the roller away from that hell which had been a peaceful trading post.

Something flashed away from the forward thrust of the machine as they turned about. Twany yellow. That was no animal! Rees' jungle trained eyes registered its difference and he pulled up quickly, thumbed off the sonic.

But there was no chance of hailing what he believed he had seen. The terrible cries from the post, muffled as they were, still rang. And his own call might bring lurking Ishkurian scouts down upon them. There was a low bush shaking to the right, the fugitive might be sheltering under it. Rees drew Gordy up to face him.

"Listen," he looked directly into the boy's eyes, "this is important, Gordy. Over there, under that bush, I think one of the Salariki children is hiding. If I go over I may frighten it into running. Do you think you can crawl in and bring it out?"

"Rees, what's happening? Rees, that noise—" Gordy shivered in the young man's grasp, his small face registering shock and fright.

"Gordy, that bush over there." Rees shook the boy gently. They could not leave any survivor of the post. And for him to beat the bushes would only drive the terrorized alien child deeper into hiding. Gordy was the only way to locate the Salariki cubling.

Gently Rees turned the boy around, pointed to the bush. Then he shook Gordy again, thankful to see a measure of comprehension dawn in the child's face. With drawn blaster in one hand and the other on Gordy's shoulder, Rees eased them both out of the roller and towards the bush. Still some feet away from the objective he released his hold on the boy, gave him a push in the right direction. Mercifully that yammering screaming had stopped. What they heard now was only the blatting of the natives.

Gordy went to his hands and knees, crawled under the dropping branches of the shrub. There was an agitated shaking and Gordy's plump buttocks, his scuffed boots reappeared. He was retreating backwards, tugging at some recalcitrant captive, both hands clasped about two small wrists while fingers with claw nails writhed for freedom.

Rees made a swift swoop, felt the rake of those nails, cruel and sharp across his cheek and chin as he gathered a spitting, wildly threshing small body up in his arms. Gordy, without being told, was already streaking back to the safety of the roller. And Rees followed, to put his fright-maddened captive down in the seat between them. He fended those raking nails with his forearm while he activated the sonic and set the roller on its way again. Only then, when they were in motion, did he take a closer look at the rescued.

She crouched all together, her point-tip ears flattened against her rounded skull, her mouth half open as she hissed silently in the heritage of her long ago feline ancestors. The fine, plushy, fur-hair on her head and along her backbone and outer arms was roughened and standing erect. Her orange-red eyes, set aslant in her broad face, were slitted and wild.

Rees had no way of determining Salariki ages. She might have been younger than Gordy or older. Her torn garment was a short kilt held about her waist by a jeweled belt from which still hung a few scent bags suspended on beautifully patterned ribbons. The ribbons for others were torn and fluttering free. So, by her dress, she was still a young child, and a favored one, probably one of Sakfor's daughters. Salariki females did not circulate freely except among their own people, and Rees had no idea of the number or ages of those composing Sakfor's late household. The Terran did know that a man of influence living off the Salariki home planet was allowed more than one wife, usually marrying two or three sisters from the same family clan.

The Salarika's head turned slowly as she surveyed Gordy, Rees, and the interior of the roller. A red, sharply pointed tongue licked out across her face and flipped in between her teeth again.

"She's got fur on her." Gordy put out an investigating finger but he did not quite touch the soft golden down covering the outer side of the arm next to him. "She sure smells nice, doesn't she?" His nose wrinkled as the heavy scents from those waist bags grew stronger in the machine. Apparently he was so interested in the newcomer he had forgotten the sights and sounds of the immediate past. Rees nodded.

"Salariki people love perfumes, Gordy. Those are their principal trade items." He could have bitten out his tongue at that slip but Gordy had not apparently noticed.

"What's her name, Rees?" the boy continued.

"I don't know," the young man was more occupied with finding a way through the mass ahead. To keep the machine to any open path was to invite immediate discovery. And what had happened at the mission? Had his decision been the wrong one? Had he thrown away the lives of three Terrans when he had chosen to go fruitlessly to the post? Sweat beaded Rees' face, rolled in glistening drops down to salt his lips and drip from his chin.

"What's your name?" Gordy asked in Basic. "I'm Gordy Beltz. I live at the mission."

The Salarika licked her face again and then raised one hand. Blood oozed from between two of her fingers. She applied her tongue there also.

"Rees, she's hurt! Her fingers're all bloody!"

Rees glanced sidewise. "A bad scratch, Gordy. But it's stopped bleeding. I'll see to it as soon as I can." He hoped that the Salariki followed the usual off-world custom and inoculated their kind against alien diseases. But he must reach the mission, he must.

"We're almost home," Gordy announced a short time later. "I see the big crook-tree. Mom, she'll give you something for your finger," he assured the Salarika. "Does it hurt much?"

Those almost noiseless hisses no longer issued from the alien. Her examination of her companions continued, but her hair was no longer standing erect and she appeared to be settling down. Rees doubted if she understood Basic. But he believed she had sensed the good will of the Terrans and their difference from those devils back at the post.

"Rees, what are you stopping here for? Why don't you drive down the road?" Gordy's questions were strung together. His face was paling once more as the young man pulled the machine to a stop well away from the mission buildings.

Rees dared not drive in until he knew conditions ahead. It would be better to avoid the usual approach and take a more concealed way from the copse of farb trees. Those would screen any scouting expedition clear to the laboratory building.

"Rees, Dad's going to be awful mad at you, running this roller across a planted field, he had doman seeds put in here last week." Gordy's hands clenched on the edge of the instrument board. "Please, Rees, what's the matter?" His momentary interest in the Salarika forgotten, he was beginning to shiver once more.

"Gordy, be quiet!" Rees maneuvered the roller along, trying to keep it screened from any enemy that might lurk about the mission. He thought he could get the machine well in unseen. Of course, so far he had seen no sign that the natives had been here. But they might well infest the jungle, be closing in about the clearing ready for an attack.

Rees brought the jungle car to a halt and turned in the seat to face both children.

"Now listen, Gordy, this is very important. We have to get your Dad, your mother, and my Uncle Milo, take them away from here or else gather them in one place where we can fight. Do you understand that?"

Gordy's hands were knuckle-white in that grip on the edge of the panel. But his nod told the young man that he was taking this all in.

"You are to stay here, in the roller with the Salarika. She's afraid and if she's left alone she may try to run away again. Then we might lose her in the jungle. So I'm trusting you to see she stays here, Gordy."

"While you go to get Mom and Dad, Rees?"

"Yes. And if there are native hiding around here they mustn't see us so don't leave this machine!"

"You can send a message on the com, then the Patrol will come and take us away," Gordy's hold on the panel eased.

"Yes, we'll do something like that. But you stay right here with the Salarika, Gordy. I'll be back as soon as I can. Now see this button? It controls the sonic. I have to turn that off when I get out. You press it down to put the curtain back up again. And keep it up all the time I'm gone."

Gordy nodded solemnly. Rees hoped he would follow orders. With that sonic up the children had a measure of protection. It reacted against Ishkurian ears in a painful manner—but that was scanty enough.

"I'm going now. And Gordy, even if Ishbi or Ishky come—don't go to them." Rees had no way of knowing if the mission natives were among the raiders, but he dared take no chances that they were still friendly.

"Yes, Rees."

The young man got out, watched Gordy thumb on the sonic, and then sprinted for the side of the nearest building. The cloying scent which had filled the interior of the roller, rising from the Salarika's clothing, began to clear from his nostrils. He stood braced against the rough wall for a long moment, using both ears and nose to give him warning of trouble.

Only the chirrup of insects, the bubbling call of the hoobra hens, the sigh of breeze through shrubbery, all peaceful sounds. But no welcoming hum from the laboratory—the a-motor was not running. And Rees tensed. He slipped along the wall, no windows broke its surface here, he would have to go around to the courtyard side before he could really see anything of the mission's interior.

At this hour Beltz should be in the lab, and Rees' uncle either there or in the house. Gordy said his mother was sleeping off one of the fever attacks. Three people to locate and warn. Mrs. Beltz first? Or the men in the lab? But they would have screens up there; a small protection but still enough to give them warning. The woman was alone; Again Rees must choose.

He was still against the wall, masked by one of the bushes. As far as he could see from here there had been no change in the garden courtyard since he had crossed it more than three hours ago.

Then the warning hit him full force, carried by a puff of wind ruffling the long spikes of leaves about him; the reek of native body odor, musky, nauseatingly strong. That was the smell of a Croc who was heated, excited. Croc—a forbidden epithet here, but one Rees knew. Croc stink here, and strong!

The Terran studied the peaceful scene, trying to guess at the source of that stench. It could be that one of those horny bodies crouched very close to him now. Or the smell could be only a lingering reminder of the recent visit of an Ishkurian aroused to the fever pitch of some strong emotion.

To reach the Beltz cottage, he would have to keep between hedge and lab wall, past the storeroom, hidden most of the way. Crouching low Rees began the ordeal of that venture. So far his nose could not pin the Croc smell to any one section. And he had seen no disturbance in the courtyard. His training in hunting craft, all he had learned during those months with Vickery, would now be put to the test.

Rees scuttled from one clump of lace-thong to the next. Then his hand went to the sill of the window which must open on the Beltz' sleeping room. To go around to the door meant advancing into plain sight. And he could endure the pain of passing through a sonic long enough to get in. Cara Beltz should still be sleeping after that shot. He would have to rouse her.

He was head and shoulders over the sill and then he lurched

back. The Croc reek was a deadly miasma in that room. He did not need more than one sickened glance at the bed to know what had happened. Stomach heaving, Rees crouched back into the bushes, using the control he had been taught at the academy to master his body so it would not betray him by sounds of retching. At least she must have been still asleep when they got to her and probably never knew. He could cling to that hope.

There was no reason to try the lab now. The absence of motor hum was only too well explained. What about the com? Could he summon help by that? But that warning last night had been firm and final. You had to reach the port by 'copter then—and on your own. No rescue missions to be flown. And their 'copter had not returned. As for the one at the trading post, the Crocs would have destroyed that, they weren't stupid.

However, in the house were other things which could mean life for fugitives. His own trail bag and its contents—he must make a try for that. Rees mastered the involuntary shaking of his body, studied the courtyard once more while he mapped out his next movements.

He did not make those until he had decided just what and where he must go. Then he went into action with swift sureness to reach another window, that of his own room.

Crocs had been here all right. Rees took in the incredible confusion of the looted room, the paw marks and scratches where they had tried to force palm locks of the cupboards. But Ishkurian body heat was radically different from Terran. They had not been able to activate those controls. Short of chopping down the walls the storage cupboards were safe.

Rees pressed his hand over one of those smears, his flesh shrinking from even such a remote contact with the murderers. From the now open cupboard he snatched the bag he had packed so carefully and he gathered up three spider silk blankets too, as well as the long bladed dagger which had been one of his father's gifts. Good as dura-steel was, it could not penetrate Croc hide, but there was other life besides the natives to be met in the jungle. And the jungle would have to be their refuge.

Opening one of the blankets Rees dumped all his gatherings into that and knotted the whole into an unwieldy bag which he hurled out of the window. Outside again he stood above his loot to listen and sniff.

Why the Crocs had struck and then gone so soon puzzled him. There had been no fires here, no evidence that they had amused themselves after the beastly fashion they had at the post. A quick kill of the Terrans, then a fade away. Why?

Sakfor's post had been a relatively primitive structure, his storehouses easily raided. The mission was a more complex system of lab, warehouse, living quarters. Had the Ishkurians perhaps been afraid of the lab and its equipment? Or did they intend to return at their leisure for a more prolonged looting?

The natives working at the mission whom Dr. Naper had promoted to tasks about the lab did have some elemental technical training. Those three at least knew the value and the use of much of the equipment. And there were things in the lab which could be turned into far more formidable weapons than the dart guns and throw ropes of the jungle people.

Rees did not know why he thought about that now. But it stuck tight in his mind, a kind of "hunch." And in the Academy hadn't they always stressed the value of examining the basis of such a hunch? Somebody might have wanted the mission left intact, somebody might be able to turn off-world machines, off-world ideas against the off-worlders who had imported them. He must remember that, and he prepared to face just such a problem.

But there was nothing he could do here to wreck the installations. In fact, the two Ishkurian technicians knew more about what was in the lab than Rees did. And he had to get back to the roller before it attracted any attention.

Gordy saw him coming and snapped off sonic. Slinging his bundle back into the storage space, Rees settled himself once more behind the controls.

"Where's Mom?"

Rees flinched as much from that question as from the touch of Gordy's hand on his arm.

"She's gone, Gordy, so has your Dad, and Dr. Naper."

"Where? But Mom wouldn't go without me!" Gordy's protest was sharp, fear-filled.

"She was sick, remember, Gordy. She must have been sleeping when they left. We're going on to the big plantation by the mountains, maybe we'll meet the 'copter and them there."

Rees could not bring himself to tell Gordy the truth, not there and then with Gordy's own memories of Kassa and the trading post still raw and horrible. And he had to think ahead further than just a few minutes, or an hour. The post, Vickery's hunting camp where he had been gathering the animals sold to off-world zoos, the mission; as far as Rees knew those were the only off-world holdings this far west.

The proxlite mines had closed down two months ago when the first broadcast had suggested off-world withdrawal. But between them now and the mountains, the range which sealed away the plain and the Nagassara space port, there were two plantations. One of them, Wrexul's, was large enough to maintain its own private police force. If the fugitives could reach that and the off-world staff had not already left—A black collection of "ifs" but that was all Rees had to hold to.

The immediate problem was to find some place to hole up until dark came. In the night he would dare to use hopping power and really make speed. To keep to the jungle floor was to leave a trail a half-blind, jungle-foolish tourist could follow. And to hop in daylight was as revealing. Yes, a hiding hole for now; and after dark run east for Wrexul's!

CHAPTER 3

THE ROLLER WAS CONCEALED between two points of rocks, crouching as might a spurred yandu in a tree den. Rees had driven back along that camp trail which numerous hunting expeditions had beaten down, and then lifted the machine by one carefully timed hop into this pocket. Lace thongs made a protecting gray-green curtain about them when he had pulled those elastic branches into position, following a pattern which Vickery had early taught him during their trapping. He plunged in the sense alarm making them safe from any surprise attack. And, with a stone wall behind them, the flamer facing the only entrance way, they were in the best fort he could improvise.

Rees looked at his watch. Four hours and a little more since he had left Uncle Milo at the breakfast table. Four hours, enough time to end a world.

"Rees, I'm thirsty." Gordy tugged at his sleeve.

Water? Food? There were always survival rations stored in the roller. But how was the water? To check the tank had been one of the first morning jobs, he had had other things to think about today.

Rees knelt on the seat to read the gauge. About half full, which meant they must use that supply sparingly. But there were other ways of obtaining water in the jungle and they should keep the contents of the tank for emergencies.

"I want a drink!" Gordy persisted.

"I'll get you one. You stay here, turn on the sonic again after I get out but stay inside, understand?"

The young man worked one of the plastic canteens out of its hold hook and tucked the jungle knife into his belt. Both the Salarika and Gordy watched his preparations with round-eyed interest.

He slid out of the roller, wiggled between two of the lace thongs, and then paused, to listen and sniff. What he sought should be found not too far away. Rees rounded one of the protecting rock piers and plunged into the misty, gray-green of the jungle world, his boots sinking inches deep into the powdery earth.

A ghost-wing fluttered by, its pale, almost completely transparent wings making it seem the shadow of the living creature which no Terran had yet been able to classify either as a bird or an over-large insect. Rees stood statue still to check that flight. And he was rewarded when the ghost-wing settled on a bulbaceous growth swelling a loop of vine about the rough trunk of a thorn-rump.

That would be on a thorn-rump, Rees thought ruefully, measuring the distance between the ground and the vine by eye and guess. Luckily the tree was old and so there was a goodly stretch of open space between the dark purple thorns. He could climb, though it was a chance he would not ordinarily take. Setting the knife blade between his teeth and thrusting the canteen into the front of his shirt, Rees gingerly took finger hold on the threatening thorns, pulled himself up until he could hook one hand over the vine near that promising swelling.

Seen this close the growth was not a part of the vine, but a parasite rooted on it, globular, with a fantastic spread of hairlike purple foliage sprouting from its lower end. The ghost-wing emerged from among those waving fronds, fluttering out in panic. Rees made a one hand stab with the knife into the side of the globe. The purple filaments writhed up and about his wrist. But he had braced himself in advance for their scratching and he knew he was immune to the particular poison they dug into his skin.

Restoring his knife to teeth grip again, Rees now pressed the mouth of the canteen tight to the hole he had made in the globe, boring in with all the strength he could exert. The bulb shrank under that pressure and the purple threads hung limp about an emptied husk, the liquid contents of which now splashed in the canteen. Rees dropped back to the floor of the jungle, a good supply of drinkable water now in hand.

His return was a backward crawl, for as he went he erased with a branch the marks of his boots. Luckily the powdery soil was easily smoothed. Then he was again in the roller with the eager children. As he let them drink the Terran wondered about the Salarika's immunity. Gordy was safe against jungle virus and the results of most insect bites. But was this small alien also protected by some form of inoculation or mutant control? They would have to chance it that she was.

She drank thirstily enough and he tried again to talk to her in Basic. Though she watched him with close attention, she did not answer, and he thought that if she did understand his words perhaps she could not speak that common stellar tongue.

However she allowed Rees to examine her torn hand. The blood had been licked away and the scratch looked clean. When the Terran tried to cover it with a plastic band, she shook her head violently and pulled away, licking at it again with her tongue in a methodical up and down fashion. Rees guessed she was following her own species' way of dealing with such hurts. It was better for him not to interfere, what served one people did not always aid another.

"Why are we staying here, Rees?" Gordy demanded. "If Mom and Dad are waiting with the 'copter by the mountains I want to go on now!"

"We can't go until dark," Rees returned, summoning patience. To stay cooped up in the roller for the rest of the day would be hard on Gordy, probably on the Salarika child, too. But they dared not leave its safety. How frank could he be with the boy? Rees' own father had treated him as an adult, but then he had been Survey.

When his mother had died Rees had been only a little older than Gordy was now, but already the veteran of two prelim settlements on newly discovered planets. And he had continued to accompany his father as a matter of course, that life was a part of Survey training, until, at the age of twelve, he had mustered in at the Academy.

Specialization in service families had reached the point that children were born into their fathers' and mothers' occupations. That was why the wrench had come as a major break for Rees when Dr. Naper had taken him from the Academy and tried to refit him into the mission pattern of life. He could not subscribe to Uncle Milo's abhorrence of Survey's basic tenets. Just as he could not and would not agree that Survey's opening of new planets only tended to increase the colonial rule of the Empire and perpetuate what Dr. Naper and those of his association considered the most pernicious aspect of Terran galactic expansion.

But Gordy was of a mission family and relatively far less tough and less prepared for just what had happened today. Was he still young enough to be elastic, or would memory re-hab be his lot if and when they escaped?

"If we move now the Crocs might find us." Rees tried to explain.

"You mustn't call them 'Crocs'," Gordy corrected him. "That's a degrade name."

A degrade name! There it was, mission conditioning. Rees frowned impatiently. He'd like to force the mission high echelon personnel to sit through a tape film of what had happened here three hours ago. Sure, any one with a fraction of good sense did not intentionally degrade any intelligent alien race. But neither was it right to disregard the fact that in dealing with aliens, Terran, or even humanoid standards could not remain the measuring sticks of judgement. On the side of the mission there had been such a determined indoctrination away from normal human wariness in dealing with X-tees that to question any "native" motives was close to a venial sin. Rees supposed that what had just happened here would be explained and excused by those policy makers in a way to satisfy everyone but the dead, the tortured dead.

"The natives," Rees corrected. "Gordy, this is important—the natives don't like us any more. If they see us—they'll kill."

"Like what the Patrol officer said on the com?"

"Just as he said on the com," Rees confirmed.

"I want Mom and Dad!" Gordy's lower lip protruded stubbornly, now it quivered.

"Well, they aren't here!" Rees' exasperation grew. He knew that this had been a day of shocks for the boy, but the mere fact that they were still alive meant something. Though, he corrected himself silently, Gordy had no way of recognizing that.

"Tonight we'll turn on the hopper, head for Wrexul's plantation. Now let me switch on the hummer and you and the Salarika curl up back there and see if you can sleep."

"Travel at night," Gordy considered the possibilities that offered.

"Stay up all night and maybe see an air dragon, Rees?"

"Truly. But you won't be able to see any air dragon unless you get sleep enough so you *can* stay awake tonight." Rees accepted the diversion gratefully.

He spread out two of the blankets on the floor of the storage compartment, gave each of the children another drink, set the small hummer, once used to quiet newly captured animals, to lull them to sleep, pleased that the girl seemed content to follow Gordy's example. Then Rees settled himself down in a corner of the driver's seat, on his knee the recorder which was one remainder from the good life with his father.

Commander Tait Naper had never been on Ishkur. But he had had training in handling widely varied alien beings. And his private note tapes, left behind when he had taken off on that last voyage, were a rich inheritance for his son. They held distilled experience hints from his successful career. Rees thumbed the button now, though the key words for his own need: jungle, hostiles, escape, and waited for the re-run beam to reach his mind.

Fifteen minutes later he snapped off the recorder. None of the specific information the beam had planted in his mind was closely applicable to the here and now. But a general idea or two . . .

"Eye of the spider," he repeated softly aloud. "If you would fight a spider, you must attempt to see through its eyes, think with its mental equipment, foresee its attack as it would make one.

The spiders in this case were the Crocs and Rees would have to strive to think Croc in order to out-think Croc, a rather confused estimate of the task, but a correct one.

What did he know about the Crocs, the educated ones at the mission, the servile class that did the heavy labor, the guides and hunters with whom he had worked in Vickery's camp? These were three types, reacting in three separate ways. You could tongue-click and clapper Croc speech, the audible speech. But no off-worlder could mind-touch as it was certified that Crocs did with one another.

Yes, you could learn something of the outward forms of Croc life: the fisherfolk of the sea shore, the hunters of the jungle, the handful of those who had chosen to learn something of off-world education and galactic civilization. But you did not really know what went on in those sloping, reptilian skulls. To use the eye of the spider here—the task was close to impossible. But Survey never accepted the term impossible.

Rees closed his eyes, tried to evaluate as he had been taught; if he had only had more training! He was in the position of a man ordered to build a Spacer, with a full list of materials to draw upon, and only a beginner's knowledge of engineering. His concentration became close to physical pain as he forced himself to study the problems of getting under a rough, armor plated skin, seeing through the "eye of the spider," trying to foresee the moves of the Crocs against the fugitives.

Again it was the absence of sound which alerted Rees, as it had when he had awakened hours earlier that morning. The sonic! His hand was already reaching for the proper button on the control panel. Could the roller power unit be failing?

But as his finger rammed home on the button, that faint vibration began again. No power failure, a turn-off. Gordy! Rees hunched around to peer into the storage compartment behind the driver's seat. But Gordy was there, stretched out full length, short arms and legs flung wide. Gordy was there—the Salarika child was gone!

How had she known? But then she'd watched Gordy turn the sonic on and off. Why had she gone; after food, water? Rees had fed the children, and the half full canteen was within easy reach. No, the canteen was gone, as was a fish spear which had lain along the back of the storage space—water, a weapon of sorts. Their fugitive from the post must be following some definite course of action. Was she going back, trying to find others of her family? That was far more probable than the idea a child would strike into the jungle for any other reason.

Rees rubbed his hands across his forehead. She couldn't have been gone very long. The breaking of the sonic had alerted him. How much of a homing instinct had her feline ancestors bequeathed her? Enough to guide her through the miles of jungle to the post? Not that she could make such a journey. The jungle was safe only when traveled by a hunter; any off-worlder must go in a machine equipped with the ingenious multitude of detective and protective devices this one possessed.

But how could he hunt down a small Salarika who probably was determined against being found, with a thousand good hiding places to hand? There was only one answer, and it was a danger for all of them—the roller must be used. The sense detector in it could be used to nose out any living thing with intelligence above a set quotient. Rees had it connected now as a Croc warning but it could as easily put him on the trail of the Salarika.

He leaned forward to study the dial. That was set to register at the mark Vickery had put there months previously, reporting on Croc mental radiations, meant to keep track of foot hunters on a drive. What would Salariki thought beams be? Closer to human, Rees guessed. The Crocs were a reptilian species; Salarika were mammals, warm-blooded and off-world. He moved the pointer with infinite care and then his heart beat faster with excitement. A tiny spark of answer. He could use the tracer though that meant hunting with the machine.

Rees activated the motor, his eyes moving quickly from what lay ahead to the tracer dial. The spark fluttered faster, then settled to a steady dot of fire. He was on course. The path weaved away from the rock pillars, heading on the slight down slope. That was a direct route back for the post. If they only had a common language and he had been able to explain the danger. He could now believe that the cubling was certain she had been virtually kidnapped, taken by force from her own kind. Perhaps, as a female, she had had so little contact with off-worlders of other species that she associated Rees and Gordy with the raiding Crocs!

Now that the Terran was sure of the direction of her trail he could try something else. Rees set the prowler to hop, cleared a large path of vegetation and settled down in the midst of a stream where water circled about the treads. They were ahead of the fugitive now, instead of trailing. And she would come to them.

Only she did not. Rees' frown grew. The spark on the dial remained constant. The Salarika was making no move. Had she witnessed their hop, was she remaining hidden to wait out the hunt? Well, he dared not waste the time in such games. This called again for Gordy's aid. Rees snapped off the hummer, reached back to shake the boy awake.

It required a moment or two to make Gordy understand. And when he did, he stared up the slope where the bush was thick and shook his head dubiously.

"I don't see, Rees, how we can find her there. There are so many places she can hide."

"Our noses will have to do it for us." Rees stepped out of the roller, almost knee deep into the water, and then swung Gordy from the machine to the up slope bank. "She's still wearing those perfume bags. Here, sniff this!" He had dosed himself with the inhaling powder which made him sneeze and had an even more violent effect on the boy.

"That hurts!" Gordy complained, rubbing his nose vigorously with the back of a grimy hand.

"Only for a minute," Rees assured him. "Take some deep breaths, Gordy." The inhalant had only a temporary effect and it could not be used again for hours. But the perfume of the Salariki clothing should be easy to pick up when their sense of smell was so intensified.

They started up the slope together, Gordy still rubbing his smarting nose. Suddenly he looked up at his tall companion. "I can smell, lots of things—different things!"

The sense of smell, so blunted in his species during their evolvement on their own world, was probably not yet as keen as that of an average animal, but it was far more effective than usual. And they were favored because the breeze was towards them—down hill. The wind must pass over wherever their quarry was in hiding.

"Over here!" Gordy jumped to the right, skidded down on one knee and scrambled up again. Rees moved to join him.

The boy was right. That scent which had hung about them so heavily in the roller was on the down breeze. They could not be too far away. But there was something else, a reek that was no perfume. *Croc!* grabbed for Gordy.

He held the boy fast as he drew a deep questing breath. Salariki and Croc all right. But the Croc stench was old, certainly nothing as strong as the taint left at the mission. An excited Croc had been there, but was no longer lurking nearby. Rees released Gordy but the boy did not move away.

"I smell . . ." he began and Rees nodded.

"Yes, but it's old, maybe since yesterday. Come on."

Rees broke through a stand of bushes, to face a dark hole in the ground. He cried out and threw himself flat, to wriggle forward and look down into a trail trap dug for one of the large beasts the jungle natives considered the best of eating.

The pit was dark, only a small portion of its covering had broken under the slight weight of the Salarika girl. Rees wondered if she had jumped from above to the seemingly secure surface of this place and her landing had snapped the roofing of the trap.

She was inside right enough, on her feet, her back against the wall, her forearm streaming blood where the flesh had scraped a upward pointing stake set to impale a captive. Mercifully she had escaped with only that hurt. Her yellow eyes were alight in the dark as she looked up at him, voicing a faint wordless plaint.

"Gordy!" Rees turned his head as he edged back from that danger section. The Crocs always undermined the edges of such a pit against any escape efforts. His own weight here might bring about another slip which would entrap them all, hold them prisoners for the Croc hunter. Gordy would have to act as his tool now.

"Is she down there?"

Rees nodded as he slashed and dug at the roots of the bushes about the hole. Those were long and tough, pulled up fairly easy when the fastening tendrils were loosened. They would make a rope of sorts and Gordy must do the rest under Rees' direction.

✴ CHAPTER 4 ✴

REES WORKED FAST. With the root lengths freed from the soil, he jerked and tore off the smaller side tendrils until he had a length of reasonably supple line, tough enough to stand the strain of Gordy's weight. He explained carefully to the boy what must be done, made him tie by himself twice over the necessary knots. To Rees' relief, Gordy was an apt pupil, appeared to understand just what he must do and why.

Then, with one end of the root rope tied about his middle, Gordy crawled out to the break and dropped into the pit. As Rees had feared the saw action of the root cord on the brink of that drop sent another portion of the concealing covering cascading down into the pit below. But Gordy swung free well above the danger of the stakes.

Rees looped the rope about a sapling, lowered it hand over hand until Gordy hailed that he had reached the bottom. The rope went slack. Gordy was unfastening it. Then there was a jerk, a series of them as the boy knotted it in turn about the Salarika.

"Take your time," Rees called softly. "Test the knot, Gordy."

"I will," the promise arose out of the ground where dust motes still danced upward. "Ready!" Gordy's pipe was echoed by a pull on the rope. Rees began to haul it. At least that second cave in seemed to have taken all the loosened earth with it. Though the rope still sawed the lip of the pit, no more of the soil gave way. A small hand waved suddenly above the surface and the claw nails of the Salarika dug into the ground as the child helped to pull herself over and out.

Rees drew her to him, loosened the knot Gordy had tied, and threw the rope back. The Salarika crouched against his legs, tonguing the gash in her arm, shivering throughout her small body. But Rees had to get the boy out before he could make a closer examination of her hurt. When Gordy was back on firm ground once again Rees knelt beside the little alien, gently drew her hurt arm across his knee—and then froze as he saw those pricks in the grayish skin, pricks already marked a brownish tinge.

"Ka thorns!" Rees whispered. One of the most devilish devices in a Croc hunter's armory. And one for which there was just one antidote. Rees bit hard on his lower lip. He had an aid kit in the roller, but he could inventory its contents too easily, just as he could also visualize that shelf back in the lab where stood a slender container of green fluid, the one outstanding achievement of Dr. Naper's Ishkurian research; an answer to the poison of Ka thorns, as well as to several other fatal jungle-fostered deaths. The Salarika in his arms was going to die, almost as painfully and horribly as had the rest of her family back at the post. And there was nothing he could do about it, nothing but think of that container and its contents, which might be as far away as Terra itself now.

Gordy must have heard that whisper. Now he laid his hand on Rees' shoulder, his eyes big and wide. "The medicine, Rees, that's good. You can give her that, make her well. Dad said it always works!"

They had all been so proud at the mission of that discovery. But it was lost now, along with the men who had made it. Just as the child who now lay across his knees was lost. If he only had the container out of the lab!

To return would be the wildest folly. They had only one hope for escape, to head quickly for the eastern mountains and the plantations at their feet. The charge in the roller motor, Rees could not be sure it would last that far. To go back to the mission where even now the Crocs could be crawling . . .

A hand with golden fur across its back raised towards his face. Again sounded that pleading whimper he had heard from the pit. Rees got to his feet, cradling the slight, soft body against his shoulder. He was a fool, a mad fool, but he was going back. The roller was, in its way, a small moving fort, and he knew the territory about the mission as well as if every portion of its expansion was imprinted on his brain.

Back in the machine Rees settled the Salarika on the blankets once again and then started the motor. The stream in which the jungle car rested angled slightly to the right, its course must run in the general direction of the mission. Rees squinted at the position of sun and shadow about him. He had about an hour, he judged, until the onset of twilight. If he could conceal the roller, visit the mission at dusk—

"Where are we going, Rees?" Gordy wanted to know.

"Back for the medicine," the young man replied, his plans crystallizing. Hide out the roller, so leave the children in a measure of safety, he knew where to do that. He would make the rest of the way on foot. His blaster carried a full charge and he would be prepared for an attack. Which the victims of the morning Massacre had not. If the lab had not been looted . . .

The Salarika was moaning pitifully three quarters of an hour later as the Terran stopped the car under the overhang of bushes he had planned as a base. He forced her to drink from the canteen, getting as much of the liquid down her as he could. Then he gave Gordy his orders. No leaving the roller, the sonic curtain kept on, and to stay out of the driver's seat, back on the blankets with the girl. There was a chance that even if the Crocs sighted the jungle car they might think it deserted and leave it alone. Crocs did not like machines, none of the hunters and guides had ever chosen to ride in it when they went hunting with Vickery. And Rees knew that part of the feeling against off-worlders was rooted in the importation of such travel devices.

Rees slipped into the brush, watched Gordy lock on the sonic, and then made his way to the blocks of the mission buildings. He circumvented the 'copter park, sniffing. Croc stink, yes, but already fading. The Terran began to believe that the raiders of the morning had not returned. The beaker would be on the lock shelf under a force shield, in his uncle's lab office. And the force shield, as were the cupboards in the living quarters, was sealed to a palm lock. Luckily Dr. Naper had taken the precaution a month earlier of setting that lock to the pattern of every adult Terran living there, otherwise Rees' errand would have been fruitless.

The lab door was in full sight of the courtyard. Any scout from a Croc band would be able to sight the Terran before he got in from that direction. But there was another entrance, one only desperate measures would force on him. Rees crept behind the living quarters, got down on his hands and knees, running his left hand over the ground while he still grasped his blaster in the right. His fingers found the grip under the sliding gravel and he jerked up the trap door giving on the water tanks. Smells, none of them too pleasant, arose from below, but they were not Croc.

He found the ladder, edged down into moist dark, holstering his weapon so he could feel along the wall with one hand as he clung to his support with the other. A lever to be pulled back, answered by a round opening on the cramped repair tunnel to serve the pump system. Rees scrambled into that, wriggling along on his belly, fighting down the almost panicky fear he always had of tight, dark quarters. If he had not given Permal a hand down here, much against his will, last month, he would not even have known of the existence of this under-the-floor slit which ran the full length of the lab building.

"Two, three . . ." His shoulders scraped from wall to wall, his hair brushed the roof over him. He was counting in a whisper the outlets. "Four!" This was it. He would come out in the lab, then he had only to get around the corner into the office.

The exit seal was stiff. Rees beat against it with his doubled fist, his impatience becoming fear as the outlet stubbornly refused to yield. He could retreat to the third opening. There, it was giving!

Light lanced in at him. No hum of motor, but the wall lights were on. And Croc stink, also other smells, the reek of chemicals, of burnt stuff.

Rees knew that the exit was under one of the stationary sinks which would afford him partial cover as he crawled out. And as soon as he was free of the repair tunnel his blaster was back in his hand.

Though his view of the room was greatly foreshortened, the Terran could see the wreck of the lab. Broken tubes and containers, smears of chemicals, covered the floor.

Avoiding crushed glass, Rees crawled free of the sink, crouched to listen. Three strides would take him to the door of the office. He stood up. Several yards away was a huddle of stained rags. Rees averted his eyes. No use to investigate that closer.

On the office threshold was a wide sear of brown fluid. Croc smell strong enough to churn Rees' already queasy stomach. One of the raiders had fallen there. In the last few moments of his life Dr. Naper had accounted for one of his murderers, made such an impression on the enemy that the body pinned by darts to the desk inside was headless. The Terran's skull would be as preserved as that of an enemy warrior dead in battle. After one sickened glance Rees kept his attention strictly on what had brought him there. The beaker was still intact, the brilliant emerald of its contents seeming to glow. He inserted his forefinger in the waiting hole below that shelf, twisted right and then left, to brush the sensitive spot within its core with his flesh.

A ghostly shimmer of light as the force field flashed off. Rees caught up the tube and then the record tape box by it. Uncle Milo and the mission might never have any other monument but that discovery, and to take this with him would be his last gesture for the project of which he had been so unwilling a part.

Back down the tunnel, holding the tube in his mouth for safe keeping, the tape box digging into his chest as he inched his way along. Luck seemed to be his and that gave him a prick of doubt, it was too easy. The "hunch," that odd form of awareness which could not be defined but which was inbred in his kind, fostered by his early education, was delivering a warning which became stronger as he emerged from the tunnel into the tank. The blackness in there was complete and again fear bit at him. What if he could not raise the trap door again, was trapped in here? He could always go back through the lab. Yet his sensitive inner alarms told him that something had gone wrong, that he was now in a pinch of danger. He did not know what or why threatened. Go back or on? Try to leave the lab through the courtyard, or raise the door here—perhaps to find himself facing a ring of waiting Crocs.

Rees climbed the ladder, braced himself under the door, put his palm to that barrier and tensed. Then he sent the door hurtling up and out with all the strength he could put into one vigorous shove. It slammed down on the ground, showering sand and gravel. His blaster was out and ready, but he was facing nothing at all save the creeping shadows.

Up and out, a heave and a roll, bringing him free of the tank and under a fringe of bushes where he lay, trying to control his hurried breathing, listening, smelling.

Neither ear nor nose added anything concrete to back that inner warning bell. If the Crocs were on the hunt, they were not yet near enough to betray themselves after the usual manner. Rees got to his knees and then his feet. He put the tube under his shirt with the tape, to give an ever present notice of their presence against his stomach muscles.

Too easy, far too easy. He was thinking that as he went, just before he stumbled, even as he fell forward, that he had been tripped up by a skillfully aimed throw stick. With a writhing which wrenched his back painfully, Rees turned just as he hit the ground, brought his blaster up to fire. A split second, that was all he had to deflect the beam of his weapon. For the body lunging at him, a short hand axe swinging up, was not the brown scaled monstrosity of a tribesman, but a lithe, furred, silvery creature. He smelled the aroma of Salarika perfume as his attacker half fell on him, the axe coming down.

Pain, and dark, soft slur of words. Rees lay in a torment hardly aware of himself save as a focal point for pain.

"Come, come . . ." Flashes of more pain as his body was shaken. He blinked at a world which tilted about him crazily, and then was able to see those slanted green-blue eyes staring into his, as if by the very intensity of that demanding glare they could arouse him to coherent understanding.

Nails which were closer to claws pricked the skin on his shoulders as the hands of the Salarika supported him in a sitting position. The scent of the alien was familiar. Rees blinked again. No, this was not the cubling he had left curled sick and in pain back in the roller. Golden fur was blue-silver here. And the newcomer was an adult, equaling him in height if not in body structure. For the stranger was also a female, delicately made. However, her grasp was steel strong and she seemed well able to hold up his limp body.

The fine fabric of her upper robe was fringed into rags from her gemmed waist belt down and only three of the encircling wealth of scent bags still dangled from frayed ribbons.

"Zannah, where is Zannah?" Her voice was a low purr which arose from the depths of her throat, her eyes cold slits.

Rees tried to collect his thoughts in spite of the pain in his head.

"Zannah!" the Salarika woman repeated sharply, a hint of hiss in her Basic.

"Little, little girl?" Rees asked groggily.

"Yiss." This hiss was more strident. "Where isss sheee?"

"Roller—back in the roller," the Terran managed to answer.

She was already on her feet, her nostrils expanded, her head turning slowly as she sniffed, until she faced the direction from which he had originally come. Then she took two or three springy steps before she turned, impatience expressed in every line of her body, to look at him. Rees tried to stand, swayed wildly. She darted back to catch him. The Salarika might have given the impression of delicacy, but her strength as she lent it to his support was all he could have asked of a Terran male.

Just how they did make their way back to the roller Rees was never quite sure. His companion retraced the path he had taken, towing him with her, and the Terran was sure she found the way by scent. The first thing he was truly conscious of, was landing on the seat of the machine while his companion crowded over and past him to the children in the storage compartment. He caught at her plush-furred arm.

"Ka thorns—" Rees had difficulty in finding the right words. "Take some of this, moisten cloth, lay it on the wound, quickly!"

Clawed fingers caught the tube and he leaned forward to rest his head on the arms he had crossed on the control half-wheel. Rees had to rest so for a long moment until the weaving world about him settled into stability and he could fumble at the aid kit. The Terran mouthed the tablets he had sought dry, swallowing convulsively to force them down. Then his headache dulled into a bearable throb, and his vision cleared. A delicate exploration by finger tip told him that over his left ear the scalp was broken, but the blood there was already congealing. Either his own efforts at escape or a belated realization of his identity on the part of the Salarika had saved him from a cleft skull.

"Rees, you are hurt!" Gordy leaned over his shoulder, inspected the damage with wounded, surprised eyes.

"Not too bad. Look in the stores, Gordy, get four Viv-ra-packs and open them."

Rees continued to sit and let the tablets work while the boy brought out the small tins. One Rees left in Gordy's hands, one he put on the seat beside him. The other two he offered to the Salarika woman. The child lay in her arms, a cloth with bright green splashes on it wrapped around the injured arm. Rees indicated the pressure point on the ration pack.

"Press, it heats and then opens," he told her. She nodded.

"Where do you go?" she asked as she put one can to Zannah's lips.

"Without a 'copter our only chance will be one of the big plantations, probably Wrexul's."

"This machine can take us there?"

"I don't know, we can only try. Tell me," he must have an answer to his question, "Why this? You could see I wasn't a Croc." He raised his hand to his head well away from the tender area about the wound.

"I did not see until just before I struck. I scented—Zannah." One of the nails flicked a scent bag at the child's girdle. "I knew that one of the children was gone, might have been taken by the snake-ones. There was their stink about also, very strong."

"So you thought I was a Croc that had taken her? Anyone else escape from the trading post?"

She shook her head. "I am Isiga, second-companion in the house of Lord Sakfor. The snake-beasts, they came to trade as usual, and their stink, it made me sick, for I have only been on Ishkur for two moons. So I went into the far part of the garden until they would go. Then I heard the screams and there was burning between me and the house, they had set fire to the oganna bales waiting there for shipping. So I hid in a tree place. Afterwards . . ." Her ears were skull flat, her fur-hair roughened and partly erect. "They hunted but they did not find me. Then I crossed Zannah's trail also and knew that she had run from that evil.

"But with her were other scents, those of you people. So I hoped that she had been found and was at the mission. But when I came here I found again that the snake-beasts had struck. I think by then," her tongue swept across her lips, "I was not clear in my mind. All I could see was the snake-beasts and what they had done and could do again to the little one. So when I caught her scent, if only faintly, and gave the rally cry to which she did not answer, then I believed I was to avenge one already dead—"

"Anyway you didn't carry that through all the way," Rees commented wryly. "It's getting dark. As soon as I think we can get by without being sighted, I'm going to set this car on hop and head for the mountains. If we continue in luck we ought to be able to raise Wrexul's by dawn."

"That is well," she gave prompt assent to his plan.

❖★ CHAPTER 5 ★❖

AS REES GUIDED THE ROLLER toward the eastern heights his thoughts continued to play with the wonder as to why they had not met the Crocs once more. The natives had struck the mission and post with vicious ruthlessness. Then, they had seemingly vanished into thin air—or the jungle. Croc hunters were expert trackers, tireless on any trail. How had the fugitive off-worlder been able to avoid them so far? Rees' efforts at concealment would have been easy for them to spot. And he did not believe that the natives had been so sated with bloodshed that they would willingly allow the escape of aliens.

Maybe time had something to do with this lull which made him so uneasy. The First Fasts: normally this was the season of native withdrawal to the inner sanctuaries of the High Trees, a district of which the off-worlders had heard but where no non-Ishkurian had ever penetrated. Because this was a period of intense Ishkurian preoccupation with their own affairs had been the very reason the withdrawal of the last Patrol policing force had been scheduled for this date, when most of the natives would be out of contact. Had the massacre on the fringes of stellar civilization been only an isolated gesture before the Crocs began their annual pilgrimage? Rees hoped so, but he could not be sure.

There was a stir beside him. Isiga slid fluidly across the barrier between the driver's seat and the storage space to join the Terran.

"The children sleep," she reported, "Also, it is well with Zannah."

"Why didn't you traders leave when the red alert came from Nagassara?" Rees asked. Mission and trading post had had little contact. But he knew something of the Salariki temperament. Sakfor's stubborn remaining past a warning was a puzzle; the aliens of the trader's species were noted for prudence and wariness.

A small sound came through the dark a hiss of feline anger. "Lord Sakfor was made a promise from the lips of the High Tree Ishgil. Traders were needed, so it was said. There would be nothing for us to fear."

"Apparently that was not true." Rees kept his eyes on the dials before him. In the dark he had to depend much upon the auto-pilot.

"So someone shall learn the result of such split tongue talk!" The cold confidence in that was a threat, or rather another kind of promise. Salariki civilization was based on a feudal organization. Such a tragedy as this which had struck down Sakfor's household would, on the trader's home world, instigate a blood-feud to be taken up by his kinsmen of all degrees. But there would be none to answer such a rallying on Ishkur.

"You think," she was indeed reading his thoughts now, "that one female of a household can not draw a knife and call for the rightful deaths of the enemy. For the moment, no. But the time will come. I am now Name-Head."

She was right! Rees was startled. Under certain conditions, which seldom materialize except in extreme instances such as this, the living adult survivor of a family, whether male or female, became the Name-Head of the victim clan. It was within providence that the woman beside him could demand vengeance from the Truce Court of her own planet and even so set an inter-world war ablaze.

"First," Rees pointed out, "we ourselves will have to be safely out of this."

"You believe that these Wrexul people will still be at the plantation?"

"If they haven't voluntarily withdrawn, and there was no hint of their doing that the last I heard, they would be in better shape to meet an attack than any other off-world holding this side of the mountains. They fortified their headquarters buildings last season and have a private force of off-world police."

In the reflected light of the instrument panel he caught a shimmer as she moved and the silvery fur-hair on her arms gleamed.

"And if the Wrexul staff are gone?" she asked.

"Lady," Rees gave her the proper form of address, "you had better pray to what God or Spirits of Power you own that they *are* there. We have an energy charge in this machine which, with luck, will last to lift us that far. After that, well, there is no way of crossing the mountains in a roller. And I do not think such a journey is possible on foot."

"I thank you that you speak plainly with me," she said after a short pause. "But tell me this also, you have much experience of jungle ways, you are certain we could not travel on foot?"

"Not with the children. I am not even certain a trained Survey Scout could get through, with the Crocs out hunting."

"Our future lies then on the edge of a knife blade, and if the blade cuts . . ." Again that shimmer of silver, she had given a very Terran shrug. "Listen now, Lord Rees . . ." He was startled at that formal title. Though she had just assumed the head-ship of her own clan, she was granting him equality on the terms of her own world, a rare concession for one of the aloof Salariki. "If such a failure is upon us I would wish this, that we go as best we can into the high places, for I have heard that the snake-beasts do not favor the cold and snow in the peaks. Then, should there be no chance of any future for us, we take the warriors' way, going so Behind the Seas, our bodies undefiled. Or do you of Terra not believe that such a course is right and proper?"

"To me that sounds proper," he assented, "if it must be done. We of Terra believe that much; that children and women should not be allowed to fall into the hands of such as the Crocs while men still live."

"Yet there was a woman of your breed at the mission," Isiga pointed out. "And she died so."

"There were divided minds at the mission. Some believed that because they had lived here for many years and treated the Crocs with kindness and fairly, they had nothing to fear."

"Kindness! Fairly!" Her head went up, she made a hissing accusation of each word. "What is kindness, fair treatment, for aliens? To the Salariki kindness is first for his companions-of-the-inner-court and the cublings he fathers there, then to his clansmen. He does not waste good will lightly on strangers without the court-yards. Fairness, yes, that he practices with all, as long as the Peace Flag flies and no man arms for war. Kindness, fairness—to the

Salariki those words have one meaning—to Terrans another—to the snake-beasts yet a third. We walk in the patterns set by our ancestors, how can we change to other trails and expect to discover no pitfalls in them? Those who believed the snake-beasts thought the same thoughts, they were fools!"

"Well, they have paid for their folly," Rees said heavily.

"Yet I do not think you were of a like mind. Why did you stay?"

"Because Dr. Naper, the head of the mission, was my chief-of-clan." He put into Salariki idiom the relationship with his uncle. "I was a warrior of the household."

"Then it was fitting that you stayed," she agreed instantly. "Yet you were not one of them in thought, for they were not a people going armed and ready for war."

"You seem to know a great deal about them." Rees was rather puzzled. Dr. Naper and the rest of the mission personnel had certainly not fraternized with the post. And he himself had been so much of the time off in the jungle with Vickery, trying to escape an atmosphere where too often his beliefs gave offense, that he had not had much contact with the post either, having seen Sakfor only twice since the Salariki party arrived six months previously.

A sound which might equal a Terran chuckle came from his seat companion. "In this place if a pat-gru flower blooms a sun before its time there is talk of such a wonder for half a moon. Do you not think that curiosity led us to speculate concerning the only other off-worlders within reach? We knew what food you ate, what beds you rested upon, what clothing you wore, and what thoughts you held or, at least, how you expressed those thoughts in deeds and words. Thus we knew well that those of the mission did not believe in walking a road of warriors. Thus, how easily fighters were able to gobble them up!"

Rees was stung. Isiga only repeated what he thought to be the truth. Terran could criticize Terran but to hear that scorn in an alien voice made him begin a retort he choked off in midword.

"But the Salariki al—"

"The Salariki also were victims? You speak that which is right. So we may see that both of our peoples have been fools, each in our own fashion," she replied. "Now we can only prepare not to fail again. Ah!"

A silver finger tip beckoned his attention, pointing to the right. They had taken to the course of the river as soon as the sky had darkened into night, using the faintly phosphorescent water, cascading from a source somewhere in the eastern mountains, for a guide to ground the roller's touching between soaring leaps. The jungle vegetation, discovering no rooting room on the rocky verges of the stream, was a black mass well to either side of the water's path. Here and there sparkled a lamp-bush, eerily green-blue, drawing to its deadly trap by that light the night flying things it fed upon.

But the color in the night to which Isiga pointed was no lamp-bush. This was a leaping burst of flame, flame consuming some highly combustible fuel, such as the energy blocks necessary to power a roller or 'copter.

Rees hazarded a guess as to the source, one which shook him in spite of the bleak forecasts he had forced earlier on himself. "Ffalow's!"

"The relay station for the Patrol flights over mountain," she added to that identification. "But would there have been any supplies left there to burn? I thought they had closed that down two weeks ago."

"They might have left a cache, as an aid to the mission, or to your post. Uncle Milo didn't say anything about such. But he was so opposed to the idea of withdrawal for the mission that he wouldn't have done so, even if the District Officer had notified him."

"The blocks would have been carefully stored and protected."

"Exactly!" The Terran snapped agreement. "The Crocs are moving east. That fire couldn't have been set more than a few moments ago."

"They go to Wrexul's to raid everything off-world this side of the mountains." It was as if she thought aloud.

"I'd say that's it," Rees agreed. "They know, or think they know, that there won't be any force sent out this way from Nagassara. They probably plan to clean up quickly and then go on their pilgrimages."

This could well explain where the Crocs had gone. Suppose the natives had put only a limited force of jungle fighters into the field? The raiders had begun with the mission, then jumped the post, were now moving purposefully eastward. If so the roller now had to pass a Croc task force, pass through or over natives who were firm in their design to wipe out all off-worlders this side of the mountains.

"So we must pass them." Again Isiga's mind matched his.

"Yes."

Eye of the Spider, see through your enemy's organ of vision. Needful, yes—but possible? Rees shook his head against a surge of fear. He *couldn't* insert himself inside a sloping, armor-plated Croc skull, see through a pair of those slit-pupiled eyes. He didn't even know if the murderous forces moving east were jungle aborigines, or those who had had enough contact with off-worlders to have garnered a paper-thin patina of stellar civilization, enough of it to have their mental processes slightly twisted into more recognizable patterns of plan and follow-through.

Rees' knowledge was speedily augmented. Above the roller, but a little ahead, a cleaver of white light cut the night, sliced towards them as might a headsman's knife.

Completely blinded Rees gripped the control wheel fiercely as the roller bucked, rode up to an almost vertical position on the back wave of the force flash. He feared that they would flop over upside down. Then that buck became a sideslip to the left, carrying the machine away from the river towards the jungle. Rees fought to level out, to bring the roller out of that erratic and broken hop to ground safety.

Roller treads bit on a solid surface. Then they bounced into the air again, slammed sidewise against a whip of vegetation which gave under the blow, so the machine slewed into the mat of growth. Behind him Rees heard the screams of the frightened children. Then he realized another pair of hands had joined his on the control wheel, that Isiga was lending her strength to his in an effort to ground them.

Somehow they hit the level once more, or approximate level. Still unable to see more than the fiery flash before his eyes. Rees judged that the nose of the roller was higher than its stern, for their bodies were jammed hard against the back of the seat.

"A force beam!" Isiga's cry made sense. The Terran felt her fur-hair brush against his arm and shoulder as she turned to the children. Then her voice was a soothing purr as she spoke to them.

Rees cupped his hands over his eyes. For a moment of icy panic he was shaken. Was he really blind? Or had the flash only dazzled him temporarily? A force beam! Some one of the Croc mop-up squad had the know-how to use, and the possession of, a Patrol weapon. Had the Ffalow's station still been manned—and over-whelmed in a native rush, so the off-world weapons had fallen into Croc claws? Force beams were strictly security limited weapons. How *could* the Crocs have them?

But *how* natives had gotten that piece of armament was certainly no problem of the fugitives; what they did with it was. Rees groped out, caught at a furred arm.

"Listen!" he demanded urgently. "We did come down on the left bank of the river, didn't we?"

"That makes a difference?" she said quickly.

"I'm sure that beam was grounded on the right."

"We did move to the left. What is the matter with you?" Her voice rose a note or two.

"Eyes—that flash—I can't see yet."

A sharp hiss of breath. Then her arm moved. Rees felt a faint touch of air against his lips, guessed she was passing her hand back and forth across his face.

"Temporary." He hoped that was true. How had she escaped similar blinding? Perhaps her head had been turned so that she had not looked directly at the flash.

"How are we fixed?" he asked in the next breath.

Isiga moved about in the seat, once leaning across him as if to see what might lie on the far side of the roller. When she spoke her voice was even, giving a concise report.

"We rest on flattened brush. But there is a tree of some size leaning from the front part of the machine so we are not level."

"Behind us?"

"More brush."

"No trees?" Salariki eyesight at night was far better than Terran, as he knew. She must be able to see in greater detail.

"None of any size."

Rees moved one hand in a sweep over the instrument panel. If the roller itself just had suffered no harm from their rough landing . . .

"I am going to try backing," he told her. "But you'll have to watch and guide me."

He fumbled for the right button, pressed it down. The roller lurched from side to side, shook in a way which told him that much of the surface of both treads must be supported on broken bushes above the ground level. Now the machine rocked back and forth, but it was also creeping in retreat, the tree support in front holding them less high. There was a crackling of brush all around. How long did they have before the Crocs swam the river to bag their victims?

And how badly was the roller damaged by the backwash of the beam? Rees clung to one small hope—that the attackers might have seen that erratic crash landing and that it appeared, from a distance, worse than it really was. The natives might now believe they were firmly grounded. If that were true the Crocs would take their own time about following them, sure of their own ability to track down and take any survivors.

The jungle car rested on an even beam now, its treads getting a grip on something solid through a mush of leaves, twigs and splintered branches. Also the brilliant pinwheels before Rees' eyes were fading.

"Now," the Terran appealed again to his companion, "any clear sky around except straight up?" The roller was no 'copter, it could not be jumped from a stand into a vertical rise.

"Not here."

To go out of the jungle to the open of the river bank was to offer themselves as an easy sitting target for the beam operator. They could plow ahead, waiting to find a clearing big enough to afford them the necessary hop run.

"Where's the most open ground path?"

Again he felt her move on the seat, guessed she was making a careful survey of their surroundings.

"Trees ahead and to the right. Only brush to the left but that way will return us to the river bank."

"Behind?" The roller was responding sluggishly.

"Yes, it is better that way."

They began a painful retreat, the machine swiped and beaten by branches and vines. Rees became aware that the sonic curtains had failed and a pounding on its button aroused no answering hum. Insect life—Rees flinched as a pin-point of fire lanced the side of his neck just above the shoulder meeting. But this was no time to worry about such minor matters.

"Wait!" Isiga's hand clamped down on his forearm, until her nails cut his skin. "A little, just a little more and you can turn. No trees there, just bushes and many vines."

No trees maybe, but vines could be worse in their way. However, he could only try. Rees waited for her cry of "Now!" and swung the control wheel. The roller obeyed awkwardly and they crackled on, beating a path through the resisting jungle wall.

☄★ **CHAPTER 6** ★☄

"GET YOUR HEAD DOWN, keep the children back there, well under cover!" Rees ordered and crouched lower on the seat. The whipping lashes of brush and broken vine swept across the top of the roller as they crunched a path onward. The young man blinked frantically. Shadows against shadows, a faint difference in the quality of light, the pinwheels fading. He gave a sigh of relief; the blindness was only temporary as he had hoped.

"The dials, to the left, second on the panel on your side," he got out breathlessly, his words shaken from his lips by the jolts of the roller. "Any change of the indicator?"

"The bar points straight up."

"Bang on it with your hand!" Rees rapped out, afraid to accept that without a test.

"Now the bar swings," she reported a moment later, "but it returns to the same position."

"Then it's still working—and we aren't followed yet."

But why not, Rees thought. Unless, unless their over-the-river crack-up had looked much worse than it was to any Crocs watching. The enemy might deem them grounded; either dead or else easy meat for more leisurely follow-up, to be picked up later after they had wiped out the last off-world pockets in this section. He said as much to Isiga.

"Since I, too, thought we were finished," she observed, "perhaps they are not to be blamed in judging our descent fatal. How long now to Wrexul's?"

"I don't know. If we could appeal for a com cast we could ride a finder beam in. As it is we'll have to depend on the spy-scout, and make sure it doesn't guide us to a Croc raiding party. But Crocs with a force beam! They can break . . ." He stopped short, aware at last of what that fact could mean.

"A force beam," Isiga finished for him a greater calm than he believed he could summon at the moment, "could also burn a path through the Wrexul defenses, is that not so?"

"Yes. But if our people knew that the Crocs were so armed, they could do something."

"What?" she asked bleakly.

What indeed? A well defended post such as Nagassara port itself, that could stand up to a force beam, put up a counter-force cast which would send the power of the attacking beam back, to burn out the caster and those who sighted it. But not even Wrexul's would possess protection of that type here. The defenders would not be expecting to front one of the top Patrol weapons in the hands of jungle fighters. Also, primitive jungle hunters would not know how to use it, certainly not with the accuracy which had downed the roller. Someone in that band had had training in modern off-world weapons.

"Wrexul's is our only chance," Rees said dully. "We can't lift over the mountains in this machine." He was beginning to doubt if they were going to roll any distance further here either. The roller was handling in a way which could not be explained by the rough terrain through which they were boring a path. The sonic was out. What about its other protective measures?

"Wait!" Isiga's voice was sharp. "That dial, the bar on it moves now!"

Rees gripped the half-wheel tighter. "In what direction, to what degree?" To him the faint glimmer of the instrument panel was too blurred to read.

"It swings right . . . ten points . . . now more . . ."

"That means the Crocs are across the river. What's ahead of us?"

Her hand was on his shoulder to steady herself as she stood up in the rocking machine, using her better-than-Terran night sight on the path before them.

"Ahh! Pull up—quick!"

Rees obeyed, and the roller lurched as he applied the cut-off, slewed around in the crushed brush. The flamer! If he could use the flamer! He fully expected to front a Croc attack out of the dark.

"We are near to the edge of a drop," Isiga reported. "How deep a one I do not know, but it is wide. Can we hop it?"

Rees' fingers went to that other button, thrust hard. The machine spurted, but there was no answering surge strong enough to raise it from the mass of vegetation where it rested. He was right, more than the sonic had suffered back there in the crash.

"The hop power is out," he said. What to do now? Try to swing around so he could rake the brush with the flamer? All he had been trying to remember this nightmare day and night about the spider's eye was at last beginning to pay off. He'd be taking the biggest gamble of his life, a bigger one perhaps than he should have. But it could be their only chance.

"Get this," he spoke incisively having made his decision. "I'm going to turn, with my back to the drop. You empty the storage compartments, fill the canteens from the tank, take all rations—you can pack it all into those blankets—get the children ready. As soon as we stop, take them and the supply packs out of here. Head to the right, along the edge of the drop. Wait . . ." he unfastened the blaster belt with its comfortably filled holster. "Do you know how to use one of these? Three pressures of the firing button gives you maximum, and you'll need that to burn through Croc belly armor."

"And you?" She took the weapon from him.

"I'm going out in a blaze of fire power as far as the Crocs are concerned. It's the pattern they follow when they are cornered in battle. They'll come up, get the flamer in the face. And then the roller will buck back into the drop and blow up. If any of them survive that toasting, they'll think we all went up with the machine. I'll join you as soon as I can."

"This machine is too disabled to aid us farther?" Her cool acceptance of their danger was a steadying support.

"Yes. It might conk out completely at any moment. Now get moving!"

He helped her gather the canteens, the packs of rations, the aid kit, two bush knives. Then he handed Zannah out into her waiting arms, saw Gordy stumble after, the small boy manfully lugging the second blanket bundle. They were gone and Rees was alone, grimly hoping his choice was the right one. With any luck he should be able to make their pursuers believe that they were all trapped in the disabled roller.

Gingerly he maneuvered the jungle car about, and his suspicions concerning the future were amply proven by the stiff, limited responses to its controls. Once the motor cut out entirely and Rees thought it was gone, until it answered haltingly to his frantic coaxing. He was turned around now, his back to the gulf masked in the darkness, the flamer facing the way the Crocs must come. Luckily his eyes had recovered to the point where he could read the spy-scout dial. Its pointer had swung well past the half-way mark. The Crocs were coming, fast now.

They couldn't carry a beamer, not over this broken ground, unless they had it mounted on a lift platform. And if they also had one of those . . . Rees smiled, a stretch of thin lips which did not in the least denote humor. That would have to come straight along the swath the roller had cleared. The flamer would take it, the beam it transported, and any firing crew riding it, dead center.

The Terran made two other preparations and sat quietly to wait. He regretted the loss of the sonic. The undergrowth flattened in the passage of the jungle car must have been the valued home of countless insects. All Rees could do was trust in the strength of the repellent he had smeared on his skin moments earlier, but that did not guard him against all stings, bites, and the crawling exploration of creeping things he could not see (and did not want to anyway). Waiting; that bit, too, worse than any insect. He began to count mentally, try thus to estimate how far Isiga and the children could have traveled since they left the roller.

Rees' eyes adjusted, and not a moment too soon! Not even Crocs, jungle wise as they were, could mask that object hanging well above the road of the roller, appearing as a blotch against the sky. It swung on and the diffused radiance of a half crushed lamp-bush gave Rees an idea of its outline. So they *were* bringing in the beam on a lift!

The Terran pushed the flamer button. A tongue of raw red fire licked out. It must have caught the lift platform and its burden square on. But Rees did not wait to make sure. His arm shielding his eyes from the glare, he spun out of the seat, clung to the door with one hand, just long enough to kick at the starter. Then he hit the ground and squirmed to his knees, scuttled over a rocky surface which bruised the skin of his palms.

Roller treads grated on the rock as the car groveled backwards. Fires were blazing around as the flamer slewed back and forth, tonguing out in a fan-shaped sweep before the retreating machine. Then that spear of fire pointed skywards as the car teetered on the brink of the drop. Rees, yards away now, dared pause to glance back.

Down it went, toppling back into the gulf. And some of the enemy had survived. The rasping, coughing screeches of the Crocs made a harsh clamor. The Terran took to his heels, hoping that they would congregate on the edge, even start down towards the wreckage. He had hit them hard and they would be swept out of prudence, wanting to take his head. The skull of a valiant enemy was a far better trophy for the High Tree of a clan than that of a victim cut down in a massacre.

Rees gasped as a pain caught him under the ribs. Now he must depend not only on his own speed and agility, but on Isiga's night sight. If the Salarika kept to the edge of the gully as he had ordered, he should catch up with the fugitives before too long. But as he scuttled faster to put as much distance between him and the crash as he could, Rees still waited for the finale he had planned.

That came with more force than he had deemed possible. A crackle of light fiercer than the native sun lit up the Ishkurian landscape, even though its source was at the bottom of the drop. Rees stumbled on, a sound rising from his lips, not quite a laugh. Any headhunters caught in that explosion of a heated motor fed a full stream of energy would no longer be interested in skulls—not even their own!

The leaders of that Croc party must have been operating the force beam on the lift. And Rees could probably count on their having been killed by the flamer. Now if there had been any survivors of the roller explosion they would not be out to track off-worlders. Rees had copied the pattern of their own people when facing overwhelming odds; get the enemy and end one's own life into the bargain.

Only, now he was beginning to worry about Isiga and the children. Surely they could not have gone any farther than this. He slackened pace, trying to see more than the splotches of lamp-bush. Then another light brought Rees to an abrupt stop.

Well overhead, but coasting down on a flight track which would connect with the ground just ahead of him, was a red line, or rather a pin-pricked outline of a monstrous head, jaws agape and every fang a small pulsating coal.

In the roller or even in the open with a blaster, Rees would have been able to face that menace with the confidence of the superior armed. But his knife was no protection against an air dragon in the thing's own territory. This was a creature of the Ishkurian night, using its light celled head to dazzle and terrify its prey into helplessness. And it was on the hunt now but Rees realized he was not the quarry.

The others! All the jungle had come into terrified wakefulness at the noise of the battle. Screams of disturbed flying things, of the small dwellers in the mass of vegetation were a loud uproar, through which the Terran could not hear the ominous flap of those wide skin-and-ribboned wings. He could only watch that wicked, red-outlined head as the thing approached in a purposeful glide.

Isiga had the blaster, and he knew her sight was excellent. But if she used that weapon to finish off her attacker, she would also advertise to any Croc that the fugitives were still alive. Their sacrifice of the roller would mean nothing and they would be easy prey for trackers.

Rees' feet continued to carry him forward, though he had no glimmering of idea as to what he was going to do with two bare hands against those red coals of teeth and the tearing foretalons which hung below the too-well-defined head.

The air dragon was at tree-top level now, the smaller trees which rimmed the gully, not the towering giants of the true jungle. Those jaws snapped with cruel visibility. The hunter must have caught some flying creature bewildered into flight. But the morsel was too small to satisfy it. Now it hovered, perhaps some ten feet above the ground, the red outline of its head jerking back and forth. Rees gave a gasp of relief, his left hand pressing his aching ribs. What the air dragon sought was under cover.

Unfortunately these things did have some intelligence, that and a habit of stubbornly settling upon one prey and that alone in a night's hunting. The air dragon would continue to patrol above, waiting for its intended meal to break from the protecting cover. And its very presence there, especially in a jungle already awakened and alert, would be a signal to summon others, the ground beasts, those that feasted on the remains after the flier had sated his more fastidious appetite and was gone.

The skull-rats, the progies; those would gather. And a pack of either would flush the dragon's game into the open. Rees had heard Vickery's stories of such combined hunts and knew that the animal collector did not exaggerate in the least. To stay was death of one kind; to move was death of another.

He estimated the circling course of the dragon. It flapped back and forth leisurely, not in the least concerned over the eventual outcome of the action. Rees was as certain as if he could see them clearly that the prey it sought was Isiga and the children. They must be—Rees studied the swing of the red tipped head above—under some bush or thick branched tree, a little to the left and even nearer to the edge of the drop. Perhaps the Salarika had been trying to reach that when the dragon had swooped too near for her to longer expose them to its pounce.

Rees took to cover. Belly flat he wormed a way towards the spot he had fixed upon as the core of the dragon's interest. He must move quickly, before the skull-rats or the progies came!

Then he was flattened under a thin curtain of cover, aware that that red pitted outline of a head swung about, was not pointing towards him! If he were only close enough! There was one action they could combine upon. Or if Isiga could use the blaster with an expert's ease and a narrow beam. With Vickery he would have tried such a move at once but now he must be sure.

Something thudded out into the patch of open cut so invitingly and menacingly on the very lip of the gully. It winked with the reflection of pale light on metal as a spark in the bush from which it had been flung fastened on it in an off and on beam no stronger than the body light of some night insect. The blaster! Isiga must have seen his arrival and was now signalling to him the position of the weapon.

Rees swept out his hands to either side of his body, raking in the muck of old leaves and twigs, hunting for a fallen branch he might use to reach the blaster. There was nothing to be found save some wood so rotted it crumbled to evil-smelling powder in his grasp.

The blaster was there in the open, the air dragon alert and ready overhead. Its circle was tight above the clearing. The longer Rees waited the less he would be able to nerve himself to what he had to do now. The Terran set his teeth, tensed his body.

He did not really leap, rather he threw himself low, as he might have done in tackling a runner, concentrating on that weapon. As his hand fell upon it, he flopped over on his back, swinging the blaster up so that it pointed skyward from his chest. And he stared wildly up into pure nightmare.

The monstrous head was not just a red outline now. All its horror bloomed in the sudden beam of a handlight. And that ray dazzled it for just the second Rees must have to thumb the blaster to narrow beam and fire. He saw the pencil of energy leap at the gaping mouth and then kicked into a roll which carried him on toward the bush from which the hand light had come.

A clawed foot raked, scraping along the Terran's side, tearing clothing from his body. But the strength of that stroke flung him on and away. Rees heard a scream of terrifying volume as he came up hard against fur and flesh and lay gasping for air.

Somehow he squirmed up into a sitting position, the blaster again ready. But there was nothing out there to aim at, neither in the air or on the ground.

"What?" he began.

"It went over and down." Fingers fastened on his shoulder. "You are hurt?"

Went over where? Rees tried to make sense of that as the hands swept down his arm to his scraped side, touched some scratch there to stinging life. Into the gully! That's what she meant; the air dragon must have been so severely wounded it had fallen into the gully!

"You shot a dragon!" Gordy's voice was a breathy cry of triumph. "It's head went all smash! That's just what it did!"

"And you have taken no great harm." Her hands were busy applying some substance to his side in swift, competent strokes.

"We've got to get out of here," Rees assembled his wits to the point where common sense was again in command. He still did not quite believe that this had really happened, that he had pulled off their second wild gamble of the night.

"Down the gully," Isiga told him, "there is a sheltered way. I had just found it when the dragon came. And there are signs of a path, we can not be too far from the plantation."

"Then let's get going!" Rees urged.

☽⋆ CHAPTER 7 ⋆☾

"NO SIGNS OF LIFE." Rees lay flat, his chin supported on an arm stretched across before him. A screen of scarlet-tipped grass stood between him and the sharply sloping drop toward a barrier which caught and reflected the greenish sunlight. He could not be wrong; the sentry towers at the four corners of that enclosure, the size and substantial structures the wall protected, said this was Wrexul's. But nothing moved from one of those buildings to the next, the place had a deserted look.

"The 'copter park," Isiga was beside him, her silver fur-hair and grey skin blending better than the Terran's torn clothing and pink-tan hide with the color of Ishkurian soil and grass roots, "there is nothing there."

Rees had already noted that disappointing fact. The off-world staff could have sealed their headquarters, taken off in the 'copters, trusting to luck that the trouble would be settled and they could return. From what Rees could sight every building was closed, the gates shut. And he imagined that persona-locks were on. A barrier tuned to Terran body heat would permit his entrance and Gordy's—but he was dubious about the Salariki. He said as much to his companion.

"We should go there, even if your people have left?"

"They didn't take the com with them. And that must be on direct beam with the port. If I could make contact with the authorities a 'copter could be sent be on robo-control."

She nodded. "But what if the snake-beasts behind us have another force beam?"

Yes, what if their brush back by the gully in the night had not knocked out the full enemy force? The rest of the Ishkurians could be ringed around down there, just waiting for a chance to get into the plantation stronghold. There was a wide swath cleared of all vegetation, fire burnt to the soil, about the four sides of the barrier. That had clearly been done since the last full rain, the black ash was still to be noticed. Someone had ordered that destruction as a reasonable precaution against any creep attack. In order to get to the gates Rees must cross that open. And only the gates, one of those two, would pass him as soon as his body heat activated their controls. Then, once in, he must locate the control room, clear the persona-locks for Isiga and Zannah. Or else head directly for the com, send his message and return here to await the arrival of a rescue 'copter. Rees outlined the alternative plans to the Salarika.

"You believe that this 'lock' is set against us, that neither I nor Zannah could pass it?"

"Wrexul's had a straight Terran staff. Your people seldom sign wage contracts with Terran firms."

"That is true. Is it now a matter of time?"

"Not too closely, I hope. And down there, with that barrier in working order, the Crocs couldn't get at us. Not unless they do have another force beam."

"So many guesses, and so easy to make the wrong one," Isiga commented. "But for this I am willing to throw the quass sticks and take what count of red Fortune offers. To be within walls which hold off snake-beasts, that would make one's heart beat less fast, smooth one's hair sleek again."

"Then stay right here, all of you," Rees cautioned; "When you see me return to the gate, then make a run for it. I will cover you with the blaster."

He shouldered the larger pack of their supplies and began to run. Under his boots the slope seemed to stretch itself, making a longer dash through the open than he had estimated when under cover above. Rees skidded against the surface of the barrier, his shoulder meeting it with force enough to jar painfully along his tender side.

Was the gate on persona-lock? The Terran waited breathlessly, clinging to that hope. Certainly the staff would not have set the combination to any but a general Terran body heat. There was too much chance that any one individual might not return. But at least Rees had not been burnt to a crisp at contact, or given a brain washing sonic blast. And he was sure the Wrexul people must have left some warm and fierce welcome for any Crocs daring to nose around.

There was a click, hardly louder than the sounds made by some grass insects. A portion of the wider gateway to his left slid back. One-man heat, one-man door, that figured. Rees leaped through and the panel went back into place behind him.

The control room, which should hold the com also—which—where? Rees surveyed the buildings and tried to guess their uses. Finally he chose one which was attached by a short corridor to the living quarters. Its outer door must also have been set on persona-lock because when he was still a foot or so away it folded into the frame.

This was a power room right enough. And one showing signs of hurried abandonment. A cup stained with dregs of Terran coffee sat on a shelf beside an instrument panel, a scarf trailed from the back of a built-in seat. Rees made a hurried examination of the board beside the coffee cup. While the mission had never used a persona-lock, in fact Uncle Milo had dismantled part of it three months ago to take out the pack motor for the repair of a lift beam, Rees knew what he was searching for. And that dial with its attendant row of buttons was easy to find.

One second to press full release, then he was running back to the outer gate. He waved his hand high over his head.

Gordy came down the slope first, carrying the other bundle. The boy stumbled once, went to a scratched knee, and when he got up, smeared the back of his hand across his dirty face. Isiga, carrying Zannah, padded light-footedly up behind the child, the encouraging words she used to spur him on reaching Rees merely as a singsong purr. The Terran sprinted out as they neared, swept up Gordy, in spite of the boy's indignation, and somehow hustled them all inside the barrier. It was necessary now to close the gate by hand. He slammed it and ran to re-set the lock.

"Food," Isiga pattered along after him. "That's what we need. And have you found the com?"

"Not yet. I'll look for it now." But as Rees went slowly about the room his steps dragged. He staggered once, steadied himself with a hand against the wall. That last spurt through the gate lugging Gordy—it was as if that effort had used up all the reserve of strength on which he had been drawing so heavily since they had left the mission. How long had it been since he had dared to relax, to rest? More than one Ishkurian day. And even now he dared not think of sleep.

"You sick, Rees?" Gordy blinked at him owlishly.

"Just a little tired. Don't you want to go with the Lady Isiga and find something to eat?"

"Where's Mom, Rees, and Dad? You said they'd be here with the 'copter. And I haven't seen them. There's no one here but us. I want my Mom."

For a moment Rees was unable to understand that; his fatigue was like a mental fog. Then he recalled dimly the excuse he had used to cover the tragedy for Gordy yesterday morning.

"They must have gone on again, Gordy." He knew he was fumbling, not handling this well. But he was too tired to be very imaginative. "We'll call a 'copter and go on to Nagassara."

"I don't believe you!" The boy stated, frankly hostile. "I want my Mom and I want her now!"

Rees lurched over to sit down in the chair from which the scarf trailed. The wisp of soft material fluttered to the ground and Gordy pounced upon it.

"This isn't Mom's," he told Rees accusingly. "She hasn't never been here. I'm going home right now, I'm going home!"

"You can't!" Rees' control was on the ragged edge of breaking. He could not deal with a frightened, stubborn child on top of everything else, not now. "Isiga!" He shouted, knowing that he did not have either the will power or the energy to leave the seat and hunt out the Salarika in person.

"You can't make me stay here." Gordy backed toward the door, his face a sullen scowl as he wrung the soft scarf between his scratched and dirty hands. "You can lock me up, but I won't stay! I'm going back to Mom and Dad. Dad's going to get you, Rees Naper, for bringing me away. He said I wasn't to go around with you. You're a bad man, you fight."

"So I fight," Rees repeated grimly. "Well, it's a good thing I know how, whether I like it or not. Listen here, Gordy, you're just tired and hungry and I know you want your mother. But we must get to Nagassara. The Crocs. . . ."

"Dad said 'Crocs' is a bad word!" Gordy's voice was shrill. "You say bad words and you tell lies and I'm not going to stay here!"

He whirled and dashed out of the doorway. Rees got to his feet and stumbled after. The persona-locks—Gordy could pass by them—leave either gate without interference. Rees must reach the child, keep him from leaving the plantation fort.

"You, you let me alone! I'm going home right now!" Gordy struggled in Isiga's grip, hitting and kicking, his voice now a scream of pure hysteria. But, as Rees had discovered earlier, the Salarika's hold was strong. And she not only continued to restrain the boy but bent over him with a soothing croon.

Her eyes met Rees' and he read reassurance in them. This was now woman's business and the Terran trusted the Salarika to handle the rebel. He must go back and hunt for the com.

He had located the unit and was seated before the call mike when she slipped in to join him.

"Gordy?"

"He has eaten, now he sleeps. Also I have put a catch on the door. But his purpose is firm. We shall have to watch him. He does not know that those of his inner court are dead?"

"No, how can you tell a child a thing like that?" Rees appealed. "I had to keep him in the roller, away from the mission. So I told him his mother and father had gone, that we would catch up with them later."

"Such evasions always lead to complications," she pointed out. "But, yes, I can understand how you found it too hard to speak the truth to a little one. Perhaps, when he wakes and is quieter, I may be able to tell him something. He is now too angry and frightened to listen."

"I suppose so. The sooner we can raise Nagassara the better!"

"There are those there who are his kin?"

"No." For the first time Rees considered Gordy's future. "No, there's no one and I don't think he even has any close kin off-world. He'll be the responsibility of the mission foundation."

"And you, you have other kin?"

"No. My father was a Survey Scout. He did not return from Rim run. Dr. Naper was my uncle."

Her green-blue eyes regarded his thoughtfully. "We heard that you sought animals in the jungle with the tamer of beasts. You did not work at the mission?"

"Hardly!" His old bitterness was sour and heavy. "Uncle Milo took me away from the Survey Academy, he was strongly opposed to the Service. But he could not make his ideas mine. So now I am neither one thing, nor another!"

"And what will you do when we reach Nagassara?"

Rees shrugged. "I don't know. Join the militia maybe. Hunt up Captain Vickery anyway. We have to get there first."

She flexed her slender fingers, casing and uncasing her claw nails, and there was a spark centering each slit pupiled eye.

"Yes, that is true, we must reach Nagassara before we can earn a future. But, Lord Rees, keep this in your mind; I am now Name-Head of a clan, a trade clan. In Nagassara you may have more than one chance. Are not Free Traders explorers too?"

Rees blinked, not really taking in the meaning of her words. Nagassara was the width of a mountain range and more away. What did any future beyond the immediate one of trying to reach there mean now?

He pressed the key of the com. The call light sparked on the board. Wrexul's personal call symbols he did not know, so he resorted to those of the mission. And such coming in on the Wrexul beam length would alert any operator at the port to the fact that this was a distress call.

Tip-tap-tock. Rees beat out the pattern. But the plate to receiver remained obstinately blank. The com was alive, sending. Why no answer? Cold squeezed Rees' middle, added to the leaden weight fatigue had hung on his arms and shoulders. Was—was Nagassara already abandoned, had the last spacer lifted? Or had the Crocs erupted all over the planet and crushed the stronghold of the off-world government?

"No answer!" Isiga's fingers hooked, claws fully out, as if she would tear the symbols out of the plate by force. He could hear her heavy breathing through the beat of the key.

"Could—could they have gone? She put one of his fears into

words as desperate moments lengthened into minutes—two—four—six . . .

"I don't see how." Rees bore down the sending key. "There may be a mountain storm, those cut the beams at times. It must be that, it has to!"

He stared at the blank mirror face of the receiver as if by the demands of will alone he could bring a responsive flash to it. *Tip—tap—tock.*

"Identify!" Imperious, demanding, that single signal on the key. Two Terrans, he gave their names and place of origin; two Salariki, cut off without transportation at Wrexul's, an appeal for a robocopter. He reeled that off, began to repeat the message with the same ragged speed.

"Naper—give name of X-Tee instructor, Survey Academy five years ago."

Rees stared blankly at the symbols on the mirror, wondering for a dread filled second or two if he had cracked under the strain, as the message had no earthly, or galactic, connection with the S.O.S. he had broadcasted. But the symbols remained there without alteration when he asked for the reason.

"This is no time to play games!" The Terran burst out, banging his fist on the edge of the panel.

"Not games, I think," Isiga said. "There is some need for them to be sure that you are who you say you are. Can it be that the snake-beasts are using coms to call out either would-be rescuers or to gain transportation into Nagassara?"

Rees relaxed. That made some sense. But Crocs using the com units that way? Only they had been armed with a force beam, too, he had to remember that. They were not just up against primitive jungle runners after all.

"X-Tee instructor—Zorkal." Luckily they had asked him to name Zorkal and not, say, the astro-math man. But Zorkal had given Rees extra instruction when he had discovered how keen the young Terran was on X-Tee.

"Set your field guide beam on C-2-59 over Y," the mirror told him, apparently satisfied now that he was Rees Naper in the flesh. "You will have to wait. There is a flash storm in Nass Pass and we can not send the Robo until that clears."

"A storm!" Isiga's voice was close to a sigh. And Rees could have echoed that sound of frustration in a far more vigorous outburst if his weariness was not so complete.

The Nass Pass could be storm blocked for minutes, hours or days. And it was very true that a robo could not fight the winds there and get through with only a ride-beam to bring it in. Rees set the guide as directed and then let his hands fall into his lap. He was literally too worn out to move. Then Isiga's warm clasp on his bowed shoulders roused him a little.

"Come eat, sleep," she purred close to his ear. "You will have time if there is a storm."

"You need rest also," Rees suggested. But he was standing up under her surprisingly strong pull, staggering to the door where she steered him.

She had found supplies left by the plantation staff, produced a meal Rees ate his way through, hardly aware of what he chewed and swallowed, or why, while she sat opposite him at the table drinking some liquid of her own choosing in delicate sips from a cup she held in both hands.

He was in the jungle clearing of Vickery's camp, facing the three walls of cages. And in each cage crouched a Croc, their snouts high, their teeth bared. The horrible stink of their hatred and anger choked him. Now the cage controls were weakening. Rees knew that without actually seeing the give of the latches. And there were no weapons at his belt, nothing but his two bare hands with which to face their charge.

To escape—to escape he must get into one of those plated bodies, see through those red eyes. But how? How did one become a Croc? Yet he must, he must!

Rees was sitting up, gasping, his heart pounding heavily within the wall of his chest. He flailed out with an arm, grazed a body which dodged that blow. Then his gaze steadied on Isiga. He must have been dreaming!

"The robo—it's here!" He got up from the bunk, ready to go.

Rees wavered. Her tone, eyes—the expression in them brought him into full wakefulness. He drew a deep breath and the air seemed to catch in his throat. That smell, that couldn't be any hazy hold over from his dream! Less heavy than the stench of his nightmare, but unmistakable for what it was. Rees whirled to face the window open above the bunk. The breeze pushed in through the sonic unchecked. It was the cool wind of early evening and the gray shadows of dusk fogged out there.

"They've come," he said in a half whisper.

Croc stink; he would never forget it as long as he was able to breathe.

"Have they shown themselves yet?" Rees' head swung back to Isiga.

"No. But that is plain that they are there." She waved a hand at the window and the wind.

"And there must be a lot of them."

"Gordy is gone."

Rees didn't take that in at once. He had been too busy listening, thinking about the force which must now ring in around the plantation fort.

"Gordy . . ." The Terran repeated absently and then the meaning of her report sank in. "How long?" he snapped.

"Zannah says only a half hour perhaps. We searched the rooms first."

Rees ran, heading for the gate, that gate through which only a Terran could pass, which should have meant their safety and escape. But which to Gordy could mean . . . No, not that—please, not that!

CHAPTER 8

"GORDY!" Rees yelled with the full force of his lungs. There was a faint echo resounding from the higher land, but no other answer. And the gate was closed.

Rees pulled up. "He could be hiding," he said to Isiga who had run along behind him. She shook her silvery head.

"We searched as I told you. Zannah also says he went to look for his mother."

The boy could be anywhere in that wall of vegetation beyond the burned strip. And with the Croc smell this strong. To try to track a missing child in the jungle which was the enemies' own hunting ground was the rankest folly.

Eye of the Spider! Rees froze. He knew, now he knew what was going to happen as clearly as if his brain did occupy one of those armored, saurian skulls, look through the red alien eyes. Gordy was a key, a key to be used to open Wrexul's.

Perhaps the Crocs had already tried to cross the barrier, found the persona-locks past their breaking. Some scout, left on sentry at one of the high points cupping in the stronghold, could have witnessed the fugitives' entrance, marked the ease with which the Terrans had passed the gate. The Ishkurians might have been just waiting for some such chance, and Gordy had given it to them!

Rees turned, began to walk back to the building at a slower pace.

"What is it?" Isiga matched her steps to his. "What is it that you have thought of?"

"Gordy, they won't harm him yet. Because he's their key to the gate!"

"The lock!" Again her voice was a hiss of anger. "They will use him to open the gate for them."

"So they must bring him back to us," Rees held to that fact which was the only one holding a fraction of hope.

"And what do we do?" she wanted to know.

"You and Zannah must wait at the 'copter park, ready if and when it comes. Maybe we can find weapons."

"No, for those I have already looked. There are none left."

"Maybe no apparent ones but I want to see what is in those store rooms." Rees headed purposefully for the windowless building he had marked down as the warehouse.

"That is time locked, I think. I could not open it."

"A lock can be shorted," he snapped.

The dusk was deepening. Night came fast here in the foothills and the darkness would provide cover for the Crocs using Gordy. Lights, they needed floods to cover the whole inner area. Wrexul possessed a flood system, the standards and lamps were in sight.

Rees set about preparing for the attack he knew was on the way. Even if the robo arrived now, they could not leave. Or he could send Isiga and Zannah. But he would have to remain until the natives moved in with Gordy. The robo could be sent back again.

The control room gave him the power of turning on the floods and Rees made a glittering day within the perimeter of the strong-hold. He tried to keep his mind on what he must do, tried to forget what could happen to Gordy. But the tightness in him was a physical pain by now.

Now the store rooms! Rees, carrying tools, went to work, making the necessary adjustments to wiring, watched the portal open. Bales, boxes that were the last crop ready to be shipped, supplies from off-world. He tore open boxes, read labels with feverish haste. In the end he brought out his selected loot, rolling two bales into the open before he tore at the sacking bagging their contents.

"Oganna!" Isiga came to him. "What is it that you would do?"

"This." Rees pulled the closely packed leaves apart, the oily drops gathered on their surfaces, pasting them together so that separating them was a task. "Spread these around to wall in the 'copter park. Pile them thick."

"Yes," her eyes held the feral spark of a hunting cat's. "Yes!" She snatched up an armload of the stuff and sped away. Zannah pattered out of the shadows, her injured arm in a sling. But in the other hand, she, too, picked up a bundle of the oganna and hurried after Isiga.

The flood lights which made day about the barrier were dimmed here by building shadows. Rees did not believe any Croc watchers could be sure what the activity of the off-worlders meant. Croc eyes did not adjust well to bright light. The enemy must now be considering ways and means of putting out the floods.

He went on with his leaves, piling them up, watching Isiga and Zannah working to outline the square on their side. Only directly facing the space before the outer gate did Rees leave a break in that low wall of odorous vegetable material.

"That is the last." Isiga came to him, brushing one hand vainly against the other in a useless try to rub away the sticky oil. She saw the gap and glanced from it to Rees with sudden understanding.

"Do you dare?"

"It is that I must," he told her bleakly.

Her fingers arose to her lips and then she jerked her hand away before they touched her mouth. But those wide feline eyes narrowed.

"Come!" She beckoned him back to the living quarters. There she caught up one of the spider silk blankets. To tear one of those was, Rees had thought, close to impossible. But somehow the Salarika achieved that task, using a knife and her claw nails. She coiled the strips across the table and brought out a basin. Water splashed from the wall tap into that container. Then she knelt before the aid kit, chose tubes and boxes whose contents she had sniffed. Powder and liquid went into the waiting water and was mixed thoroughly by sloshing the bowl back and forth. That done she turned to Rees.

"Your clothing," she indicated the remains of his shirt, the scuffed boot-breeches, "off. I do not know how well this will protect you but it will be better than nothing at all."

He stripped quickly as she soaked the parts of blankets in the basin. Then she went to work deftly to wind the sopping material about him from foot to neck, leaving the binding of his head, with only a narrow opening for eyes, nose and mouth, to the last. The liquid had turned a bright purple-blue and Rees guessed that he must now present a weird appearance, perhaps startling enough to actually work in his favor as a momentary surprise for the Crocs when he had to face them at the breakthrough. He flexed shoulder muscles, had Isiga loosen the bindings about the upper part of his body, ready for any action he must take.

At a trilling cry from the outside, Isiga looked around.

"They come, Zannah says."

But Rees did not need the small Salarika's warning. The smell was enough—sickeningly heavy. Yes, Crocs were on the march.

"Get to the robo landing, keep under cover!" He gave her the blaster and picked up his own weapons, if one could call a sleek coil of hagger hide rope a weapon.

Isiga dodged out the door, caught Zannah's hand and ran. But Rees' path led him towards the gate. He had earlier marked down his post there and he reached it now after a zig-zag route. So he crouched at last between two of the supporters of the flood nearest the barrier. Crocs would head for that, to douse the light, as soon as they were through the gate.

Hooting—harsh barking. The Ishkurians were certainly making no effort to hide their presence outside, attempting no sneak attack. They must know how few and weak their quarry were. And here they came!

A brown plated head, revealed in detail in the light, raised a snout pointing at the gate as might a hound what had treed a quarry. And, riding on the Ishkurian's shoulders, Gordy! Rees' heart gave a lurch of relief. The child was still unharmed!

The Croc's scaled hands went up, he stopped a trifle to allow Gordy to slide from his plate ridged back. Rees' breath came out, in a hiss close to Isiga's expression of anger. That was Ishbi from the mission. No wonder Gordy had accepted such an escort readily. The native whom the boy had known as a friend for at least half of his short life, Ishbi who was a link with his home and family, Ishbi whom Gordy would now trust sooner than he might Rees himself.

Gordy walked forward confidently. He paused by the gate to look back and Rees saw Ishbi's head jerk in a movement approximating a Terran nod of encouragement. Other Crocs emerged into the open behind Ishbi, a wedge of them carrying some burden. Gordy was to open the gate and they would insert a prop to keep it so until they could all pour in. Simple, neat, and it would work. Ishbi had enough familiarity with the mission installations to head straight for the power and shut off all controls there.

The door in the larger barrier opened and Gordy walked boldly through. A concentrated rush from the wedge of hovering Crocs sent a log crashing into that opening. Now Ishbi, holding two giant slabs of taluc bark on either arm, took a running leap, skimmed along the log. The taluc bark smoked and the native threw them from him as he hit the inner side of the fortress wall. There were others coming the same path with their temporary shields covering them for that instant when they must pass the portal and cut the protecting ray operating there.

With the log providing them passage over the ground wire and the improvised shields, swift and daring runners could make the passage. However, they were not all to be so lucky as Ishbi and his first follower. The third native to make the jump gave a snorting cry as a convulsive leap took him through, only to lie writhing on the ground. There was a halt in the advance. Ishbi barked an order and turned to Gordy.

But the child was staring wide-eyed at the dying Croc. With a cry he began to back away. Ishbi made a grab for him and Gordy, looking up, must have seen something in the suarian countenance looming above him which was utterly disillusioning. He backed farther, his hands raised as if to fend off the big Ishkurian.

Rees went into action. The rope snaked out in a loop which encircled Gordy and pulled tight. Rees jerked, the distance between them was short enough so that the boy would not be hurt and it was the only way to get him quickly out of Croc clutches.

Gordy screamed, high and shrill, and Rees hauled him in. He held Gordy, rope and all, before the surprised natives were fully aware the Terran boy was out of reach. Gordy, his arms still pinned to his sides by the loop, fought and kicked in Rees' hold, but he was too hampered to break loose.

This was the worst, the dart and dash the Terran must make into the shadow of the nearest building, with two Crocs loose and perhaps more ready to attempt crossing the log bridge now that they were inflamed by seeing their prey directly in view.

Rees cringed within the wrapping bandages as he sped, expecting at any moment as he held to that zig-zag path to feel the bite of an Ishkurian dart in his back. Perhaps it was his weird appearance in that purple covering which gave him a few seconds grace when the Crocs sighted him. If they were expecting a Terran or Salarika to show, then a purple thing of totally alien species would be momentarily startling. And the majority of Crocs were not quick thinkers.

Even so Rees was hardly able to believe he had actually made his first run without opposition when he crouched in the door of the com unit building, Gordy still wriggling and screaming wildly in his hold.

"Gordy!" The young man put his face closer to the boy's, hoping that the sound of a familiar voice, a chance to see his features through that opening in the head bandages would prove his identity. "Gordy, it's Rees, Rees Naper!"

But Gordy had past the point where reason could appeal to his mind, he was completely hysterical. Holding him tight, Rees steadied for another rush. Ishbi leading that invading party was bad luck. The Ishkurian could recognize the guide beam, turn it off and ground the robo. Yet Rees could make no stand here, not with Gordy so wild and without a weapon.

He reached around, pressing the struggling child tight to his chest, and caught up the waiting blanket he had left there. That was also wringing wet with Isiga's preparation. Gordy gave a gasp as Rees wrapped the clammy folds about him, then subsided into a limp weight. Once more Rees broke into the open.

There was a crack behind him and the flood by the gate went out, shattered by some well flung dart. But the ensuing dark was an aid to the Terran now, not a danger. He ran for the 'copter park. Fire, a green-yellow fire ran along the ground there, stiffened into a four walled square of odorous flame. Rees marked the narrow gap before him, knew he must risk the tongues licking out on either side. He measured the distance ahead, put his face down against the bundle which was Gordy, and ran at the best speed he could muster for that slit passage to safety.

Heat scorched his hands, face. Rees raised his head. Isiga crouched in the square, the blaster barrel steadied on her forearm laid across her knee. Rees dropped Gordy, grabbed for the weapon.

"Have—to—get—back," he told her in labored gasps, "must—smash—beam—control."

Her ears were flattened, her lips curled in a cat's snarl of spitting rage. He caught the blaster as she released it. Already the flames from the oganna leaves were fifteen or more feet high, their heat spreading inward. With his palm Rees pushed the Salarika away from him toward the middle of the square. She pulled at Gordy and obeyed Rees' gesture, while the Terran turned again to face the gap, hardly sure now where the opening was.

One arm over his face, the other holding the blaster as tightly as he had Gordy, Rees set himself for another dash. The three would huddle down in the open, covered by wet blankets, hope that the robo would come in before the fire died. If he could reach the beam and render it safe from interference, a danger he should have foreseen.

Rees leaped, cried out as he met fire. Then was beyond its breath. His bandages were no longer so wet. A charred strip fluttered free from his waist as he ran.

There ahead a shape moved, shadow against shadow. Rees fired with the blaster ray set on a wide fan, was answered by a hoarse croaking cry. Now he was in the control room, the light on as he had left it. But a brown serrated back, a snouted head, were between him and the panel. Once again the Terran fired, saw flame crisp across the Ishkurian, go on to cut the panel in two. The light in the room crackled and went out. Only the flickering dance of the burning oganna leaves gave any radiance. He had finished the main power set.

But the robo guide beam was equipped with a secondary impulse. And it would continue on that emergency changeover for at least an hour. Time and the duration of the storm would battle for their future. Rees had done all he could to safeguard their one slender hope. It remained for him now to try to save himself. With all controls off the Crocs would stream through the gate unchallenged. But they could not cross that flame wall, not until it smoldered into ashes. And oganna had a long burning period.

Rees slipped away from the control room. The smell of the burning leaves was heavy and aromatic, removing one of his safeguards, the ability to scent the enemy. Croc cries were harsh in the night and then, as if by command, they were suddenly stilled. He thought the natives were combing the buildings, circling that core of flame, attempting to herd their prey inward.

But the Terran still held one advantage, the ability to cross the fire wall, or so he hoped. Hurriedly Rees ran his hand down his body. Those protecting bandages had dried, but they still covered him. And he had no choice, he had to pass the gap for the third time. Death that way, painful as it was, would be better than any the Crocs would deal out to a prisoner.

Now to locate the gap once again. These waves of flame were confusing, and the slit had been a narrow one even in the beginning. To choose the wrong place meant complete disaster.

Behind Rees there was a noise, a guttural grunt. He fired at the sound and ran. Once more he flung his arm up to shield his face as he took off in a leap designed to carry him through the spot he believed was the thinnest in the wall of fire.

Then he was rolling over and over, his bandages smoldering in half a dozen places. When he was really aware of anything beyond the pain and heat, he knew that he was lying flat, most of his body bare as Isiga worked feverishly to tear those charred strips from him. Burns smarted, but he must have been lucky, very lucky.

"Can you move?" The Salarika bent over him to ask. "We must get back out of range."

Rees turned his head and saw what she meant. Darts were arching through the flames, catching fire in the process, to rain down on the pavement of the park. He rolled over and tried to creep out of range, but the pain in his hands, under the pressure of his weight, was too great for him to stand. Somehow Rees got to his feet, leaned heavily on Isiga as she towed him to the blanket heap which was the children. There she pushed him down and held a canteen to his lips while he drank greedily.

"Listen!" Her head went up, ears aprick. Now he could hear it too, the warning landing whistle of the Robo coming in to set down. They caught the green wink of its lights as the flyer made its vertical descent. Rees stood blinking as the tripod feet of the cabin touched the pavement. He wavered forward with an outstretched hand, and then moaned with pain as his seared fingers proved that that vision was indeed real, that they had beaten the nightmare after all.

Seconds later he waved Isiga into the pilot's seat, saw the children huddled behind her.

"They'll have her on robo-beam in reverse," he said. "Use the lift button, and then the all-clear so the beam can pick us up."

Rees pointed out the proper controls, his hands so painful with the slightest movement that he had to grit his teeth against crying out. But in spite of that torment he smiled weakly as they rose straight out of the hollow of flame into the clean, cool air of the night. The spider had woven webs and caught victims, but not all, not all!

There was going to be a future in Nagassara or off world for them after all. Isiga's hands dropped from the controls as the robo pilot took over smoothly. She leaned toward the Terran, concern in her cats' eyes. But Rees continued to smile as they rode out on the beam lifting to the mountain pass where the day and the future were arriving close upon one another.

THE
X FACTOR

For Helen Hoover,
whose weasel-fisher people
gave me the Brothers-in-Fur

⟡⋆ CHAPTER 1 ⋆⟡

EVEN NIGHTTIME on Vaanchard was disturbing. It was not a time of peace in which one could hide. There were gemlike glints in the garden path, a soft luminescence to the growing things, new scents and—

Diskan Fentress hunched over, his chin almost touching his knees, fingertips thrust into his ears. He had closed his eyes to his surroundings, too—though there was no way to filter those scents out of the air he breathed. His mouth worked; he was afraid he was going to be thoroughly and disastrously sick, right here where his shame would be public. Not that anyone would let him see their disgust, of course. The elaborate pretense that Diskan Fentress was one of them would continue and continue and continue—He swallowed convulsively.

The greenish moonlight had reached the edge of the path now, awaking the glints to crystalline brilliance. A new fragrance tantalized his nostrils, but not aggressively. Diskan could not imagine anything in this garden as aggressive. When created and brought to perfection by the Vaans, a pleasure place was subtle.

Diskan fought a silent struggle against his heaving insides, against the terrible bonds this garden and the building from which he had fled, this city, this world, had laid upon him. His trouble reached back farther than just his coming here to Vaanchard—to a day when Ulken the Overseer had brought a stranger down to the pond back on Nyborg, had called Diskan out from the murky water, where he stood up to his middle, green slime smearing his bare body, and had spoken to him as if he were a—a *thing*—not a man with feelings and a mind, if not a body, like his fellows.

Now Diskan's breath came in a ragged sob. His eyes might register the path and the strange growth, if he wanted to look, all the elfin glory of the night, but *he* saw the past now.

His troubles had not begun by the pond either, but back down the trail of years. His mouth shaped a grimace, half a snarl of frustrated rage. Way back, that beginning—

He could not remember any time when he had not been aware of the truth, that Diskan Fentress was a reject—a badly working piece of human machinery that could be turned only to the simplest and dirtiest of jobs. He did not know how to use the outsize share of strength in his poorly coordinated body, breaking when he wanted to mend or cherish. And his mind functioned almost as badly—slowly and stupidly.

Why? How many times had he demanded that in the past, ever since he could think and wonder at all! But he had learned quickly not to ask it of anyone but himself—and that impersonal power that might or might not have had a hand in his misfashioning.

Back on Nyborg he had—would they say—"adjusted?" At least being used for the brute-strength jobs left him mostly to himself during the day, and that was escape of a kind, something he did not have here.

Then, in spite of shrinking from that memory, Diskan thought again of the scene by the pond. Ulken, filthy, coarse, but still judged infinitely higher in the community scale than Diskan, standing there, a sly grin on his face, shouting as if his victim were deaf in addition to all the rest.

And the man with him—Diskan closed his eyes, licked his lips before he swallowed again, willing himself not to—no, no!

That man, lithe, of middle height, all feline grace and ease, his fine body well displayed in the brown-green uniform of Survey, the silver comet of a First-in Scout on his breast! The stranger had looked so clean, so close to the ideal of Diskan's haunted dreams that he had simply stared at him, not answering Ulken's shouted orders— until he saw that *blackness* on the Scout's face, just before the Scout had turned on Ulken. The overseer had shriveled and backed off. But when the Scout had looked at Diskan once more, Ulken had grinned, maliciously, before he slouched away.

"You are—Diskan Fentress?" Disbelief, yes, there had been disbelief in that, enough to awaken in Diskan some of the old defiance.

He had waded out of the water, pulling up fistfuls of coarse grass to rub the slime from him.

"I'm Fentress."

"So am I. Renfry Fentress."

Diskan had not really understood, not for a whole moment of suspended time. He had gone right on wiping his big clumsy body. Then he answered with the truth as he had known it.

"But you're dead!"

"There's sometimes a light-year stretch between presumption and actuality," the Scout had replied, but he continued to stare. And a small hurt, hidden far inside Diskan's overgrown frame of flesh and bone, grew.

What a meeting between father and son! But how could Renfry Fentress have sired—*him?* Scouts, assigned for periods of time to planet duty, were encouraged to contract Service marriages. This grew from the need to breed a type of near mutant species necessary to carry on the exploration of the galaxy. Certain qualities of mind and body were inherited, and those types were encouraged to reproduce their kind. So, Renfry Fentress had taken Lilha Clyas as his wife on Nyborg, for the duration of his assignment there, a recognized and honored association, with a pension for Lilha and a promising future for any children of their union.

In due time, Renfry Fentress had been reassigned. He then formally severed the marriage by Decree of Departure and raised ship, without knowing whether there would be a child, since his orders were a matter of emergency. Eight months later Diskan had been born, and in spite of the skill of the medics, it had been a hard birth, so hard that his mother had not survived his arrival.

He did not remember the early days in the government creche, but the personality scanner had reported almost at once that Diskan Fentress was not Service material. Something had gone wrong in all that careful planning. He was like neither his father nor his mother, but a retrocession, too big, too clumsy, too slow of thought and speech to be considered truly one of a space-voyaging generation.

There had been other tests, many of them. He could not recall them separately now, only that they were one long haze of frustration, mental pain, discouragement, and sometimes fear. For some years while he had been a small child, he had been tested again and again. The authorities could not believe that he was as imperfect a specimen as the machines continued to declare.

Then he had refused to be so tried again, running away twice from the creche school. Finally one of the authorities, after a week of breakage, sullen rages, and violence, had suggested assigning him to the labor pool. He had been thirteen then, larger than most full-grown men. They had been just a little afraid of him. Diskan had a flash of satisfaction when he remembered that. But he had known better than to try to settle problems with his fists. He had no desire to be condemned to personality erasure. He might be stupid, but he was still Diskan Fentress.

So he had gone from one heavy work job to the next, and the years had passed—five, six? He was not quite sure. Then Renfry Fentress had come back to Nyborg, and everything had changed—for the worse, certainly for the worse!

From the beginning, Diskan had been suspicious of this father out of space. Renfry had shown no disappointment, no outward sign, after that first moment of blank survey at their meeting, that he thought his son a failure. Yet Diskan knew that all this existed behind the other's apparent acceptance.

Renfry's attitude became only another "why," giving Diskan almost the same torture as the first "why" had always held. Why did Renfry Fentress take such trouble to search out a son he had never seen? When Diskan had been born and his mother had died, the Scout had been traced by the Service as was the regulation, so that he might express his wishes concerning the future of his child. And the answer had come back, "Missing, presumed dead," an epitaph for many a First-in Scout.

But Fentress had not died in the black waters of space, where a meteor hit had doomed his ship to drift. Instead, he had been picked up by an alien explorer, outward bound on a quest similar to his own, the hunt for planets to be occupied by a rapidly expanding race.

And among the people of his rescuer, Renfry had found a home, a new wife. When he was again able to establish contact with his own people, he had received the now years-old report of his son's birth. Since his new marriage, happy as it was, could have no offspring, he had hunted that son, eager to bring him to Vaanchard, where Renfry had taken his optional discharge.

Vaanchard was wonder, beauty, the paradise long dreamed of by Renfry's species. Its natives were all grace, charm, intelligence governed by imagination—a world without visible flaw, until Renfry brought his son to shatter the peace of his household, not once but many times over!

Diskan dropped his hands from his ears, suffering the discomfort of sound. He held them up to survey the calloused palms, the roughened fingers. In spite of soothing lotions, the fingertips could still snag fine garments, window hangings, any bit of fabric he touched. They could smash, too, as they had tonight!

There was a smear of blood across the ball of his right thumb. So he had more than memory to remind him of what had happened back there, where the bell-toned notes were rising and falling in a wistful pattern of music that was not human but that sang in the heart, was a part of the body. Light, sound, and, now that he had unplugged his ears, he could hear laughter. It was not aimed at him. They were so kind, so intuitive. They did not use laughter as a weapon; they did not use any weapons. They only overlooked, forgave, made allowances for him—eternally they did that!

If he could only hate them as he had hated Ulken and his like! There was a fuel in hatred to feed a man's strength, but he could not hate Drustans, nor Rixa, nor Eyinada, their mother and now his father's wife. You cannot hate those who are perfect by your standards; you can only hate yourself for being what *you* are.

The movement of his fingers enlarged the bead of blood on his thumb. It trickled sluggishly, and Diskan licked it away.

"Deesskaann?"

The lilting song of his name—Rixa! She would come and find him. There would be no mention of shards of gem blue on the white floor. No one would ever mention again a priceless wonder that had been reduced to splinters in an instant after centuries of treasuring. If they had raged, if they had once said what he knew they thought— that would make it easier. Now Rixa would want him to go back with her. *No!*

Diskan stood up. The carved bench swayed. He watched with a second of detached acceptance—was that about to crash into ruins, too? Then he stepped behind the seat, moving with the exaggerated care that had been a part of him ever since he had come to Vaanchard, knowing at the same time it would be no use, that he would trample, smash, blunder, that wreckage would mark any path he would take through this dream world.

He could not retreat to his own quarters; he had done that too many times in the past few days. They would look for him there first. Nor could he continue to hide out in the garden with Rixa on the hunt. Diskan surveyed the lighted building. Music, the coming and going of forms before all those windows, no hiding place unless—

One darkened room on the lower floor—He made a hurried count to place those two windows. He could not be sure, but they were dark and drew him, as a hurt animal might search out a hollow log for temporary shelter.

The tide of his misery ebbed a little as he bent his mind to the problem of reaching that promised retreat undetected. Clumps of bushes dotted the ground, and he could avoid the one glowing statue. Under the music and voices from the house, he heard the trilling call of a night flying varch. A varch! With a little luck—

"Deesskaann?" Rixa was on the path not far from the bench.

He made for the next bush and crouched behind it. Now he centered a fierce concentration on the varch, visualizing the wide green wings with their tipping of gem dust, which created a filmy aura when it flew, the slender neck, the top-knotted head. Varch—Diskan thought varch, tried to feel varch.

Suddenly that call sounded to his right, beginning as a trill and ending in a squeak of terror. The green body flashed out of the shadow, winged toward the path. Diskan heard a second startled cry—from Rixa. But he was on the move, slipping from one bit of cover to the next, until he stood under the nearest of those dark windows, reaching up for the sill. No mistake now—no clumsy fall. Please, no break—just let him get into the dark and the solitude he must have!

And for once, one of his formless prayers was answered. Diskan spilled through the window to the floor, the sweep of curtains veiling him. He sat there, panting, not with physical effort, but with the strain of steeling himself to master his body. It was several seconds before he parted the curtains to inspect the room.

A single low light let him see that he had taken refuge where indeed they might not look for him—the room that was Renfry's. Here were kept the travel disks from his Scout trips, the trophies from his star wandering, all mounted and displayed. It was a room that Diskan had never before had the courage to enter on his own.

On his hands and knees, he crawled from behind the curtains, to sit crouched in the middle of the open space, far from anything he could brush against or knock over. He laced his heavy arms about his upthrust knees and looked about him.

A man's life was in this room. What kind of showing would *his* life make if the remnants of his passing were set on shelves for viewing? Broken bits and pieces, smudged and torn fabrics—and the slow, stupid words, the wrong actions that would not be tangible but that made smudges and tears inside himself and others. Diskan's hands went up again to his head, not to muffle the sighing music, the hum of voices from beyond walls and door, but to rub back and forth across his forehead, as if to ease the dull ache that had been ever present during his waking hours on Vaanchard. But he did not seem stupid to himself, at least not until he tried to translate into action or words what he thought—as if inside him there was a bad connection so that he could never communicate clearly with his own body, let alone with those about him.

There were things he *could* do! Diskan's mouth for the first time in hours relaxed from the wry twist, even shaped a shadow smile that would have surprised him had he at that moment faced a mirror. Yes, he could do *some* things, and not, he thought, too clumsily either. That varch now—he had thought of the varch, and then he had thought of what it must do—and it had done it just as he wished, and with more speed and skill than his own hands carried out any of his brain's commands.

That had happened before, when he was alone. He had never dared try it before others, since he was rated as strange enough without that additional taint of wrongness. He could communicate with animals—which probably meant he was far closer to them than to his own kind, that he was a slip-back on the climbing path of evolution. But the varch had distracted Rixa for the necessary moments.

Diskan relaxed. The room was still, the sounds of merriment more muffled here than in the garden. And this chamber was less alien in its appointments than any other in the huge palace dwelling. The rich fabrics at the window were native, but their colors were not so muted here. They were warmer. And save for one lacy spiral object on the wide desk-table, there were none of the fragile native ornaments. The rack of travel disks might have been taken out of a spacer—perhaps it had been.

He studied that rack, his lips shaping numbers as he counted the disks, each in its own slot. More than a hundred worlds—keys to more than a hundred worlds—all visited at some time or another by Renfry Fentress. And any one of those, fitted into the autopilot of a spacer could take a man to that world—

Blue tapes first—worlds explored by Fentress, now open for colonization—ten of those, a record of which to be proud. Yellow disks—worlds that would not support human life. Green—inhabited by native races, open for trade, closed to human settlement. Red—Diskan eyed the red. There were three of those at the bottom of the case.

Red meant unknown—worlds on which only one landing had been made, reported, but not yet checked out fully as useful or otherwise. Empty of intelligent life, yes, possible for human life as to climate and atmosphere, but planets that posed some kind of puzzle. What could such puzzles be, Diskan speculated, for a moment pulled from his own concerns to wonder. Any one of a hundred reasons could mark a world red—to await further exploration.

Keys to worlds—suppose one could use one? Diskan's hands dropped again to his knees, but his fingers crooked a little. That thinking, which was clear until he tried to translate it into action, picked at him.

A blue world—another Nyborg or Vaanchard. A green—no, he had no desire to face another alien race, and his landing on such a planet would be marked at once. Yellow, that was death, escape of a sort, but he was too young and still not desperate enough to think seriously of that final door. But those three red—

His tongue crossed his lips. For a long while he had drawn into himself, refused to initiate action that always ended in failure for him. There was a key to be used only by a very reckless man, one who had nothing to lose. Diskan Fentress could be considered as such. He could never be content on Vaanchard. All he asked or wanted was what they would not grant him—solitude and freedom from all they were and he could not be.

But *could* he do it? There was the tape, and outside this house, not too far away, was the port. On that landing space were berthed small, fast spacers. For once his background would be an asset. Who would believe that the stupid off-worlder would contemplate stealing a ship when he had no pilot training, when the control quarters of a small ship would be so cramped for his hulking body? It was a stupid plan, but he was stupid.

Diskan did not get to his feet. Intent even now on making no sound, no move that might betray him, on all fours like the animal he believed he was, he reached the tape rack. His big hand hovered over the three red disks. Which? Not that it mattered. His fingers closed about the middle one, transferred it to a belt pocket—but that left an easily noticeable gap. Diskan made a second shift at the rack; now that gap was at the end of the row, in the shadow. If he had any luck at all, it might not be noticed for some time.

He was rising when he heard it, the click of the door latch. Two steps would carry him to cover. Dared he take them? But again, for once, body and brain worked together. He did not stumble over his own feet, lurch against the table to send the ornament crashing, or make any other mistake; he got safely behind the window curtains before the door opened.

☽★ CHAPTER 2 ★☾

NOTWITHSTANDING the half light, the figure that entered shimmered. Frost stars glinted from a wide collar, from a belt of state. Drustans! Diskan flattened himself still closer to the window frame, felt it bite painfully into his thighs, tried to breathe as shallowly as possible. Rixa was bad enough, but to confront Drustans, her brother, would be a double defeat.

The Vaan youth moved with all the grace of his kind to the desk-table and hesitated there for an instant. Diskan expected him at any moment to wheel, face the window, and draw the skulker out of hiding by the very force of his will. There would be no change in the grave concern of his expression, of course. He would continue to be correct, always able to do the proper thing at the proper time and to do it well.

A small smolder of dull anger still glowed in Diskan, perhaps fed by the fact that in this room he had been able to make a decision, to carry it through without mishap. To surrender now to Drustans would be a special sourness.

But if the Vaan had come for Diskan, nosed him out in some manner—and Diskan was willing to concede that these aliens had powers he did not understand—then Drustans was not making the right moves, for his pause by the table had been only momentary. He went on now to kneel at the tape rack.

Diskan's own hand pressed against the belt pocket. Did—could Drustans have picked, out of the air, the theft? Yes, the Vaan's hand was at the slots of the red tapes! But why—how—?

Drustans plucked out one of the disks—the very one Diskan had moved to fill the empty space. Still on his knees, the Vaan tapped the disk with a forefinger and studied it. Then he tucked it into a belt pocket and, as quickly and silently as he had come, left the room.

Diskan drew a deep breath. So, he had not been after him but had come after the tape. And that could mean trouble because of the switch in disks. Suppose Renfry had sent his alien stepson to get the tape for reference. There were at least three men here tonight who would be interested in information on "red" planets—a Free-Trader captain, Isin Ginzar; an attaché from the Zacathan embassy, Zlismak; and another retired Scout, Bazilee Alpern.

And once the mistake was discovered, Renfry would come here—which meant either Diskan must move at once, tonight, or he faced just another ignominious failure, with more shame and humiliation. He could replace the disk in another slot, let them believe a mistake had been made in filing, which was easy enough—but he could not make himself cross those few feet and put back his key, relinquish his plan. He had accomplished this all himself, thought it out, done it. And he was going to follow through—he had to!

There was nothing he wanted to take with him from this house but that which was already in his belt. It was night. Once out of the garden, he could easily get to the space port. He knew the geography of this small strip of territory well enough. And, Diskan realized, if he did not attempt escape now, he never would; he could not nerve himself to another try.

He swung through the window. The garden was a triangle, its narrowest point extending out from the house, and that point gave access to a side street. He looked down at himself. There was a smudge across the breast of his tunic. He was never able to wear clothing for more than a few moments without collecting stains or tears. Luckily, he was dressed very plainly for a feast day, no frost-star collar, none of the splendor Drustans and the other Vaans considered fitting. He might be taken for a port laborer, wandering lost, if he were sighted.

With caution, Diskan worked his way to the spear point of the triangle. The house was very much alight, but it was close to midnight, and they would be serving supper in the banquet hall. Rixa must have long since given up the search for him in the garden. He must use well what time he had.

Somehow he scrambled over the lacework of the wall, meant more as a frame for the garden than any barrier. One sleeve tore loose from the shoulder, and now he had a smarting scratch, oozing blood, above his elbow. His dress boots made no sound on the pavement. Their soft soles were thin enough to let him feel the stone. But that did not matter—he had gone barefoot so long that his feet were tougher perhaps than the fabric of the boots themselves.

This way—to the corner, then to the first side turning—and that led straight to the port. He would enter quite far from the small ships he wanted, but once he was actually at the field, he could manage. This sudden small self-confidence was heady. Just as in the old tales, you obtained a talisman of sorts and then you were invincible. He had his talisman in the belt pocket, beneath his hand, and now there bubbled inside of him the belief that the rest would follow, that he would find the ship and escape—

Such a spacer would be on two controls, one for manual and one for travel tape. Diskan scowled as he tried to remember small details. All ships took off by pattern, and he dared not ask the Control for a particular one. So, he would have to risk the other way—feed in his tape, set on auto-control, go into freeze himself—and just hope. And the steps for that—? Well, Renfry, striving hard to find a common interest between them back on Nyborg while they had been waiting for exit papers, had talked about himself and his work when he discovered Diskan uncommunicative. And Diskan had listened, well enough now, he hoped, to get him off Vaanchard.

The field was lighted in one section. A liner must have just set down within the hour, as there was activity about one sky-pointing ship. Diskan watched closely and then moved forward, walking with a sureness of purpose. He paused by a pile of shipping cartons and hoisted one to his shoulder, then set out briskly on a course that angled toward his goal. To the casual glance, he hoped, he would be a laborer—one of those selected for the handling of cargo for which machines could not be trusted.

He dared not stumble—he must keep his mind on those slim small ships in their cradles ahead. He must think of his arms, of his feet, of his unruly body, and of what he was going to do when he got inside a space lock. He would mount to the control cabin, strap in, feed the tape disk to the directive, then set the freeze needle, take the perlim tablets—

Diskan was under the shadow of a trader before he thought it safe to dump his burden and quicken his pace to a trot. The first two of the smaller ships were still too large for his purpose, but the third, a racer made more for use within this solar system, between Vaanchard and her two inhabitable neighbors, was better—though he did not know if it could be used to voyage in deep space.

However, such a ship could be set for maximum take-off, to wrench him out of the influence of the control tower. And speed was an important factor. For such a ship there would be a watch robot.

Theft was not a native vice on Vaanchard, but all ports had a floating population of which a certain portion was untrustworthy. No racer was ever left without a watch robot. But Diskan had some useful information from Nyborg, learned by watching his companions at the labor depot. Robots were the enemies of the strong-back boys. When rations were scanty or poor, the human laborers had learned ways to circumvent the mechanical watchdogs at warehouses— though it was a tricky business.

Diskan glanced at his big, calloused hands. He had never tried to dis-con a watcher before. That was a task he had believed he was too clumsy to handle, but tonight he was going to have to do it!

He studied the ship in the launching cradle carefully. The port was closed, the ladder up, and the watcher would control both of those. But a watcher was not only there to check invasion; it was also attuned to any change in the ship. Diskan swung down into the cradle, put where the port inspectors had their scan-plate. He forced himself to move slowly. There must be no mistake in the false set of the dial he wanted. Sweat beaded his cheeks and chin when he achieved that bit of manipulation.

Up out of the pit—to wait. A grating noise from above marked the opening port. The ladder fed out smoothly. This was it! Diskan tensed. The watch robot, once out of the ship, would sense him instantly, come for him. A watcher could not kill or even do bodily harm; it only captured and held its prisoner to be dealt with by human authority.

And Diskan must allow himself to be so captured to serve his purpose. There was a clatter; the robot swung down the ladder and turned quickly to rush him. A thief would have run, tried to dodge. Diskan stood very still. The first rush of the machine slackened. It might have been disconcerted by his waiting for it, wondering if he had some legitimate reason to be there. Now if he had known the code word of its conditioning, he would have had nothing in the world to fear, but he did not have that knowledge.

A capture net whirled out, flicked about him, drew Diskan toward the machine, and he went without struggling. The net, meant to handle a fighter, was loose about him. He was almost up to his captor when he sprang—not away from but toward the robot. And for the first time that Diskan could remember, his heavy bulk of body served him well. He crashed against the machine, and the force of that meeting rocked the robot off balance. It went down, dragging Diskan with it, but his arm was behind its body, and before they had rolled over, he had thrust one forefinger into the sensitive direction cell.

Pain such as he had never known, running from his finger up his arm to the shoulder—the whole world was a haze of that pain. But somehow Diskan jerked away, held so much to his purpose that he had dragged himself part way up the ladder before his consciousness really functioned clearly again. Those who had told him of this trick had always used a tool to break the cell. To do it by finger was lunacy on a level they would not have believed possible. Diskan, racked with pain, stumbled through the hatch.

Sweating and gasping, he got to his feet, slammed his good hand down on the close button, and then swayed on—up one more level. The wall lights glowed as he went, obeying the command triggered by his body heat. He had a blurred glimpse of the cradle of the pilot's seat and half fell into it.

Somehow he managed to lean forward, to fumble the disk out of his pocket and into the auto-pilot, to thumb down the controls. The spacer came to life and took over. Around Diskan arose the cradle of the seat. His injured hand was engulfed in a pad that appeared out of nowhere. He felt the stab of a needle as the tremble of the atomics began to vibrate the walls.

Diskan was already half into freeze and did not hear, save as a blur of meaningless words, the demand broadcast as those in Control suddenly realized an unauthorized take-off was in progress. He was under treatment for an injured pilot as the racer made its dart, at maximum, up from Vaanchard on the guide of the red tape.

To a man in freeze, time did not exist. Measure of it began again for Diskan with a sharp, demanding clang, a noise biting at his very flesh and bones. He fought the pressure of that noise, the feeling of the necessity for responding to it. Opening his eyes wearily, he found himself facing a board of levers, switches, flashing lights. Two of those lights were an ominous red. Diskan knew nothing of piloting, but the smooth beat of the Scout ship that had taken him to Vaanchard in his father's company was lacking. There was instead a pulsation, an ebb and flow of power on a broken beat.

Another light turned red.

"Condition critical!"

Diskan's head jerked against the padded surface of the cradle. The words were mechanical and came out of the walls around him.

"Damage to the fifth part. Going on emergency for landing! Repeat: going on emergency for landing!"

Substance spun out of the wall to his left. In the air it seemed a white mist. Settling on and about his body, it thickened, became a coating of cushioning stuff, weaving him into a cocoon of protective covering. The trembling beat in the walls was even more uneven. Diskan knew that an emergency landing might well end in a crash that would erase ship and passenger on the instant of impact.

His helplessness was the worst. Simply to lie there in the covering spun by the ship to protect human life and wait for extinction was a torture. He struggled against the bonds of his padding—to no purpose. Then he yelled his need for freedom to the walls pressing in on him as his screams echoed from them.

Mercifully, black closed about Diskan then, and there was an end to waiting. He was not conscious of the fact the ship had entered planetary atmosphere, that the journey tape guided a crippled ship down to the surface of the unknown world.

The spinning ball of the planet lost the anonymity imposed by distance. Shadows of continents, spread of seas now showed on its surface, appeared waveringly on the visa-plate above Diskan's head. A dark world, a world with a certain forbidding aspect, not welcoming with lush green like Vaanchard or with brown-green like Nyborg— this was a gray-green, a slate or steel-hued world.

Orbiting, the spacer passed from night to day, to night, in a weird procession of telescoping time. There was a sun, more pallid here, and five moons shedding a wan reflected light on saw-toothed heights, which formed spiny backs of firm land above morasses of swamp and fen, where the shallow seas and land eternally thieved, one from the other.

There were eyes that witnessed the passage of the ship drawing closer to the surface of the world. And there was intelligence—of a sort—behind those eyes, assessing, wondering. Movement began over a relatively wide space—an ingathering such as was not natural, perhaps an abortive ingathering, or perhaps, *this* time—Eyes watched as the spacer, poised uneasily on its tail of flames, began the ride down via deter rockets to a small safety of rock and earth.

The descent was not clean. One tube blew. Instead of a three-fin landing, the spacer crashed, rolled. Vegetation flamed into a holocaust during that crazy spin. Death of plant or animal came in an instant. Then the broken hulk was still, lying on mud that bubbled and shifted around it, allowing it to settle into its glutinous substance.

For the second time, Diskan roused. The dying ship, in a last spasmodic effort, strove for the safety of the life it had guarded to the best of the ability its designers had devised. The cocoon of which he was the core was propelled from the pilot's seat, struck against a hatch that lifted part way and then stuck. The stench of the mud and the burned vegetation brought him to, coughing weakly.

Wisps of torn white stuff blew around his head and shoulders. The fear of being bound and helpless, which had carried over from those seconds before his last blackout, set Diskan to a convulsive effort, which scraped him through the half-open hatch, meant for the emergency escape.

He went head first into the mud, but his shoulder and side jarred brutally against stone, the pain bringing him around. Somehow he scrambled over stuff that slid and sucked at him until there was solid support under his flailing arms, and he drew himself up on an island in the midst of that instability.

Clawing the remains of the cocoon padding from his head, Diskan stared about wildly. The spacer was three quarters under the sucking mud, a flood of which was now tonguing in the hatch through which he had come. Diskan tried to gain some idea of his present surroundings.

The wind was cold, though the smoldering swamp vegetation still gave off a measure of heat. But the fire ignited by the ship was already dying. Not too far away Diskan saw white patches, which he thought might be snow, on a rising spine of rocks. He had known winter on Nyborg and winds as chill as the one now lapping about his body. But on Nyborg there had been clothing, shelter, food—

Diskan gathered up the torn stuff of the cocoon and drew it about his shoulders, shawl fashion. It made an awkward-to-handle covering, but it was a protection. The ship! There should be a survival kit in that—means of making fire, iron rations, weapons—! Diskan slewed around on his rock perch.

There was no hope of returning to the ship. The flood of mud had poured relentlessly into the open hatch; to try to return was to be trapped. Suddenly he wanted solid land, a lot of it, around and under him. And the best place for finding such a perch was the snow-streaked rocky spine.

It must have been late afternoon when the ship crashed, for though there had been no sunlight, there had been the gray of a cloud-cast day to light the scene. But by the time Diskan, exhausted, smeared with icy slime and almost hopeless, reached his goal, it was well into twilight, and he dared not try to move farther, lest a misstep plunge him into the bog into which the ship had now totally disappeared.

He crawled along the broken rock of the ridge, at last wedging himself into a crevice, where he pulled the cocoon fabric about him. The first moon was up, a round green-blue coin against the sky, and its following sister was above the horizon. But neither gave light enough for further travel over unknown territory.

There were reddish coals on the other side of the mud pool, marking the blaze. Diskan longed for a few of those precious sparks now. But there was no fuel to feed them here and no way of crossing to the burned-over land. He squirmed as far as he could into his shelter, misery eating into him.

So—one part of his mind jeered—you thought luck would change when you used your key, that you could make a better future. Well, here is that future, and in what way is it better than the past?

Diskan coughed, shivered, and chewed on that bitter thought. He had his freedom, probably freedom to die one way or another—by freezing tonight, by slipping into the mud tomorrow, by a thousand and one traps on an unknown planet. But another thought warred against the jeering voice—he *had* survived so far. And every moment he continued to live was a small victory over fate—fate or *something* that had crippled him from his birth. He had this freedom—yes— and his life, and those were two things to hold fast to this night as if they could give him warmth, shelter, and nourishment.

☽⋆ CHAPTER 3 ⋆☾

DISKAN FEARED the insidious chill as the night wore on. He crawled at intervals from the crevice to stamp his numbed feet and beat his arms across his chest. To sleep in this creeping cold was perhaps not to wake again. And each time he so emerged from his poor shelter, he strove to view by the light of those hurrying moons just what lay about him.

The rocky point rose in a series of outcrops back and up in a miniature mountain chain. As far as he could tell, the rest was bog. Twice he heard a howling from the path the rolling ship had blasted, and once a snarling, growling tumult, as if two fairly well-matched opponents struggled. Perhaps the flamed land held food that attracted scavengers. Food—Diskan's middle reacted to the thought. He had often known the bite of hunger in the past, his big frame requiring more substance than had been allowed on several work projects, but he could not remember ever feeling this empty!

Food, water, shelter, covering against the wind and the cold—and all must be found in a world where even one mouthful of an alien plant or animal could mean sudden death for an off-worlder. The rations that might have sustained him, the immunity shots meant to carry the shipwrecked through such a disaster—all were gone.

Howling again—and closer. Diskan stared out across the mud pool to that shore where the embers smoldered. There were shadows there, too many of them, and they could hide anything. How long

217

did night last on this world? Time had no meaning when one could not measure it by any known rule.

It began to snow—first in a few flakes that filtered into his crevice to melt on his skin, then more thickly, until Diskan could not see much but a curtain of white. But with the coming of the snow, the wind died. He watched the storm dully. If this drifted, it would cover the bog and make a treacherous coat to hide the mud.

A sharp cry jerked Diskan out of a half stupor. That—that had come from the outcrops behind his refuge! He listened. The swish of the falling snow seemed deafening, as deafening as his fingers had been in his ears back on Vaanchard. Moments passed. The cry was not repeated. But Diskan knew that he had not been mistaken—he had heard a living thing give voice out there. A hunter—or the hunted? Had that been the death cry of some prey?

Panic was colder in him than the chill born of the rock walls about his shivering body. Every nerve cried, "Run!" And yet his mind fought down that fear. Here he had to face only the narrow opening to the white world; he could defend that opening with his two hands if necessary, whereas in the open he might speedily be pulled down.

Time can dull even the sharpest fear, Diskan discovered. There was no second cry. And, though he listened, there were no more sounds out of the night. Finally, before he realized it, there was a slow end to night itself.

Diskan knew it first when he was aware he could see farther. The snow was spread in a wide cover, broken by patches of dark which must mark the liquid surface of the mud. That rocky far shore lost some of its shadows and was growing clearer by the moment. Though no sun showed, day was coming.

He pulled at the tattered stuff of the cocoon. It was as white, save for a mud stain here and there, as the snow. And he thought he could knot it into a kind of cloak. His fingers were cold and twice as clumsy as usual, but he persisted until he had a crude rectangle he could pull about his shoulders, anchoring the ends under his belt. The mud through which he had wallowed on his escape from the ship had dried on skin and clothing into a harsh blue shell, which cracked and scaled as he moved but which might give him additional protection against the cold.

Most of all he needed food. Recklessly, he had scooped snow

from about the crevice and sucked it so that its moisture relieved his thirst. But, as he wavered out of his crack of shelter and down to the edge of the mud pool in a very faint hope of seeing some part of the ship, he faced only a blue surface rimmed with brittle ice-coated stalks of vegetation on one side and a blackened smear on the other.

It was a small thing to catch the eye, a wisp of yellow-white from the black scar. Smoke! Diskan took a quick step forward and then paused. There might be a still-burning coal over there, but traps lay in between.

"Steady—" he told himself, and the spoken words somehow were as comforting as if they had come from lips other than his own chapped ones. "Slow—steady—"

Mud cracked and fell from his shoulders as he turned his head, tried to assess what lay to the right and how far toward the burned ground his present solid footing extended. Stiffly, forcing himself to study each step before he advanced, Diskan climbed around the rocks. The cold of the stone was searing to his hands until he halted, worried loose some strips of the cocoon material, and tied them about his palms. Meant to insulate, it served for protection, though it made his hands more bulky and threatened his holds.

He pulled to the top of one of the rocky pillars and had his first less limited view of his present surroundings. The spine became part of a larger ridge, perhaps the main body of land. Diskan could see the blackened scar of the ship's crash ahead of him. There were spots of the ominous blue mud and tangles of frozen vegetation, but there were also scattered rocks, which provided stepping stones.

"Slow—" Diskan warned himself. "To the right—that block there—that mat of brush—it ought to hold. Then that other rock— Easy now! Hand hold here—put the foot there—"

He could not have told why it was easier to move when he gave himself such orders, as if his body were apart from his mind, but it was. So he kept on talking, outlining each footstep before he took it.

The patches of white snow, he learned, marked more solid footing, but caution made him test each. And once a stone, hurled ahead, proved that caution wise, for the rock cracked through the surface and a blue earth mouth sucked it down.

He had set foot on the black crisp of the burn, felt and smelled the powdery black ashes his weight disturbed, when a cry startled him, brought his attention to the sky. A winged thing swooped and fluttered, the morning light making its coloring a vivid streak, for it was rawly red, with a long neck that turned and twisted in a serpentine fashion, a head with a sharply peaked comb or topknot. And it was big. Diskan estimated that wing spread to equal his own height.

With a second screech, it planed down—but not at him. It headed on into the heart of the burn smear. Then there came another cry, and a second red flier appeared, to settle at the same spot. Diskan hesitated. The smoke lay in that direction, but he did not like the look of those birds, if birds they were. And several of them together could offer trouble.

More squawking ahead. There was a small ridge between Diskan and where they had landed. Now a squall—the same as he had heard earlier in the night—sounds of what could only be a fight. Diskan went on, and from the top of the ridge he looked down into a battle-field from which the morning wind brought a stench that made him gag.

Things lay there where the flames had struck them down. The bodies had been so crisped that he could not tell more than that they were the bodies of large creatures. On the side of the biggest, one of the red fliers had taken a stand, its long neck writhing as it strove to strike with a sword-sharp beak at a smaller four-footed creature that snarled, squalled, showed teeth, and refused to be driven from its feasting. These were four, five—eight at least of its kind—and they moved with a rapidity that seemed to baffle the birds.

Then one of the defenders grew too bold or too reckless. That rapier beak stabbed and stabbed again. The creature fell back in a limp curl, between the bones where it had been tearing at charred flesh. The victory appeared to hearten the red flier. Its neck curved, and it opened its beak to voice an ear-splitting honk. From the air it was answered. Three, four more of its kind flapped into view.

The animals about the carcasses snarled and complained, but they retreated, their rage apparent in every move. With two of the fliers, they had been ready to contend, but a flock they dared not confront.

As they withdrew under the fire of the now attacking fliers, Diskan got a better view of them. But whether they were warm-blooded animals or reptiles, he could not decide. There was certainly a growth of what seemed coarse yellow-green fur down their backbones and the outer sides of their legs, and a bush of it upstanding on their heads, but their projecting snouts, their strongly clawed feet, and their whipping tails were sleekly bare, as if naked of fur but covered with small scales. They were as vicious in appearance as the fliers, and though they were small in size, Diskan had no wish to face a pack of them.

Luckily, their path of sullen retreat was in the opposite direction, up the other side of the cup that held the burned bodies. But though the darting fliers barred them from the ridge on which he stood, Diskan also edged back. He stumbled down through the powdery ash to the hollow from which the smoke still ascended. A handful of what seemed to be stones lay there, and two of them showed a red tinge. Diskan stooped and blew gently. The red deepened—a mineral that the fire had ignited and that continued to hold the heat? He sat back on his heels. Here was the means of fire—warmth—not only to be used here and now, but to be taken with him to a less populated section of the country, if he could find the means to transport one such coal. His resources in that direction were limited.

Under a coat of cracking mud, he wore the tight breeches and ornamented tunic of Vaan festival dress. That did not even permit a ceremonial hunting knife at the belt, as was the fashion on Nyborg. All he had was two belt pockets, one of them empty since he had used the tape.

Pocket! Diskan pulled open the pocket covering. Then he plucked at the raveling patches that served him as gloves, bringing loose a fluff of broken threads. Insulation—of one kind—and there was that of another, too. He went to the edge of the mud pool, worked his threads into the evil-smelling substance of that quaking earth, and, with care, smeared the mixture into the interior of the belt pocket, making sure all of its surface was thickly covered.

Moments later he was ready to go, his hand cupped over the now bulging pocket where that glowing bit of mineral was safe. He had fire, the first weapon of his species, now at his command. And he wanted to get away, as sounds from over the ridge suggested that the ground pack of scavengers had been reinforced and was once more giving battle.

Diskan made his way back to the rock spine. Food—he might

have been lucky enough to knock over one of the scale-fur things or a flier—but he was not too sure. And to arouse the rage of either species, presenting himself as a possible meal, would have been folly. But judging by the numbers he had seen, he realized this was not an empty land. He could find other prey.

He passed the crevice of his night camp and began to climb to the promise of wider land beyond. As he crested a slope, he caught a strong scent—not the stench of the scavengers' feast, but certainly not that of vegetation either. It was not disagreeable, and it attracted him enough to want to learn its source.

Diskan's kind had long since lost their dependence on the sense of smell—if they had ever possessed it to the extent of the other mammals that had shared their first home world. What might have been a quickly identified beacon to one of those was an illusive trace for his questing nostrils. But he continued to sniff as he went.

He found the source at a narrow cut between two leaning rocks. On the gray surface of both those pillars was a silvery smear, which glistened in the now strong sunlight. Diskan thought a liquid had been sprayed there, to trickle for an inch or so in fast freezing drops. But between the rocks lay something to capture his attention at once.

The creature was dead, its throat ripped wide, the frozen blood a clot of red crystals. Unlike the scavengers, it was entirely furred, the fur as gray as the rocks about it, so that it was the wound he had first seen. That it was a hunter was manifest by the fangs in its gaping mouth, the claws on its feet. The head was long and narrow, with ears pointed and extending backward. It was short of leg but long of body, well adapted to the rocky country in which it had died. And it was meat!

Diskan jerked the body loose from the ground, finding it lighter than he had thought it would be. He had his meal, thanks to the unknown hunter who apparently had not lingered to consume the kill. With a strip of the cocoon material, he tied two of the limp legs to his belt and went on in search of a camping spot.

It was not too long before he found that. A stiff pull up through a small gorge brought him to an ice-encased stream. And along the bed of that grew the brittle winter-killed growth of more than one small bush and struggling tree.

The withered leaves that clung to a few branches were silvery in color. Diskan wondered as he broke up wood for his fire if that were the normal shade of vegetation on this planet. He coaxed flame from the smoldering mineral and then examined the body of the animal. He had no knife, no way of cutting or cleaning it, of even skinning the creature. There was no resource but to toss the whole thing into the blaze and let the fire work for him.

It was a grim and nasty business, but hunger drove him. And he licked his fingers afterwards, the pain in him stilled for a while— though he wondered if his system could assimilate the alien flesh or if illness and death would come from that eating. From the fire he raked the blackened skull and studied it. The strong, slightly curved teeth caught his attention, and with a rock he smashed the charred bone, breaking out the largest teeth. Two were the length of his little finger, all were sharp, and he thought that they might have future possibilities. Diskan opened the second pocket on his belt and brought out its contents.

A flash writer—he smiled wryly—just what he needed now. His name check plate—for a moment he fingered that, half inclined to toss it away. The code on this thin strip of metal would have brought him food, clothing, lodging, and transportation anywhere on Vaanchard; here it was useless. But he would not discard anything until he was sure. A ring—Diskan turned that around. Its deep purple gem did not flash fire in the sun; it was somber and dark, Diskan's own choice of adornment, though he had hardly looked at it when he had taken it from the box back on Vaanchard. Custom dictated that he wear it. He had squeezed it onto his little finger, the only one the loop would fit, and then dragged it off again, too aware of how incongruous it had looked on his hand. It was as useless here as all the rest.

Now he could add to his treasure six teeth, blackened by burning, which might or might not be more serviceable in his present plight than all the other things. He put them back in his pocket, the teeth on top.

His clothing, under the coating of stains and mud, appeared to be standing up well to the rough travel of the morning. Diskan inspected his calf-high boots carefully. There were scuff marks, a scoring or two, but the soles were surprisingly intact. And his cocoon cloak, while a thing of dangling tatters, was still protection.

He was alive; he had food and fire, and he was free. Diskan leaned his back against a piece of water-worn rock and looked at the drift, which suggested that this ice-bound stream had a turbulent past. The riverlet's valley appeared an easier path into the interior of the higher land, and there was plenty of firewood here. He had put aside a haunch of the late meal to provide food for later. And the sun, while not really warm, seemed to concentrate in this cut so that a few of the snow patches were melting.

Save for the dead animal, Diskan had seen no sign of life in this part of the country. Perhaps the feast by the burn scar had drawn most of the hunters. So much on the hopeful side.

On the other hand, this climate was hard, since he was unequipped for it. And this could be only the beginning of a far more severe season, with a long period of steadily worsening weather to be faced. He had no weapons, no knowledge of how long his lump of mineral would continue to smolder or of how much native fauna there was to protest his invasion of hunting territory they considered their own.

Dwelling on the worst would get him nowhere, and the more one permitted one's imagination to summon up difficulties, the darker all shadows became. Diskan began to search through the driftwood about him. It was all bleached, but one piece was enough different in color to attract his attention. He knelt and worked it loose from the frozen soil.

He held a barkless length of what might have been a branch. Thick as his wrist, it had a smooth surface that was not gray-white but a dull green, with the grain marking showing up in a darker emerald. One end was a thickened, knoblike projection, from which stubs of other small growths jutted. The other end was splintered into a sharp point.

Diskan swung it experimentally. Somehow it balanced well in his hand. The knob head could be a club, the splintered end a short, thrusting spear. With a little work, say some way to fasten the teeth to those stubs and a little honing and sharpening of the spear end, he would have a weapon—outlandish and very far removed from a blaster, a stunner, or any of the arms known to stellar civilization, but still a weapon.

Knotting the seared meat to his belt, the bulb-spear in his

swathed hand, Diskan strode away from his dead fire. He walked firmly, his head up, his eyes searching the country around him. There was no fumbling in his hold of that weapon, no shambling uncertainty about his pace.

❧★ CHAPTER 4 ★❧

THOUGH THERE WERE NO CLOUDS to screen off the sun's rays, shadows laced the cleft through which the stream issued, and Diskan saw that the walls of that cut rose slowly on either hand. It grew more chill between those barriers, and the frozen growth was scarcer. He had a choice, to halt here for the night where there was still fuel for a fire, or to go on into the unknown on chance. Finally, he decided in favor of the halt.

He had his fire going and was gleaning more fuel for its night feeding when he straightened, his hand going to the club he had thrust through his belt. The sensation of being watched was so sharp that he was disconcerted when he swung about to perceive nothing but the rocks, the frosty earth, and the broken brush. As far as he could tell, there was no hole in the surface of either cleft wall large enough to hide a sizable enemy in ambush.

Yet he was sure that there was something—or someone—lurking there, watching. Diskan pulled his weapon from his belt, making a show of using it to pry a length of drift from the iron-hard hold of the frozen soil. He hoped his sudden about-face had not betrayed his suspicions. It might be a small advantage for him if the hidden one believed he was still unconscious of its presence. But Diskan gathered his wood now with his left hand and kept the club ready in the right.

Twice more he tramped back to the side of the fire to dump loads. He was trying to locate the source of that spying. No hole in the cliff faces, no growth large enough to mask anything of a size to

226

be feared. Or was that true? There were reptiles, insectile things, small, but still deadly, to be met on other worlds. The same might well be true here. Only Diskan could not associate his feeling of being under observation with the idea of a reptile or an insect. He chose a water-worn rock and set his back against it. Keep it up—this act of unconcern—and do not, he told himself fiercely, do not use what you know to judge what may be met here!

He rubbed his thumb across the knot end of the spear-club. A piece of wood. What kind of defense could it offer against any attacker? Diskan picked at the projecting stubs—three of them shooting at angles. He had had a hazy idea of connecting the teeth to those stubs. But how could they be fitted so? Always he had made a botch of any hand work that required exact fingering.

"Take it slow—" he said, his words a muttered whisper. "Just take it slow—" He blinked into the fire, thinking.

Always—always there had been a pushing at him from without. The impatience of all those quick ones through whose world he had shambled, stumbled, blundered, had beat at him. He had never traveled at his own pace—not that he could remember—except those times when they had left him alone to do some dirty job. And even then there had been surprise supervision from those who made manifest their belief that his efforts would always fall far short of their demands.

Diskan fed the fire as he deliberated over the events of the immediate past. And he grinned with a new confidence at the flames. Why—he must be an outlaw now! He had stolen that ship—and he had no notion how many laws, rules, or regulations he had broken since he had plucked that tape from the storage rack. On the other hand, he had escaped the ship, survived a freezing night, found a road to higher land, had fire, a weapon—though there was that watcher out there. A seesaw balance that the slightest mistake would swing against him—permanently—

Being an outlaw did not bother him. In a way, he had been one since his birth—an outlaw or an outsider. He felt no guilt over the ship. If he had the past hours to live over again, he would do just the same. Past hours! for the first time Diskan was startled to recall that he had no idea how long a voyage the tape had covered. He could have lain in freeze for months. But for him the escape from

Vaanchard was only a day or so behind. No use bothering with time—all that counted now was day and night here.

Night was coming. Was that what held the watcher quiescent all this time? Was it a hunter that struck at night? Diskan measured his pile of wood. He had had little sleep the night before, and he was not sure he could keep awake very long now. And if the fire died, the chill might be as dangerous as that watcher. Already the sun had gone from the stream valley, and shadows made dark patches that advanced stealthily toward his oasis of flame and warmth.

Movement! Diskan held the club with a steady hand. Surely he had seen a shadow flit from one rock to another. Animal? If so, could he—

For the first time, he thought of how he had handled the varch. Might he deal with an intruder so? But he had known something of their habits. And he had had failures on Nyborg, trying to handle feral beasts unfamiliar with human-kind.

But—Diskan could not build a mind picture of a shadow. He lacked a goal for his reaching thought. There were the fur-scale creatures, the red fliers, the dead thing that had furnished him with food. He concentrated on a mental image of each in turn and reached—to meet nothing. A shadow was no proper target.

Beyond the limit of Diskan's sense, there was a stir—a heightening of concentration. The shadow quivered, nerve alerting muscle. A sense for which the man had no name went into action. The shadow waited, first eagerly, then impatiently, and then with a dying hope that became resignation. A head moved; jaws opened and closed on something inert. So, the other way—the slower way of contact. A slim body flowed about the rock, dragging a burden with it.

Diskan sat very still. The shadow had taken on substance. A dark blot separated from a rock, advanced toward him with a curious bumping up-and-down movement. Even though the twilight was thickening in the valley, Diskan could make out the outline of the creature's head—and it was misshapen. And then he saw that it was dragging along the limp body of another animal, bumping it over the uneven ground.

On the very edge of the fire gleam, the burden was laid down and the carrier arose in a slender furred pillar. Points of red, bright as any gem on a Vaanchard collar, were steady in a head hardly bigger than the neck that supported it. The creature was large enough so that, holding itself erect on its powerful haunches, its bobbing head could have nosed Diskan's shoulder with him standing. And its whole stance spelled not only power but also complete confidence.

The fur, which was a thick and gleaming coat on its body, was dark, save where the firelight brought small frosty sparkles running along the surface. The front paws, now held against a slightly lighter chest, were equipped with claws of a formidable length.

Diskan did not move; at that moment he could not. Those fangs, showed in a gleaming fringe below the lips, made the threat, and Diskan recognized it. Yet there had been nothing in its approach to suggest that it was about to hurl itself at him. Was it the ruler of this strip of country, so supreme in its ownership of a hunting territory that it did not view him as an enemy to be feared? Curiosity was strong in many creatures. Hunters on Nyborg used fluttering strips of bright cloth tied to a stake to draw in fesil for the kill, since they could not stalk that fleet-footed animal with any hope of getting close enough for a stun blast.

His scent, the fire, his trail could have drawn the attention of the thing now watching him with such cool appraisal. And if he made no threatening gesture, it might withdraw, once its curiosity was satisfied. But it settled back on its haunches with a little wriggle, as if it intended to keep its position for a while. Diskan knew very little of animals, save what he had learned through his own untrained observations. But as his first surprise wore off and the newcomer made no move, his own curiosity grew stronger.

It had come on four feet, and he thought that was its normal form of progress. But it also seemed at ease in its present erect pose. And there was something odd about the way it held its forepaws.

The fire needed attention, but dare he move? Any gesture on his part might alarm his visitor—cause it to attack as a startled animal could. Or it might go, and Diskan was suddenly aware that he did not want that either, not until he could learn more about it.

Hoping that once again he could move with sure ease, he put out his hand. But it was the old curse that made him misjudge distance and knock down a pile of branches. Hand grasped club in a spasm of reaction as he waited.

But the visitor did not move. The sinuous head was erect, the red eyes still regarding Diskan. He grabbed for the nearest sticks and thrust them crookedly into the flames. The fire shot up, drawing a flickering veil between him and that silent watcher. When he could see clearly again, the animal had withdrawn a short distance and was again rising on its haunches. But the limp body it had brought still lay where it had been dropped.

Diskan eyed that and his visitor.

"You forgot your supper—" His words sounded too shrill, a little ragged, but to his amazement he was answered.

How could you describe the sound issuing from between those rows of fangs—not quite a hiss, nor a growl either. A soft sound, which, Diskan thought, could be a warning. Again he tensed, waiting for some move of aggression. It was then that a very odd thought flashed into his mind. That animal—it acted as if it expected some special response from him!

What? Had it delivered a formal warning recognized by its own kind—a kind of "get out of my territory or take the consequences" challenge? His ignorance was a danger. How much intelligence watched from behind those red eyes, assessing and reasoning from what the eyes reported? Humankind had long ago learned that intelligence and humanoid shape were not always allied. There were humanoid animals—and nonhumanoid "men." What did he have here?

Diskan's formal schooling had all been at the creche. His resentment and fear of the impersonal authority exercised there had turned him against learning, and they had written him off as waste material. He had fought mental training as he had fought all the rest of the system in which he did not and could never fit. What he knew had come later, in scraps and bits of observation and pick-up information, when he had realized that he had willfully flung away the good with the bad. Now he had little background to base his guesses upon—and he had no confidence in such guessing.

Suppose he now confronted intelligence. Would it be an intelligence so far removed from his own type that communication was impossible? How could you say this creature "reasons," is a "man," and that one is what his own species declared an animal?

"I mean you no harm—" The words sounded silly even as he mouthed them. To a creature who might communicate in hisses and growls, they could have no meaning. There was a gesture, universal among *his* kind—would it convey anything to the visitor? Diskan raised his hands, palms out and on a level with his shoulders—the old, old "See, I bear no weapons against you; I come in peace."

There was no answer; the red eyes did not even blink. Diskan dropped his hands. That had been as stupid as his oral appeal. Of course the gesture would mean nothing. Yet he had a strong urge to persist, to try to make contact, for the more he considered the creature's behavior, the more he was sure that it was not the ordinary curiosity of a wild thing—not even that of a hunter that feared nothing within its own country—that held it there. Could he approach it?

Diskan shifted his weight, about to rise. Then he remained still, for his visitor had swung its head around. It no longer faced him. Instead, for a long moment, it gazed over its shoulder, down the now dark ravine. Then it dropped to four feet, and with a litheness almost serpentine, it simply flowed between two large stones, to vanish into the night.

Although Diskan waited, trying to catch any sound above or beyond the crackle of the fire, he heard nothing. Yet he was certain that the creature had been alerted, or summoned, and that it had left with a very definite end in view. When waiting did not bring its return, Diskan moved beyond the fire to the prey it had left behind. Again he picked up one of the long-eared, short-legged animals, its throat torn. But this was not frozen. It must have been killed only a short time ago.

Well, his visitor's loss was his gain. Here was more food—though he wanted to devise a less messy way of cooking it. Some experimentation with the sharp end of the club-spear proved that its point could function as a knife. And with that poor aid, Diskan was able to worry off the skin and clean the beast. He impaled it on a piece of drift and roasted it to make a better meal than the burned meat that had sustained him that morning. He left a portion untouched and on impulse carried that to where he had last seen the creature, laying it on the ground there. The stranger might not care to have its food seared, but he would make the offering.

Diskan kept awake as long as he could, feeding the fire. The heat, reflected against the rock he had chosen as part protection, made him drowsy, and at last his head fell forward, to rest on his knees. But the club-spear lay under his hand, free and ready.

A furred head moved from the shadows into the open. There was no need for its owner to sniff at what lay there. Lip wrinkled up over fangs in distaste; the burned flesh was decidedly not to its taste. Then the head rose a little, and eyes noted the fire, the sleeper on its far side.

So, some contact, the furred one thought. This—this other had accepted food; that much it had responded. It was a matter of waiting. The carrion eaters downstream—it would be a long time before they would again follow this trail! Satisfaction, hot and complete, blanketed other thought for a second. Watch—watch and make sure this one followed the right trail. Perhaps, only perhaps—

Stern admonition against such speculation followed. Remember the other failures. But this one was different. His general shape is the same, to be sure. Shape—what matters shape? This one responded differently.

The silent discussion the furred one had with itself came to an abrupt close. The furred body coiled into a circle with muzzle rested on strong hindleg. Something lighter than sleep, but resting body and mind, claimed the watcher for a space. Diskan's sleep was far deeper as the fire smoldered to gray ash.

He was pulled out of those depths, feeling cold and stiff. The fire was a black dead ring, and it was snowing again. The wet of the melting flakes was on his face as he looked blearily about. Stumbling up, Diskan stamped his feet, their numbness alarming him. He swung around to where he had left the meat offering.

Snow had drifted over it, but he could still see a greasy end of bone protruding. He walked over to pick it up—frozen hard, and there was no sign that it had been touched. He could not have explained why he was disappointed. He should be pleased, Diskan told himself. The visitor had probably not returned, and his food supply was increased by so much.

The snow was growing thicker. Might be well now to get out of the open, keep on down the narrowing end of the ravine where the walls arched toward each other almost like a roof. He made a bundle of unburned wood, bowing his back under it, and club in hand, pushed on.

Around him the white surface was unmarked by any track, though Diskan kept a lookout for any trace of a paw trail. He had been right about the cover offered in the narrows; the drive of the snow failed as he advanced. However, the footing here was not so good. Evidences of raging high water through this gorge were present in tumbled stones and bedded drift that protruded just enough to provide trip traps. Diskan's pace grew slower and slower.

It was dark in here, too. He could look up to a slit of sky, but yesterday's sun was missing, and the heavy clouds turned day into twilight. Once he paused to consider the advantages of retracing his way into the open, where the brush would give him fire and he could hole up for the storm to pass—always supposing that it was not of the variety to last several days. But even though he faced about and took a step or so along that back trail, Diskan discovered it made him increasingly uneasy to retreat, and finally he plodded doggedly on.

An increase of falling snow marked the beginning of an opening from the gorge, and he came out into a space where the water was no longer a stream but a small lake. Ropes of ice threaded down a cliff face to his left, marking a falls. The same gray dead growths grew here, but there was also a small stand of trees that were not leafless. Instead, they presented a brilliant patch of color.

Neither scarlet nor crimson but a shade between the two, which Diskan could not name, the wide leaves rattled against each other as the wind blew. He caught a metallic note; the leaves might be some hard substance. More of them lay in bright patches under the trees. Diskan saw some, detached by the present breeze, fall—as if their weight bore them directly to the ground, not fluttering away at the wind's pleasure.

The red wood was on the opposite side of the lake, but it drew Diskan, as if its color was a warmth. He crept across a bridge of ice-rimmed rocks, seeing below the frozen surface the water swirling to the stream that had guided him. When he came to the first of the trees, he noted that each of those brilliant leaves was coated with a transparent shell of ice, making hard winter gems. And their sharp edges could cut—he drew back from that danger.

As he opened his belt pocket for the coal, Diskan examined the small lump anxiously. To his eyes, it seemed just as it had been when he had first picked it up—its power to ignite in no way diminished.

But it could not continue so forever, and could he find another such? He had seen it only as a coal and had not the slightest idea of how to search for its like in the natural state.

Diskan dropped his bundle of wood. He need not have lugged that along; there was plenty here. But again prudence had dictated that he go prepared. Fire first, and then food, then—

Sometime he would have to set on a goal, not wander aimlessly. Find a place for a semipermanent camp, then hunt and—Diskan shook his head. Fire now. Go easy—one thing at a time.

☌★ CHAPTER 5 ★☽

RED AND SILVER—as if fire and ice had combined weirdly to raise such walls, for this was a city, and through it moved shapes which were only fluidly flowing shadows, never to be clearly seen. Yet they went with a purpose Diskan could dimly sense, though it was not any purpose of his or his kind. Moreover, the urgency that was motivating the shadows reached out to him, enfolded him, making him uneasy, not knowing the why—only that he was drawn deeper and deeper into the heart of fire and ice, there to witness, or to partake, in some crucial rite.

Sometimes as he followed those shadows, a piece of the city would loom clearly before him for an instant of sharpened sight, and he would glimpse a bit of carving, a doorway, a flight of steps that were real and solid amid the dream. But though he fought to reach such, as they seemed islands of safety in the curious liquid life about him, yet he was always borne swiftly by on a river with a current he could not oppose.

Then sound joined sight, a sound he could not define any more than he could define the nature of the shadows. And that sound was a part of him, striking to his very bones, knitting him into the city and its purpose, until Diskan knew the birth of panic. More wildly he fought to break the pull of the current, to win out of the flow.

Sight, sound, and now scent—a scent about which there was a faint familiarity. There, in one of the patches of clear visibility, was a pillar—or was it a tree, a tree with bright red leaves? Diskan made a mighty effort. If he could throw his arms about its bole, he could free himself from the current.

Did his reaching fingers feel the texture of bark? The sound beat in his ears now like the pulsing of his own heart as the city became a wild swirl of red and silver, silver and red, until the colors made one.

But still his fingers held something—Gasping, Diskan came to himself. He was standing calf deep in the snow, his roughly mittened hands clasping the trunk of one of the trees, while the frozen leaves overhead chimed in the wind. Under the racing moons, the ground was light in its snow blanket. He could see the sharp division between shadow and open.

His fire burned as a single red eye. Yet from it curled a plume of smoke that was not the yellow-white of normal burning. It was visible against the snow bank because of the tiny dancing red motes caught up in it. They sparkled in small flashings of light as they ascended.

Diskan pulled out of the snowdrift and staggered back to the fire. There was a scent to that smoke, cloyingly sweet, and it lapped out a tongue to meet him. Coughing, waving a hand before his face to clear the motes from him, he circled to the other side. There was evidence of what had been fed to the fire, skeleton now, but still to be seen—leaves from the grove.

He picked up a branch and stirred those skeleton leaves into broken ash. The glowing bits gave forth one last burst of spark motes. Diskan gulped frosty air into his lungs. Everyone dreamed, of course, but the fantasy from which he had just awakened was unlike any other dream he had ever had. It had been so real, in spite of its vagueness of detail. Had the leaf smoke been responsible for it?

Warily, he searched through the pile of firewood, putting aside any which might have originated in the nearby trees. Then he coaxed the flames to full life again, sure of danger in such dreaming. He had been quite far away from his fire when he had awakened. What if he had wandered farther yet and succumbed to the numbing cold before he roused?

Yet as he squatted by the fire, Diskan could not erase memories he had carried out of the dream. Unlike those from ordinary dreams, they did not fade but grew sharper as he dwelt upon them. Those momentary clear glimpses he had had of the city, of a carven block set in a wall—The markings on that block, he had seen them only in the dream—A doorway that he *knew* gave upon stairs, he had not sighted—

Diskan shook his head. Beyond those bits, nothing. Yet there was a vast importance to them. He would never forget them, purposeless as they might be.

The day broke clear with the coming of sun instead of another fall of snow. Diskan ate the last of the meat. Though it would have been prudent to save some scraps for the future, once he had begun to gnaw the hard flesh, he finished it.

By the time the sun was well up, he had discovered that the valley about the falls and the lake was a prison. To climb up the ice-coated surface of the cliff by the falls was a feat he dared not attempt. Beyond the wood was another sharp rise, so he was in a cup with only one entrance and exit, the stream gorge he had followed the night before. Yet every time he turned to that, he was stopped as effectively as if he ran into a barrier. What or why that was, he did not know, just that *that* trail was closed to him.

That left only the valley walls to explore. By midday, he settled on what he deemed the best ascent, a place behind the grove. There was more of a slope there than elsewhere. His old dread of his clumsiness was in full force, and he was sweating in spite of the cold as he dragged himself up to a ledge about three times his own height above the valley floor. Remembering the most elementary precaution about not looking down, he scraped along the ledge, hugging the cliff, studying each step ahead before he planted boot on it.

Not too far away, that scanty footing widened under a broken patch of rock, offering the possibilities of a rough ladder. He gained that point and surveyed the way ahead. The roughened surface did not rise straight up but diagonally. Only when he pushed a little away from the cliff surface to look up, Diskan could see a snow hang there. To have that start a slide—

Diskan caught the tip of his tongue between his teeth and tried to breathe more evenly. His imagination had been only too quick to produce a picture of instant catastrophe. And it was in a spirit of defiance against his own body that he reached up for the first hold.

He had never doubted his own strength, only his use of it, but the climb was an ordeal that tried every bit of stubborn endurance he possessed—not by its difficulty, for the hand and foot holds were there and he found them, but by his abiding fear of not using them properly, or making some awkward slip through his own clumsiness.

Now his field of vision was rigidly limited to a few feet, but he was always aware of the overhang of snow that could sweep him in an instant from the path he so painfully traveled. The pads of cocoon material bound about his palms absorbed the perspiration on his hands, but his face was dripping with sweat, his fair hair plastered to his skull. And now and then he had to rub his head against his arm to clear his eyes of the stinging salt moisture.

A study of the way ahead showed that he must edge along an almost horizontal crack that sloped to the right. But it was here that the menace of the snow hang was the greatest. Diskan's arms trembled with effort, and it seemed to him that his body was more and more sluggish. But there was no retreat now.

He grunted and pulled to the right, into the crack. A four-inch surface, surely not wide enough to be deemed a ledge, was under the toes of his boots. And above, at shoulder level, there were hand, or at least finger, holds. With his body pressed tight to the frigid stone, so that his cheek was scraped by the surface of the rock, he could move, inches at a time.

Inch out, pull over, inch out, pull over—the nightmare journey went on and on. He was shaken out of his terrible absorption in winning those inches, one at a time, when he felt a wider surface under his boot soles. The crack ledge was broadening! With a gasp of relief, he moved faster and then slowed under sharp control. This was no time to take a chance!

The poor bit of hope he had carried with him from the valley floor was swept away in an instant as he rounded a spur of the wall. The ledge widened—to a good-sized shelf—then ended! Nor was there any hope he could see of another way up that last pull to the top of the cliff. Diskan collapsed, his lips trembling a little as he faced defeat.

What was worse, he was sure that he had no retreat either. He could not control the shaking of his hands, a shaking that spread up his arms and into his body, while he tried to control convulsive shudders born of fatigue and tension. He pulled up his legs and drew in upon himself in a ball of fear and despair.

A fine sifting of snow filtered down to powder him. That overhang—would the wind bring it down? Diskan roused from his fog of misery. If he could not go forward, he would *have* to go back, and he had better try that before inaction and cold froze his nerves and muscles and he could not do it at all.

He pulled up to his feet, turned to face left, and was feeling for the first step back when he saw a dark blot flattened against the cliff as he was. Fur fluffed under the exploring fingers of the wind, but clawed feet clung tightly, and those eyes—not reddened now by fire gleam but in their way still gem-bright—were on him. The creature of the wild was coming along the ledge path.

Diskan could not raise his club now, and even as he watched, the dark blot moved and gained a good length in his direction. It paused again, still eying him. That stare robbed Diskan of what small confidence he had managed to dredge up. He pushed back onto the wide portion of the ledge and shouted, in what was part defiance but more surrender to unavoidable fate.

He fell, scrabbling wildly for a hold to keep from going over the edge. Then the animal landed beside him, half on him, and he heard the roar of the snow giving way. Diskan always wondered how that rush from the heights missed sweeping them along, but the center of its force was farther to the left, over the section where he had traveled one inch at a time. Snow buried him, but he was still on the ledge when the fury of the slip was past, its final crash in the valley loud in his ears.

He felt hot breath on his cheek and smelled a scent like that of the smears on the rock where he had found the body of the first kill. Diskan looked up into those eyes only inches away from his own as he lay on his back. Breathing hard, he kept still. That fanged mouth was too close to his throat, and he remembered the wounds that had torn the life out of its prey.

Then that furred head snapped back, and the creature pulled away from him. But Diskan did not move until it had withdrawn to the other end of their small perch. With all the caution he could summon, he sat up, his back against the cliff, his feet out over space.

The animal did not move. It had risen on its haunches, erect as it had sat across the fire. And its attention was divided between the man and the situation in which they found themselves. Diskan shivered. The snow slide had carried away the threatening overhang, but he knew that he could never turn his back on the animal to shuffle along the narrow crack.

When his companion in misfortune made no other move, Diskan relaxed a fraction. He eyed it measuringly. In the firelight and during his first glimpses of it here, it had seemed dark. But now the wind ruffled the long fur on its back and shoulders, and there were frosty streaks revealed, as if, close to the skin, the silky hairs of the pelt were far lighter in shade. The color was a slate gray with a blue cast, a shade or so darker than the rocks behind it, lighter on the belly and the inner sides of the legs. All in all, it was a handsome animal, even if its movements suggested a power approaching viciousness.

"Where do we go from here?" Diskan asked at last, his voice breaking the silence sharply.

The narrow head snapped about. Then it turned again with what seemed calculated deliberation—so that the animal looked at the cliff face that kept them both marooned.

For the second time, it looked to Diskan, then back to the cliff. The man frowned. To read any meaning into those gestures was sheer imagination, but it would appear the animal was striving to force his attention in that direction.

"No road there," Diskan returned. "I've already looked—"

Once more the head swung back, eyes on him, drawing his gaze to them. Diskan broke that contact with a little cry. He did not know what had happened then, only that he feared it and that he wanted no repetition of that strange sensation.

For the first time, the animal uttered a sound, a hiss that held overtones of anger as far as Diskan could guess. Then, with the same deliberation of its head turns, it crossed to the edge of the ledge, turned, lowered its hindquarters, and hung so, wriggling its body, for several seconds. It might have been searching for claw holds it knew were there—then it vanished from sight.

"What—?" Diskan crawled to the place where it had disappeared, fighting a dizzy feeling as he looked over.

The animal was climbing along the rock face, working its way with assured purpose and a better rate of speed than Diskan dared try. Having reached a point some distance from the ledge and below it, it began to climb again. When it was on a level with that outcrop, it hissed at Diskan, and he could no longer deny his belief that it strove to show by example the road out.

"I don't have any claws," Diskan protested. "You're better equipped for this than I am." But there was a way along there—Only, with the animal now gone, he could retrace the other way.

The animal was climbing again. A burst of speed brought it to another ledge, and it reared up there, watching the man. There was something so superior in its attitude that Diskan was stung.

"All right—here goes!" Why he was making this insane effort, he did not know, but to turn tail and edge back under the watchful eyes of the animal—he could not do it! Where the furred one had gone, a man was going to follow.

Part of it was bad. As he pointed out, he had no claws, and his fingers and booted toes were far less effective than the natural equipment of his new companion. Once he slipped and thought that his finish, until his fingers caught another hold. After an eternity of struggle, he crawled up to the second ledge—to find it empty. Only in the snow along its steadily widening surface was the firm print of clawed feet leading to the right. Diskan humbly followed. He might have passed the exit from the valley—another rock crevice—had it not been marked for him. The scent was stronger this time than it had been by the kill, for the glistening streaks on the rock were still wet.

Diskan squeezed into that crack. It was a very tight fit, and his cocoon cloak caught on projections and tore yet more, as he took some painful scrapes. Then a last jerk brought him out in the open at what must be the top of the valley wall.

Wind had swept the snow from the more exposed positions, and the animal prints held only in the hollows. The surface of this upland was broken, all spires and points. Diskan could look down into the lowlands, where there was a wide sweep of bog, the blue of mud lakes startlingly visible against the gray and white of the rest of the country.

Food—Diskan thought of his stomach for the first time since beginning the climb. There might have been something worth hunting in the valley. Up here there was nothing at all. To go down now into the bog country would be a wise move. He started to pick a path along the heights.

A flash drew his attention to the left, away from his goal. It was something not natural to this rocky land. He could not have told why he was sure of that. Not fire—what would fire be doing here unless he was not alone in his occupancy of this planet? In spite of his hunger, he turned away from the slope that ended in the bog country, to hunt down the source of that flash.

Pattern—those blinks were coming in a pattern! Diskan broke into a trot as he came to a relatively level space. Pattern meant a signal!

He skidded out onto a small open square and stood looking up at the thing that had drawn him. Sometime—very long ago, he thought, as he noted the weatherworn edges of the stone—someone, or something, had chiseled and cut one of the natural rock pinnacles into a squared column. At a little below its crest, an oval of white opaque substance gave forth, at intervals he could time by counting, flashes of clear light.

Five counts, then a flash, three counts, flash, ten counts, flash, eight—then the whole pattern over again. This was a signal. The why Diskan could not tell—for some long vanished aircraft, for communication between distant points of land? But it was very old, and it was the work of intelligence.

So, it could be that he was not alone, that more than his animal visitor had once moved with purpose along this rocky spine.

Diskan walked around the column. In a patch of snow on the other side was a single clawed footprint, a signature and a signpost. And beyond, as timeworn as the columns, were the traces of a way, cut here and there through the rock, leading along the crest of the heights.

It was stupid to turn away from the bogs with their promise of food, as stupid as anything he had ever done, Diskan told himself. But his boots had already trod on that pawmark, and he knew that he was going to follow that very ancient road.

❦★CHAPTER 6★❦

AT TIMES IN THE GROWING TWILIGHT, Diskan could not be sure that he was still following any path at all. But then he would sight a marker, a side of rock smoothed to make the passage easier, a flattened length under foot. And the road was descending, not along the bog side of the ridge but on the left where lay higher ground. He sighted other valleys like that which held the lake, level bottoms covered with banks of snow, a few with groves of the red-leaved trees.

It was into the widest of these valleys that the ancient road curled. And the end of that path was marked by two pillars, squared as the one that had borne the signal light. On their crests were lumps, the meaning long since battered away by time. And beyond lay nothing but unbroken reaches of snow. To the left and right, running along the base of the ridge, was a tangle of vegetation, a promise of shelter.

Diskan saw tracks there, not those of the clawed feet, but smaller and rounded as if what made them walked on a foot close to a hoof. Only he was not to follow that, for out of the still air a voice spoke.

The words were unintelligible, but they were words, and that they were meant to catch his attention, Diskan did not doubt. Almost on reflex, he threw himself into the cover of the brush, hugging the earth, staring out into the dusk. He was sure that the call had come from before him, somewhere out of the valley, and not echoing down from the rocks at his back.

There was silence, twice as deep. Diskan lay, watched, and waited. Half unconsciously, he began to count under his breath, as he had with the light flashes on the heights. He had reached thirty when again that spoken sound rolled across the open. On the third repetition, he was sure of one thing—that each time the sound had been the same, that the strange words had been repeated and the tone was mechanically level, as if some machine rather than any living thing had voiced that warning or greeting or summons.

Which of the three it might be had vast importance. To disregard a warning might be high disaster. To answer a summons could be going into peril. But a greeting was something else. And was that broadcast as old as the beacon above? The words were spoken with a crisp, sharp authority. Diskan could not connect it in his mind with the evidences of age at the signal pillar and along the road.

Here was a screen of brush. He could move behind it along the valley wall. If he had been sighted and that voice directed at him, sooner or later that which spoke would come hunting. Diskan moved, his club-spear to hand, his attention fixed on the open.

The broadcast continued to sound at the same intervals as he worked his way from one piece of cover to the next, and it did not vary. But Diskan's uneasiness was not lulled by that fact. The words might be mechanically produced, but that did not mean that he could be sure he was not under observation.

It began to snow again, and he welcomed that together with the dark. Both made a curtain behind which he could move faster. The wall of the valley was curving, and he believed that the voice sounded closer.

He rounded a spur and looked out into another stretch of open. But here there were no bushes, save for some withered stalks very close to him. And the look of those—Diskan pushed out his club and caught the nearest stalk. At a very slight pressure on his part, it snapped, and he pulled it to him.

Burned! It had the same appearance as the seared vegetation he had seen near the crash of the spacer. He rubbed the charred stick between thumb and forefinger and eyed that open space narrowly. Level—unusually level—more so than any other site he had seen in this new world. A good place to plant a ship. Was that it? Could this be where a spacer had finned in and then lifted again? Snow covered any rocket scars, but it was just possible his guess was right.

Once more that unintelligible message rang through the still air, though now it sounded somewhat muffled, as if the falling snow deadened the broadcast. Diskan stood up, daring now to take the chance.

He plunged forward, across the narrowest end of the open expanse, blundering into more burned brush on the far side. Then he saw through the dim light a half bubble that was a familiar thing from his own past. That was a temporary shelter such as he had seen in the tri-dee tapes. It was windowless and doorless, but somewhere along its surface, an entrance would yield to the heat and pressure of a hand. This was a rescue cache, established as a refuge for the survivors of some ship crash. Perhaps more than one spacer had fallen into a mud bog on this unknown world.

And Diskan could understand the need for that broadcast now, even if he did not know the words. It was a set signal to draw any survivors to the refuge. And surely, since the call still sounded, the cache cabin was not in use.

With numb fingers and his teeth, Diskan ripped the cocoon windings from his hand and set it against the surface of the cache at waist level, slipping it along the bubble as he began circling the shelter. Unlike a more permanent erection, any seal would be attuned to the general body heat and not to a palm pattern of an individual man or men. When he found the lock, it should yield to him. Then, food, clothing, arms—perhaps everything he needed—would be his.

How long had this stood here broadcasting its call? And why had it been left? A ship downed here, sending out an SOS—then arrival of a rescue force, perhaps a Patrol cruiser—unable to find any survivors, but evidence that such had existed, had they set up the cache and blasted off, expecting to return later? He could string those guesses together into a plausible explanation—except for the fact that the broadcast was *not* couched in Basic, as it should be for a Service rescue cache.

Diskan had a poor education, but Basic, as well as native planet speech, was hypo-taught to every child as soon as he began to talk. And there were no spacegoing people now, human or nonhuman, who did not use Basic as the common tongue, though it might be necessary for some aliens to resort to mechanical means for translation. So, why not Basic for the beacon call of a cache?

His questing hand suddenly slipped into a hollow his eyes could not distinguish in the fabric of the cache. It did not feel large enough, that hollow, but he pressed his bare palm as tightly as he could into the narrow space. He had found the lock—now for the unlocking.

A slow glow spread up the walls. Then, as abruptly as a snap of fingers, a narrow slit opened before him, and Diskan edged through—into light, heat, smells. The wall closed behind him as he stood looking about the refuge.

Food—he wanted that first. Diskan took a step or two away from the now resealed door, and then his legs gave out, and he swayed and fell. The light was dazzling; it hurt his eyes. He levered himself up on his hands, to blink at the array of containers jumbled all together, as if hastily dumped.

Pulling himself to the nearest, a broad cylinder, Diskan forced up the snap lid. More containers, rammed in carelessly. Among them he recognized one, pried it out of the confusion, and triggered the small button on its side.

Minutes later he was gulping a reviving liquid that tasted like a richly flavored stew and that was intended, Diskan knew, as Sustain food for survivor use. Having finished its contents, he returned to the unpacking of the cylinder. But as he handled each tube, can, and box he pulled from that inner disorder, his surprise grew, and with it an uneasiness.

Some of these supplies he knew, but most of them he did not. Not only that but the unknown items varied among themselves, too. He was sure that the strange identification symbols differed greatly, so that he might now be sorting over rations for a score of races, even of species. Did that mean that the survivors these were intended to succor had been a mixed lot—alien, human, and grades in between? But only a crack liner would carry so widely differing a set of passengers on just one voyage.

And the loss of such a liner would have been news reaching even to Vaanchard. Or—Diskan frowned as he set out that bewildering array of containers—or had such a crash occurred as he voyaged in freeze through space?

But a liner carried a thousand or more passengers. This cache could not contain supplies for that many. Had one lifeboat with a highly mixed crowd set down here? That might be it. Only—why not then broadcast in Basic? It did not fit.

And none of the rations he did know bore the seal of the Patrol—which they surely would have done had this been a Service cache. The way they had been slung into this cylinder, not packed, but crammed—Diskan began to sort them. Surely there was more than one unknown tongue on the labels. He pressed the heat-serve button on a second tube and ate its contents slowly, while he studied the display. When he had finished, he restored the unknown rations to the cylinder.

Then, methodically, he began to rummage through the other containers of the cache—to discover that all but three of those were palm-sealed to a personal print code! Then this could not be a Service cache or all contents would be free to anyone managing to make the shelter! This was a cache, right enough, but intended not for any survivor of a space disaster—no, for some special survivors.

Some of the things he had uncovered he could use. There was a parka-coat of Orkanza hide with an inner stuffing of insulating Corn moss—a little tight across the shoulders, but he could wriggle into it. Boots of the same Orkanza hide made watertight by sal-fat grease were too small. Regretfully, he had to set those aside. Pushed down under them was a tunic. Diskan spread that out across his knee, and his uneasiness sharpened.

This was a dress tunic, a refinement of Ozackian spider silk—or something quite close to that fabulous, and very expensive, fabric. There was a tracery of embroidery about the high collar and around the breast latches that made a lacy pattern composed of hundreds of minute gems threaded on the silk. Only a Veep would wear a garment such as this. Yet there was a spot on the front, a stain that was greasy to the touch, as if food had been carelessly spattered there.

Diskan folded the tunic and put it with the boots. He found two sleep bags, both too small, but which, put together, would give him a better bed than he had known in many days. But—there were no weapons, no tools, unless both were in the locked boxes. He had food, a new coat, and a big puzzle.

He tried to pry open one of the sealed boxes, using the sharpened point of his improvised spear, only stopping when the wood seemed likely to crack. Primitive as that weapon was, it had to serve him, since the cache could not offer better. Diskan padded the two bed rolls together and then set about moving some of the containers so that anyone entering the shelter would take a tumble to announce his arrival. He stretched out on the bed with a sigh of satisfaction.

In spite of the light still glowing in the walls, he slept—but not to wander in a dream city. Outside the core of warmth, the snow continued to fall, blotting out his own tracks to the cache.

But in the night, others were astir; communication traveled, but not by spoken word. Forces met, moved, parted. Impatience, anger colored the discussion. And then watchers settled into place around the cache and what it held—so important to their purposes.

Diskan stirred, rolled over, blinked at the shaky pyramid of boxes of which he had made his alarm. The light of the walls remained the same—but something was different. He sat up and looked around the bubble with more sharply focused attention. As far as he could remember, it was the same. Surely no one had tried to enter, or that box pile would have fallen.

Quiet enough—that was it, quiet! The broadcast that had drawn him here had ceased to function. He no longer heard that murmur of sound, reduced to a hum by the walls of the shelter. Perhaps his entrance had stopped it.

Why that was making him wary he did not know. But now, trying to remember what had happened up to the point of his falling asleep, Diskan was sure that that murmur *had* continued after he had entered the bubble. So, his entrance had not automatically silenced it.

He had never believed that he possessed too vivid an imagination, but now it seemed to him that the silence of the broadcast could act as a signal by its very absence. Suppose, just suppose, that somewhere else on this world there was a settlement or camp, in automatic communication with the cache—so that when it was entered, the camp was notified. A cache could also be a trap!

Diskan went to the pile of rations and then took up the torn cloak of cocoon stuff, tying it into a bag into which he crammed the supplies. The thought of a trap had settled so in his mind that he thought it a fact. Why it had been set, and for whom, did not matter; getting out of it at once did.

With the parka tight about his shoulders and chest, the bulky bag and his club in his hands, he set his palm to the door. The slit opened, and he came out into day and snow that was knee deep.

No matter what, he was going to leave tracks through this unless another storm covered them. There was a grove of trees before him, not the red-leafed kind, but a mass of a bare-branched, thick-standing species. To get into that grove could mean losing all sense of direction. He must keep in the open and head for the heights from which he had come. In and among those rocks' spires would be a good many hiding places.

Having made his decision, Diskan struck out through the puffy snow. It was far harder than it had first seemed, this tramping through drifts. The snow was damp and heavy, clinging to his legs, working into the tops of his boots, caking on the edge of the parka. Twice he fell when footing suddenly sank under him. But he kept going, past the space where he was sure an off-world ship or ships had set down, heading for the rock wall and those eroded pillars marking the ancient road.

He was perhaps two-thirds of the way to that goal when the beacon voice spoke, startling him so much that he lost his balance for a third time and toppled into a drift high enough to engulf him. As he fought his way out, he listened. Were those the same words he had heard the night before or were they different? Diskan discovered that he could not depend upon his memory. They could be different— first announcing his coming and now his going.

But to put on more speed was impossible; he could wade at hardly more than a strolling pace. And twice, when he halted to breathe, he studied the way ahead anxiously. There seemed to be any number of pillar-like formations, all crowned with lumps of snow. Then he knew he was lost.

All right, he did not really need the pillars. At any climbable point, he could find a way back up the slope, and from there he could watch the cache throughout the day. Then, if there were no visitors, at nightfall he could return to shelter in it. Up there, he could watch his own back trail, be sure he was not hunted.

To any Patrol officer, he would be a prisoner, but he was sure that the cache was not Patrol. Perhaps to anyone else, he could pose as a survivor from a lifeboat landing. Diskan smiled. He had all day to think up a good story and settle all its details so deeply in mind that he could reel it off with convincing force. He began to climb.

Three times he moved before he found what he deemed the perfect lookout. Though he had no farseeing lenses, the valley spread out below this perch as a white map, broken only by his own trail. He triggered open a ration tube and ate. Of course he could not see the cache from here—but he did hear the broadcast droning through the crisp air.

But it grew monotonous, this staring at the snow and his tracks through it. Diskan wished he did have lenses and could see what lay beyond the tangled wood he had feared to enter. Now and again he watched the sky, once stiffening as a flying thing swooped, until he saw it was no machine but one of the red birds.

As the hours he could not measure wore on, Diskan began to believe his fears of the morning rootless. The voice continued to sound; there was no sign of anyone coming along his trail. There might well be no one but himself of off-world origin on this whole planet. It was cold up here; he might be wasting a whole day to no purpose. Yet he did not want to go back to the cache—not now, anyway. Time enough to return when night closed in. He could do it cleverly, using the same trail back—

It was hard to just sit here, waiting. He studied the part of the valley he could see clearly. It might be wise for him to move along the heights and come up to the cache from another direction. Diskan repacked his supplies into a bag of smaller compress, shouldered the bundle, and began to move, trying to keep to cover, as if he were a Scout moving through enemy territory—though he could not put name to that enemy, nor explain why he was convinced of the need for not revealing his presence.

But he had watchers who knew a kindling of triumph. Their quarry was on the move again—in the right direction.

☙⋆ **CHAPTER 7** ⋆❧

DISKAN MUST HAVE BEEN on the trail for some time before he saw, beneath the patches of snow and the spotty growth, indications that he was again following a road—not a trail such as animals would make, but one fashioned of blocks of pavement, no longer aligned, yet present. Even in this state, it was easier footing than the cliff edge, and he could make better time, though it struck away at an angle from his course.

The broadcast reached him now as a booming noise in which he could no longer separate the words. And to that, the wind whistling among the rock pillars made a shrill accompaniment.

But the squall that halted him, almost in midstep, was neither voice nor wind. The road entered a cut between two rock spurs, and facing him at the far end of that cut—

Diskan went into a half crouch, his wooden weapon in both hands, the splintered point foremost. The thing was big, much larger than the creature that had accompanied him before. It stood erect, on two stumpy hind legs, so thick with fur that they looked straight. In contrast, its belly was naked and a dull, unhealthy-looking yellow, with small flecks, as if it were coated with scales. Like the scavengers, the creature was, to Diskan's off-world eyes, an unwholesome mixture of animal and reptile.

The head narrowed from a brush of upstanding ragged skin to a snout, where fangs curved up to make a white fringe about yellow lips. But the worst was that it moved forward on its hind legs, its action grotesquely human, its well-armored forepaws raised a little in front of its chest as if it were about to attack him with fists.

That armored snout opened to emit, not the squall Diskan had heard, but a very reptilian hiss, its breath forming a steamy cloud. It was fully his height, or perhaps an inch or so more. And Diskan had no doubt that once within reach of those claws, he had only a slight chance of survival.

Still facing the beast, he withdrew step by step. Luckily, the thing seemed to be in no hurry to close the distance between them. It matched him step by step, and save for the hissing, it gave no sign of active hostility. But he knew he had good reason to fear it.

Back—now he was out of the beginning of the cut, in a place that gave him more room to dodge any rush. He was sure he dared not turn his back and run—such a move would merely bring the enemy to attack. Whether the thing was fast on its feet, he could not tell, but it was fighting in its own territory and had the advantage.

There was space to Diskan's right between two rocks, a narrow slit offering a bolt hole. Diskan backed toward that. The bushy head was sinking between the thing's shoulders. Its hissing climbed to a high note and was almost continuous. It was working itself up to a charge, he was sure.

He was in the crevice now, the wooden spear centered on the beast's midsection. The footing was rough here; he had to glance down now and then to assure himself. And each time he did that, he gave the enemy a second or two of advantage.

Again that other squall. Seemingly out of air a dark body appeared between Diskan and the menace. Back arched, thin tail whipping back and forth in rage, fangs bared, snarling in a rising crescendo of sound, was the furred animal, or one of its kind.

The hissing of the attacker was terrible. And the creature struck with a speed Diskan had not granted its rather clumsy-looking body. Claws curved down, but not into flesh as their owner had intended, for the furred one had dodged with lightning speed, sprung somehow under that blow to strike in turn at the naked yellow belly, opening a spurting slash there. Huge feet stamped, kicked, but the smaller animal had another chance at the big one and opened a second dripping wound.

Only this time it was not so lucky. Claws caught in its fur and swung it off the ground, up to the level of waiting jaws, in spite of its writhing, its flailing paws. Diskan acted. It did not occur to him to leave the two beasts locked in battle, making good his escape. Instead, he leaped forward, his puny weapon ready.

He could not get close to the struggle, but he thrust as true as he could for one of the wide eyes in that head now bending over the fiercely fighting captive. The spear did not go home as he had hoped, but its point raked across the eyeball. The creature gave a fearsome cry and flung up its head.

Diskan stabbed again, trying for a spot beneath that high held head. He had some dim idea that might be a soft place in the creature's body armor. His spear met opposition and did not even penetrate that deceptively naked-looking skin, but the force he had managed to put into the thrust ended the hissing in an explosive grunt.

The beast tried to drop its captive, one paw going to its throat, but the furred one had a hold with teeth and claws about one of the forearms. As the creature kept trying to reach for its throat, its attacker's raking claws scored the flesh of its upper chest with great effectiveness.

The hissing had stopped, but to Diskan's surprise, the snouted head continued to toss in frantic movement. Then it finally tore the furred one loose and threw the animal from it. The heavy furred body struck Diskan, bearing him to the ground.

Claws tore his parka but did not reach his skin, as the creature spat, snarled, and strove to free itself from their involuntary entanglement. Moisture spattered Diskan's face—blood from gashes in the furred one's shoulder. It scrambled away from him and turned again to face the enemy with the same hunchbacked stance from which it had launched the battle. But its tail did not whip so swiftly; there were red splotches on the rock beneath it.

The two-footed thing had both paws to its throat, its snout still pointed skyward. It stamped on, not as if hunting them but as though it were trying to escape a torment. Reaching out, Diskan pulled the furred one to him, out of the path of that thing lurching along blindly.

It blundered on past them and was brought up full face against a rock. There it stood for a long moment, its body jerking convulsively, before it went down, its chest heaving, its forepaws beating the air. Diskan relaxed his hold on the other animal. It no longer struggled but lay against him quietly, watching what could only be the dying struggles of the enemy.

But what had killed it? Diskan wiped his hands down the front of his parka. None of the slashes the furred one had inflicted had looked like mortal wounds. And his first blow had not penetrated the eye. He had not even cut the yellow skin when he had aimed at the thing's throat.

Those forepaws now lay limply over the belly; the chest no longer heaved. Diskan thought it must be dead, or close to it.

The furred one got to its feet, giving a little cry of pain when a front paw touched the ground. But it moved in spite of its injuries to the side of the dead thing, sniffing at the upturned snout and then at its throat—as if it, too, were undecided as to what had put an end to the peril.

Diskan retrieved his club-spear before he ventured to approach the body. He had to struggle against revulsion before he could touch that unwholesome corpse. At the point where his weapon had thudded home on the neck, his fingers found a softened area. Had he by lucky chance broken the thing's windpipe, left it without air to fill its lungs? What mattered most was that it was dead.

The stench rising from the body was such that Diskan drew away and scrubbed his hand in a snow patch to wash from it the feel of the skin he had touched. Then he looked to the furred one.

A deep crimson tongue was licking as far as it could reach along the slash in the animal's shoulder. Another tear bled on its flank. Diskan scooped up snow in both hands and brought it to the injured animal. The steady licking stopped, and those solid, pupil-eyes regarded him. Then the tongue swept out over the snow, back and forth, until it rasped on his palms. He brought more, until it went back to licking its wounds.

Diskan hesitated. Night was coming. He wanted to return to the safety of the cache. Yet he could not walk off and leave the hurt animal here alone. In the freezing night, death could strike. But neither could he carry it across broken country.

A small whine—the furred one was on its feet, gazing at him. And for the second time, Diskan stared into those eyes—to experience once again that odd sense of mixed identity. This was not the same as his contact with the varch, with the beasts of Nyborg, when he had used his projected will to move them to his purposes—and this he did not want! He strove to move his eyes, not to go on into a place where fear ruled.

He began to walk along the ancient road, the furred one limping beside him. Diskan was aware of their movements, but as one who moved in a dream. And he could not break the rhythm of those strides he took. This was a reversal of his usual contact with animals. As the varch had flown to his order, so now he moved to that of the animal beside him.

The battle of wills ended in nothing but exhaustion for Diskan. He retreated in mind even as he obeyed in body. An out-and-out struggle won him nothing. All right, obey—just as he had in the past whenever he saw that rebellion only brought more trouble.

Now and then, as they paused to rest, the animal leaned against Diskan's thigh. Of his own accord, he gripped the loose roll of skin and fur at its shoulders, steadying it whenever it rested so. The tongue-licking appeared to have halted the rush of blood from its wounds, but it moved slowly, in obvious distress.

Together they went through the pass that had been defended by the dead thing. And now the timeworn road descended in a series of wide and shallow steps, cracked and eroded, but not too steep to provide fair footing. Diskan stood at the top, that part of his brain that had retreated from the domination and control of his movements registering what his eyes reported.

Here the spine ridge of the uplands had been cut almost in two by a section of bog running well back. The rim of the cache valley beyond must be a single, almost knife-thin wall, lying now well to his left. The steps of the descent grew wider as they neared the level of the boglands, and from the last step there was only a fall to the water-soaked lowlands. It was late afternoon, but the shadows were not thick enough to veil what stood out in the embrace of the water and mud—square cubes, rectangular blocks of dull black, spaced in a definite design, as if the roofs of some long-drowned city protruded from the grave and engulfed it.

Yet no matter how hard Diskan stared at a building, how he tried to concentrate on its size, its general shape, its position among the rest, there was a queer sensation of not seeing—of an intangible haze between him and the ruins, an unsubstantial aura about it.

Those lines of blocks went on and on, fanning out from the foot of the giant square on which he stood, to vanish well out in the bog. He could not sight the other edge of what must have been an ancient metropolis.

The furred one stood away from him and limped down the first step. Diskan, still under control, followed. This city repelled him, and he struggled to free himself, to return to what now appeared the sanity of the cache.

They halted on that last broad step. Was the furred one intending to leap the last drop, to go out into the morass of sunken buildings? But it settled down with a grunt, lying wounded side up, its eyes on him. Diskan sat down as abruptly, aware that they had reached a journey's end, for the compulsion was gone. He could turn and crawl up the flight of stairs, keep on to the valley of the cache—except that he was too tired, his body aching, his head swimming a little, to try it.

Their present perch was certainly exposed. Snow had drifted across it, and if there was a wind, they could be frozen. He had reached that thought dully when the animal raised its head and looked down into the ruins. There was something so urgent in that movement that Diskan followed its gaze. What was coming had already reached the edge of the platform, a sleek round head there, another, a third—

They climbed up, balanced on their haunches, eyeing their fellow and then Diskan with those compelling, unwinking stares. Soundless communication? One of the trio advanced and squatted down beside the wounded one, its head moving back and forth as if by sense of smell it examined the slashes. Then it set to licking the wounds.

The other two vanished with that flashing speed Diskan had seen his companion use in battle. He had brought the creature to the aid of its own kind; they or it had released him. He could no longer question the fact of their intelligence. However, their interest in him had preceded the fight in the pass. Could it have been that the wounded one had deliberately entered into that battle on his behalf?

Diskan watched the two with dull wonder. He could see no difference in them as to size or color or fur. They might have been twins of one birth. The wounded one gave the impression of now resting at ease, confident that its comrade's attention would restore it.

A flicker at the edge of the platform, a head rising. In the sharp-toothed jaws of the newcomer were sticks, several of them. The animal crossed the stone and dropped its burden not far from the man. And it was not alone—two more, carrying gleanings from the swamp edge, followed. And they came and went, adding to the pile.

Diskan was past wonder now. He brought the offerings to a place not far from the wounded animal and built a fire. Miraculously, though he was not impressed by such miracles anymore, his fire stone still held life. And the flames arose as the wood gatherers continued to appear with more fuel.

He opened his bag of rations. To offer its contents to the busy furred ones would be to exhaust his provisions in perhaps one meal, but he hesitated as he picked out a tube, glancing at the wounded one. His concern was unnecessary. A head, held high because of a wriggling silver thing gripped in the mouth, appeared in the firelight. The captive was tossed down before the patient, who, with a thump of the paw, stilled the offering and then proceeded to dine.

Diskan ate, fed the fire, and watched the comings and goings of the furred ones. Since he could not identify individuals and they moved on and off the platform so constantly, he could not tell how many there were. The one who had come to nurse the wounded one remained, crouched beside its patient, now and again licking the slashes, while the others came and went, some singly and some in twos and threes.

With food in him and the warmth of the fire thawing out his numbed body, Diskan began to feel stronger. Testing his companions, he went to the stairs, ascended a step or two. They paid him no more than passing attention. He was certain he could leave if he willed. But why do so now? He had fire—and they were still bringing fuel, as if to feed it all night long. They had made no hostile move.

And—Diskan realized suddenly—he did not want to leave—to leave them! He had been alone since the ship spat him forth in that final attempt to save his life—except for the visits of the furred one or ones. Once he had wanted to be alone, away from the pity and rejection of his own kind. But here—here he could not turn his back on the fire and the animals and strike out into the twilight merely to hunt the cache, which was a deserted shelter for his own species.

Diskan hurried back to the fire. His boot struck something lying beneath the snow and sent the object flying into the full light of the flames, where it glistened. He picked it up.

A stunner! He stared down at the weapon in disbelief. Meant to temporarily paralyze, not to kill, but secondary weapon of all spacemen, it was the weapon he had hoped to find in the cache, not here on the open rock. This was a precious find. Diskan quickly read the charge dial. It was half expended, if the guage was to be believed. So this had been fired, and then dropped—

From the weapon, he glanced at the animals. Had it been fired at them? They had not seemed hostile. But there could be reasons for their apparent harmlessness. Now he had a weapon far more effective than his club-spear.

Diskan hunkered down closer to the fire, searching the butt of the stunner for any mark of ownership, but it was discouragingly bare—just ordinary issue. Another trace of the cache people?

He turned to where he had found it, kicking loose the snow. Nothing else, and the weapon could have lain there for days—months. Carefully he put it inside his parka, so it rested heavy and cold against his middle, his confidence growing from that weight.

Once more he settled beside the fire, sleep pulling at him. The wounded furred one and its nurse had curled up together, and the others had disappeared. Diskan's head nodded. He pulled out the stunner, and curled his fingers around it as he lay down.

He watched the fire drowsily, hardly conscious of movement to his left. It was just another fuel carrier, bringing bigger branches this time. Odd color about them—leaves—the frozen leaves of the wood in the lake valley—red leaves—

And the animal—it was feeding the fire, pushing those leafed branches straight into the heart of the blaze. Diskan tried to rouse, but he was too sleepy—far too sleepy.

❍⋆ CHAPTER 8 ⋆❍

XCOTHAL—Diskan walked through water, sweet, ever-flowing water, sometimes calf high, sometimes, when he came to an intersection of streets, knee high. There was a scent to the water, fresh, sharp, astringent, very good in his nostrils. Xcothal at feast time. But he could only see dimly as if he moved in a dream—and he wanted to see it clearly, all the beauty and light and color!

Around him splashed and romped the brothers-in-fur, the companion ones, as eager as he for the feasting and playtime to come. Their thoughts sometimes meshed with his, so that he savored the pleasure of the water paths, saw and felt as he would not see and feel by means of his own body. This was Xcothal the great, and he was moving to its heart where a wonder beyond all wonders waited.

But the others—not the brothers—the others? There were shadows; yes, he caught glimpses of them, never long enough to give them substance, bone, and flesh—to make them real. And Xcothal was not a deserted city. It held life other than his within its walls, its streets, which were brooks and streams. He wanted to meet that life, be one with it, with a longing so intense that it was a pain! Yet though he turned and watched, there were only shadows.

Carven faces on the walls, runes running. Those he could almost read and knew, in his failure, that had he been able to read them rightly, the shadows would be substance. Always so close, always to fail!

Yet the brothers-in-fur were not shadows, and that thought

sustained Diskan to try and try again. Perhaps when he reached the wonder, then it would all come right. But that was so far! He walked through the water; the buildings passed him on either hand, too blurred for him to be truly sure of their form, knowing somehow that he could never enter them even if he turned aside from this street.

His first mind-filling joy was fading as the pain of longing and loneliness grew sharper. The brothers-in-fur, they knew. They had ceased their play, had come to him and pressed against him now and then reassuringly, the touch of their damp fur a caress. But he knew—knew now—that this was not the true Xcothal. This was but a dream, though it might be a way-dream sent to him for a purpose. And in his eyes tears stung for a loss that grew heavier as he went on and on through a shadow Xcothal in search of shadows—an endless quest.

Dawn made the sky a silver bowl. The fire still smoldered in a circle of dark forms on the stone platform above the swamp. Diskan moaned and flung out an arm, as if he tried to grasp something that was fast fading from him. There were tear stains on his cheeks. His eyes were still closed. About him those others stirred, got to their haunches, all facing the fire.

So far he has gone.

It is not enough! Sharply impatient.

Do not hurry this. Would you lose all by haste?

He is like the other one—the female. So far but not enough.

Perhaps. But it can be that the Place will unlock the door.

Never enough. Sadness, misery of loss.

We shall not put aside trying. Let him wake now. Put on him the wish; let him seek that which must be found, in his body this time. That way is dangerous; there are the swamp traps.

So? Are we not here to watch and direct? The female and the others, they walked in safely, did they not? And this one is certainly not less than them. Perhaps he is more, much more. Wake him; set on him the wish; follow where he cannot see us. Is this agreed?

Seconds of silence and then: *Agreed.*

Diskan opened his eyes and looked up at the sky. The enchantment of the dream still held him. He expected to see the color of those buildings and to feel the softness of the air that had enfolded him as he walked the streets of water, not this chill and austere sky. Then the dream powdered into nothingness and he sat up.

The fire was there and by it still a few sticks, but the animals that had shared its warmth were gone, even the wounded one. He sat alone, looking out over the dark ruins.

"Xcothal," he said aloud. That was Xcothal, or what Xcothal had become with the dimming power of many centuries pressing it down into a rising tide of mud and water. Somewhere, in the heart of that waste, was what he must find. He went to the edge of the platform to look at the frozen swampland. Patches of dull blue, breaking the surface of the ways between the blocks of the buildings, warned of mud holes. Not an easy road, but the one he must follow.

Diskan ate, checked the stunner, picked up his bag of supplies and the club-spear. Then he jumped from the platform to the level of the city.

There was a sharp cry; birds wheeled up from roosting space on the roof of the nearest building. They were white and black, the colors sharply contrasted. Now they skimmed ahead of him, uttering their cries to alert the silent city against an intruder come to disturb its drugged sleep.

Diskan picked his way with care. Frozen and dried vegetation was his guide from step to step, with now and then the solid footing of some stone blocks tumbled from their original settings. But, where in his dream he had been upheld by a sense of joyful excitement, now he traveled in a somber cloud of uneasiness and with the feeling of loss.

Doorways gaped at him, opening upon dark interiors. He had no desire to explore any of them. On the walls were faint traces, much worn, of the carvings he remembered, and even more obscured lines, which could be the runes he had wanted so to read.

Brothers-in-fur—the animals that had gamboled beside him on that other walk through Xcothal—Diskan kept watching for them. But no paw print, no glimpse of a dark body, gave him companionship now. He glanced back once, to see that the shoreline, marked by the steps, was well behind. Then the street curved to the right, and a building hid them from view.

Pools of water, even though roofed with ice, slowed him while he found a way about them. Luckily, the blue mud holes were few along this street, and both times he had come to them, there had been room at one side for passing. It was when Diskan paused by a fallen wall to scoop up some of the snow to allay his thirst that he saw the first indication that there might be other life within that dreary waste.

Ice had been broken at the edge of a pool, and in the mud of its verge were prints, frozen iron hard now. Diskan bent over them.

"Boots!" He identified the marks aloud and then started as the word echoed hollowly back to him. But those were boot prints right enough and beyond them another mark, as if the maker had fallen and braced his weight on his hands to rise again. A hand print—the five fingers well defined in the mud. But a small hand—Diskan set his own down beside the mark for comparison. A hand print, and boot impressions, and the stunner he had found. Some off-worlder had come this way before him. And judging by the size of the hand print—a small off-worlder.

Diskan set a brisker pace. A single man lost, disarmed? There was nothing to fear from him, and perhaps it meant company in his desolate place. Perhaps a shout might bring the stranger? Yet Diskan hesitated. He shrank from arousing the sullen echoes. A shout could be a cry to end the world.

Now why had he thought that? To end the world—how *had* the world of Xcothal ended? In that dream, he had seen the city in its glory and power—now he wandered through it dead, with the signs of great age upon it. There were centuries, maybe even thousands of planet years, between that "then" and this "now." Yet, the brothers-in-fur had existed then, and they had certainly been with him in the now—unless they were an illusion, too.

Diskan shivered. Of what could he be sure? Never before had he been forced to look outside himself and guess what was real and what was not, because he had been only too well aware of the real, and that for him was ever present with pressure and rejection. Vaanchard had been real, Nyborg had been real, and the creche had been real. But here the real and the unreal flowed together. He could stamp his foot on the frozen mud, feel the jar of that contact throughout his body, thus making sure of the truth of where he stood. But last night he had been as sure of the soft water about his legs—in these same streets.

And he had traveled with the furred ones in both the real and the unreal, so how could he be sure of either any more? Perhaps today was also a dream—perhaps Diskan Fentress lay encased in the mud-filled spacer. He jerked away from that path of thought. No—for the second time he stamped. *This* was real! This was now and it was real. And, judging by those tracks, another of his kind had found it real before him.

He set out again, down the street that no longer ran straight but curved. And as he went, he watched for any signs of the one who had gone that way before him. The size of the city began to impress him. He had been walking at a steady pace for a considerable time, and still the street continued to stretch on and on with only one change— the buildings were growing higher as he advanced. Where none had been more than two stories tall when he had entered the city, now they were double that, and fewer had broken walls. Ahead, he could sight still higher erections. The blue mud patches had vanished, and the coarse mats of brittle grass and vegetation were thicker. Now and again Diskan saw the black and white birds perched on the upper windowsills watching him inquisitively. They must accept him now as harmless, for they no longer flew ahead cawing a warning.

However, the very fact that the birds were quiet nibbled at his nerves. Save that they did move, sidling along their perches, they could be less-worn carvings to ornament the dead city. Diskan glanced up at them now and then. They had an attitude of interest, showing no fear but rather confidence that whatever was about to happen would not involve them.

What was about to happen? That expectancy was a part of it all, a waiting growing in intensity, willing him to do something, be somewhere.

The day was dull and cloudy, though there was no more snow. Perhaps the sun could have made the canyon between buildings less dour. Deliberately, Diskan halted, dropping his supply bag, seating himself on some steps leading up to a doorway with a sense of defiance. He ate, slowly, drawing out the meal as long as possible. His vision of Xcothal, which had lingered beyond the dream, had worn away during the day, as if he had rubbed it off against these age-old stones. As he gazed about him now, he wondered how he could ever believe this city had been alive.

And who had lived here then? Those shadows that had remained shadows with no definite shape? Why—it could just as well have been dead in his dream or at least uninhabited, save for the brothers-in-fur—

A sound, echoing. Diskan's hand went to the stunner, but he did not draw that weapon. A limping paw had dislodged a stone to announce the coming of the one who now moved to meet him, for this was the one who had fought in the road pass.

And the eyes were on Diskan. He shrugged and picked up his supply bag. There was no reason for him to fight that summons, one he felt was imperative. He moved on, his dream reviving as the brother-in-fur limped beside him. There were others, too. Diskan did not need to see them. Their presence was as tangible as if he could lay hand on their fur.

On and on, the buildings always rising. The city, speculated Diskan, must be not unlike a pyramid. Odd that he had not noticed that fact from the ridge top on his first sighting of the ruins. He could now count more than ten stories before the weathered and broken rooflines showed. But ahead was a yet taller building.

This was it, the place he strove to reach in the dream! Why he was sure of that, he could not tell, but he was. They came out in the open, into a square, or rather a circle, into which fed street after street, as the spokes of a wheel might join the hub. The centermost building was unlike the rest in that it, too, was round, a stairway encircling it, to lead to a covered arcade. Diskan crossed the open and began to climb the stair.

Now those who had accompanied him unseen were in the open, following him in a dark pack, soundless in their pacing, keeping always a little to the rear, in numbers he could not reckon.

The arcade presented him with a choice of doors. Diskan took the nearest and stepped into a gloom so great that he was blinded for those moments it took his eyes to adjust. Then a thin filter of light from above showed him that he stood in a wedge-shaped room, narrowing at the far end. That was all, bare walls, bare floor, nothing!

He looked to the one who had limped beside him.

"What do you want?" he demanded, and his words echoed.

They wanted something of him, and that demand for action unknown battered him. He must *do* something—perform some act they were waiting for. Only they gave him no clue, and the tension built in him until he cried aloud:

"I don't know what you want! Can't you understand? I don't *know*!"

The shout relieved some of the pressure, or were they releasing him from the burden of their need? There was a stir. Diskan glanced over his shoulder. As silently as they had come in his wake, they were retreating, leaving him here alone. Alone! He could not bear being alone—not here!

Diskan dropped his supply bag, his club-spear.

"No—!" He was on his knees, reaching for the limping one with more than entreaty, a determination that, come what might, he would keep that one with him.

There was angry hissing—eyes blazing into his, a rejection so utter and complete that it froze Diskan until the animal had limped out of range. Then that one, too, was gone, and he was alone.

All the pressure he had half sensed since the morning's awaking was off him, but the void it left was so frightening that Diskan could not find the strength to move. Something great and wonderful, without description in any words of his, had been waiting here. And through his own stupidity it was lost. Logic told him that was not true, but emotion hammered back it was—it *was*!

He was reaching for his club when he saw some marks in the dust on the floor, for the longer he sat there, the more his sight increased. Not clear prints—but someone, or something, had been there before him. Dully, for the want of a better purpose, he began to follow them.

Outside once again, in the covered way to which the steps led. Soil had blown in here through the centuries. There were clumps of withered grass rooted in the larger deposits. And the tracks—much sharper now—boots! Two pairs, maybe three—and a place where another had trod across that trail. Three—four others here! With a chance, they might still be!

Diskan broke into a shambling trot. The trail circled the building to another doorway. He hesitated by that. Night was almost here. He had no liking for the interior of the building in the dark. What memories, what ghosts could walk here in a man's dreams? He dared not dream again of Xcothal as it had been.

But there was light beyond, a thin diffused gleam that came from no visible opening. It might have been born from the air itself. There were tracks leading straight across the rooms. Mechanically, Diskan followed them, to be confronted by a bare wall into which they vanished.

Shaken, he put his hand to the blocking surface. It moved, so easily that he went off balance and fell into a corridor, also dimly lit. Here the dust had not gathered so thickly; there was only a smudge or two to point the trail. And the corridor was circular, apparently following the line of the outer wall.

Diskan took to thumping the wall on his left, seeking another of those masked openings. His guess was proved right when a second swinging stone moved, and he looked into a well-like space. Up and down that curled a stair. Down he would not go—the gloom hung there. But up—from the floor above he might have a full view of the city and learn where he now was in relation to the swamp shore from which he had come. Diskan climbed, not finding it easy, for the steps were steep and narrow, and there appeared to be no more openings or landings until he came to the top.

He felt his way about that space, with no idea how far he now was above street level. Another door stone opened into a much wider corridor, its right wall broken by arches through which he could look into the clouded evening sky. Wind blew in freshly, and Diskan went to stand there.

The city spread out below; yet between him and those buildings and streets, there was a curious haze, not a fog or mist such as he knew elsewhere, but more a distortion of sight, so that one moment a building could look so, the next seem altogether different. Diskan was forcibly reminded of Xcothal as he had seen it in his dream. There was no color, none of the feeling of happy rightness; yet the Xcothal he surveyed from this perch was not the ruined city.

That distortion did not frighten him; on the contrary, it soothed the sense of loss that had ridden him since his failure to fulfill the plan of the brothers-in-fur. Diskan continued to watch the shifting scenes below until a vast fatigue weighted his eyes and he shuffled back, to drop with his shoulders the inner wall, his hands resting on his knees. His eyes closed. Dream—he was willing to dream again. Perhaps he would find the answer so.

But tonight there were no dreams.

★ ★ ★

Shadows flitted through the streets, held council together.

He is not to our purpose—as the others were not. Forget him.

Yet he dreamed clearly. Of the others, only the female dreamed, and as she dreamed, she feared, awaking to call on the powers of her own kind for protection. He dreamed, and in his dreams he was happy; thus he is unlike the others.

Have you thought this, wise ones? We may not again find what once we had, but this one could be shaped to our purposes?

A hard task shaping. And in the process of shaping, that which is shaped may break.

Yet let that not deter the shaping. How think you, one and all?

Long has been the waiting—we are only half of the whole. This one has been the most responsive yet. Let shaping be tried. Do we agree thus?

We agree.

Diskan slept soundly as the shadows separated and went to accomplish purposes of their own in the streets of Xcothal.

᪣⋆ **CHAPTER 9** ⋆᪣

THE BLACK AND WHITE BIRDS wheeled and circled outside the arched openings. Diskan watched them apathetically. He had not moved from the place that night and fatigue had chosen for his rest, though the sun was bright and the day sky cleared of all clouds. He felt emptied, without any wish to move, to think, to be—

But now life sparked within him. Dragging himself to his feet, Diskan walked slowly back to the stair that had brought him to this perch above the city. Wearily, he circled down, around and around that spiral, slowly, as the descent made him dizzy. There was a great silence within the walls of the building. Was it a temple, a fortress, a palace? One of three—or all—he would never be sure.

Diskan came out in the lower hall. Now much plainer to read were the tracks he had followed the night before. For want of any other employment, he began to trace again those others' passing.

Shoulder high on one wall—a blackened streak. No stunner left that! Blaster raying, though he was not too familiar with the traces of those lethal weapons. And just beyond that scar a door stood open. Diskan drew his stunner. Against a blaster that was hardly better than the club-spear, but it was the best he had.

The room beyond startled him. In this building he had seen no signs of ruin and decay, but now he fronted walls that were holed, riven in great gaps, with a crumble of debris out on the floor of the chamber. And each of those holes gave upon blackness, as if there were great open space beyond.

Fire marks—sears of blast. This chaos, Diskan realized, was not the result of time, but the work of man, energetically tearing into fabric of the building—searching for what? He began a cautious circuit of the chamber, detouring about the rubble, longing for a lamp with which to explore the darkness beyond.

A chattering. Diskan swung the stunner, thumbed the button, and saw a mass collapse limply. He turned over with the toe of his boot the body of one of the scavengers such as he had seen at the burned ground.

He stopped near some claw-marked stone, from under which came a dark oozing, now dried. Diskan dropped his supply bag to examine the fall of stone more carefully. Gingerly, he began to lever the top of the mass apart, then leaped away as it cascaded from him into the gap of the broken wall.

Sound reached him from the shaking mound, a clicking. Diskan readied the stunner, watching for another of the scavengers, but the limited light revealed instead a head, shoulders, an outflung arm. The man was dead, had been so for some time. What Diskan could see of his clothing suggested a spacer uniform, and there was the glint of an officer's insignia on his upstanding collar.

On the wrist of the outflung arm was a wide bracelet inset with a dial. The face of that glowed, and from it came a steady ticking—a com device of some sort. And it was recording or broadcasting—or whatever—even now. On impulse, Diskan pulled the thing over the cold hand and brought it into better light.

A dial, without any symbols or figures he could read, only a single needle that swayed as he moved the bracelet, swinging so that its delicately arrowed head always pointed in the same direction, to his right now, but ever to one wall as he tested it by turning. A direction finder of sorts. Intrigued, Diskan tried to slip it over his own wrist, discovered the supporting ring too small, and finally attached it to his belt.

He returned to the dead man. Two blocks Diskan could not move imprisoned the body, but he cleared away enough of the rubble to see what had brought the man down. Not the fall of the wall, which had partly entombed him, but a blaster burn across his body breast high. The condition of the chamber was now clear; it had been a battlefield. Slowly, Diskan piled the largest stones he could find back over what he had uncovered for the only burial he could give the stranger.

Now he wanted to get out into the light of day. He struck at the limp scavenger with the club before he left, thus making sure it would not return to its digging. As he went, Diskan watched the device he had taken from the body.

The needle still pointed in one direction, and it seemed to Diskan that the clicking accelerated. What could it be attuned to? Others roaming this pile, carrying on some desperate struggle of their own? Diskan had no wish to be involved. But still the swing of the needle intrigued him, and he followed its lead along the outer corridor.

Then that hair-thin guide pointed left. Diskan searched the wall for an entrance, and the stone gave under his hand. Before him was a hole blasted in the surface of the far wall. The clicking was a steady purr, but that purr warned him. He had no wish to walk into blaster fire. Slowly, Diskan backed away and let the outer door slide into place behind him. This was another mystery of Xcothal and one he did not want to solve.

Walking firmly, he went out of the building into which the animals had brought him. When he was on the stairs in the outer air, he breathed deeply. He must get away, free himself from the dead city, from his failure here. The quarrel of off-world strangers was none of his. He felt a curious detachment, as if he had no tie with his own species any more.

He had drawn heavily on his supplies. Could he work his way back to the cache? Diskan closed his eyes for the moment, trying mentally to picture the route he had come. It was simple. He might not be trained to track, but there was nothing difficult about this. He strode confidently down the stairs and looked for the opening into the street that had brought him here.

Then his confidence ebbed a little. All those wheel spokes of open ways looked exactly alike. He had come in there—no, there—or had he? He could not tell by the buildings; they were all the same.

The morning's sun had melted the snow patches that might have held tracks; he had no guide save chance. But that was the way to the ridge. Diskan turned to face it. And surely, once pointed in the right general direction, he could find his way. Let him see the ridge as a landmark and he was safe.

He entered the street he had chosen. Too bad he had not been more observant yesterday. But during the last part of that journey, after the animal had joined him, he had been aware only of his companions, the one beside him and those he could not see. And of those, there had been no trace since they had left him in the wedge chambers.

If this was not the street he had traversed yesterday, it was very like it. The sun glistened on what Diskan thought was a runnel of ice and then saw was a track, a shining mark running straight from one building to another. He poked at it with the spear point, and the wood skidded on a slick, slimy surface, rising with a ball of noxious material on its tip. Diskan thrust it again and again into a hummock of grass to clean it. He hurried on, not liking the looks of that trail, if trail it was, and certainly not wishing to investigate its source.

The birds and the animals had been in the city yesterday, but now he began to see disturbing traces of other possible inhabitants. A second slime trail, wider, thicker, and more disgusting than the first crossed the street. And this time Diskan had to take a running leap to clear it. Perhaps the creatures who made these were night crawlers. If so, the sooner he won out of the city, the better. It had lost for him all the appeal of his dream; its sinister aspect was growing, so that even when the sun shone brightly into its streets, the buildings seemed to exhale gloom from their open doorways, setting up a fog of fear.

Diskan broke into a trot, glancing from side to side, and now and then over his shoulder. There was no movement, no sight of anything. But that very stillness was part of his discomfort, for it hinted at things lying in wait behind a window, within the shadow of a doorway. Allowing him to come, to pass, then following—Twice he stopped short, faced about, stunner ready, certain that he *had* heard some betraying noise, that danger prowled at his heels.

He consulted the device he had taken from the dead man. The clicking was very faint, barely audible when he held it to his ear. And the needle pointed back to the center of the city. He was sure the peril he sensed had nothing to do with his own kind. This was of the city, yet not of Xcothal. An empty shell had been left, and into that emptiness had crawled other things that had no kinship with those who had built the shell, who were, in fact, the opposite of those first intelligences. This was no city of promised light, color, and joy, as he had seen it yesterday, but a graveyard, given over to all that opposed his dream.

More slime tracks, and one so wide that he feared he could not leap it. The noisome odor was stronger; the tracks could perhaps be fresher. Then Diskan knew that he had chosen the wrong road, for the street widened into a great pool with a center of blue mud. And that mud blew a bubble as he watched, the dull skin swelling out and out—to break, spewing bits of yellow stuff over the surface of the lake.

The yellow substance was light enough to be airborne, floating in motes. Some of these sped together as steel attracted to a magnet. And when they met, there was a spark of fire, a small flaming coal, which fell to melt a bit of ice or set flame to a tuft of dried reed. And there was a stench worse than that from the slime tracks.

No safe way of crossing that lake. The ice crust was thin, and Diskan did not trust the footing along its shore, which lapped against the walls of the buildings. Back—back to the hub circle and choose again, and Diskan had the feeling that something was satisfied, amused by his retreat.

At the circle, he sat down on one of the steps of the center building. Here the sun shown warmer, more brightly. When he looked down any one of those streets, it was to meet obscurity, akin to that which had bewildered him when he had surveyed the city from the arched walk at the top of the tower structure. Yet this was different, for then he had a sense of expectant enchantment, whereas this warned, repelled, set up a barrier. Diskan weighed the bag of supplies. He could ration what was left. All these supplies carried various sustaining ingredients that allowed one to stretch them thin and still have an adequate level of nourishment. But he wanted out—away from those now-sinister streets, back to the natural rock and marsh he could understand.

Deliberately, he studied the four streets to his left. Down the first he had just returned. But he had retained enough memory of yesterday to limit the possible exit to one of those four—or the three he had not tried. Now he selected the center one of the trio and set out for the second time.

Slime trails again, but these had hardened in the frosty air. For the rest, this way was exactly like the first.

He held to a brisk walk. It was past midday, and he wanted to be out of this maze before sundown. To be caught at night in one of these dark ways was a risk he did not want to take, and he must make good time now.

A lake, with blue mud for its center—Diskan did not believe what he saw. He rammed the spear point against the ice surface at his feet, and it pierced the pane over dark fluid, releasing an evil smell, proving its reality. He was back again! But he had not taken the same street—he could not have made that mistake!

Holding fiercely to that belief, Diskan retreated for the second time. The street that had brought him here before—that had been the first of those probable ones, and this had been the third! He knew that was true. Yet as far as he could see, he stood now just where he had before—

Back to the hub. Panting and sweating, he squatted once again on the steps and counted those streets with a finger. He had been right! Here was the ration tube he had sucked dry and left lying to mark where he had rested. *That* was the first street, *that* the third! And since they radiated out spokewise, why, one could not run into the other without some curve he would have noticed. Yet he had found the lake the second time.

Diskan put his head in his hands and tried to consider the problem carefully, logically, only there was no normal logic in this. So, he must have counted wrong some way. Only he had not, one part of his brain shrieked—he had *not*! This was the old frustration, the old defeating knowledge that somehow he had not performed some function with the right responses. Thoroughly shaken, Diskan was almost afraid now to lift his head and look at those streets so much alike, so much a trap for him.

When he did raise his eyes to survey them with a control he fought to hold, the obscurity had deepened. Why, he was hardly able to see down any length farther than the first three or four buildings. Diskan gave a gasping cry, caught up supply bag and club, and began to climb the steps of the core building. For all his determination, he could not face the murk of those streets. And to come a third time to that lake would be more than his sanity could stand.

He pushed in the first open door and looked about the deep gloom of the hall into which the animals had brought him. Full circle! It must have been near this same hour yesterday that he had stood here. Then he had been keyed to desires, pressures from without. Now he was alone—very much alone.

Diskan gazed at the blank walls, his eyes always returning to the point of the wedge where the dusk was thickest. Yet he had no uneasiness of spirit such as had frightened him in the somberness of the streets. What had been the purpose of this chamber? It was so large, companies of worshipers could have gathered here. Was it a fane? Or hundreds of councilors could have debated together if this was a place of government. A court might have held vast formal ceremonials down its length. Now all was silence, dust, shadows. No trace of carving, no matter how worn, none of the vague impressions of what might be runes ran along the smooth surfaces of the narrowing walls, no altar, no dais, no throne raised from the floor.

He began to walk toward the narrowed point. At his belt, the device ticked more and more loudly. His glance told him that the needle pointed ahead when he held it on his palm. But here was no rubble or battle sign.

Suddenly, Diskan spoke. "What do you want of me?"

In a measure he had begun to feel as he had the day before—that a demand was building, becoming more imperative, that he was being given a second chance at some test, the importance of which was past his assessing.

He was midway down the chamber now. Did the shadows gathered at the point have substance? Were the animals returning? No, he could not see them, turning, pacing, moving in to meet him. Nothing so concrete awaited him. Still some sense tricked him, or his eyes, into that belief in movement, in the appearance of a pattern forming there, woven to a purpose he could not guess. If he could only follow the lines of that pattern, he might understand! But though he concentrated, tried to force such understanding, it did not come— only that movement he could not trace. And at last it dwindled into nothingness and was gone.

"*Tell me!*" His voice arose in a despairing cry, echoing through the hall. But when those echoes died away, there was only a dusty silence and a loss that hurt.

Diskan waited, hoping to see again that weaving which was only half on the borderline of his sight, to catch from the air about him some helpful hint of purpose, to learn the step to be taken, the unseen door that must be opened. Nothing—Whatever had brought a small measure of life for a portion of time to this age-old hall had died, as a fire might fall to ashes, its flames unfed.

He turned at last, his shoulders hunched and bowed, his pace a tired shuffle. This last and perhaps greatest of his failures left him drained of all purpose and feeling. He went out to the hall, and because he had no place else to go, he found again the inner stair and climbed to his perch of the night before. Below was Xcothal, but this time he had no desire to look out upon its ruins. He feared what he might see in those streets as the night closed in.

As one who nurses a pain that cannot be soothed, he rocked slowly back and forth on his haunches, his arms folded over his middle.

"What do you want of me?" That was no shout, only a ragged whisper, but he repeated it over and over, until his mouth was dry, his voice husky. And there was never any answer, not even the cry of a bird.

He did not sleep; he could not. The sense of danger arose about his post as the fumes of the mud lake had billowed up with their choking stench. No test of courage could be harder to face. In the darkness, Diskan fought back, and he had so little to fight with! But the hour came when, because he could not live with his own fear any longer, Diskan crawled on hands and knees across the cold stone to look down on the city, the pit from which that terror arose.

Dark such as he had not imagined—yet the longer he watched, the more he saw that there were degrees of darkness in a way he could find no words to describe. There was a flowing, an ebbing there also—not to be defined—a life that was not his life, nor the life of that other weaving in the chamber. This was a thing that had entered unbidden, that strove to knit itself into the ruined walls, to remain, unless that which had once been came again.

That which had once been! Xcothal—

"It is past—" He did not know why he spoke that protest in a frozen whisper.

Past! Past! Perhaps his word had been taken up by an echo; perhaps it was only the sigh of a breeze below his lookout. The coiling of the dark upon the dark grew swifter, reached higher about the hub building. Diskan made himself watch it. His body shivered and his nails cut deeper into his own flesh, although he was not aware of that small pain through the larger that filled him.

Xcothal—he clung to his dream, strove to batter aside the tide of darkness with the color, the life, the beauty it smothered and buried. Xcothal should not be taken! That which had dwelt here could not be so lightly overcome, banished—Xcothal—Diskan stared into the night and fought—throwing away all logic, all reason.

He only knew that, in summoning his dream and holding it, he was waging a small engagement in the midst of a battle, and he held to his post grimly. What had been dark waves beating on shadows began to change. He did not know when he saw that first spark of light flash into being, a pinpoint in the streets. But there came another and another—minute sparks of light whose origin he could not guess. They followed no pattern, a cluster here, a line of individual points there, a solitary beam in the midst of heavy dusk.

They did not move as did the whirling lashings of the dark but endured as outposts. And at length, no more appeared. Diskan unclenched his fists. Again on his hands and knees, he went back to the wall. He did not want to sleep; he did not need it. There was a tingling awareness of the night, such as he had never experienced before, running through his veins, warming him so that with impatient fingers he pulled at the throat of the parka, opening it farther.

Something—he did not know just what—had happened, as if a machine long idle had been triggered into action once again, and ripples spreading from that action were lapping on, out and out. Was this what they had wanted of him, the brothers-in-fur? No, swift on the heels of that came the denial, and he knew it was the truth. He had failed then, but now—

Diskan did not notice the device hung at his belt. On the dial the needle quivered, fluttered; the clicking was a solid purr that did not reach his deaf ears. All that was real for him now was what lay out there in the night, stirring, moving. And this time—surely this time—he was going to learn what it was!

✪ CHAPTER 10 ✪

NOT A SOUND but a vibration in the air, through his body, was transmitted by the stone on which he crouched. A summons? After it, a quiver, as if each and every heavy stone in these walls strove to answer, only had no way of giving voice. Diskan waited tense, yearning—

Again!

His body obeyed without any command from his brain as he stood up. In his veins, the blood flowed more quickly; he felt alert, ready for anything that might come. The deadening fog of fear had been rent into tatters, was shriveling from him.

In the dark, needing no physical sight as a guide, Diskan found the stairs, began to descend. Beat—once again! A heart awakening into life—Xcothal's heart? In his eagerness, he stumbled, almost fell, and that mishap taught him caution. Round and around, down, always waiting for that beat of life within the core of ancient death.

He was on the threshold of the wedge-shaped chamber when it vibrated for the fourth time. And he saw the furred ones moving up the steps, slipping around and about him, as if he had no existence in their eyes. There was no reckoning the number of their dark shapes in this pale light. Diskan only knew that they were many and that they came from all directions, pressing with purpose up the outer steps, toward the wedge chamber. The brothers-in-fur! But they could not be alone—there must be the others!

Bewildered, Diskan drew to one side just within the doorway, his eyes searching for what he felt must be there, though what he sought, he could not explain. The interior of the huge hall, which had been so dusky, was now growing lighter. Sparks hung in the air here and there, always above the mass of furred bodies, reared up on their broad haunches, their heads all turned to the narrow far end, as if fixed in a hypnotic stare on some point or thing he could not see. There were so many of them!

Now their heads moved, a rhythmic ripple that ran back like a breaking wave to Diskan's place by the door. And following that ripple came the vibration, stronger now, a beat that shook the building, the living things in it, as if the very earth heaved.

Ripple, ripple. With a start, Diskan became conscious his own head had joined in the slow bend forward and back. The sparks in the air grew brighter. They were of different colors, gems tossed aloft to hang in brilliant array—green, blue, orange, scarlet, violet, shades in between, dazzling to watch.

From over the heads of the animals, the lights moved out and away, drifting to the bare walls. But where they touched the stone they melted, spread in glistening runnels and shooting trails of jeweled fire. And they were not still, those runnels and trails, but moved, interweaving, loosing, weaving again another design, as had the dusky shadows. Only this was the splendor of which that had been the dying ashes.

Diskan shaded his eyes with his hand from what was close to searing brilliance. He longed to watch, and yet he could no longer do so. He was on his knees, his head moving in time with those of the animals about him. And from them, a vast wave of ecstasy, which was also expectancy of some greater wonder to come, rose about him.

Boom! Boom! Xcothal awakening—the past returning to flower again.

Yes! Yes! Diskan's lips shaped the words he could not voice aloud. To know—to be in Xcothal in this hour! This was what he had sought without understanding. He stood on a threshold; take only one step and wonder beyond reckoning was his!

A scream—

The fabric of lights, of rapport with the animals, was rent as if a knife had slashed it. Dazed, Diskan shook and shivered. He fell forward, and that saved his life, for over him a blaster bolt blazed, to strike the wall and scar it with a core of crimson destruction.

Diskan twisted, still too much under the spell to know more than that it had been broken. He stared up, bemused, at the smoking evidence of that shot. Then he was knocked down and rolled over by furred bodies launched at him. And by the time he fought his way free of those, his wits were back.

Had he really been attacked by the animals? Diskan thought not as he sat up, back against the wall, well out of line of the doorway from which that blast must have come. His companions in that ritual had merely removed him speedily from the line of fire.

Fire from an off-world weapon! Now a piercing buzzing from his belt! Had the device guided the enemy here? Diskan unhooked it and almost threw it from him, his grief and anger at the interruption turning into a smoldering rage. No, he would hunt that other down! He had been close to dying in that ray, yes. But what was worse, he had lost that which had been almost within his grasp here. And for that there was no pardon! This thing he held in his hand, it could perhaps guide him to his attacker.

However, as he scrambled up, the animals pressed about him, imposed their bodies as a barrier between him and the doorway.

"No!" Diskan strove to elude their guard. "Let me through!" He thrust against them. Then he remembered the stunner, dragged it out, and sprayed widely with it.

That cleared a path as the animals went down, temporarily paralyzed. Diskan ran into the night, the com device in one hand, the stunner in the other. Free of the chamber, he paused. To charge ahead into a blaster was stupid. Logic took over, forced control that his rage had broken. Do not run into death—hunt, trail, use what cunning he had.

He studied the dial on his palm. The needle swung to his left, in the general direction of the ruined chamber in which he had found the dead man. Here it was dark; his sight was still dazzled by the lights that had snapped into nothingness at the firing of the blaster. But the dark could be a cloak as well as a disadvantage. Also he remembered the way well enough. With his shoulder against the wall, Diskan crept along the curve.

The buzz of the device was less strong; his quarry must be well ahead. But the needle pointed fixedly on. And he would find him—most certainly he would find him!

Behind him forces he did not sense stirred.

He was close; he must not get away. So close we were, brothers!

Let him go; he is useless to us now. To himself he has returned. Perhaps he is not for our shaping.

Close! There was a chorus of that, beating down doubts.

Until he comes again to the threshold by his own wish, he is useless. Let him seek now his kind; let that be the test.

There was opposition, ready and hot, but it was overruled.

If he goes to his death, then that is the ordained pattern, and we cannot change it by all the arts. We cannot be whole with that which is flawed. He must aid in his own shaping, or the shape will be imperfect. Let him go free to do what is in him to do. Only when he has freed himself can he enter the portal we open to him. We watch, we wait, but we cannot move until he is again with an open mind and heart.

So close—Wistful, regretting.

Close, yes. But now, waiting—Our renewal is delayed; we cannot change that, for any recharging will take time, much time.

Diskan entered the room with the broken walls, his eyes turned away from the pile of stones that was now a tomb. In the dim light of the room, he could see the needle pointed to one of the wall rents. Crazy to go in there without a torch, without any hope of seeing what lay ahead, while the one he hunted could be in ambush. But, crazy or not, he was going!

An incautious step among the rubble, and he fell heavily. As he lay there for a moment, he heard a sound ahead, and the com buzzed more loudly. His teeth clenched, Diskan crawled on, taking that one small precaution against a blast.

Oddly enough, as he thrust head and shoulders through the hole, he did not come into absolute darkness such as he thought existed beyond the walls. Instead, once past that barrier, he found gray half light, and he was not far from another stair. But this curled down and not up.

Reaching that, Diskan lay flat, his ear pressed to the floor. Faint sounds—feet on the steps? The enemy was moving away. But to be trapped on the stair, a target from raying from below—

He waited until the sounds were so faint that he could hardly distinguish them. And then he swung over, planted his feet on the steps, and began to descend, but with caution.

The buzz of the device was faint, a click instead of a steady beat. When he held it to his eyes, the needle changed with every curve of the stair.

Round and around, down and down. He was already certain he must be well below the level of the streets without. There was damp rising from the stairwell, and with it an unpleasant odor of decay, such as might issue from a swamp. Perhaps there was some underground outlet on the marsh bog that had come to partially swallow Xcothal.

He had to slow his descent; the rounds of the stair were making him dizzy. And once, during one of those pauses, he heard a sound from behind. Diskan pushed against the wall, his head up, peering up the corkscrew.

Outlined in the dim light was a round furred head. The animals! At least one of them was trailing him. He had used the stunner freely back there in the chamber. Had his art turned friend into enemy? But when he halted, that one halted, too, did not strive to draw closer. After a long moment, Diskan relaxed. In a way, this was a return to his first days on this world of mysteries, when he had been dogged across the ridge by just such a follower. He began to descend again.

How deep was that curl of stairway? He had not tried to count the steps, but at long last, they brought him to a firm footing from which a passage ran. And here the swamp had thrust exploring fingers.

The dank air was filled with evil odors. There were unwholesome, faintly glowing growths on the wall in leprous patches, others noduling up from the floor. Diskan had never seen a place he liked less. Yet the device told him his way lay ahead, and he could see traces of another's passing—broken fungi growths and smears on the slimy floor.

Those ragged wall growths made it difficult to see clearly. Diskan picked a very slow and cautious path, listening always—for the sound of footsteps before him, to the buzz of the com, for the animal behind. The latter he did not hear at all, but the ticking of the com approached a steady purr once more.

It was lighter down here than it had been aloft, from the luminescence of those monstrous and contorted growths. So foul was their general appearance that Diskan took every precaution to avoid any direct contact with them. But he inadvertently brushed the back of his hand against a spike of fleshy stuff broken by the passing of the one he trailed.

He might have put his hand into flames, the pain bringing back a swift memory of the hurt he had taken to dis-con the watcher robot. Then the powers of the ship had healed his wound. Now he could only rub his knuckles across the skirt of the parka, hoping he was removing the irritating ooze, not smearing it in. There was an angry puffing at the base of his fingers, and he felt sharp stabs of pain when he tried to flex them.

More of the broken "branches" hung ahead, making him squirm and twist to avoid their dripping poison. Why had the enemy not used his blaster to burn clear a passage?

Diskan knew very little about those weapons. Legally, they could be worn and used only by off-worlders on planets certified dangerous, and by those of the Service. The ordinary galactic citizen had no reason to use them. He presumed they were charged much the same as the stunners, with a measure of energy that would become exhausted. And if the man ahead had not used his now to burn off this fungi for a clear passage, it could mean that his present blaster charge was low.

For the first time in hours, Diskan examined the pointer on the stunner. He had used it on the scavenger and had sprayed his path clear with it above. And it had read only half charged when he had found it. Now that small black line rested very close to the red "empty." So if the enemy lacked weapon power, he was hardly any better off. Still, he had no intention of retracing his way up into the open.

What had brought the man he tracked down into this hell hole? Flight from a stronger party? If so, where had that enemy gone? The animals? No, the dead man aloft had been blaster-killed, and up in the great hall, the blaster had been aimed at Diskan, not into the mass of furred ones among which he had knelt. So the other must have believed him part of the threat that had driven him into hiding.

Ahead was an open space cleared of all the growth, save for some shriveled tendrils and ash on the floor. A blaster had been used here systematically, to clean a long stretch of wall on both sides of the passage. And carvings had been laid bare by that burning—not eroded into faint shadows as they had been above, but deep and clear, though discolored by the countless years the fungi had rooted over them.

Not pictures but runes, truly runes! Only the sweep of those markings held no sense as they followed curves not lines over the walls, both horizontally and vertically, in such an involved massing that it was very difficult to separate any one mark from the rest.

Four blocks, two to a wall, faced each other. And smashed before one lay a mass of glass and metal, which was surely off-world in origin. Beside it a broken coil of voice tape, snapped and snarled upon itself, coiled in a never-to-be untangled knot. Diskan's com device was purring in a rising beat. He avoided the tangle of tape and reached the part of the passage beyond where the growths began again.

"Grufa na sandank—forwarre!"

That shout could have come from anywhere ahead, but Diskan thought it sounded close, too close. And the words had no meaning. He took shelter behind a bulge of fungi. That could have been nothing but a warning. The high voice had held a note of hysteria, which was a further deterrent to plunging headlong up the passage. This place was enough to turn a man's mind. Diskan could well believe that whoever shouted might ray anything or anyone who had him cornered.

"Who are you?" Diskan tried to make that sound calm and natural. He spoke Basic and waited for an answer he hoped might make sense.

"You make no fools of us, Jack Scum. Come on and you'll be rayed!"

Basic was used for reply this time, but that did not make any more sense as far as he was concerned.

"I don't know who your Jack Scum may be," Diskan called. "I don't know who you are either. I am a wreck survivor landed here by chance. My name is Diskan Fentress."

"Wearing a Jack coat?" There was scornful disbelief in that. "You have to the count of five; then we shall fire the wall growths. The smoke of their burning will stifle you!"

"Wearing a coat I found in a survivor cache," Diskan returned hurriedly. So that was why he had been rayed up there. His parka labeled him one of the enemy. "I tell you—my spacer cracked up here. I've been wandering around—"

"I don't believe you. Kal nadra sonk!"

"All right, I'm going." He stepped back into the cleared space. This business of the smoke from burning wall growths being suffocating could be true, but if his guess was right, they would not waste blaster fire.

He glanced around. Carefully, in the middle of the passage well away from the walls, stood one of the animals, its head up, watching him. It moved a step or two, limping, and Diskan knew it for the one that had shared the fight in the pass. It came on slowly to stand beside him, facing down passage. And Diskan had the feeling that again they were ranged against a common foe.

A murmur from beyond, not loud enough for him to distinguish words, just enough for him to guess that there were more than one waiting up there.

"No—you cannot! Please, High One, come back—please!"

That high voice, again strung to nervous protest. There was movement ahead. A figure lurched, apparently out of the wall, with another and slighter one dragging back at it. The larger took a step or two in Diskan's direction, then crashed on the slimed floor, pulling the other with it. Diskan sprang forward, using the stunner, knowing this was his chance.

Both of the figures lay still, caught in the bonds of the beam. A moment later he was standing over them, stooping to search for their weapons.

A Zacathan! The soft folds of the neck and head frill spread out behind the alien's head. His yellow-gray skin almost matched the color of the growths. The large reptilian eyes stared up at Diskan, though there was an oddly unfocused quality in them. Above the alien's waist the tight fabric of a protecto-suit had been cut away to allow bandaging of his torso; then plasta-skin had been poured over the wide folds.

His smaller companion also stared at Diskan as he rolled the body over, but those eyes were very aware, filled with fear and loathing. A girl, her hair tumbling out of a net, her protecto-suit smeared and scraped—and in her belt what he was seeking, the blaster. He transferred that before he looked around.

There was a gap in the wall, a rough-hewn doorway. They must have come through there. He moved to explore the space beyond. He found two supply bags, a bedroll spread out, an ever-burn lamp, and a jumble of other things piled against the far wall—but no one else.

Diskan lifted the girl and carried her in, to drop her on the bedroll. Then he made the same trip with the Zacathan, whom he stretched out on the floor. The alien's skin was harsh and dry to the touch; he was manifestly fevered, perhaps seriously hurt.

With his hands on his hips, Diskan looked from one to the other. Survivors from a crashed ship would not be wearing protecto-suits. Those were the issue of some government service to be used by planet explorers. He did not know how long he would have to wait before they came out from under the effects of the stunner beam and he would be able to ask some questions, but now he had plenty of time.

☾★ CHAPTER 11 ★☾

THE FURRED ONE stretched out across the doorway, now and again gazing out into the passage, listening perhaps, Diskan thought. He himself prowled the room, inspecting the material piled there. Then he triggered a tape reader, which had a spool set in it.

"Report 6A3, Mimir Expedition. Fifth day since we holed up. Hist Techneer Zimgrald suffering from his wound, has been alternating between unconsciousness and fevered raving. Necessary for me to go above to see whether we are still being hunted. Will record again upon my return. Julha Than signing off."

"Julha Than," Diskan repeated, peering down at the girl, who watched him with those hating eyes. "I am Diskan Fentress—" Could he be sure—? He thought that there had been a change in her icy regard when he repeated his name. On impulse, he struggled out of the tight parka so she could see his Vaan tunic, spotted and worn as it was.

"It was the truth I told you," he added. "I survived a spacer crash; my ship was swallowed up in a mud bog. And I found a cache—that's where I got this coat."

As long as the stunner held, she could not answer, but she would have to listen, not being able to thrust her fingers into her ears as he had in the Vaanchard garden.

"I don't know what has been going on here. I found a dead man under some rubble in the room this passage stair heads from. He was wearing this, and that is what led me to you—after you tried to ray

286

me." Diskan held the device in her line of vision. "Believe me, I'm not after you. I have no reason to fight—"

He thought that he had at that moment when he had stormed out of the chamber after the fleeing sniper. However, that rage had cooled. Now he could understand the mistake about the parka. He turned away from the girl and went to kneel beside the Zacathan. There was nothing he could do for the alien. His medical knowledge was nil; he had had no intensive briefing in first aid such as all members of an expedition were given. Doubtless the girl had already done all she could for the alien.

Diskan was impatient for the stun effect to wear off, to ask questions. Once more he turned to the tape reader. There were other disks fitted in below the speaker. Diskan awkwardly freed the tape in the flow bars and took the first one from the small rack to snap in its place.

"Report 2B1." He thought he recognized the girl's clipped speech. "The firing of the wall growth produces a nauseous and perhaps dangerous effect. We have withdrawn to the side chamber, leaving the port-blast on remote control. There is good evidence that the deductions are correct, that the 'Place of Great Riches' lies near here and we may well uncover the clue in this wall search. Captain Ranbo and his two crewmen have gone for more heat-unit charges and to secure the ship during our work here. Julha Than, Second Tech, reporting."

Click, click, click, and then the voice began again:

"Report 2B2. Heat unit in the port-blast exhausted, but use was successful. Wall shows excellent series of carvings—see vid tape 884. First Tech Mik s'Fan has gone to explore ahead. Have received two progress signals from him. Captain Ranbo and his men have not returned yet. We cannot use the in-probe without the stepped-up beamer they are to bring. Using this period to make detailed scan-vid record of uncovered walls."

Again the clicking interval. Then another voice, harsher, with a hissing intonation—without doubt, that of the Zacathan. And this dictated portion was couched in a technical code that meant nothing to Diskan. That flowed on and on until the tape was exhausted. Diskan put the rewound disk back in its slot and selected one from farther along.

"Report 5D5. No reply from First Tech s'Fan in eight planet hours. Have set recall three hours ago, putting it on urgent. Have tried to reach Captain Ranbo also. No reply since the garbled message of an hour ago. The animals are on the stairway and seem hostile, keeping us from ascending. Hist Tech Zimgrald does not want to incite them, for the reasons he stated in his earlier report. Since they test, even by our crude methods, about 8 over X or more, he is striving to establish contact by the Four Rules. They do not move against us, but neither will they permit us to leave here. Have set both ship call and summoner on full and locked them."

There was an interval and then Julha's voice, not precise or controlled this time, but high in tone, her words coming fast and slurred:

"Report 5D6. Message from ship, cut off after a few words. Ship under attack; no answer from s'Fan. The animals are still guarding the stair, making no move at us—"

The message broke off, and there was nothing more on the tape. Diskan pulled out the next and threaded it in.

"Report 5—5D—" Plainly, Julha had been uncertain of the proper numeration. Her voice was strained, and she spoke haltingly.

"After the animals disappeared, we went up the stair. No sign of anything amiss above. The trail markers were still up, but we tried twice to get out of the city and found ourselves lost. Have no explanation for this. At nightfall, returned to the tower-temple. Animals gathered in the usual way in the great hall. Tried to enter, but two barred the way. We have returned to base camp here. No messages recorded while we were gone. I asked the High One to put me under hypo-sleep again tonight—the dreams have been growing worse. He wishes me to allow them and record by brain-read, but they frighten me so I cannot stand that. No animals on the stair. We shall prepare emergency packs and try again tomorrow to leave the city. Cannot see how the markers became so confused. Hist Tech Zimgrald will now add to this report—"

The Zacathan in his own code completed the tape. Diskan looked once again at the girl.

"So you couldn't get out of the city either," he commented. "What happens to those streets when one tries to make the ridge? Does it affect everyone? And you had markers to follow—"

Her eyes were no longer wary or fearful. She was surveying him now as if he were a problem that interested rather than repelled her.

"Now"—Diskan reached for the neighboring disk—"what happened next?"

"Report 6A1. Set out at dawn for a new try to return to the ship. Saw party of three coming in—watched them from town lookout. The High One believes them to be Jacks. Remained on the upper walk. As they drew near, we noted animals about them, but in hiding. We kept to cover, but thought it best to withdraw to lower levels. Can only be old story of the treasure drawing them for a grab. If so, we may be alone, and Captain Ranbo and his men are—are already dead." There was a pause before she continued to record. "Hist Tech Zimgrald wishes to record that he believes this to be a Defense One action. He is unsealing arms, and we shall each carry them. The call for Mik s'Fan has dead-offed, and we have no unit to step it up. As far as we know, we are now alone—"

"We were—"

Diskan jerked around. She had moved on the bedroll and levered herself up with the use of her arms, manifestly fighting the muscle weakness left by the ray. "Please, help me up. Get the High One on the bed here. The bleeding must not begin again—I have no more plasta-skin or curb shots!"

He aided her to sit with her back supported against the wall and then hoisted the Zacathan carefully to the improvised bed.

"The Jacks shot him?"

"In a way. They had begun to burn holes in the walls up there. They plainly knew something of what they were hunting for—some of the ship's people must have been made to talk. The High One was trying to watch them, and there was a break—he was caught under a wall fall. I think they believed him dead, and that was when I saw their captain, wearing that—" She pointed to Diskan's discarded parka. "Why they didn't come on down here, I can't tell. But they hurried away. I got the High One from under the stone; he didn't seem so badly hurt then. Somehow we came down the stair here, but later he collapsed, and ever since—" She spread out her hands in a gesture of helplessness.

"And the dead man up there?"

She shivered, covered her face. "Later, I went up—He came after me, and I fired—I never really knew what happened."

"But they did not come down here?"

"No. I—I thought you were one of them. The animals—they come and look at us, then go. I thought you were going to use them against us. I've—" Julha gave a shaky laugh. "I've tried to talk to them, but it's no good. They are intelligent, you know; the High One is sure of that. But we haven't been able to establish any method of communication."

"You say these Jacks knew what they were after. Just what is that?"

Julha did not answer immediately but caught her lip between her teeth, as if to muffle any speech while she thought it over. Then she must have made her decision in favor of trusting him, for she began to talk swiftly.

"This planet was recorded about twenty years ago by a First-in Scout—Renfry Fentress." She stared at Diskan round-eyed. "Fentress—you?"

Diskan shook his head. "My father."

"Yes, I did not think you could be that old, unless you were mutant. Well, he vid-pictured the ruins as part of his report. And the Zacathan archivists became interested. They have the legend repository for this section of the galaxy, and every once in a while they think—and usually they are right—that they can uncover pieces of the Forerunners' history by exploring the base of such legends. This was one of those times.

"And, as most always, the rumor got out it was a treasure hunt, especially since the High One Zimgrald was put in charge of the expedition. He's made two very rich and exciting finds in the past— the Shining Palace of Slang and the Voorjan grave sites. Both of those were fabulously rich, though their archaeological value was beyond price. These legend hunts are always a gamble—

"Anyway, the Zacathans got exploratory rights here, with all claims to archaeological finds. They assembled a mixed staff according to regulations. I'm a Second Archaeological Techneer from New Britain, Mik was from Larog, and Captain Ranbo and his men, our two lab techneers, were all on loan from Survey."

"A small expedition," Diskan commented.

"Yes, but we were just to do the prelim survey, and then the real field force would come in, if and when our reports made it worthwhile."

"And you thought it would be worthwhile?"

"The High One did. We don't understand the whole process of legend tracing. The Zacathans are so much longer lived than we, and they have techniques of learning and mental storage we cannot equal. I know there is something here that excited the High One greatly. And I am sure we were traced by these Jacks because they are determined to loot what we do find. They can sell such treasure in any of a hundred or so undercover trading centers!"

"But—where did they go?" Diskan sat back on his heels. "I found a place where a ship or ships had planeted, and near there was a survivor cache—with its broadcaster on."

"But didn't that broadcast tell you who they were?"

Diskan shook his head. "Not in Basic."

"Then our people didn't leave it for us!" She folded her hands together. "I thought—perhaps they had to take off and had left it. Only they would have set a standard signal call."

"No. I got this coat there. And there were a lot of sealed containers, personal locked. Must have been a dump for one special crowd."

"Then, wherever they went, they intend to come back. But where did they go? And our ship—it must have gone also. Why?"

Diskan considered those questions. Suddenly, he knew that for the first time in his life, he was thinking swiftly and clearly, able to translate thought into speech unhaltingly. And he had a lift of new self-confidence.

"You said another ship was going to follow you here. Would they be waiting for some signal?"

"Yes—oh, yes. They were to conclude the work on Zoraster. And if our report was negative, they would then return to home base."

Diskan nodded. "There you have one possible explanation. Your ship could be used to deliver such a report. They might have this Captain Ranbo or some other member of his crew under hypo-control. Your second ship gets the negative and takes off for home base, leaving the Jacks free from interference, with plenty of time to clean up here."

"And they could be coming again—now!"

Diskan had picked up the com device from where he had laid it beside the tape reader. "What's this? And how does it work to track someone?"

"We use those to check on our people while exploring. There's always a chance of an accident, a need for rescue. When we're in the field, one of those can be tuned to an individual." She took the dial from him, examined it closely, and then looked up, a shadow of fear in her eyes.

"This has been select-set for me!"

"And they must have found it on your ship?"

She nodded.

"And so they could have one set for him, too?" Diskan indicated the Zacathan.

"I'm not sure, not without a lot of adjustment, which they may not know how to do. It works differently with Zacathans because they are telepathic."

"But if they do have one, they'll head straight here."

"Yes, but we can't get him up those stairs!"

"No, only there is the passage running on from this room."

"Mik went that way—" Julha's voice was very low.

"We may have a lot of time," Diskan told her, "we may have very little. But staying here, we have no chance at all. Have you any high Sustain? Enough to get him on his feet?"

"But moving him that way—it could kill him!"

"And staying here might kill him, and us, too. Or—knowing who he is, they might not want to kill him. He'd be a tool for them—after they broke him properly." Diskan was brutally frank, and he saw her flinch from the thoughts his words brought to mind.

"The young man is entirely right—" Delivered in a slow hiss, that statement drew their eyes to the Zacathan.

Though he still lay stretched on the pallet where Diskan had placed him, his eyes were now focused on his companions with the light of full understanding in them.

"High One!" Julha came away from the wall. He raised one four-digit, talon-clawed hand.

"He is right," Zimgrald repeated slowly. "These scavengers would like nothing better than to have such a key as me to turn in many locks. Thus, they must not have it—ever. Were it not that I can be, I believe, of some small service to our general purpose still, I would make sure of that myself. I do not think that I am unduly concerned with my own future when I say this to you. There is that here which perhaps can be swayed to your aid—if I can remain with you to aid— Your true help lies there—"

With infinite labor, he turned his hand to point to the furred one, still lying across the threshold.

"There is a way through these ruins that those know and use. Learn it from them, and you can hide indefinitely from any hunters. Haaa—"

The call he uttered was low, hissing, and directed to the furred one. The animal's head swung around, and it favored the Zacathan with one of those unwinking stares by which it, or its kind, had disconcerted Diskan in the past. Now the creature got to its feet and limped over to the Zacathan. Reptilian man and furred one matched stares for long enough to make Diskan uneasy.

"I cannot touch thoughts with it directly," Zimgrald reported at long last, "but it is my hope that it now understands that we are in peril here and must go hence. Whether it will be our guide, I have no assurance."

"Even with Sustain, High One, you cannot climb the stair," Julha protested.

"That is also right. Therefore, we must take the other road— along the passage."

"Mik—" Her lips shaped the name rather than uttered it aloud.

"Mik, yes, he went that way and he did not return. But for all of us, there is little other choice. To climb those stairs might be walking straight into the arms of the enemy. Whereas"—his yellow lips curved in a half smile—"we may leave behind us here that which will discourage followers—even if only temporarily. There are tools that can be weapons at need. Now, do you do thus—"

From the pallet, he gave quick yet clear directions. Things were sorted out of the general mass of the piled supplies and combined to his liking, though Diskan found that a measure of his old fumbling awkwardness returned. When the girl grew impatient at his ineptitude, the Zacathan sent her to make packs of the supplies they must carry. Under the alien's patient and concise exposition, Diskan became more sure.

In the end, he had a framework of tubing, to which had been attached by wire the high-voltage ever-burn lamp. He did not understand just what the contraption would do, but the Zacathan's reliance on the queer assembly was high, and Diskan was sure that Zimgrald was certain of its efficiency.

This was placed across the passage, a frail enough barrier. The furred one watched Diskan's actions with concentrated interest. When the young man returned to the room, Julha was on her knees by the pallet, about to administer a Sustain injection to the Zacathan.

"It would be good to know," Zimgrald remarked, "how much time the Armored Spirit allows us before disaster swoops like a grahawk. But that is another of the puzzles past our solving. Do not hesitate, little one. I am as eager to be away from this hole as the twain of you!"

His reaction to the reviving injection came swiftly, and when he got to his feet, he moved with only a small hesitation. Diskan swung the larger pack to his back; the girl took up the smaller. They went into the passage where the furred one lingered. As they came out, the animal turned and limped along the unknown way, Zimgrald at its heels with Julha, while Diskan brought up the rear. He glanced back once at the framework of the device he had set up in the corridor. According to the Zacathan, it would deter pursuit; Diskan had no idea how. He only trusted that it would.

☙ ⋆ CHAPTER 12 ⋆ ❧

ZIMGRALD CARRIED A TORCH but did not snap it on. The diffusion of light from the growths appeared to satisfy the Zacathan. Diskan could see no other sign that anyone else had trod this way before them. He began to marvel at the recuperative powers of the Hist Techneer, for Zimgrald was keeping a gliding pace equaling a fast walk for his two companions, while a little to the fore limped the furred one as guide.

"High One." Julha touched the shoulder of the Zacathan. "That Sustain shot, it will wear off—"

"All the greater reason, little one, for us to make speed now." There was an almost cheerful note in the alien's voice. "Do not concern yourself; our bodies are not alike. I shall perhaps surprise you with my ability to keep the trail. Fentress—" He raised his voice a little so the name boomed back at Diskan.

"Yes?"

"What is your knowledge of this world?"

"Very little. My ship crashed at setdown and rolled into one of the mud pools. I had been in freeze and so was lucky, for the emergency ejector got me out. There was a rising ridge of solid ground, and I came along that. Then I found the survivor cache—"

"And the city. But not without guidance. Now that is the truth, is it not? Guidance such as this." One of the four-digited yellow-gray hands gestured toward the furred one.

"Yes—"

"But you are the son of the Scout who first discovered Mimir. You must know more—" There was pressure behind that, Diskan knew. Perhaps the Zacathan had his own suspicions under his outward acceptance of Diskan.

But Diskan was not going to spill all his own past history at the bidding of this alien, even if that would settle the other's doubts.

"A First-in Scout visits many planets during his service. Not even he can remember them without a tape—" The minute he said that, Diskan knew he had made a mistake.

"A tape—ah, yes. You crashed on Mimir. Yet this world is far from any transport lane, Fentress. It is not on any commercial or open-travel voyage tape. There would be no normal reason for you to visit Mimir."

"I came for reasons of my own!" Diskan snapped.

He could see the pale oval of Julha's face as she glanced back, though Zimgrald had not turned his head. And Diskan thought that, even in this dim light, he could see the wariness again in her eyes.

"Reasons that might have something to do with those who seek us?" The Zacathan continued to probe.

"No!" Diskan hoped that the very explosiveness of that reply would carry the accent of truth. "Until my ship planeted here, I did not even know Mimir existed."

"Yet your ship came on tape if you were in freeze." No hint of suspicion, yet Diskan knew that he must satisfy the other or those questions would chip away at him.

"Yes, my ship was on tape, but I did not know the tape destination. It was blind chance that it was Mimir. I'm not a pilot; the ship was on auto. I don't even know why it crashed. I wasn't curious until it started the ride down and failed. Why the ship was on tape is my business, but I'll swear by any power you want to name that it had nothing to do with what you have met here!"

To his own ears that sounded a little too quick, too emphatic. Under the circumstances, he was not sure that had he been Zimgrald, he would have believed it. He was sure that Julha did not, for she walked faster, close to the Zacathan, lengthening the space between them. And perversely, Diskan allowed her to do that. Let them believe it or not—he had told the truth.

"You have satisfied my curiosity acceptably, Fentress. These odd-ities of blind chance do exist, as no one can deny. The X factor—"

"X factor?" Diskan repeated. Had the Zacathan meant what he said? Did he believe that Diskan was speaking the truth or was he only willing, for now, to accept the explanation, cloaking his doubts?

"Yes, the X factor—that which comes of itself to throw askew equations, speculations, lives, history, that unknown twist or turn of small events that changes a man's personal future, the work he would do, or the future of a people and an empire from one possibility track to another. One may have a problem close to smooth solving. Then the X factor arises to make the simple complex, all calculations wrong. Thus, to Mimir you may be the X factor, and to you Mimir may be the same. So I believe.

"This chance we cannot control or understand may have delivered you here at just this time. Ah—" There came a sound not unlike a human chuckle. "How interesting life may become without warning! This Mimir is a world of many puzzles; perhaps we shall add to that number. Now—what have we here?"

The passage ended. Julha gave a little cry, which held an under-current of fear. Diskan moved up to join them.

There was a vast expanse broken only by lines of huge blocks supporting a ceiling above, rising out of a weird marsh.

Though Zimgrald switched on the lamp, sending its powerful beam down the aisles between the pillars, it revealed nothing but pools of murky water, the fungi growths, a nightmare of swamp. The furred one lowered its head to sniff at the edge of a pool reaching to their feet. It hissed, spat, made a lightning-swift dab with a forepaw. There were ripples on the surface of the water, sending bobbing several padlike plants floating there. Then the Mimiran animal sat up on its haunches to look at the off-worlders. In warning? Diskan wondered.

Dare he try contact? He knew the danger of that reaching out, or thought he did. Why did it come to mind again now and with so strong an urge? He pushed aside fear and tried to reach the brain behind those burning eyes.

There was a sensation of dizzy spinning, of being caught and whirled about by a power much stronger than he was. Diskan heard himself cry out. He was in a panic because no effort of his could free him from the spin.

"Diskan!"

His head bobbed loosely on his shoulders; he swayed in the grip of the Zacathan on the very edge of that poisonous pool. Still the furred one sat upright, watching, reaching. Reaching, that was it! Of his own free will, Diskan had opened a door and through it something had reached for him, almost sucked him out into an unknown so appalling that he shuddered with the sickness the thought of it aroused in him. Had he been lost in that unthinkable, he would never have returned.

With the Zacathan's hands still on him, Diskan backed away from the animal, feeling as weak as if he had survived, just barely survived, some indescribable ordeal.

"What happened?" Zimgrald's voice in Diskan's ear was very steadying, as if he leaned his whole trembling body against a solid and sustaining support.

"I—I tried to make mental contact with—with that!"

His hand rose almost of itself and pointed stiffly at the furred one. The outthrust fingers might have been a stunner he was aiming in his own defense.

"Contact? You are a xeno-path?"

"I—sometimes I can make an animal, or a bird, do as I wish. Before I was afraid, but I did it now, I don't know why—!"

"And you found far more than you expected." No question, a brisk statement of fact. "Yes, these are telepaths to a high degree, though not of any order I have had previous knowledge of. But, again, this is luck. If you can establish better communication with them than I have been able to do—"

Diskan twisted free from the other's hold. "No! Never again! I tell you, it—it would take me!" He tried to explain, and his old inability to fit words and thoughts neatly together made him stammer. He was ready to defend himself from such a risk with a stunner—with his bare hands if need be!

Then common sense reasserted control. The Zacathan could not *make* him try contact, not unless the alien put him under some form of hypo-control. And he would make sure that did not happen. Diskan was about to voice that defiance when they were startled by a sound echoing down the passage from which they had just emerged.

Zimgrald's features, with their lizard cast, sharpened; his neck frill arose in a wide fan behind head and shoulders.

"So, they found our surprise." His words were close to a hiss. "We have very little time after all!"

Julha caught at the Zacathan's arm. "High One, what do we do?"

The Zacathan's frill fluttered and began to refold. "Why, little one, we splash forward—or rather we pick the best footing possible." He looked at the furred one. "This one knows what we want—escape. It will, I believe, continue to aid us. Certain emotions are strong enough to project in themselves—fear, hate, love—and fear we shall depend upon now to do our pleading for us. But it is best we move on. That surprise will deter them from the trail for a space, but it is no lasting barrier."

But they did not go forward, out into the swamp. The furred one dropped to all fours and headed right, along the wall through which the passage had entered. Zimgrald appeared quite content to follow the animal's lead. A hand on Diskan's arm, he pulled the young man forward, Julha on his other side.

Once again the Zacathan switched off the lamp. Diskan was about to protest when he saw the wisdom of that action. The far-flung beam might not only advertise their coming to some unknown menace ahead, but it could also be sighted readily by those following.

Here the luminescence of the growths was not quite so concentrated as it had been in the passage, but there was enough radiance to show them their footing, and the animal's, a few paces in advance.

"What is this place?" Julha ventured after they had gone a short way.

"Who knows?" Zimgrald answered. "For some reason, the city builders needed it. These piers must support a goodly portion of buildings above. But the why of this cave? Who can tell that?" His frill lifted a little as he shrugged. "In its time it had a use or it would not be. This city has always been wedded to water—"

"Yes," Diskan broke in dreamily, "the flowing streets, the cool, clean flowing streets—"

"Yes," prompted the Zacathan gently. "What of these flowing streets?"

For a second of time Diskan was back in his dream. "Sweet water, scented water—water of the streets of Xcothal—" His voice trailed off as he came out of that half spell and knew that both of them were listening to him alertly.

"You have dreamed?" Not gently now—a demand, quick and pressing.

"Once I walked in Xcothal with the water washing about me." Diskan gave the alien the truth.

"And what did you learn of Xcothal when you walked thus?"

"That it was beauty, color, light—a very fair place."

"And that you would walk there again if you could?"

"Yes—" At that admission he felt the Zacathan's grasp on his arm tighten and then relax.

"So they reached you—with that they reached you! You see, little one." Zimgrald spoke to the girl. "The dreams are not evil; they were reaching—"

She shook her head emphatically. "No! Those dreams were horrible; they threatened! I did not walk streets of water in beauty; I fled through dark hallways and ever they hunted me!"

"Who?" Diskan asked. "The Jacks?"

Again she shook her head, with even more force. "No, I never saw who—only knew that they wanted me. And it was very bad. We did not dream alike, though I, too, was in a city—"

"Xcothal—" Zimgrald repeated the name thoughtfully. "This name for the city, it is from your dream?"

"It is. And this is Xcothal—but not the one I saw then."

"Living flesh for a moment laid across the crumbling bones. You have some strange gift, Fentress, one that I envy you. In my mind I can build a picture when I look out over tumbled stones and long deserted buildings. Training, memory, surmise all give me bits to fit together into a picture, but I know that never is the picture the full truth. Sometimes it may fit close, but a line is wrong here and a curve there—"

Diskan had an inspiration. "The X factor?"

Zimgrald chuckled again. "Undoubtedly—the X factor. It is missing for me; it may not be for you. Perhaps you can evoke the picture that fits perfectly!"

"I'm no archaeologist."

"What are you, Diskan Fentress?" asked the Zacathan.

The old bitterness shadowed his reply. "Nothing—nothing at all. No—" The desire arose in him to shock, to break the Zacathan's calm. "That is not the truth. I am a criminal—a subject for stabilizing treatment if I am found!"

Julha missed a step, but Zimgrald gave a small sound like a snort.

"I do not doubt that either, Fentress; you are so proud of it, as a definite victory for you. But why do you consider it a victory? What life-vise are you fleeing in such haste? No, do not fret—I shall not pick below the surface you have chosen to shell you in. Only you are far more than you guess. Do not crawl into the mud when you can soar. Ha—do you notice anything about the atmosphere now, children?"

The quick change of subject left Diskan tongue-tied, but Julha responded.

"It is warmer!"

"I thought so, though the Sustain has given me protection against any chill. Now why is this so?"

Not only was it indeed warmer—the warmest Diskan had known, save directly by the fireside, since he had landed on Mimir— but the rank air carried another taint. Zimgrald sniffed, drawing in deep breaths and expelling them several times, before he gave a small nod.

"Warm springs, perhaps. A natural phenomenon, but hardly to be expected under a city, though we should always disabuse our minds of the 'expected.' There is never just *what* we expect. Our friend waits—"

The Mimiran animal had indeed halted at the foot of a broad stone, slimed here and there with splotches of evil-looking growths, angled to their left and lifting at an incline out into the open marsh. Zimgrald surveyed what they could see of it.

"A bridge of sorts. But watch the footing. On stone, those slime patches can be highly treacherous."

"They were!" Julha darted forward, to pick up and bring back a gleaming object. She held it out to Zacathan. "Mik dropped this!"

"A refill tube for a hand beam." Zimgrald identified it. "Yes, we might reasonably suppose this to be s'Fan's." He clicked on his more powerful lamp, bringing into brilliant focus that rising arch of stone and its approaches. Well up the incline was a smear. A body crushing one of the growths in a fall could well have left that sign.

"Mik!" Julha clapped her hands together. "He must be ahead of us—on this very way! He could still be alive, he could be!"

"It is possible," Zimgrald agreed. But inwardly Diskan doubted that the Zacathan was any more hopeful of finding the missing explorer than he was. "No, child." The alien put out a hand to restrain Julha. "Hurry here we do not! We cannot risk any accidents. See, observe the caution of our guide—"

The furred one had started up the bridge, if bridge it was, but as the Zacathan pointed out, the animal advanced with caution, weaving a crooked way that took it around those slime patches. And, gingerly, the three fell into a single line, to track in the same way.

As they went, the chemical fumes grew thicker, rising from the swamp. The reek reached them in puffs, as if exhaled in regular gasps. Once up the first approach, the ramp ceased to climb but leveled off and ran, as a rampart or road, straight out between two ranks of the thick block supports, into the general gloom of the cavern.

For spaces, the slime patches failed and the furred one hurried. Then would come another line of splotches, and they went back to their weaving in and out among them. Diskan thought that their guide not only feared the slipperiness of those smears but also knew that contact with them was dangerous. He remembered the stinging burn from the growth he had brushed against back in the passage and decided that such caution was well merited.

"Where can the end of this be?" Julha asked at last.

Time was only relative to action, Diskan knew, but they *had* been walking this raised road for what seemed a long period. He glanced back several times, trying to make out the wall from which they had come, but the limited light from the fungi made shadows close in behind them, and he could see very little. Meanwhile, the ramp stretched endless before them.

"The end, little one, is when and where we find it." Zimgrald answered her with a tired slur to his words. She must have noted that at once, for she caught at the Zacathan's hand, held it in both of hers.

"High One, you tire! We must rest, eat, see to you!"

Diskan half expected the Zacathan to deny that, and he was disturbed when the alien nodded agreement. Was the other beginning to fail?

"As always, little one, you speak with good sense. Yes, let us rest, for a short space only. And eat. Those are good thoughts to put into action."

They sat down in one of the spaces free from the slime, and the girl opened her pack, taking out ration tubes of a like brand to those Diskan had found in the cache. But she made the Zacathan swallow a tablet before he sucked at what was a mixture of food and drink in the container.

Diskan hesitated and then twisted in half the tube he held, the material of it coming apart under his strength, hardened by those years of physical labor. Keeping the oozing top section, he held out the other to the furred one.

The animal arose and limped to his side. Erect on its haunches, it held the tube to its mouth and squeezed out the contents with the claws of its forepaws. Now Diskan saw why something about those claws had puzzled him at the time he had first sighted one of this species. Claws and paws, yes, but the dexterity was that of a hand, not human perhaps, but still a hand.

He glanced around to find Zimgrald watching him. "They are not animals." The Zacathan might have been speaking Diskan's own thoughts aloud. "What are they? That is a very important question—what are they?"

And another important question, Diskan wanted to add but did not, is what do they want with us?

◦⋆ **CHAPTER 13** ⋆◦

THE WARMTH OF THE UNDERGROUND world was lulling. Perhaps the exhalation of the swamp carried a drugging quality. Diskan had no desire to go on. Neither did either of his companions appear eager to take to their feet again. Julha was watching the Zacathan carefully.

"High One"—she broke the silence first—"is it well with you?"

The edge of his neck frill stirred. "Do not fret, little one. This old creeper will be able to creep yet farther, if for no other reason than curiosity, which will not let me rest until I see what lies at the end of the trail. It is in my mind that this was once a place of water. They loved water—those who have gone, long gone, before us. But why it must wash the deep foundations of their walls and towers, that is only to be guessed at—"

"An amphibian, water-born race?" Diskan hazarded.

"Perhaps. There are such—or were such—just as there are races who fly or creep. Yet our friend here"—he nodded to the Mimiran animal—"is not of the water."

Greatly daring, Diskan risked a question of his own. "What do the legends say of Xcothal?"

Zimgrald smiled. "Very little. A hint—such an old hint—of treasure to be found in a city of the sea—"

"Treasure!"

The Zacathan's frill was rising to frame his lizard, shadowed face. "Ah, that is a word that makes the blood run faster, does it not? But

I believe that Xcothal's treasure is not that which one can hold in his two hands, count into boxes, feast the eyes upon. Oh, all races have their wealth, sometimes gathered into piles and stores. But if there was wealth such as that here once, I believe the years have seen to its scattering, and those Jacks will not find what they seek, not even if they dismantle Xcothal stone by stone—the which they are certainly not prepared to do."

"Treasure—knowledge?" Diskan speculated.

"Just so—knowledge. Always remember this, youth. Beneath the wildest tale from a people's past lies a crumb of truth. Sometimes that crumb may be very small and much distorted by rumor and legend, but it is there. And if it can be sifted free from all the accumulation of the years, then it is worth more than all the precious metal and gems a man may heap up to feast his eyes upon, for the feasting of the mind is the richer experience and lasts the longer. The hunters behind us pursue their 'treasure,' which may long since have ceased to be, but I do not believe it is the same I seek here."

"But royal tombs, storehouses—"

Zimgrald nodded. "Those can be found—and looted. And I may be wrong also. I have never claimed infallibility, my children. Look, our guide is growing impatient. I would say it is time we were once more on the tramp."

Diskan aided the Zacathan to his feet. For all his brave words to Julha earlier, it was plain that Zimgrald was failing. Their rest and food might have given the alien a return of strength, but how much longer he could keep going was a question. And as far as Diskan could see, there was no end to their present road.

The Mimiran animal, having seen them rise, turned and moved on, its head carried well up, as if it sought some airborne scent. But the odors from the waste below, Diskan thought, were enough to make anyone breathe less heavily. He kept a back watch for the enemy, but if the Jacks had passed the booby trap, they seemed in no hurry to catch up with the fugitives. Only the thought of the hunt made Diskan speed his pace until he was treading close on the heels of the other two.

"There is no need for pushing. The High One can go no faster," Julha snapped.

"I am afraid reason supports the thought that there is," Zimgrald told her. "We would present excellent targets for an attack, and I do not wish to leave this roadway unless there is no other choice."

With that, Diskan was in hearty agreement. He had the stunner with a close-to-exhausted charge and the blaster he had taken from Julha. But to stand up against a determined Jack rush with no more defense than that was sheer suicide.

A man did not turn Jack, preying on traders and colonists on frontier worlds, unless he was already an outlaw to the point of no return. And to get what they wanted, these looters would have no scruples at all. They might keep the Zacathan alive—until they had what they wanted from him. And Julha, as a woman, would be an extra bonus. Him they would burn down without a thought, and he would be the lucky one. But how could the Jacks be so sure as to center a major grab operation on Mimir? Was it just Zimgrald's reputation that had brought the pirates here—the fact that the Hist Techneer had made two outstanding archaeological finds in the past? That was a gamble nearly to the point of being stupid—and stupid the Jacks were not. Those who were died early and were not equipped for a planned raid the way these were. All they had done here bore the marks of a carefully thought out operation.

On the other hand, the Zacathan had been telling the truth a few minutes ago when he had said that the treasure he was after was not material. So, what did that mean? What secret from the past was so rich a find as to bring on a grab?

"What do they want here?" Diskan demanded out of his thoughts.

"Loot!" Julha said scornfully.

"But our young friend means what kind," Zimgrald said. "Yes, that has been a small puzzle among the larger for me also. They are very well prepared, these Jacks, and they have had detailed briefing on our plans. They are very sure that they are in quest of something worth such a major effort, as if they have had success promised to them. Yet I do not know what could be worth the risk and expenditure of this grab."

"You?" Diskan asked. Could it be that—a highly successful Hist Techneer to be kidnapped and kept on ice? But that would be pure speculation of the kind that was too great a gamble for Jacks with their need for a quick profit and an even more speedy getaway.

"Flattering." A chuckle warmed Zimgrald's voice. "But, except for how I may aid them here, I think not. The law of averages would dictate that no man can continue to make big finds year after year. No, what they seek is here, unfortunately for us. They believe that we have the secret, and that makes us important. Otherwise, they would write us off and go treasure hunting—to leave us wandering about this pile, marooned and helpless."

"Rrrrrrugggg!"

Julha cried out. The Zacathan's frill shot up and fanned. Diskan's hand went to the butt of the blaster. The furred one, who had been silent during their whole journey through this stinking pit, had uttered that nerve-rasping cry. It stopped short and reared on its haunches, its clawed forefeet advancing a little, its muzzle gaping to show fangs. There was no mistaking that stance—it was facing danger.

Diskan shouldered past the Zacathan and Julha, shucking his pack as he went.

"Get down!" he ordered with a thought of blaster fire sweeping the ramp road. He was in a half crouch, trying to pierce the gloom ahead, to distinguish the menace there.

After that first battle cry, the Mimiran animal was silent, but Diskan could hear the faint hissing of its breath.

"Zimgrald," he cried, "use the lamp!"

The broad beam might betray them, but it would also reveal what lurked there. That was better than supine waiting for danger to come to them, perhaps in a fashion for which there was no defense.

Yellow-white was the glare behind him, making his shadow and that of the furred one great black fingers across the stone. And it also showed, only too clearly to off-world eyes, that which squatted in the middle of their path. Diskan shrank back a step before he steadied. That thing was far worse than the monster he had faced in the pass. With all its alienness, that had been akin to beasts he had known on other planets.

But this repulsive thing was akin to nothing outside of an insane nightmare. The front portion had reared up above the main bulk and was weaving to and fro, an obscene pillar, tapering, having no features Diskan could discern, save a puckered opening, which moved with the swaying, opening and closing.

Glistening trails of slime oozed down the gray hide and puddled about the fat center portion of the thing. This or its kind must have left the tracks he had found in the outer city.

Diskan's revulsion was tinged with fear. The thing was huge, twice, maybe three times, his own not inconsiderable bulk. And for all its lack of visible eyes or other sense organs, he believed it was not only aware of them but also able to spot them exactly. Every indication was that it greeted them with hostile intentions.

He brought up the blaster, leveled it at that swaying head, and then judiciously moved the sights down to the fat roundness of the mid-body. After all, there was a good chance that the thing could be better hit in that more stationary part.

"Wait!" Zimgrald's order came just as Diskan was about to press the firing button, and such was the authority in it that Diskan obeyed.

The furred one had made one of its quick darts—not ahead at the slug thing but sidewise, against Diskan, carrying him to the right. Now the opening in the weaving pillar puckered into an outward pout and from that spouted a dark stream of liquid—too short, for it splashed against the stone merciful inches away.

Diskan fired, but his aim was poor, and the ray only clipped the pointed "head" of the creature. It writhed, looping the upheld pillar of its body in a fantastic whip of coiling and uncoiling skin and muscle. Sometimes it twisted back on its bulk in a way to suggest than any bony framework existing under those unwholesome rolls of flesh was not rigid.

"Wait!" For the second time Zimgrald rapped out that order.

But this time, Diskan was in no mind to obey. He strove to center the blaster on the middle of the bulk, only the movements of the creature were more frenzied, convulsive in their rapidity and force. Had that slight burn really done all the harm the thing's writhing now suggested?

There was a sound, as if someone had torn a length of fabric. Across the middle of the frantically threshing bulk, skin and flesh parted in a break that grew wider and wider as the motions of the creature sloughed it apart. The pillar gave a last titanic upthrust and then fell forward limply, to lie full length on the stone, revealing fully what was rising from the bag its actions had broken open, for it was as if the whole slug had been an encasing bag and the prisoner in it was now emerging. What it was was difficult, even in the light, to make out clearly, for it moved jerkily, pressed together, as if trying to hide from the lamp. Legs, yes—for one was flung suddenly aloft. A jointed leg as long as Diskan was tall, covered with a thin red skin that gleamed with shell sleekness. Then, like the slug before it, the creature gave a convulsive wriggle and straightened up.

Diskan heard a choked cry from Julha, a hiss out of Zimgrald. The thing was fully and fearfully clear, its elongated body poised several feet above the surface of the stone, supported on eight legs, the middle joints of which were taller than its back. There was a head, a round ball with eyes, or at least patches that resembled eyes, and a long tube it kept extending and then snapping back in a roll.

The slug had been repulsive and had stirred fear in Diskan, but looking at the thing now kicking its feet free of the shriveling skin, he knew this was a deadlier enemy. He fired.

The tube had snapped forward, a stream of liquid issuing from it. Then the searing blast caught the creature head on, and Diskan might have rayed directly into a cache of explosives, for the thing literally blew up. Scarlet flames scorched out of the midst of a sharp bark of air displacement.

Diskan staggered, blinded by the glare. He was unconscious of the pressure of a furred body against his own, shepherding him away from the edge of the drop. And the horrible smell set him gagging and choking.

"Zimgrald!" he managed to get out between gasps. "Do you see it?"

It must be dead, it had to be. But Diskan could not put aside so easily his fear that that horrible, insectival head might be still pointed at them. Why the impression of danger had been so intense he could not tell, but that they had escaped something far worse than any other danger on Mimir, Diskan was certain.

"Nothing—there is nothing—" Even the Zacathan sounded badly shaken.

Diskan rubbed his smarting eyes; he could see a little now. But to believe what his eyes reported—that was something else. Where that menace had been, entangled in the wrinkled folds of slit slug skin, there was, as Zimgrald had reported, nothing. Both slug and what had come out of it might never have been! The stone was bare.

"Did—did we just imagine it?" Diskan stammered.

The lamp beam moved. Now a slick smear caught in it, glossy in the light. Where the slug had spat at them, the trace of that remained. No, they had not dreamed it. But the bewildering effect of that last shot dazed Diskan.

"We did not imagine that—or that!"

Far back along the road they had come was a short cry.

The fireworks must have put the Jacks on their trail. The Mimiran animal was already padding on, over the battleground so strangely vacated. Diskan took the rear guard again. Zimgrald switched off the lamp and with Julha trotted after the furred one.

Diskan shouldered his pack and held the butt of his weapon close to his eyes, striving to read the amount of blaster charge remaining. Zero! He tapped it with an anxious finger, trying to make the indicator shift, but it remained the same. He restored the now useless weapon to his belt and brought out the stunner, though what use that might be against another transforming slug he did not know.

The knowledge that the hunt was now behind kept them going along that endless ridge of stone. Then the Zacathan called softly, "We are descending!"

That was true, and they had to watch their footing carefully as the thick patches of slime again splotched their way. But at last they were down, to be fronted by a wall with swamp water and growths all about it. The furred one turned to the right again, leading them to what Diskan could see only as a blank barrier. Then—it disappeared! He did not slack speed as he saw Zimgrald and the girl do likewise. In turn, he reached the slit giving into a passage running between an inner wall and an outer one. Here was no light at all, and he blundered on, knowing their full trust rested on the furred one.

It was very narrow, that passage. Diskan's shoulders brushed the chill wall on either side, and sometimes did more than brush, so he must turn sidewise to edge through. The warmth of the marsh was gone; the cold he had known outside on Mimir was biting.

"Another turn here, to the right—" Zimgrald warned him from ahead.

Diskan's outthrust hand saved him from coming up against a dead end, and he wriggled into that second runway. But there was a faint patch of light ahead, and the outlines of the rest of the party showed against it.

On they went until that gray brightened into a hint of sunlight, and at last they came out in the open with the crisp air about them. Zimgrald leaned against a block of stone. Both his hands were pressed to his bandaged body, and he breathed in heavy gasps. There was no doubting that the Zacathan was close to the end of his ability to keep going. What they needed now was a hiding place, and surely somewhere in the ruins of the city they could find that!

But, were they in the city? Diskan looked around, striving to find some landmark. The black bulk of the ruins was there, but now about them—between that and their present perch—was a stretch of blue mud-spotted marsh. Before them a kind of causeway, rough and broken, ran to a ridge. The same ridge that had brought them to Xcothal? Diskan could not be sure of that. They might have gone clear through the city and come out on the other side for all he knew. But the ridge, if they could reach it, promised some form of shelter. And the square of stone on which they stood under the whip of the wind was not a place to linger.

"We have to keep going—" Diskan moved to Zimgrald's side.

Julha half supported the Zacathan. She looked at Diskan with hostility. "He cannot!" she retorted. "Do you want to kill him?"

"I don't," Diskan replied shortly. "But this wind could—or those after us. We have to get up there"—he pointed to the ridge—"and as fast as we can."

The Zacathan nodded. "He speaks the truth, little one. And I am not finished yet!"

But he was close to it, Diskan knew, and that causeway was no easy path. He put the stunner away to leave both hands free and stepped forward, drawing the alien's arm about his shoulders.

"Down here." Diskan half carried Zimgrald to what looked the easiest way. "Keep right behind me," he flung at the girl. And those were the last sounds he made, except grunts, during that grueling journey. For once, the body hardened by years of labor did not fail him with awkwardness. He went slowly, but he made no missteps, and he moved Zimgrald along, even when more and more of the alien's weight sagged against him.

The trick was, Diskan speedily learned, to keep your eyes on the space immediately before you, to shove out of your mind all thought of the length of the track ahead or that at any moment the Jacks might explode onto the platform behind you, with you providing a fine target for a stunner—to freeze you until the enemy could collect you at their leisure. No, Jacks must be pushed totally out of mind, and the world *had* to narrow to the steps just ahead.

He was breathing heavily now, Zimgrald a dead weight. Under Diskan's ribs was a band of pain; his legs and back ached—Push that out of mind, too. Now, up the stone—there—Here was smoother walking. Now, up the next one—two strides—up the next step— Steps? Diskan's memory moved sluggishly. For the first time he allowed himself to look farther than the footing immediately ahead.

Rocks all around, and there was a line of steps before them—two, three—before another smooth stretch. They had reached the ridge!

✧★ CHAPTER 14 ★✧

"IN HERE!"

Dimly Diskan saw the girl waving vigorously up ahead. He staggered on, the pain under his ribs eating him, Zimgrald's weight almost more than he could support. Once more he made the effort and brought them up and between two rock pillars into a pocket where the wind did not reach and where Julha was brushing out the drifted snow.

He tried to lower the Zacathan to the ground but stumbled and fell with his burden, the alien sprawling half over him. Then for a time Diskan simply lay until jerks at his arm brought him back to a greater degree of consciousness. Julha leaned over him. Her eyes were fierce, as hating, he thought dully, as they had been at their first meeting.

"Get up! You must get up and help me! He is worse—help me!" She slapped Diskan's face with force enough to rock his head painfully against the frozen earth. Then her fingers hooked in the hood of the parka as she tried to tug him up.

Somehow he got his arms under him and braced his body off the ground, but the effort left him panting. He rolled back against the cold rock and blinked stupidly at the frantic girl.

The Zacathan now lay on his back with a plasta-blanket from one of the packs pulled up about him. His beak-sharp nose jutted out from a face where most of the flesh seemed to have melted away, so that the bone structure was sharply defined. His eyes were closed, and he was breathing through his mouth in small gasps.

313

Close beside him was one of the hand-port heat units—and its broadcast, though aimed directly at the Zacathan, also reached to Diskan, so that, half unconsciously, he moved his stiff hands into that welcome warmth. The pack the girl had carried and his own were open, their contents strewn around as if she had plundered both in a hurried attempt to find what she needed. And a medic-aid container was there.

"I tell you"—her hands were at her mouth, her eyes very large and fixed—"he is worse! I have no more Sustain. And he needs Deep Sleep and build shots. I don't have them!"

Diskan continued to blink. The warmth and the drugging fatigue, which made every movement an effort almost too great to bear, put a hazy wall between him and Julha. He could hear her words; they made sense in a dim way, but he did not care. He wanted to slip down, to let his leaden eyelids close, to just rest, rest—

The sharp sting of another slap brought him part way back.

"Don't you sleep! Don't you dare sleep! I tell you—he'll die unless he has help. We have to find it for him!"

"Where?" Diskan got out that one word dully.

"That cache—you said there was a survivor cache. There would be medic supplies there, all kinds. Where's the cache?" Her hands clutched the breast of the parka. She shook Diskan.

Cache? For a second the mist cleared from Diskan's fogged mind. He remembered the cache. There had been a lot of things there. Yes, there could have been a medic kit; he had not been looking for one when he explored. But the cache—he had no idea where that was now or where they were either.

He reached out, scraped up snow from a rock hollow, and rubbed it across his face. The chill of that on his skin brought him further awake.

"Where is the cache?" Her impatience needled him.

"I don't know. I don't even know whether we are on the right ridge or not."

"Right ridge?"

"We may have gone completely under the city and come up on the other side. If that's true—"

She sat back on her heels, her expression very bleak. "If that is true, he has no chance at all, has he?" Reaching out, she drew the blanket closer about the Zacathan's throat. "But you aren't sure of that?"

"No."

"Then make sure! Get up and make sure!"

Diskan grimaced. "Have you a packet full of miracles to shake out for us? I don't know this territory at all. It could take days of exploring to find out where we are. And, frankly, I can't get on my feet—not right now."

"Then I will!" She jumped to her feet, only to sway and catch at one of the rocks. She clung there, and her eyes filled, the tears slipping out to make runnels down her face.

"To collapse when he needs you?" Somehow Diskan summoned sense enough to point out to her what should already have been obvious. "We can do nothing, either of us, until we have rest, food— That may be hard for you to accept, but it is the truth."

Julha turned her head away and wiped at her cheeks with the back of her hand.

"All right!" But her agreement was delivered like a curse. "All right!"

On her knees again, she rummaged among the packs until she had found the ration tubes. One she tossed in Diskan's general direction, and he eyed it for several long seconds until he could muster enough strength to reach for it. Then he held it a space longer before he triggered the heat-open button. But once the tube did open and the aroma of its contents reached his nostrils, he found it easy to raise it to his lips.

It was hot, it tasted good, and it began to do its work against the haze of fatigue. When he had swallowed the last drop, Diskan looked around far more alertly. And it was only then that one thing about their improvised camp registered. One of their company was missing.

"The animal—where's the animal?" he demanded.

Julha was attempting to drip bits of the ration into Zimgrald's mouth. She shrugged impatiently.

"The animal? Oh, that has not been with us since we came across the stones to the ridge."

"Where did it go?" Why it was important to Diskan he did not know, but to learn that the furred one had left him gave him a curiously naked feeling, as if some support he had come to depend upon had been snatched away.

"I don't know. I haven't seen it since we came here. Does it matter?"

"It may, very much—"

"I don't see how."

"It brought us out of the city. It might be depended upon to help find the cache—"

"But I haven't seen it. It never came to the ridge."

Had it returned underground, Diskan wondered, considering some duty done when it had brought them into the open? And what of the Jacks on the trail behind? Julha might have been reading his thoughts, for now she said:

"The Jacks—what if they come here? We can't move him—"

Diskan brought out the stunner.

"The blaster charge is exhausted, and this is just about gone, too. But it is all we have. Let's see—"

Somehow he was able to pull to his feet and make a slow inspection of their present hole-up. He had to admit the girl had chosen well when she had guided him into it. There was only one entrance, a narrow slit that could be defended forever if one had proper weapons. And while the space was open to the sky now graying into dusk, the rocky walls were twice his height.

He lurched to the entranceway. The rock outside was bare, which stilled his fear of tracks. What snow Julha had brushed from the pocket had been spread away by the wind. They need not have a fire with the porto-heat unit. Yes, there was a good chance that in the night they would escape notice by any trailers.

"Listen!" He swung around. "I have the device they could have used to track you. What about Zimgrald. Can they now have one on him?"

"Not unless he wished it. I checked with Zimgrald, and Zacathans broadcast on another beam; their personality pickups can be intentionally scrambled, ours cannot. He scrambled his as soon as we knew what was happening."

Diskan was grateful for that information. The Jacks no longer had the girl's device; they had none tuned to him and none for the Zacathan—which meant they would have to do any tracking on the same level as a primitive hunter. And night was coming fast. Diskan did not believe that the Jacks would risk a scramble through this wilderness of rocks in the dark. He said as much to Julha.

"So we may be safe from *them*," she countered, "but the High One must have help!"

"There is nothing we can do tonight. A fall here could mean broken bones, and injuries for either of us would be fatal. In the morning I'll climb to higher ground and scout. If I can sight any landmarks I know and we are on the ridge land of the cache, then we can make plans."

She eyed him levelly and then picked up the stunner. "Well enough, or—not well, but what must serve. Do you sleep for a while; then I shall—"

Diskan wanted to protest, but common sense told him she was right. In his present state, he would fall asleep on watch. So he lay down in the heat of the beam near Zimgrald and was asleep even as his head turned on the ground.

When he roused again, with Julha tugging at him, there were no moons racing across the sky but a heavy roofing of clouds from which snow fell. The flakes hissed into drops on the warmed stones and ran in small streamlets down the rocks.

"How is he?" Diskan leaned close above the Zacathan. The shallow, gusty breathing continued. To his eyes, there had been no change in the alien's condition.

"He is alive," Julha said thinly. "And as long as he lives, there is hope. When he grows restless, put a little snow in his mouth. It seems to give him relief." She pulled the hood of her suit up and settled down beside the Zacathan.

Diskan held the stunner she had passed to him, watching the falling snow. If this was the beginning of a really bad storm, they might find themselves prisoners in this rock cleft in the morning. And yet Zimgrald manifestly could not last much longer without aid, aid that might or might not be found in the cache.

It was apparent that the Jack ship had returned—or had it? The party that had hunted them through Xcothal might have been left here to make sure of Zimgrald and the girl. If so, then the cache was for their convenience. But then Diskan did not understand the need for the broadcast that had guided him there. It certainly seemed that it had been set to pull in strangers. Who? Any of the archaeological expedition who had escaped the initial attack of the Jacks, as had Julha and Zimgrald? Or had the Jack ship, plus the spacer they had taken over from Zimgrald's people, both lifted so swiftly they had not been able to pick up all of the Jack crew planetside?

In any event, now that cache could well be the bait for a trap. The Jacks would expect desperate survivors to make a try for it. Thus, there was no chance at all for him to do as Julha wanted, to get in and out with medical supplies, escaping all detection. On the other hand, his thoughts flinched away from that alternative—that they must sit here and watch the Zacathan die, knowing all the time that there was a chance they were too prudent to take.

Diskan knew that there would be no arguing with Julha. Either he would make the try or she would. Of course, they might be so far from the right ridge that there would be no question of locating the cache at all. Diskan stood up, made one of his periodic tramps to the cleft entrance, and stared out into the dark—not because he expected to see anything there but because the action kept him awake and alert.

When he came back to the circle of heat by the unit, there was a small movement from where the Zacathan lay, and Diskan hurried to him. The alien's eyes were open and his lips moved. Hurriedly Diskan scooped up snow and strove to put it in Zimgrald's mouth. He did that three times before the Zacathan turned his head, refusing more.

"Julha?" The whisper was very faint.

"She is asleep," Diskan whispered back.

"Good. Listen carefully—" The labor of that speech was so intense that Diskan shared it vicariously. "I am—going—to—will—hibernation. I am very weak—so this may be self-killing—but it is—one—way—"

Hibernation? Diskan did not know what the Zacathan meant, but he dared not interrupt with any question.

"In my belt—" Zimgrald's hand moved under the blanket. "Get—mirror—"

Trying not to disturb the covering, Diskan felt under it. His hand was caught by taloned fingers and guided to a belt pocket. He brought out an oval of yellow metal so highly polished that even in the very faint light of the unit he could see it was a mirror.

"Julha—tell her—hibernation. Take care—"

"Yes?"

"The animals—they—have—the—secret—Open—a door—to them—if you can. Now—hold the mirror—"

Zimgrald must be slipping into delirium, Diskan thought, but obediently he held the mirror up before the Zacathan's eyes. The alien's gaze fastened on the surface of that oval in an unblinking stare. Time passed, the snow hissed down, and still those eyes held upon the mirror. Diskan's fingers cramped and then his arm. He must move!

Very slowly he attempted to change his position without lowering his hand. And as if that slight movement on his part had been a signal, Zimgrald's eyelids dropped, closed. The gusty breathing stilled—

Startled and frightened, Diskan touched the Zacathan's cheek. The flesh seemed as cold as his fingers. Dead! Had Zimgrald died as he sat watching? Diskan dropped the mirror, and the metal rapped against the top of the heat unit.

"What is it?" Julha sat up. She gave a little cry and bent over the alien. "Dead! You let him die—"

"No!" He tried to find words of explanation, of the right kind to pierce the fury he could sense was growing within her. "He told me to get this"—he picked up the metal mirror and held it out to her—"said he wanted hibernation—"

"Hibernation! Oh, no—no!" Swiftly Julha stripped back the blanket and felt the arching chest three-quarters covered by the plasta bandages. "But he did—he's gone into willed sleep! And nothing prepared, nothing!"

"What is it?" Diskan asked.

"The Zacathans—they can self-hypnotize themselves into trances for indefinite periods. But it is a great strain, and with his strength already so depleted—Why did you let him do it?"

Diskan arose. "Do you think my refusal would have stopped him? I do not read him as being of less will than either of us. How long will he remain like this?"

"Until he is brought out of it. But"—she tucked the covering back around Zimgrald—"perhaps it is better so. In the trance he knows no pain or ill. And when you return from the cache with what he needs—then we can rouse him." Diskan guessed that doubts of doing that successfully were very strong in her.

"Yes, the cache—"

If they could find the cache, *if* they could find it unoccupied, *if* the supplies there contained what they needed, *if* it was not a trap— all the ifs that had occurred to him during his time of sentry-go over- loaded the scales against them. Diskan had as little hope of carrying through such an expedition as Julha had of ever rousing the Zacathan.

She was busy now attempting to roll the alien's body more tightly into the blanket and spoke to Diskan impatiently.

"Help me! He must be kept warm while he is in trance."

When that was accomplished to her satisfaction and the unit set closer to a body that, as far as Diskan could tell, was that of a dead man, she began repacking their supplies.

The sky was gray, and the snow had ceased to fall so heavily. Diskan knew that he must satisfy her with some move.

"I'll go upslope," he said. "We ought to know more about the country before we make any definite plans—"

"I'll stay here. The wrapping, the heat must not fail. I'll tend the High One until you return. You see"—she hesitated and then continued—"there is a kin-debt between us. He took sire-oath for me before my birth, for my father was once his assistant and killed on one of his expeditions. Thus, Zimgrald came to my mother and offered her the protection of his house under sire-oath. She accepted, so I became a hatchling of his line. Always has he been as my father— though he is counted as a very great personage. And it was my good fortune to be able to serve him on this venture—the first time I have been able to offer him anything in return for all he had done for me. Thus, I cannot let him die—we are kin by the bonds of the heart if not the body." She spoke as if she recited aloud her thoughts, and Diskan believed in the truth of what she said.

"Keep this!" He held out the stunner. "I'm going up now—"

He squeezed through the cleft entrance and climbed the slope, avoiding all the snow patches he could. The light was better, and by the time he reached the top, he could see enough to give him bear- ings. It all depended upon this ridge's position in relation to the city.

The pull to the heights was not easy, and it took longer than he expected. But at last Diskan lay belly down on the crest of a small spur and surveyed the marshlands. There was the city, endless blocks swallowed up by a haze. He could see the causeway that had brought them to solid land. Along that nothing moved, though the black and white birds drifted in the sky over the rocky ridge land.

Slowly studying each few feet of the country as carefully as he could, Diskan turned. Then—that was it! The wide stairway down which he and the wounded furred one had come after their battle in the pass! This *was* the same ridge land—they had that one small advantage! And to his right, somewhere back in the saw-toothed ranges, was the cache. Against all good reason he was going to try to reach it. Julha would give him no other choice.

CHAPTER 15

"THE RIGHT RIDGE!" Julha's eyes glowed; she was transformed. "Then we can do it—save the High One. But you must hurry—"

Diskan knew she would not accept any argument now. In her mind, she had skipped over or pushed aside all possible dangers. In her mind, he had only to take a short walk, collect what they needed, and hasten back. If it were only that simple! But Diskan did not believe he could convince her that there were real dangers to be faced.

He tried to think of the few small things that did ride on their side of the balance. He had the parka taken from the cache; he was not wearing a protecto-suit, which the archaeologists used as a uniform. Thus, unless the Jacks really knew about him, which he doubted, he could pass for one of their company at a distance. And the cache had not been sealed. If he could cover the country between here and there by day, try to raid the cache at night—But it was with no real hope of success that Diskan made those vague plans.

Picking up one of the supply tubes, he put it in the front of his parka. The stunner rested on top of the bag. For a long moment, Diskan considered taking it. Then, regretfully, he knew that he must leave the weapon for Julha, that he could not deprive her and the unconscious Zacathan of that one small means of defense.

"Are you going now?"

He read only impatience in that.

"Yes. If I'm not back in a couple of days—"

"*Days!*" She caught him up.

"Yes—*days*. I can't jet across this ridge, remember? If I'm not back—do the best you can for yourself," he ended bleakly, knowing that to the girl he existed only as a means of aiding Zimgrald. It would be—be warming somehow if she could spare just a little thought for him. Outside the crevice, the day was dreary, and the snow came in gusts. Here was a pocket of warmth, but what was more, companionship, the knowledge that his own kind existed. His own kind? When had he ever been one with any—human or alien? Julha only gave him the same treatment now that he had always received. He was strength—to be used without thought.

Diskan scowled and made for the crack entrance—to face bared teeth, to hear a warning growl. The furred one was back, blocking that exit, though it did not appear to do more than warn. As Diskan persisted, it retreated before him, still growling, its whole stance a threat.

He came fully out of the crevice. The furred one crouched on the ground, its whip of a tail lashing, as it snarled and hissed. Yet Diskan was certain that its anger was not directed at him but at his actions. He took another step. The animal leaped, striking against him with enough force to send him staggering back against a rock, but those fangs did not snap. On the ground again it crouched, ready for another spring.

"No!"

The furred one stiffened, then fell, only its eyes alive and watching him with such intensity of purpose that Diskan was more than a little alarmed. Julha had followed him out; now she lowered the stunner she had used.

"Go on! I used only a small charge, so go quickly!"

What if the creature had been trying to warn him against some danger? Diskan climbed a point of standing stone and looked around. He could see the dark line of tracks where the furred one had come from the marsh below. But, save for the birds, nothing stirred there.

"Go on!" Julha's voice rose. Her arm was out, her hand raised as if she would push him away.

Diskan jumped down and caught up the helpless animal, now a limp weight in his arms.

"What are you doing?" the girl demanded harshly.

"I'm not leaving it here to freeze," he told her bluntly. "It guided us out of that place—"

"But it attacked you just now!"

"It tried to keep me from going out. It didn't use either teeth or claws. You let it stay here, understand?" For the first time, Diskan barked a direct order at her as he put the furred one down in the hollow of the crevice not too far from the Zacathan, where the heat would keep the immobile creature from the cold. Then, without another word, he went out, to begin the climb upslope for the second time.

It was a long day and a hard one. Diskan did not sight any living thing to share the white and gray world, save one or two flights of birds, high in the sky over the marsh. There were tracks in the snow but none he could identify as belonging to the furred ones, and certainly none of them were made by off-world boots. However, he kept to cover and crossed bare rock with the caution of one who has hunters sniffing at his trail.

In the later afternoon, he studied the valley of the cache from a concealed vantage point. Nosing into the sky was a ship. In lines it was not too far different from the slim government spacers Diskan had seen many times. But there was no Service insignia above the door hatch. That was closed only by the inner door, and the long tongue of the entrance ramp was out, its lower end on the soil.

Not too large a ship. Diskan tried to estimate the number that might make up its crew, but he knew little of ships, and the Jacks might put cargo space to use for extra fighting men. The best thing was not to guess at all, just be prepared for the worst.

One thing—the broadcast of the cache beam no longer sounded. It could even be that, having returned, the Jacks had dismantled that entirely. He could not be sure until he circled to that side of the valley. And the coming dusk would give him protection for that maneuver.

The impossibility of any success was like a dead weight on his shoulders, a cloud over his thinking. Diskan had never been the quick-witted improviser, and he had no hopes of suddenly developing any such ability now. The only course before him was to move along the valley wall and see what *did* wait to be faced in or about the cache.

If he had been cautious before, Diskan now became so tense that he fell twice, both times lying for long moments, fearing he did not know just what. Every time he dared look at the spacer, there was no change, no sign of activity about the ship. Snow had drifted about the foot of the ramp—filling in shallow depressions that must mark footprints, leading off in the general direction of the cache. If snow gathered about there without melting, the ship had planeted long enough ago to let the ground cool from the deter rocket blasts.

Twilight drew in, and Diskan put on more speed. The rough footing was too difficult to cross in the dark. But the snow was falling again, and if he could get down to the level of the valley floor, it might cloak his movements. Somehow he made that descent. There were no lights showing. Perhaps the invaders were in their ship, or they might be roaming Xcothal. Diskan devoutly hoped that the latter was so.

He was able to sight the glow of the cache walls—so it had not been dismantled. But this was now a case of extracting an egg's contents without cracking the outer shell. If the bubble structure had occupants and he walked in on them—The whole expedition was hopeless. But squatting here behind a bush, with the snow plastering him and the wind slowly congealing flesh and blood, was no answer either. Something stubborn within Diskan would not accept retreat.

So he slunk around the cache, approaching it in a gradually narrowing circle. No tracks—so no one had come recently. Probably he could walk right up and in—His feet were growing numb—these boots, stout as they had seemed when he began this venture, were not made for tramping through snowdrifts. And his fingers were so cold that he held them in his armpits to bring back a feeling of life.

Now he was opposite the door. He put out one of those cold hands, touching the bubble surface, ready to activate the lock.

"Jav tiltmi's lure—?"

The snow had muffled the sound of any advance. Diskan started with shock; then a hand caught his shoulder. The speaker was level with him. The shock that had momentarily stunned Diskan's thinking processes held just a fraction too long. He tried to spin out of that hold but instead was thrown forward by an impatient shove, going on through the now opened door into the lighted interior of the cache.

Too late—there were two men there, both facing him. Diskan jerked back, to come up against the one who had pushed him in. He was too slow and clumsy. Before his poorly aimed blow got home, the other struck, with sure science. And the lights, the room, the world, vanished for Diskan.

He was floating on a sea, easily, contentedly. There was a murmur of sound somewhere, at first lulling, part of the soothing rock of the waves. Then there was a ripple of uneasiness that troubled his content, shook him. Words—someone was talking. And it was very important that Diskan learn what those words meant, who was talking. He began to concentrate, with an effort that was difficult to maintain, to separate one word from another.

"—landed in a mud bog and sank. I came ashore—on the rocks. It was very cold and it was nighttime. There was a fire, where the ship crashed, before it rolled into the mud—"

That—that was the way it had been! The spacer crashing—and he had come ashore on the rocks, watched the fire and wanted its heat. It had been like that! He was Diskan Fentress who had run from Vaanchard by a stolen tape and had landed on Mimir. But who knew all this? For the voice was going on, detailing all that had happened— not only all that had happened but also what had been in his mind at the time. And who knew that? Diskan Fentress knew. The uneasy ripple was now a sharp stab of fear. That was *his* voice, going on and on, talking in that swift gabble, without his mind or will, only his memory dictating the words.

But how could that be? He was not willing that run of words. In fact, his mind was listening, not speaking. He could not define the process any better than that.

A babbler! He was either under the influence of a babbler device or some drug that worked in a similar way! And he would continue to follow the past in detail for anyone listening—without the power to delete a single experience of the past few days. Which meant that those listeners who had put him under would learn of the escape from Xcothal and the place where Julha and Zimgrald now were—as well as if he took the enemy by the hand and led them directly to the right spot. They might accept a running report, without demanding too much in the way of detail, on his early experiences on Mimir. But Diskan did not doubt they would take him through the ruins step by step, and the drug or machine would bring to the surface of his memory details so trivial that he had not even realized he had noted them at the time. There was nothing he could do about it—nothing! He would have to lie here helplessly and hear himself betray those who counted on him.

The monotone of the voice continued, not seeming in the least to belong to him, and Diskan tried to think. He was as much controlled as the robot watcher had been back at the space port—until that watcher had been short-circuited.

Diskan thought of his fingers. Move—move, fingers! If he could move them, then there might be hope of—But his body did not obey any command he sent. He could not even raise his eyelids to see where he lay, who listened to his babbling speech.

It was no use—they had him! They could use him to the full, and after that it would not matter in the least what they finally did with him. The despair sent his mind reeling, seeking complete unconsciousness and oblivion.

But Diskan was not to reach that welcome blackout for which he strained. Instead, he once more became aware of his words, and they were such as to deliver a counter shock.

"—the natives guided me north. They have a settlement well beyond the ruins. Aliens, but can be reached by alpha power—"

But that was nonsense—natives? The furred ones? They had no settlement that he knew of. And what was alpha power? This was no memory of his, disclosed by a babbler. Completely confused, Diskan listened as intently as he could.

"Readily accessible, willing to make contact. They know the ruins but consider them taboo. However, they will not object to off-worlders visiting there, since they believe that any curse will fall on the intruders, not on them."

"Treasure." Another voice, faint but audible. "What about the treasure?"

"Natives have traditions of two rich burial sites. Asked me if I was among those who strove to disturb the Elders. Said that such would bring upon themselves the wrath of the shadows, but that was not their concern. The places are in the city—under the center tower. Showed me from the outside. You go—"

Directions, detailed directions, for reaching the hub of Xcothal and a place within the tower. But that part of Diskan's mind now listening and alert had no memory of all this.

"And the archaeologists, what of them? Have you seen them?"

"The natives spoke of them, said that the Shadows swallowed them up. They defied the guards set by the Elders. There is no need to defend what lies there, the natives say; the city can take care of its own, how the natives do not know."

"All right. He's given us what we need. Bring him out of it, now!"

What they did Diskan did not know, but there was a click somewhere within his mind, as if one intricate piece of machinery was brought into place against another. He opened his eyes and looked up at the two men watching him. Neither one was a racial or planet type Diskan could recognize. The skin of one had a blue tinge, and his coarse, brindled hair grew down in a sharp point until it almost met his bushy brows. He wore a space officer's undress coverall and had a blaster prominently belted about him.

The other had on a well-cut, well-fitting travel tunic, breeches, and boots of an inner system man. He was something of a fop, following the latest fads, for his skull had been completely denuded of hair and the bare skin tattooed with an intricate design, which a filigree skull cap of gold emphasized. Diskan had seen his like at the space ports, a Veep from some decadent trade world, but to see such a man here was a surprise. His type was as much out of place on Mimir as Diskan had been on Vaanchard. Now he smiled, though the goodwill suggested by that stretch of thin and colorless lips did not reach, nor was it intended to reach, his slightly protruding eyes.

"We have to thank you, Fentress. And your report has cleared one minor mystery, as to why the tape we were at such pains to obtain from your father's collection was so far wrong as a guide. Luckily, we tested it before taking off; otherwise, we might have lost a vast amount of highly valuable time.

"You *have* cost us some of that essential time, young man. But tonight you have given us that which makes up for such delays. You realize that we have had you babbling?"

Diskan nodded. He was still trying to take stock of the situation. There was a third man present, wearing inner system dress, but of a less elegant cut. A medic's symbol on his tunic meant he must be the private medic of the Veep; perhaps his drugs had provided the babble.

"Good. We had thought to learn a rather different story from you. But that is not important now. These natives, you say they will not oppose entrance to the city.

"Yes," Diskan improvised.

"These planet taboos are sometimes helpful then. A lucky situation. They are willing to let us provoke any curse and are so not inclined to prevent exploration."

"A trap, Gentle Homo? They might have planted such a tale," broke in the medic.

"Of course. But we need not spring any trap ourselves, need we? We have those who can do it for us, including our young friend here—unless, of course, he *wants* to be reprocessed in some correction lab. And do not believe that I shall hesitate in turning you over to the authorities to do just that, Fentress, unless you agree to be sensible. Your flight from Vaanchard puts you directly into the 'unreliable personality' grouping, and you can be given to the Patrol whenever I choose, with a cover story locked into your memory pattern to satisfy our purposes. It is always best to get on a footing of complete under-standing at once, isn't it?"

Diskan knew very little of what could be done to a man's brain. What this Veep threatened could be possible. They might be able to plant false memories, just as they had been able to make him babble, ship him off Mimir, and turn him over to the Patrol as an escaped criminal. Only, they thought he had really babbled, that they knew the truth of what had happened to him here, and they did not! What had fed all the false information through his lips? These "natives"— the furred ones? He could only take action now as it came and wait for an explanation.

"All right." He had hesitated before giving that agreement, but perhaps that was natural. Apparently the pause raised no doubts in the Veep.

"Yes, of course you will cooperate, all we need you to. Now I suggest a period of rest; we need not begin our expedition until tomorrow. You, young man, will remain where you are. If you wish to escape undue fatigue, accept my word that you are under muscle lock stass and that beam will not be lifted until we are ready for you to move. To try to raise so much as one finger will be a failure. Scathr nur gloz—" He switched from Basic to another tongue and picked up a fur-lined cloak, shrugging it about his shoulders, pulling a visored hood up to cover his head and most of his face. The medic did the same, and they passed out of the range of Diskan's vision.

The blue-skinned space officer came a few steps closer to stand over the prisoner. With one boot he toed Diskan, whose body moved stiffly as if all joints were locked into place.

"You babbled, you swamp worm." He spoke thoughtfully. "And loose babble cannot be faked. But these natives—we didn't see any. How come you found them so neat—like you were in a straight entry orbit?"

"They found me—" Again Diskan improvised.

"And maybe they're going to find us." The Jack's hand went to the butt of his blaster. "Let us hope they keep to this 'you blast your way and I'll blast mine' policy. If they don't, there may be some blasting they won't like. And you could just be in the middle if we come up against any cross—"

He toed Diskan again and then went off, leaving the prisoner with a frustrating collection of unanswered questions.

ۚ★CHAPTER 16★ۗ

DISKAN LAY IMMOBILE, his eyes closed but his mind very busy. They had had him babbling, and he had talked all right, but some of that information had been false. And he still could not understand how that had happened or from where that information had flowed, seemingly to convince his captors. The "natives"—who? He was certain he was being used to funnel the Jacks into Xcothal; that was apparent. But this business of the curse and the city that had its own defenses—which the Jacks would dismiss as superstition.

And the Veep here—What did the Jack believe lay hidden on Mimir—something so rich as to attract backing from an inner system grandee, actually bring him to share the operation? But perhaps he thought his pirate employees would develop sticky fingers if not right under his eye. What Julha and Zimgrald had told Diskan made sense, that the Zacathan's name was associated with two famous archaeological finds in the past, thus making his presence on Mimir a gamble good enough to draw an ordinary Jack raid—but not this setup under a Veep! Such a man could back a grab, but to come along himself meant so big a haul as to be worth the risk.

That reference to the tape from his father's collection. Was it the tape he had seen Drustans take from the rack? But Diskan could not accept that his father, or the Vaans, had had a part in any Jack grab. Diskan tried to remember who else had been there that night. A Zacathan from the embassy, a Free Trader, and there had been other off-world guests. But he had paid so little attention to any of them, had been so buried in his own hole of misery, that they had been only fleeting faces to which he could not now set names. And Drustans' connection with any one of them? No answers there.

But one thing Diskan did know—with the Veep in the open this way, his own life, and that of any witness, was no longer worth a puff of breath once his usefulness was over. The Veep might talk of having Diskan in a vice because of his flight from Vaanchard and the stolen spacer, but a dead man was even easier to control. He could be simply left anywhere on this planet; if found later, he would be accepted as an unfortunate survivor from a wreck. And Zimgrald and Julha, if they were located by these, could expect no other fate either. Perhaps already all the rest of the archaeological expedition's personnel were dead.

For the moment, and a very short moment that might be, the Zacathan and the girl were safe. Diskan had not babbled about them, thanks to the false information for which there was no sane accounting. The Jacks would probably head for the city in the morning, using him and the other hostages they had mentioned as shields to test any trap in Xcothal. And in the open, he might have a chance for escape, if a very slim one.

Natives? His thoughts kept circling back to that. The furred ones—it could only be the furred ones. And there was one way— Diskan shrank from that; he would have shivered had such motion been possible to his stass-locked body. This was far more difficult than that climb up the unstable cliff, the march across the underground bog, the fight with the slug thing, the carrying of Zimgrald to the ridge. Diskan had never feared so much the risking of his body, but this meant the risking of something else, a part of him he did not want to gamble. Yet, twist and turn though his thoughts did, they always returned to one solution, probably the only one.

Diskan at last faced the truth of that and made himself accept it. Then, before panic swept away all courage, he did it. The lame furred one, he concentrated on that one, building up in his mind the clearest picture he could mentally paint of the furred body, those compelling eyes, as he had seen the Mimiran animal last, before Julha had struck it down with the stunner. Surely the effects of that ray had worn off now, and it never dulled the mind when used on a low-charge.

In that mental picture, the furred one's eyes grew larger and larger, flowed together to form a great dark pool or tunnel or space into which Diskan was drawn, faster and faster, whirling in, spinning around.

He could not break away now because he was not summoning the other, as he had summoned animals on Nyborg, the varch on Vaanchard, but was being summoned instead. And that feeling of utter helplessness in the grip of relentless power was so terrible that he was absorbed instantly in a battle to keep some rags of his identity, not to be diffused in a darkness where Diskan Fentress would cease utterly to exist.

The dizzying whirl *could* be fought, he discovered. He was still himself, a small hard core of man. Content to keep that, he relaxed a small portion of his resistance. Now it was like hearing himself babble, having no control over either words or the memory that produced them. Communication was in progress all about him. He could catch a word, a thought, tantalizing in its almost intelligibility, but never enough to make sense. Babble—could this have been the influence that had so skillfully planted the false information in his mind?

A feeling of growing impatience. He shrank from that. This was the old sickening frustration of being the one completely out of step, of being trapped in a round of stupid action when mind and body did not mesh. But to his loss of confidence there was this time a prompt response, an understanding that amazed Diskan. And there clicked into his mind a picture so vividly presented that he might be viewing it with his eyes. What *were* these furred ones that they had such power?

On the last of those stone steps he had once descended to enter the bogged streets of Xcothal lay a pile of driftwood. A fire to be built and then the addition of branches to which frozen red leaves were still attached. This must be done before they entered the city. It was imperative!

Diskan assented, how he did now know. And then he was whirling again, sick and dizzy, being ejected from the dark pool of the furred one's eyes. But he brought with him something he had never known before in his life and did not realize even yet that he had, though it steadied his spirit, quickened his thinking, and was an

armor against what might come. For the first time in his life, Diskan
Fentress knew a kinship founded in trust.

Consciousness spoke to consciousness, picking up another mind
here, there, across feet or leagues, causing a stir as wind might ripple
a pool; yet this was a far more purposeful ripple.

*Response, brothers, at last! A seeking to answer our seeking. Give
now the power and see what is the final fashioning. We have tried this
one, will try again. Perhaps at last we have a shaping to serve our
needs! The uniting—ah, brothers—think upon the uniting after all this
weary space of time.*

And the others?

*After the manner of their spirits, let them advance or retreat or be
served as they would serve. The lizard one, the female, they are not for
our shaping. Among these new ones—who knows—perhaps we shall
find more. But there is one, this one, my brothers, who lies ready.
Concentrate upon the shaping. Let the word go forth!*

So he was to build a fire on that last step and add the leaves to it,
Diskan mused. The furred one willed it so, and from it would
come—? Then he remembered Zimgrald's last words before the
Zacathan had willed himself into a trance.

"The animals have the secret—"

Diskan had thought those words born out of fever, but perhaps
not. What secret? That of the treasure? What treasure? And what had
the leaves to do with it? The first night when he had dreamed of the
city, long before he had known that it existed in reality, he had been
in the valley of the red-leaved wood, had used some of those to feed
his fire, had awakened under branches that still bore them. Leaves,
the spark-filled smoke—some drug to summon up the far past in a
dream?

Was he being ordered to return the Jacks to the Xcothal that
was? Yes, that was what the furred ones wanted. And it might just
work. If he could keep his own sense and the rest of the party were
drugged—! But what reason could he give his captors for building
such a fire? Order of the natives before going into a sacred city?
Would the Jacks or the Veep accept that? No use worrying now; he
would have to take such problems as they came. With a confidence
he had not known before, Diskan decided that tomorrow's action

would have to be improvised and that tonight he could do nothing. As if he let go some anchorage with that, he drifted into sleep.

The next day was one of the bright, clear ones that appeared to alternate with storms on Mimir. As the party set out from the cache, to be joined at the ship by the Veep and a man wearing the badge of a personal guard, together with the medic, Diskan wondered what this world was like in a warmer season. The bogs must be twice as treacherous and the waterways bad traveling, but these valleys in the ridgeland might be pleasant—not that he was ever likely to see them so!

Three Jack crewmen all well armed, the Veep and his two, and one of those a professional guard not only expert with the usual weapons but also in all the various forms of unarmed combat as well—that was their party. No wonder they had released Diskan from stass and allowed him to travel unhampered by any bonds. To try a break from such company was simple suicide.

At first, Diskan was uneasily aware of the guards at his heels, but by the time they reached the traces of the ancient road on the crest of the heights, his apparent docility had had its effect. The Jacks kept close, but they no longer watched his every movement, now giving more attention to the countryside. And a wary watch that was. The space officer's distrust of the "natives" must have been shared by his crew.

But perhaps they felt a little of what Diskan knew to be a fact. This rocky ridge was not empty of life as it had been on his return to the cache. Though he saw no paw prints in any snow patch nor caught the least hint of any scout, yet they were under observation, and many watched them on their way.

"These natives"—the Veep, cloaked and mask-hooded, moved up beside Diskan—"where is their village?"

Diskan stabbed a finger in the direction toward which they now headed. "There—"

"And they will make no trouble when we enter the ruins?"

Diskan allowed his expression to go stolid. If he had babbled long and loudly enough about events leading up to his landing on Mimir, and he must have, then the Veep would be expecting dull acceptance from him now. He had never tried to play any part, but he had only to think himself back to the days on Vaanchard and the rest would be easy. However, here was a chance to do a little preparation for future action.

"Why should they, Gentle Homo?" he asked. "It is their belief that that which guards the ruins will protect itself without any aid from them. They only say that the watch fire must be built to insure that it does not issue forth from the city in its anger at being disturbed."

"A watch fire?"

Diskan knew that the eyes behind the visor of the cloak hood were measuring him with dangerous intentness. The Jack officer had one kind of cunning and the force to back his decisions. This Veep had higher and more dangerous powers of the same order. He was not a man to be easily fooled.

"A fire must be built at the entrance of the city. This is very important to them. They did it when they took me in. I think it warns off what they believe lurks there—but the fire only acts so for a space."

"And you saw nothing dangerous during that visit?"

"Only tracks—" Diskan thought of the slug paths.

"Tracks? What kind—off-worlders'?"

Diskan shook his head. The Veep had been quick to ask that. But the Jacks had been exploring in Xcothal—twice, maybe more times. Why this pretense that they had not come to the city before? And where were the other hostages the Veep had spoken of last night? Diskan almost broke step. Suppose the Veep already knew about Zimgrald and the girl and intended to pick them up now?

"Strange paths on the earth," he answered mechanically, while he imagined what might happen, "marked with slime. Some were very large—"

The Veep nodded. "Some native swamp creature, only to be suspected. But those Imbur's men have already reported. They seem to be nocturnal and need not be feared. And that was all you saw?"

"Yes," Diskan answered absently. For the past few moments, a sense of not being a prisoner alone among his enemies but a scout of another force had grown so strong that he began to fear he might betray the confidence building in him now.

"And they do not fear that this treasure will be found and taken from the city, these natives?"

"It is not their concern." The words arose easily to his lips as they had when he had babbled, and Diskan let them come, content to listen himself to what might be a subtle message concealed in a spate of vague information. "They consider it a matter of the Elders, to be handled by the guards *those* set,"

The Veep beat his gloved hands together as if his fingers were chilled. "Their confidence would seem excessive under the circumstances." That might be his own thoughts rather than a remark addressed to Diskan. "Of course, they may not have dealt with off-worlders before."

Diskan did not have to turn his head to know that the eyes behind the visor slits were trying to penetrate to *his* thoughts, watching for any clue as to whether Diskan knew of the archaeologists.

"I do not know—only what they told me."

"Told you?" the Veep repeated. "They speak Basic—but that would mean that they do have off-world contacts."

Diskan waited for a clue, but he dared not be silent too long. Then he replied; "They think messages—in mind pictures."

Had he been right to disclose that much truth? Nothing from the hidden watchers either assured or protested.

"Telepaths!"

Yes, the Veep could accept that. There were several known telepathic races, and, Diskan recalled with a chill at perhaps having made a bad mistake, one was the Zacathan. But he had said it and must now wait on results.

"Telepaths." The Veep was smiling now, the lips showing under the edge of the visor definitely curved. "Well, another link in the chain. No wonder the High One chose to do his hunting here with so small a party. Also, perhaps why these think they have nothing to fear from explorers in their city. Remote controls—But I am afraid, Fentress, that our ingenuity can overcome even such alien preparedness. We have our defenses and offenses. Also, we shall have you and others to spring any traps."

Diskan understood the other's confidence. Every one of the party, except himself, was strung about with weapons and various devices. Some must be detection and location units. They had had those on all morning. He did not believe that either the Veep or the Jack officer would have started before taking every precaution possible to galactic science and ingenuity. Yet, they had *not* detected the watchers, and he did not believe that they knew he was in slight contact with the hidden ones. Therefore, Mimir's people did have that which could baffle off-world defenses.

"They say that the city *can* protect its own. I don't know how." Diskan tried to make his voice heavy and sullen. And perhaps he was successful, for the Veep laughed.

"No, you wouldn't, would you, Fentress? Ah, rendezvous as ordered, and right on the proper tick of time."

Three figures moved out of rock shadows into the full sunlight. One was a Jack, armed like his fellows, The other two—Diskan thought they walked with an odd jerkiness, as if each step were taken to order. But he could have shouted his relief. Neither was Zimgrald or Julha.

As the parties joined together, he got a good view of the other captives.

"Drustans!" That cry of recognition was startled out of him.

But his Vaan stepbrother was—was gone! This stranger shambling along on curiously stiffened legs, his features frozen blankly, his arms tight to his sides, as if held there by invisible bonds, was far from the lithe, graceful, supremely confident person who had increased Diskan's sense of inferiority and clumsiness every time he looked at him. And the other with Drustans—a Survey crewman by his uniform—walking with the same stilted gait, his face expressionless, his eyes locked on something inward—

"Yes, a family meeting." The Veep's smooth voice purred. "Unfortunately, Drustans came to know too much, so we had to bring him with us when we left Vaanchard. He had played several roles for us—that of research expert, and then hostage, and now to research again—or should we say scouting? Ah, perfect, Fentress. I think you once wished to be a First-in Scout, following in your father's orbit as it were. Well, now you are about to realize that dream, a little late. I would also advise you to note the present condition of these Gentle Homos. They caused us difficulty—at first. But now they agree perfectly to all our plans. They will carry out any order, including turning on each other—or you—should the need for drastic discipline arise. So far you have been more cooperative, Fentress. Continue to be so and you will not have to be reduced to the same type of amiability."

The other prisoners were under some form of mental stass control, Diskan decided. Perhaps the condition was by now permanent, and they were past any aid. He had heard of such induced robot compliance, though the practice was deemed worse than willful murder on any civilized planet. A threat of this was to be feared.

He went on, Drustans falling in on his left, the other prisoner on his right, their jerky pace bothering him as he tried to keep step.

"With such a foreguard," Diskan heard the Veep say, "we need have no fears."

What did the off-worlder expect? That this road was mined, that they were walking into an ambush? Did the Veep really know about the watchers and this was his answer to any menace from them?

No!

A reassurance out of nowhere, but reassurance. The watchers were free to move as they wished; the off-worlders would not see them. Ahead was the narrow pass where Diskan had fought the beast at the side of the furred one. Two of the red birds arose, flying sluggishly, well fed. The stench of old death was wafted back to them. One of the space crew, blaster drawn, cut past Diskan and his companions to investigate, and then waved them on.

"Some kind of animal, dead," he reported.

"Which we do not need to be told!" snapped the Veep waspishly. "Faugh—!"

They passed the partially stripped bones. The beginning of the stairway was not much farther, and below Xcothal. At a word of command, they halted. The Veep scrambled to a higher point, using far-seeing lenses to view the ruins. Xcothal was the same today as it had been that other time, Diskan noted. Near to hand, the buildings were clear-cut against the frozen marsh, but farther out a curious haze distorted the sight. He should be able to see those higher buildings at the core, the tower of the hub, from here. Yet there was only a mist rising in the direction where he was sure they stood. He watched the Veep adjust and readjust the lenses, as if, even with those to aid him, he could not get a clear sight of the bones of Xcothal.

Diskan looked down the stair. On the wide platform of the last step, it was just as they had pictured it for him—a pile of drift waiting to be ignited. Among the yellow-white of the branches bright splotches of scarlet, the leaves—

That was his part of the action. Put flame to that and it would all begin. What was "it"? Diskan did not know, but the anticipation swiftly filling him was born of confidence and that trust he could not define.

Light the fire and then—

& CHAPTER 17 *&*

THE VEEP HAD GIVEN UP his survey of the city and had dropped down to join them. As he slid the lenses back into their carrying case, he looked down the giant stairway to the platform where the firewood waited. Then he glanced over his shoulder at Diskan.

"All there waiting for us—very convenient." His comment was a silky purr. "We announce our coming, and they make the arrangements to greet us. How simple do they think we are?"

"That firewood is not just for our use," Diskan returned. "They do the same when they enter the ruins. It is their custom."

"And perhaps a means of defense, Gentle Homo." The medic spoke for the first time.

"A defense for *us* to use?" The Veep laughed. "It would seem that we do have samples of simple wit among us after all."

"The smoke from the fire, Gentle Homo, might have some importance," the medic persisted. "If the natives themselves build such fires, it might be most wise to follow their example."

"Smoke?" Again the Veep laughed. "Even with the wind blowing in the right direction, how far would that smoke reach? And we have only his word that they do it—"

"Given under babbler influence," the medic retorted.

The Veep stared down at the waiting wood. "I don't see any reason for it—"

Then the Jack officer cut in. "Lots of things that don't seem reasonable to us, Gentle Homo, do to aliens. Maybe it's a rite of some

341

sort. If so, it won't do any harm to follow it. Might bring them down on us if we didn't."

"We are grateful for your bending your past knowledge to the present problem, Murgah," the Veep replied sharply, "but I do not think we shall build any bonfires—"

Diskan tried not to let his consternation show. He was under their constant surveillance; there was no way of starting the fire—or was there? He tried to think it out, appealing dumbly to that support he had sensed during the hours of ridge travel. Contact still held; his "reach" met it. But there was no answer to his silent question. Either the furred ones could not, or would not, supply him with the next move. Diskan was on his own.

"March!" The guard behind Diskan underlined that order with a prod of blaster barrel in the small of the prisoner's back. His two stassed companions had already started to descend. They would go down that stairway, out into the ruins. He had to get the fire going— he had to!

There was one way. He was driven to it by desperation. The three of them—himself, Drustans, and the controlled Survey man—were still in the lead. There was no one between Diskan and the brush-wood. He eyed the stone treads before him, counted them, tried to judge their height and from which one of them he must make his try.

They were about the fifth tread from the platform. Now—and he must make it look natural. There was no use ending up crisp in a ray without achieving his goal. It was funny. So many times in the past he had fallen over his own clumsy feet without wanting to—now he must do it on purpose! His fingers already probed under his parka. Luckily, he had been warming his hands there from time to time. This guard would not suspect a familiar gesture. The latch on his belt pouch—would it never yield? Hot, burning—his fire stone was still active! That had been his one fear, or the greater one among many small ones.

In his bare hand it was a searing pain, almost as bad as the wound he had taken in his fight with the watch robot. Now!

Diskan tripped and fell forward, fighting any impulse to save balance. He landed hard on the solid stone of the platform, and the force of that drove most of the breath out of him, was a shock that brought him close to a blackout. But he held to his purpose. Roll now—he had to roll and make it look right. A moan—yes, he could moan and try to get to his feet—

Only that abortive scramble brought him instead to the pile of firewood. He flung out his arm, allowed his tortured fingers to open so that the stone fell into the central mass. Then he wavered back, his arm over his face, and allowed himself to go limp. There was a clatter of boot heels on the stone; there were cries from behind him.

But also there was a sudden crackling, a flash of heat, as if no natural fire had been laid and waiting. Diskan stole a glimpse. The whole pile was bursting into flame—it might have been soaked in some combustible chemical. And from it, spark-filled smoke arose, not straight up into the air but puffing out from the sides in clouds. The first cloud was already about him. Diskan breathed in a spicy aroma that seemed to clear his head, taking away the pain in his hand, the shock of the bruises he had taken in his fall. He saw the guard come charging into the cloud and then—

Color, light, running water, fresh and scented, rising about his legs. Xcothal streets in festival time. And with him the brothers-in-fur marching or rather weaving their joy dance around and around. Those shadows with whom he had sensed a deep oneness before, they were darker, had taken on more substance. He caught tantalizing glimpses of forms—beauty, grace, strength. If he could only see them better!

Rich fabrics hung from the windows and made soft ripples of color down the walls. And the wind about him was a gentle caress, as sweet in its scent as the water continually flowing about his tired feet, for he was tired, Diskan knew, happily tired. He had come a long and arduous journey, and this was the end of it—this was home!

Pleasure, completion—he could put no other name to the emotion that united him with the brothers-in-fur. The shadow people, they were growing more and more real; there was one walking to his left—

No—these others were not shadow people! They were men like himself—though Diskan could not make out their faces. A kind of sparkling aura wreathed about them, moving spirally about their bodies, so that he caught only glimpses of a swinging arm, wading legs. Yet he knew they were his kind. And they did not belong, like the shadow people. They were not a part of Xcothal as he was a part.

No brothers-in-fur kept pace with them or wove the thal pattern between them. They were intruders!

Diskan wanted to attack, to expel them forcibly from the peace and happiness of Xcothal, but the brothers wove the thal pattern for him to walk within, and to break that was sacrilege.

In their own time, brother! The assurance came to him. *In their own time and their own way they shall be judged and dealt with. Think not of them now.*

Yet to see those dark shapes stalking along his own path spoiled his homecoming. He could not abandon mind and heart to the thal pattern as he should, and that was dangerous. The warning came from the brothers:

Drift with the thal, right, left, in and out, thus, and thus, and thus.

Though his lips did not move and no sound issued from his throat, Diskan felt as though he were singing, not words but a melody that was born of the rhythm of the thal. And as he so sang, he could hear the others—not the intruders, not even the brothers-in-fur, but the shadow ones—who must become real, they must!

The water was rising higher about him; he was coming to the heart-core of Xcothal. Surely in this place the shadows would put on the robes of reality and he would be one with them as he must be. There was the tower, and from it issued the call, so that the shadows were massing there, flowing up the circular stair into *That Which Was, Had Been, and Would Ever Be!*

But the intruders were coming, too, and whenever Diskan glanced at them or thought of them, the shadows dwindled, the song dimmed, and he was not as sure of the pattern of the thal. Why must they come?

In their own way, they, too, must see—what they wish to see. And from that seeing will grow the judging. Patience, brother, patience. To all there is an end.

"But not to *That Which Is!*" he protested

So *do we hope, brother. Prove it so, oh, prove it so!*

Diskan flinched under the force of that appeal, under the burden they had dropped upon him without warning. But what did they want of him? What must he do? He was without answers.

Do what comes to you. Act as you must, brother.

Face that which must be faced as your nature would have you.

Advice that meant nothing. His feet were on the steps now; yet still he moved in the thal pattern. Only the shadows were gone; those who moved with him were the intruders, still masked by those sparkling veils. Those and the brothers-in-fur—for he was their key! That much came to him in a flash. For long they had been locked away from their hearts' desire; on him depended their futures also. Yet when Diskan sent out a call for enlightenment, there came no answer. He understood; this action was his alone. They had given him all the aid that was theirs to give; now he walked, as did those others, to face a test and a judging.

He was in the wedge hall, but it was far different from the way he had seen it last. There were walls of silver over which advanced and retreated, glowed and dimmed, thal patterns. And—some of those he knew!

Diskan traced with his eyes a running, twisting curl of red-gold, and then he smiled. You wrought with your thought, thus and thus, and—brilliance almost blinding. The glowing surface dripped small shining motes to cascade to the floor in a glittering pile. Material that could be used—

Treasure! These had come seeking a treasure, had they not? Glittering toys of no real value. Let them have this treasure of theirs—

Again Diskan wrought with his will. The drops—gems? It did not matter. They were toys—could be used thus—

The drops formed into a design and remained so. A diadem of crimson and gold rested on the pavement. Diskan laughed. Toys—with some beauty—made to please the eye. But that he could make them so—!

The flash of wonder that crossed his mind set him to act again. Treasure—let him show these others treasure such as they sought, which was in no way the treasure of Xcothal! This time he willed a belt, dripping a fringe of blue-green jewels.

Yes, yes! Do what must be done, brother. Treasure.

"But this is not the treasure!" Diskan protested. "Toys for play-things, to amuse and adorn. They are worth nothing beyond delighting the eyes for a space."

You are right to offer them to these others. Make them, brother!

Diskan obeyed, though his first exultation waned. They lay

spread across the floor, what he had fashioned by his will from the energy of the thal. And they were nothing, for could not anyone amuse himself so?

Not so, brother. Now the testing—watch!

Those sparkling clouds that clung about the intruders thinned, vanished. Diskan recognized them all as memory lanced the spell of Xcothal. There they stood, the Veep, his personal guard, the medic, the three Jacks, the stassed prisoners and their Jack guard, while the color and the thal patterns receded from the walls. There was a chill, a withdrawing that Diskan felt as a pain. Even the brothers-in-fur were gone.

Only the glittering array on the floor was still the same—or was it? To Diskan's eyes the gems now had a hard, repelling glare. Had—had he really willed them out of the thal patterns or was that a dream also? Could they be real?

The Jack guarding the prisoners gave a hoarse cry and leaped forward, grabbing at a trail of necklace. He choked and crumpled up, his fingers only inches away from the prize. The Veep's guard held a stunner well to the fore, while his employer pushed back the hood of his cloak, gazing a little blankly at the wealth before him, as if he could not believe in its existence.

He stooped as if to pick up the blue-green jeweled belt and then drew back. Straightening, he turned and beckoned to the stassed Survey man.

"Get it," he ordered in a voice hardly above a whisper.

The prisoner jerked forward and stooped in turn. His fingers moved with stiff clumsiness, but he picked up the shimmering length and held it, his eyes betraying no interest. After a long moment, the Veep reached out slowly and drew it away from the captive's clutch. Back and forth it passed through his hands, a rippling glory of gem light.

There was a new expression on the Veep's face. He was plainly excited, entranced. "It's real—real I tell you!" His voice climbed to an echoing cry.

The other three Jacks looked from the massed glitter on the floor to the private guard and back again. There was avid hunger in Murgah's eyes, but he did not advance to the lure. The limp body of his man lay between as a warning.

Only the Veep's guard was intrigued, too. His long years of training and control held; he continued to watch the three Jacks on their feet, but he also stole glances at the loot.

"*Real!*" The Veep repeated, and that word hung almost visibly over them.

Diskan tensed, warned by a concentration from the unseen pointing in upon them. He shot a quick glance to his left. Drustans and the Survey man were the only two apparently oblivious of the display. The Jacks were plainly straining at the leash—and that leash was their respect for the Veep's personal guard. How long that fear of his ability would hold them in check, Diskan had no idea, but that they *would* make some move he was sure.

The Veep's first bemusement was wearing off. He ran the belt back and forth through his hands, but now he studied it critically, as if he knew some fault existed, that it merely remained for him to find it. Then he raised his eyes to Diskan.

"Where did this come from? Our scouts did not find it here earlier!"

"Look about you," Diskan replied. "This is not the same city that they visited." He expected the Veep to demand an explanation of that.

Instead, still holding the belt, the man walked back to the entrance of the wedge room. He stood outlined in the door, gazing into the open of the hub. His guard stepped back a little to give him room but still kept a position from which he could cover any advance on either the treasure or his employer. Then the Veep returned.

"You are right," he agreed in his usual controlled tone. "This is no longer a ruin. So what has happened, a time twist? Or are we now mind-controlled?"

"The smoke!" The medic broke in. "Back there—that smoke!"

The Veep shook his head impatiently. "I am drug blocked, so are you, Sherod. What is it, Fentress?"

"I don't know. But this is the real city—" He did not know why he added that.

The guard moved, edging back, his stunner still and ready, while he worked his way crab-fashion to the door as the Veep had done before him. Once there, he pressed his shoulders against the wall, giving a lightning survey outside. When he turned again, there was a shade of expression on his face for the first time.

"What is this?" he asked of the Veep, and his tone was sharp, with none of the usual diffidence.

"I have not the slightest idea. This"—the Veep waved the belt in his hand so it was a glittering whip—"feels real, looks real—and I'm blocked against any ordinary hallucination. But how much we dare depend upon our senses here and now—What about it, Sherod?"

The medic shook his head. "I did not think it could be done—such illusion fostered. They *must* be illusions—"

Murgah laughed, a harsh crackle. The blue skin about his mouth showed deep brackets. "One way to find out. We take this with us, and we leave—fast!"

"I'm inclined to agree with you, captain." The Veep nodded. "And, as an additional precaution, the harvesting will be done by our non-friends." He gestured to Drustans, the Survey man, and Diskan. "You—gather it in!"

The Survey man was closest, and he went down on one knee to pick up the red and gold diadem. Drustans moved to the right and leaned over. Diskan's inner tension sparked. He threw himself to the floor as a crackling ray burned across the space near where he had stood. It caught the Veep's guard, and he had only an instant in which to scream.

Diskan, still rolling, was brought up against stiff legs, and Drustans fell upon him. The Vaan's arms flailed out awkwardly, and another weight came down on the two of them. Diskan, his face ground painfully against the stone, was helpless for a space to struggle free. He heard other cries of pain and smelled the overpowering odor of rayed flesh.

Grasping for a handhold to draw him free of the struggle over him, Diskan closed his hand on a sharp object and dragged it to him. Then he gave a last mighty heave and rolled the weight off him, sliding forward to the wall.

By the time he pulled around, the battle had become a hunt. Stabbing lances of fire from the door, two other rays answering from the chamber. Men ran, dodging into the open. Diskan sat up. In his hand he held a gemmed knife, which he regarded with dull surprise.

The stunned crewman was now dead. One of the rays had caught him during the melee. And not too far from him lay the Survey man, also burned. By the door huddled the Veep's guard. And two figures rolled over and over, still struggling, within arm's reach of Diskan. To all appearances, they fought in a kind of slow motion, which was almost amusing.

Of the rest who had been in that chamber, the Veep, Captain Murgah, and one of the Jacks were gone. Who hunted whom, Diskan did not know. What mattered was he was free. He got to his feet.

The fighters rolled apart. One lay on his back, his hands and feet moving as if he were still engaged in that struggle. Diskan bent over him. Drustans! How the Vaan could have put up a fight at all when stass-controlled, Diskan had no idea. Sherod lay beyond, around his neck a gem-set necklace pulled tight.

"Get—away—" There was the light of reason in Drustans' eyes now as they met Diskan's.

Diskan did not answer, but he pulled the Vaan to his feet and steadied that lighter, slender body against his own.

"Get away—out of the city!" the other insisted. He wobbled to the door and would have fallen had not Diskan caught him.

Out of the city—Diskan had left this city once before. And then, too, he had aided a wounded man—Zimgrald. Zimgrald and Julha! From faint, far-ago memories planted in a misty past, they snapped into urgent life in Diskan's mind. Zimgrald, Julha up in the rocks, with death drawing in as a dark cold—

"All right." He swung an arm about Drustans' waist and pulled the Vaan along. But it was like wading through water-washed sand in which there was no stable footing. Diskan had to fight that within him which cried, "No! No!"

And he fought, though his breath came in painful sobs and he dared not look around him at the Xcothal that had been—that was now for him.

☙★ **CHAPTER 18** ★☙

"LET ME GO—for now let me go!" Diskan did not know whether he was crying that aloud or through that other way of communication. "This is what I must do!" Abruptly, as if some decision he had not shared in had been made, that backward drag on him ceased. He was down the curved steps into the hub, Drustans staggering beside him. And the city was strange, for it wavered, as though one mist-edged picture fitted over another not quite exactly. Sometimes they stumbled between lines of dark ruins. Sometimes the water washed their feet, banners lined the walls, and the shadow folk came and went on their own mysterious business.

Would they win out of here? Diskan had tried this before and found all streets led to the same pond, but this time he went with a kind of inner certainty. Only what about the Jacks and the Veep? And those others who had been here earlier, in the ways beneath the tower? All might now be prowling these dark streets.

"Where are we going?" Drustans asked, breaking Diskan's concentration of listening, staring, seeking out what might lie hid in any darkened doorway, any side lane.

"To the ridge—if we can make it."

"You think that the natives might help?"

"They have helped—"

"You mean—the illusions?"

Illusions? No, Xcothal was no illusion, but Diskan was not going to argue that now. He was eaten by the need for speed—he must reach the fugitives hidden on the high land and then—then what? Diskan did not know what would happen after that, but that he was following a necessary sequence of action he was sure.

This time there was no befogging of the trail. Even the haze that always hung to confuse the eyes when one looked out over the ruins lifted. No more half matching of a city with its bones. Xcothal's rubble was clear in the light of the moons, that pallid light so bright that Diskan could see the many tracks breaking the white surface of the snow, tracks all leading into the city—boots and paws. The furred ones had been numerous, and they still gave him escort now, though he could not see them.

He is going from us!

In this he is right. It is what he must do—a shaping of his own kind, which is needed, a road he must walk for himself.

Brothers! For the first time Diskan tried to join in that communication which was not for voice or ear but which nonetheless existed.

For a long moment, there was no reply. Then an upsurge of clamor as if many thoughts shouted all together.

Brother! And the joy in that was a fire to warm frozen heart and long-chilled body.

"How many are there—of these Jacks?" Diskan asked Drustans.

"I do not know. They kept us prisoner on the ship. We saw only the guard and those with whom we have just been. Diskan"—his voice slowed—"do you not wonder how I came here?"

"As a prisoner, of course. Did you think I believed you one of them?"

A shadow of an expression Diskan could not read crossed the Vaan's face.

"I was stupid." Drustans' voice was sharp, almost as if he resented Diskan's faith in him. "I believed a story concerning a need for verifying factors on a journey tape. So I took it, but it was not the one they wanted—"

"No. Because I had already stolen that," Diskan returned. He wanted to laugh, to shout, to run. What did it matter, all that which had happened on another world, in another time, to another person? The bubbling in him was something such as he had never known in all his drab days of life. This, this was freedom! It no longer mattered that he was big, clumsy, slow-witted—all those other inferiorities he had hugged to him. Yes, he had treasured his faults, using them to wall off a world he feared. He had no envy of Drustans now. He simply did not care about the Vaan or the life he represented any more.

"They tricked you, but I did it on my own," he said now. "I stole a tape, and a ship—which is now at the bottom of a bog hole. I'm probably certified 'unreliable'—"

"But we can question any such judgment!" Drustans broke in. "You will have a hearing, a chance for defense. Present circumstances will be in your favor—"

"A hearing if and when we get off this world," Diskan pointed out dryly.

"Help is coming; they knew that." Drustans spoke with his old confidence. "That's why Cincred was pushing so fast. The Patrol is hunting him. He had to scoop up any treasure and get off Mimir as quickly as he could. Once he spaced, he believed they could not trace him. Or, if by some chance they did, the authorities could not really prove anything. He could unload the loot with contacts not too far away. There would be plenty of suspicion, yes, but no illegal act could be brought home to him."

"They can get him now—they'll have witnesses."

"And when we get back to the spacer, I can set a beam call to bring in the Patrol cruiser!" Drustans began to trot.

It sounded very simple and quite easy. But surely this Veep Cincred would not have left the ship without a guard, and Diskan mentioned that.

"True. But still we have a better chance now than we had even one time-unit ago. And perhaps—"

"Perhaps the Veep and the Jacks are still sniping at each other, yes. Only there are others to consider—"

"The natives?"

"No. Two survivors of the archaeological expedition."

They had reached the space below the steps. Diskan leaped, caught hold of the platform edge, and scrambled up and over. Drustans, the stiffness of the stass hold gone, pulled up beside him.

Brother, the hunt begins behind you.

Diskan was on his feet to look back. Nothing stirred down the city streets, but he did not doubt the truth of that warning. Either the Jacks or the Veep were there, if not in sight.

"We're being trailed now—"

Drustans spun around, intent upon the ruins. "I do not see them!"

But before the words were fairly out of his mouth, they did see a flash of blaster fire, cutting along a wall, leaving a glowing track on the aged stone. Not aimed at them but still on the trail they had just traversed.

Diskan made a decision. He caught the Vaan's upper arm.

"There's a badly wounded Zacathan here, and a girl. I haven't the training to operate a ship's com and you have. Will you try for the ship while I attempt to aid those others? If there is going to be any ray battle up this slope, they can well be caught in it!"

"What if we all go together?"

"No. You can move faster alone, and you know the ship. Wait— Julha has the stunner. That isn't much defense against a blaster, but it is a weapon and you won't have to go up against any ship guard barehanded."

Diskan was already on the way, taking the steps in great strides, searching ahead for the point at which he must cut off to find the crevice. The moonlight was so clear that he could almost have been walking in the brilliance of midday. Here—this was it!

"Julha!" He dared to call, not wanting to walk into a stunner beam. There—that was the opening to the crevice. A hiss from the shadows, then a whine—the furred one! It knew him, was welcoming—

Diskan and the Vaan crowded into that pocket so well protected by rock walls. Julha stood before the bundle that was Zimgrald. She looked at Diskan and then, beyond him, to Drustans, and her expression was one of vast relief.

"You have found help—" She swayed forward, but Diskan caught at her wrist, twisted the weapon from her loosening grasp, and thrust it at Drustans.

"Get going!" he ordered the Vaan. "And—"

Can you protect this one, see that he safely reaches the ship? He asked it of those others.

This is asking what is not of our concern, this meddling in the affairs of those who are not brothers. It was a silent protest.

It cannot then be done? Diskan's disappointment was acute.

Silence; then the faint impression of a conference he did not share in.

This is a thing that must be done for the good of that which lives in Xcothal?

This is a thing as right as thal patterns! Shall I swear it to you?

No need. Send this one who has no ears to hear the truth, no eyes to see. We shall take a part in this game, but you know the price.

Does one talk of price when one reaches for one's heart's desire? was Diskan's swift reply. Then he spoke aloud:

"You are going to have company, Drustans. How much they can or will do for you, I don't know. But they will aid as much as they are able."

Both the Vaan and Julha were eying him strangely. Drustans spoke first:

"The natives?"

Diskan nodded and dropped one hand to rest it for a moment on the head near his thigh. "The brothers-in-fur. Now go!"

Julha protested, but the Vaan was already on his way, the stunner in his hand, the furred one streaking to pass him.

"Where is he going? What do you do now?" She caught at Diskan and tried to draw him away as he stooped over the Zacathan.

"In a very little while," Diskan told her, "they are going to come out of Xcothal fighting. And I don't fancy being caught in any blaster crossfire. We move, back toward the ship, and Drustans is already on his way to get help—"

"Our people have returned? But they would come at once for Zimgrald! Didn't you tell them he is here? No, you can't move him!"

"I can and will. The only ship now planeted is a Jack one. There is a chance, a slim one, that Drustans can get on board that and signal in a Patrol cruiser he believes is trailing these Jacks. Now, don't ask any more questions—get going!"

Diskan spoke harshly with a purpose. She snatched some things from their packs while he picked up the Zacathan, grunting as he stood under the alien's weight. With the girl before him, Diskan came out of the crevice and started the climb to the old road.

Shadows flowed about the rocks, but he had no fear of those, saying quickly to the girl:

"Don't be frightened. The furred ones are with us. They will give any alarm." The limp body he carried was heavy, but this night he felt as if he could do anything, that he now possessed all the strength and energy in the world!

They wound among the rocks to the crest of the ridge.

"Back in the city," Julha cried out. "That was a blaster. Who are they fighting? Our people—Mik?"

"Each other," Diskan replied briefly.

"Why?"

"Because they discovered what they were hunting—"

"The treasure! Oh, no!" She was distressed. "The High One, the finding should have been his—"

"They found *their* treasure," Diskan corrected. "It was what they wanted of Xcothal. I believe that Zimgrald sought something else here. Xcothal has more than one treasure to offer—"

It had—it had! He held that knowledge to him to warm, to strengthen, to arm him against anything that might come out of the night to try him now.

And he was not really aware of the passing of time until the girl stumbled and fell, and he was alerted to that by the furred ones.

"I cannot go on," Julha told him in a small voice. "Do you, and I shall catch up."

"There is no need. For the time, we are safe. Here—"

It was another rock pocket, but it did not face the marsh and the city; rather it faced that distant valley where the ship stood. The watchers were all about them in a protecting screen. Julha knelt by the Zacathan, her hands touching the beak-nosed face of the tranced man tenderly.

"He still lives and sleeps," she said.

"And while he lives, there is hope." Diskan repeated her own earlier words.

"Please, what happened? Did you find the cache, and who is that man who came with you?"

Diskan cut the story to its bare framework, but when he came to the scene in the wedge chamber, when he had wrought the treasure of Xcothal for those determined to have it, Diskan hesitated. Who would believe unless they had seen, unless they had done as he had? Was all that, too, only an illusion? But *he* knew it was not! Only he could not tell that part of the story. It lay too close to the secret of his own treasure, which was not to be shared, could not be shared.

"They thought they had found what they sought," he told her.

"Part of the illusion." She nodded, and since she had made that a statement instead of a question, Diskan need only keep silence.

"And that set them at one another," he continued, giving her the rest of it as it had happened.

"Then"—her hand went out to smooth the covers about the Zacathan—"they did not really discover anything at all! It is still waiting for the High One. When this is over, he can take up his search!"

Diskan tensed. More prying, more delving—to break open the heart of Xcothal?

Not so, brother. To those who have no eyes, no ears, there is neither sight nor sound nor being. Perhaps later there may come those who have the sight and hearing—and to those Xcothal will open a door, many doors. But to others—nothing. And they will tire of their fruitless searching and go, ceasing to seek what may not be found—by them. The swift, wordless answer came.

"Perhaps he may," Diskan agreed, but he thought that Zimgrald—even if he survived his hurt—might never return to Xcothal.

"And if he does," he continued, "you will aid him?"

Her hands moved as if she were shoving away some burden she could not bring herself to assume again. "If he asks—I will. But—"

"But you hope he will not ask—that is the truth of it? Do you hate the city so?"

"I—I think I fear it. Something slumbers there. To wake it—"

"Would change a world!" Diskan said softly.

"But I do not want that change!" she whispered.

"Then for you it will not come. Do not fear; it will not come—"

She raised her eyes. "You—you are different. And you know something, do you not?"

Diskan nodded. "I know something. I have seen the world change—"

"And you were not afraid." Again it was a statement, not a question.

"Yes, in a manner I was afraid, very much afraid."

"But you are not now."

"No."

Brother—from the sky—it comes!

Diskan could see it, too, a star with no fixed position, making a fiery sweep across the sky. That was a ship, orbiting in, near to tailing down. The Patrol?

"A ship!" Julha had seen it now and was on her feet. "Help for us?"

"I think so—can you go on now?"

"Yes, oh, yes!"

Diskan took up the burden of the Zacathan. Now that it was so near the end, he was plagued by last wisps of doubt. What he was going to do was to close a door firmly, and once closed, that portal could not be opened again. In spite of the sorrows of the past, it was hard to make so radical a change in the future.

Julha was half running, half trotting, but Diskan's pace was far slower. This could be the last walk he would ever take with his own kind.

One comes!

"Diskan?" A call out of the night.

"Drustans—here!" That call had come from some distance away, giving him a few more moments.

He put down Zimgrald. Perhaps of them all, the Zacathan could come the closest to understanding this—a twist of the X factor no man could control once it entered his life. But still there were those last-minute doubts, a feeling of being pulled in two directions, until he lost some of the brave certainty that had filled him most of this night.

"Why are you waiting here?" Julha came running back. "The High One—is he worse?" She threw herself on her knees beside Zimgrald, her hands busy about his wrapped body.

"He is the same—"

Perhaps some tone of Diskan's voice drew attention away from the alien. Diskan was peeling off the parka, then unbuckling his belt, dropping them both beside the recumbent form of the Zacathan.

"What—what are you doing?"

"I am going. You are safe, Drustans will be here very soon. The Patrol ship is planeting—"

"You mean—because you are an outlaw, you are afraid they will force you into rehabilitation? But they can't—they won't, not after we tell them all you have done here! We shall testify for you!"

Diskan laughed. He had almost forgotten that he must be judged a criminal—unreliable, subject to punishment by his kind or by her kind. He had moved too far down another road.

"I am not afraid of the Patrol," he said, still amused. "No, Julha, I am returning to Xcothal because that is now my world—"

"But what you saw there is all illusion!" she cried. "An empty ruin is what it really is. You will die there of cold and hunger."

"Perhaps"—one of his doubts came to the surface—"perhaps you are right and I am walking into an hallucination or dream. But it is mine, far more mine than this world of yours in which I now stand. I am going back, perhaps, as you say, to die among broken ruins and tumbled stones. But to me Xcothal is not dead—it lives and in it thal runs, sweet waters flow, there are things that can be shaped by the mind as your world shapes them by hands. And there are those who await me there with a welcome I have never known in your world—"

"You can't! You'll be rayed by the Jacks—" She gave another argument.

Diskan shook his head. In spite of the cold, he was fumbling with the catches of his tunic, pulling off the garment that had always seemed too confining to his big arms and wide shoulders.

"I will not enter *their* Xcothal." He dropped the tunic. "Good voyaging, Julha. When the High One recovers, tell him he was very right. The furred ones—they are the key if one can use them. And there is a treasure in Xcothal that surpasses all the wealth of the worlds beyond. Tell him I have proved it!"

"No!" She tried to catch him as he turned. But then he was running among the rocks, paying no heed to his footing even in the rough country, not aware of the cold about his bare upper body. And around him bounded in plain sight the furred ones, leaping and playfully springing upon one another in their exuberance.

In time, Diskan came to the stair and descended it with great strides. Then he stood on the platform, impatiently tearing from him the last bits of clothing that were of the past, the last ties with what had been.

Before him was a straight running stream of water, sweet water, which was the road, and through that moved the shadows. But these were shadows no longer, for he saw them at last for what they were— bodies like his own—not aliens—though even with different shaping they could not be strange. And in their eyes recognition, welcome for the unlocker of doors, the one uniting brothers-in-fur with brothers-in-flesh—who might lead also to the surmounting of still farther and stranger barriers—

And with a shout of greeting, Diskan leaped forward, into the sweet water, the color, the life that was Xcothal, the Xcothal that had been and now was again!

☄. ★ CHAPTER 1 ★.☄

THE SHADOW DEATH struck Mungo Town just after harvest, as if it had purposefully waited to give the greatest pain, the harshest of deaths. Perhaps there *was* a method in that time selection. What can an off-worlder know of a new colony's lurking dangers in spite of all the assurances from Survey testers that another planet is waiting free and open to settlers? No one knew of Voor's menace until the fiftieth year after first-ship landing, and then it was only a handful of outpost villages and holdings which were hit and the reasons given were practical and believable.

Bad water, contaminated food, attacks of heretofore unknown dangerous animals—you can read these explanations all in the official files if you have a morbid interest in how part of a new colony began to die. The next year it was worse. Then death came to Voor's Grove a few days after the planting. There were four survivors—two infants, one three-year-old girl, and a woman who never gave coherent answers to questions, but crooned unendingly to herself, until one night she managed to elude containment at the medic's center and disappeared. They tracked her as far as the edge of the Tangle and that was that. Once in the Tangle anyone must be written off.

So it was on Voor. But colonists are a tough lot and people who are crowded off one of the League's Chain Worlds do not have much choice, after all. There were two whole years after the Grove strike when there was no trouble at all. People do forget—even after they

363

have gone through the rigorous pre-settlement training. There were always the preferable believable excuses, as I have said.

Those did not hold after Mungo. You can wipe out twenty or so people, but when the death toll comes to two hundred and twenty—it is not that easy to find logical explanations.

That was how I came to be a Voorloper. I grew up in a trek wagon and could inspan the gar team before I could heft a shoulder weight of trade goods. I was second generation from first-ship. First-ship people always have a certain standing on any colonial world. They were those willing to gamble the most, and usually they end up either dead or prosperous enough to carve out their own holdings and make them pay. On most worlds that is true. On Voor those who survived became lopers—they knew the score.

My mother died at Mungo's Town and my father, Mac Turley s'Ban, after he returned to find the ruin there, inspanned his smartest gars, loaded his trekker, threw me in on top of what he believed would best suit a loper's needs, and took off. I was about six then and now I can't even remember what it is like to live rooted and not as a loper. There are still holdings, but they don't push out northward any more—mostly they stick to the southern portion of the big land, on that side of the Halb Canyon river. The north has some settlements—mostly miners after Quillian Clusters. Those keep up forcefields at night, and that solution is too expensive a drain on any ag-man's credits. For some reason none of the brains the League has sent can understand why the Shadow doesn't spread south. For the last few years they have not sent out any "experts on X-Tee" any more. We aren't rich enough a world to pull such help. Our potential, my father once said, would not pay off fast enough.

He always had that set to his jaw whenever he met a League man. In fact I've known him to sit lock-toothed all evening when a couple rode into our camp and tried to question him. He would even get up and disappear into the wagon and leave them there with their mouths half open, looking as slack brained as a goof-monkey. After a while he got a reputation and even a holdings man never mentioned Shadows when he was around.

I don't know what he'd done before he earthed in on Voor in the beginning. He never talked about the old days, just as he never mentioned my mother. Once or twice, when I got old enough to really notice things, I wondered if he had been enlisted in Survey himself. He seemed to have a lot of strange scraps of learning about trekking. Then from the first he made notes on a recorder. In fact the only off-world thing he ever got for himself (except stunner shells) when we went Port Side once a year for our stock was a case of tapes.

Though some of those were for me. Even though we were on the move all the time, he saw that I was not dirt stupid. I had to learn, and I will say this, I really liked it. First it was all practical stuff—filling in what he didn't show me. He listened to that, too. I learned to repair a stunner, a food synthesizer, a hand com. We did jobs like that at holdings now and then.

Then there was history—of the League, and of several different worlds. I never understood why he picked those special ones and I knew better than to ask. They were a queer mixture—no two alike, and none near Voor as far as I could tell—at first. Later I began to see what they did have in common—Astra, and Arzor, and Kerdam, Slotgoth—they had all begun as Ag worlds—just like Voor. Only it turned out later that they had a lot of Forerunner remains on them—and some queer things had happened there as a result.

I was not too good with the tech tapes. It took me a long time to become as competent a craftsman as my father demanded. He had a lot of patience, and it was as if he was making very sure that I was going to be able to use my hands well enough to make me a good living before he was through with me. I did learn, too. But I was better with animals. I could handle the gars, as I have said, when I was too little to climb onto one. Somehow they liked me—or else I had that kind of a gift—

My father talked sometimes about natural gifts. He made sure that I understood men were not all alike. Of course, I don't mean just aliens and Terrans (that any one with a tenth of a brain in his head already knew) but men—Terrans themselves—had different talents they used—when they knew how. Once he started to talk about Psi, then shut up quick and got that locked look on his face. It had been healing he had been explaining to me then. I wished he'd go on—but he never mentioned that again.

There were the healers. Mostly they were girls or young women. I had seen them do some things in the out-back which were not explained on any tape. My father appeared to dislike them, or else there was something about their talents he distrusted. He was always uneasy when one of them was anywhere near him. Once I saw him deliberately turn and walk away when a healer at Jonas Holding was going to speak to him.

She was a nice looking young woman radiating a kind of peaceful feeling. Even being near a healer could make a person feel warm and comfortable inside. I saw her stand and look after my father and there was a sad look on her face. She even half raised her hand as if to lay a healer's touch on something which was not there at all.

However there were other gifts my father did discuss—such as psychometry, where you could hold something in your two hands and tell through your own feelings about it who had made it—where it came from. Then there was foreseeing—though my father said that was rare and not always to be trusted. There were some people, too, who could read thoughts—tell what a person was thinking—though he had never met anyone like that—just knew about them from tapes, and things he had seen once or twice.

Aliens had a lot of such powers, but they did not always work between Terran-human and them. Our brains were too different for that. Though sometimes those aliens who were the farthest from us in body structure seemed closest in mind.

My father would never use any weapon stronger than a stunner, and he never had a blazer in the wagon. He was strong about that— but he made me a good marksman with both stunner and tangler. We did have times when we needed those. I had a sand cat charge me once and its foreclaws dug gouges out of the earth about a finger's length from my boot toes when I brought it down. We just left it sleeping there. My father never killed for pelts the way some lopers did. He was very firm about that even when the Portsiders wanted him to bring in jaz fur and he knew right well where a colony of jaz nested. It was not because jaz were too easy to kill—a jaz at nesting time was something a wise loper kept away from. They hunted men with a cunning which made them a nasty kind of danger if you got up among the Spurs.

Yes, my father gave me an odd education—both by tape and by example. He had a different rep among the other lopers, too. About every two years or so, he deliberately crossed the Halb, he said to visit the mines. We did trade with one or two. But I got to know early that was not the main reason we took a chance most lopers did not care for—in spite of the mine transport paying off so well.

Because we never headed straight for the mine territory. Instead we'd circle around, always stretching on each trip a little farther north. Then we'd visit dead holdings. Though my father told me early we were never to mention that. At first he would go in among the deserted buildings alone; he'd even suit up—he had a full Survey suit such as they wore on the first-in trips on other planets. He always ordered me to stay back at the trek wagon with the com. It was also his order that if he did not report every so many time units I was to inspan and get the hell out as fast as I could make it, making me swear on the Faith of Fortune I wouldn't try to come in after him.

My father was a true-believer and he raised me so. At least I was believer enough to know that you did not break that oath—ever— that a man's own faith in himself would rot and fade away if he ever did.

After a while he did not suit up if the holding was one he had visited before, but he still did if it was a new one. When he came back he would dictate into a tape just what he had noticed—even the smallest things—such as what kind of weeds were growing now in the old gardens, and whether anything had been looted out of the houses—nothing ever was. The strangest thing was that there were never any animals or birds to be found anywhere near a holding which had been cleared out by the Shadows. But vegetation always grew very rankly there. Not the imported food stuffs which had been specially conditioned for planting on Voor, but weird things which were not even of the native Voor growth we knew. My father did drawings of that—only he wasn't too skilled at the job; but he described it carefully, though he never brought back any specimens.

After every such visit he did something else which would have made any Portside official think he was ready for reconditioning. He would make me tie him up, wrists and feet, and put him into a sealed sleep bag. I was to keep him so for a day and a night. Again he made me swear that if he started to talk funny or fought to get loose I was to inspan and get out—leave him there there all fastened down and not come back for maybe two, three days. I had to swear I would because he was so demanding about it. Though I think I would have risked breaking *that* oath if I had ever had to. Luckily it never happened like he feared.

I knew what he searched for—though we never discussed it—some answer to the riddle of the Shadow doom. It was not for the benefit of Voor at large, but because he had within him a burning desire to bring to justice, if such a thing were possible, that which had ended his stable life.

Voorlopers are solitary men. A number, like my father, were refugees from blasted northern holdings who had survived because they were away when the doom struck. Others were misfits, loners, men who could not root themselves in any place, but were ever wandering in search of something which perhaps even they could never understand. They talked very little, their long stretches of lonely travel taking from them much of the power to communicate with their fellows, except over such elemental things as trade.

If one chanced upon a holding at the harvest festival he might linger, watching the festivities with a detached wonder, as one might view the rites of an alien people.

There were several who traveled in pairs but my father and I were the only two of close kinship I had knowledge of. They had no women. If they assuaged a natural hunger of the body it might be in one of the Portcity pleasure houses (even on such an undeveloped world as Voor a few of these existed, mainly for the patronage of the ship's crews). However, no woman ever rode in a trek wagon.

Women are jealousy guarded on Voor as they are on most frontier planets. The ratio is perhaps one female to three males, for pioneer life did not generally appeal to unwed women. Those who came were already hand-fasted to some man. Remarriage came quickly to widows, and daughters were prized, even more than sons, since a man might tie to his holding some highly desirable male help could he provide a wife for one of the unattached.

Only the healers came and went freely. Their very natures were their safeguards and they were valued so highly that, had any man raised his eyes to one covetously, he would have signed his own warrant for outlawry and quick death thereafter. Healers did wed when their powers began to wane, for those powers were at their strongest from the beginning of adolescence until they were in their third decade. Then they had their pick of husbands, for there was every hope that any daughter of such a union might inherit the gift.

We were at trade in the northmost of the holdings—Ratterslea—and I had then grown to match my father in inches, though I was still not his match in strength, when I first heard directly of my mother. I had taken a packet of thread and needles (a favored betrothal gift on Voor) to the Headhouse where Ratter's wife received me in guest style, the tankard of fall ale and the bread-of-traveler set out on a tray she held herself, rather to my surprise, for I was no son of any holder, nor an off-worlder.

She was tall, and in her hip-length smock of bright cloth with its many bands of embroidery to show off her skill, her breeches and boots of well-tanned gar hide, smooth as the thread I had to offer, she made a fine figure of a woman. Her hair was the color of darth leaves when the first breath of frost wind touches them—ruddy and yet gold—and it was bound about her head like those bands of ceremony worn on other worlds by great rulers—those they term "crowns."

In her sun-browned face her eyes were a strange, vivid green and they were eyes which searched and probed, so that I, who seldom said even a word to any woman, felt very ill at ease and wondered if I had in truth washed all the road dust from me before I had dared to come.

"Greeting, Bart s'Lorn." Her voice was rich and deep as the shade of her hair.

I was a little startled at her words for though I was very used to being called "Bart," yet this was the first time in my memory that I had been also greeted by my full clan-family name. "s'Lorn" was strange to me—it was the first time I had heard the reference to my long dead mother.

"Lady of the Holding," I produced my best guest courtesy, "may fortune smile upon this rooftree and your daughters be as handmaidens to that fortune. I have that which you have ordered and it is our wish that it find favor with you—"

I held out the packet but she did not look to it. Rather still she studied me and I grew yet more uneasy and even wary, though I was sure that in no way could I have offended her or any under her roof.

"Bart s'Lorn," she repeated the name and there was something in the tone of her voice which I was stranger to. "You are very like— male though you are. Eat, drink, bless so this house—"

I was yet further amazed, for such a greeting is given only to a close kinsman, one who is esteemed and very welcome in either good times or bad. Since she did not take the packet from me, I placed it on a nearby table and did as she bade, even as if I had been a youngling of her own household and not near a man grown. Carefully I broke the bread-of-the-traveler into two portions. One I dipped within the tankard, end down. Though at that moment my mouth seemed dry and I was indeed far from hunger, I put the moistened portion between my lips. Steadying the tray with one capable hand, my hostess did the same with the other piece of the thin round, thus sharing food in ceremony with me.

"Yes," she said slowly when she had swallowed that traditional mouthful, "you have very much the look of her, Voor born though you are."

That bite of moistened bread which I had taken seemed to stick within my throat. I gulped it down hastily.

"Lady of the Holding, you speak of s'Lorn—that name my mother bore." There were questions in plenty pushing into my mind and as yet I could not sort out which were of the greatest importance. At that moment it rushed upon me how much I had always longed to know of the past and yet had never dared to ask of my father.

"Sister's sister she was to me." The relationship my hostess claimed was one by marriage. In some clan holdings it was as close as that of shared bloodkin. "My sister was Hagar Lorn s'Brim, and her sister—she pledged to Mac Turley s'Ban."

I bowed. "Lady, forgive my ignorance—"

"Which is none of your fault," she countered briskly. "All men and women know of that which came to Mac Turley s'Ban and what a wound it gave him, which has not healed even to this day. Did he not send you here, not coming himself, for he will have no speech or meeting with those who once knew him in happiness and full strength of clan." She shook her head slightly.

"He has made of you a holdless, kinless one. Does this ride hard on you?" Again I met her eyes and felt that measure of being weighed and searched, as if she would have each thought and feeling out of me, plain before her as a reading tape is spread.

It was my turn to stand straight and proud. Holdless and kinless I might be in her eyes, but in my own I had a place I knew at that moment I would not trade for all the land and gear which made up the wealth this prosperous holding displayed with pride.

"I am a voorloper, lady. My father has, I think, no reason to find me less than he wishes—"

"And *you* wish?"

"Lady, I think that I could never be other than I am."

"Well, it is true that a gar trained to the hunt cannot be harnessed to the plow—else the spirit be broke. Also perhaps the Shadow has touched also on you—"

"The Shadow!" Even here below the Halb that word had an evil ring.

"There are shadows and Shadows," she returned. "Enter, Bart s'Lorn, now that we have met at last, let me know more of you."

She ushered me through the great hall where there were many about their tasks: a girl at the loom, another carding the fleecy hair of those small gars which are bred for their coats, older women busy at oven and open stove. They all looked at me with frank curiosity and appraisal and I put on an outward show of what I hoped equaled my father's habitual aloofness. Though I marked one girl who sat on a chair, not a stool, before the fire and who did not look at me at all, rather gazed as one who could see beyond wall and room, dreaming with open eyes. Her hands were idle and lay limp, palm up upon her knees, and her upper smock was of dull green, shorter than those generally worn, more akin to the riding dress of a traveler.

She we passed and came into the far end of the room where there were two cushioned chairs. On one of those my hostess seated herself, waving me to the other. Straightway she began questioning me and such was the authority in her voice I found myself answering, not through polite courtesy, resenting inwardly that any so attempt to enter my life, but rather as if indeed she *were* bloodkin and had such a concern for me that she had a right to know such things.

Though the holding was far from Portcity, she was plainly one well learned in many things and with a taste for some of the same ways of life my father honored. She had questions concerning him also, where we went and what we did.

At first I tried to evade her directness, thinking that our concerns were none of hers in truth. Then she spoke to me emphatically:

"He would not have so sent you to me, *me* of all this world, had he not wanted me to know this, Bart. For he understands from the old days what manner of person I am and what moves in me, even as it has made of him a rootless, roofless man. For I, too, was at Mungo's Town—though I was also gone when the Shadows came."

In all the ways she had surprised me since our meeting, this gave me the greatest stroke of amazement. I had not known in all my years any others who had lived in that ill-omened place.

"Shadow dead—all of them—" her face grew then near as grim as my father's could upon occasion, rounder of cheek and chin though it might be. "You alone—why—"

"Not I alone—there was my father!" I corrected her.

She shook her head. "He was on journey that night, he came back. You lay in the bed—not crying—rather as if you slept though your eyes were open. It has happened elsewhere. Always it is a child who lives—or sometimes an elder whose memory does not thereafter return. Tell me, what can you remember—the farthest back of all memories!"

Her demand was sharp. It was one my father had never made, perhaps because he did not want—or dare—to do so. That he had been away from the town when the Death had come—that much I had always known.

What did I remember? Had she not so caught me perhaps I would not have automatically obeyed her command and tried to recall my first clear memory. I had heard men, and women, too, boast that they remember this or that happening which reached back to the time when they crawled on all fours or were carried in arms. What did I remember?

With real effort I closed my eyes, for to me memory most often presents itself in pictures as if I were running through some reading tape of my own devising. What then did I see?

There was a hot sun blazing over my head, I could feel it even as the ground swayed, far down and away, for I was perched on the wide back of an animal which ambled peacefully along, snatching, as it went, mouthfuls of leafy brush which was high enough on either hand so it could so graze without bending its head to the ground. My two hands grasped tightly the stubby mane of the gar as I stared about at its horns. It was a wagon beast and was yoked to a fellow that also mouthed at leaf and stick with flabby, mobile lips.

There was the yoke before me, such a yoke as I have handled many times since. So I rode in the sun and yet though I could feel the heat of that upon my head and shoulders, still I was cold, I shivered. And I was afraid. Yet what I feared so—no, my mind flinched from remembering. I could not recall.

A man came up beside the gar, a man so tall that even that great beast did not make him seem either small or lacking in strength. He swept me from my perch as if he knew that the fear was eating at me, held me to him, so that my head lay on his shoulder and my face in hiding against his body. I clung to him with desperation.

Though now I forced, and searched, and strove for the first time I could truly remember to recall the past, that was my first memory. I was five planet years old, on my first trek. Behind that—lay nothing.

I was not even aware that I must have been repeating aloud the description of the picture in my mind until I heard the woman near me catch her breath.

"Nothing farther back? Nothing of—of her?"

Did I begin to shiver again? I was not sure. Suddenly there was someone standing beside me on the other side, and a tankard was pressed into a hand which I found I had lifted as if to ward off some blow.

"Drink," said a soft voice and I sensed that special calming which is the healer's heritage.

I raised the tankard and drank, but first, over its rim, I looked at the one who had brought it to me. It was the girl of the green smock, she who had sat by the fire dreaming, or seeming to dream, and who alone in that hall had, as I believed, never seen me. Now she watched me alertly as the liquid she had brought me filled my mouth and I swallowed.

Was it sweet, or tart? Surely it was not of any ordinary brewing. I thought that somehow the taste of sun-ripened berries, of autumn ripe fruit, as well as the sharp freshness of spring water had all been caught in it, mixed with a subtlety to leave no one flavor or taste in full command. It was cool and yet it warmed. I forgot that cold which had begun to form an icy core within me. No, not forgot it perhaps, just knew that it no longer mattered, had been pushed far off so that it concerned someone else but not the me who was important, alive, and here and now.

"You are a healer," I stumbled awkwardly, stating the obvious.

"I am Illo." She added no clan or house ending to that single name. Some healers did indeed acknowledge no roof, no holding. Those were wanderers, serving those in need from place to place—in their own way like the lopers—yet far more involved with their fellows than we in that they cared deeply for strangers, whereas we stood aloof and could not summon such emotions even if we wished.

"She is also shadow touched," said my kinswoman. "Have you heard of Voor's Grove?"

All the Shadow tales were known to the lopers. "You were the girl then?" I said to her directly.

"Drink first," she bade me, nor did she answer until I had indeed finished to the last drop what brew filled the tankard and turned it upside down in the fashion of a feaster after a toast, to show that I had honored the words spoken.

"Yes," she said then as she held out her hand for the empty tankard. "I was of Voor's Grove, the first holding to be set in the north plains, planted and raised by Helman Voor, for whom this world was named. It may be even that I am of his blood kin," she shrugged. "Who knows? I do not remember—I cannot remember. I am Shadow touched."

♦★CHAPTER 2★♦

IF I FLINCHED AGAIN it was inwardly, for I held tightly to that outward calm which I patterned after my father's way of facing the problems of this world. Instead I asked now, with a boldness for which I was proud:

"What really is Shadow touch? Of all on this world a healer must best know the answer of that."

She wore a considering look on her face. Not, I thought, as if she were weighing whether she might trust me with any true answer, but because she was seeking to choose words which could explain something very difficult to make clear. Then she questioned in turn:

"What are the Shadows?"

Only it seemed that she did not expect any meaningful reply from me, for then she added:

"Until we learn that—then how can we also open the door in here," she touched forefinger to her broad forehead, uncovered, for she wore her hair fastened tightly back as most healers do, "where must lie the explanation for this curse."

Beside the lady of the holding she was slight, though tall. Her body was as spare as the lead wand of a loper, and had nothing about it of the ripeness of a woman bred to mother a child. Her skin was browned near dark as mine by sun and weather, and her features were a little sharp, their angularity made more apparent by the gauntness of her cheeks. Still she carried the calm and authority of her talent in her, so in her own way she was good rival to her hostess, for I did not believe that she was rooted here.

375

Now she looked at me directly again.

"There comes a need—"

I could make little sense of that and, when I would have asked her what she meant, she had turned swiftly and went back down the hall taking the tankard I had emptied with her. Now I glanced at my hostess.

Between her eyes a frown line deepened. She stared after the girl a long moment before she brought her eyes back to me once again.

"Where does Mac trek this season?" she asked abruptly.

"We go to Dengungha." I named the mine settlement he had sought out on the map before we left Portcity. It was the farthest north now of any settlement, closest to the waste of the Tangle. Beyond it lay only ruins—the ruins of Voor, of Mungo—neither of which we had ever visited during our wanderings. Our trek wagon carried some off-world equipment for the mine—a small cargo, one which would barely pay for our supplies. I had thought it strange that we shipped so little, but my father offered no explanation, and he was not one to be questioned unless there was definite reason.

"Dangungha," she repeated. "Then where—?"

I shrugged. "My father is trek master, his the trail plan."

Her frown had grown deeper. "I do not like it—there is—but it is true that one does not question Mac's coming—or going—one never did. He is a man to keep his own council. Only one ever could speak freely with him—"

I thought I could guess—

"My mother?"

"Yes. We thought him a dour, secretive man. Only when he was with her it was as if he threw away all defenses and came fully alive. You would not have known him, seeing him as he is today. She was his light—and much of his life. He is Shadow touched now, even if he himself never came under the curse in body or mind. I wish—" her voice trailed away into nothingness and I sat in courteous silence, though I began to wish that I were free of this hall. For to me it seemed like a cage, pressing in upon me.

There was the good smell of fresh bread, of other things which meant a well-run household. But such caught in my throat as if I smothered in them. I wanted the outside where there was no hum of talk, no clatter of loom, of pans, no bustle of work strange to me.

My hostess roused from her thoughts. "There is no reasoning with him. That we learned years since. He will go his own way, though to take you with him—"

Now a spark of heat flared in me. "Lady, I want nothing more than to be my father's son."

Once more she looked into my eyes and there was a sternness in her face as she answered me:

"Only a fool would say that was—is—not so. You must go your way in spite of all. The Faith of Fortune," between us she sketched in the air the sign of a blessing, "be with you Bart s'Lorn. You need the best that fair-wishing can bring you. We shall say your name before the Hearth Candle here each night."

I bowed my head and indeed she moved me with that solemn promise. I, who had no roots, nor had ever wanted them, did not know until that moment what it might mean to be so treated, as if indeed I were blood-kin with those ready to stand at my side, or at my back, were evil to rise in my path.

"Lady, I give you the thanks of the heart," I fumbled with courtesy words I had never had reason to use before. "It is a very kindly thing you do."

"Little enough." That set sternness was still in her face. "Little enough, for there is no turn in a chosen road. Give to Mac my good-wishing also, if he will take it, or if he ever thinks of the past which once was. He is—No, I shall not say such words to you. I do him no wrong in my thoughts, only I hold for him a very great pity."

She arose then and I got to my feet as swiftly, sensing that she would dismiss me. Still she walked again by my side down the hall and saw me through the door with full guest honor. I did not look back after the farewell words were said between us, for, oddly enough, I still felt uneasy and afraid. Not as I had when we had spoken of the Shadow—that was a thing which all men found ill to discuss—but rather I feared the hall itself and the abundant life there, a strange and alien life which in some way was vaguely threatening to my own.

My father had not chosen to outspan in the visitor's field, but had camped down by the river, some distance from the holding buildings. I had started down the footpath which led to the water and so on to our wagon when someone came from behind to match step with me.

I glanced up startled, for I had been deep in my thoughts. It was Illo, the healer, and her stride was free and near as long as mine, that of a traveler who had been on many trails in the past. There was a pack resting against her shoulders, a weather cloak folded and strapped to the top of that. She wore the thick-soled boots of a tramper, and in one hand was her healer's staff, a straight cutting of qui wood which had been peeled and smoothed so that it seemed to shine in the sunlight as if it were a rod of pure brilliance such as lit Portcity buildings.

"How can I serve you?" I asked quickly, for healers never come to any one save for a purpose. They do not walk idly, nor do they seek out conversation save when they have something meaningful to impart.

"You travel north. So do I go also. My way is long, and—" now she returned my glance, "perhaps there is little time. The truth being I would ask passage with you."

Such a temporary arrangement between loper and healer was not unknown, usually when, as Illo said now, there was a need for speed on a long trip. But the miners at Dengungha were all off-world men and they clung always stubbornly to a belief in their own medics. There would be no call for a healer to seek them out.

"I do not seek the mines—" She was not reading my thought, of course. It must be well known by now where we would travel once we had crossed river. "There is another place."

Illo did not name it, and it was not courtesy to ask. Though I could not recall any holding now to the north—unless some party had gathered more courage to front the unknown during the months just behind us, and trailed into the forbidden land for a ground-breaking.

However, though a healer had the right to ask passage, I could not see that my father would take kindly to this addition to our party. Yet there was no refusal he could give and not offend all custom. She said nothing more, only walked beside me to our camp.

My father sat on his heels beside the fire. Close to his hand lay a pipe and from it trailed still a small thread of smoke. He had been indulging himself in his one great extravagance, for the dried stuff he smoked was from off-world and could only be obtained by near ruinous bargaining with some shipsman. What he took in such trades from time to time he guarded so well and used so seldom that a small pouch of it would last him for many months. Also he used it only, I had come to know, when he was low in spirit, or else under that dark cloud which made him, sometimes for days, even more silent and aloof.

He had a reader out and there was a coil of tape set in it. But he was not using it, rather looking into the fire as if whatever message he would know was better found there.

A loper learns quickly certain measures for protection. Our hearing, I am sure, is better than that of any who are holding born, or off-worlder. Though both my new companion and I wore the soft, many-fold soled boots which favored the feet of those who traveled, yet he became aware of us and glanced up.

That his mood was no good one I could see at once. The frown which he turned upon Illo was dark. He got slowly to his feet, a little stiffly, but standing as straight as her staff should she set it pole-like in the earth.

"Lady—" even that word as he said it had the grating sound of some tool seldom used, even a little rust bound in a setting.

"I am Illo," she said. The healers never used honor words by choice. "I would travel beyond the river," she came directly to the point.

My father's frown grew darker and now he looked to me in accusation. I knew that it was in his mind then that I had, without reference to him, made some promise to this girl. Only again she must have understood at once.

"There have been no promises made to me," she said coolly. Nor did she glance to me. "You are trekmaster, so I say to you—I have need to go beyond the river."

"Why?" my father asked starkly and boldly. "There are no holdings there—now—"

"And the miners have their medics?" she completed his thought almost before that "now" was out from between his lips. "It is true, Trekmaster. Still—there is a need for me to go beyond the river. And—since there are no holdings, I come to you. All men know that Mac s'Ban alone travels there."

"The land is cursed." There was no friendliness in him, even though that inner peace which the healers cast (perhaps without willing it, merely because they are what they are) must be touching him as it was me. It would appear that his stubbornness was proof even against that.

"All men know that also—even the off-worlders," she agreed. "Do they not put force fields about where they hack and despoil the earth? Yet I say and mean it—there is a need for me in the north."

No man on Voor could stand against such a statement. A healer could sense the need for her services, and, having once had that call, there was nothing save her own hurt or death which could hold her back from answering it. Nor would any man stand against the compulsion which moved her when she so would journey. My father might hate to give her wagon room because of those dark depths and sorrows within him, but he could not say her no.

We broke camp with the dawn. My father had not asked me anything concerning my talk with the Lady of the holding, nor had I volunteered even her greetings, for the fact that we were three in camp instead of two made him as unapproachable as if there was about *him* a forcefield. Maybe there was—one of his will.

The gars came to the yoking at my whistle as I had long since trained them to do. They never wandered far in their grazing and lopers often said that we had the best-trained animals on the plains. There were six of them, prime beasts, for we tended them many times better than we treated ourselves. Against the brittle, sun-dried grass of the land their dusky blue-gray hides were plain to see. And they were beginning to grow the heavier coats of winter wool.

As we did not use them for holding tasks my father had never allowed their horns to be blunted, for there were beasts abroad eager enough to taste gar meat, and he insisted they must be able to defend themselves. There were three bulls, massive creatures with a wide curl of horn, two sprouting from above their eyes, the third and sharpest from the nose. The other three were their mates, for the gars, like the human kind on most worlds, were monogamous, and also they mated for life. It was well known that a gar whose mate was slain or died of some accident often grieved and would not graze until it, too, wasted away.

Our wagon was port built under my father's orders and design, much of it finished by his hands and mine, and less than two years old now. It was of bals wood which, cut green, can be shaped—then, when dried under the sun for the right number of days, becomes metal-hard. Such could stand years of heavy use and yet not show scratch nor dent.

It was divided into sections, two for cargo—one small, one for that of bulk—while the front and third portion could serve as a home in storm time. Though most lopers have an ingrown desire to sleep in a bag under the trekwagons themselves when it can be done. We do not like walls, as I have said.

The river crossing was a ford, easy enough to make at this time of the year, since only the spring rains brought it high and fast enough to offer any mishap. On the far side there was a faint trace of road but my father turned from that and struck out across the width of the land itself.

If one were a bird or one of the fluttersnakes from the Tangle—one could perhaps have seen more than just a very distant blue shadow in the far distance. We lopers did not travel by set trail or roads in this part of the continent—if any other lopers ever took to the north except my father and I. There was a com receiver in the wagon which could set up an automatic guide to Dengungha but it was apparent my father was not going to depend upon that now.

I waited, as I walked beside our lead gars, for some question or even direction from Illo. However she paced steadily at our long learned stride—or near its equivalent—with no more words than my father had to offer.

Gars for all their bulk can even run should the situation demand such effort from them. The stampede of a wild gar clan is no safe thing. However their usual procedure is a steady trot which a man can match without undue effort, if he is trained to it. Our beasts always kept to that in the north, unless brought to a halt at order. It was as if they neither liked the land nor trusted it no more than we did and so preferred to keep in motion. Whereas in the south they often slowed to catch up mouthfuls of any brush or tall growing grass to munch wetly and noisily as they went.

We veered west steadily, though I knew well enough that the mine lay due north, and westward there could be nothing at all save one evil tongue of the Tangle which licked out into the plains, forming a curve as if to entrap therein any foolish enough to venture so near to its vile mass.

Men had flown over the Tangle with Survey instruments in the early days of Voor's first discovery. It registered life, but what kind of life no out-world built com or pick-up had ever been able to distinguish. From the air—I had seen the picture tapes—it looked like a thick, puffy, grey blanket—like smoke perhaps. Yet smoke would move, billow, thin or thicken and the Tangle did not.

From the ground it was an impenetrable mass of vegetation, so thick grown as to defy anything but a flamer to cut one's way in. Since there was plenty of empty land for which a settler did not have to fight, the Tangle was not so warred against. People had been lost in it, yes, flitters downed. If there had ever been any survivors of those crashes they had certainly never won free. As for getting out a guiding rescue call by com—that was impossible. A faculty the experts could not pin down made every com instrument go dead when one went so low as to skim just above the billows.

Yet now we were headed in a direction which could only eventually bring us to the Tangle's edge. As far as I knew there were not even any holding ruins in that direction and I could not understand what my father desired. When we nooned and ate our journey meat and drank from the wagon cans we had filled at the river, the brightness of the sun was dimmed by gathering clouds.

I saw Witol, our lead gar, a tough old bull on whose instincts any man might well depend (if he were Voor wise at all) lift his heavy head from grazing and turn west and a little south, his huge nostrils expanding as if to catch the slightest change in the wind which had risen with the gathering clouds. He snorted loudly and his team fellows also stopped their eating, likewise turning to face the west.

My father, who had been hunched silently moments earlier over a mug of res-tea which he had no more than sipped, got to his feet, and, like Witol, looked west into that wind. I did likewise, for the chill in the air grew sharper, and, though our senses are so much more the less than the beasts who accompanied us, I was at last able to catch a scent.

It was something which could not possibly come from the open land before us. Only once had I picked up such an odor and that had been when my father's wanderings had led us well down the Halb into a place of swamps, unusual to find on the Big Land. There the same stench had struck us as that wet and slimy land had lain until the hot touch of midsummer sun. It was sickening—as if the wind now blew across some matter long gone into decay.

Illo moved a step or two out, away from the wagon, from the uneasy gars whose snorts had become grunts signaling rising uneasiness so that I went among them quickly, rubbing their big heads between the horns, making them aware of me. For gars seem, in spite of their awesome bulk, to depend upon our species when confronted by the strange and threatening. But the healer had her hands now raised to mask the lower part of her face, her eyes showing bright and intent above her interlaced fingers.

Though I strained to see, for our distance glasses were in my father's belt pouch and he had not taken them out, there was nothing but the rolling land and the wind blown grass. Illo turned her head a little and looked to my father.

"It—*they* move—"

His head jerked as if she had slapped him. In spite of the dark tint the sun had set upon him I saw a flush burn along his cheeks. He reached out and his hand fell upon her shoulder, tightened. He even shook her, until his control almost instantly returned and he moved away from her quickly, as if she herself were the source of some contagion and he wanted to put safe space between them.

"What do you know?" His tone was savage in its harsh demand.

"I am from Voor's Grove." She had dropped her masking hands. There was no sign of outrage on her face, her calmness remained complete.

He might have forgotten all the rest. To him now she could be the only important thing in the world.

"What do you remember?" Some of the harshness had faded from his voice, but the demand remained, even more intense.

"Nothing—I was only three. I do not even know why I and Attcan, Mehil lived—though they were only cradle babies then. There was Krisan also. But surely you know of what happened at Voor's—you who are ever seeking to find the secret of the curse."

"You are a healer—you have talents—a gift—" it was as if he now pleaded with her.

She shook her head. "But no more memory than does your son. It is only this to know—some children, always Voor born, second generation, survive the Shadow curse. Do you not think that the medics, the off-worlds' experts, have not tried, poked and pried, sent me into talk-sleep—done everything known to their science to wring an answer from me."

"They did that to you?"

Illo looked surprised. "Did they not also test your son in that same way?"

"No!" His denial was vehement. "No child should—why were they allowed to do this to you?"

She lost none of her serenity. "Because there was no one to speak for me and say they could not. Perhaps I should even be grateful to them, for it may have been their proving which released what you call my 'gift'. It is known that such a talent often manifests itself suddenly after illness or some injury. But what happened long in the past does not matter now—what does is the message this wind carries. Somewhere the Shadows must prowl."

Now he did take out the distance glasses, and, using them, turned his head slowly right to left and then back again even more slowly.

"Nothing—nothing which can be seen. There is no holding now in this way—"

"Not now," she agreed. "But bear you only a little more west and then north again and Voor's Grove will lie before you."

For the first time my father looked uneasy, as if she had caught him without any ready words.

"I am sorry, healer—" his voice was hardly above a mutter.

"There is no need for any distress. It is there I would go—"

"Why?" I asked that from where I stood with my arm laid across Witol's wide back. The smell of his hide had driven out for me that wind borne stench of corruption.

It was a breech of custom, of good manners to ask such a question of a healer. Still I could not hold it back. In our wanderings we had visited near all of the forsaken holdings of the north, but never had my father returned to Mungo's, nor did I expect him to. What lay at the place of her past life which drew her now?

"Why?" she repeated. She did not look at me, or even at my father, rather into the distance, as if she needed no glasses but already could pick out there her destination. "Why? I do not know, but it is a call—one I cannot ignore."

"There can be no one there," my father pointed out. "It is not good to see what was once—"

He had hesitated but she finished the sentence for him calmly:

"A part of my life? I cannot remember. Perhaps if I returned there I could. What they did to me has left me with the need to know, only until now I did not feel that so strongly. Now it has become a call, like to such which the talent makes a part of us when there lies sickness and suffering somewhere and no help to hand. I cannot turn back—"

Though the clouds had grown heavier the wind had fallen away. I could no longer smell that stench. Loper that I was, and so weatherwise, I dared to speak up to my father:

"There is a storm coming—and we have no shelter."

Storms on the wide plains can be deadly—a strike of lightning out of the sky can kill man and beast. The torrent of autumn rain is always chill, and, more often than not, brings a burden of hail. I have seen such stones bury themselves half into the earth by the force of their fall, they being near large enough to cover most of my out-stretched palm.

The gars were bellowing now, turning their backs to what wind there was. Witol threw up his head, sounded a summoning call. I leaped aside away from him, knowing that no voice or hand, no matter how accustomed he might be to it day by day, would hold him now. We were only lucky that we had out-spanned and that the half-maddened animals would not drag the wagon with them.

They went, their ropey tails up, their eyes rolling in growing terror. My father wasted no time in worry over whether we might round them up once again, or whether they would run on until exhausted, or perhaps come to earth with broken legs caught in some grass-hidden hole. Once more he caught Illo by the arm, to draw her swiftly to the wagon, pushing her up to me, where I had leaped to the foreseat, with as little ceremony as if she had been a bale of such goods as could take rough handling.

We near tumbled back into the living section with hardly time to scramble out of my father's way as he threw himself after. Then we were both up, he and I, making fast the flap covering, moving along the sides of the wagon from one section to the next to test each cover latch and pushing the heaviest part of what we carried into the center as a makeshift anchor against the fury on its way.

The dark was now that of night. We did not light any lamp. Such, too, might become an added danger if what we expected came to pass. And it did.

That wind which had come early was but the gentlest of breezes against the force which slammed against the wagon, its roar enough to make anyone deaf. There had been a change in the direction of the fury; it blew from the west yet seemed to be altering towards the north. Under and around us our transport shuddered, shook, seemed to cower closer to the earth. If we had only had time we could have dug out beneath its wheels, letting it sink lower to the ground for anchorage. But that time had not been granted us.

The screech of the wind, which arose higher and higher in the scale like the scream of a woman under torture, was endless. I did not hesitate to crouch on my knees, my hands over my ears to shut out what I could of that fury. The wagon moved—swaying first from side to side until I was sure we could crash, then ahead, as if the wind had some intelligence and so had taken us prisoner.

I was thrown forward and landed against another form. Our arms reached out, caught at each other's bodies. I was locked with Illo in an embrace of stark fear when the hail struck with the same punishing force as the wind which bore it.

✦★ CHAPTER 3 ★✦

THE WAGON CONTINUED TO ROCK. Also it was again moving forward as if the wind was exerting full force against it. Though the grasslands might seem, under their covering of growth, to be flat surface, they were not. There were dips and hollows, small rises here and there, so that our transport now trembled on the edge of being completely thrown from its wheels and I could not understand how we continued to remain upright.

I had known autumn storms before, ridden out many of them. However the force of this blow exceeded anything in my memory. All one could feel was the helplessness of uncontrol, over even his own person. While always the sound of that blasting wind, the battering of hail over and around us, continued.

Were we being driven back towards the river as the gars had earlier fled? I could not be sure, but I believe that that was not so. The wind instead of battering us south was bearing us west and north— in the very direction we had been heading. Yet what could anyone make sure of in this chaos?

How long that thundering, howling storm possessed us as prisoners I could not tell. The dark continued. In time I loosed my hold on Illo and strove to push aside those containers which, for all their travel lashing, had broken loose and thudded into our bodies with force enough to crack ribs or break bones, if they were to hit squarely.

My first efforts were blind, more the instinctive reaction of one who had always lived on the edge of peril and whose body reflexes took over even when his thoughts were awry. Then I began to gain hold of myself as it came as a clear stroke to cut through my own haze of fear that, though my father had entered the wagon in good time, he was not joining me in doing what could be done to secure the lashings.

I called him, and the roar, the thud of hail made so much sound I could not hear my own voice. Having done what I could to relieve us of immediate danger of being crushed, I crept on hands and knees through the thick dark to the fore of the wagon where I had seen him last come through the opening and turn to lash down the flap door.

The wagon was still rocking forward, and I held one arm out to fend off anything which might yet be adrift. With my other hand I groped ahead, striving to find—to touch him.

My fingers brushed trail leather, closed upon what could only be his upper arm. But he did not move at my touch, and there was a looseness—The wagon made another of its threatening side dips and his body slid, until I managed to reach and support it.

He lay with his head heavy against my shoulder now, my questing hand felt stickiness draining down his face, and it was plain he was unconscious. Light—I must have light—!

Now the wagon itself was filled with the smell of spilled saloil. We used the lanterns of the trek people rather than the very costly unit rods from off world. There was no place outside Portcity or one of the mine compounds to recharge those. To try to spark a light with oil free-flowing might well add a final disaster to our situation.

I attempted to discover the extent of his hurts by touch alone, but I dared not examine him fully lest some unwary pressure of my hands might make his situation worse. Though I bent over him until our faces near touched I could not, in this uproar, hear his breathing, though my finger tips located the throat pulse and there was an answer there. Was it strong and steady as it should be? I doubted that. There was nothing to be done—nothing until the storm blew out or finished its play with us in some drastic fashion.

Illo—a healer! She would know—could give aid—Where was she?

The wagon lurched, tipped forward. I was jammed heavily

against the fore part of the wagon, my father's inert weight lying half across me. The cargo! It had been well stowed. However, the lashings and bolted rods which held it were never meant to take this kind of punishment! I thought of two of the crates—they contained machines too heavy to transport by the miners' flitters and so consigned to our slower service. If those now broke loose they might even smash forward from the rear compartment to crush us. I struggled to free myself from under my father's body so that I might loose the door flap—make sure there was a small chance of escape.

Only there was no time. Whatever hollow lay before us now was deeper, more precipitous than any ordinary dip in the plains. The tilt of the wagon assumed a sharper angle. Then—the fore part hit.

We were stopped in the mad race which the wind had urged us into. Continued wind pressure now at the back might flip the whole transport entirely over. I held my breath waiting for that to happen.

Dimly I became aware that the pounding of the hail had ceased, and though the wind continued to batter us it lacked the last ultimate fraction of strength to send us end over end. I drew a deep breath, my whole body tense as I tried hard to listen. Had that continual roar dulled my hearing, or was it that the storm had spent the worse of its attack and was dying at last?

It was true that the wagon had stopped, slanted sharply towards the fore. As far as I could tell the cargo in the back was not battering down the two partitions between us. I shifted with care from under my father's weight, edging around his crumpled body to fumble with the lowest of the second flap lashings. Light—if we could only have a fraction of light!

The flap edge gave and I dragged it up. What came into the battered mess of what had been our home was a grey twilight, but steadily growing stronger.

My father lay beside me. There was a dark stream of blood down the side of his face spreading from the hair on the right side of his head. He was struggling to breathe, and now, with the dying of the storm fury, I could hear moans bubbling from his lips. Only there was red froth showing also at the corners of his mouth, spreading down his chin.

Illo crawled forward. She lifted a hand to signal that I try to straighten him out, then edge back that she might see his hurts.

Fortune had favored us in this much—we had her gift to depend upon now.

Her finger tips touched very lightly that matted patch of hair. Having seen healers at their task I knew that, though she knelt with closed eyes, having to steady herself against the angle of the flooring with her other hand, she was "seeing" after their strange fashion the extent and nature of his injury. Then her fingers slid down to his chest which I had quickly laid bare and once more she traced back and forth with the slightest of touches.

So much had the wind now died I was able to hear his labored breathing as well as those moans of pain. Now I heard the words I had so anxiously waited for:

"He is badly injured." She did not try to spare me and for that I was very glad. "There is a crack in his skull, and his ribs are broken. He must be aided, and quickly—My pack—"

She looked into the welter of stuff on the floor. I was busy with the rest of the lashing of the door flap. It was plain that broken bones could not be tended in this place. We would have to move him to where his body could lie straight and she would have the room to work upon him.

The flap open, I looked out. The day was now light—though there was no sign of sun. Immediately facing me was a hillside down which washed streams of water as thick as my wrist. When I thrust head and shoulders out to see more, it was plain that the wagon had come to rest, almost as a stopper might be pounded into a bottle, in one of those grass-hidden gullies which are to be found in the plains to carry off the water after just such storms.

That water which flowed down the walls was now rising about the fore of the wagon itself, fast enough to suggest that in a very short time it might wash high enough to lap into our present perch. We must get out and that quickly—but to try to carry an unconscious man through the rising flood was impossible. I made this report to Illo. She nodded, but did not raise her eyes from my father's face.

I crawled around them as best I could and up the slope formed by the other part of the wagon. The latch on the second compartment yielded easily enough. Beyond, though a few of the smaller containers had jammed themselves to this end (doubtless most of their fragile contents was now useless), I had no barrier against my drawing myself along by hand holds on those same shelves to the hatch of the end cargo section.

It all depended now on how well our restraints had worked there; I could open the hatch to find it barricaded by those machinery-filled crates which I could not shift by myself. Thumbing the lock-bar I discovered that just that had happened. There was a solid surface of crate facing me and no way from this side that I could hope to push it aside.

Back I went, fear riding on me, for I knew that for my father it could well be a matter of time, very little time. I stopped in the first cargo compartment only long enough to shoulder a coil of rope, though I had very little hope of being able to use that as it could be done only if there were two or three men to bring full strength to bear.

"No way out back there." Just as Illo had been frank with me, so did I return the same truth in my report.

"We must hurry," was her only answer. That was one I had already guessed for myself.

I dropped down into the rising water, the wagon holding the major push of the current away from me. Now I could clearly see what had happened. We had blown into quite a deep crevice. There was thick brush on both banks and sight of that gave me my first fraction of dim hope. It would depend entirely on how far down those roots reached and with what tenacity they clung to the ground in which they were now buried. If the streams of descending water loosened the soil, what I planned was near impossible.

Though the brush resisted my climb, I had the wagon itself to pull against. The front wheels were nearly under the rising water now, but the back ones rested deeply up slope and I could drag myself through the whipping, briary stuff which laced my skin with a network of clawed scratches, until I reached the back of the wagon. There I loosened the latch and flung it wide open, to see that it was the largest and heaviest of the crates which jammed entrance at the other end of the section.

Now I tested the brush, paying no attention to the saw-edged leaves, the thorns which cut into my hands. My choice was one near the lip of the gully. There was no water running there within a good space on either side, and, in spite of all my sudden jerks and longer, deliberate pulls, it did not stir. I would have to chance dependence upon its support.

Back I crawled into the compartment, making fast one end of my rope with loper's knots which would hold even a maddened gar. A gar! Never in my life have I wanted anything as much as Witol or one of the herd to stand waiting at that moment. But they were gone—I hoped they had reached some shelter before the full fury of that wind and hail had struck.

With the other end of the rope looped well about me I went again to my bush. Its inner trunk was thick, perhaps as large as my thigh, but I had to slash and cut with my belt knife to slice away the branches which were so close springing one could not reach that trunk without such clearing. Then the rope was around the trunk. I tested it the best I could, before I swung my whole weight upon it, throwing myself deliberately down slope. I brought up with a gasp of pain. Nor had that moved the crate barrier.

"Loose the end for me."

Gasping for breath I swung half way around, one hand on the up-tilted wheel to steady myself. Illo, her breeches plastered to her legs, her browned hands reaching out, had joined me before I knew it.

Two of us might do it. We could but try. Now she was only another pair of hands as far as I was concerned, an addition of strength. At my nod as I still fought to get back my breath, she took from where they were tucked into her girdle a pair of gloves and drew them on. As a healer, I guessed, she could not risk the sensitivity and skill of her fingers in the rasping punishment mine had taken. That done, she did not hold back any from twisting the rope with closed fists. Above her I settled myself for another effort.

"Now!"

The quick jerk, to be followed by a pull in which I knew we put both our strength. It moved! Loosed out of its tight jam against the door the crate appeared to give easily now, and I saw, as I turned my head, the edge of the obstacle visible in the wagon opening—then it tottered, fell forward into the brush, splintering and breaking the mass of greenery with its weight.

I threw the rope from me, was already up within the wagon bed, heading for the compartment door. Illo was on my heels as I pushed through the second section to reach our living quarters. There I found she had already accomplished what I would have believed impossible for her strength, for my father was a big man, spare of flesh perhaps, but heavy of bone. He had been straightened out upon a length of board she had loosened from the side of a bunk, for those could be dismantled at need for extra space. His body arranged as best she might, it was only necessary now for me to once more use the rope, setting one end of it with her hold, to bind my father's blan-keted body to that board.

Half carrying, half dragging him so we retraced our way just as the first waters of the rising stream licked across the forepart of the wagon. It might be injurious to move him, but now that was the lesser of evils. Lowered from the wagon end and still immobilized on the board, we transported him on through the brush to the lip of the gully, though twice we had to lay down our burden so I could knife-hack a passage for us.

When we reached the torn earth of the edge over which the wagon had plunged I was so beat by weariness that I had only strength enough to see our burden over and lying face up in the matted, water-soaked grass under the clearing sky. I longed to throw myself down beside him, but there was that which must be saved from the wagon lest the water sweep away what might come to be our future means of life.

Three times I made the journey down and up, each time spurring myself to the descent and climb. Up there now was Illo's precious pack which she had already opened as she worked over my father, food, damp blankets, our stunners and tanglers, two night torches, a com which might or might not work after the way it had been bounced about during our wild journey, and anything else I chanced upon which would serve us.

It was plain that without the gars there was no hope of pulling free the wagon. At least none that I could see. There was always the chance that the com might have range enough to reach Dengungha—of that I could not be sure. The miners had a flitter, and, though I had little idea now of where we were in connection with their settlement, on this plain there should be some way of raising a signal for help which would guide air borne rescue to us.

The heavy pelt of the rain was luckily over, but it had left the grass in which we made now an uncomfortable camp site soaked and flattened by the burden of water which had fallen. I had the emergency heat unit from the wagon, though its active life was so limited we could not hope for it to last long.

Illo asked my aid in strapping my father's ribs with bands cut from one of the blankets. She had also bandaged his head. Now, wrapped in near all the coverings I had managed to pull free from the water rising so steadily in the fore part of the wagon, he lay beside that single unsteady flame. His face was grey rather than pale beneath the weathered brown, and I could not bear to look at him often. At each time I did a fear I would not allow myself yet to face arose in me like some choking illness.

I set up a lean-to of planks torn from the inner fittings of the wagon, thatched as well as I could manage with the brush I slashed free. The clouds had scudded south to allow a watery emergence of the sun. I climbed to the highest of the small rolling hills which lay beneath the blanket of grass and turned the distance glasses on the land around, hoping against hope to pick up sight of the gars.

There was nothing, save a bird or two wheeling and dipping back and forth across the sky. We were left with only the chance that the com might summon aid, and I trudged back to the lean-to and got it out.

Such off-world artifacts were always prized and kept in the best repair possible. These were too costly when shipped by Spacers for the average Voorsman to own. Though I knew how to repair one, there were certain materials which could not be substituted by anything known on Voor. The men of the holdings worked well with their hands—in wood and stone. There was some primitive and experimental work done with metal—the forging of large tools and the like. But small precision objects which were the result of centuries of technological know-how could not be duplicated.

It was with the greatest of suspense that I opened the com carrying case to inspect how its contents had fared. The round of metal, with the mike disc lying upon it, had been packed as best we knew, so I had to pull out wads of grass-cotton to free the disc and dial. I could see no breakage as I worked the thing carefully out of its soft nest. Then I pried loose the back of the inner case. Wires, works, I traced what I could see without taking the unit apart. My spirits arose a little as I could detect no fracture. Now it depended upon the range.

Where the wind had driven us I could not tell, though when I had used the distance glasses I had been sure that the ominous smudge which marked the Tangle was far more visible. Perhaps we had been blown on to cover more distance than we could have covered in several days at the usual trek pace.

Illo had been tending a small pan to which she had fitted a long handle so she could hold it well over the flame of our heat without scorching her fingers. She seemed entirely intent upon her task and did not even look up as I readied the com and raised the mike, repeating into it the call letters which had been assigned us in Portcity and which must be on record at Dengungha. Three times I uttered those and waited for a reply. What came back to me was a crackle so loud and disturbing that I had to lay the mike down upon the box; that outburst of sound was enough to hurt ears already assaulted by the storm's long roar.

Patiently I went through the same procedure twice more, with no better result. If there was not any fault in the com, then there must be some freakish effect left by the storm itself which interfered with reception. Regretfully I had to fit the com back into its case.

Illo appeared satisfied with the bubbling contents of her pan for she set that aside until she hunted out a bag of small grass-cotton puffs. Wetting one of those in the pan's contents, she sponged my father's lips, gently forcing his mouth open so she could squeeze her improvised sponge and so get some of the liquid into him.

He no longer moaned. The very inert limpness of his body frightened me, though I determined not to let her know that. What liquid she had managed to get into his mouth was dribbling out again at one corner. Now she did look up at me.

"When I do thus," once more she held the sponge ball above his mouth, "you rub his throat—gently—downward. We must get him to swallow some of this. It is strengthening, a barrier against the shock and chill which follows bad wounds."

I followed her orders. My father's flesh was indeed cold under my touch. Resolutely we worked, I under her orders, until he did swallow and she was able, by patient concentration, to get perhaps a third of the contents of the small pan into him.

"We shall let him rest now." Her own hand rested for a long, measuring moment on his forehead below the bandage.

"He—how is he?" For the first time I asked, dreading even as I did what she might answer.

Slowly she shook her head. "These are bad hurts. I think that one of the broken ribs may have entered into a lung. As for the crack in the skull—we know so little of what may happen after such as that. However, he lives, and, as long as he holds to life, then we can also hold to hope. I wish we could get him to some cover better than this—"

I got up, frustration and anger at what had happened building up in me, so I must keep a sharp rein on my tongue and swallow the words I wanted to say. It was none of her doing, or his, or mine, that this thing had happened. Still something in me wanted to make me lash out and scream with rage that it was this way. Once more I left our sorry camp and tramped back to my small hillock which certainly raised me very little above the rest of the plain.

In the gully the water washed high now, hiding the fore of the wagon, which shook now and then as the current tried to break or bear away this barrier against its even flow. I turned my glasses along the path of the gully itself. It was truly a flow from the north. Perhaps it even traced its beginning back to the mountains beyond the Tangle where Survey ships had flown to map from the sky, but, to my knowledge, no one of my race had ever gone. They were stark, those mountains, sharp, jagged peaks, showing like teeth between the gaping jaws of some monster. Dire, and dark, and not for humankind.

There was, as I watched the flow of water in the gully, storm wrack coming with it now. Brush such as grew along the banks, uprooted when the waters gnawed the soil from about their roots, bounced and wavered along. Some of the stuff came to rest uneasily against the wagon, building up more tightly the damming barrier that had begun.

Now there was other movement in the water. My hand flew to stunner butt and I had that out of my holster when I saw, and knew it was no vision, an ugly, armored head rise above the surface, round, unblinking, but dead white eyes, regard the brush and the wagon.

This was certainly like no creature I had seen before, not of the grass plains. I took a running leap from the hill, was down at the gully's rim as a webbed and taloned paw, larger than my own hand, slopped up from the water, drew arching claws down the wagon's body, seeking some hold.

That it found. A second paw now wavered aloft hunting similar anchorage. I pushed right to the edge of the drop, my weapon ready. The thing had already opened jaws wide enough to near split its head in two and those were tooth ringed—I could be well sure it was a flesh eater.

The monster did not move clumsily in spite of the bulk of its body, for beneath the longish neck the rest of it was wide, out of proportion with the head, while the legs appeared much too slender to support it. This thing, I thought, must spend much time in the water. Now it hauled itself to the top of the wagon, and, lifting higher that ugly head, gave voice to an ear-rasping grunting.

"What is it?" Illo came up beside me.

"I don't know. But—"

The head shot around, made a dart in our direction. The eyes looked blind, white balls only, without even the faintest slit to suggest a pupil. Yet it was evident that the thing saw us, judged us either enemy or prey. Still grunting it drew itself wholly out of the water, showing other hook-clawed legs, and started to climb along the upward slant of the wagon.

I centered the stunner on its head, set the charge on full, and fired. I might as well have flipped a twig for it did not even shake its head as if momentarily dizzy. Yet a gar, a sand cat, a jaz would have been plunged into instant unconsciousness.

The clawed forefeet were already raking into the brush from which I had hacked our escape path. Perhaps on land we could hope to outrun it, or dodge, but not with the unconscious man lying beside the fire. I might have fired too soon, my aim a fraction off—

This time I made myself concentrate only on that weaving ugly head. There was a point directly between the white eyes—I settled on that for my target. Then Illo's voice broke through my strained concentration.

"Aim for the neck, where it joins the back!"

What did she know about it? She by her own words had never seen this thing before.

"Aim there!" her voice had the crack of an order. "Its brain—I cannot sense a brain at all!"

Her words did not mean much. But a straightforward shot had not brought it down. I had once seen a gar paralyzed when a stunner merely clipped its backbone. Could that trick work here?

Though every instinct told me that I might be wrong, I changed, in that last instant, the angle of my ray shot. I did aim where that weaving neck sank into the foul, scaled and flabby bag of body.

Full strength, and I held it past the first shot, refusing to let myself remember I could so exhaust the whole charge completely.

The neck snapped straight up into the air as if, instead of a ray, I had laid across it the lash of a whip to torment the flesh. Then it looped forward, falling limply, so that the head dragged along the brush as the body itself, the taloned paws relaxing their hold, slid down and down, slipping at last from the wagon into the stream, where it sank beneath water now brown with silt.

❂⋆**CHAPTER 4**⋆❂

THERE WAS A BRIEF SWIRL OF WATER against the pull of the current and then nothing at all. If the thing was indeed a water dweller it could lie hidden there, so covered now was the surface with floating debris of the flood and a film of mud, only to emerge once again to attack. We must move away. But to do that—

When I spoke my fear aloud Illo nodded. "This thing—I have never even heard of its like before," she said slowly as she stood still gazing at the flow of water as if she expected any moment to see that hideous head rise again. "At least in the south. It might be a dweller in those swamp lands perhaps—but where—"

I was facing north-west. During my travels as loper I had seen many strange creatures. In fact it had been one of my father's concerns to record any new living thing, were it flyer, crawler, or growing plant, which we came across. So detailed had been this work of his that it had first led me to wonder if he had not, in that unknown past which he never shared with me, been connected with Survey.

Not that he shared officially any of his knowledge with the authorities at Portcity as far as I knew. It was as if he was driven by some need of his own to learn all which it was possible to gather about Voor. However, like Illo, we had never heard of nor seen anything like the monster of the flood.

As for a swamp—there were some in the south, yes. Still none so large a spread of country to give living space to this size creature. While to the north—

I had raised my head now, gazed beyond the swiftly flowing, ever rising waters which were now rocking the wagon even more dangerously, so that it canted to the right and might well be shortly engulfed. The stream, though born of the fury of the storm, lay in a bed which water had already carved, and it came from the north-west— that same direction in which the Tangle made its stain across the healthy plains.

Was that mass of entwined vegetation a cover for a swamp? It could well be, though so thick a growth seldom was a part of any swampland I knew. And the beast we had fought off was of a size unsuited to the density of that maze men had not been able to force any path through as long as planet record existed.

Yet so sinister was the reputation of that massed growth I could well accept that it might give living room to any number of monsters. Not that that had any meaning for us now. We must concentrate on getting ourselves and my father to some civilized shelter. If we could not raise the mines with the com, then we must somehow trek south, back to the holding where we had been only days earlier.

I set about once more securing from the wagon such materials which might be of use. Spare of frame as my father was, we could not carry him between us and achieve any great distance, except at less than a usual walking pace. I believed that we had no time for that. Still there were other ways which we could attempt, and I salvaged gear, venturing gingerly time and again into the rocking, tilting wagon.

Water already washed into the front compartment and the wagon was near on its side as the stream gnawed steadily at the bank in which the back wheels were embedded. I had given Illo the second stunner and she had stationed herself to watch for any more water-dwellers.

The clouds had finally all gone and the sun made a dim showing, but it was already far down the horizon. I had so little time. Also I was so tired that my hands shook as I strove to unfasten lashings, bundle up all I could, perhaps bringing a lot which I had no need for in my desire not to miss anything which would be of value.

There was no lifting out the cargo. That, unless we could contact the mines and gain aid there, must be written off as a total loss. But the small stuff I bundled out hit and miss, passing up the awkward armloads I gathered to the girl who piled them about her sentry post.

I worked until the wagon gave a warning lurch so that I leaped clear just as it went over on its side while water boiled up and in. Somehow I won back up the slope and fell, gasping for breath with a band of permasteel seemingly fastened about my middle, drawing always inward as might the jaws of a slowly closing trap.

Illo had already carried some of the goods back to our improvised camp. Much I knew I could not deal with now. It was all I could do to stagger towards that flare which had now become a beacon, there to collapse again, my body one ache from head to foot.

I remember drinking from a pan Illo handed me, thinking dimly that we must set a guard for the night. Most of the grass plains had few predators, and all of those, as lopers knew, were not only night hunters but afraid of fire. However, there was still the water—and what could come out of it. Only I could not make any effort to so much as reach for the stunner which was thrust into my belt, even keep my eyes open. Instead fatigue settled on me in a smothering blanket, drew me in and covered me, as might the Tangle itself.

I awoke—The stars were brilliant overhead; the orange-red of Voor's moon was a ball hanging near directly over me. It was one of those instant awakenings which come to those who live always on the edge of the unknown, whose instincts and inner warning systems have become trained to signal alerts as potent as any a starship might possess.

There was the light on the ground—Three of our salvaged camp lamps had been filled, trimmed, and set out, burning sturdily. Beyond them lay an unsorted mound of all I had pulled from the wagon. After I had given out, the girl must have brought much of it here. The girl—!

She sat hunkered down beside the plank which served my father as a bed. The lamps gave her face a deceptive ruddiness. Her eyes were closed, but the hand lying beside her held grip on the other stunner.

I was ashamed at my own failure. At that moment my pride was cruelly hurt that I, who was supposed to be the toughened loper, had failed what was surely a good part of my duty. She had even pulled over me one of the gar fleece blankets. That I now hurled aside in my flare of temper at my own collapse.

Yet that temper only raged for an instant. Something had awakened me; my plains knowledge assumed control. I could hear the water in the gully, though that did not sound to me as if it were now made by any rushing stream. Perhaps that storm born flood was subsiding.

My loper's belt was about me, slung with those tools and aids any trekker must depend upon. Beside the stunner holster, the weight of my knife was against my hip as I stood up. My hand rested steadily about its hilt as I slowly turned my head from east to west, and then faced around to look north.

There was the night wind, yes, but it did not sing tonight through the long grass which had been so beaten down by the storm. Nor did it carry with it that strange odor which had been a part of it before the coming of the storm. If some scavenger prowled beyond the reach of our fire, the visitor made no sound.

For a moment or two I had a sudden leap of hope—the gars! Had Witol managed to find his way back, perhaps heading as herd leader the others of the team? I whistled softly that call which the massive beast always answered if he was within range of hearing.

There was no snorting, no sound of those hooves thudding on the plains ground. Yet there was something—a sound, a feeling had brought me out of sleep and now held me tense and listening. If my father—I knew that my hard-learned knowledge of the loper's world was nearly only the beginning of a child's first reading tape compared to his. I had seen him so alerted many times in the past, and always there had been excellent reason.

Sight was not going to serve me beyond the lantern glow; smell and sound had brought me nothing—yet. I crossed to where Illo huddled, stooped and drew the stunner from her lax grasp. With that at ready, saving my own for an emergency, I began a slow circuit of our improvised camp, stopping every few paces to listen, to stare out into the country with its moon-painted patches of light and dark.

Nothing to be detected. The grass was so heavy with water that it was beaten towards the ground. Anything trying to reach us through that would have made both sound and movement which I could easily pick up. There remained the stream. I unhooked my night torch from my belt. Its charges must be carefully conserved as there was only one small box of them which I had managed to drag away from the flood. Still I thumbed the control button on high and aimed the wide beam of frosty light down into the gully.

The weight of the wagon, its forepart pushed by the stream, had broken one of the embedded rear wheels, so now it lay on its side. Were my father whole and the gars to hand, its repair and return to the trek would have been a hard job but not an impossible one. Under the present circumstances I could not hope to draw the vehicle out again.

That river which had been such a force had greatly subsided. Though its surface was still opaque with silt and muddy swirls, the current had lessened and was no longer high enough to give cover to any such beast as had threatened us.

Though the dropping of the water would certainly have partly uncovered the bulk of the creature's body were it still inert from the ray, there was no serrated, scaled back showing. The thing had either been borne well down stream, or had swum away of its own accord. To my most searching survey nothing lay there but the wreck of the wagon and the steadily lessening flow of water.

I had made a circle about our camp without result. Yet—I knew. There was something which had awakened me, something out there somewhere—waiting—

I thought of what my mother's kinswoman had said—Shadow touched. Oh, I had heard the expression before but then it had not meant—me. What had happened when the death had come to the northern holdings? Why had a child here, some infants there—all second generation—escaped whatever doom it was which had blasted whole settlements out of existence? Why should we not remember?

Once more I reached back in my own mind—No, there was only riding the gar under the sun, my father tramping beside the beast. I could not even clearly remember him; the gar was far more vivid in my mental picture.

Was that because riding was strange and wonderful, an exciting thing for a small boy? The settlements and holdings used gars, yes— but those were lesser in size, in strength, in all that which might impress a small child, than the animals a loper trained and lived with most of his life.

I thought of my father's constant interest in the deserted and ruined sites where the Shadows had struck—risking his life to explore such. Why did men speak of "Shadows"? If there were no survivors who could report on the nature of the danger—then who had given them that name?

Again I searched memory and could find nothing to answer my own question. I had heard of "Shadows" as a danger, as doom and death, all my life—still, in spite of all my father's searching I had never been told why that unknown menace in the north had been so named. It was as if there was some inward flinching away in me which kept me from such speculation, a barrier—

As I slipped once more around our camp I not only searched the night-covered land for the reason for my waking, my uneasiness, but another part of my mind was busy—for the first time I could honestly remember—in asking those questions. Three times I went around just within the farthest gleam of the lanterns.

Instead of being able to reassure myself that nothing waited in the water-drenched, moonlit land, my feeling that we were under observation of some sort grew deeper. I found myself hunching my shoulders against my will, as if I expected a knife to come whistling through the air to strike into my flesh, a blaster to crisp me, skin and bone. I waited for a long space each time I stood at the edge of the gully, my torch beam striking down at the water which was reduced so rapidly now in its flow it was as if the ground itself was a sponge soaking up that fluid in huge quantities.

At last I turned aside from my self-appointed sentry's beat and went directly to where my father lay, covered with one of the blankets. In the light which was less glaring than my torch, his face was drawn, the bones seeming to stand out beneath the skin as if in these short hours some deadly illness had eaten through his resistance. And— His eyes were wide open. Not only open but aware. They met mine with intelligence, a compulsion which brought me to my knees beside him. I might have at that moment been no older than the small boy in my memory of the past.

Illo had washed the blood from his face, bandaged his wounds. The blanket was pulled up to his throat, masking the broken body. Pain must have made those lines so deep there now, but he had forced it away from him, under his control. I read that, and I do not know how I did it.

I saw his lips move with effort. There was a beading of sweat across what forehead the bandage did not cover. Driven by what lay in his eyes I leaned very low above him so my ear was close to those struggling lips. "North—to Mungo—" his words were a mere wisp of sound. "North—I—I—must—lie—in Mungo. Swear this, swear it!" Somehow he had gathered the strength to make those last four words ring out, above the tortured whisper, clear and strong as he might have given the signal for the gars to be on the move. There was a bubble of red again showing at a corner of his mouth. He coughed thickly, rackingly. The bubble burst, and blood spewed forth. But his eyes never loosed their hold on mine. His lips worked again—but there was only that terrible, tearing cough which brought out gouts of blood instead of the words.

"I swear—!" There was no other answer which could ease him in this time; that I understood.

The bright glint in his eyes still held strong and clear for a long moment after we made that pact. I reached beneath the edge of the blanket, found his hand and held it. In him there yet remained some strength, for his fingers tightened in my hold, gripping mine with a force I would not have believed he was still able to summon.

He did not try to speak again. But he kept his eyes open and on mine and we held that grasp. Was it for long? There was no measurement of time. I am not sure when it was that his head moved a fraction on the folded blanket we had used to pillow it, when he looked beyond me at something else. For that he did see something in that last moment I shall always swear. What it was remained his secret, but I think in some manner it was a comfort, for the pain lines lessened, and there was a new peace—an expression I realized I had never seen on my father's calm face before. He was in that moment younger, eager, a man I did not know, that it had never been for me to know.

I still sat by him as the moon dropped low in the night sky, but what I guarded now was nothing—an outworn coat, a forgotten and unneeded garment. My father was gone and left in me an emptiness which grew deeper and wider, making a space into which I thought I might even fall and never climb out of again. I had had no life which had not held him always there—what could I do now?

I started. The touch on my shoulder then was as if a blaster had seared across unshielded flesh.

"He has taken his own way, that lay in his mind from the beginning."

I looked up at the girl, my anger hot enough to burn away the uncertainty of moments earlier.

"He had strength—he would not have—done what you say!" I denied her words fiercely. For I had seen once or twice in my roving life those who died of what seemed minor illnesses or superficial hurts because they had no wish to live. My father was not to be numbered among them. I think at that moment my rage boiled up in me, fed by the hurt of my own loss, might have led me to strike out physically at her.

"He was tired—very tired, and he was one of those who know—"

She did not draw away from me. Her face and voice still held the calm of her calling. That serenity began to react on me as it always did when one came in contact with the healers.

"One who knows what?" I demanded.

"It is given to some of us to understand and know when the great change draws near. He was a man who has been driven many years by that which he could not accept—he had already begun to believe that he must reach beyond our life to understand."

Her words dropped into my mind one by one as one might cast pebbles into a pool and watch the ripples spread outward to the edge of the surface and then break and go. That my father was a driven man—yes, that I had always known since I had grown into the age when one's world does not center only upon one's self as it does for a child. That he was ridden ever by the puzzle which remained beyond his solving, yes, that, too, was true. But that he would surrender—No! I bit back the harsh outburst which I might have used to greet that. What remained to think on now—at this present—was not that he had died—doubtless of such hurts not even off-world medical wonders could heal—but that he had asked a promise of me and I was sworn to fulfill it.

How was that task to be accomplished? I did not even know for sure in what direction Mungo's lay or how far away. But that I would do this—that I must.

"I have sworn to him that he will lie in Mungo's—or what is still left of it," I told her. Somehow I shook my mind free of the frozen grip upon it, began to think of ways and means. Days of travel might lie ahead. I had no transport—even if I could raise the mine or the port on the com, I knew that I could get no one who would be willing to help.

Very well, alone I would do what I must. So I set to work. But when she saw what I brought out of the jumble of supplies Illo came forward, and, without a word, set about helping me. My father's body we sealed into the protect suit he had used all these years for exploring the Shadow-blasted ruins. There was a keg of plastaseal in the broken wagon, part of the shipment for the mine, used to repair their shelters there. Now it proved the outward seal, the encoffining for the body, until even the white suit was completely hidden by a swiftly stiffening green casing which under the sun became dura-hard.

Just as I had half thought out the transport for him alive, so did I now follow the same idea for him dead. The planks from the bunks I also sealed together with what was left of the plasta—forming a platform on which the enclosed body could be safely lashed.

I worked away most of the day, dealing with what supplies and tools I might use or improvise. Nor was I aware, as I worked, of anything but the job at hand, driving myself to its doing. Only when I had fastened the last rope and smeared the remaining drops of plasta over those knots, did I stagger to the side of the fire and take in shaking hands the bowl of food Illo held out to me. I was halfway through gulping its contents when I heard the sound which brought me to my feet, the food dribbling to the ground as the bowl turned over in my grasp. Faint and far away, yes—! I had no doubts that that was what I had heard.

Now I dropped the bowl entirely, put fingers to my lips to aid in a distance piercing whistle. Gars—that could have been the bellow of some wild herd bull, for there were such, drifters from the ruined holdings. Only, once a team was well united, it was the nature of the great beasts to keep with their masters in a strong relationship, and our gars had been unusually united, even for their breed.

That they could have traced us over the wildness where the stream had driven the wagon, that, too, was not unknown. I had heard tales of gars who had traveled from one holding to another seeking the breeder with whom they had been identified in training as calves. That was why few of them could ever be sold away from their trainers.

It was close to sunset, but there was light across the land. I fumbled for my distance glasses after I had whistled for the second time. Now I could pick up greyish specks in the distance—three of them. Where the others were—remembering the fury of the storm, the beating of the hail, perhaps I could expect no more than those.

Illo moved in beside me. "Yours?"

"I will wager it. But there are only three—"

"Not enough to raise the wagon," she commented.

I shook my head, my attention all for those distant dots which were growing larger by the moment. They were moving fast, at a trot, their horned heads now and then dipping groundwards as if they scented some trail. But there was no mistaking that larger bulk in the lead now—Witol! One who followed was his mate—Dru—and the third—he was a youngster whom we had put to the yoke only this season, a calf sired by Witol—Wodru.

With the gars I could well carry out my plan. Only, as I turned back to the fire confident that they would soon be shouldering their way to our camp, I remembered for the first time Illo and her own quest. I was bound to the task my father had set for me, but as trekmaster he had given her passage with us. The cargo we carried for the mine would be no problem—I could use the com as a set signal for the men there and give in that fashion a pick-up point so that they could find what might be salvaged. Illo's transportation was another matter. I must now take on the responsibility of seeing her safely to her own destination.

"Will you go on?" I asked bluntly. "Have you any map or guide?"

She looked up at me over her shoulder, for she had gone back to kneel by the fire and add to it some of the brush culled from beneath the growth where the rain had not left it sodden.

"Trekmaster's bond?" she held out her hands to the small flames. "No, I do not hold you to it, Bart s'Lorn. Such can be dissolved by mutual consent."

"I do not consent," I told her sharply. "With the gars we can pack enough supplies surely to see you to where you would go—"

"Very well then. Suppose I say now that I go to Mungo's—"

"Why?" I challenged her. "Because you know that I must journey there? But that is folly. I can see you to whatever holding—"

"Holding?" she interrupted me. "There is no holding or settlement— save that of the off-worlders—this far north—now."

"But you said—you had call, that you were needed. The off-worlders—?"

Her lips curved in a faint smile. "Would they drink my potions, allow my hands to draw any illness from them? They have no belief in such. Yes, I was called—but not by any messenger such as can be seen or heard. I told you—I am Shadow touched. As your father there is a need in me to know—to discover what I cannot remember. So—Mungo's fell to the Shadow doom as did Voor's Grove. Therefore, perhaps I can learn the nature of what I wish there as well as in the place from which I came."

I did not like it. Still it cannot be that any man says 'no' to a healer who declares that she has a call for aid. That she could not help my father was no reflection on her skill—for there are hurts past any healing. It was true that if I did not have to linger on my own journey to see her to her destination it would be the better. Still I was not satisfied within myself, though I could raise no adequate argument against such a journey.

The gars reached our camp and then I saw a thing which I had witnessed but once before in my life, for the three beasts, led by Witol went to the crude sled on which my father's body lay in the coffining I had devised and there stood for a space, Witol at the head, Dru on his right, Wodru on the left. The great team leader raised his three horned head and gave a cry which was not his usual deep-throated bellow, rather a keening which I have heard from those of his species when one of their own herd or team lay dead.

Three times did the gar sound his cry and then he turned, the other two falling in behind him, and they walked slowly and purposefully to me, Witol lowering his head now so that I could lay my flattened palm on the smooth hide between his great eyes as was also customary when one of his kind chose to serve a man of his own free will.

For near ten years of my life I had known Witol, yet never had he given me this salute. We had often speculated, my father and I, as to the intelligence of the gars—now I believed I had proof that they were indeed more than just the bearers of burdens which off-worlders classed them as being. Now I spoke to Witol and the others, greeting them by name as gravely and with as much courtesy as if they had been the people of some holding, thanking them for the offering of their service.

Thus we slept that night within the light of the lanterns, but more secure, for the gars could and did keep patrol. I thought earlier that I might never sleep well again, that memory would come to plague me with the knowledge of all I had lost. Only that was not so—perhaps the fatigue of my body won the battle with my mind, for I sank into a darkness which even dreams did not trouble.

☽∗ **CHAPTER 5** ∗☾

AMONG THE GEAR which I had salvaged from the wagon were two things which I made use of in the morning. Though I was left with no way of transporting the heavy crates which had been ordered by the off-worlders, still I, now by force of circumstances made trekmaster, must take what precautions that I could concerning the consigned cargo. So I set on the top of that small hillock beyond the lip of the gully a detect taken from the miner's own order. Sooner or later they would be in search, and that sound broadcast into the sky would register on the instruments of their flyers though it would not summon any other wanderers.

With the detect I left a tape recording of what had happened to us so that my father, even in death, would be cleared of unfair dealing or refusal to carry out a contract. Since loper's pride demanded this by their small but rigid code, I made sure this was done to the best of my ability.

We worked through the morning dividing all I had brought from the wagon, choosing that which was the most useful for what might lie ahead. I set aside tools, such off-world gadgets, which, if they failed in the wilderness of the plains, would be only useless burdens. For example, we needed no coms, for there would be no one in the north land to pick up any cry for help. So what we took were the necessities to which a loper could pare his packing when it was necessary.

There were the trail rations—the hard cakes of pressed and dried

411

meats and grains produced nourishing food. I made another raid upon the wagon, detached two of the water carriers which were slung on the upward side I was still able to reach. Illo strained the rapidly dwindling water of the gully through a length of cloth and filled both of these as well as the supply would let her. Together they made a single load, one slung on either side of her back, for Dru.

Blankets folded into packs held extra charges for the stunners, our two tanglers, some simple tools, such as the hatchet which I had used to clear the brush in the gully, a coil of the rope which was so thin and could be looped into small lengths and yet remain so tough even my belt knife had difficulty in slicing it through. We decided against the lanterns, taking instead all units for the two torches that my father had worn on his belt and my own. Illo shouldered her own compact pack, and I had another like it put together with all I could think of which might be of use in the field. There was a second sling of packs for Wodru, and Witol bent to the harness I had cobbled together for the sled which held my father.

We ate a hasty meal when the sun was noon high and then started onward. One thing I had taken with me which might be considered as unnecessary burden were those tapes my father had dictated after each exploration of one of the deserted holdings, together with the reader. They had no like, I was sure, anywhere on Voor and if we could learn anything more of what lay before us, it might come only from those.

Across the gully we went. Nor did I look back at the wreck of the wagon. It was as if that part of my life was now finished, complete, and there was no need to think of any loss—save the greatest one of all and that we carried with us.

Our goal was that distant shadow of the Tangle, the ugly blot of which stretched across the far horizon. I had a map of my father's make, which I carried in my belt pocket, and I knew each marking on that as well as I knew the lines appearing on the palm of my own hand. For I had been with him when most of them had been set down. I had shown this chart to Illo before we broke camp and she had pointed to the northwest where there was only vacancy.

"Voor's Grove lies so—" she spoke with such conviction I did not doubt her. "Where is Mungo's?"

To my knowledge my father had never returned to that lost town once he had taken me out of it. Still he had marked it and in a separate way with a small sign like the blade of a drawn knife done in red. To my plains-wise observation it lay a little to the east from where we had crossed the gully. Nor would it be as close to the Tangle as Voor's Grove.

On this wide land there were few marks one could sight on as guides. The Tangle was the most obvious one, being the end of any march or penetration in this direction. So that we need only head on towards that and then prospect a little from our main trail to strike Mungo's. Or so I hoped—and made myself believe.

The gars moved onward at a steady pace which was not difficult for either of us to match. I had made no provision to lead any of the animals as a loper sometimes sets guide rope to the fore yoke of a wagon. Somehow I accepted that Witol understood what we chose to do and would himself willingly follow the same path.

The grass was lifting upright once more under the pull of the sun as the heaviness of the rain damp was loosed. As it brushed against us and the hides of the gars, we were soon wet to our knees, with patches of damp well up the animals' legs.

By mid-afternoon we came to a wallow-cupping and this brimmed full with the bounty left by the storm. The three gars drank their fill from one side of that already dropping level of water, while we did the same from the other. Nor were we alone. There was a scuttling in that grass, a fleeing of small things we could not see. In the muddy rim about the wallow was such a tracery of tracks it looked as if this had been a point of meeting for both birds and animals. I picked up those of species I knew, inspecting the mud patch carefully all the way around for any prints which might be left by the few predators hunting in the grass lands. Luckily I saw no claw prints of the scrowers—those sharp-beaked screaming furies who could outrace a running man and were ready to feed on anything smaller or weaker than themselves.

However it was only wise to put as much distance as possible between us and that pool before the coming of night. For that which would drink by day was in the main harmless. The true hunters emerged after dark. Witol might have been able to read my mind, for, once his thirst and that of his companions was quenched, he quickened pace to a trot and I broke into the loper's run to keep abreast of him. Twice I glanced at Illo, but she seemed able to keep up well with the other two gars and I was fast losing any fear that she would be a drag upon me. She could have well been trained by the same schooling as I had known for so many years.

There was no shelter on the plains. One felt naked, I discovered, without the wagon which had always served as the center part of any camp I had known. Still we must select a site before the coming of dark, having no lanterns to give us that small protection our own species find from fire or light as dusk closes in.

At length I settled on place backed by a ridge, one of those small conformations which the height of the grass half hid. That grass itself I hacked away to bare a stretch of ground. The sun had dried it sufficiently that it might be heaped into small mounds on which we could spread our blankets. Only I would set no fire to be a signal in the night.

The gars, loosed of their packs, grazed in a circle, now and then lifting a head with nostrils expanded to catch the rising night wind which carried no sickly taint in warning. We sat side by side, munching each on a single pressed cake of the journey food, discovering that every bite must be chewed a long time before it was soft enough to swallow.

During all the journey we had exchanged very few words. Now I wanted desperately to forget—if only for a short space—the mission which sent us north. Perhaps I should bring out the tapes and their reader, listen to my father's words in preparation for what might face us tomorrow, or the day after, or the day after that. For I could not calculate as to how long it would be before we would chance on what was left of Mungo's. Only, in that hour, I dared not do that. To listen so might break through the metal-hard resolve which kept me going. So, in a kind of desperation, I asked a question:

"You travel like a loper—have you gone far?"

She retorted with another question:

"This north land is not strange to you, is it?"

"No, if you have heard of my father you must also know what men say—said—of him. That he hunts what he cannot find and pushes into places better left alone."

"I know. That is why I sought him—and you—out. You ask if I have traveled far—yes—both in body and in mind—"

"I do not understand—" If one traveled in body, then certainly one's mind also went the same distance, I thought foggily. I was becoming aware now of my fatigue. Perhaps I still could not think clearly as I had before the storm had struck and changed my life.

"What do you know of healers?" She sat crosslegged on her blanket-spread sleeping mound. The sun was down but we still had twilight so I could see her face. That was smooth of expression; now it seemed to me as if she wore a mask, and what lay behind that mask might be very different from what men thought.

"As much as anyone who lopes Voor. What you have is a talent which cannot be learned, for the seeds of it are in you at birth. Though you must also stay with an elder of your kind from childhood, learning all she may teach, so that your talent is refined, as the miners reduce raw ore into metal."

"Well said," she answered. "All of it true—to a point. Only this we also know—that our healing does not work with an off-worlder, for a man, woman, or child must believe before the cure begins. While the off-worlders who visit us, even some settlers of the first generation, cannot accept what we have to offer. Therefore, a part of our talent grows out of Voor itself, has roots here and perhaps this gift has other purposes of which we are still ignorant."

"So you seek for an answer to such another purpose in the Shadow doomed places?"

"A year ago," she did not answer me directly, nor even look at me, instead turned her head a fraction so that her eyes were on the fast-falling dark and the grazing gars who were near formless bulks moving slowly in their circle about us. "I was at the holding of Bethol s'Theo—I had gone there on a call reaching me while I was beside the sea gathering the kor weed from which we make a soothing drink for the very young. Only another had been close enough to answer the calling first. She—her name was Catha and she also came from the north and from one of the Shadowed places—it was named Uthor's hold."

She paused as if expecting some word of recognition from me but I could not give it. We had visited seven of the Shadow ruins. Two had been old and even my father could not put name to them, though he grasped quickly at any hint of lore concerning such.

"The one for whom the call was made was not born in Bethol's hold, nor was his name even known. He was found on the shore after a great storm, and the belief was that he was thrown or had crawled out of the fury of the sea. Yet no one ventures out upon the sea at that season—and at other times there is no reason for going far beyond the shore with the fishing fleet—"

She was very right. On other worlds there were stretches of sea between masses of land. I had seen such configurations on the tapes my father used to teach me something of the past of our species. But Voor was different—here was one great mass of land which extended completely around the world and the two seas framing it were narrow and dangerous, rent by sudden storms which churned them into death traps. Men only traveled on land—as yet so thinly settled there was not much need for the stretching out—and there was always the Shadow menace to be feared in new places.

"His hurts of body were not so serious," Illo was continuing. "Catha laid the healing on him and those wounds closed cleanly, were beginning to renew fresh, unharmed flesh. But his mind was rent worse than any blow to a skull could have made it. So—just as she reached into the wounds to drive out the infection and bring healing, so did Catha enter his mind—"

I drew a sharp breath. There was something in me which recoiled instinctively from such an action as Illo described. Now the girl turned to me full face, and there was no longer a mask upon her features, rather her mouth was stern set, a spark shone deep in her eyes, a spark which might have been the seed of anger.

"Where there is a need, there the healer serves. Does it matter if it is a shattered body—or a shattered mind?" she demanded.

"Perhaps that is so. Still—would you if you could throw open your mind to another, make *all* your thoughts plain? I cannot believe that many would say 'yes' if you asked them that."

She sat silent for a long moment and then nodded slowly. "So one who is not a healer would answer so, to that I will agree. But minds can be healed, and if we know this to be true, then should we not also use our talent to accomplish that? Think about it, Bart s'Lorn. Would you want to go on living with a broken mind, babbling incoherently, perhaps rising to a fury which would set you to kill the innocent?

"However, Catha did try to apply to this man the healing power of the mind. I was there and I followed where I could, giving also of my strength and will. And she was succeeding," excitement had crept now into Illo's voice, "I tell you she was doing what she willed. Then—it came—a shadow, a darkness—it struck—both at the man—and at Catha—so that she herself had to withdraw swiftly into unconsciousness. The man lay screaming of monstrous things which he saw gathered around him, tormenting him. Catha remained for hours in her own withdrawal sleep. When she came again to knowledge—she was changed.

"In her there was a purpose as strong as any healing power. She knew something she would not share with us—even with me who had tried to sustain her. She went to the man and she—killed!"

I was as startled as if the Shadows came down upon us. For what Illo had said was against all right, all reason, all sanity. No healer could kill. One could use her talent to ward off physical danger—but to kill—no!

"It is true," the girl cried now as if I had denied her story. "For I saw it. She killed, and then she went out of the holding, and she would speak to no one. Also—there was that clinging to her as might a journey cloak which made all whom she met turn aside and give her room. Nor was she seen or heard of again. Until—"

"Until—" I prompted when she had been some time silent.

"Until I dreamed. I think that she learned something in that broken mind, something of so great a horror that when it came alive or awake at her striving to heal, it was a threat to everything which moves a healer. She fled from it at first, and then she knew that it had risen because of what she had tried to do and perhaps she alone could put it to flight. So she turned against her nature and it died. After that she must seek—"

"For what?" I was deep into the spell of her story. No man knows his world wholly, nor does he so know himself. What seemed an act of blasphemy might have been indeed one of courage as upstanding as a feast candle flame.

"For the answer. I tried to find her for I feared that after her act she might choose to die also. Twice I had word of a woman seen by Voorlopers—though never close enough that they could hail her. She was heading north. Then—I was at Styn's Settlement where there was a child with a broken leg and there the dream came. I saw Catha as if she stood beside my bed, clear and bright.

"Her face was anxious as if she faced some great task and she looked to me. It was a calling, a true calling, though it came in a way which I never heard tell before that a calling might. I waited two days until I knew that the child was healing and then I started north—"

"And you think this was all a thing connected with the Shadows?"

Illo shrugged. "How can I tell? Save the calling is still with me and it leads north. I thought first of the only Shadow doomed place I knew—that of Voor's Grove. So it was there I planned to go—but it may not be any place I yet know. And Mungo's Town was also Shadow rent."

"What do you believe this Catha is doing—or trying to do?"

"Again I do not know. Only I cannot deny her—or the calling. Have we not all long hunted some answer to the Shadow doom? Fifty planet years have those of our blood settled here. The first years—they were good—you have heard the stories of those, many times—all children listen. Then—something happened—there are no records of what it was or where the ill began. One by one the northern holds and settlements were Shadowed—died—except for such as you and I—a few children—babies—who were Voor born—who lived—but could not remember. If Catha has found a beginning or even a path which will lead to the answer—"

"Such a search is madness!" I interrupted her sharply. "You know what doom the Shadows bring—" As had my father who had also spent his life in such a search.

"Who or what are the Shadows?" She asked the same question which had lain earlier in my own mind. "Did not your father ever seek answers just as Catha has done? You went willingly with him—"

"Not all the way. He would never let me enter the ruins."

"True. But all he learned there he shared with you, did he not? You see, before I dreamed I went to Portcity and there I asked access to such of his recordings as are known. He left very few there—only answers the authorities demanded from time to time. I listened, I watched. Perhaps he—and now you—know the most of any now living on Voor."

"Which is very little—no more than you could have read in the official tapes."

"Yes, and those tapes which you brought with you," she sat quietly, her hands resting palm upwards on her knees as if she mutely asked for something which could fill them.

Why had I clung to the tapes? I had told myself that they might provide us with a guide—to what? Not Mungo's, for we had never returned there. To my own private questions? I had heard them many times over and never been the wiser.

"I don't know!" My voice was over-loud; in answer I heard Witol grunt heavily out of what was now the true night darkness, as if he too questioned me in some way. "I know nothing more than the tapes."

"You were very close to your father—did he never try to awake your memory?"

"No!" my reply was as quick and hot. "He never asked—he never let the Portcity medics see me when I was little—" That much I could remember, of staying hidden in the wagon whenever we were forced, when my father could not prevent it, to visit that stronghold of the off-worlders. It had been three years or more before he took me with him into the town. In some way I understood he had feared for me. What had he known from his own days off-world that had made him so reluctant to have me questioned?

"Me they tried," she said then and there was a cold note in her voice. "They decided I was memory blocked—"

"But—but that is off-world technique!" I protested. "Do you mean that the Shadow doom is not of Voor—?"

"It is of Voor," her reply was flat. "There is probably more than one way of closing a child's memory—a small child's. Great terror can do it naturally, drugs perhaps—even interference such as one who has the healer's knowledge can use for evil. I think your father knew, or suspected something—that is what he went searching for, always protected in a safe suit. How did he even get such as that? They are not common issue on Voor where it has been generations since the First-In Scouts downed ship here and found—at that time—nothing of a menace."

"I don't know where he got it. He—he just unpacked it one day and used it."

"Used it needlessly—if his reports were correct."

"Yes."

Suddenly then her hands flew upwards, covered her ears. She bent forward as one who has a sharp pain thrust through mid-body.

"The calling!" she cried aloud. There was fear in her voice.

"Now?" I was on my feet, staring out into the dark, turning slowly.

There was no longer any crunching sound from the grazing gars. Instead I heard the thump of a hoof beating hard on the earth in half challenge, such a sound as Witol made should he meet the lead bull of another loper team—a warning as well as a recognition of the other's equal status.

"Never has it come thus before—" her voice trailed away. "We are right—our course lies ahead."

"I go only to do what my father asked of me." My voice sounded sullen in my own ears. I was not going to be drawn into her mysterious quest for a healer who had betrayed her kind by killing. I did not want to know what lay behind the wall in my memory, even if that was what *she* sought.

"Well enough—" the pain and startlement had gone out of her voice. With the moon yet to rise I could not see more of her than a formless lump on the improvised bed place. "Follow your path as I must mine, Voorloper. Still I believe that those trails are one and the same."

I heard rustling movements as if she were settling herself to sleep. Now, though still uneasy, I lay down and pulled my own blanket over me, pillowing my head on the edge of my back pack. Over me the stars were bright and clear. I thought of the off-worlders who wandered among those as we Voorlopers wander the plains of this world. *They* were pent in a ship, I lay under the open sky. If they sought strange things and mysteries to beckon them on, so did I have the same, whether I willed it so or not.

The gars had returned to grazing. Whatever had brought that warning stamp from Witol no longer seemed to trouble him. Resolutely I tried not to think of what lay on that crude sled beyond our night resting place. My father was not there—

He had never followed any formal religious practices, though he was a believer. In fact he had pointed out in his education of me that tolerance of the beliefs of others was the mark of a properly taught man, and that one did not force any faith—such must be found each by himself for himself. Yet he had believed also that this life was not the only one which a certain element within us knew. Why had he been so determined that his body be returned to the spot he had avoided all these years? Last night I had been so numbed by my loss I could not have asked those questions. Now I began to realize that what I had known of my father had been perhaps only a small portion of the real man, and that brought a hurt of its own which lay heavy in me.

I must have dreamed that night for I awoke heavy hearted—with a dull pain behind my eyes and a feeling of some danger which I had faced or had sought to face. Illo seemed in no better mood, and there was little talk between us as we broke camp and, once more taking up our burdens and apportioning theirs among the gars, went on. Though first I stepped to the top of that grass-entwined ridge and used the distance glasses.

The dark mass of the Tangle lay there right enough, still forming a low-lying cloud which met the earth at the horizon. Immediately ahead it was farther off and I guessed by comparing what I saw with the lines on my map that I had by luck, chance, or something which perhaps had greater influence than either, chosen rightly. We were headed directly towards Mungo's.

We made good time, also, for the gars fell at once into their distance-eating, long-legged stride. No large head dipped now to catch up a mouthful of grass tops as they went. Rather Witol pressed on, the others followed, at a lumbering trot which soon made me lengthen stride to keep up with him, making no matter of the sled he drew and which skidded from side to side, caught momentarily on some tuft of grass, to be jerked free again by a slight movement of those heavy shoulders.

The sun pushed up the sky and once or twice we paused, drank sparingly of our water and shared part of the second tank with the gars. Loper that I was and used to tramping, I found that this push was greater than I had known before. Still I had no wish to slacken pace. If Illo was drawn by that "call," I had a similar spur within me which demanded speed and yet more speed.

In mid-afternoon we sighted with the naked eye the beginning of Mungo's ruins. Winds and rains, perhaps as punishing as the storm which had driven us across the grass lands at the height of its unleashed fury, had had their way here unchecked. Walls were rubble, the outer ramparts of the settlement looked to be no more than a tumbled hillock. There was the darker vegetation arising about it, that strange, warped vegetation which was the sign of the Shadow doom. Trees which were not wind-twisted awry, but unnaturally so wrung from their sapling birth, clung among the fallen blocks and rotted timbers.

There seemed to be more vivid life there than in the grey-brown of the plains where the grass had been bleached and aged by the sun and was now dying in the autumn chill of the night frosts. The growth marking the town was still dark, still swelling with life, as if it were encapsulated in another season. Yet the swelling plants, the crooked-trunked trees were forbidding.

Our fast forward trot slowed the closer we came to those fallen walls, that choked dark green—a green which in these sites was spotted with black in places, as if a blight-like rot fed upon it from the first moment that each leaf uncurled, and yet was never able to consume all it had fastened upon.

At length the gars stopped and the three drew together in a line, facing towards the haunted ruins. I knew their reaction of old—not one of the animals would approach such remains beyond a certain point. Only men went forward; perhaps only my species was foolish enough to venture so.

$\partial_\star$ CHAPTER 6 $_\star\sigma$

I UNHOOKED THE SLED TIES from Witol after shucking my back-pack and freeing the other gars from their burdens. Illo helped in my task without breaking the silence which had fallen between us when we at last sighted my goal. She had said it was hers also—but I determined that the venture which I had sworn to carry out would be mine alone.

Though I had viewed those other ruins my father had prospected down the years and this looked no different, still it was the one which had been my own birthplace, in which I had lived, where something unbelievable had happened. I was frankly afraid, still I knew that I must pass that fear if I could not overcome it.

At last I faced the girl squarely.

"This," I said with all the force I could summon, trying so hard to make my voice have the unyielding authority my father knew so well how to summon, "I must do alone."

I had so much expected a protest from her that I was oddly deflated when she stepped back a pace, plainly joining with the uneasy gars, and answered me:

"This is for you, yes."

I took the cords of the sled in my hands, put all the strength I could muster into drawing the burden behind me as I turned away abruptly to face the sprawling sore which had once been a settlement of my own kind, and in which lurked the unknown which all the beliefs of Voor made out to be our greatest enemy. Night was not too far off and I wanted to have done with my task before the dark closed in, though I had my torch ready to hand, newly furnished with a fresh unit.

It took both strength and will to pull my burden on. I did not look back, rather narrowed and concentrated all my energy and thought on one thing—the speedy fulfilling of the promise I had made. The closer I approached what had been Mungo's Town the more something deep within me fed the beginning of panic. Only that I dared not acknowledge. More than the stubborn weight and heaviness of the sled made me breathe quickly, as a man pants in a grueling race. I set my teeth and pulled viciously, until the cords bit into my wrists and hands, and found that small pain was steadying.

The vegetation did not present too thick a barrier—in fact there was a kind of opening directly ahead of me, as if at one time or other the growth had been cut back to clear a path. Though the very suggestion that that had been done was enough to feed my uneasiness, I had no choice with my bulky and awkward burden but to make that gap my entrance.

The fleshy growth was even less natural looking close by. A small branch I had to fend away broke with a pulpy, squashing sound, while from the mangled leaves which the sled crushed there arose a rank odor, not unlike that which the wind had borne before the coming of the storm.

I tried not to breathe in deeply. Not only were the scents offensive, but I feared they might be poisonous in some way. However, as I advanced, the vegetation thinned, while the ruins it cloaked appeared less broken. In what had once been small gardens about individual buildings were other plants and these, in spite of the lateness of the season, bore flowers—large expanses of petals bigger than I had ever seen before.

Still there was an odd resemblance between them and the much smaller blossoms which holdings still cultivated in the south. Save that these were of angry, vivid oranges, brilliant scarlet, the deep crimson of spilled blood.

There was no wind to reach exploring fingers here—yet—those blossoms moved! Their heads, which appeared near too heavy to be supported by tall, spindly stems, swayed, dipped, arose again. All were wide open and their darker centers had the unpleasant seeming of—eyes—

I battled with imagination and pulled my burden on. Though I had fulfilled my sworn oath in part I was now at a loss. Where should I leave this sled—and what it bore? I paused to turn slowly, looking around me.

Memory was still locked. I could not tell in which house I must once have lived. Though the buildings here appeared near untouched and bore no marks of erosion by storm and season. Where—?

Because I had no clue as yet I pushed on, finding the sled more and more of a burden, needing ever great strength to draw. The settlement apparently followed the plan of those I knew well—a cross-hatching of streets with houses set pleasantly apart, so that each had garden space about it. If the pattern was consistent, just a little farther should bring me to the center of the one-time village, where the meeting hall must stand. Now I conceived the idea that the hall would serve as well as any place in which to leave the sled—it was the heart of Mungo's Town as the planners had seen it.

The doors and windows of the one-story dwellings gaped black—lack of usual glassite coverings there being the only sign of decay. I had no desire to enter any and explore. In fact I averted my eyes and kept them straight on the road before me, for the movement of the flowers grew more disturbing by the moment.

My shoulders ached fiercely and the sled appeared to catch more and more on stones or plants, dragging back like a living thing being pulled against its will. I had to pause and exert effort every step or two to bring it on. Only a little farther—The toe of my tramping boot caught and I sprawled forward without warning. I flung out one hand instinctively to stop my fall and puffy leaves exploded under my weight, shooting out thin streams of sap. Then I was face down and near screaming with pain, for that sap, spattering on my skin, burned like acid. I could see blisters already rising, even in seconds. The sticky liquid had struck, too, along one cheek and the side of my neck, but luckily had not reached my eye. I got to my feet as best I could, and grabbed with my other hand for the canteen of water at my belt. Working free its plug with my teeth I splashed the contents over my burned skin, taking more in the palm of my unburned hand to fling at the fiery torment on my jaw and throat. Easement came almost as quickly as the pain had struck.

Get out—that was a shout filling my mind now—get out!

I kicked about me to clear a path ahead and my efforts uncovered what had brought me down. A blaster lay there, its metal pitted with holes, though it had not been eaten by rust. Another kick sent the weapon flying back into concealment, I pulled at the thongs, and was out into the wide space around the hall.

Here alone there were no dancing flower heads, no acid-sapped vegetation. Instead—I stood staring in disbelief. If such had been in those other ruins my father had described on tapes, he had not been able to mention it.

For what I was looking at was bones—skeletons huddled together along the walls of the hall. Almost as if the whole village had been lined up by a ruthless enemy and blasted down all at one time. Such signs of violent death were difficult to comprehend for a moment— though I had seen death before, but never a slaughter on such a scale. There were no signs of the bleached bones of blaster fire which was my only knowledge of any weapon which could hit so widely and suddenly as to wipe out a whole village.

I forced myself to move forward. There were no other relics visible. The ground under them was barren earth, unmarked by any scorching. Metal objects, a buckle, the hooks on any settler's belt—even perhaps an ornament—nothing of such showed—

The bodies lay in some order. Had they been gathered so by a survivor? Only as far as I knew *I* had been the only survivor and no five-year-old child could arrange this. Had my father, perhaps someone else who had returned later, arranged the dead in such a manner—but why?

I worked my way around that line of bones, and, taking out my hand torch, entered the hall itself. Perhaps the answer could be found here. In spite of the open window spaces, the vanished door, it was dim within until I turned my torch to full and began a slow sweep about the room.

There were benches, in rows covered with dust. At the far end of the room a platform one step high had given a stage of sorts. I knew that this was like all village halls—it was the center of education, of entertainment, of the necessary meetings to discuss common policy. There was nothing here—

I stumbled a little as I went back into the open. The night was coming fast. I was filled with a need to be free, out of Mungo's Town before darkness fell. There were shadows gathering—Shadows!

What *was* the Shadow Doom? Who had first called the menace so? That one must have known *something* to be able to impart a name to the danger. I walked closer now along the line of unknown dead. There were only bones—twice I noted smaller skeletons which must have been children. Why had they died and I survived?

This did not look like the result of a plague—then the unburied dead would have been found in their houses. No, this more resembled an execution!

That thought arose against my fear. For an execution meant an enemy—one which or who must have form and substance, who could be fought—made to pay! Was this what had ridden my father all through the years? Had he come back to look upon the dead and guess—likewise guess enough so that he spent the rest of his life in search?

Yet he had found nothing, and he had been closer to the actual outrage than I was now. If he had only told me more! My blistered hand hurt as I formed a fist. I needed badly a spur for definite action, for a chance to fight back.

Instead I turned at the end of the row of the dead and went back to the sled. I pulled this onto the barren earth where even my own boots had left no track. Carefully I lined up that improvised transport and its sealed burden with the rest who lay there.

For the first time I wondered if my father had had another reason to send me here—not just to return him to lie among those with whom he had had some tie in years past—(which of those skeletons might be my mother? I flinched from that thought as if it were a blow). No, could it be that he meant me to confront the horror which had happened here and react just as I was doing, determining that, when he had been forced to relinquish the search, I would take it up? If that were so—then he was succeeding. Though I had heard of the Shadow Doom all my life, had seen its effect on my father and others, it had never been as real to me as it was at this moment.

I hurried back the way marked by the torn vegetation, wanting to be out of the town. Still I was certain that I would return—I had to know! For the first time I could share with Illo the demands of her own search—if the woman she sought, this healer named Catha, could give me any answers, then those I must have!

Illo had not been idle while I was gone. She had established a small camp at the nearest point the gars would advance towards the village, even hacking off armloads of the grass to form such beds as those we had rested upon the night before. The spread of the ever-present plains grass was not as thick, nor did it grow so tall here. There was evidence that these had once been fields and straggling through the choking grass, putting up a valiant battle for growing room, were clumps of grain now harvest yellow.

Though the gars were at graze, devouring such clumps with greedy relish, I noted that they followed the pattern they always had used when we were encamped near ruins. Two would eat for a space, the third stand with head up and pointed towards the remains of the town. Though they exchanged the post of sentry through such timing and selection they appeared to agree upon among themselves, there was one ever on watch.

I quickened pace as I saw the loads piled and Illo's work. The blisters on my skin were once more smarting and I wanted her verdict on my hurts. She was swift to see my injuries, and, when I told her how they had occurred, she searched her pack to bring forth a pot of greenish ointment which, after she had washed the blisters carefully once more with water, she spread over the burns leaving them free from pain with the redness of the skin beginning slowly to fade.

Water was our need. We had that which had been carried in the wagon containers on gar back but it was not enough to last long for both the animals and ourselves. The settlement must have had some close and well-enduring source of water. Though that would have been pumped through pipes into the ruins (and I, for one, would not set to my lips any liquid which bubbled within that place of death) still the ultimate source should be beyond the village itself. I summoned Witol with my whistle and he came to me, a generous wisp of the grain stalks bobbing from his moving jaws.

It was well known that gars could scent water where a man with his inferior senses could easily die of thirst, and what I asked of the lead bull now he had done many times before. Letting him scent the liquid left in my canteen I made the hand signal for "seek." After a moment of rumination, he swallowed his mouthful and began to trot to the east purposefully.

I took Illo's canteen and one of the wagon cans—it now being light enough that I could carry it. We crossed the lines of more grown over fields where I could trace irrigation ditches, the kind used in plains settlements during the dry months of mid-summer. Witol held up his head, his nostrils wide open. Now he uttered a grunt from deep within his throat as we came upon what had once been a reservoir. The soil had been dug away and the deep pocket left, spread with several coatings of plasta, made a smooth bowl which cupped now enough water to reflect the sunset, and ran in a small stream through an underground duct which I believed entered the village.

The source was partly rain and what else arose from a spring occupying an opening in the plasta on the side away from the ruins. I kicked off my boots so that I might better walk over the slick of the plasta and went to fill the containers, Witol drinking noisily from the pool. The water was cool near the spring and sweet. Since the gar showed no repulsion I could believe it good.

I had been so immersed in my own thoughts since I had come out of Mungo's that I hardly realized that Illo and I had said very little to one another. Save that I had described to her the plants which had led to the poison effect on my skin, some necessary exchanges concerning matters of our camp, we had not spoken together. However, when I returned with the water container full resting on Witol's back, and twilight thickened, I resolved that I must tell her of my discovery.

That night we dared a fire. There was no time in the past when there had appeared to be any danger beyond the ruins, as I could testify from my own experience, and anything stalking prey on the plains would not come near one of the Shadow-taken settlements. There is something about fires, that earliest weapon of our species against the power of darkness, which provides us with a comfort to the spirit as well as the body. Looking into the flames I could even imagine that all I had seen that day was part of a dream. Since that was not so Illo must have a full accounting.

I spoke stiffly, bluntly, with an attempt at preserving a lack of emotional involvement. The bones, white, stripped, nameless could not convey to me as much of an impact that bodies would have. When I finished my story, my companion in this quest was quiet for a long moment. Then she asked, as if it was something she must do, though she hated the need:

"You—you knew none? There was no return of memory?"

"Nothing—I—" my hesitation was of a space of a breath only, "I looked—there was nothing, not even a bit of metal to identify one from the other. Though I think that all the villagers must have been there. Why not me? I saw what must have been other children—"

Her face wore that impassive mask-like look. "How old would you guess?"

I moved uneasily. "I could not say—none were very small."

"And you were five," she mused aloud. "I must have been nearly four—there were two who were babies—and one woman—but she was brain hurt and disappeared into the Tangle. She broke the bonds the medics laid upon her and they later tracked her to that."

"But the babies—what became of them?"

She cupped her chin in her hand, rested the elbow of that arm upon her knee where she sat on a pack of the gear we had not needed to open. It seemed that she, too, looked now into the fire for comfort.

"Brother and sister—twins. They had a kinsman who was off-world and who had come with the thought of staying at Voor's Grove. When he heard what had happened he took them and shipped out. I never heard what happened to them after."

"There were eight settlements and holdings in all which were overrun," I totalled them up on my fingers. "Mungo's, Voor's—Stablish's in the far west and, a little south of that, an off-worlder one, only that was not a real settlement, rather a semi-permanent station set up to study vegetation cross-breeding. Then eastward, Welk's Town, Lomack's, Robbin's, Kattern's. We, my father and I, went to Welk's, Lomack's, Kattern's, the off-world station and Stablish's. How many others had survivors—children?"

"Why—" her mask cracked and her eyes showed a flicker of astonishment. "Only—only you and I! That is all. You know, of course, of the birth lag—"

That had been another peculiarity of Voor which I had half forgotten over the years since my father had had me read the records. The birth lag—colonists were encouraged to have children as soon as possible if the conditions on the settled world were favorable. But on Voor there had been a strange effect which had at first caused some concern, and then, as the years passed, and more settlers came, had been accepted as the norm for this world. No children had been born during the first six years after landing. Then an established pattern of cycle births, for there would be a few years in which the number of births was approximately normal for our species on the home planets from which they had come. Again would follow birth lags of increasingly shorter intervals. Until now that oddity did not exist— at least not in the south. And since no one settled in the north now, if it still differed that did not matter.

"What if ages five or six—and under—meant immunity—" Illo continued. "You may have been the youngest—the latest born at Mungo Town. I was the first of another grouping at Voor's. We have never known what caused the lag—just as we don't know what caused that—" She pointed through the twilight to the settlement. "All the other settlements and holdings could have been caught by chance during the long lag—so no survivors."

Her reasoning made sense. Then our own chance of survival had indeed been very small; we were the only two of our kind. Whether that could mean anything or not, I was in no position to argue.

"What are you going to do now?"

I knew, though I had not yet put my resolve into words. "Try to find out."

That had become the future for me. I could return to Portcity, yes—start over as a loper, back-packing on my three remaining gars—making the rounds as a small trader. Or I could join some holding—an extra pair of hands was welcome anywhere on the frontier. But I would not. I *had* to know—if such a thing was possible to learn at all.

The girl regarded me steadily. "Your father had years of searching what did he learn? You may be running now into something worse than you can remember—because you don't remember!"

I thought of those ordered rows of the dead within the town—the

suggestion in that of a reason, a definite pattern behind this depopu-
lation of the north. There was something utterly dark and cruel in the
way those bones lay along the wall—something I could not live with
in my memory.

"They were killed, deliberately, for some purpose. It wasn't an
illness, or animals in attack, or—" I tried to reckon up the dangers
which could wipe out a town. "The Survey reports all say that Voor
has no intelligent life above the 6-plus level. If there has been a Jack
outfit in hiding here that would have recorded, no matter how many
distorts they tried to use. Even a distort records—something."

Illo shook her head. The firelight flickered, sometimes seeming
to make her eyes show with a spark of fire of their own, or so it
seemed to me. I wanted to look at her just because she was alive,
clothed in flesh, able to talk, to think, to be—not like that—I tried to
shut down hard on the picture which kept creeping out of the dark
into some line of vision which was in my mind and not directly
before my eyes.

"All of those explanations—they have been worn into tatters."
She raised one hand and brushed back a wisp of hair from her forehead. "None of them, except perhaps a plague, would account for the
radical change in vegetation. I know herbs, most of the wild grasses,
the plants. The knowledge is part of my training. This afternoon,
while you were gone, I went close enough to view what grows over
there. It is all different—it reminds me of the Tangle in some ways—
still it is not of that either. It is poisoned—you have your own
experience with it to prove that." She gestured at my hand, shiny
with the balm she had spread over it.

"What about you—your calling?"

She shook her head. "It—it is gone."

"What do you mean?"

"Just that. And I have never known a calling to end so before. I
think—I think she is dead—"

"Your Catha?"

"Yes." The single word brought silence.

"So you will go back then? I can give you Wobru—a water tank—"

"No!" Her word of denial was emphatic as that "yes" had been
earlier. "I must know—just as you must. There is some reason why
we survived—"

"You said it yourself—by chance we were the right age."

"Beside that." She made an impatient gesture with one hand. "You are not a true believer, are you?"

"A true believer in what?"

"One of the Assembly of the Spirits," her voice was as impatient as her gesture had been.

"No. But surely you aren't either." I knew the Assembly—they occupied three settlements in the south, keeping very much to themselves and having only necessary contact with others. Their lives were narrow, ruled by what my father had termed "taboos." His own acceptance of differences between men had been very liberal and his distrust of fanaticism had led him to impress upon me the fact that some of the worst disasters in the history of our species have been born from judging strangers by standards we held too rigidly. In my father's eyes there was a simple code of right and wrong which guided any man. And he had acknowledged some power beyond our knowledge at work in the universe.

The Assembly in their rigid beliefs were, as the miners and other stations manned by off-worlders, the few places not welcoming healers. That she would mention them now startled me.

"No," she agreed. "I am not one of them. How could I be, as you say? But they have certain interesting beliefs—such as the one that we are intended for specific roles in life, and, from what is so ordained, we cannot escape. We may deliberately turn aside from a road because we dislike what it entails for us, yet the side turning we choose will eventually curve back to bring us to the same end. In this matter—"

"That is *their* belief!" I countered. "It is only chance that you and I are survivors—there is no mysterious 'spirit' or fate guiding us along." That was one idea I would not allow myself to accept. The decision which I had come to in Mungo's when I had seen that open graveyard had not been dictated to me; it was my own, or rather one I had taken up because of the man who had been the center of my world. Whatever had left the sign of its—or their—cruel passing must be made to answer—if it was humanly possible to make this so.

In a way, though I believed in her story of Catha and the calling which had brought her to join us, I was glad that Illo was not to be our guide now. I accepted what I could see, hear, touch—I was not a healer, and if I were to succeed in finding the murderers of Mungo's it must be by my own senses and not depending on something which was not a part of me.

"You believe in yourself?" Her question cut through my thoughts and surprised me.

"As much as I can." I was honest with her. I had never really been placed on my own before, I realized that. Any decision I made now, any mistake in judgment or action, would be my own and I must face the results alone.

"That was a fair answer," Illo nodded. "So do I also. I believe in my own training and say this much—we are meant to do this thing. Also, though the calling has failed, we should still point north. You returned to Mungo's and have made one discovery there which your father has not recorded. I say now let us go to Voor's Grove—No," she did not give me any time to protest. "Your story began here and returning has seemed of little use in unraveling it. Do not deny me the chance to return to *my* beginning; perhaps we may profit from it more than you can now guess."

I had to admit that I had no other goal, and surely I could learn little more from Mungo's. Why not agree? Voor's Grove also my father had not visited, there was just a chance—

So I agreed because I had nothing else to offer.

⊙★ **CHAPTER 7** ★⊙

THAT NIGHT I was not ready for sleep. Instead I unpacked the reader and my father's tapes. Though I had heard them all before—some many times, for when we were on the plains he oftentimes took out one or another and sat listening to his own words replayed, a frown of concentration on his face as if he must always bolster memory, make sure that there was no clue he had perhaps over-looked. Yes, I had heard them before, but now it was my turn to concentrate, to strive to find a loose thread that I might pull on to reduce this tangled web to order.

Illo listened with the same absorption. We heard descriptions of just such plants as I had encountered that afternoon—of the fact that, though the buildings on the perimeter of each deserted site had seemed to be in very bad condition, those farther in did not show the same signs of erosion. I waited eagerly for some mention of a central hall, or any indication that my father had found there evidences of massacre such as was at Mungo's. But there was nothing at all which suggested that he had ever discovered the remains of a single body.

If he had done so, why had he registered all else in minute detail and left what was a most important discovery unvoiced? There was something else—

Though he had spoken of the alien-seeming vegetation in detail, he had never described the nodding flowers. I played each tape to the end as the red moon climbed the night sky. The gars had come closer to the fire. Wobru and Bru were lying down, chewing their cuds

435

rhythmically, but Witol was on his feet and disappeared at intervals. I knew that the bull was on sentry go and that I could trust his senses farther than my own.

"You have learned anything?" Illo asked as the last of the tapes came to an end.

"This much—if there were skeletons in other places my father did not mention them—or the flowers—"

"Flowers?" she pounced upon that. "What kind of flowers?"

I described the blossoms and how they had seemed to move though there was no wind. It was a small thing, but how could I rank the importance of any hint?

"They moved—" she repeated. "Bart, have you been to the Tangle edge?"

"No closer than this place. There was never any reason to head that way."

"But you have seen the picture tapes taken by Survey, by the off-world teams after the Shadow doom began?"

"Thick, grey, just what men name it—a tangle of vegetation too massed to get through except by burning. Even that does not work— the stuff is said to grow overnight and if one ventures in too far the trail closes up behind him. It dampens out coms and range fingers. They will not operate near it. That's why no one can go in—" I summoned up my general knowledge of the Tangle as I had heard and tape-read.

"Also—it moves," she said then. "As your flowers in the town— it quivers and sways even if there is no wind. That is part of the tan-gling process, for in its ever movement it twines and winds stem and leaf together, sometimes to remain so tied permanently."

That I had *not* known. At my questioning she said she had once been in Portcity and had heard the report of a man who had been sent on a rescue mission. Some off-worlders in a flitter had flown too low over that trap and had vanished into it.

"I wonder," she sat now with forefinger to her lips as if she would chew upon it, as one did upon a sliver of journey food, "can there be an alliance?"

"No one would be fool enough to bring seeds or plants from the Tangle to bed on the plains!"

"Perhaps no one brought them. Remember the storm? What

could the force of a wind such as that carry in it? I wish there was some detailed record from one of the doomed villages of what happened just *before* the Shadows. Could there have been some signs of approaching trouble which no one thought to notice—"

"Such as a new flower popping up in a garden plot?" I wanted to scoff, yet still I was caught by her reasoning. Perhaps my father had had a somewhat similar idea; he had spent so much time in the tapes describing the vegetation. Also now I remembered something else— that when he wore the protect suit he had always shed that well away from the camp site and had brushed it over with disfect powder. But that had been for the first two or three times he had gone so exploring; after that he had not even used the suit.

"Such as a flower, a new flower, in a garden place," she agreed.

Illo knew more of growing things than I did, that I was willing enough to allow. A healer must have a wide knowledge of plants, which harm and which can help. I knew that in her pack she had small boxes of dried leaves, of crushed-to-powder seeds—all of which had their uses. While the blisters still on my hand and cheek, though they had lost the sting of pain under Illo's treatment, were warning enough that poison grew and flourished in Mungo's. At this moment I was ready to open my mind to any theory. Though I could not equate any inimical plant with what I had seen. Poison in such might produce a plague, yes. But I was still certain that there was some cruel thought behind the doom. Perhaps not thought as we reckoned it—still intelligence, however alien that might be in form.

I packed away the tapes and we both lay down on our grass and blanket beds. Illo had said very little, but I guessed that she was thinking much. I hoped I would not keep seeing, even in dreams, that which lay so close to us behind the nodding flowers. Did they still nod at night, I wondered? This was so still a night, without even a breath of wind stirring in the grass,. As if something lay behind its defenses in the dead town—waiting—No, I must not allow my imagination to stray so.

It was a restless night for me. I must have slept very lightly for twice I roused to hear the gars changing watch. I realized that night not how much I knew, but how little. I had thought that I was well equipped for a Voorloper—yet now I needed more—so much more.

The gars were brisk in setting out the next day, glad in their own way, I was certain, that we were turning our backs upon a place they shunned. Witol now carried the water cans filled to their cap pieces, while Bru was free of burden. She took to ranging ahead, crisscrossing our chosen direction of march. It was as if she were playing scout. I had never seen a gar behave so before, but then, mainly, they had marched in yoke with the wagon and not gone ranging free on the trail.

There was no trail in the grass to be sure. The sky today was overcast. I kept watch on the scudding clouds. Another bad storm might well mean our deaths when we had not even the shelter of the wagon. However, the animals showed no signs of uneasiness, and I knew that they would betray those well ahead of a drastic natural change.

To the right that distant threat of the Tangle marked the horizon line; we were heading due west in the general direction of Voor's Grove as well as I could place it. By all accounts that would be yet two days journey away.

There were formations of migrating birds across the sky and their cries reached us above the constant rustle of the grass which made up part of the wind's song. Our pace was steady but we did not push, as now and then we rested while the gars grazed. We did not talk even when we so paused. Illo wore her mask face and I had an eerie feeling that I, the gars, perhaps even the plain over which we trod, was not really visible to her, that she was deep somewhere within herself working out some problem. At our third rest I dared to ask her if she had picked up her call again. She shook her head.

"There is nothing. Perhaps I shall never know—" her voice trailed away and I could add the missing words for myself. She would never know what had happened to Catha. I guessed, though I did not say so, that what had come was death.

In mid-afternoon I sighted a small herd of lurts—the first life other than winged we had seen since the storm. The natural inhabitants of the plains must have gone to cover then or else were so scattered and mauled that they had been driven from their regular territories. Witol bellowed and the small graceful creatures fled in great bounds. We do not know why the gars will warn off the wild grazers—perhaps they have a kind of jealous desire to protect food which they might just need.

However the sight of the lurts running free meant that this was truly a deserted land. The most timid of creatures, they would not even share territory with other wildlife larger than themselves.

"This is good country." We had paused at the top of one of the low ridges. Illo shifted her pack a fraction and then went down on one knee and parted the heavy growth of grass. I thought she was looking at the richness of the soil, but instead she dug a moment with her fingers among the grass roots and then held up something which caught glittering life from the daylight as it swung back and forth in her grasp.

"This—have you seen its like before? You have ranged far—" She held her find out to me.

There was a chain of metal links. At first I thought that exposure had given it that bronze-blue color. Only when I took it from her, it was not pitted, and I believed that the smooth surface was not in the least touched by time. If that were its natural color the material was like nothing I had ever seen. Which meant little—it could have been dropped by some off-worlder, perhaps a prospector, the metal forming it an alloy from another world.

The chain was beautifully fashioned, a work of art, the links fastened one to another as the scales of a sku lizard are set on the skin. It was broken, but mid-point along its length, when it had been intact and the clasp locked, there was a plate set in as part of the chain, curved a little to continue the line, it must hold to fit closely about the throat. That plate was about the width and length of my shortest finger, and, as I wiped it clear of the remains of the soil from which Illo had freed it, I could see that it was deeply incised with a bewilderingly ornate scrolling which resembled somehow an unknown script.

"Off-world," I commented. I peered around at the grassy slopes which descended gently from where we stood. Perhaps it was my experience in Mungo's but I found myself hunting for some sign, unpleasant, of whoever had once worn it. I would not have been surprised to see a skull peering open-eyed at me from behind one of the tussocks.

"Perhaps—" She sat back on her heels and set about dividing the grass, pulling at it. Was she also hunting such grim remains? If the same thought which nibbled at me struck her I wondered that she still explored so.

"This is an alloy—I think." I wanted her to stop that search. "We have no art, no skill to produce such a thing on Voor."

"It is older than the coming of Voor—" Her search had proved fruitless. She looked up, not to me, but at what I held.

"You mean it dates back before the coming of Survey—?" Voor had been the First-In Scout who had mapped this planet for the League and because he had been close to retirement, on his last out-range of exploration, it had been given his name. He had chosen to settle here when his service years were ended.

"Yes."

"But that is impossible!" I twirled the chain between my fingers and was surprised that she would make such a statement. Or why—

She wiped the last of the earth traces from her fingers and arose.

"You know little about us—the healers." There was affront in her voice, her lips were thin set and her eyes were as unfriendly as if I had shouted "Liar!" at her openly. "We have gifts. I—and several others of my craft—can hold a wrought object thus," she set her palms together with exaggerated gesture, a little cupped as if the chain did so lie in her grasp, "and know what a thing is in truth—something of its age, of those who made it, used it—perhaps even how it reached where it lay until I saw it."

I would have denied that this could be done, then I hesitated. Who knew what could be done truly with the mind? There were off-world strains who had odd gifts. Terran blood had mutated and changed as those from the home planet reached out to the stars, found rooting on distant worlds, developed from the use of alien soils and atmosphere changes which grew ever stronger, became a more permanent part of each generation under those foreign suns. Though I had never been off-world, I had seen enough of the many types (and those were only a very small number who ever made Voor a landfall) at Portcity, visitors, members of the commissions come to investigate the doom, miners, starmen, to understand that we, who had common ancestors long ago, were now sometimes different species altogether. There were also those who had never been human by our small standards at all—the Zacathans, the Trystians—others.

So it was never wise to state absolutely that this or that talent could not exist. Even the settlers of Voor had come from several different worlds and so had bloodlines which might have branched untold planet years back, giving their descendants unusual attributes.

"Let me psyche—" She took the chain deftly out of my hold, did indeed cup it between her hands. Her eyes were closed, I could see her whole body tense in the act of complete concentration.

I had felt nothing save the smooth surface of the chain. Though the idea clung to my mind that the scrolling on that foreplate did have a definite and important meaning—almost as if it were an identity disc such as are worn by starmen in some services.

An identity disc? Not impossible. There could even have been a ship's crash—or the coming of a single LB, escaping from some catastrophe in space before Voor made this world his last official landfall. That fitted plausibly. Only that would put back the age at least a century, perhaps more. No metal or alloy I know of could have existed uneroded—unless—

Forerunner!

We are late comers into space, even though we have been for centuries now star voyagers. Still there had been those who had sought the star lanes, mapped and held them, long before our first crude rocket had lifted from Terra and man had eyed the stars with a covetous desire. Galactic empires had risen and fallen and of them we knew so little.

The Zacathans had their records. In their long lives (so much longer than the years any of us might aspire to) they had made it their purpose to search out, to catalogue all of the alien remains which could be found. There had been many such finds—the Caves of Astra, the half-melted and blasted cities on Limbo—even greater discoveries. Machines so intricate and obtuse that our best trained techs could not begin to understand them. Some had kept on running, even on deserted worlds—for how long—a million years—a billion?

I remembered my father's other abiding interest, the gathering of such material on Forerunner finds as trickled through to the records of Portcity, his stories at our lonely campfires of what had been found—and how we had only barely touched the edge of that knowledge which the forerunners had lived with for eons. However, there were no known Forerunner ruins here—or at least none which had been discovered.

It was easy to build and speculate on such a hint. We had our

First-In Scouts—perhaps the Forerunners had had such explorers also. One had landed on Voor—or whatever name he had given this world in his turn—come to trouble in some fashion and—

Illo's face broke the mask which fell on her when she withdrew into her healer's trance. It twisted as if she were in some actual pain and with a sudden movement she hurled the chain from her. I gave a cry of half protest and fell on my knees, scrabbling through the grass with my hands until my fingers found that smooth length.

The girl had not yet opened her eyes, but her tormented expression appeared to intensify. She shivered so violently that she near over-balanced and did waver from one side to the other, until, having reclaimed her find, I reached her side and threw my arm about her shoulders, drawing her close until I could steady her against my own body. I could feel still that shivering of—fear—revulsion—?

She raised her hands and covered her face. Now she was sobbing, harsh, hurting cries like those of an animal in pain. I heard an answering deep lowering from Witol, bellows from Bru and Wobru. The gars gathered beyond the slight rise on which we stood, their horned heads raised as they stared at us with their large eyes.

"Illo—what is it?" Perhaps some of the warmth of my body, the quiet soothing I strove very hard to put into my voice, reached her.

She lowered one hand, caught fiercely at my arm with a grip so hard that her nails bit through the leather of my sleeve so that I could actually feel pain in the flesh beneath. There were no tears on her cheek; though her breath came in those ragged, breast-tearing sobs, her eyes were now open—and dry. She stared straight before her and there was a look about her as if she were in truth being drawn away in some terrifying fashion, that though I held her and had not and would not let go, still she was leaving me.

Dropping the chain once more to the ground I seized her by both upper arms. I shook her with what was close to a brutal assault. Her head wobbled back and forth on her shoulders. She gasped, cried out. Only that sobbing dwindled, now she did not move to shake off my hold. Instead she took a stumbling step closer, her arms came up about my body and she held to me as tightly as if I were the only safe-guard against being swept away by some peril I could neither see nor understand.

For a very long moment we stood thus. Her shivering lessened, her head had fallen forward against my shoulder, and I heard her ragged, forced breathing growing less urgent, more normal.

For the second time now I dared ask:

"What is it?"

For a second or two I was afraid that my question was going to arouse once more whatever inner storm had gripped her. She did shiver, and her hold on me tightened. Then she raised her head. Her mouth trembled but somehow she mastered whatever force had so rent her.

"I was—I was—" she shook her head in a small helpless movement as if she could summon no words to explain what had happened in that space of time which she had held the necklet and tried to understand any secret it might know.

"They—" she began again, "they did not think—think as we do. My head—it was as if someone ran through my head opening doors—letting out all kinds of things—things I could not understand—that I never knew that I could contain. It all came at once! Bart—whoever wore that—there was some terrible danger and he—she—it—" She shook her head from side to side. "I don't even know what it was!" Her voice was near a wail. "But there was fear—terrible fear which ate—ate right into me. And—how one who was like us—even like—If I could only have understood, had time—it moved so fast—"

She loosed her hold on me with one hand and put it to her forehead. "So fast—and I could not follow its thoughts—they were like the flash of blaster flame—hurting—eating—in my head. But something happened here or near here—when that was dropped. And it was bad—worse than we, any of us being as we are, can understand."

Though she did not seem able to make better sense than that, the words she did find to attempt to explain steadied her. She loosed her hold on me utterly and I saw her self possession return as she spoke. She looked down to where the necklet lay.

"Bart—I dare not touch that again. But it has a message—we—someone with more training or talent than I—could understand—unravel. It is important, that much I know. Can you carry it?"

I stooped and picked it up for the second time. In my hands it was nothing but a loop of strange metal bearing, part way down its broken length, that curved bar. I felt nothing but the smooth surface. And I said so. Illo nodded.

"Put it away—safely. When—if—we get back to Portcity that must be sent off-world—to one of the League centers for sensitive learning where they have the trained handlers who deal with Forerunner things. It may be one of the keys such as men have always longed to find—if it is given to the right person who has a mind trained and safeguarded well enough to be able to put it to use."

I coiled the chain into a small ball and stowed it in my belt pouch. She watched me fasten the loop of that closely as if wishing to make very sure that her discovery would be safe. How much of what she believed was the truth I could not tell. But that she thought it was correct I had no doubts at all.

We left that ridge and tramped on, the gars scattered back into their usual line of march, no longer watching us as intently as they had when Illo had tried to learn the secret of the thing. Neither of us spoke of it, yet I was oddly aware with every stride I took of the rub of the purse back and forth against my thigh, and of what lay within it.

I had to keep a tight curb upon my tongue for I wanted very much to question her. Perhaps, I told myself, such questions might even be good, helping her to sort out whatever stream of wild impressions had overcome her. Yet it was not right, I thought, to put her to such a task now—not unless she opened the subject. Which she did not do.

Once more we camped on the plains. This time with no fire, since we were out of the range of the ruins which had a certain "safe" area about them—no animals venturing any nearer than our gars would go. It was the gars who again played sentry for us. Illo was not silent this night. Instead she talked almost feverishly, as if she must hear the sound of voices—using that sound as a barrier against something else.

She spoke of her wanderings as a healer—she seemed to have ranged distances by choice rather than settled long at any hold or settlement—going up along the coast, striking inland—visiting Portcity to renew certain supplies and talk with ships' medics. For off-worlders though those were, they were more keenly interested in any planet form of medicine and healing than the mine medics. She said that many of them compiled records of unusual healing processes from world to world—and she had found them most willing to tell her what they could of worlds where there were also healers not unlike herself in training—people who could diagnose illness often by touch alone and subdue pain and conquer disease by drawing it out of the body by their wills.

That she had an inquiring mind I already knew, but now I saw that she had a deep thirst for knowledge, save that as all healers it was not a knowledge which depended upon machines and technology, but rather upon what lay within a man or woman—dormant sometimes— to be tapped by those lucky or learned enough to be able to open the right door.

The right door—what she had said about that feeling in her brain when she had tried to psyche the chain returned to me. Opened doors with that behind them spilling out in no pattern which she could understand. Such a thing—it could lead to madness. I resolved in that moment that if it were possible I would never let her touch the chain again. She had been strong enough this time to throw it from her before the chaos it bred in her mind had conquered. There might come another time when her thirst for the unknown would lead her to a second try and she could not again be as strong-willed or fortunate.

✵✭ CHAPTER 8 ✭✵

VOOR'S GROVE indeed lay in the shadow of the Tangle. It surprised me that knowing, as they must have done, the sinister qualities of that menacing wilderness, the settlers here had drawn so close to such impenetrable mystery. Or perhaps in the days when the settlement had been first decided upon the Tangle was not considered such a menace, that men believed they might fire or dig it out of their way, altering the land as they had done successfully on other worlds.

Also, since the abandonment of the settlement, the Tangle may have grown unchecked, but then that result would differ from what had happened elsewhere. For in past years a careful check upon it had shown the growth to be static, that it neither expanded in summer seasons or retracted when the plains droughts and frosts hit hard, as they did in a regular cycle of planet weather.

Plainly Voor's Grove had been well situated as far as its founders, unaware of the Shadow doom, had decided. It lay at the uniting of two rivers—those which came together to form the greater flood of the Halb as it flowed east and south. One of these streams reached westward and north—the other came directly from the northern mounts, breaking from under the curtain of the Tangle as no other that I knew of did.

River trade in the plains lands might have built up well—had the dream of settlements here not been broken. Unfailing water in the dry years was a thing to be prized. The settlement had been placed on the vee of land where the two rivers boiled on to their uniting.

That water which flowed from the west came with a swifter current and was fairly clear. But that of the second stream moved far more slowly and was turgid, brownish and opaque. I remembered the armored thing which had been storm washed to the wagon and I would not have ventured to ford that stream no matter how shallow it measured.

Luckily there was no need to venture into what might be a water trap. There had been a bridge once, built of the same stone, brought in from the mountain quarries to the west, which formed the walls of the ruins. Enough of that span remained to give us footing.

Voor's Grove itself, even though thickly cloaked by the same poisonous-appearing vegetation as Mungo's had been, was, I could see, much the larger settlement. It was older, too, by about ten years, and had been meant by its ambitious founders to be the capital of the plains lands—hence its name.

Once more the gars would not come near, halting well away as Illo and I approached the tumbled, water-washed stones of what had once been the bridge. For all its greater size it presented the same picture of ruins and growth gone wild as had the settlement in which I had been born. I studied my companion carefully as she surveyed what we could see.

"No memories?" I could not help asking, for she was frowning as one might who was attempting to recall something which remained as only a trace at the very edge which thought could reach.

She shook her head instead of answering me, but now she moved with some purpose. Shucking her back pack she opened it and searched among the contents to bring out a skin bag which I had already seen—from which she had taken the salve which had brought me relief from the poisonous sap. She opened that and, dipping in two finger tips, brought out a gob which she proceeded to rub over her face and then both of her hands. When she had done she looked at me.

"This will save us from another accident such as you faced in Mungo's Town—"

Save—us? Then she expected me to accompany her into Voor's Grove. Perhaps for a second or two I thought of refusing, but I could not. My curiosity was far too aroused. Would we find the same signs of a massacre here?

I rubbed away until those portions of my skin which would be exposed were well covered with a film of grease carrying an odd but not unpleasant scent. It had drawn the pain from my blisters which were fast healing so they showed now only as reddish marks.

I dropped my pack beside hers and checked my belt equipment. There were tangler and stunner, both of which were fresh charged, my long knife, the pouch in which rode that enigma we had discovered in the grass, my torch—though it was still early afternoon and we should not be so long in there that I would use that. Yes, all the defenses any loper could carry were close to my hand.

Relieving the gars of their burdens, we stacked that packed gear at a point directly opposite the remains of the bridge and then set out to see what might lie within Voor's. Illo took the lead, moving out while I steadied the water carriers against the other gear, before I could call to her to wait.

She balanced lightly and skillfully from one stone to the next, twice having to jump to cross gaps in the masonry. The brown water swirling below had an oily look to it, as if it were not really water but the exudation of some unpleasant growth. I watched it carefully before I began the crossing. There was no movement to be sighted on the surface or under it. However the tumble of stones could well give good footing to any such monster as we had seen pull itself up on the wagon. So I stood there on sentry duty, my hand on the butt of my stunner, alert to any movement, until Illo was across. As a healer she wore no weapons—had refused the other stunner, and had only the long-bladed belt knife which was a working tool for any traveler. That would be useless against the scaled and armored thing.

Once she was across she turned a little and I was quick not to let her believe that I held back where she had led, setting foot on the first pile of stone to follow. Some of those stones, as I made the same jumps over the gaps, appeared unsteady and I wished I had had the foresight to bring with me the rope which had lashed the burdens on the gars. Linked so together, if one of us tumbled into the noisome appearing water the other could lend a hand.

As is mainly true when one fills the immediate future with imagined forebodings, we had no difficulty after all in winning into Voor's Grove. Directly ahead of where the bridge had once given access to what must have been the main street of the town that

spotted unwholesome vegetation was thin. We slashed a path with
our knives, to find that it had formed only a slight wall and we were
now without a barrier.

"The flowers—!" I pointed to where those did indeed stand in
place of the once familiar gardens which must have divided dwelling
from dwelling.

As in Mungo's the brilliant blooms had looked almost like flames
shooting from eternal but hidden fires. But—They were quiet. Quiet
until we moved forward. I caught Illo's arm, held her so for an
instant.

"Watch them!" I ordered.

They were still no longer. Instead they swayed, dipped, turned
their wide expanse of gaudy petals this way and that. I had an
unpleasant thought that somehow they were alive with a life we did
not understand, and that their present movements were struggles to
loosen the earth's grip upon their roots so that they could advance
upon us.

"They sense us—" her voice was quiet, she did not attempt to
move out of my hold. "That must be the truth—that they sense our
presence."

At least none of them grew near the open passage which was the
main road of the settlement. My thought that they could in any way
move to attack us was childish folly. One cannot reasonably give
such motive and desires to a plant—or at least I could not.

"What are they?" the girl was continuing. "Sentries—guards—?"

She made as if to move from the middle of the road, closer to the
nearest bed of those bowing, straining splotches of color. I held her
back.

"I do not know what they are—but I feel we are better to remain
at a distance."

"Perhaps you are right," she conceded.

Once again, as we approached the heart of the town, we could see
that the ruin was not complete here. Houses stood sturdy enough
though their once grey-white walls were stained green in places as if
some mould or algae of sorts sought to defile them. For this vegetation
was evil. I was as sure of that as I was of my own person. It was
rotten, though that rot was not visible to the eye—it was the flowering
of foul decay.

Suddenly Illo stopped short, her head swung about and she looked to a house on her right. It was no different from any of the rest we had passed—the same stained walls, the same mass of nodding, weaving flowers.

"What is it?"

"That—no—" she put her hand to her forehead. "For a moment, just a moment, I thought—Only I could not hold that thought. No, I can't remember!" Her voice arose a note or two, was a little desperate.

I suppose I should have suggested that we enter that dwelling, explore it. Perhaps it had been her home—But I could not possibly have forced myself, or allowed her, to cross into the territory of the flowers in order to reach the gap of the door.

We went on. Our pace was slow and I was sure that, even as I, she was listening, trying to make herself receptive to sound, sight, feeling—

The road brought us out, as in Mungo's Town, in the heart where stood the meeting hall. This one was different from that of the smaller town, for it had a series of booths erected to one side. I saw there piles of pottery, rotted streamers of cloth, the wares of merchants, now far gone in disintegration but making it clear that when the doom had come it had fallen on a market day, or perhaps a fair when traders from down river had gathered here to bargain.

That expanse of gravel about the hall was empty—there was no line of skeletons. I drew a breath of relief. Perhaps, judging by the fact that my father had never reported such a find in his explorations and since the signs of certain death were missing here, Mungo's had been an exception to the general state of the deserted villages.

Illo left my side, walked purposefully toward the hall. "The place of records," she said as I hurried to join her.

For the first time I realized the important omission of my exploration of Mungo's. Of course—there was a small record room in each hall! Why had I not remembered that? I might only plead that the sight of the dead had driven it out of my mind. Also that I had been absorbed in the task which had sent me into the doomed village, the answer to the promise I had made. To leave my father's body with the other dead—that of his friends, his family—had been the purpose which had obsessed me.

The hall was the same as that I had seen, there was more

ornamentation here as became the meeting place of a village which aspired to become a city. I saw painted on the walls the star symbols of four planets—those from which Grove people must have originally come. There was also a plaque which caught the eye because it was stark black and on it inserted in a glowing silver color, untarnished, was an inscription.

"To the memory of Horris Voor, opener of worlds, all honor.

May this, the last of his discoveries, prove his quiet resting place.

Earthed the rover, furled the star wings—

Peace comes at the end."

"Peace comes at the end," I repeated and a sound, which was not laughter but a cry to challenge all which must have happened here, followed my words.

Illo had gone to stand closer to the plaque, now she put a finger to trace some of those shining letters.

"He wanted life for his people; what did they gain here?" She shivered.

"Death," I concluded for her sourly. "He must have died before the doom came."

"I hope that he did," she returned. "I hope he died still believing that he had given a gift to the homeless. See those symbols," she gestured towards the inlays about the edge of the plaque. "You know those worlds, you must have heard of them. Would you care to live on any one of them?"

"*No!*" I did not know them of my own knowledge, I had never been crowded, imprisoned, hopeless, on a world where breeding had gone unchecked, or one which lived under iron dictatorship, or one where the need for the very bare necessities of life was so great that each day was a slavery of unending toil. Yes, the people from those worlds must have looked upon Voor as a kind of paradise. What kind of a hell had it really proved then to be?

"I wish—" she said very softly and I believed I knew her wish though she did not speak it aloud. From which of those worlds had her own kin come? Had she had a family—how big—brothers, sisters—?

At least they had known who I was when I had been found; I had had my father. But Illo had no one, and by her own account she had been at the mercy of those who had tried to stimulate her child's mind, to perhaps even shock her in order to answer questions. That she had survived and become the person she was, was perhaps as great an achievement as any of Horris Voor's when he had discovered a new world to open to the homeless, the restless, the oppressed.

"The records," her tone was decisive now as she turned her back firmly upon the wall.

As was true of every building I had seen from the outside, even the record room here had no door. I looked carefully at the wall. There was a series of small holes which had perhaps once held hinges. Doors and windows, gone—though the rest of the building or buildings about were intact, seemingly in good order. There were even those remnants of trade goods in the booths. Why—doors and windows?

Illo stood in the middle of the small side chamber. The walls held the racks for tapes, a number of them. Not only the records of the village would be here, but information tapes for learning. Or such should have been there. But every rack was empty. The reason occurred easily enough.

"Whoever came here, found you and the rest—they must have taken the tapes—"

"But then they would have been kept at Portcity. And those other doomed villages and holdings—there were no tapes from them on file either."

She had a point. If such tapes existed my father would certainly have used them. He had made his own records of the places he explored. However, though he went every time we visited Portcity to the record office, now I never remembered his asking for anything to do with the other sites prior to their abandonment. Missing tapes— who would want them and why?

In Mungo's the villagers had died. Had it been different in other places? That woman who had been found here in Voor with a broken mind—the one they had traced after her escape to the Tangle. Had she known something after all, something which the experts had not been able to get out of her with their probing in the short time before she had managed her flight?

"Who would want tapes?" I asked myself aloud.

"Some one—or thing—" Illo's mind made the same leap mine was making, "who wanted to know more about—us."

"This was an open planet," I objected to my own conclusion.

"There was not even a trace of Forerunner artifacts ever found. Our detects registered no intelligence higher than that of the gars and maybe the mountain corands."

"What if there was a distort—" she said slowly. "The Tangle—it acts as a distort—we've learned that much."

Always the Tangle! I did not want to believe that the solution lay within that. No one would ever be able to penetrate it—not unless one of the huge hell-burst machines, which had long ago been outlawed for war on any Confederation or League world, could be found and brought here, its devouring fury unleashed on the grey blot. But then, if the Tangle *did* contain any intelligent life, enemy or not, we would never learn it. What a hell-burst was loosed against it consumed, until nothing was left but the bare rock bones of a planet and clouds of ashy dust.

"If our answer lies in the Tangle—" I shrugged.

"If it does—" but she did not sound defeated. When I stared at her, my attention drawn by something in her tone, I saw that she was gazing thoughtfully at those empty racks.

"There has to be intelligence!" There was a sudden new energy about her as if, having been shown a problem, she was now eager to be about its solution. "Have you ever been to the Tangle—to the very edge of it?"

"No. There was no reason—and—well, I don't even know of any loper who has. I've read the records at Portcity—they were enough."

"Not always. Most of those records were compiled by off-worlders."

"*Trained* off-worlders," I reminded her quickly.

"Yes, trained. But they are trained to depend on equipment. You have loper instinct—you must have. Could an off-worlder take out a trek wagon and travel without a guide, a gars-trained man?"

"He'd probably end by sending a distress call," I returned. All I knew of off-worlders were the miners and the ship people, and some merchants settled in Portcity. None of them could live off the plains, steer a course cross-country—or set a gar team on the trail. I used off-world equipment—but it was simple stuff—and I depended first on my senses more than any machine. In that she was right. Just as she might be able to heal a case some off-world medic would mark off as hopeless.

"So? Since the days when the settlements were first alive here there has been very little *our* people have tried to learn about the Tangle. The truth is—we have been afraid of it."

"With very good reason. Nobody lost in there was ever found— there were the two mapping flights from Alsanban, they sent out their last reckoning over the eastern end of the Tangle. Then Hertzo's flyer and the Recki Company one—"

"Off-world—all of them."

"Lausur wasn't off-world," I pointed out. "His expedition made a sweep for forty days along the forepart back in 30 A.L."

"True. They made an edge sweep, but that was all it was—an edge sweep—"

"Sanzori!" I stared at her. "It was after Lausur that Sanzor was doomed!"

There might be nothing at all in the sequence of those two happenings, in fact no connection between them had occurred to me before, nor had I ever heard anyone speculate upon the fact that the doom of the first farthermost holding, a small one whose fate had then been ascribed to plague, had occurred just after Lausur's return from his long march, his tentative attempts to penetrate into the Tangle.

"If something was alarmed, made fearful—" Illo said slowly. "If to them—or—if we were as alien as that flood monster seemed to us—Lausur's march might have been taken as a threat, to meet with a counter."

"But it was two years before the next Shadow doom," I was trying now to remember my history. Luckily such facts had been well drilled into me.

"We might have been under observation—the fear or anger we aroused growing as we pushed farther north, closer to the Tangle. The first of the flyers crashed or was swallowed up during those two years—that was a Survey one. It would have had a great deal of equipment on board—"

What she said was making more and more sense, a kind of dark pattern. Threatened territorial rights was a very ancient cause for war. An animal—or a man—might fight before his own strip of country was invaded, or just at a suggestion that such an invasion threatened. And, supposedly if menaced by something wholly alien to himself, perhaps even in thought processes—fear would generate even higher to feed the anger.

"But why didn't someone figure that out—they've had plenty of time—years of it!" I near exploded.

"They were conditioned—conditioned to believe in reports, in the findings of machines—delicate and mainly accurate to be sure—but still machines, devised by men to help along our own process of thought, not perhaps wholly alien ones. Could such machines detect what their makers might not even be able to image exists?"

"The mine colonies have not been troubled. But they have the force fields. No village could afford to set up one, they would have no way of living inside. But if they strike at us—why not at Portcity—at the big places which are growing stronger—those south of the Halb? More settlers are coming in and settling in the south every season."

"It may just be," Illo was frowning a little, "that they cannot for some reason act at that distance—"

I noted that she now said "they" and not "it" or "something" as she had before. Our enemy was taking on a kind of nebulous shape which it had lacked. That this was all guesses was true, but at least it provided us with a starting point.

However I did not see yet how we could hope to explore the Tangle—or why we should try. There are born into our species certain fears, rages, desires. These may be overlaid by the conditioning we receive during youth, still they can be awakened, and, once awakened, can drive us to action.

I had spent all I could remember of life trailing my father, who was, in turn, driven by an obsession concerning the Shadow doom. He had died because of an accident of nature, yes, but in his dying he had bound me to the same search, for the sight of the deaths in Mungo's had helped to shape me, too. Illo had come to the same path by more subtle means, but she would not, I knew, be turned aside.

What we could do at the Tangle I did not know; there was no solving its mystery. At least I could see none. Only piece by piece between us, we had built reasoning which would send us there.

Illo left the empty records room, came back into the open. I took a quick turn along that line of booths, peering at the remains of what had lain in each. There had been no attempt to cover over, put away, any of the wares. Improvised display counters had been fashioned of piled up transport boxes, and their tops were crowded with merchandise. Though time and weather had dealt hard with most of that.

I picked up a belt knife, to discover its length of tressteel, metal which could withstand years of constant use and exposure in the ordinary way, pitted, part of its length a lace of fine holes. A fast inspection of other metal wares showed that they all bore like signs. I clanged the knife down on the box on which it had lain. It shivered in my hand, splitting into small pieces.

The hilt I tossed from me and then wiped my hand along the leather of my breeches at the thigh. That easy collapse of a metal which I well knew and had used all my life, trusting in its endurance, shook me badly. There had been that necklet which had lain for a long time in the grass and yet had shown not the slightest sign of wearing—except the brown links which had parted. Yet here the hardest of metal forging which I knew had not endured for even twenty years—far less—for Illo had come out of Voor Grove and she was younger than I. This fair must have been in progress on the very day the Shadow doom struck.

"You—the two babies—the woman—" I strode back to join her for she had not followed me but rather remained at the door of the hall, surveying the whole of the scene which she could sight carefully by a slow turn of the head, "were you all found together?"

"No." She shook her head. "It was a Voorloper who came. He was bringing an order from the port for—for—I cannot remember the name. But he saw what had happened, knew it when his wagon beasts refused to enter. I think he was a brave man for he came alone, knowing that sometimes the children were spared. He found the babies together in one house—I was trying to lead Krisan out, pulling at her hand. Only I was like one as witless as she then, crying, and babbling some strange words—He said later I was—singing—"

"Singing?"

"So he told it. He had to put restraints on Krisan for she would have run from him and she screamed terribly. I—I can remember that—only we were free of the town then. I was in the wagon wrapped in a blanket. Krisan lay on the floor of the wagon, rolling from side to side, trying to get free. First she screamed and I was very frightened—then she grew quiet all of a sudden and later she sang,

sang and called—but her words were all strange and I was so afraid of her. The Voorloper headed across country to the mines and they took us out by flyer—only that night she chewed through the restraints—they had left her hands and feet roped because she was so wild. And she went—they trailed her to the Tangle—and reported her lost when they saw she had burrowed into that.

"The Tangle—it must be the Tangle!"

I showed her the broken knife and I saw her astonishment—"But that is tressteel—" she exclaimed.

"And it breaks like rotten wood! Those devilish flowers—look at them!" A flutter of color had caught my sight. I whirled.

The flowers still moved a little, but not as they had. Only all their heads were pointed in our direction. Illo's suggestion that they could be watching us stood to the fore of my mind. How dared I deny that anything—even the least probable—could be true? I had lived on Voor all my life, been born here—but I was the alien—and there could be a thousand, a million secrets which my kind could not, dared not, penetrate. If we were wise—

"The Tangle—" Illo said with the same resolution she had had when she insisted that a calling for need had brought her north.

"The Tangle—" I repeated heavily, knowing that there was no other way I could go—but this was indeed a road I might not have chosen but one I must follow to its end.

❦★ CHAPTER 9 ★❧

We had traveled along the edge of the Tangle now for a full day, studying that massive barrier of intertwined vines, thorn edged bushes, thick branched, low growing vegetation. There were no flowers here—no sinister blooms which swung without air to stir them, petaled eyes to watch. Though the plants varied in shade, all were a darkish green-grey—near black and utterly unwholesome—at least to my eyes.

Oddly enough the gars had not held off as we drew near this alien stretch of country, as they had when we approached the Shadow doomed villages. Though they did not graze near the barrier, they seemed content to accompany us.

"Not a single break—" I pointed out in the later afternoon—

For some reason the Tangle appeared to radiate heat. I mopped my face with my arm, feeling as if I had been trudging miles under a midsummer sun, when I knew well that we were not far from the time of the frost bearing winds out of the north. What would those do to this mass of growth—or was it impervious to cold?

We had not attempted to touch it. Those finger-long spines on most of the outer rim bushes were enough to warn one off from such folly. If I packed a blaster instead of the tangler and stunner I might have experimented a little. But from all reports one could not even ray a way in. This whole expedition was folly and the sooner we admitted that the better.

Though one part of my mind kept assuring me over and over of

458

that folly there was something else which kept me pacing doggedly on, scanning the Tangle. I had not the slightest idea of what we sought, yet I went. Illo, a little ahead of me, would stop every few steps and face the brush and vine wall, her expression that of one listening.

We camped that night a little away from the somber blot which seemed darker than any land ought to be. It was after we had eaten and drunk, crouching close to a very small fire fed from twists of dried grass which I fashioned out of my loper knowledge, that she said suddenly:

"The necklet—"

My hand was at my belt pouch—there was only one necklet. Now, in spite of a firm feeling that this was a dangerous thing, I brought it forth. Only to discover that it had another attribute, one which nearly made me drop it. We had found the chain under the sun, in the full light of day. Now dusk turned swiftly into dark, and in that dark the broken circlet glowed! I flinched. Yet the metal gave forth no heat, only that steady gleam of blue, enough to tint the fingers which held it.

"Give it to me!" Illo ordered.

"It—it may be a carrier—" I moistened my suddenly dry lips with tongue tip. There were alien metals said to radiate and that radiation reacting against a human body—acting upon human flesh—This had ridden against my body for hours—a couple of days. What could I have absorbed from it? For the skin of my pouch could not have shielded me from any radiation.

"It may be far more. Give it—!" Her voice was sharper, her fingers reaching to pluck the chain from my grasp.

"No!" I coiled my hand tightly around it. "If there is radiation—"

"Who could better judge such than a healer?" she asked.

She was right. Still, remembering how this find had affected her before, I did not want to yield it.

"What do you think that this has to do with the Tangle?" I hedged.

"Perhaps nothing, perhaps everything. It is old—it may go back to a beginning. It belonged to another people, perhaps *they* had a way, knowledge—Don't you see," her tone was near fierce now, "we must have a key, a guide—"

"To what? We have no way of knowing—"

"We must learn." She snatched then, her fingers pried at mine, and, rather than struggle with her, I had to allow her the chain.

She held the metal links closer to our pocket of fire. When the flame light touched the metal its own radiance dimmed. Illo slipped the chain back and forth, pulling at each link as if she wanted to test its strength, as a man tests a rope to which he is about to entrust his life.

"There is no radiation—as we know it," she reported. "There is energy, yes, but it is of another kind."

"What?" I wished mightily now that I had hurled that find from me back on the plains, sent it to be hidden once more under the thick growth of grass.

"Energy akin to an esper talent," she returned calmly. "You must know that when a sensitive uses such he radiates energy. That has been measured in a healer's work."

She spoke the truth, so much I could accept. However, that an inanimate object, such as this chain, could contain such energy—that was another matter. Illo still slid the links back and forth between her fingers. Then she laid across her palm the curved plate covered with intricate engraving which was as much a tangle of lines as the growth barrier we had been tramping by all day.

"Not yet." Slowly she opened the fingers she had curled around that plate. "But it will!" There was triumph in her voice, a light in her eyes which not just a reflection from the fire. "This—this *is* a key! Let me sleep with it and I shall know more." Once again her hand closed tightly over the coil of metal and I knew that she would not yield it to me. Still I was more than just uneasy to see that in her grasp.

A key—to what? I looked over my shoulder at the black blot which was the Tangle. The growth arose, a wall against all my kind. If this chain were a key to the opening of that wall—Only such a thought was folly.

She did not speak again, her mask was back in place, and she curled up at once on her grass bed. As she settled her head I saw that the hand holding the chain rested against her cheek. It was wrong— the act meant danger—both thoughts were fast fixed in my mind. Only I dared not move to take that from her. I could have been some- how caught on the edge of her own concentration of her talent, which walled her off from any interference.

I walked away from the fire to where the gars grazed. Witol lifted his big head and whiffled at me, the snorting sound he made as a greeting. I drew my hand along his warm back where the patches of thicker winter hair were already growing, some near long enough to catch my finger tips.

Witol was part of the sane world I had always known. There was comfort in standing so beside the big animal, smelling the scent of his hide, feeling his hair under my hand. This was real. But picking at me eternally—since I had entered into Mungo's—sharper and sharper now, was an emotion which was part fear (I faced that squarely) and part something else, of which I was not yet sure— curiosity, a loper's desire to learn a new trail, a need for revenge on whatever had made this wide country a land of death for my kind? Perhaps a little of each.

I knew that I would go on in the morning, follow the useless path along the Tangle, hunting what never existed—a way in. Why—? This was like some tale from a story tape in which an impossible quest was laid upon some unfortunate and he was compelled by non-human pressure to continue to the end.

Voor's world. The planet had once seemed so open and welcoming—but perhaps my kind were never meant to—I shook my head vigorously as if I could so flip away that insidious conclusion. Each and every world which my species had colonized had had one problem or another. That quality of need for mastery, which was a birth-part of us, was always so awakened into life to set us hammering some very hostile planets into earth-homes. No world was ever a paradise without any danger. In fact such might have been far worse a pitfall for my kind than the worst stone-fire-airless hell. We would only have atrophied there—become nothing.

I scratched the upstanding tuft of coarse mane-hair between Witol's ears and he snorted happily, butted me with near strength enough to knock me from my feet. Our fire was like a fading eye— and weariness reached into me. Anyway our exploration would be limited by our supplies, as I had already made clear to Illo. We must turn south as soon as the water in the tanks Witol shouldered during the day reached a level I had scarred across the sides.

Back at the fire I added the last of my twisted faggots of grass, and then stretched out, my blanket over me. Though that curious warmth which had been with us all day still seemed to reach out even this far into the plains.

I shifted unhappily on my bed. Though I was tired enough to sleep, and to a loper strange places were no deterrent to rest—as long as they were in the open (for we of the trails find it difficult to rest easy within confining walls)—still my busy thoughts would not still. I turned upon my back and lay looking up at the stars. So had I seen those on many nights. Only then I had not been—alone—I had tried to keep from me that feeling which had struck, attempted to over-come me, at my father's death.

Now I fought that battle once again. From the time I had been small—the time I could remember at all—he had worked to prepare me for this kind of loneliness. There are many accidents and ills which whittle away at the numbers of lopers. A man may be asked for at Portcity, perhaps spoken of when one loper met another on the trail—but his fate never known. I had been taught as best my father could manage to be self reliant. If he had mourned my mother, others dead in Mungo's Town, he had never done so openly. As I have said he was not a follower of religious belief which was built upon a formal creed and ritual. Yet he had said at one or two rare moments that he believed the life essence we knew was but a part of something else which had an existence beyond our comprehension, and that we must accept death as a door opening and not a gate slammed shut.

Illo had had less than I during the years since Voor's Grove had been doomed. No one of *her* kin had remained to keep her in touch with normal life. I thought of what she had said about her ordeal when they had tried to make her remember. That she had made a place for herself with her talent testified to her courage and the sta-bility of her mind.

So my thoughts wound back to what she was doing this night— sleeping with the touch of that ill-omened thing she had found. Suppose I moved now—tried to free the chain from her while she slept—or did she even sleep? Was she in some kind of trance? Should I—could I take it—?

I wanted to do just that, yet I found that such an act was impossible. Though I struggled against that unseen compulsion there was no chance for me to move. Slowly, though my thoughts still spun, I closed my eyes and slept.

There was the Tangle straight before me, and behind—or rather in me a compelling force sending me straight ahead at the fearsome thorny hedge which was its outermost defense—thorns to pierce the flesh viciously, blind the eyes. I threw up my hands to protect my face, fought to free myself. Still I strode on as if my path was as open and free as the plains.

I must be right against the thorns now, I had surely covered that small stretch of open ground. I dropped the hand I used to shield my face. There was before me light—a light which waxed and waned as might an earth-bound moon—save that it was not ruddy as Voor's moon might be. Then, as my eyes adjusted to that flickering light, I saw no moon disc; rather a pillar, as if some humanoid form had been set alight and was moving. Of the Tangle there was no sign— only that light which glided away, drawing me after it—

My heart beat heavily, I was gasping for breath as if I were running, and in me there was such expectancy, such a drawing that—

"Bart! Bart!"

Out of somewhere came a force to fasten on me, making me reel back and forth. Something held me back when I must go. That figure ahead was gaining ground—if I lost sight of it—

"Bart!"

I was pulled, lifted—I was awake!

Illo knelt beside me, both her hands were tight on my shoulders as if she had been dragging my weight up—or away—

"I—let me go—"

"Not that way!" She spoke crisply, nor did she loose her hold. She kept her link between us as if fearing I would lapse into some unconscious state again.

I blinked, shook my head.

"You are here," she said slowly, accenting each word, as she might if a child had wakened crying in the night. "You are here—and *now*—"

Though what she meant I did not understand. Gone indeed was that throbbing light. Behind Illo's head the sky was grey, lightning— the sky I had seen many times.

"I—I was—the Tangle—" My words twisted, as if, when I attempted to find those which best explained the vividness of that dream, I could not find the proper ones.

"Not *that* way," she repeated. "That is what *they* want—we go *our* way, not theirs."

She loosed her hold on me at last and I sat up. This was the camp we had made. There were the banners of a new day showing above the horizon. The fire was burnt out, still I felt no chill. On the other side of the pile of ashes the three gars stood, their large eyes watching me, seeming to hold a measure of that same studying look which Illo kept upon me.

"They? Who are *they*?" I demanded.

She did not gesture with her hands, rather she turned her head a fraction to point with her chin.

"I do not know—save that there is a form of intelligence somewhere in there—one I cannot tap. Which is aware of us—though—though it fears and so it weaves traps—not this time to catch bodies but minds. Here—"

She reached to her belt, holding out the chain. It was a complete circlet now, I saw that somehow she had bent together two of the broken links to make it whole.

"This you wear—"

I made no attempt to take it from her. "Why? I don't want—"

"Only you can use it. It is adapted to a male principle."

"Use it how?"

"I said it was a key—it is. One which that waiting there has reason to fear, or at least dreads. No," she silenced some of my unasked questions, "I received no more impressions than that. It must be worn by a man, and it will get us in—"

"Through that?" The thorned brush of my dreams was perfectly visible now. "We'd need a blaster—"

"I wonder." She sat back on her heels, her attention turned to the brush wall. "How does this vegetation react to a stunner?"

"React to a stunner? There could be no reaction to such a weapon. The power of that reaches into the nervous system, completely relaxes all muscles. It affects only animals and men. A plant has no—"

She arose, still facing the Tangle rather than looking to me. "We do not truly know what such a growth as this may have. That which attacked the doomed places is surely alien. What if this is even more so? Will it cost you anything to try?"

I had the two charges in the weapon, a dozen more looped in my belt. There was also a bag of them in the gear Wobru had been carrying. It would not be any great loss to prove to her that such a thing was impossible.

"I'll try," I promised. "You learned nothing more from that?"

The necklet was still in her hands. She glanced down at it and then thrust it vigorously in my direction. "Fleeting impressions—none I could fasten upon. The last thoughts of he who wore it were so chaotic I could not read them. Only that he had been sent on a mission when some evil struck, so that he could not fulfill his duty. That overrides much of the rest—his last despair at failure. But it has much to do with the Tangle, that is a matter I am certain of. Also he was on his way there when death took him—and only a man can pick from this what is needed."

The last thing I wanted to do was to take that necklet, fasten it about my throat. Perhaps it was because I so shrank from that act my pride was aroused. Illo was used to dealing with things of her talent—the "unseen." She could accept this all as something which one must do, even as a Voorloper would inspan his wagon before he drew out from a camp. To her my squeaminess might seem without any base except craven fear of the unknown.

Well, I admitted to myself, that I did have. Still there was enough determination left in me so I must prove to myself, if not to her who might not understand, that I was not to be defeated by the unknown before I put up a struggle. Realizing that I must do this quickly, without stopping to consider what might happen, I caught the necklet from her, worried open the clasp and set it about my neck, making tight the fastening once again.

It fitted so well, lying just at the base of my throat, that it might have been fashioned for me. The collar of my hunting shirt was loose, since in this strange warmth I had not tightened the lacing thongs. So there was nothing between the smooth metal and my flesh. That inscribed foreplate lay directly in front.

A sudden thought crossed my mind—on some planets there were animals trained to serve men, animals with not the same grade of intelligence as the gars, or ones not so amiable. Those creatures bore the seal of their ownership—collars—some patterned with the name of the owner. Suppose—suppose this was such a collar and I had so voluntarily accepted subservience to a will I did not know and perhaps could not even understand? But I did not mention this to Illo.

She reached up when the necklet was in place and touched, with only fingertip, that plate at the base of my throat. The metal was not cool against my skin, instead it seemed to have the same temperature as my body.

"Duty—" she said the one word slowly, as if meditating on what it meant. "He was in such anguish of mind because of his duty—he tried to fight off death because he had not fulfilled what he must do."

"Could you tell who he was—or," I hesitated and then added, "*what?*"

She considered that question for what seemed to be a long moment.

"He was humanoid—I think—At least this fits you so well it might have been made for you. But his mind—it was different. Only his emotions were plain to read—that because they so rent him at the end. It all happened very long ago." She made a queer little gesture with both hands as if scattering something on the ground—perhaps fragments of all those lost years which had clung to the necklet until she decided it must be used.

We broke camp, loading the gars. Instead of ranging ahead today, the three beasts fell into single line behind us. They could have been in yoke to a small wagon. Nor did they break that line to graze. Illo, for I left the guide point to her, did not advance directly toward the portion of Tangle by our camp. Rather she set out again on a parallel route westward.

We had been tramping so for some time and the sun was already well up, when she halted abruptly, faced the Tangle wall. To my eyes this portion differed in no way from that we had surveyed along the way we had come. Yet she stared straight at the thorned brush and ordered:

"Try the stunner—here!" She stretched out one arm, her index finger pointing at a bush which overtopped my own head by a good half length of my body.

I drew my weapon, feeling slightly foolish, for I believed that its charge would only be wasted. However, I must use it, if for no other reason than to prove that fact to my own satisfaction as well as to her.

My pressure on the firing button was steady; I had set the power to top force. Now I swung the barrel of my weapon slightly, playing the invisible ray up and down the bush she had indicated. Nothing— just as I had thought. However, as I let the stunner slide back into its holster, she was running toward the bush.

"Thorns—!" I warned her.

She had already put out her hands, though I noted she did catch only the tips of the branches where their armament was the least. Then—

Had I not seen it I would not have believed that it might happen. Illo had given a jerk. The brush moved forward a little in answer to her tug, then wilted. That was the only word I could use to describe its sloughing downward, the seemingly instantaneous withering of leaf, the limpness of branch. There was a gap in the wall!

"Again!" She shouted that at me, her face flushed, her eyes alight. No mask on her now, she was all aroused eagerness. "Again!"

So I followed her orders; an inner bush withered, taking with it to the ground a huge matted mass of vine. We had the beginning of a path. However, the outer portion of the Tangle had yielded in the past to something far more potent than any stunner—blaster fire— only to regenerate, rising from the roots thicker, more deadly than before.

I reached the edge of the gap, threw out my arm and caught her, dragging her back.

"Wait—it may grow again!"

Her face showed a flash of anger, but she did not try to pass me. I had no idea how long it had been before the regeneration on those earlier expeditions. Still certainly it could not have been too long or the process would not have so impressed the would-be past explorers.

We waited. There was no change in the withered growth. I was as suspicious as I might have been with a stunned sand hound. For I could not shake off the feeling that perhaps this was a game—if you will—being played by something that was well prepared to defend itself and had successfully done so for generations.

No sign of life came, no movement of branch or even straightening of crumpled leaf. Illo turned on me:

"Would you wait away the day?" she demanded.

I wanted to say "yes, if need be." Yet I did not. As far as I knew from past records, and my father had indeed combed those, playing the tapes over and over again, the stunner had never even been considered as a weapon of possible use against the Tangle. Why should it have been? It could be that so simple a discovery would have made the expeditions free of its secrets long ago.

I checked the charge in my weapon carefully. About a quarter of it had been expended—and I did not know how far we might go—or what else could lie before us. Voorlopers are a mixture of the daring and the wary—that is, they must be if they continue to live. One part of me wanted to push forward, the other was uneasy—this answer was *too* simple.

"We must go!" Illo twisted away from me, started forward, planting her boots firmly on the first layer of wilted vegetation. I roused from my indecision and hurried on, elbowing by her, to once more spray the growth, watch it wither, grow limp, and sink to form a carpet. There was a snort from behind. I looked around and saw, to my true amazement, that Witol was coming too, his herd mates behind him.

Now I was aware of something else, as I stood and sprayed to open the way. There was a rustling through the Tangle, though I could not, in the pocket the stunner had opened, feel any breeze. I moved with the utmost caution, looking from side to side. The nodding flowers which had studded the villages of the dead were in my mind. Those had moved without any wind's help also. Was it the leaves, the branches, those strangling vines, which set up that sound here?

Nothing encroached on the path the stunner opened. In fact, I thought, though I could not be sure, that the growth seemed to edge back. If it had not before come in direct contact with the ray I wielded, it now had enough sensation, or intelligence of a sort, to fear contact. Surely the path *was* wider than the space I had rayed, wide enough so Illo and I advanced abreast and the gars had no trouble in single-filing behind us, not even their burdens of gear scraping so much as a leaf on either side.

We advanced slowly, for after each spraying I determined to wait a space to be sure there was no swift renewal of life. I had to refit the stunner twice with fresh units. When I looked back it was down a long tunnel, the other end of which had near disappeared. We could not keep on so forever. Either we must find some natural clearing in this nightmare of an alien wood, or carve us one in which to rest.

That dank heat which had reached us even as we had only skirted the edge of the Tangle was far more oppressive here. Sweat ran down my face, lay under my shoulder pack to fret my shoulders. The half-healed scratches from the fight when I strove to get us and our gear out of the wagon stung furiously. Luckily there was not what I feared we might find here—no noxious insects swarmed about us to sting or bite.

Our progress became a set pattern: ray, wait, advance, ray, wait, advance—

Until—

A mass of the Tangle fell in the usual way to the ground, that ground which gave off a sour smell of its own. The disappearance of the growth left something standing—something which no stunner could possibly affect—a pillar of black stone—and it was no natural spur of rock either.

✦ CHAPTER 10 ✦

NOR WAS IT A PILLAR WE FACED. For, as the last of the foliage melted away, I heard Illo's breath go out in a hiss and I was startled into raising my weapon to give another blast which was not needed. What stood in our path, slightly larger than life size, was a statue carved of dull black stone, but with such fidelity to detail it might have been a living creature frozen by some means to act as a guard against further intrusion.

It was humanoid in contour though there were differences. The hands which had been raised to cross on the breast had six fingers, the face was more markedly oval than any Terra-human's, while the nose extended well out, having a definite hook of the broad tip. There was no sign of any representation of hair save on the very top of the head where there stood erect a crest looking not unlike flaps of skin a lizard might own.

Though the whole of the body was done in exacting detail, there were no eyes represented in that face, only dark pits where such should have been. Also there were no sexual characteristics such as were common to my own kind. It could have been masculine, feminine, or neither. But that it had been fashioned to represent in mirror-exact fashion a living or once living creature I had not the least doubt.

As I continued to study the face, that impression of menace which had been born in my mind from its sudden appearance and its being set in that alien form faded. I felt instead a brooding sadness, as if it had been placed as a memorial, rather than intended to warn off those who managed to enter the Tangle this far.

The stone of which it had been carved had no counterpart in any I had seen on Voor. The entwined mass of vegetation, the passing of what must be an untold number of seasons, had done nothing to dull or erode the work. It stood now uncovered, as clear in all its lines as if it had been only recently set in place by the artist who had conceived it. It was not beautiful by our standards, no, but still it had a power—a purpose—for it conveyed stronger and stronger that hopeless feeling of what I now believed to be defeat, resignation to extinction.

"They knew—" Illo's voice was hardly above a whisper.

I understood her meaning. Yes, whoever had wrought this monument had known that there would be no future—no way to go except to an ending. The more I looked upon it the more my own spirit sank, the greater appeared our folly in trying to penetrate a wilderness of the alien which was never meant to be invaded by our kind.

"No!" Illo caught at my arm. "Do not let it do that to you! Do not let it make you think-feel failure!"

She could not have read my emotions, she must have judged them entirely by her own reaction to that sombre, brooding monument to despair. Perhaps that was its weapon! Perhaps it formed a trap, not for our bodies, or even our minds, but our spirits. Still it took almost all the determination I could summon to walk forward, approach that silent statue.

More and more it did not appear to be a work of art, rather something which had once lived and now had been left, unable to completely die. I found myself staring mainly, as I advanced, at those pits in which eyes should have rested, half fearing, half believing, that I might see there sparks of life, even if such had withdrawn from all the rest of the frozen body.

The dead black color—had that been selected because the creature itself had been that color in life? For that it represented a living species, even a living or once living person, I no longer doubted. I found myself passing to the right while Illo broke her grasp on me and went to the left, the statue for an instant between us.

Heat—a surge of warmth reached me from that stone. I had no wish to put out a hand and touch it—I could not have forced myself

to make such an investigation. Only the black figure might have been
a torch radiating heat outward.

I heard the grunting of the gars. They had come to a stop. I swung
around, to blast with the stunner the growth on one side, giving them
greater room to pass the figure by. They seemed reluctant to move on
for the first time since they had so followed us into the Tangle. Witol
raised his head and bellowed, as he might when delivering a challenge
to some audacious bull intruding on what he considered his own
territory.

Would the animals turn back? I felt that no urging of mine would
influence them, that now they moved by their own volition and
could not be controlled by my commands. So I waited.

Witol challenged for the second time. There was something in
the massed walls about the small space the stunner had cleared which
gave back, in odd, hollow echoes, his cry. Reluctantly the bull
lowered his head and paced on, his two companions falling in single
file behind. I saw him swing his head to one side so that even the tip
of his horn might not touch the figure. However, he had chosen—
and in our favor. Once more I began my task of raying open a way
before us. Still the vegetation answered with withering, crumbling of
limb, curling of leaf.

"Forerunner—surely—" Illo kept her voice low. She might have
feared some listener. "Have you heard of or seen its like before?"

I tried to remember the tapes which my father had collected and
poured over. There had been many Forerunner civilizations; men
realized that as they spread outward to take over planets which had
once been colonies, or the homes of unknown races now vanished.
There were worlds which were nothing but one huge, deserted city,
the tall buildings based on every inch of available land—their original
populations too great for us to fathom—all emptied by time. There
were worlds which had been burnt off, turned into radioactive cinders,
or half devastated, with glassy craters where cities or points of military
installation had stood.

Wars which had been perhaps galactic-wide in that remote past
had swept away races, species. It must have happened over and over
again—civilizations which built, reached for the stars, grew powerful,
established federations or empires, then fell apart in wars, in plagues,
in slow decay when stellar commerce failed and no star ships came.

My own species was very young compared to stellar time. Though we were spreading fast, building, trying to wrest from the reminders of the past we found more and more of their secrets. There were many Forerunners, yes, and at different times, on different worlds, or in different sectors.

The Zacathans with their great storage banks of historical knowledge might have a clue to that figure, but if so it was on a tape my father had never found. Only, and now a new excitement came to life in me, a Forerunner find—a big one—that would mean complete freedom for both Illo and me. For the finder's fee for such was untold credits. We could go anywhere, do whatever we willed—if this was Forerunner.

"They faced certain death—" Illo's thoughts had not swung so wide or in such a selfish direction as mine. "They had and expected no hope—"

I had tried not to think what that mourning figure had meant—its defeat was too plain, enough to dishearten us.

"In their time," I commented. "Their time is past."

She did not answer me at once. I think she was still caught up by the emotion that lost statue had engendered. Perhaps because she was a healer, trained to be attuned to the ills of others, it had struck far more deeply with her than with me. For a loper learns early that good and ill both exist, and sometimes the ill outweighs the good, but both must be accepted and dealt with to the best of one's ability.

As the stunner cleared our path I half expected to uncover more such relics of the unknown. But we were well beyond that statue, which was either a warning or the monument to the death of a people, before the growths melted away to disclose now the beginnings of walls. What we had come upon by chance was a gateway, one which lacked any sign of door or barrier, while the walls stretched away on either side to be swallowed up quickly by the Tangle. There was an arch overhead, a shallow one with only a slight upward curve.

Illo once more caught at my arm. "Look!" Her other hand swept up toward that arch. That had been fashioned of the same dead black stone—as were the walls—but it was not smooth. Instead it was carved in a twisted, intricate design, one in which you could distinguish nothing but curves and lines which led nowhere. Save that the longer you studied them the more the idea grew upon you that this was no abstract adornment but had a meaning. Perhaps it was an inscription in a language which expressed its symbols in a way totally alien to those we could ever understand.

"The necklet!" My companion reached up to catch the edge of my skin shirt, dragging that down and away from the ornament I had so reluctantly put on that morning.

"There is a sameness—" she declared.

I fumbled one-handedly, the stunner still at ready in the other, trying to loose the clasp so that I might compare. Only that fastening would not yield.

"Unfasten it—" I ordered Illo.

She slipped the chain about, as I bent my head and stooped a little, so that she might be able to more speedily find the clasp.

"It—it is gone!"

"No it isn't—I can feel it—" I objected.

"Not the necklet—the fastening!"

"What!" I rammed the stunner into her nearest hand and began feeling along the chain for that clasp. There were no slightly larger links—nor did I feel the place where she had mended the chain so that it could be worn—that place where she had squeezed two of the broken links together. It was as smooth as if it had been sealed on me.

I caught my fingers in it then and strove to tear it off. All that happened was that the links cut into my neck with knife-edge sharpness and I had to stop.

"You can't see the clasp, or the mended place?" I demanded.

I could feel the chain once more slipping about, this time in her touch.

"Neither is there! But I don't understand—"

What I understood was an impossibility. There was no way for the clasp and the repaired breakage to so meld into the chain as to be now undetectable. Yet I could not believe that she was deceiving me, and certainly my own fingers had not been able to locate any irregularity in the necklet either.

"Perhaps it was made to respond so—to body heat or the like," Illo said slowly. "I have heard of the Koris stones—is it not true that they only come alive and take on their jewel brightness and fragrance when worn against bare skin? Might there not be an unknown alloy of metal which fastens of itself under the same conditions?"

True or not, I was unhappy that the alloy had answered so to *me*. I had not been easy when she had first suggested my wearing the chain. I was really disturbed now.

"Take my belt knife and see if you can cut through it," I ordered.

She drew back from me and her answer was blunt and instant. "No!"

"No? Why? Do you think I am going to keep wearing something I can't rid of—"

"Which you must *not* get rid of."

Her voice held such authority that I simply stared at her in open disbelief.

Since I could not very well use the knife myself, I was to go collared to her pleasure. My resentment, fed by fear as I will freely admit, then flared.

"Explain to me why—" I strove to keep my voice even, not to let explode the anger building in me.

"I cannot. I only know that in some way, which we shall learn, you must bear this—"

My teeth snapped together, I would not allow her to guess my fear. Instead I thumbed on the ray of the stunner which I snatched back from her, spraying ruthlessly and recklessly ahead at what lay beyond the arch, clearing a way for us within the only partly visible walls.

The ray diminished with my continued attack, until I realized that, in my rising fury, I had exhausted the current charge. That sobered me. For we had no idea how far this mass extended, nor how much longer we would have to call upon the stunner for service.

I snapped in a new unit, but did not look at or speak to her. With every breath I drew I was aware of that chain making me, as I believed, a slave to some force which was the worse because I did not know what it was or in what way it would next show that it was master.

There was a nudge against my shoulder, imperative, delivered with a force which nearly sent me sprawling forward to land face down in the wrack of the plants I had mown down. Witol's mighty bellow, the loudest I had ever heard from his thick throat, echoed about our ears. He edged by me, his burden of the water tanks on which we depended scraping, pushing me, sending me against Illo.

Head down, the bull pawed the ground, sending bits of wilting leaves, slimy under soil, flying behind him. His eyes glinted redly and he was the picture of growing rage, as if he had caught fire from the same emotion which had earlier possessed me.

Bru echoed his bellow with her higher call, striving to draw even with her mate. While Wobru momentarily arose on his hind legs as if longing to lunge forward, but found no way he could make room for himself beyond the broad backs of the two older gars.

What had so aroused Witol and the others I could neither see nor guess. To my closest survey the unsheared brush ahead still presented exactly the same appearance as it had all along. Nor, when the echoes of the gars' cries died away, was there anything to be heard. Only Witol and his mate had passed under that archway and there was nothing left for us to do but follow.

Without realizing until after I had made the gesture, my hand went again to the chain about my throat as I passed under that arch. What warning or greeting did that fanciful involved script hold? What relation might such have to the badge I wore now in spite of myself?

The gars had paused, Witol's nose near touching the bank of Tangle which had not yet yielded to the stunner. I worked my way around the side of the gar, trying to avoid touching any unwithered stuff, any thorns. Once more I sprayed ahead, widening the ray to the farthest extent the weapon would allow, then, in turn, swinging it back and forth to make a broader path.

So on we went, nor did there appear as yet anything else which that growth concealed. If the wall was guarding a village, or even the buildings of a holding—then where did such stand? The vegetation fell to reveal nothing but a mass of the same beyond.

Witol halted so suddenly that I bumped against his massive shoulder. He did not yield and now I could not push past. His head swung low, and one of his horns caught in the matted stuff which lay dead or dying on the ground. He tossed and the vegetation flew, he pawed and earth glistening with slime appeared. Only that broke also as he deliberately dug one horn down into it, tossed, pawed. Great chunks of tainted soil flew out and away. There arose so putrid and foul a smell from his efforts that I gasped. Illo held one hand to close off her nose.

There was something—under that coating of diseased soil (for all I could think of was that the very earth itself here bore no relation to the clean dirt of the plains). Witol's efforts uncovered a smooth surface, one which was still streaked, it was true, with greasy, evil smelling clay—but one which certainly was not normal ground.

Witol worked industriously, first with one large cloven hoof, and then the other. Wobru shouldered aside his mother and came behind the greater bull, beginning in turn to paw at earth his sire had already disturbed. While Illo and I watched with amazement, the gars, laboring together as if they were teamed, cleared a space which was growing larger by the instant. Now and then Witol turned his head to me to grunt. His meaning was so plain that I, who had always commanded the beasts, now obeyed his orders, sweeping the stunner—killing and then stepping aside to let the gars clear away the debris.

We were no longer in a tunnel of vegetation. Rather we stood in a clearing which was roughly square, swept nearly clean through the efforts of the animals, floored with a metal which I judged to be the same as that of the necklet I wore.

Though the poisonous and foul growths of the Tangle had covered it perhaps for eons of time, the surface showed no sign of rust or erosion. What might be its purpose and what had led the gars to act as they did were both mysteries I did not attempt to solve. Illo stooped but did not quite touch that flooring.

"It is not pavement, I believe—" she studied the expanse carefully. To my eyes there was not a single sign of any break in it—the whole piece was a giant plate.

The gars had finished their cleanup and now stood quiet, the heads of all three hanging low, their noses near touching the plate. Were they in search of a scent? Were they looking for something? I had passed the point of amazement now; I was not sure of anything. Before my eyes the beasts I had always taken for animals, of some intelligence, but still animals, had engaged in action which suggested that all our estimates concerning them were very wrong, that they were far more than prize stock to serve settlers on Voor. It was at that moment I began also to wonder whether they were not, as a species, far older and longer evolved than we had ever guessed. Had their long-ago ancestors indeed known the race who had set this plate they now revealed to us?

Illo cried out, stumbling a step or two towards me. I met her and we clung together. That platform which had appeared so intact, so solid, was sinking, and we were being carried downward with it.

I tried to reach the edge, drawing the girl with me. Witol took a ponderous step or two, setting his large body broadside to cut me off from any escape. Before I could push around him we were already too deep, so that even a leap would not have allowed me to catch the edge of the break.

The gars stirred and I heard Wobru grunt uneasily. I say heard, for, as we sank, there was a darkness closing in about us. That patch of light was still above us—now far above us. Our rate of descent seemed to be more swift than we were aware of—otherwise no light appeared to pierce into the depths into which the platform carried us.

Illo held onto my hand with a grip so tight that her nails cut into my skin, but I made no move to loosen it. Just now it was good to have that touch, to reassure myself that I was not insane or hallucinating, that this was really happening.

I now had to turn my head well up, back on my shoulders, to watch that fast disappearing square of sky which I could not hope to reach. While all about us was a darkness which was heavier and more solid than any moonless night could be. There were no stars here to reassure us with their light.

"Bart!" Illo had turned a little in my hold. I looked down and saw her face. There was a curious bluish light across it. "The necklet—it is afire!"

Afire! I felt no more heat than that subtle warmth which I had been aware of since I first put the chain on. The circlet fit so tightly to my throat that I could not see it, but I could catch a radiance which appeared to stream out across my breast and shoulders.

I loosed my other hand, temporarily thrusting the stunner back into my holster, and in turn worked free the torch from its thongs at my belt. My fingers found the "high" button and a moment later the ray swept out and around.

We were descending into a well, the walls of which were coated by the same alloy as formed the platform on which we stood. That fitted exactly to the walls, sliding down them with no sign of any space between. There were no visible openings, not a seam to be detected along those walls—as if the whole tube had been cast as a single great piece. Nor was there any chance of a hand or foothold on that smooth surface. Unless the trap which was this platform could be controlled in some manner, we were perhaps to be buried alive in an installation which was a total mystery.

I looked to the gars. They stood as quietly as if they were waiting in sedate sequence as they always did to be inspanned before a move-out. Why—and what—and who—?

I did not voice such question. Illo knew no more than did I, and I could expect no answer from Witol. However I kept the torch sweeping about the walls, seeking some opening, some hope of escape. Still we continued to drop smoothly down.

The open patch at the top was now smaller than my hand; I could not even estimate how far beneath the surface we had come. There flashed into my mind scattered bits of the information my father had culled from the Forerunner archives. There had been apparently some races or species among them who had had a liking for under-surface life, building strange and unknowable installations in caves, in burrows they tunneled, as if they were more at home in such places than on the surface of the worlds they chose to visit—or to colonize.

Perhaps this race, if it were not native to Voor (though a vanished native civilization could not be ruled out) had been of that type. There must come an end to our journey soon. This, I had come to believe, was not a trap for prisoners (or at least I hoped that was so), rather an entrance to some place of importance.

The end did come—as the platform suddenly passed the tip of an opening in one wall, pulled on, down and down, until there was a wide door open before us. Then it came to an abrupt halt.

I half expected the gars to take the lead in disembarking, I do not know why. However, the beasts showed signs of uneasiness, snuffling and moving their feet as if they were not quite sure of the stability of the platform, though it no longer moved.

There was nothing to do but to go on, through that doorway which seemed a cup of pure dark, hoping that somewhere beyond there might just lie some means of returning to the surface. I said as much and Illo agreed.

Now that we had reached the bottom of the well, she appeared to have regained her confidence—or at least put on the appearance of doing so. I had to admit to myself that action as represented by the waiting doorway renewed my spirits also. Shoulder to shoulder we stepped from the platform into the waiting corridor or tunnel. Once more the gars fell in behind us as they had when we had broken our path into the Tangle.

I swept the torch from side to side. This appeared much like the shaft we had descended—or its lesser twin—being laid upon its side. The same smooth, seamless walls, no breaching of those, no sign of another doorway, of any exit except the one we followed.

"Switch off the torch a moment," Illo said.

I did not know what she wished to learn, only I did as she bade. Then we discovered that the light I carried was no longer necessary. Though perhaps not as bright as the radiance from the necklet, there was a dim glow to which our eyes adjusted, enough so that we could walk without difficulty seeing ahead. I was glad to save the torch and fastened it back in my belt, taking once more the stunner. Not because I expected to encounter any more of the Tangle's foul mass but because with it in my hand I found a certain reassurance, an illusion perhaps that I might still be in some control of the situation were we to discover—what? Some alien form of life—some mechanical installation—which had been left to run through endless time by its vanished creators? I did not know, nor did I try to speculate, I only knew I felt safer with the stunner in my fist.

The road seemed endless. So much so that once we stopped, drank from our supply of water, sharing that in small measurement with the gars, eating our trail bread. I gave a cake of this to each of the beasts and they chewed noisily, apparently finding it to their taste. At the back of my mind stirred the thought that once our supplies were gone—No—that would I face when the time came. We would be as prudent with both food and water as we could, and I would not say aloud what might be the end of such blind wandering.

At the end of the corridor was a door. This was closed, though I could see the slit which marked it clearly when I once more loosed the torch and had Illo hold it that I might examine the barrier. There was a cup-like pocket to my left but no latch that I could distinguish. I fitted my fingers into that depression and strove to push, but the barricade remained immovable. Was it locked and we prisoners?

There was one other thing to try. Once more I braced myself and used fingers as best I could, this time pushing towards my right instead of inward. For a long moment I thought that my guess was a failure. Then, perhaps as the result of centuries of disuse was overcome, it did slide reluctantly, taking all my strength to force it along. I discovered that a series of sharp jerks were better to stir it a little at a time, accomplishing more in that way than any steady pull. The panel was open at last, and with its opening light spilled through—a light which was almost as bright as day in the upper, outer world.

❦⋆CHAPTER 11⋆❧

LIGHT STREAMED FROM ABOVE, steady and clear, while between us and its source reached a flight of broad, shallow steps. The surface of each step was inlaid with color, brilliant color. The designs were—faces!

There was nothing inhuman or alien about these representations as there had been in the face of the statue guardian we had passed in the Tangle. These were of people who might have lived in any holding or village. While each varied from the next, possessing such life-like features I could only believe that they had been originally fashioned to resemble once living personalities, still they had been carefully set so that anyone climbing the stair, no matter where he would put his feet as he went, would tread upon one or another of them.

There was something unpleasant in their cast of countenance, a slight exaggeration of this feature or that, the beginning of a sly smirk, a leer of the eyes. On close examination one could well believe that whoever had wrought this stairway had done it in a mood of hatred and vengeance. To tread upon the helpless face of the enemy—that was a conception which in itself was a token of so strong a fury that it shook one.

Illo went down on her knees, put out her hands to touch the nearest of the faces on the bottom step. It was as if her finger had fallen on a coal of living fire, so did she instantly jerk away.

"They—there are skulls—or a skull here, Bart—under the pattern face, a real skull."

As I knelt beside her I could see nothing but the surface. It must have been her fine-tuned healer's touch which had read the horror beneath the covering.

"Their enemies—how great was their rage—!"

"These could not be our people." My mind pictured instantly for me those lines of skeletons at Fors. Those bones had been intact, the skulls all there. This place was old, it had existed, I was certain, long before the coming of the First-In Scout of our kind to discover Voor.

"No—much older. But like us." She looked up at the doorway above, from which that light streamed. "We must go on—but to walk so—" she shivered.

I studied the faces carefully. Yes, they were all unlike, all realistic representations. But still human—as human seeming as I was.

"This happened a long time ago," I assured her. Though what "this" might have been I could not understand, save that the stairway might have been erected to celebrate a final victory, a crushing defeat—for who—the builder, or those they had pictured? Had one race or species been driven from the surface of Voor, taken precautions to exist here, then wreaked its vengeance on visitors in such a monstrous form? Or was the answer just the opposite: the aliens had won and celebrated their victory with an everlasting portrayal of the conquered? In any event the artist who had designed this had shown with merciless accuracy all the meanness, cruelties and evils my species was capable of in those subtle lines on the faces.

"Long ago—" she echoed. "But they tried—to seal them in—their enemies. The skulls—it is evil! Evil!"

I stood up, and, when she did not move, I stopped and drew her to her feet.

"There is nothing to be done now. I do not believe that more than bone was sealed here—"

"We do not know." She turned her head a little so her eyes met mine. There was a deep horror in them. Plainly she was shaken as I had seldom seen her. "How can we understand what happened here once? A tomb is a quiet place in which nothing any longer sleeps—it is but a place of memories for the living, and, as years pass, ceases to be even that. Such a thing as this keeps old hates terribly alive." She shivered. "We do not know what they believed—and belief is a very potent weapon—as well as a guard—"

"*We* do not believe!" I thought I knew what she hinted at and it shook me for a moment, but only for a moment. Such a suggestion was something I refused to accept. If one did not believe then this threat had no existence.

"Yes—" Her voice was still shaken. She no longer looked at me, her eyes turned once more upon the steps, though her hand lay on my arm and she did not draw away from me.

"Peace—peace be unto you! To those who wrought and those who died in the making—peace! For all is gone—and now forgotten. Rest you both in a final and unending sleep of peace."

It did not seem strange that she would speak so. I had none of her talent, still I had been disturbed when I looked upon the paintings made to be trod upon many times over. Now I did not look at them; I would not allow myself to gaze from face to face.

Close together, her hand remaining on my arm, we climbed that stairway. I heard the hooves of the gars clinking on the stones as they came after. Nor did we look down again at what we trod upon. Perhaps Illo was trying as hard as I was to force from her mind, as we went, the possible meanings of that staircase.

The quality of that light ahead impressed me. It was a very long staircase, with rises so shallow, steps so wide, I began to wonder if we were not indeed once more approaching the outside world and if what beckoned us on was not true daylight. However, as we reached the head of the stairs, and looked ahead through a very wide portal, we did not see the open land, neither the plains nor the rank growth of the Tangle.

Illo's startled cry of wonder matched my own exclamation of amazement. We might be stepping into one of those experimental stations such as I had seen on tapes, where plant life studies were in progress. Raised sections of the same alloy stood in straight rows. Each formed a trough or bin filled with soil. Some gave rooting only to dried stalks and skeletons of plants, others were rankly luxurious with still living growth.

Overhead floated a cloudy, misty covering which drifted in patches, as if indeed miniature clouds had been imprisoned here. Those moved, slowly, though now and then one paused over one or another of the bins to loose a shower of moisture.

Above those drifting cloudlets spread a criss-cross network of what looked to be bars. Some of these held a core of light. Others were dark in random patches. The light which some did supply was not unlike the sunlight of the outer world, just as the warm humidity of the place was that of a mid-day in the south at the season of sowing.

Still there was nothing resembling a conventional garden in this display. Those plants nearest to us which were alive were strange to me. As we advanced farther into what must be a very large chamber, for we could not see the other end, we passed close to that first planting of living vegetation.

I cried out, jerking Illo away just in time. Out of what had looked not unlike a clump of ferns had arisen a whip-lash of tendril, moving also with a whip's agility, to fall just short of where the girl had stood a moment earlier.

The tendril-vine (or whatever it might be) struck out again, while the fern-part from which it came rocked and swayed, as if so eager to seize upon any intruder that it was attempting now to move its roots to reach us. We skirted that warily, brushed against the side of another planting place which held only the dead, while the tendril continually flailed after us.

"Keep away from the planted boxes." My order was unnecessary after that display. Illo would have lingered to watch the continued struggles of the thing, but I pulled at her again. The sooner we reached the other end of this place (if it had an end at all) the better. I was, however, careful to steer a zigzag path, passing beside the beds where there was nothing living. I thought of leading the gars. Though whether the tendril could have held one of the large beasts to any purpose I did not know. It could, of course, have some other method of subduing its prey—say poisoned thorns—as far as I knew. When I looked back I saw that Witol and the rest, pacing again in a straight line, were following our own maneuvers, and my inward questioning about the intelligence of the animals once more arose.

We were at the side of the fifth of the planted boxes away from the entrance when I came to sudden halt. For what faced us were the same flowers which had appeared to watch us in the Shadow doomed villages. Their colors were not as strident here, and they were smaller. But that they were of the same species there was no question. Also, as we neared their position, they had deliberately turned their heads to face us, and that bowing, weaving which was caused by no wind began.

For some reason here they seemed even more sinister than those others had in the open—perhaps because this was their own place (how long ago had they been planted and by whom?) where in the destroyed settlements they had been left unchecked or culled. Their unusually fleshy stems made a slight whispering sound, brushing against one another as they kept up that continued movement.

Once more we made a careful detour about their station. There came then a whole section of boxes holding nothing but the brittle bits of the dead. Above this a matching section of the bars held no light. We walked more freely here and the gars pushed forward too, since they did not have to avoid the planted boxes.

I had no way of telling the time or how long we had been on the move—first into the Tangle, and then coming to this underground forcing house. However I believed that we all must rest. Illo agreed to that, not knowing what might lie ahead. Here among the empty earth boxes would be a safe place to camp. The gars, relieved of their burdens, lay down since there was no grazing for them. I spared each a cake of our own dried provisions and shaved a fourth into slivers which Illo and I chewed as we sat with our backs against one of the boxes.

Just as these had no lights above them, so did the drifting clouds of moisture appear to avoid passing directly over us. For which we were glad as we did not fancy being suddenly rained upon. As I settled on my back and stared straight up into that "sky" I thought I could just distinguish, very far above the network of the light lines, a dark ceiling.

Illo did not settle down at once. Instead she burrowed into her pack, and, having turned over a number of small bags and bundles, she brought out a packet of what looked to be long, dried twigs. These she separated with care. Putting two to one side, she broke up a half dozen more into small lengths and then went to the gars, holding out first her palm on which rested some of the twig bits to Witol. He sniffed with an energy which nearly blew them away, then put out a purplish tongue, sweeping up what she offered. His companions seemed as eager to take their share.

When she came back she held out one of the two remaining twigs to me.

"This is arsepal. It has many virtues. Wild animals seek it out for themselves to chew upon. It strengthens, clears the senses, is a preventive of infections. I wish I had more of it. But I think it is well if we now follow a prudent course and do all we can to arm ourselves against any ill."

The root was aromatic, its scent, as I held it close to my nose, clean and clear against the dank, near-fetid odors wafted from the growing beds. I chewed upon it and discovered, though it seemed to have no particular definable taste, it made my mouth feel clean. Also, once moistened by saliva, it softened, was easy to chew small and swallow.

She was not so quick to sample her own portion but continued to sit there, looking away from our small refuge by the dry and the dead towards the massed boxes before us where things grew far too luxuriantly to make me easy of mind. At that moment I did not want to look ahead, only lie and let the tiredness seep out of me in sleep— if one dared sleep in such a place.

"What are you thinking of?" I asked at last, mainly because I could not reach for that sleep with her still sitting there, a half-chewed twig in her fist and her eyes set on what I could not see. For I was sure she was no longer just watching the plants themselves.

"Of the link—" the words came from her with a force which aroused me. "What is the link—between what we have seen this day and the Shadow doom? Who first named it Shadow doom—and why? They might as well have spoken of lead death—of the Unknown—of—of—" her sentences trilled away as she still stared at what I could see, and perhaps, more at what I could not.

I had no answer for her, she did not even wait for one, but her words plunged on:

"Those flowers—they are the first proof of link. What reason for their being in the villages?" She flung her arms wide as if she would grasp something and pull it to her. "I want to know! I must know!" Then that trance-like stare broke and she glanced at me as if she saw me once again as a person. For the first time she smiled, her calm mask breaking so that in this alien place she was all human, not even a healer any more.

"When I was little," even the tone of her voice was changed, it had lost that faint hint of intoning, "I used to read story tapes. There were all the old, old adventures which are still always new—probably because way back in time somewhere they did hold once a kernel of truth. There was always the lady in great distress, menaced by all manner of evil, from monstrous beasts to dark-hearted men. But through all her trials she never lost heart, always knew that good would finally triumph.

"Then there was the hero, a mighty fighter and doer, who did not know the very name of fear, and to whom danger was a challenge he went eagerly to meet. The two of them were plunged into all manner of action through which they fought with sword, or wit, or plain strength of arm until evil was overcome and good put on a victory crown.

"Sometimes I wondered what it would be like to be caught in such an adventure—" She paused and I cut in:

"So now you are and discover that the truth is somewhat different—one's feet ache from walking, one can feel the cold of fear, also that you do not have the support of knowing that it will all come right in the end. Yes, adventures are not what the tapes would have us believe." I deliberately settled my head on the pillow of my pack and closed my eyes. In truth I realized that I was no hero and certainly could not make a good showing as one, no matter how action might call for such an effort. I thought that there might be a hint of mockery in her talk—though I believed that was a show on her part, meant probably to bolster her own spirits. At that moment I was selfish enough to want to try and refresh my own. The last things I wished to consider were the attributes of a proper hero.

I was even tired enough to sleep, willing to depend upon the gars for sentry duty, since I knew that they never slept soundly, but spent their rest halts and nights in light doses, awakening at intervals to graze—even though there was no grazing here.

Night and day must be all the same here. I came awake later aware of a weight resting half against my arm. Bemusedly, not yet fully aroused, I turned my head a fraction and saw that Illo was huddled down beside me, not the width of a camp fire away, and her head had rolled against me. She was deep in sleep, her breath coming in slow even rhythm. Her face, however, had a frown line locked between her brows as if questions without answers still haunted her.

Gently I moved away from her, allowing her head to rest on the edge of my pack, as I slipped out from the half-weight of it. The light was the same; the gars still knelt chewing their cuds which must be near vanished by now. Witol opened his big eyes as I came up, and closed them again, having assured himself, I supposed, that all was well.

However, slowly I became aware that the peace which had appeared a part of my sleep no longer existed. Just as the nodding flowers had given us the feeling of being watched, so I sat up and looked around, surveying the long vistas of the aisles between the boxes, planted, or full of the dead, with a growing uneasiness. There was something here—even if the gars on which I had, perhaps foolishly, depended for sentries did not appear to sense any trouble.

Though I studied all, I could see there was no outward change— only the misty pseudo-clouds were ever in motion, all else was quiet and silent. Still that sense which is sharp in one who has lived on and with the plains got me to my feet, moved me to the next aisle to peer up and down—and then to the one beyond.

Here the lights glowed and that dangerous growth was vigorous. So I kept a careful distance from it, drawing the stunner, hoping that if I came under any attack I could face that as well here with the same weapon as had defeated the Tangle.

Here all was very quiet. Here I could not hear the breathing of the gars, the slight rustle Illo might be making turning in her sleep. It was as if I were totally alone, caught in strangeness, hedged about by alienness which was threatening because it had no possible meeting point with my own species.

In those moments that I stood there my view of this place shifted. I had considered it a forcing house for plants—perhaps an experimental station, such as my own kind used on other worlds to test the possibilities of adapting natural food products to strange soils. Only that logic was based on my observation and information. What if there was an entirely different reason for the forcing of the plants?

At that moment there crept into my mind, thin and weak at first, as might a first root break out of a seed casing, another conception altogether. There were no armies on Voor. My kind had never had to band together against a concrete and visible foe. I had never even seen any of the Patrol, the armed might of The Federation, except when once a cruiser on a routine outer fringe world flight had landed a squad at Portcity, mainly to pick up some records a disabled Survey ship had jettisoned there.

Since the Shadow doom had always remained just that—shadowy, unknown—one did not think of it as a trained force, an army. What the Voorloper had to fight he faced alone—weather such as the sudden storm which had been our bane, a handful of hostile animals, the mishaps of a sudden illness where there was no medical aid. These dangers would be small against—

My whole body tensed, my fingers ached a little with the tight grip I kept on the stunner which was ready, which, without my conscious volition, swerved slowly from side to side as if I were prepared to sweep free a broad path with my ray. Yet here was no tangle of jungle—there were the orderly networks of aisles leading to infinity. I wrangled my distance glasses loose with my left hand, keeping the stunner ready in the other.

Boxes, some full, some dead, a numberless procession of them, and that was only along the one aisle. I could not sight the far end of the place in which I stood because—

I blinked, wiped the lenses of the glasses against my thigh, put them to my eyes again. There *was* a definite limit, far from here—but no wall. Rather a thick mist, as if the small cloudlets overhead had their birth there, breaking from a greater mass which touched the floor.

And—

I began to back down the side aisle which had brought me away from my companions. I had not just imagined that! My eyes were too distance-wise to be deceived. The foggy mass was on the move, in our direction!

At the same time I made sure of that, I was swung back against on the boxes, hurled off balance by a ring of fire about my throat. The glasses fell from my grasp as I threw up my hand to tear at the necklet. But I did not lose my hold on the stunner.

With that circle of pain eating into my flesh I was no longer Bart s'Lorn. Or rather I was he battling what I could not see, hear, feel, but which was in me. I must go forward—this was needful—I was—

Food?

The conception was such a shock that it broke the hold of the pressure on my brain. That small recession of struggle let me marshal my forces. I turned and staggered back, wavering from side to side, slamming with bruising force from the boxes on one edge of the walkway to those on the other.

The necklet did not feel hot to my fingers, but there was my own blood welling from the frantic scratches of my nails striving to pull it open.

"Bart—?"

Illo was pulling herself up to her feet with one hand on a box where brittle stems turned to powder at her touch. "Bart—!" Her eyes were large, staring at me as if I had suddenly put on a monster's mask. Then she fairly sprung away from the box to meet me; with both hands she caught mine as I clawed so futilely at the necklet.

It was Illo—truly it was Illo—not that other—that other with her mouth twisted open to voice a hideous scream. Dark hair—light hair—one face over another—and then gone again. I was going mad—the whole world was twisting around me, assuming one shape which melted into another, and then another—

There was a hag! No, she was not old—young, young and evil, and her mouth gaped open to show teeth ready to tear wolfishly at my flesh. No—she was old—old with all the evil knowledge gained during a vicious life in those burning eyes, and she had a knife—a knife to match that which was already sawing at my throat.

She led the pack. I must get away—run—I brought up my fist and sent it crashing into her face. Then the face was gone. I could run— run to meet *them,* the others—those who waited—who needed me.

This was like trying to run through a viscous flood rising higher and higher about my legs. I was wading now. The level reached my knees, clung about my thighs. I could not see it! I threw out both hands, strove to cast the invisible off. My hands met nothing. Still it was there, slowing me down, holding me back so that they could catch me.

They—they were everywhere! There was no escape! My heart pounded in great jolts, trying to break through the cage of my ribs, tear its own path out of my body. The pain at my throat—my head was being forced up and back, a garrote might be slowly closing about my neck.

I screamed like a tortured animal:

"Almanic! Almanic!"

He was here somewhere. I had been loyal—I had carried the summons to the kin—I had obeyed orders—thus I deserved his help.

The tide of the mist—the death mist—rolling forward to meet me. Food—the cursed creations needed food. They had taken and taken—and taken—

"Almanic!"

It was hard to keep my feet with that sucking flood rising about me. Ahead I could see them—the Outer Company—the defenders—I must reach them before the gate closed—I must!

Those others—storming at my heels, creeping in from the sides. This was their place, they knew it. The things they had spawned from their own black delving into the forbidden reached greedy tendrils for me.

A lashing out—I was jerked back, not by the cord about my neck, but that which hurled from one side, which tightened about my waist, crushing in about my body until pain was a red mist rising in my head, blotting out everything.

"Almanic!" I cried in despair. The gate was closing. I had fallen to my knees. There was none who dared leave his place and come to aid me. Too few—they were needed, needed to hold the sanctuary. To sacrifice themselves if the need came. I must watch all hope shut away.

But the eaters would not get me! Or else they would get my body when it no longer mattered. My key—my life key! My hands up to that.

"Ullagath nu ploz—" Words which would release me, by their tones alone, to a final dissolution. *They* could come upon me now but what would lie to their hands would be of no use to them—They must have their meat alive!

"—fa stan—" I must remember! Why did the proper words fade in and out of my mind? I had known them beyond any forgetting since I was old enough to wear a key as a man and a warrior. "—fa stan—"

What was next? By the Will of the Fourth Eye, what was next? I must have it! Now—before they cut me down, bound me, drew me back to serve their bestial appetites.

"—stan dy ki—" It was coming again—I must hold on. I realized dimly that my shoulder was jammed against a wall of some sort—

that around me was an awful stench of death and decay—that that pressure about my middle was pulling tighter and tighter, until pain ran hot fingers up into my brain—I could not remember! I must!

"—ki nen pla—"

Someone was calling. Not the one of the Outer Company. They had gone, the gate was closed.

"Bart—!"

I shook my head. It troubled me, that word—a name—yes, it was a name. But it had no meaning! I must remember—

The pressure about my waist gave way. I sprawled forward, crashing hard against an unyielding substance. I could not remember— I would be meat, meant for the half-men! With a last dying hope I sought the bar resting against my throat. If I could only remember! Instead, I plunged into the dark—perhaps the Power was merciful after all, and I had gained death without the ritual, I thought, as I surrendered to that engulfing wave.

CHAPTER 12

I WAS MOVING, but not on my feet—rather I half sat, half lay on the back of a living creature that bore me forward. There was a mist—a cloud which had seeped into my mind. I could not think. Who was I? The citadel had fallen and the half-people had loosed the growing death—fed it horribly. No! I dare not think! Let me slip back once more into that nothingness of non-memory—non-mind!

This body being borne forward—was not mine. Let me be free of it! Free—

I tried to move and found that I was a prisoner—in bonds. The half-men had taken me!

Then from my forehead there began to spread a coolness, driving back the fire which ate at me, in me. Very, very far away I heard sounds rhythmically repeated. Sounds?—words? Words which had no meaning—alien words. The half-men would lock me with their word spells, even as they had bound me with their living ropes. I tried to close my mind to those words—so to keep the ill in them from me. What was the chant of protection? I could not remember it! That was gone, stripped from me, as a prisoner is stripped of all weapons. And still those sounds continued:

"Return—Bart, Bart, Bart—return!"

The coolness spreading into my head, waning, pouring over, smothering, the chaos whirling in my brain which would not let me think!

"Return—you are Bart s'Lorn! You are Bart s'Lorn. Awake and remember! Return—Bart s'Lorn!"

Bart—that was a name—a name I knew once. When and where? Who had he been? Some comrade-in-arms—kinsman? Who—who?

If I could grasp the memory of Bart then I would have a key—A key—there had been a key, too—A key! A necklet which I wore! But that was mine—given me when I had become a man to serve—to serve—

My head was filled with pain worse than any hurt of body, as if a war raged in the very channels of my brain itself—as if two fought there in desperate battle.

"Bart s'Lorn! Wake, Bart—wake!"

The cool pressure on my head—that was not of the evil of the half-men. It was beneficent, healing—Healing? There had been one who was a healer. For just a moment it was as if a face, serene, untouched by any of the raging conflict I knew, was clear in my memory—a young face—the face of one who was a mender, not a destroyer.

"Bart—"

I was not only thought—I was also body. My body contained me—it must obey my commands. I was a person—I was—With a great forcing of will I made the body obey me. I opened my eyes.

The world about me was dim, fogged—as if the parts of this body answered only sluggishly to my will. See! I ordered—see, for me—now!

Now the fog broke. I could see! I was riding on the back of a large animal. Only I was not alone. There was one who sat behind me on that broad back, whose hands were up, pressed against my forehead. It was from them that the blessed healing coolness reached into me.

More and more of the space around us cleared to my sight. We rode down an aisle between beds of vegetation, keeping an exact middle path. For from those beds arose whips of vine tentacles which reached vainly to ensnare us, flowers the color of open wounds leaned far forward seeking to engulf our flesh—to feed—to smother—to kill!

"Bart!" She whom I could not see, who rode behind me, called that name yet once again. The touch of her hands upon my head tightened, but not with that terrible compelling pressure I had known in the earlier assault which had sent me whirling thankfully into the dark.

I drew a deep breath; I began to understand at last. Though I had been—somewhere else—and I had *been*—been another—I was truly who she now hailed: Bart s'Lorn. Even as I knew that, the other identity in me made a last despairing attack, but this time her touch gave me strength to hold.

"Illo!" I cried her name, and that was another key, unlocking more of the past. My task was like trying to patch the holes in a tattered strip of weaving, so that the design would once more be whole and right.

"Bart!" There was a joyful note now in her answer. Though I could not see her face, I thought that she was triumphant—that I had fulfilled some task she had longed for me to accomplish by my own efforts.

Task? For a moment only that other gave a last shadowy cry of thought—the task—duty—*I had failed!* Only that was not so—I was here, in the here and now—I was Bart s'Lorn!

Slowly I found words, but, as I spoke aloud, my voice sounded weak as might that of one who had been ill a long time.

"What happened?"

"You were not yourself," she answered promptly. "I do not know what or who possessed you. You said that we must reach the Gate before we were taken. One of the vines caught you. I stunned it free—and then we got on Witol and we rode. I have been trying to draw you back. And who is Almanic? You called that name many times."

"Almanic—" I repeated. Yes, once more a shadow thought curled quickly and was gone before I could seize it. "I think he was a friend but also a war leader. I believe he was the one who ordered me—No, not *me*—but perhaps he who once wore this necklet—to do something. And the wearer was too late."

I was still weak inside, but I could now see clearly. We were still transversing one of the aisles, though here all the boxes were planted with vigorous growth, growth which moved and twisted as we rode by. I knew the reason for that unnatural life and it set me shivering.

"What is the matter?" Illo demanded instantly. Her hands were no longer pressed against my forehead, but rested, one on each of my shoulders, as if it were necessary that she keep close contact with me.

"They fed—these things were fed—on—flesh and blood! This was the place—no, I cannot remember!" Nor did I want to. Save that, in me, the cold horror grew stronger and stronger. I had to fight with all the will power I could summon to keep myself from sheer panic.

"Do not try!" Her command was sharp. Once more her hands were on my forehead, and, with her healer's skill, she drove away that evil out of me.

I looked steadily ahead. There had been a thick mist there—surely I remembered that now. The cloudlets still floated overhead, but the fog which had been so dense when I last remembered surveying the far part of this garden (if one can call such a forcing place that) was gone. I did not know how far we had come, but before us now was a doorway—a closed doorway.

There were plants as tangled there as they had been in the splotch of upper jungle. I had a queer, fleeting impression that once they had swarmed here as a tide, trying to beat a way through that portal. A great patch of them spread out from that to the right, forming a thick river of growth which reached up and up, past the network of lights, a column steady now with the matted substance of seeking vegetation standing against the wall to reach out—up and out!

However it was toward the door they guarded we headed.

As at the open portals we had seen there was a curved arch carrying the intricate unreadable script of the unknown. I eyed the mass of vegetation warily.

"The stunner, where is it?"

"Here," once more her hands dropped from my forehead. A moment later she reached around before me with the weapon. I checked its charge. The unit was full.

"I used the last of the other one." Illo explained, "to ray that vine which was squeezing you to death. It is recharged but we have only two more charges."

I made the setting carefully, adjusting it from wide to a narrower beam. Witol paused just beyond the reach of the waving vines and branches. Here the plants were far more active, greedy, demanding. They were larger, too, with a bloated look to them.

Squeezing the button I sent the first ray at a particularly active vine which had twice lashed at us, only to sprawl short by just a fraction, not knowing whether this weapon would still serve us. The vine jerked as might a man who had taken a hit. Then it looped limply down, and those behind it also started to wither. Encouraged,

I played the ray back and forth across the whole width of the door, watching the mass droop and die.

Our path open, Witol walked forward of his own accord. Then, from the center-most point of the door arch, there suddenly shot a finger-thin beam of blue light. It struck, full on my throat, at the necklet.

From out of the air above us sounded a voice, with the inflection, I thought of a question. Password—? Was escape to be locked against us by the safeguards set eons ago?

The necklet was once more warm. While from somewhere, perhaps out of the nightmare of that other mind which had invaded mine, I picked words—two of them—meaningless sounds—still I was as sure of their importance as if I had been taught them from earliest childhood:

"Iben Ihi!"

There came a groaning, a shivering of the door. The leaves grated apart slowly, so slowly—opening to us. Twice I thought it was stuck and would move no farther. Perhaps Illo and I could have scraped through that thin slit but the gars, no. And there was no thought of leaving them.

On it went by jerks, the scraping loud. At last we had space enough. Witol walked forward without being urged, and we came out of that place of evil growth into a long corridor which inclined upwards at a gentle slope.

The corridor was not clear. Men had died here, or things with the bony likeness of men. They lay full length upon the floor or in piles along the walls as if they had leaned there until time had sent their bones sliding down. Armor of metal were about some of the bodies, and I noted all I could see clearly wore about their neck bones collars like that which chance had set upon me.

There were weapons, too, or at least I judged some rods, a few still clasped by finger bones, to be those. We did not stop to examine this battlefield. I had a vast reluctance to look at the dead, an aversion to disturbing their rest. Even Witol picked his way with care, striving not to touch one of the sprawling piles of bones.

Our way was lighted by a soft diffusion of gray, though I could see no torches, none of those criss-cross rods of illumination which had been in the large plant chamber. Witol was unable to quite avoid touching one outflung skeleton arm. At contact the bones crumbled into a white powder, an armlet of metal fell, with a soft small clang, to the floor. Though the air was fresh enough there was such a feeling of both age and despair about this place that I was in a hurry to be past the ranks of the dead, to find the end of our road, only hoping that would be a door to the outer world.

For the first time since we had entered this way Illo spoke:

"What were those words—those with which you commanded the door? I have heard off-world tales of doors and enclosures where a barrier is set to open only to certain sounds, some only if one certain imprinted voice utters them. But this is no off-world place of our time—"

"I do not know. Somehow they were just in my head," I had to answer. Her surmise concerning the reason for the opening door sounded logical to me. There is no guarantee that what has been discovered by one race or species in the past may not be recovered by those who follow them long after. Doors, safe keeping boxes, and files, on my world at Portcity could be sealed by the thumb of their owner thrust into a sensitive opening, one attuned only to that owner.

At that moment I was willing to believe that those who had fashioned this installation (whatever they had intended it to be) could have sealed the secret of some of their doors into the necklet. That confronted by the voice demanding the proper password some locked-in simulator had produced in my mind the proper words. So far we had been amazingly lucky. I could only hope (for what that hope might be worth) that this luck would continue.

The slowly rising ramp was not long and was topped by another door. This one lacked that arch and inscription, but as Witol advanced, with more confidence than I could summon, it too, as if in answer to our very approach began to open with the same grating reluctance the others had shown.

I heard Illo's soft gasp of wonder as the opening split middle of that door grew wider. We were looking into a place lighted as had been the garden hall, but with a less strident, more eye-easy glow. And what did we see? Was it the equivalent of one of our villages, or a large holding, of even Portcity? Or was it simply one large complex of living and working quarters all linked, still quartered here and there by passages, such as that which lay beyond the door?

The buildings were not of the metal which had been in common use elsewhere, but rather of another substance, almost as if one had gathered great gleaming jewels and hollowed them, giving them doorways. They were of different shapes, which added to the gem simulance. Some were square and tabled with recessed step cutting, some carbochon, ovals, or drops, other sharply pointed, diamond fashion. Colors played across them, ebbing and flowing, though each had one color particularly its own and the ebb and flow was the darkening and lighting of shades of that color.

Though I have seen tapes made of the pleasure worlds, and some of the remains of fabulous Forerunner finds, I had never seen the like of these. It was like viewing a dream world. One felt that a single step forward into the valley which ran ahead might break that dream, shatter those fantastic jewels into nothingness.

There were no clouds overhead, nor any visible grid been set, in scattered pattern, circles of crystal, as if to represent the stars of the outer world. None of these were bright enough to emit any true light, and I guessed that that must be diffused from the buildings, or even the walls of this huge cavern.

Whether the city holding hollow had been formed by nature or by the efforts of intelligence I could not guess, but it seemed to be a half-sphere, the walls we could see sloping up in that fashion. There was no sign of any growing thing, again in sharp contrast to the perilous way we had come. The silence was awe-inspiring and complete. So complete, that the hoof clicks of Witol and the other gars sounded far too loud, somehow wrong, as if this wondrous place should have been left to drowse eternally, dreaming—

I had half expected to see more evidence here of whatever disaster had struck down those defenders within the outer portal. However the way or street before us was bare. If any dead remained, they lay within their homes and I had no desire to explore there. In fact both Illo and I were content to stay on Witol's back as the bull paced proudly forward.

Our feeling of intrusion slowly died, but not our sense of wonder at the beauty of the place. There was no sign of any aging, no evidence here of disaster or defeat.

Illo spoke very softly, as if any voice might disturb some sleeper: "Their end—it came well."

When I made no answer, she said:

"Can you not feel it? The peace? All that was dark and evil shut out forever?"

My hands without my conscious willing went to the necklet. That was still as warm as the skin on which it lay. Far back in my mind swirled once more that terror and horror which I had carried with me into the darkness—swirled, died—was gone. I could feel now as she did that there was nothing here—not the dead awesome silence of Mungo's Town and Voor's Grove, the menace of the Tangle—that other stranger and more fearsome terror which had lain in wait among the planted boxes. No—there was not an emptiness which made a man feel estranged and alien—there was peace—utter peace.

Illo's sensitivity, born from her talent, had felt it first, now it spread to me. I did not believe that this wondrous jeweled city had been deserted by those who had rejoiced in its beauty. Rather they had made a choice, withdrawn into their homes, accepted freely, with thankfulness and wistful longing, that final peace.

Witol paced on, but the clicking of gars' hooves could never disturb the sleepers here. We passed between the ever-changing hues of the walls until we came to one structure which bore no color at all. It was crystalline, yet its shape was wrought in facets as a gem might well be treated to best display its finest qualities.

The gar bull came to a halt. Looking about I judged that this crystal of many flickering sparks of fire was the center of the alien city. For here the streets, or ways, between the smaller structures converged to join in a circle about it.

Three spires of the flashing substance arose above all other of the buildings and there was a wide open entrance before us. I slid from Witol's back, reached up and drew Illo down with me. That we had reached the heart of all the mysteries which had been set to plague us and our kind—I was as sure of that as if I had shouted aloud some question and had been answered with the weight of true authority.

We would discover no sleepers here, of that I was also sure, as I went up the two broad, wide steps which raised the diamond walls above the rest. With Illo's hand in mine I stepped confidently forward into what? A temple raised to some unknown force for good (for such a place as this could not house evil), a meeting place of assembly like our village halls, the palace of some ruler? It could be any one or all three.

We passed within where sparks of light appeared to dance in the air. There was something else too, which made me alert, clear of mind, free from all fatigue of body, insecurity or doubt. This was how man was meant to feel—always and ever!

I turned my head a little. Illo's eyes met mine. In them was my wonder mirrored, heightened, made into pure joy. We gazed at each other for a long moment. Something in me demanded that I hold to this, hold fast—for this was a moment which meant much. It would mean even more if one had that in him which could rise to the greater heights—the mountain tops of self-knowledge and confidence these others knew. Only—even as I realized that, I knew that my species was not made for such heights. We were as cracked jugs into which poured spring water, fresh and clear, only to have that dribble forth little by little, leaving us empty ever more.

Hand in hand we went on between lines of flashing pillars until we came to the center-most heart of the place, even as it was the heart of the city. There was a bowl of opaline substance, around its sides also traveling rainbow fires. Only here those were softened, made less dazzling, less brilliant.

We looked down into that and saw that in the very bottom, where that bowl was the deepest, there was liquid, a small, still pool of it, perhaps one cupful, or at the most two. As the bowl which held it, it showed many colors which skimmed its surface, now blue, now gold, now green, now red—now all mingled together in a burst of radiance.

Illo dropped my hand and fell to her knees, her hand stretched forward, reaching down, until her forefinger tips touched the water. She sang, low, soft, words I could not understand. Yet I never wanted her to stop, for the singing was the color, the brilliant, ever changing color, and the color was the singing. Though what I meant by that I could not make plain even to myself.

Slowly I, too, knelt. My hands were once more on the necklet. This time, as I fingered the plate set against the hollow of my throat there sounded a chime. Unlike Illo's singing that did not mingle with the color, but was apart, and it gathered in it both paeans of triumph, despair of defeat.

The necklet fell forward, was loose in my hand. I held it so, knowing what I must do with it. There could be no troubling of this peace. The last loose thread of the pattern must be returned to the weaver and bound fast. I leaned forward, allowed the necklet to slip into the pool.

No longer was the water still. The liquid began to churn about, rising as though I had taken a kettle ladle and stirred it so. Rise it did, higher and higher; faster it flew about the sides of the bowl, until one could not see water at all, only streamers of color whipped about, beaten into one another, emerging once again. Nor could I turn my eyes away from that whirl, though I knew the sight was setting a compulsion on me, preparing me for—

I was in a garden and there was a woman singing as Illo had sung, soft and low, and very happy. She was setting out small plants one by one, packing rich earth about their roots. There was the warmth of sun in the air and I was very happy. We were going to the fair and I would be able to buy some toy for my own self. I had my precious coin in my belt purse. I could feel it through the stuff of that purse whenever I pinched, and I pinched many times over.

If she would only hurry—this was no day for planting in the garden—it was festival time. I ran to the edge of the street to look and listen. The street was very wide, the houses tall—or else I was small.

Then—

It was as if a dark cloud had crossed the sky. That cloud broke into pieces, and those pieces were dropping, raining down upon us. I was afraid and I cried and ran, ran inside the house, and hid my face against a cloth on the table. I heard cries, gasps. Then I knew there was something in the room with me. Fear struck me into a small tense statue. I dared not look—yet I must—it was forcing me to look—No!

Maybe I screamed, perhaps my throat was too taut with terror to let me make a sound. It was calling me, making me—I had to—

I turned, bringing handfuls of the table cloth in my grasp.

What stood there—for the second time in my life I attempted to blot it out—but this time I could not do so.

Those flowing, swirling outlines of the figure tightened, its substance became more opaque. Yet, though it had a pseudo-human form, it was not a person. Young as I was I knew a jolting terror of what I saw forming under my eyes, making its own body from bits of leaf, the flyaway seeds of plants I had played with in the garden, other seeds, some still in their pods, nuts in their shells and out—

It stood hunched a little, and it had hands, now tightened, thickened so that the fingers, crooked like claws, were as solid as my own. Thorns instead of nails crowned each of those fingers. Only it was not just the threat of those reaching for me which caused me to scream, to back until my small body was flat against the wall so I flung up an arm to ward it off.

I called for my mother, for my father. My throat was raw with the force of my screams. No one came—only that—that *thing* which had holes in its face where the eyes should have been. Still, even if there were no eyes, it could see me. It stretched forth one arm, that thorn clawed hand, but it did not try to touch me. Rather those fingers crooked in a beckoning gesture.

I had folded my body closer to the floor, a small animal, nearly stark-crazed with fear. It did no good to scream any longer, I knew that dimly. Now I was so stricken with fright I was easy prey; still it came no closer. Twice it beckoned. I did not move. There was a prickling feeling in my head, I knew that it was calling me, expecting me to follow, to come to it.

My body even stirred as if to obey. Now I balled myself, my face hidden on my knees, my arms wrapped about my head and shoulders. I was retreating from that horror, retreating into my own self, deeper and deeper. I would *not* look!

The special horror of the thing which I felt dimly, even as I made the plunge into an inner darkness, was that it had made itself—made its form out of things I knew, had handled, had played with. It was to me as if the wall of a room had formed a mouth to suck me in— window eyes to watch me. All my world in those moments took on a fearsome otherness I was not prepared to face, and which was so utterly alien I had to blot it out of my mind as well as hide it physically from my sight. For to have the familiar change before one's eyes into a frightening otherness was such an ordeal that perhaps even an adult would have found hard to face.

Darkness, and then suddenly it was light and I was under a warm sun, riding perched high on a gar's back. By the side of the beast paced my father, his face set, white under the weathering, the lines upon it the signature of some horror looked upon and never to be wholly faced. I had returned again to memory—my first memory. Yet now I had, at last, reached behind that to know a fraction of what shock had veiled from me all these years.

⚬★ **CHAPTER 13.**⚬

I BLINKED AND BLINKED AGAIN. There was no gar—nor my father. A sense of loss filled me for a long moment, then seeped away. I stood and watched liquid churn up and up in an opaline bowl of a pool. My past retreated farther and farther, to become a picture of something which had happened to another person long ago.

Yet, though my memory was still incomplete, out of some hidden corner came answers—slowly—one by one. The colors in the pool met, mingled, became other shades, darker, lighter, took on patterns. I had seen such lines and swirls before—yes! My hand flew to my throat. Then I remembered that that alien chain was gone, that I had hurled it into that same pool where it had sunk into hiding. Only those lines of color were much like those which had patterned the foreplate, those which had been over the doorways through which we had passed.

The designs had meaning. What they would tell was important, imperative for me to understand! Some buried emotion in me raged and fought for that understanding. I dropped to my knees and flung out my hands. Spatters of foam, raised by the faster and faster passage of the water being stirred around and around, struck my fingers, dripped from my outstretched palms.

I withdrew those wet hands, brought them to my face, my fore-head, pressed flesh against flesh with the water in between. Straightway I became aware of a sharp scent filling my nostrils, making even my closed eyes smart and begin to tear.

However that same water—or the scent of it—cleared my head, shook me into such a sharp awareness as I had never quite known before. I dropped my hands, shook my head from side to side, yet again blinking my eyes to clear them of the tears that scent or strength in the liquid had induced.

I stared down into the massing and the flowing of the color. This was part of a talent, or else some strange science of a race long forgot, utterly alien. So that the messages they had left—the warnings— came through to a mind such as mine only in fragments and broken phrases.

Piece by piece I fought to catch a hint here, an almost entirely clear reading there. My people depended upon tapes for their records; what I was watching now was something like those in its results but very unlike in substance. There were so many holes that I had to bridge the message by leaps of imagination, by flights of guessing.

Two races—one from space, a remnant fleeing some unexplained disaster out among the stars. Each of another culture, so divided in ways of logical thought pattern that communication between the natives and the star-rovers was near impossible.

Yet those natives had taken in the refugees, tried hard to make their settlement prosper. Greed, drive for domination, were taints the star-rovers carried like foul diseases in their blood. The taking over of knowledge peculiar to the people of this planet consisting in the main of their extraordinary talents for shaping and control of plants, their oneness with all forms of life on their world. The newcomers seizing upon their knowledge, yes, but not learning the strict controls imposed by a high moral sense.

Experimentation to adapt the growth of this new world to the service of the newcomers—experiments which were used in excess and misused. Plants which became like mind-changing drugs—an unruly and anarchic people addicted to them—the need for more and more—

War, for the natives learned too late the manner of the race they dealt with, the horrors which could be loosed with forced mutation gone mad.

Plants deliberately fed—on flesh, on blood, on living bodies. The result of such deaths—the Shadows. Things with tenacious life but which were greed, hunger, born from engorged plants as near wisps of nothingness, needing to build new bodies by their will from fragments of leaves, seed, even earth dust. Development of raging hunger, until that changed into a potent weapon to draw to the feaster, walking, living food!

Immortality for the shadow being in a fashion. Development at last of creatures so alien that they had no possible contact even with that which had been their own source. Resting dormant between the feedings, yet awaking when the food, the rich feasting again landed in Voor. The gathering of energy—slow at first—then richer, fuller, stronger as the Shadows went forth, bursting from their seed cases where they had lain waiting for time, past our counting of years.

Shadows who had no substance until they could make themselves bodies, but with wills so compelling that they could call to them, bring into their nesting boxes their food.

The natives—so great had been their horror at what they had unleashed, they had chosen a final withdrawal, leaving only a record which might never be read—the record lying before our eyes—an accusation and a warning.

"So—that is it!"

Words startled me, broke the chain of communication between me and what was to be read in the pool. I looked to Illo. Her face was starkly pale beneath the weathering brown; there was such a sickness in her face that I moved quickly to steady her where she also had knelt to stare into the pool.

"They—they—ate our—own people!" The horror in her voice was a sick cry. Her mouth twisted as I pulled her into my arms, her face now hidden against my shoulder.

I felt my own stomach churn, a sourness rising in my throat, I could not put out of my mind that line of skeletons. Then they—*they* had been so long from food, so starving—they had not brought back their prey as they had done from other settlements but had—*feasted* there! I retched, fought my nausea. Illo was shuddering in my hold.

"Don't!" her cry was muffled against my shoulder. "Don't!"

I hoped she had not in some manner (nothing seemed impossible to me here and now) read my thoughts. Perhaps she was fighting terrible memories of her own.

"Did you remember?" I asked between those waves of nausea which I battled.

"Yes—" her voice was very faint. Her fingers dug into my shoulders, scraped together, in a frantic hold, handfuls of my jerkin.

"Why not us—?" The one question which the pool had not answered. Why had we escaped?

"We—we were—we were fed on the food of this world from birth, we were *of* Voor—there was a kinship—a faint kinship— between us and—*them!*"

I shuddered. If her answer was the truth I could easily come to loathe myself.

"No!" again it was as if she could read my thoughts. "Not for us in truth. They—*they* chose to change. But they could still recognize— maybe without knowing it—those bred here. Perhaps they wanted us to join them—to renew—to be with them!"

I remembered that *thing,* its thorn-clawed hands which had not torn me but rather had beckoned. Dim kinship? A need to add fresh life to its dreadful company? Had that indeed moved it?

"One of them could have taken me—easily," I said slowly. It had been a thing all shaped from bits and pieces of vegetation, but it had looked solid enough. And certainly the activities of it and its fellows—I swallowed once, and again, still fighting that need to vomit.

"It had chosen." Illo turned her head a little so she could look up to me. There were tear tracks down her face. "In the past it had chosen—perhaps such a choice always had to be made. They could invite—but such as we had to make the choice." She spoke as if she had complete belief in what she said. Whether that was the truth or not we might never know.

"This can't go on." I made myself turn from memories of the past. Sick as I was, resolve now filled me, pushing out the horror, stiffening my purpose.

Blasters? No. Those had been already tried and had failed—The things which we had sought, perhaps must seek again, to fight, were indeed shadows. The stuff of their bodies—when they needed bodies—could be summoned at their wills. But who can blast a shadow? The whole of the Tangle perhaps might be rooted up and destroyed by some weapons from off world. I did not doubt that the

Patrol could bring in superior devices we had not even heard of. But none would prevail against shadows.

"Look—" Illo's grasp on me tightened, she drew me closer to the edge of the pool.

The intertwining race of colors and shades there was thinning. There remained only one bright thread clear running—the blue of the necklet's glow.

"Watch—" but she did not have to tell me that.

In and out, convolutions and spirals, in loops and double loops, it wound and unwound. Again there was so much I could not understand, that I could only guess.

Those who had withdrawn to their gem-bright city, had locked their gates, and then chosen of their own will to pass on into another existence, had left this message. Warning? Suggestion? It was both, though I could be sure of so very little of it.

Then it had been beyond their abilities to do this thing themselves without becoming like the vile things they fought. Long dead now, they could not be degraded, used—Yet the Shadows retaining wisps of memory, their abiding hate for those who had defeated them, sentenced them to a long dormant waiting until our own people had come—the Shadows would answer a call, catch at a chance avidly, thirsting to feast on what was no longer there but which to them was no memory, still existed.

Swarming in upon this last safe citadel so long inviolate they could be—eliminated. Or so the message came to me as I watched, more quickly to Illo—perhaps because her talent made her far more sensitive, while the necklet had in a measure built a lesser bridge of communication for me.

The girl pulled free of me and sped across the innermost chamber, back the way we had come. I followed her, not catching up until she stood on the top of those two wide steps which led to the pillared chamber.

"Look!"

The gars had come up to us, turned, their heads low, tossing from side to side as they do when about to defend themselves against attack. Her gesture pointed beyond them.

There was a swirling in the air, visible only because some particles of glittering dust, perhaps all that time had shaken from the jewel buildings, writhed and danced in the air. There were no leaves, no bits of vegetation here which the invisibles could draw to them, yet they fought to shape something with what little did exist.

I could not number them, for there was no one swirl completely apart from the other. Illo hesitated only a moment and then swung about—I knew what was in her mind—there had been a final defense which the natives had set to protect their death sleep.

"The pool!"

That defense must have been activated by now, I realized that perhaps we would be caught in what was to come. What Illo would do I had no idea. That instinct which is in all of us to search for some way out when danger faces one did awake in me.

"Witol!" I caught at the nearest horn of the bull, "In!"

He bellowed, pawed the stone underfoot as if determined to stand his ground, then came, herding his mate and Wobru before him. We fairly fled between the rows of pillars back to the pool.

There were no longer any blue streamers racing across it. Still the liquid had not sunk back into the small cupfuls we had found there at our first coming. Rather the whole was taking on a red hue, a red shot through with sparks of orange and yellow—if fire could become water, then that was what we saw.

The flow reached the rim of the pool, the center going higher, forming a great bubble. Those orange and yellow lights disappeared, the stuff was thicker, viscid, darker red. I could think only of a giant welling of blood—

"Watch Witol!" Illo drew my attention from that terrible flood with a cry.

The gar bull had not paused at the pool, but was trotting on, still herding his two companions before him, uttering short bellows. I caught Illo by the hand and ran after the gars who now broke into the gallop which they could show when there was need, my strides lengthening as I attempted to catch up. All my Voorloper sense returned to me then. "Trust your gars" was the old and well-attested cry of the plainsmen.

We passed down another line of pillars, were in the street once more on the other side of that central shine. Witol galloped, Illo and I ran. The gars were mute now as if they did not want to waste their breath.

More of the gem houses flashed by us. What goal Witol might have I could not guess. Having no solution myself I was content to trust his instinct, always so much sharper than my own.

We came to another gate, another door. This time I had no necklet to guide me. But that same cry I had uttered to bring us here came to my lips again.

"Iben Ihi!"

The grating noise was louder, the portal showed only a few inches of opening then froze. Witol seemed to go mad. Lowering his head, the bull drew back a little and charged, the sound of the impact of his horns against the door ringing in echoes and re-echoes through the city of the dead.

The force which he had used must have jolted free the ancient mechanism for the door sprang open just as I thought his assault might have jammed it past any further effort. Witol whipped through that aperture with a speed one would not expect from his bulk, the other two crowding behind him. Illo raced, her one hand twisted in the lashing of the gear on Wobru's back; I was only seconds behind.

I looked back; the door was snapping shut even as I watched, once more sealed. We were on a ramp, a stepped ramp, leading up. The gars strained to take that incline at the same burst of speed.

Their instinct was keener than mine, yes, but now I, too, felt that warning. I had no idea what fate the long dead had left to be visited upon the enemy should they reach this final stronghold. But that it was drastic and complete I could well guess.

We scrambled and climbed. This had been no easy entrance nor exit such as the other ways. Here the smooth metallic coating had become rough stone, the stuff of Voor itself which acted to our advantage, for I doubt whether we could have climbed so fast on a smooth surface at such a sharp rising angle.

What light showed us the way ahead was very faint, once the gate was shut and the glittering of the city gone. There were only some grayish gleams at the head of the ramp. Witol had been forced to slacken speed by the steepness of the incline; he was snorting and panting now, but he did not falter.

Even as he had charged the gate, so now he drew a little ahead and butted at a mass of fallen stone which near sealed us in, except for crevices which allowed daylight through. Stones and earth flew, fell back on us. Witol made a last lumbering leap and was gone, the other two gars after him, bringing us along as we clung to the pack lashing.

I had expected to burst forth in the Tangle. Instead we were in a very narrow valley, a knife-edged cut between two ridges of rough rock. Witol, breathing hard, did not pause, though his speed was more labored, his panting near as loud as his grunts. He kept on down the middle of the narrow way, though that required scrambling over slides of fallen rock, a weaving in and out to find footing at all. There was no sign of any vegetation here—only grey rock seamed up the sides of that cut with wide bands of black which was like that from which the eyeless statue had been hewn.

If there had ever been any road here it was long since hidden under those slides. In fact so rugged were our surroundings, I would have thought that none could have ever forced a path here before.

We were at the end of the knife-narrow valley, then out into the beginning of a wider space in which there was a sparse growth of grass, when the blast came—with force enough to knock us from our feet, send rocks crashing down all along the way we had come. The gars voiced such cries as I had never heard the beasts give before; their terror was plain. They ran on in a mad way, twice more being knocked from their feet by great earth shocks. Illo and I lay where the first of those had flung us, our fingers biting into the dusty earth to provide the only anchorage in what had become a shaken and shaking world.

I buried my face in the crook of my arm, coughing heavily, for dust arose to whirl so much about us it was a cloud to hide all—even my own hand lying so close to my face. The grit stung my eyes until they watered.

This then was the final answer of those in the gemmed city—and we had loosed it. I was as sure of that as if some voice out of the dust proclaimed our deed aloud in a solemn indictment. The opening of the gate where that hellish garden grew was invitation to the Shadows to reach the prey they had always coveted. Perhaps the essence of what made up the shadow cores had no longer real intelligence, as well as no body unless they built such—but I was certain that the age-old hatred had not been lost.

Those skeletons we had found within the city gate—had they

been the last victims before somehow, with their unknown knowledge, the natives had been able to expel their enemies ? I had a half thought which again made sickness rise in my throat— volunteers? Men who had gone to such a death that satiated the victors, rendered the attackers so sluggish after their feeding, they could be better dealt with? We would never know—I did not want to.

But the city—its people driven to their final refuge had made their choice. They must not have been able to handle an attack in force—perhaps there had been only a handful of them left. Perhaps they had never lived or wanted to live on the outer surface of Voor. Only they had made sure that if their defenses were breached they would take the enemy with them. I—I had in reality been the one to breach the defenses—open the gate with the necklet which was the key.

Had the return of that to the pool not only released the final message, but also triggered the defense to ready, so that when the Shadows followed us greedy for the feast they were met with—?

With what? That there had been a mighty explosion underground was so evident it was not even necessary to speculate about that. However was any explosion enough to finish that which could not be seen, which had no substance unless it wished for it? Had we, instead of defeating the evil, loosed it instead, sent it free to roam with the wind?

My sickness grew stronger as I made myself face that possibility. My hope was a thin one—the city people had known the nature of their enemy. Certainly any final defense they would rig would be one which that nature could *not* withstand. Only hope is a tricky thing on which to build confidence.

Muffled by the dust I heard the bellow of the gars. It seemed to me that there was no fear in that sound any more—rather anger— and perhaps confidence. At least the ground had stopped shaking. There was still a rattle of falling stones, a crash of larger boulders in the vent valley from which we had emerged just in time. The dust was beginning to settle.

I sat up, trying to wipe my eyes without getting any more grit into them. My body was grey with dust. I coughed, and spit, choked, and coughed again. A figure thoroughly muffled in dust was performing like action an arm's length or so away.

Slowly I edged around without even getting up as far as my

knees, for I had an uneasy feeling that if I tried that I would not stay even so far above the ground for long. The shifting billows of dust had fallen well enough to show me that there was no longer any break in the cliff wall. That crack through which we had run to safety was so choked now with rubble that it was sealed as tightly as a stopper could be pounded into a water bottle—

A water bottle!

The need for a drink struck me like a blow. Now I did get slowly, and with caution, to my knees, arose to stand, swaying, shielding my eyes against yet moving clouds of dust, looking out into the wide open land of grass and far spreading space. Not a tree, not a hint of bush, vine or thorn growth arose there. I licked dust from my lips and then wished that I had not, for it added to my thirst.

The other dust-covered figure which was Illo also stood up, weaving a little. Before us was the open land—not only that but I caught sight, through my watering eyes, of a greyish strip set in a lone thread of greenery, as if the growth there had not yet been season killed. The warmth which had been with us so that we had come to take it for granted, even as does a man the summer sun, ever since we moved along the edge of the Tangle was gone, cut off with a blast of chill wind against our backs.

I could see more clearly now—that ribbon was water and the humps moving determinedly towards it must be the gars. There was no other moving thing, nor even tallish growth. This was a land as stripped as the mid-plains I had known for most of my life.

"Come—!" I took one step and then another, and found that truly the ground was no longer rolling under me. I could walk. I need only cover the distance now lying between myself and that ribbon and water was mine.

Laying a supporting arm about Illo's shoulders, I started that march. We wavered together for a step or two and then strength flowed back into us, seeming to come the faster as we determinedly followed the gars into the open, nor did either of us look back.

My full attention was on reaching the water I craved, and we exchanged no words as we made that leg of our journey. Not until we threw ourselves full length in an opening between the stream-seeking bushes of a thicket and laved our faces, hands, arms, drank, rested and drank again, did she speak:

"It must be gone—all of it." Though I noticed she did not turn her head to look along our back trail to that valley which had ceased to be the last door to the underworld. "That was their final plan—if *those* got into the city to destroy it all!"

I rolled over on my back and lay looking up into the dun grey of the sky. It must be nearing twilight, but the roof of clouds overhead made it hard to judge. We should round up the gars, assemble our camp. Yes—that dark thought crept into my mind once more and clung.

"How," I blurted out, "do you destroy something which is only a—shadow?"

"*They* knew." Now Illo did turn her head a fraction, reluctantly, as if she must make herself do this. "It was by their arts that the first evil came to be; I think they had a last drastic control. While they lived they were not forced to use it. I think it would have been very hard for them to destroy their city—it was part of them."

"You talk as if you know—but how *can* you!" I persisted.

She was sleeking back the damp locks of her hair which had fallen into the water moments earlier and were now plastered into a ragged frame about her face, a face which seemed thinner, older, more tired than I had ever seen it.

"I know—" she hesitated as if hunting for words to make plain, emphatic what she would say—"I know it here!" The fingers of both of her hands were on her forehead just above her eyes, rubbing back and forth as if to ease some pain—or memory of pain. "It was in me—first the calling as I told you—that was true. And when the calling stopped and I believed that Catha must be dead—there was still a need in me—another calling, deeper buried, but one, I think which would have kept me crawling forward on my knees when I could no longer walk, if that had been necessary. That—all of it is gone!"

"You—" I remembered, but now it was not so horrible, so immediate—rather as if time had raised the barrier between memory and this moment which it would have naturally done had all been normal in my world, "you were being summoned still—by Shadows?"

She was frowning and rubbing still at the frown lines as if to erase them.

"Perhaps, or perhaps something else. Perhaps it was time that certain conditions must be fulfilled. There was no real reason why we, of all travelers, should have stumbled upon the necklet—"

I sat up and drew my knees close to my chest, lacing my arms about them. Out of my inborn desire for independence I did not want to follow her reasoning. That was born of her talent, I told myself. Still there were oddities about the both of us. Alone on Voor, as far as I knew, we were the only survivors of the Shadow doom. There had been that freak storm, the worst I had ever encountered in all my years on the plains, my father's death, the task he had laid on me.

Men who worship some forces greater than they themselves can truly imagine may see patterns in the laying out of our lives, reasons for action or choices which we do not understand. As if we are tools, honed and readied for one special task, set to it, instead of blundering on by ourselves.

I looked up into the evening sky where the first faint stars began to show, We two were born of Voor, no matter our off-world blood. Creatures—people—like us had once landed here, were caught up in an evil which became a dark blight, an evil which was able to reach out and draw in turn upon some inner quality of my species. Had those refugees indeed been of my own stock or enough like us so that our heritage was a common one?

Only this time our blood had been the victims—except for Illo and me. If the Shadows could move to bend men to their purposes, could not some overwhelming *other* will, seeking ever a weapon against them, have had a hand in what we had done?

"What do we do now—?" I asked it of the sky, and of myself, but Illo answered:

"Nothing. Time will heal. We shall not speak the truth to anyone. It is gone, all of it—that garden place of utter evil in which they fed and spawned, and which I think they needed in order to live—the jewel city where now no one will tramp and pry and seek out secrets we are not meant to handle, use, or know. I am a healer—I shall heal—In time this memory shall fade more and more into a story—"

I sat up, put my fingers to my lips and gave Witol's whistle.

"I do not think we shall forget so easily," I told her. "But, yes, we must keep silent. There will be holdings in the north after the years pass and others find no more trouble. Perhaps the Tangle will fade, it may have been nourished by what lay under it. *Their* peace is locked upon them for all time—" I could still sense a little of what I felt in the city; I hoped I would not forget that healing peace ever. "You are right, this is our secret, we shall remain who we are, and none shall know the difference. After all," I was on my feet now and had stretched wide my arms as if some burden had loosened and fallen, to leave my back unbowed any longer, "what better life can I choose—Voorloper!" I shouted that to the sky in a sudden burst of relief and returning youth, as Witol and his companions came trotting up to the two of us there under the evening sky.